GRADUATE SCHOOL IN ASTRONOMY

To learn more about the AIP Conference Proceedings, including the
Conference Proceedings Series, please visit the webpage
http://proceedings.aip.org/proceedings

GRADUATE SCHOOL IN ASTRONOMY

X Special Courses at the
National Observatory of Rio de Janeiro
(X CCE)

Rio de Janeiro, Brazil   26 –30 September 2005

EDITORS
Simone Daflon
Jailson Alcaniz
Eduardo Telles
Ramiro de la Reza

National Observatory of Rio de Janeiro/MCT
Rio de Janeiro, Brazil

SPONSORING ORGANIZATIONS
Department of Astronomy-CoAA
National Observatory of Rio de Janeiro/MCT
CAPES

Melville, New York, 2006
AIP CONFERENCE PROCEEDINGS ■ **843**

Editors

Simone Daflon
Jailson Alcaniz
Eduardo Telles
Ramiro de la Reza

Department of Astronomy and Astrophysics
National Observatory of Rio de Janeiro
R. Gal. José Cristino 77
20921-400 Rio de Janeiro/RJ, Brazil

E-mail: daflon@on.br
alcaniz@on.br
etelles@on.br
delareza@on.br

Authorization to photocopy items for internal or personal use, beyond the free copying permitted under the 1978 U.S. Copyright Law (see statement below), is granted by the American Institute of Physics for users registered with the Copyright Clearance Center (CCC) Transactional Reporting Service, provided that the base fee of $23.00 per copy is paid directly to CCC, 222 Rosewood Drive, Danvers, MA 01923, USA. For those organizations that have been granted a photocopy license by CCC, a separate system of payment has been arranged. The fee code for users of the Transactional Reporting Services is: 0-7354-0336-8/06/$23.00

© 2006 American Institute of Physics

Permission is granted to quote from the AIP Conference Proceedings with the customary acknowledgment of the source. Republication of an article or portions thereof (e.g., extensive excerpts, figures, tables, etc.) in original form or in translation, as well as other types of reuse (e.g., in course packs) require formal permission from AIP and may be subject to fees. As a courtesy, the author of the original proceedings article should be informed of any request for republication/reuse. Permission may be obtained online using Rightslink. Locate the article online at http://proceedings.aip.org, then simply click on the Rightslink icon/"Permission for Reuse" link found in the article abstract. You may also address requests to: AIP Office of Rights and Permissions, Suite 1NO1, 2 Huntington Quadrangle, Melville, NY 11747-4502, USA; Fax: 516-576-2450; Tel.: 516-576-2268; E-mail: rights@aip.org.

L.C. Catalog Card No. 2006926959

ISBN 0-7354-0336-8
ISSN 0094-243X
Printed in the United States of America

Contents

Preface vii
Observatory Photo viii
Sponsors and Organizing Committee ix
Lecturers xi
X CCE Program xiii
Group Picture xv
Programs of Previous CCE—from 1996 to 2005 xvii

Chapter 1: Planetary Systems 1
P. Artymowicz

    1. Exoplanets and Theories of Their Formation 3
    2. Disk-Planet Interaction 7
    3. Transitional and Beta Pictoris-type Disks: The Origin of
        Structure 23
    4. Conclusions 30
    Acknowledgments 31
    References 31

Chapter 2: Globular Clusters 33
R. G. Gratton

    1. Introduction and General Properties 35
    2. Formation Scenarios and Cluster Evolution 43
    3. Variable Stars in GCS: The RR Lyrae 46
    4. Abundances in GCS 48
    5. The Case of ω CEN 56
    References 57

Chapter 3: The Evolution of Dwarf Galaxies 61
E. D. Skillman

    1. Dwarf Galaxies—An Overview 63
    2. Global Star Formation Histories of Dwarf Galaxies 67
    3. Mapping Recent Star Formation in Nearby Dwarf Galaxies:
        Testing Our Knowledge of the Star Formation Process ... 80
    4. The Metal Poor ISM of Dwarf Galaxies 83
    5. Starbursts in Dwarf Galaxies 93
    Acknowledgments 102
    References 103

Chapter 4: Advanced Topics in Cosmology: A Pedagogical Introduction 109
T. Padmanabhan

    1. The Cosmological Paradigm and Friedmann Model 111
    2. Thermal History of the Universe 114
    3. Structure Formation and Linear Perturbation Theory 124
    4. Perturbations in Dark Matter and Radiation 129
    5. Transfer Function for Matter Perturbations 136
    6. Temperature Anisotropies of CMBR 138
    7. Generation of Initial Perturbations from Inflation 146
    8. The Dark Energy 153
    Acknowledgment 163
    References 163

List of Participants 167
Author Index 169

PREFACE

The Observatório Nacional of Rio de Janeiro (ON) has offered annually, since 1996, four general courses in astronomy and astrophysics at post-graduate level. This 'Cycle of Special Courses', as it is called in Portuguese ("Ciclo de Cursos Especiais", CCE) cover themes on Planetary, Stellar, Galactic, Extragalactic astronomy and Cosmology. Despite of being originally directed to students of our Graduate Programme at ON, they rapidly became an attraction for students in astronomy from other institutions, both from Brazil and from other South American countries.

The X Special Courses (X CCE) took place at ON in Rio de Janeiro from September 26 to 30. This year these courses are being printed in the format of a book for the first time to celebrate the tenth consecutive year of CCE at the Observatório Nacional. We hope to extend this valuable contribution by renowned scientists to a larger community in this useful and practical way.

We wish to thank all past lecturers for their great enthusiastic participation and all students who have contributed for the success of the School that now has become a permanent academic event at ON. In particular, we give special thanks to this year's lecturers Pawel Artymowicz, Raffaele Gratton, Evan Skillman and Thanu Padmanabhan for the preparation of the texts presented in this innaugurative written edition of the Advanced School of the Observatório Nacional. Finally, we acknowledge the support by the staff at ON, the Division of Educational Activities, secretary and library for their help in all aspects of the organization. We also thank the Astronomy Department and the Head of ON for financial support and encouragement.

Simone Daflon
Jailson Alcaniz
Eduardo Telles
Ramiro de la Reza

Rio de Janeiro/RJ, Brazil - 2005

Campus of the National Observatory of Rio de Janeiro in 1920.

SPONSORS

Observatório Nacional - ON

Coordenação de Astronomia e Astrofísica - CoAA

Coordenação de Aperfeiçoamento de Pessoal de Nível Superior - CAPES

ORGANIZING COMMITTEE

Simone Daflon (daflon@on.br)
Jailson Alcaniz (alcaniz@on.br)
Eduardo Telles (etelles@on.br)
Ramiro de la Reza (delareza@on.br)

Observatório Nacional
R. Gal. José Cristino 77, São Cristovão
20921-400 Rio de Janeiro, Brazil

LECTURERS

Pawel Artymowicz (pawel@utsc.utoronto.ca)
University of Toronto at Scarborough
Toronto, Canada

Raffaele G. Gratton (raffaele.gratton@oapd.inaf.it)
INAF - Osservatorio Astronomico di Padova
Padova, Italy

Evan D. Skillman (skillman@astro.umn.edu)
Astronomy Department, University of Minnesota
Minneapolis, USA

Thanu Padmanabhan (nabhan@iucaa.ernet.in)
Inter-University Center for Astronomy and Astrophysics - IUCAA
Pune, India

X CCE PROGRAM

- **Disks, dust, and protoplanets : dynamical view - Pawel Artymowicz**
    - Protoplanetary disks and the growth of planets
    - Disk-planet interaction: resonances and torques
    - Disk-planet interaction: migration scenarios, eccentricity evolution
    - Dusty disks in young planetary systems
    - Origin of structure in dusty disks

- **Abundances in Globular Cluster Stars - Raffaele Gratton**
    - Stellar clusters: Cluster formation and evolution
    - Abundances in globular clusters: what they may tell us
      - Distances to globular clusters and impact on ages: short and long distance scales
      - Star-to-star chemical inhomogeneities: the Na-O anticorrelation
      - Lithium abundances
    - Self enrichment in globular clusters: the case of Omega Cen
    - Binaries in globular clusters: impact on abundances

- **The Evolution of Dwarf Galaxies - Evan Skillman**
    - A Brief overview of the Theory of Galaxy Formation
    - The Global Star Formation Histories of Dwarf Galaxies
    - The Low Metallicity Environments of Dwarf Galaxies
    - Star Formation at Low Metallicity in Dwarf Galaxies
    - Starbursts in Dwarf Galaxies

- **Making Sense Out of the Universe - Thanu Padmanabhan**
    - Friedmann Model and the Composition of the Universe
    - Structure formation in the Universe
    - Inflation and generation of initial perturbations
    - CMBR
    - Dark Energy

X CCE: GROUP PICTURE

PROGRAM OF PREVIOUS CCE - FROM 1996 TO 2005

I CCE - November 25-29, 1996

- Cometas: Origem y Evolucíon Dinâmica - Dr. Julio Fernandez (Faculdad de Ciências - Uruguay)
- The Milky Way and its Satellites - Dr. Gerry Gilmore (University of Cambridge - UK)
- Clusters of Galaxies - Dr. Michael West (St. Mary's University - Canada)
- A Modern View of Normal Galaxies - Dr. Reynier Peletier (Kapteyn Institute -)
- The Origins of the Elements - Dr. David Lambert (University of Texas - USA) (December 9-12, 1996)
  Organizing Committee: Katia Cunha, Paulo Pellegrini, and Silvia Lorentz

II CCE - October 20-24, 1997

- Formation of the Solar System - Dr. Bruno Sicardy (Observatoire Meudon/Université Paris 7 - France)
- Mass Loss and Stellar Evolution - Dr. Henry Lamers (SRON Laboratory for Space Research - Holland)
- Structure and Dynamics of Elliptical Galaxies - Dr. Roberto Saglia (Universitats-Sternwarte München - Germany)
- Modern Determination of Cosmological Parameters - Dr. Jens Villumsen (Max Planck Institute - Astrophysik - Germany)
  Organizing Committee: Cláudia Angeli, Cláudio Bastos, and Paulo Pellegrini

III CCE - June 1-5, 1998

- Asteroids: Formation, Evolution and Interactions - Dr. Vincenzo Zappalà (Osservatorio Astronomico di Torino - Italia)
- The Chemical Evolution of the Galactic Halo - Dr. Christopher Sneden (University of Texas - USA)
- The Formation and Evolution of our Galaxy -Dr. John Norris (Mt. Stromlo/Siding Spring Observatory - Australia)
- Surveys of Galaxy Structures and Evolution - Dr. Matthew Colless (Mt. Stromlo/Siding Spring Observatory - Australia)
  Organizing Committee: Daniela Lazzaro, Paulo Pellegrini, and Vladimir Ortega

IV CCE - June 7-11, 1999

- Galactic and Extragalactic Interstellar Medium - Dr. Rene Walterbos (New Mexico State University - USA)

- Modern Approaches on Fundamental Astronomy - Dr. François Mignard (Observatoire de la Cote d'Azur - France)
- High Angular Resolution om Astrophysics - Dr. Farrokh Vakili (Observatoire de la Cote d'Azur - France)
- Galaxy Formation in the Universe - Dr. George Blumenthal (Lick Observatory - USA)

  Organizing Committee: Eduardo Telles, Paulo Pellegrini, Reinaldo de Carvalho, Roberto Martins, and Vladimir Ortega

V CCE - June 26-30, 2000

- Cosmology from Observations of the Low Redshift Universe - Dr. Brent Tully (University of Hawaii - USA)
- Infrared Studies of Comets and Asteroids - Dr. Humberto Campins (LPL-University of Arizona - USA)
- Protostellar and Pre-Main-Sequence Evolution - Dr. Francesco Palla (Osservatorio Astrofisico di Arcetri - Italia)
- The Structure and Evolution of the Milky Way - Dr. Steven Majewsky (University of Virginia - USA)

  Organizing Committee: Daniela Lazzaro, Jucira Penna, and Ramiro de la Reza

VI CCE - July 09-13, 2001

- The Formation of Massive Stars - Dr. Claus Leitherer (Space Science Telescope Institute - USA)
- Small Bodies in the Solar System: Living in the Kingdom of Chaos - Dr. Alessandro Morbidelli (Observatorie de la Cote D'Azur - France)
- Chemical Evolution of the Milky Way - Dr. Francesca Matteucci (Universitá di Trieste - Italia)
- Galaxy Formation and Cosmology: Recent Progress - Dr. Richard S Ellis (Caltech/Cambridge - USA/UK)

  Organizing Committee: Cláudio Bastos, Daniela Lazzaro, and Ramiro de la Reza

VII CCE - July 15-19, 2002

- Primordial Alchemy: From the Big Bang to the Present Universe - Dr. Gary Steigman (Ohio State University - USA)
- Evolution of Stars in Galaxies - Dr. Georges Meynet (Observatoire de Geneve - Switzerland)
- Planetary Formation - Dr. Alan Boss (Carnegie Institution of Washington - USA)

- Modern Instrumentation in Spectroscopy - Dr. Luca Pasquini with the participation of Dr. Bernard Delabre (European Southern Observatory - Germany)
  Organizing Committee: Ramiro de la Reza, Cláudio Bastos, and Eduardo Telles

VIII CCE - August 18-22, 2003

- Physical Properties of Kuiper Belt Objects - Dr. Hermann Boehnhardt (Max-Plank-Institute for Astronomy - Germany)
- The Birth and Death of Stars - Dr. Nicholas B. Suntzeff (Cerro Tololo Interamerican Observatory - Chile)
- Topics in Extragalactic Astronomy - Dr. Chris Impey (University of Arizona - USA)
- Star Formation and the Interstellar Medium - Dr. Guillermo Tenorio Tagle (INAOEP - Mexico)
  Organizing Committee: Daniela Lazzaro, Eduardo Telles, and Katia Cunha

IX CCE - October 25-29, 2004

- Planetary Nebulae as Astrophysical Laboratories - Dr. Mike Barlow (University College London - UK)
- Planetary Observations and Landers - Dr. Angioletta Coradini (Istituto di Astrofisica Spaziale, Consiglio Nazionale delle Ricerche - Italia)
- Radiative Transfer and Mass Loss in Hot Luminous Stars - Dr. John Hillier (University of Pittsburgh - USA)
- Stellar Populations in the Local Group and Implications for Galaxy Formation and Evolution - Dr. Rosemary Wyse (John Hopkins University - USA)
  Organizing Committee: Cláudio Bastos, Fernando Roig, Katia Cunha, and Vladimir Ortega

CHAPTER 1

Planetary Systems
Pawel Artymowicz

PLANETARY SYSTEMS

Pawel Artymowicz

Physical Sciences
University of Toronto at Scarborough
1265 Military Trail, Ontario, Canada M2A 1N7

Abstract.
We provide a non-technical introduction to some current topics in planetary system origins, relevant to the understanding of a decade's worth of discovery and characterization of systems other than the solar system. We consider both the radial velocity exoplanets (planets outside the solar system) and the dust disks known as transitional and debris disks, which are natural and conspicuous parts of young planetary systems. Our emphasis is on new dynamical theories, including new concepts in disk-planet interaction and the resultant three types of migration of protoplanets in disks. Migration is considered the key issue for planet survival during the T Tauro disk phase. We also discuss a variety of observable features arising from the dust-gas coupling in the presence of stellar radiation pressure. Nonaxisymmetric features have been both observed and predicted theoretically, although detailed comparison has not yet been performed.

1. Exoplanets and theories of their formation

Theories and observations are tightly interwoven in any science, but the science of the origin of planetary systems provides one remarkable example of their mutual complementarity and motivation each provides for the other. The history of this subject is as old as physical science itself. Extrasolar planetary systems have been predicted by pure thought, starting from the prescient ideas of atoms and motion-allowing vacuum, by Leucippus and Democritus (cf. Dick 1982) in ancient Greece. The oldest and the newest theories regarding "other worlds" (planetary systems) are in general remarkably similar, each describing both their evolution, including formation from rotating rarified gas which forms a turbulent nebula ("single whirl") where refractory elements fractionate out and form planets, as well as their enormous possible diversity. But on that last point, modern theory is still catching up with the ancient predecessors, spurred into action by the remarkable success of observers who, as of this writing, within the past decade succeeded in finding 188 extrasolar planets (cf. Marcy et al. 2002, Schneider 2006).

In contrast, the theory of the 1980s that we summarize in this brief introductory section (for review see Lissauer 1993), called standard formation scenario, was tailored to the explanation of planets in one system only under the tacit assumption that our system is typical and representative of other. In this model, planetary systems form from the protoplanetary disks (also known as primitive solar nebulae, protostellar accretion disks, or T Tauri disks). Planetesimals, comet-sized primitive rock+ice bodies, formed from dust, accumulate in orbit via binary collisions, and in less than 1 Myr build protoplanets (bodies larger than 1000 km).

Terrestrial planets are finally assembled in the inner solar system within 30 Myr. A crucial role in their growth is played by gravitational focusing, which works best in kinematically cold planetesimal disks. Cooling (circularization of orbits) is provided by the nebular gas drag and by planet's launching of spiral density and bending waves into the disk.

Outside the ice condensation boundary, at a distance of several AU from the sun, protoplanets grew quicker and larger because of the availability of water ice, and grew up to a mass of several Earths, gathering around them a massive hydrogen+helium envelopes. In the "core-accretion" or "core-instability" scenario, the primitive atmosphere becomes unstable and accretes onto the core without mixing, when the core mass exceeds 8-15 Earth masses, a value in line with core masses in our system (see reviews in Mannings et al. 2000 and Reipurth 2006). Jupiter was thought to have been born: (i) at or near its present location, because of ice boundary location, (ii) on a circular orbit ($e \approx 0$), due to circular motion of the protoplanet and the disk, and (iii) with mass determined by the process of tidal gap opening in a viscous disk with parameter $\alpha \sim 10^{-2}$.

1.1 Diversity of solar systems

Although most theoretical concepts from the standard planet formation theory of the 80s are perfectly usable even today, in the hindsight we see how limited some of the predictions regarding extrasolar systems turned out to be. Ironically, the first planets ever found outside the solar system (by Wolszczan and Frail 1992, in an unlikely place: around a millisecond pulsar PSR1257+12) are of terrestrial type and although closer to their sun than our terrestrial planets are to the sun, exibit neatly near-circular orbits with two major bodies very close to a mean-motion resonance (3:2), not unlike Jupiter and Saturn (5:2). However, a theoretical expectation (Boss 1995) that the solar and extrasolar systems share the basic blueprint (giants outside a few-AU radius, terrestrial planets inside) was soon afterwards disproved by the first 'hot jupiters' such as 51 Pegasi discovered via Doppler shift or, in other words, radial velocity variation, by Mayor and Queloz (1995) to have orbital period of only 4 days. While more data (among others, about long-period systems) are needed before we can be certain that the solar systems is atypical, if not unique, in the universe, the accumulating statistics ceratinly makes that conclusion very plausible (cf. Marcy and Butler 1998, Marcy et al. 2002, review books by Mannings et al. 2000, and Reipurth et al. 2006):

• Large planetary companions (with $a < 3$ AU and at least Saturn's mass) exist around at least $\sim 10\%$ of normal stars. They can be found at any distance from the star currently observable, with a possible depletion at radii less than 0.5 AU.

• "hot Jupiters" (minimum masses $m > 0.1 m_J$, semi-major axes $a < 0.1$ AU) exist around $\sim 1\%$ of sun-like stars. There typical period is 3-4 days. There is a noticeable excess or pile-up of hot jupiters at these periods compared with a few times longer periods, although they are a small minority of all exoplanets.

• Very massive planetary companions are found with the frequency $dN \sim m_i^{-0.9} dm_i$, i.e., the logarithm of mass has a very flat distribution up to the minimum mass $m_i =$

$m \sin i > 10 m_J$ (10 Jupiter masses).[1] This decreasing tail of planet-like bodies overlaps with a low-mass tail of massive companions (stars or brown dwarfs with mass 13 to 80 m_J), but the crossover mass is as yet unknown.

- Eccentric planets (i.e., planets on elliptic orbits) are common. There is a clear e–P correlation resembling closely that of the pre-main sequence and main-sequence close binary stars. Orbits with $a < 0.1$ AU tend to have $e \approx 0$, which might be due to tidal circularization by the star. There is a weak direct correlation of e with $m \sin i$. Also, $m \sin i$ correlates positively with distance or orbital period: there is a deficit of massive super-jovian planets closer than about 0.3 AU from the stars and a deficit of sub-jovian planets at more than ~0.5 AU (e.g., Paploizou and Terquem 2005). It is hard to tell which of these correlations are primary (a physical connection acquired at birth or later such as planet migration sensitive to their mass, or eccentricity-inducing stellar flybys frequent far from the host star) and which merely a statistical consequence of the primary ones without any direct connection.
- Most transiting exoplanets have jovian-type radii, first detected in the case of HD 209458b, which has a record-low mean density 0.38 g/cm^3 (Charbonneau et al. 2001, 2006). They must be gaseous planets like our Jupiter rather than giant rocks.

Preliminary models of interior structure based on the transits were constructed. The difficulty in modeling is to know how much of the stellar radiation is absorbed (and where) by the planet. While HD 209458b must have a very small core (or no core at all), this seems to be an exception. Other radial velocity hot jupiters have mean densities in the range 0.7-1.5 g/cm^3 (Charbonneau et al. 2006). The preliminary ideas about the internal structure of three exoplanets are contrasted with the data about the solar system giant planets in Figure 1. Notice that in the case of exoplanets, by "core" we mean an estimate of the total heavy element contents, which can either reside in a well-defined core or be mixed with the gas.

HD 149026b has a very substantial core of heavy elements (70 Earth masses), and resembles a super-Neptune rather than Saturn, despite a Saturn's mass. This illustrates just how diverse the exoplanets are internally, not only orbitally. The large core of HD 149026b and the likely 'normal' core of HD 189733b exclude the origin of these planets in a disk fragmentation event (cf. Boss 2000). We feel that this should come as no surprise. Disk fragmentation model (also called Giant Gaseous Protoplanets or GGP scenario) was always appealing because of short formation time, but has had serious problems justifying its assumed unstable initial conditions.[2]

---

[1] The unknown inclination of the orbit i does not allow a unique mass determination, giving only the minimum mass $m \sin i$. Assuming randomly oriented orbits, this mass is on the average $\pi/2$ times smaller than the true mass.

[2] Disks defend themselves from approaching danger of a global breakup by growing spiral, galaxy-like wave modes, which in the non-linear regime dissipate energy of rotation and heat up the disk, thus curbing the instability (e.g., Laughlin and Bodenheimer 1994). This stabilizes galaxies at Safronov-Toomre number $Q > 1$. A very optically thick protoplanetary disk cannot cool fast enough for breakup (on orbital time scale, cf. Rafikov 2005). In fact, only isothermal disk models can be persuaded to fragment. Other assorted difficulties include: difficulty of reproducing typical sub-jovian and jovian planets (GGPs at the outset have jovian masses and are bound to grow by accretion even further during a long disk lifetime, ending up as super-jupiters or brown dwarfs); and finally, difficulty of fractionating a solid core of an exoplanet from a well mixed initial GGP.

Comparison of gas and rock/ice masses (in Earth masses, M_E) in giant planets and exoplanets (2006)

Planet	Core mass (rock+ice, M_E)	Envelope (gas, M_E)	Total mass (M_E)	Radius (R_J)
Jupiter	0-10	~313	318	1.00
Saturn	15-20	~77	95	0.84
Uranus	11-13	2 - 4	14.6	0.36
Neptune	13-15	2 - 4	17.2	0.34
HD 209458b (discovered 1999)	~0	~220	204-235	1.32 ± 0.05
HD 149026b (discovered 2005)	~70	~45	105-124	0.73 ± 0.03
HD 189733b (discovered 2005)	~10(?)	~356	354-379	1.15 ± 0.03

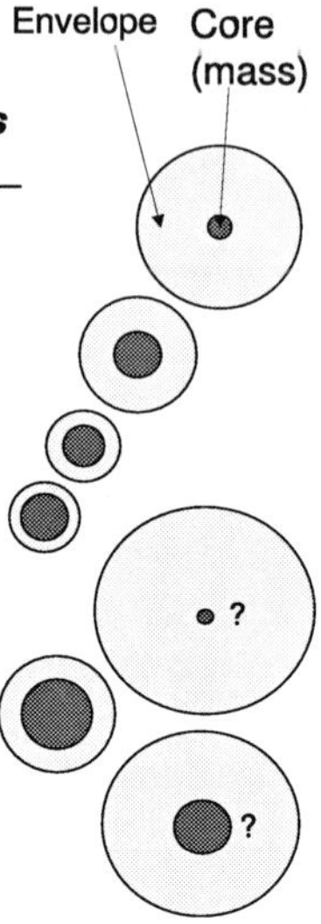

FIGURE 1.

In summary, ironically, pulsar PSR 1257+12 remains the only truly solar-like system, regarding the orbits and terrestrial masses of the planets. We now know some 50 times more(!) giant exoplanets than the giants in our system. The diversity of exoplanets far exceeded our naive expectations before 1995, and makes our system look atypical. Their orbits are too close to their stars, too elongated, or both. Chemical composition of host stars is clearly correlated with the frequency of occurrence of close giant exoplanets. (One example is HD149026b in Fig. 1, which has a star with more than twice the solar metallicity.) It is unclear why this is so, probably the metal-rich protoplanetary disks both produce more planets and enhance their delivery to the inner part of the planetary system (see Reipurth et al. 2006 for a collection of excellent reviews hereafter referred to as PPV or "Protostars and Planets V").

1.2 Dusty disks as young planetary systems

For consolation after the perplexing differences and surprises that radial velocity systems provided we might turn to another area of astrophysical research. For two decades now, and hence significantly longer than for instance the dection of radial velocity variations of stars, astronomers have studied another aspect of planetary systems: dusty circumstellar disks around main-sequence stars. Dusty disks better match the standard expectations about the mineralogy, spatial extent etc. of a planetary system like our own. These disks descend from the primordial solar nebulae that accompany all forming intermediate and low mass stars. Late evolutionary stages of disk systems, following the loss of the hydrogen+helium gas from disks, are observed as a class of infrared-emitting systems known as Vega-type, Vega-excess or β Pic-type systems. Detected by IRAS and ISO satellites thanks to the presence of a large area (up to $\sim 10^{30}$ cm^2) of solid grains much different from the ISM dust, complemented by a varying but generally much smaller amount of gas, the Vega-type systems comprise as many as 15% of nearby main-sequence field stars of type A to K (for review see Lagrange et al. 2000).

Such systems were quickly realized to represent a stage in planetary system evolution (e.g., Aumann et al. 1984, Smith & Terrile 1984), although it was not immediately clear which one (some were suggesting a stage of "snowballing" necessary to build large solid particles). An opposite view, that solids in the disks are intensely eroded and reduced to dust, rather than accumulating, now prevails (Artymowicz 1997, Vidal-Madjar et al. 1998, Lagrange et al. 2000). Planetesimals, i.e. comets and asteroids, replenish the dust via ice sublimation and mutual collisions. The disks ages range typically from a few to a few hundreds Myr.

High-resolution imaging has revealed structure in some of the disks implying a possible influence of planetary masses (more about this later). An important finding by Dominik et al. (1998) of a Vega-type infrared excess from 55 ρ^1 Cancri, a star orbited by a hot Jupiter-type planet, provided the first link between radial velocity and Vega-type systems. (Both represent planetary systems, seen from a very different perspective.) The disk has been, however, difficult to spot in the visible/near-IR scattered light; it has not been confirmed in HST imaging despite the initial claim based on Earth-bound observations (Trilling & Brown 1998; Schneider et al. 2000). Imaging of dust in the known exoplanetary systems will be a interesting future area of studies. We may notice that the prototype β Pic was also an isolated example of a scattering disk for about a decade, before improved sensitivity allowed imaging of any other objects, so current problems are temporary. We return to the dusty planetary systems after discussing the dynamics of disk-planet interaction.

2. Disk-planet interaction

The discovery of 'hot jupiters' highlighted the conceptual difficulties associated with forming such planets in situ, either in the critical core mass accumulation followed by gas accretion scenario, or the gravitational instability scenario for giant planet formation. Simply speaking, the disk-planet interaction and the resultant large-scale migration of planets became the only hope for understanding the observations. In this section, we discuss the disk-planet coupling along the lines of the most recent review by Papaloizou et al. (2006).

The idea of migration is not new, as the basic mechanisms were proposed in the early 1980s and 1990s. (see Lin et al. 2000 and references therein). In the standard theory of migration from 1990s, two modes of migration were known: type I and type II, the former applying to small-mass embedded protoplanets and the latter to gap-forming massive protoplanets. Both predicted disturbingly short radial infall times that in the type I case threatened the survival of embryo cores in the $1 - 15M_\oplus$ regime before they could accrete gas to become giant planets. At the end of 1990s, the main question became how to resolve the type I migration issue and how to account for the observed radial distribution of exoplanets.

2.1 Migration type I

When the mass of the protoplanet is small the response it induces in the disk can be calculated using linear theory. Density waves propagate both outwards and inwards away from the protoplanet. These waves carry positive and negative angular momentum respectively and accordingly a compensating tidal torque is applied to the orbit resulting in type I migration. Like other types of migration discussed later, type I migration is a differential effect, a residual of two opposing torques from the protoplanetary disk gas located inside and outside the orbit of a planet.

The tidal torque

When hydrodynamic equations are linearized about a basic state consisting of an unperturbed axisymmetric accretion disk, the response to individual Fourier component (harmonics with azimuthal periodicity or number of arms given by integer m) can be calculated and at the end summed up. The gravitational potential ψ of a proplanet in circular orbit is

$$\psi(r,\varphi,t) = \sum_{m=0}^{\infty} \psi_m(r) \cos\{m[\varphi - \Omega_p t]\}, \qquad (1)$$

where φ is the azimuthal angle and $2\pi/\Omega_p$ is the orbital period of the planet of mass M_p at orbital semi-major axis a. The total torque acting on the disk is given by $\Gamma = -\int_{Disk}(\Sigma \vec{r} \times \nabla \psi)\, d^2r$ where Σ is the surface density of the disk.

An external forcing potential $\psi_m(r,\varphi)$ with azimuthal mode number m that rotates with a pattern frequency Ω_p in a disk with angular velocity $\Omega(r)$ triggers a response that exchanges angular momentum with the orbit whenever, neglecting effects due to pressure, $m(\Omega - \Omega_p)$ is equal either 0 or $\pm\kappa$, with $\kappa \equiv \Omega$ being the epicyclic frequency in a Keplerian disk. The first situation occurs when $\Omega = \Omega_p$ and thus corresponds to a corotation resonance (CR). The second possibility corresponds to Lindblad resonances (LR): an inner Lindblad resonance (ILR) for $\Omega = \Omega_p + \kappa/m$ and an outer Lindblad resonance (OLR) outside the planet's orbit for $\Omega = \Omega_p - \kappa/m$.

Lindblad resonances

Torques at LRs (Goldreich and Tremaine 1979, 1980) are of crucial importance for the standard theory of disk-planet interaction, and provide a dominant effect for: disk gap opening, shepherding of planetary rings by satellites, migration, as well as planetary eccentricity damping in the type I situation (Ward 1986, Artymowicz 1993ab). The reason for neglecting CRs is that in the linear theory with a planet on a fixed orbit they have been shown to be subdominant to LRs, e.g., by Tanaka et al. (2002).

The torque arising from the component of the potential with azimuthal mode number m is found, for a Keplerian disk, in standard form reads (Goldreich and Tremaine 1979)

$$\Gamma_m^{LR} = \frac{\text{sign}(\Omega_p - \Omega)\pi^2\Sigma}{3\Omega\Omega_p}\Psi^2, \tag{2}$$

with

$$\Psi = r\frac{d\psi_m}{dr} + \frac{2m^2(\Omega - \Omega_p)}{\Omega}\psi_m. \tag{3}$$

where the expression has to be evaluated at the location of the resonance. Torque exerted on the planet from an outer Lindblad resonance is negative and causes its inward migration, while the torque due to an inner Lindblad resonance is positive corresponding to an acceleration and outward migration.

Let us denote by c_s the sound speed, by $r\Omega$ Keplerian speed, and by $h = c_s/(r\Omega)$ the inverse Mach number in disk, also equal to the geometrical aspect ratio of the disk, or the ratio of disk's half-thickness H to radius r. The total torque is obtained by summing contributions over m from $m = 1$ to $m = \infty$. Contributions fall dramatically above a limiting value of m equal $m \approx h^{-1}$. We can express this pressure torque cutoff condition as $\xi = mh = mc_s/(r\Omega) > 1$. For a finite ξ the true (as opposed to nominal) positions of the Lindblad resonances can be found from a WKB dispersion relation of density waves

$$m^2(\Omega - \Omega_p)^2 = \Omega^2(1 + \xi^2). \tag{4}$$

The effective positions of the resonances are shifted with respect to the standard theory. If a denotes the orbital radius of a planet, an m-armed potential $\psi_m(r)$ creates nominal positions of ILR/OLR at $r_{LR,nom} = a \mp 2a/3m = a \mp (2H/3)\xi^{-1}$, where $H = c/\Omega$ the disk's semi-thickness or scale height obeying $H \ll r$. In Goldreich-Tremaine theory LRs converge to $r_{LR,nom} = a$ for high-order harmonics of the potential. (This caused some spurious infinities in initial calculations of type I migration.) The effective resonance positions, where the potential actually excites the waves and around which the waves have their first wavelength, are given by (Artymowicz 1993a)

$$r_{LR} = a \mp (2H/3)\xi^{-1}\sqrt{1 + \xi^2}. \tag{5}$$

In particular, when $m \to \infty$, Lindblad resonances pile up at $r = a \pm (2H/3)$ instead of $r = a$.

The exciting potential $\psi_m(r)$ becomes so localized for $\xi \to \infty$ and the pressure-shifted LR positions, where the wave-potential coupling takes place within the first wavelength, so far from the peak of exciting potential (at $r = a$) that the resulting torque on planet decreases exponentially with m. Torque cutoff has good analytical approximations useful for disk plus point mass problem (Artymowicz 1993b).

Using those analytical approximations, Ward (1997) compared the torques due to individual ILRs with those due to OLRs. We show in Figure 2 this comparison for a very small planet that does not perturb the surface density significantly (Papaloizou et al. 2006). The main reason for different shapes of the ILR and OLR torque curves is that these resonances belonging to the same m are not located symmetrically with respect

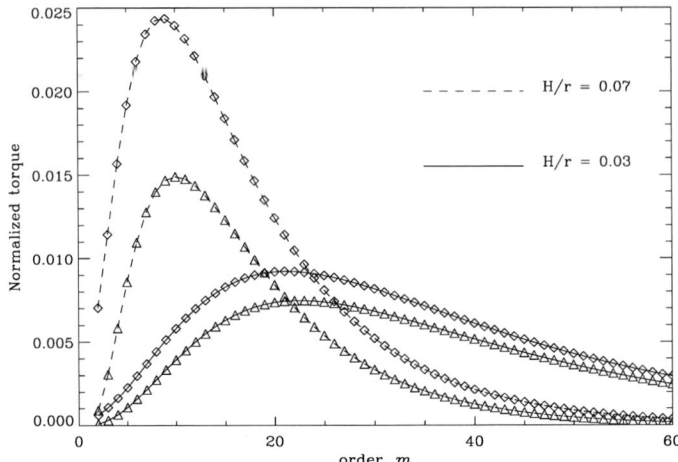

FIGURE 2. Individual inner and outer torques (absolute value) in a $h = 0.07$ and $h = 0.03$ disks, as a function of m. For each disk thickness, the upper curve (diamonds) shows the outer torque and the lower one (triangles) the inner torque. These torques are normalized to $\Gamma_0 = \pi \mu^2 \Sigma a^4 \Omega_p^2 h^{-3}$, where $\mu = M_p/M_*$.

to the planet's orbital radius. We can see a clear dominance of OLRs over ILRs, that is the dominance of outer disk over the inner disk. Virtually independently of the assumed unperturbed density profile $\Sigma(r)$, the differential torque results in an *inward migration* of a protoplanet (Artymowicz 1993b, Ward 1997, Tanaka 2002).

The most recent linear calculations by Tanaka et al. (2002) that take into account 3D effects, and are based upon the value of the total tidal torque, including the corotation torque (fully unsaturated since it is a linear estimate), give a migration timescale

$$\tau \equiv a/\dot{a} = (2.7 + 1.1\alpha)^{-1} \frac{M_*^2}{M_p \Sigma a^2} h^2 \Omega_p^{-1}, \tag{6}$$

for a surface density profile $\Sigma \sim r^{-\alpha}$. Notice that the all tidal torques scale with the square of the perturbing mass (disk response to planet scales as one power of M_p, force on planet from the disk scales as another M_p). Inertia of the planet scales as M_p, hence the acceleration and migration rate scale linearly with M_p, while the timescale as $\tau \sim M_p^{-1}$ (cf. the above equation). For an Earth-mass planet around a solar mass star at $r = 1$ AU, in a disk with $\Sigma = 1700$ g cm^{-2} and $h = 0.05$, we obtain $\tau = 0.16$ Myr.

A number of sophisticated numerical calculations with planets on fixed circular orbits have shown a good agreement with the linear theory (for review see Papaloizou et al. 2006). Only at Neptune's mass, protoplanets in numerical calculations sometimes migrate significantly slower than the linear prediction, and of course after gap opening, which occurs a higher mass, the migration slows down. However, type I is a grave danger to Earth-type planets which nominally all should travel toward the star in much less than the disk lifetime, which equals several Myr. The apparent robustness of type I migration in our theories creates potential difficulties for the accumulation scenario for the critical jovian cores.

Possible solutions to the seemingly unstoppable migration conundrum include:

(i) unusual LR location and strength if gas is strongly magnetized (Terquem 2003, but no guarantee this always helps and not worsens the situation);

(ii) the disk self-gravity modifying the spiral density patterns and thus changing the pull of the disk on the planet (has been modeled by Nelson and Benz 2003, Pierens and Huré 2003, but does not make a big difference and actually speeds up migration);

(iii) hypothetical high eccentricity of a planet might slow or reverse migration (Papaloizou and Larwood 2000, but there is little support for such an eccentricity);

(iv) detailed disk thermdynamics and radiation transfer including shadows cast by the disk around the planet on itself (a moderate slow-down of migration was found by Menou and Goodman 2004, Jang-Condell and Sasselov 2005);

(v) MHD turbulence was proposed to disrupt type I migration and replace it with a random walk (Nelson and Papaloizou 2004; however, would it not be an asymmetric random walk with precisely the same consequences?)

(vi) One tantalizing possibility is that migration type III (see below) supersedes type I. (3-D calculations of this problem are needed.)

2.2. Migration type II

When the planet grows in mass the disk response cannot be treated any longer as a linear perturbation, nor the unperturbed surface density taken as smooth power law. Nonlinear numerical hydrodynamics such as the calculation shown in Figure 3 show that a deep gap around the planet opens for standard disk parameters and planet's mass ratio similar to Saturn, and generally between Neptune's and Jupiter's ($\mu = M_p/M_* = 10^{-4} - 10^{-3}$). Several, not always compatible, criteria for this event have been proposed, so let us enumerate a few.

Lin and Papaloizou (1993) proposed two criteria, a thermal and a viscous criterion. The thermal condition requires that the planet's gravity be strong enough to overwhelm pressure in its Roche lobe radius (Hill sphere radius), $r_L = (\mu/3)^{1/3}r$, or in other words that $r_L > H$ (where we have $h = H/r$). After raising both sides of equation to the 3rd power, it reads

$$\mu > 3h^3. \qquad (7)$$

This condition used to be questionable derived from the Rayleigh instability concept, with which it has no connection; afterwards the justification involving nonlinearity of the disk response was substituted.[3] This second justification is also problematic (there are numerical examples violating the thermal criterion, where the gap exists without the criterion being satisfied. The concept of nonlinearity may either be irrelevant (viscosity

---

[3] Papaloizou et al. 2006 write that the flow perturbation becomes non-linear and the planetary wake turns into a shock in its vicinity. Dissipation by these shocks as well as the action of viscosity leads to the deposition of angular momentum, pushes material away from the planet and a gap opens.

alone may, in principle, provide for damping of *linear* density waves, or at least not very useful since weakly nonlinear shocks do accompany even an Earth-mass object, which clearly does not open a gap.) We see the status of the thermal criterion as uncertain.

The condition that angular momentum transport by viscous stresses be interrupted by the planetary tide is approximately

$$\mu > 40 \frac{\nu}{r^2\Omega} \tag{8}$$

if one follows the derivation by Lin and Paploizou (1993), where use is made of an uncertain assumption that the distance at which Lindblad torques cease to act is equal to one Roche lobe. That is not accurate, as the CR zone is in reality about 2.5 times wider; moreover if $(2H/3) > 2.5 r_L$ then $2H/3$ takes over the role of the limiting minimum distance of interaction and leads to the following viscous criterion

$$\mu^2 h^{-3} > 100 \frac{\nu}{r^2\Omega}, \tag{9}$$

which happens to be virtually equal to the side-by-side product of the standard thermal and viscous criteria, eqs. (7) and (8). Essentially, all those criteria appear to be useful and approximately correct in practice, because they are mutually dependent, and in addition even the independent criteria like eqs. (7) and (8) accidentally coincide for the parameters corresponding to the Jupiter in a Minimum Mass Solar Nebula. This may not be a general result, so attention to the correct derivation and form of the gap opening criterion is needed. In that respect eq. (9) might be preferable, as it allows for the role of both gravity, gas pressure, and viscosity. Indeed, Crida et al. (2006) analyze this simultaneous dependence on all the physical processes deeper than we can do it here.

Once the gap is open, the planet is traveling centered in it, as if shepherded by the two disk edges, following their motion with the disk material accreting slowly onto the star. The time scale of migration type II is, roughly, the viscous timescale $\tau_{II} \sim r^2/\nu \sim 0.1$ Myr from the distance of Jupiter, $r = 5.2$ AU. While still shorter than the lifetime of primordial disks, this timescale is formally longer than τ of embedded planets.

There are two important exceptions to this description of type II migration. One could be called migration type IIb. It happens when the gas in the disk immediately surrounding and interacting with the planet becomes depleted to the point that the planet is more masive than that gas. Migration slows down below the type II speed, approximately in proportion to the gas:planet mass ratio. The second exception is when the LR torques responsible for centering the planet in the gap become weaker than the CR torques from the CR zone: the centering and symmetry of type II has been observed to spontaneously break down: the situation described below as migration type III.

Numerical modeling and how to test it

Many important results on the behavior of bodies embedded in disks have been obtained through computations. The corresponding migration regime is called type II migration (e.g., Lin and Papaloizou, 1986; Ward, 1997). In fact, what comes out

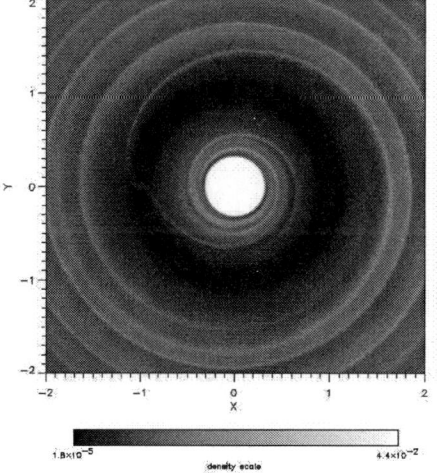 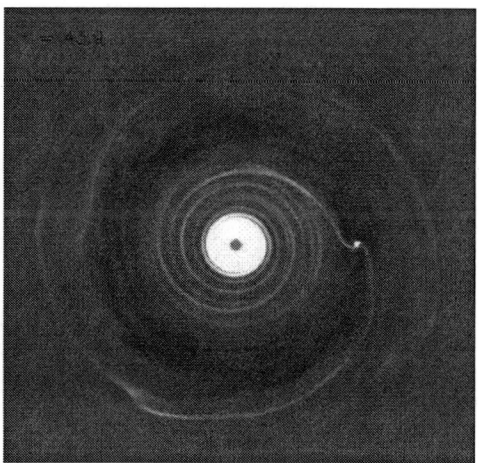

FIGURE 3. Surface density profiles for an initially axisymmetric disk model about one hundred orbital periods after the introduction of a planet, which remains on a prescribed, circular orbit. The mass ratio is a Jupiter's $\mu = 10^{-3}$. The program in the left image is ZEUS (2nd order scheme with artificial viscosity), on the right PPM (higher order scheme, no explicit viscosity). Notice different amount of vorticity and wavelets in the disk.

of the numerical calculations is often immediately interpreted in terms of standard type II migration. That, after a closer look, is unlikely. The simulated drift is likely a combination of type II and type III.

Medium-resolution hydrodynamical calculations (several hundred by several hundred cells) of planet-disk interaction in the type II regime were performed by Bryden et al. (1999) and Lubow et al. (1999). Since protoplanetary accretion disks are assumed to be vertically thin, these first simulations used a two-dimensional $(r - \varphi)$ model of the accretion disk. The vertical thickness H of the disk is incorporated by assuming a given radial temperature profile $T(r) \propto r^{-1}$ which makes the ratio H/r constant. Typically, simulations assume $H/r = 0.05$ so that at each radius, r, the Keplerian speed is 20 times faster than the local sound speed. Initial density profiles typically have power laws for the surface density $\Sigma \propto r^{-s}$ with s between 0 and 1.5. More recently, fully 3D models have been calculated using the isothermal equation of state (D'Angelo et al. 2003a). Spiral arms are weaker and accretion occurs primarily from regions above and below the midplane of the disk.

The viscosity is dealt with by solving the Navier Stokes equations with the kinematic viscosity ν taken as constant or given by an α-prescription $\nu = \alpha c_s H$, where α is a constant. From observations of protostellar disks, values lying between 10^{-4} and 10^{-2} are inferred for the α-parameter but there is great uncertainty. Some codes require also additional artificial viscosity for proper post-shock oscillation damping; a popular code ZEUS belongs to this category. All of them also have a small spurious viscosity in the form of resolution-dependent diffusivity (sharp features cannot propagate on grids

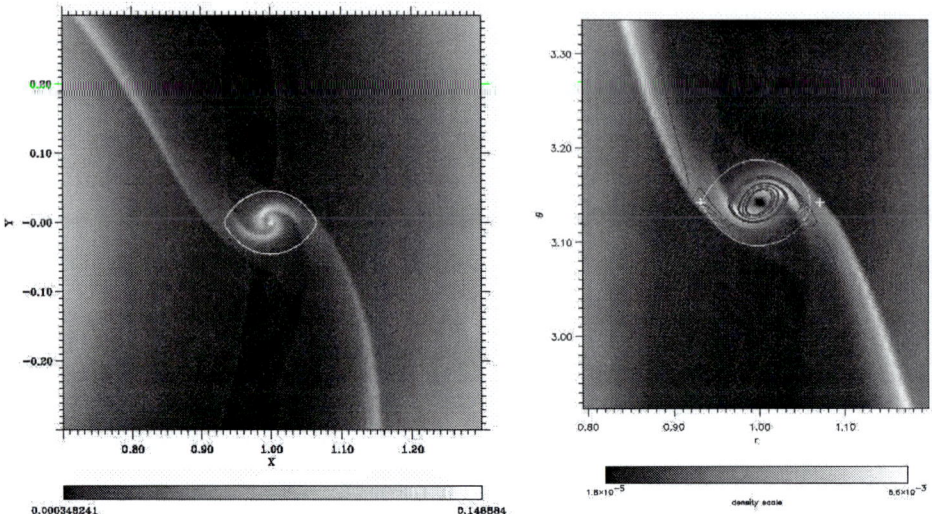

FIGURE 4. Left panel: Jupiter's vicinity in a global simulation on a variable-resolution grid using Piecewise Parabolic Method (PPM) by Artymowicz (1999, unpubl.). Surface density of disk gas is color-coded. Notice planetary wakes in the disk gap and the complex set of shocks near the well-resolved Roche lobe (white oval). Right panel: Streamlines of gas superimposed on shaded density plot in Lubow et al's (1999) calculations. The flow splits into a part that returns to the disk, and a part that enters the Roche lobe, to eventually be accreted by a planet occupying the central sink cell.

freely without being washed out with time); measured amounts of that effect are small. Full MHD-calculations have shown that the viscous stress-tensor ansatz may give (for sufficiently long time averages) a reasonable approximation to the *mean* flow in a turbulent disk. The embedded planets are assumed to be point masses (using a softened potential). The disk influences their orbits through gravitational torques which cause orbital evolution. The planets may also accrete mass from the surrounding disk.

A typical result of such a viscous computation obtained with a hydrocode based on ZEUS second-order finite differences algorithm (Lubow et al. 1999) is displayed in Fig. 3 (left panel). Here, the planet with mass $M_p = 1 M_{Jup}$ and semi-major axis $a = 1$ is *not* allowed to move and remains on a fixed circular orbit, an approximation which is made in many simulations. Clearly seen are the major effects an embedded planet has on the structure of the protoplanetary accretion disk: spiral wave patterns with tightness of the spiral inversely proportional to the temperature (i.e. $h = H/r$). It is interesting an a bit disconcerting to realize how much difference we can see between second-order, viscous calculation and a higher-order, non-viscous flow simulated with PPM. J

Figure 4 presents gas flow near the planet in two different numerical methods. The PPM model on the left does not allow accretion, while the right-hand panel presents a model allowing a fast accretion of the gas. Despite this diverging assumptions about the gas accretion, flow and gas features are similar.

Assessing the accuracy and robustness of various numerical hydrodynamics algorithms and their implementations is a difficult task. We do not know analytical solutions to realistic multidimansional problems we face in disk-planet interaction. We cannot simulate a high-Reynolds number, supersonically rotating fluids in laboratory to make a direct comparison or test the codes against experimental data, which has always been important as a method of validation of hydrocodes. We hope to achieve a numerical convergence to a stable answer when we increase the number of resolution elements (cells) to our calculation, but the problems and algorithms are complicated enough for there to be no mathematical proof of convergence to a unique, let alone the correct solution. In other words, even if each code converges, they may still converge to different, wrong flows. Often there is no unique way to implement the method, or to set up a given calculation. There is usually a choice of coordinate system, making it rotating or nonrotating, in the disk-planet problem. There is always a choice of the length of timesteps. We would like to know which choice is 'best'. We also need to be able tell numerical instabilities or problems (sometimes called features) with the code from a genuine physical processes. One example of the latter could be whether or not a planet embedded in a disk is a giant vortex generator.

To address some of the above concerns and to make a first wide ranging comparison of codes, a comparison project was organized by (but not restricted to) the European Research and Training Network "Planet formation". As many as 17 groups participated and the results have been published by de Val Borro et al. (2006). The test problem was actually a small number of different 2-D calculations with prescribed initial conditions (smooth-density axisymmetric gas nebula between 0.4 and 2.5 times a, the planet-star distance serving as unit distance), a softened-gravity planet on a fixed circular orbit (softening radius ε in the formula for planet's potential $\psi(r) = -GM_p/\sqrt{r^2 + \varepsilon^2}$ equal to 0.6 times the disk scale height H), boundary treatment (non-standard, to avoid wave reflections, of escape of gas from the disk) and other details such as a prescription for a gradual introduction of a planet into the disk to avoid persistent transients. Two mass ratios were studied ($\mu = 10^{-3}$ and $\mu = 10^{-4}$) to approximate the masses of Jupiter and Neptune relative to the sun. Left completely open were the choices of a numerical method, the geometry of the grid (if any) and some minor computational details as required by the codes. In each case, the grid resolution around the planet was to be effective the same: square grids with about 64 cells per unit of radius.

Figure 5 presents the similarities and differences between 15 different numerical methods, the names and specifics of which are described in de Val Borro et al. (2006) and the URL address cited in the list of references, but can be ingnored here). Each panel is a polar coordinate plot with radius on the horizontal axis and the azimuthal angle in units of *pi* radians on the vertical. A tiny black dot at position (1,0) represent the planet of Jupiter mass ratio, at the time of 100 P (orbital periods) from its gradual introduction into the calculation over the first 3 periods. The color scale is identical in all figures, and covers the $\log \Sigma$ between -1.65 and +1 (in arbitrary units, equal to the initial density of the disk). Some important conclusions can be glimsed from the figure. all the numerical codes do not provide the same answers. While the gap width is fairly uniform, some simulations produce a deeper gap than others. With the exception of a particle method SPH in the lower-right corner all the codes find rarified gas blobs surrounding Lagrange triangular points L4 and L5 at positions $(1, \pm 1/3 \cdot \pi)$, and the charactristic spiral wakes extending into both the inner and outer disks from the vicinity of the planet. Some codes, especially of the second-order finite volume kind, produced from 1 to 3 vortices at the outer edge of the gap (seen as red blobs at radius $r = 1.25 - 1.5$). Some codes produce so strong vortices that the vortices are accompanied by non-linear, sheared spiral wakes, and visibly distort the edge. On the other hand, survival of large vortices is likely an artifact of a 2-D modeling, which does not extend to 3-D models.

Figure 6 compares 15 axisymmetrized profiles of density, $\Sigma(r)$, at time 100 P. Most profiles are impressively similar, apparently more so than the detailed and time-dependent views of the disk alone. Torques have also been evaluated and with some exceptions are within 50% of each other. One of the reasons for this relatively good agreement is, however, a rather large smoothing constant ε used. This type of a comparative research will be of much practical value for those who try to derive general truths from a limited number of numerical models.

2.3 Migration type III

The terminology 'type III migration' refers to migration for which an important driver is material flowing through the coorbital region. If type I denoted embedded migration, type II the open-gap migration, then type III could be thought of as partial-gap migration. However, neither its nature nor rate are in any sense an interpolation of type I and II migration. Rather, migration type III can be orders of magnitude faster than either of its cousins. For brevity, we shall often just call it fast migration.

Corotational flows

In a frame which corotates with the perturbation pattern such as a planet, an inviscid gas on orbits closer to a planet than approximately $2.5 r_L$ (2.5 Hill sphere radii) describes horseshoe and tadpole trajectories in motion trapped and librating with respect to the planet. In a local approximation similar to the Hill's problem of celestial mechanics, the streamlines have an analytical approximation shown in Figure 7 (left-hand panel). These streamlines approximate the more exact streamlines shown in the right panel of Fig. 4. To the lowest order, however, the flow and its density distribution remain point-symmetric about the planet and the time-average torque on the planet is zero even if the material is distributed asymmetrically at first. This phenomenon is known in literature as CR saturation. One important result that the approximate theory of flow gives us is the estimate of the half-width of the CR region, or the separatrix distance x_s. It is very weakly dependent on migration and in practice always very close to 2.5 r_L.

Symmetry breaking and the induced CR torque

This symmetry is, however, broken as soon as the planet starts to migrate. Initial motion or gradient of density in a disk remove saturation and give rise to a new mode of migration, in which the radial drift causes the gas flow to exert on the planet a finite

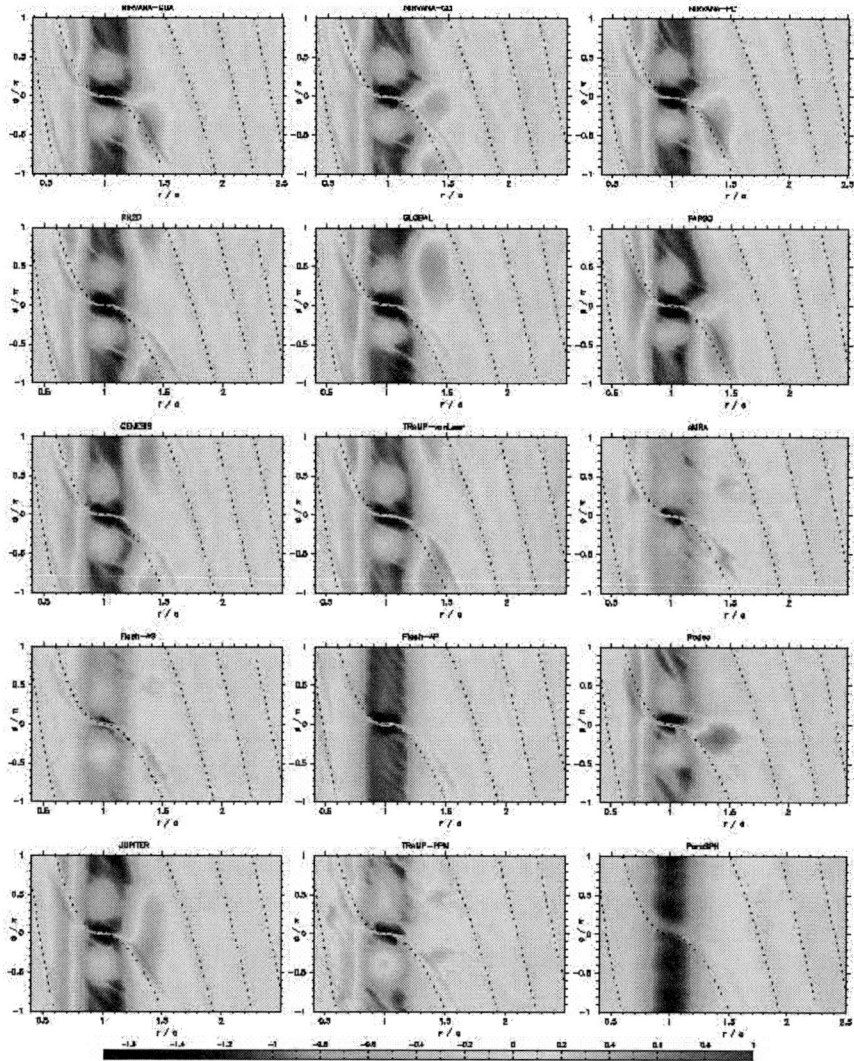

FIGURE 5. Comparison of surface density profiles in 15 numerical hydrodynamics codes (de Val Borro et al. 2006). See text for explanation.

induced torque which *supports* the migration. Whether or not this leads to a large enough positive feedback to support fast migration type III, depends on the density difference between the solid-line disk region and the dashed-line corotational regions in Fig. 7, as well as the speed of the asymmetry-causing migration. The right-hand panel of this figure shows a case of outward migration of the planet. The planet on a

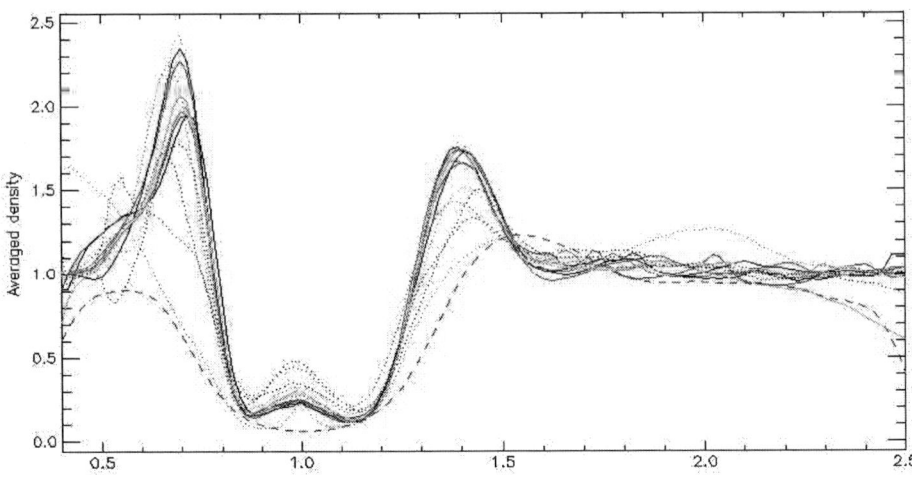

FIGURE 6. Comparison of axisymmetrized surface density profiles in 15 numerical hydrodynamics codes (from de Val Borro et al. 2006). See text for explanation.

circular orbit by definition does not have any motion in this corotating frame, but its motion in the inertial frame has an outward velocity component $\dot{a}$, so that the distant disk material in the comoving frame is endowed with the equal and opposite radial speed $-\dot{a}$. This causes the distant trajectories to bend into the shape of parabolae. Originally (at $\dot{a} = 0$) given by vertical lines following the shearing-sheet-like velocity distribution (streamlines pointing downward when $x > 0$ and upward at negative x), for finite $\dot{a}$ all of them have an equal amount of negative speed $(-\dot{a})$ added along the x axis. Identical symmetry breaking applies if the disk rather than the planet has radial motion due to viscosity, because the relative motion is still the same. What matters is how much mass crosses the CR region, exchanging angular momentum with the planet, from the outer to inner disk, and vice versa.

The sign of the effect is easy to deduce from the right panel of Fig. 7. Since the dashed-line librating region, slaved to the planet, is of lower density than the ambient disk, either due to initial conditions or the creation of a gap by a planet, or both, there is more material in front of the planet, i.e. in the direction of its motion ($y > 0$) than behind the planet. The excess material in front exerts a positive gravitational pull (torque) on the planet, thus providing positive feedback to the outward migration assumed at the outset.

On a historical and pedagogical note, it was rather difficult to visualize the possibility of type III migration purely theoretically, because all the theory used to be done in the inertial or uniformly rotating but not expanding frame of reference. It is also much easier to fix a planet on a circular or elliptic orbit than to let it evolve freely. The expectation that migration rates will be four orders of magnitude below the orbital speed certainly argued for fixing the orbit completely to avoid any drift due to numerical artifacts. In fact, when W. Kley and the present author collaborated in the mid-1990s on allowing the simulated stellar companions including planets to freely evolve in m, a, and

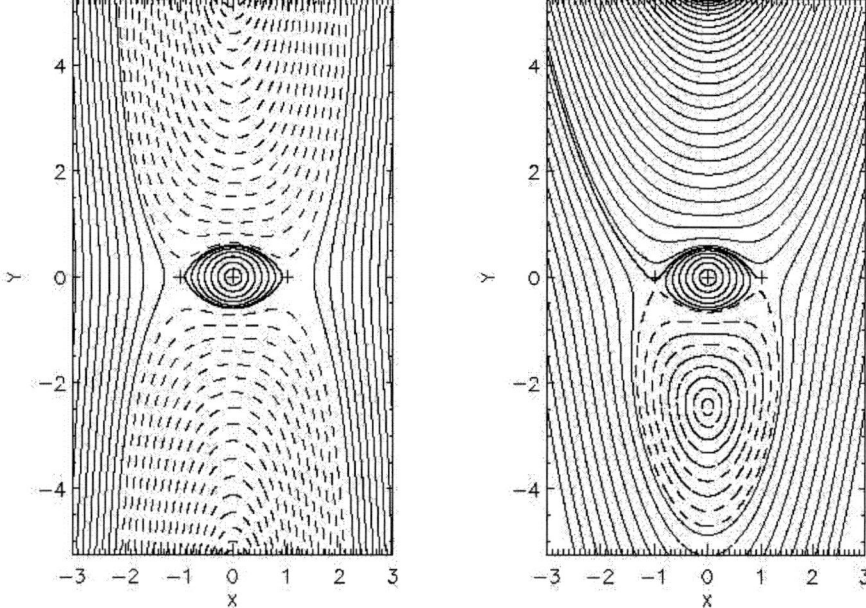

FIGURE 7. Fluid streamlines around a planet in local coordinates (x – radial coordinate, y – azimuthal; distances in Roche lobe (Hill) radii; the planet is located at $x = 0$ and $y = 0$.) Horseshoe region of closed streamlines defining corotational zone is shown by dashed lines. The left panel shows the symmetric situation in the case $\dot{a} = 0$, the right panel asymmetric trapped zone in libration w.r.t. planet for $\dot{a} = +\dot{a}_f$.

e (mass, semi-major axis and eccentricity), they stumbled upon an unexplained and quite abnormal inward migration rate of giant planets in their model, the characteristic time of which was about 50 P with very little dependance on planet's mass. The code was scrutinized briefly for programming bugs, nothing was found, and the project was abandoned. In the hindsight, it was most probably an unrecognized migration type III. Dismissing unexpected phenomena must be done judiciously. Other researchers also recognized migration type III only a posteriori. publications by other researchers, after being originally explained away as type II migration. It pays to remember that coincidence of migration rates or other results with prior expectations based on preconceived notions of what is the dominant physcal process, might be just that - a coincidence.

Masset and Papaloizou (2003) studied the limit of slow migration and concluded that the induced torque scales linearly with $\dot{a}$. They concluded that this situation leads to a possible runaway, an exponentially growing $\dot{a}$ in sufficiently massive disks. They proposed the name "runaway migration", which turned out slightly misleading. Artymowicz (2004) independently found a fast but not exponentially unstable migration. He later provided (Artymowicz 2006) a more general formula valid for torque in slow and fast migration in which the torque saturates at $\dot{a}$. In each particular disk a planet may have zero, one or two *stable migration speeds*, depending on the initial conditions of motion. For instance, inward migration might be as likely as outward migration. Here is the analysis in a nutshell.

The specific angular momentum that a fluid element near the separatrix takes from the planet when it switches from an orbit with radius $a - x_s$ to $a + x_s$ is $\Omega a x_s$ where x_s is the radial half width of the horseshoe region estemated to be $2.5 r_L$ (Artymowicz 2006, and Fig. 7).

Imagine the simplest possible situation, that the disk and the CR libration regions both have constant densities and that their difference is denoted by Σ_Δ. If $\dot{a} > 0$ but small, the CR region retains contact with the planet both in front and behind it. The orbital drift will, however, make the orbital radial jump (or U-turn) ahead of the planet (at larger y) smaller than the corresponding jump behind the planet, by a difference that we shall denote by Δ. Essentially, in our simple model the radial jump behind the planet, on the separatrix or the last librating orbit in the right panel of Fig. 7), will always be the same x_s, while the jump in front will diminish until it disappears altogether at a charcteristic value of $\dot{a}$ which we denote $\dot{a}_f$ and call fast migration speed. At that speed Δ reaches a maximum equal x_s and cannot grow further. The torque between the planet and disk saturates at the fast migration speed, which can be written as (Artymowicz 2006)

$$\dot{a}_f = \frac{3 x_s^2}{8 \pi a} \Omega_p, \tag{10}$$

while the synodic jump difference assumes the form

$$\Delta = x_s \left(1 - \sqrt{1 - |\dot{a}|/\dot{a}_f} \right), \tag{11}$$

valid for all $|\dot{a}| < \dot{a}_f$ (otherwise $\Delta = x_s$). If the planet does not migrate ($\dot{a} \to 0$) then Δ vanishes as required. The knowledge of Δ is equivalent to the knowledge of the disk-planet torque, and an induced migration rate that would result from that torque. These quantities will be proportional to Δ and to the surface density deficit Σ_Δ.

We use the nondimensional mass deficit parameter M_Δ defined as

$$M_\Delta = \frac{4 \pi a x_s \Sigma_\Delta}{\mu M}. \tag{12}$$

More specifically, M_Δ is the mass that a full CR annulus of width $2 x_s$ and area $4 \pi a x_s$ would have, if filled with density difference Σ_Δ, normalized to the planet's mass $\mu M = M_p$ (M being the stellar mass).

The final step of the calculation is to equate the assumed and the induced (resultant) migration speeds. As a result, we obtain an *equilibrium*, steady migration speed for every possible Σ_Δ. These results are plotted in our Figure 8 (left panel). Imagine increasing slowly the mass deficit. Up to the point when $M_\Delta = 1$, the planet has insufficient feedback from the disk to migrate rapidly, and since the CR torques were the only ones taken into acount, the planet has zero migration speed.

We can improve our simple theory by adding torques due to differential LRs, the same ones responsible for migration type I or II. Then the inward/outward summetry

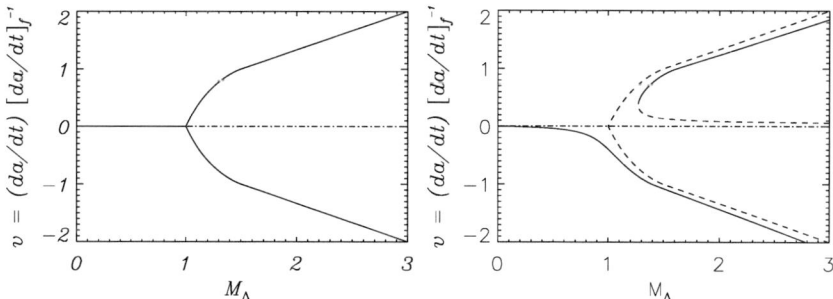

FIGURE 8. Bifurcation diagrams in a simple theory accounting for CR torques only (left panel), and a theory with the LR contributions added (right panel). The bifurcation to fast migration occurs at $M_\Delta = 1$ to 1.3.

is broken and the bifurcation diagram take the shape shown in the right panel of Fig. 8. We see that the abrupt loss of stability by the non-migrating equilibrium is replaced by a more gradual transition from type I/II migration for $M_\Delta < 1$ to the full speed of type III migration, plus the contribution from LR torques, provided that the migration starward. The outward migration, on the other hand, must undergo an abrupt jump from fast to slow migration when approaching the point $M_\Delta \approx 1.3$ from the right-hand-side. The fast migration speed $\dot{a}_f$ is the characteristic speed of incipient migration type III when the disk conditions are marginally supportive of it. Higher speeds can be achieved for more massive disks or more empty corotational regions. What are these quantities in practice? A quick calculation tells us that in order to support fast migration of a Jupiter, the disk should be somewhat more massive than a Minimum Mass Solar Nebula. Saturn should be able to migrate easily in just twice the minimum nebula. The speed $\dot{a}_f$ in the case of Jupiter is capable of changing the position of a planet by a factor of 2 in only 44 orbital periods! However unrealistic such a short time might appear, it is very well confirmed by direct numerical simulations at high resolution. Peplinski and Artymowicz (2006) substituted the time-dependent mass deficit parameter measured in the course of the simulation of a Jupiter in a massive solar nebula (4 times the MMSN). The evolution traced approximately the shape of a bifurcation diagram. The planet traveled outward at a speed higher than $\dot{a}_f$, reached the vicinity of the numerical grid boundary, lost its underdense libration region, and started migrating inward, again obeying the equilibrium speed at each radius, to within 25 percent accuracy. A snapshot from one of the PPM calculations of a large-scale migration is shown in Figure 9.

Consequences for planet formation

Fast migration, for the same disk profile and planet mass, can be directed either outwards or inwards, depending on the initial conditions. This type of planetary migration is found to depend on its migration history, the "memory" of this history being stored in the way the horseshoe region is populated, i.e. in the preparation of the coorbital mass deficit. Note that owing to the strong variation of the drift rate, the horseshoe streamlines

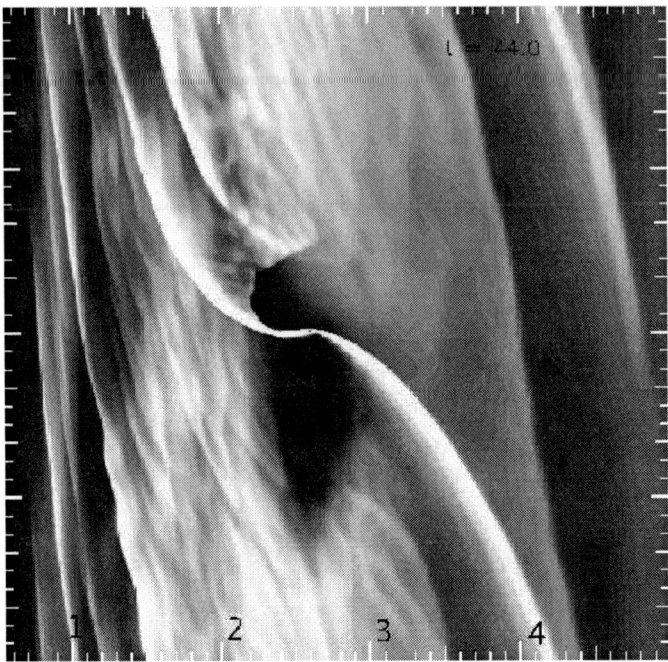

FIGURE 9. Density of gas in a PPM simulation using one variable-resolution mesh. Jupiter-mass planet rapidly migrates in a disk 2.5 times more massive than the Minimum Mass Solar Nebula (Artymowicz 2006). Vertical axis covers the full azimuthal angle, the horizontal is radius in units of initial star-planet distance. After being placed on a positive density gradient, the planet migrated outwards by a factor of 2.6 in only 44 orbits. A trapped coorbital region of low density (dark shade) is clearly visible below the planet (barely visible itself in this plot at radius 2.6). Migration speed corresponds to $M_\Delta \approx 3$.

are not exactly closed, so that the coorbital mass deficit can be lost and the runaway can stall. This has been observed in some numerical simulations, whereas others show sustained fast migration episodes for Saturn or Jovian mass planets that can vary the semi-major axis by large factors in less than 100 orbits (e.g., see Figure 9). To date, it is still unclear whether migration type III can in principle continue indefinitely (given that conditions in disk support it all the way in or out). Because of the need to take account of complex coorbital flows in a partially gap forming regime close to the planet, the problem of type III migration is very numerically challenging and therefore issues of adequate numerical algorithms, resolution and convergence remain outstanding. We cannot dwell here on the details of such calculations; they are discussed by Peplinski and Artymowicz (2006) and are the subject of active research by others.

The Minimum Mass Solar Nebula (MMSN) is not massive enough to allow superjovian planets to migrate fast. On the other hand, Saturn will migrate fast (in type III mode) in disks a few times the MMSN. This may be related to the unexplained fact that most of the extrasolar planets known as "hot Jupiters", with a semi-major axis $a < 0.06$ AU, happen to have sub-Jovian masses. The detailed scenarios accounting for the actual masses seen in radial velocity surveys need to be constructed, the challenge there is to study in detail the mass growth rate of a giant planet, based on internal restructuring and the supply of ample gas.

Migration type III has one big advantage over the standard two of its predecessors: Type I and type II motions are difficult to stop, which we discussed above at some length to show why this issue is considered a central difficulty of the current dynamical theory of planet formation. In contrast, type III motion in a partially open gap (in front or behind the planet) is extremely rapid but very fragile at the same time: any significant gradient of disk density will arrest it, be it due to varying efficiency of accretion (Shakhura-Sunyayev α), dead zones preventing midplane accretion, photoevaporation of disk parts by external ultraviolet flux, flybys of stars in the Orion-type dense stellar cluster, or other causes. Saving migrating planetary cores may not be difficult after all!

3. Transitional and Beta Pictoris-type disks: The origin of structure.

So many important processes in dusty disks aroud newly formed stars depend on the radiation pressure exerten by the star on dust and gas that it is worth for us to totally focus here on two main subjects: What drives the evolution of the disks, and why do the new observations by HST and ground-based telescopes show rich non-trivial structure, from blobs and lopsided appearance to pieces of spiral arms not unlike those we study numerically around protoplanets. Figure 10 is a roadmap to physical processes and their basic outcomes in circumstellar disks. Since axisymmetric ring formation has been discussed many times in the past, we shall almost exlusively concentrate on the possibility of gas-dust-radiation coupling to create a non-axisymmeteric structure, possibly confusing a our efforts to discover planets by their shepherding of dust.

3.1 Interactions of planetary disks with interstellar dust

At the upper-right corner of our diagram there is a spot succinctly stating that radiation pressure repels ISM dust grains, and hence the evolution of the disks is their internal matter, not a result of outside influences on Vega-type objects. Lissauer & Griffith (1989) proposed that sandblasting by ISM dust during rapid passages through atomic clouds depletes circumstellar disks; β Pic which happens to have a small velocity with respect to the clouds would be spared the sandblasting. Whitmire et al. (1992) proposed that all the nearby Vega-type stars have recently passed through molecular cloud and were sandblasted, which generated the finer dust from meteoroids. Artymowicz and Clampin (1997) revisited the issue and found that the ISM neither creates nor destroys the disks around A-type stars, mainly because the ISM grains are repelled by radiation pressure; the 'internal sandblasting' dominates over ISM sandblasting out to radii of order 400 AU, at which ISM may cause some one-sided disk asymmetries. something that we need to keep in mind right now that the imaging is revealing new objects and features.

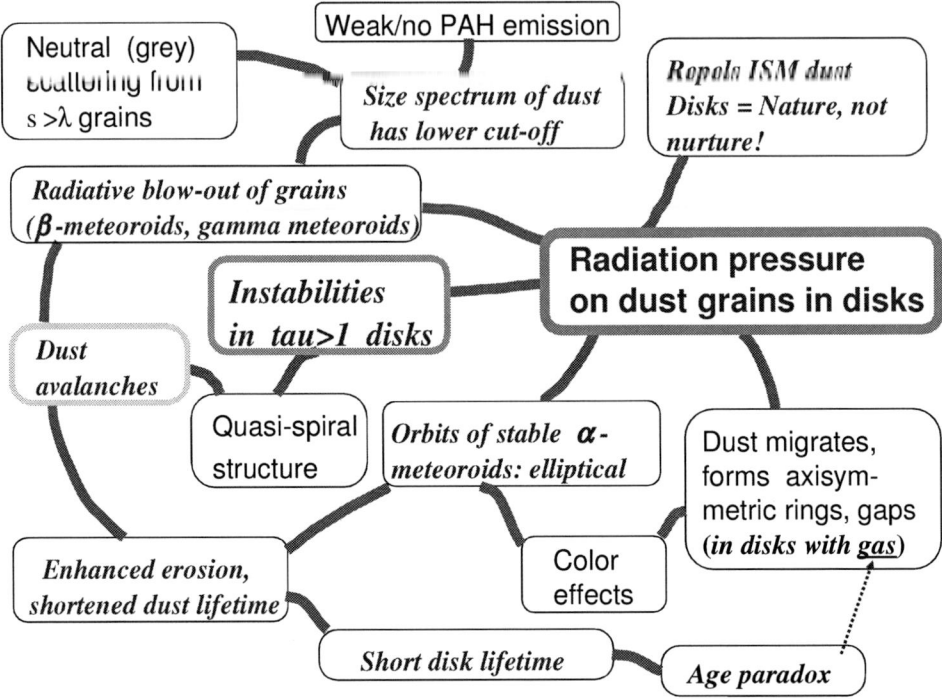

FIGURE 10. The many roles of radiation pressure in young planetary systems. Processes are written in a straight font, directly observable featured are in italics.

3.2 Size spectrum has a lower cut-off or knee

Radiation pressure equaling one-half the stellar gravity ($\beta = 0.5$) suffices for ejecting grains from a parent circular orbit to infinity, unless there is sufficient gas to counteract a rapid escape of small grains. The so-called β-meteoroids, dust below the appropriate radius s_β, for which $\beta = 0.5$, escapes. (Particles on bound orbits are sometimes called α-meteoroids.) Peak values of β much larger than unity are actually found around the known Vega stars, reaching several dozen in the case of Vega itself. In case of β Pic, common materials such as magnesium-rich silicate forsterite ($Mg_{0.95}Fe_{0.05}SiO_3$) and also water ice particles reach a peak of $\beta \sim 2-6$ for particle radius $p = 0.1 - 0.2\mu m$.

As predicted, in β Pic there is a good observational evidence that particles below 2 μm radius are indeed rare (Artymowicz 1997). This is also true of very small Polycyclic Hydrocarbons (PAH particles). The effects of radiation are quite similar in different systems (e.g., Artymowicz and Clampin 1997). Luminosity differences simply modify the blow-out grain radius but the knee is always there. However, the cut-off must be where it is in β Pic or at larger sizes in order for the scattering not to introduce noticeable reddning or blueing with respect to the starlight (particles larger than the wavelength of the visible photons are required). Interestingly, new observations of β Pic by Golimowski et al. (2006) do show for the first time a somewhat red scattered radiation at large distances from the star (> 300 AU) while a sister disk of AU Microscopii does show an opposite effect of strongly blue scattering (it is 60% brighter at B than I, according to Krist et al. (2005). Perhaps the difference lies in the lower radiative blowout size of grains around a weaker source of AU Mic. HR 4796A is a narrow disk, and does not have color effects (Clampin et al. 2003).

3.3 Collisional dynamics and avalanches of dust in disks

Estimates show the possibility of the so-called dust avalanches (Artymowicz 1996) in HR4796A and, in fact, any disk with similar dimensions and dustiness ($f_d = 5 \times 10^{-3}$ in HR 4796A). The concept of an avalanche or, in other words, a chain reaction of outflowing debris is illustrated in Fig. 3. Three kinds of particles are distinguished in the figure. In addition to α and β particles, we define the γ-meteoroids as such (very small) grains, whose dynamics is strongly affected by gas drag. Slowed down in their outflow by the drag force, γ-meteoroids do not contribute significantly to dust processing, and we ignore them for a moment (cf., however, the next subsection).

Mutual collisions of stable disk particles ($\alpha + \alpha$) and the bombardment of disk grains by outflowing β-meteoroids ($\alpha + \beta$) contribute to the creation of fresh β-meteoroids, subsequently accelerated by radiation pressure force. On the average, $N+M$ fresh β-meteoroids per collision are produced (N from cratering/erosion and M from catastrophic disruption). Since the probability for a given β particle to strike a disk grain while crossing the disk annulus with optical thickness $d\tau$ is roughly equal to $d\tau$, a toy model of the growth of an avalanche can be constructed by neglecting, among others, the need for a grain to accelerate over a finite radial distance before collisions can become strongly erosive/disruptive. The growth equation for the number n of particles in the avalanche has the form $dn = (N+M)n\,d\tau$. The solutions of the toy model are thus exponentially growing avalanches of the form $n(\tau) = n_0 \exp[\int_0^\tau (N+M)\,d\tau] = \exp[\tau(N+M)]$, with n_0 an arbitrary constant. The optical thickness of the disk along its midplane, τ, is approximately its dustiness factor f_d divided by flattening ratio $z/r \sim 0.1$. Therefore, a very large amplification factor of an avalanche of order $\exp 30 \approx 10^{13}$ may be obtained if $(N+M)f_d \sim 30(z/r) \sim 3$.

From the physics of grain collision and more detailed models of a disk at radii $r \sim 100$ AU it follows that $N+M \sim 10^2 - 10^3$ (or $10^{2.5\pm0.5}$). Therefore, a plausible *upper limit on the dustiness of gas-free disks* exists in this model: $f_d < 3/(M+N) \sim 10^{-2\pm0.5}$. This value is 4 times larger than that in β Pic but only 2 times larger than that in HR 4796A. Hypothetical gas-free disks above that limit would tend to self-destruct on exponentially short time scales unless and until they reduce their dustiness down to the limiting value. The details of the evolution are yet to be determined.

3.4 Inferring the presence of gas (Age paradox)

The dust grinding rate of dust which, in a steady-state collisional cacade, is also the mass loss rate from the largest parent bodies (planetesimals), can be evaluated in detailed modeling of a disk. Dividing the expected mass of the rocks in a typical protoplanetary disk (e.g., $\sim 120 M_\oplus$ estimated by Artymowicz 1997) by that rate yields the estimated half-life timescale of the whole disk (as opposed to the lifetime of the currently observed dust, which may be a thousand times shorter). Clearly, the disk's half-life should be longer than its age. But this is precisely the trouble with HR 4796A. We obtained a preliminary estimate of 3 Myr disk self-destruction time. HR 4796A and its disk are 8 ± 3 Myr old.

This paradox can be resolved if we relax one or more of the model assumptions. The most natural resolution is that there is an unobserved gas component with total mass at least ~ 4 times exceeding the dust mass, i.e. a fraction of Earth mass. This mass would be much smaller than the upper limit of 7 $M_\oplus$ of gas, obtained from observations in molecular emission lines. Notice that the easiest method of direct detection of gas, via its absorption lines, may not be feasible in HR 4796A because of the viewing geometry with line of sight inclined by at least 1/3 of radian, an angle several times larger than the opening angle $z/r \sim 1/10$ of a disk. Theory can thus be a valuable tool for predicting the presence of a hard-to-see gas component.

3.5 Vega-type system classes

The theoretical limit on the area of dust in Vega-type disks should modify the statistics of the observed fractional IR luminosity f_d. Artymowicz (1996) considered the pre-ISO statistics of the Vega stars and obtained a bimodal histogram of f_d. While there were many more examples (per $\log f_d$ bin) of disks with $f_d < 10^{-3}$ and $f_d > 10^{-2}$, the only two systems in the $10^{-3} - 10^{-2}$ bin were β Pic and HR 4796A. This provides a strong support for the division of Vega-type systems into "gas-poor" and "gas-rich" based on a very simple and readily available diagnostic (f_d). It would be very interesting to revisit the observed statistics with a fuller sample of disks and proper account of selection effects, if any[4]. Decin et al. (2003) recently observed a large sample of Vega-type stars with the ISOPHOT detector onboard ISO satellite, and studied the age dependence of the Vega phenomenon. After correcting some poorly known ages of stars, they've found little support for an otherwise popular idea that there should be a law of decline of the amount of orbiting dust in a planetary system seen as a power-law of dustiness vs. age. A power-law lower envelope has been found, a large spread of systems above it, but also a constant demarkation line of dustiness of order that of β Pictoris, a line that normal systmes respect and do not exceed corresponding to 10^3! According to our theory, this maybe simply a limit enforced by avalanches.

---

[4] Notice that there is no obvious selection against discovering systems with, say, $f_d = 0.03$, as opposed to $f = 0.003$ in sky surveys done in the past.

3.6 Gas-related effects in disks

The gas can have many observable consequences. For example in HR 4796A it could slow down the otherwise rapid escape of very small grains (γ-meteoroids). By the virtue of their slowness, γ-meteoroids might contribute significantly to the total area and observability of such fine dust. More generally, most gas-rich systems should be able to retain observable fraction of very small and transiently heated grains (which influences their light reprocessing and spectra) and/or PAH (polycyclic aromatic hydrocarbons). A correlation of PAH/small grain features with f_d is, indeed, present but awaits full analysis and description. Gas will also have a moderating effect on the overall dust processing rate in disks. If gas dynamics is truly important there, the HR 4796A disk may be a very promising laboratory for the study of distinctive nonlinear spiral density waves and resonantly truncated disk edges, hopefully indicating the position and orbit of planet(s). In contrast to this situation, a gas-poor disk like β Pic will not be able to maintain a sharp edge with or without planets. The dust will in general be trapped only temporarily at the outer Lindblad resonances in the circumbinary disk (binary=star+planet). A gradual gap, washed out by large velocity dispersion in disk, might then appear. Sharpness of profiles and disk features is a hallmark of the presence of gas.

Dust can migrate in disks both toward and away from the star, sometimes quite rapidly. The usual direction is inward, for the following reasons. In the solar nebula, there is a partial cancellation of the stellar gravity by the radial gradient of gas pressure, giving rise to a small decrease of orbital speed with respect to the Keplerian value $v_K = sqrt{GM/r}$; we can denote it by $\eta = \Delta v/v_K \approx 0.005$. This causes an inward migration of solids due to the headwind $w = v_K \eta$ experienced by particles, and the associated loss of angular momentum at a speed proportional to w. The proportionality constant for large particles increases with decreasing size, for they are then better coupled to the gas (have larger area to mass ratio) while still orbiting along weakly perturbed Keplerian ellipses or circles. On the other hand, very small dust grains are coupled so well via strong gas drag force that they are almost frozen into the gas and corotate with it (at a sub-Keplerian speed $v_K - w$). This causes a small, size-independent net radial acceleration (gravity being slightly larger than centrifugal force), balanced by the radial drag component. In this regime, migration speed increases linearly with the particle size because of the linearly decreasing drag force. Large-scale migration of solids in turbulent gas disks was recently modeled by Stepinski and Valageas (1997). The maximum migration speed at intermediate particle sizes, for which the stopping time (velocity divided by gas drag deceleration) is equal to the dynamical time Ω^{-1}. Migration can remove such dust from a solar nebula.

In optically thin disks dust is subject to the combined gas drag and radiation pressure forces, which modifies the migration speed to $\dot{r} \sim (\beta/2 - \eta)v_K$, where $\beta < 1/2$ is the radiation to gravity ratio, and the coefficient of proportionality is a function of grain stopping time. For example, a 25 μm radius grain in HR 4796A disk has $\beta \approx 0.2$ and has an average circulation velocity $v_\phi = \sqrt{GM(1-\beta)/r} \approx (1-\beta/2)v_K$. The orbital motion of that grain is slower than that of the gas, thus the particle feels the push of a backwind, gains angular momentum, and spirals outwards. In some cases outflow speed may be independent of particle size (over a certain size range), because the dust mobility of small (well-coupled) grains increases, while the radiation pressure drops with the grain size (Takeuchi and Artymowicz 2001). Poynting-Robertson drag can be included in the analysis but it is never dominant except in very low-density disks, e.g., in our Solar System.

3.7. HD 141569: Planets or dust mimicry?

HD 141569, a system shown in the left-hand side of Fig.2 is a quiescent Herbig-type star (type B9.5Ve) surrounded by a light-scattering (and IR emitting) disk (inclination 40 degrees away from edge-on). HD 141569 has a double-peaked Hα emission indicating a rotating gas disk close to the star, as well as gaseous CO detected at radius of order 90 AU. Details of its structure were imaged for the first time with NICMOS/HST at 1.1 μm (Weinberger et al. 1999) and at 1.6 μm (Augereau et al. 1999). The crossed dark radial stripes are artifacts of the observation method, but the division of the disk into an inner main part and an outer ring is intrinsic to the object, although over-exaggerated by grayscale map. Analysis of the 1.1 μm observations yielded the radial profile of the vertical optical thickness $\tau(r)$ times the unknown albedo, which we reproduce in Fig. 4. The profile has a moderate dip at $r = 250$ AU, interpreted by Weiberger et al. as a sign of a planet residing in the disk at that radius. If this feature is indeed due to a planet, its eccentricity must be small (which requires formation in situ), and a moderate mass (on the order of Neptune's mass; this follows from gap opening criteria). An obvious difficulty, however, arises in the formation theory because of the very large distance from the star. In the Solar System, the Kuiper belt region is 5 times closer and yet had insufficient mass (surface density) to form planets. Time needed to assemble planets at 250 AU also strongly disfavors *in situ* formation. Outward migration to this large radius remains an unlikely possibility. In fact, the gap is not deep enough to stop a predicted rapid inward migration type I (Ward 1997).

In this and similar cases one should avoid postulating planets indiscriminately to account for every morphological feature of the disk, unless supported by independent evidence. In HD 141569 other plausible explanations of the disk morphology exist, which naturally explain the puzzling differences in the appearance of the disk at the two wavelengths observed (Augereau et al. 1999 do not detect at 1.6 μm the disk part inside $r = 180$ AU, prominent at 1.1 μm).

If the disk is nearly optically thick in radial direction, shadowing of outer disk parts by inner disk parts in conjunction with a variable geometrical disk thickness might play a role, especially in the scattered light images like the NICMOS ones. At present we have no direct information on either vertical geometry or radial optical depth in this disk. Secondly, a variety of general scenarios can be constructed in which dust either originates or accumulates in a certain place in a disk, depending on dust grain size. We consider the dust migration under the combined gas drag and radiation pressure forces (Takeuchi and Artymowicz 2001) a much simpler explanation overall. If the disk is, as in the case of HD 141569A, nonaxisymmetric, a nonaxisymmeric initial distribution of dust, combined with a method of multiplying the visible area of dust, might be of help.

Grigorieva et al. (2006) produced for the first time a comprehensive model of dust avalanche traced from the beginning in a presumed planetesimal-planetesimal collision, through the time of escape and exponential growth, to the eventual decline. Collisional avalanches are expected to be triggered by a localized disruptive event, such as the collisional breakup of a large cometary or planetesimal-like object. A fraction of the dust then produced is driven out by radiation pressure on highly eccentric or even unbound orbits. These grains moving away from the star with significant radial velocities can break-up or microcrater other particles further out in the disk, creating in turn even more small particles propagating outwards and colliding with other grains. Should this collisional chain reaction be efficient enough, then a significant multiplication in the number of dust grains could be achieved. In this case, the consequences of a single shattering event in terms of induced dust production could strongly exceed that of the sole initially released dust population, possibly too small to be detected in the absence of avalanches. The outwards porpagation of the dusty grains might induce asymeric features in the disk.

The novelty in this calculation is the full treatment of size distribution and mutual collisions. A concept of superparticles is used, these are entities following the same trajectory in space and containing a large number of similarly sized particles. During colisions, superparticles proliferate beyond the capability of a program to trace all of them, therefore regular pruning or re-sorting of superparticles done so as to preserve integrals of motion, is done to keep the total number of superparticles to about 10^5 to 10^6. Amplification factors of 10^3 are routinely achieved in the system just a few times more dusty than β Pic. This would guarantee visibility of an avalanche coming from a collision of two large planetesimals. As to β Pic itself, however, typical parameters regarding the materials strength of dust grains lead to only small amplifications by a factor of 10 to 100, and so for visibility against the backdrop of a large disk would require initial cloud of dust that could only be created in a protoplanet-protoplanet collision, which makes this mechnism very unlikely.

3.8. Instabilities in $\tau > 1$ disks

Finally, disks made of dust and gas can under the right conditions develop their own spiral wavelets and even spectacular spiral arms somewhat like the spiral galactic arms. Radiation pressure acting on an overdense region in a disk (which could be a spiral arm, for instance) has the ability to compress it, if the disk has noticeable optical thickness. Then the front of the region is being pushed the most, and the back of the region is in a partial shadow of its own making. Relative to the center of the region, radiation causes a compression, which acts in complete formal anallogy to self-gravity. Therefore, a criterion can be developed along the lines of the derivation of the Safronov-Toomre gravitational instability of a disk. This model has an analytical linear solution (Artymowicz, 2006), however, it must now be studied numerically in a fully nonlinear regime. In conclusion, there are several good explanations for nonaxisymmertic features in dusty circumstellar disks in addition to the perhaps most tantalizing one, which involves hypothetical exoplanets. All of them will nedd to be scrutinized before it will become clear which process is responsible for which particlar morphology of a disk.

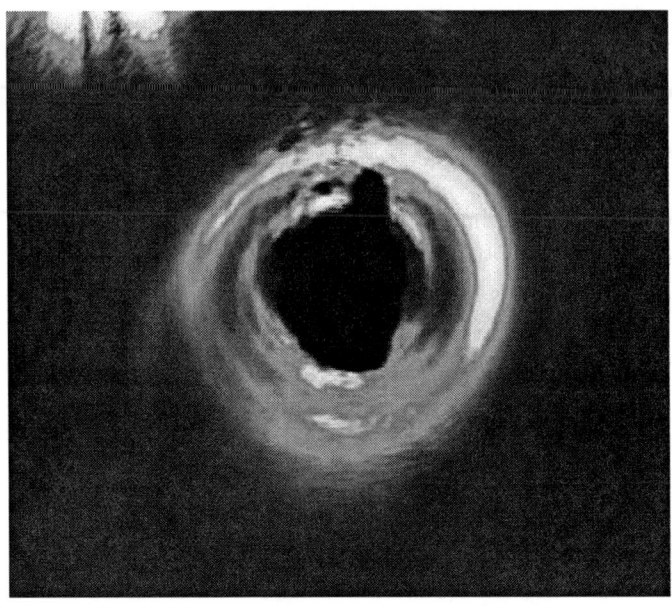

FIGURE 11. HD141569A seen in the near-IR light by HST (Clampin et al. 2001)

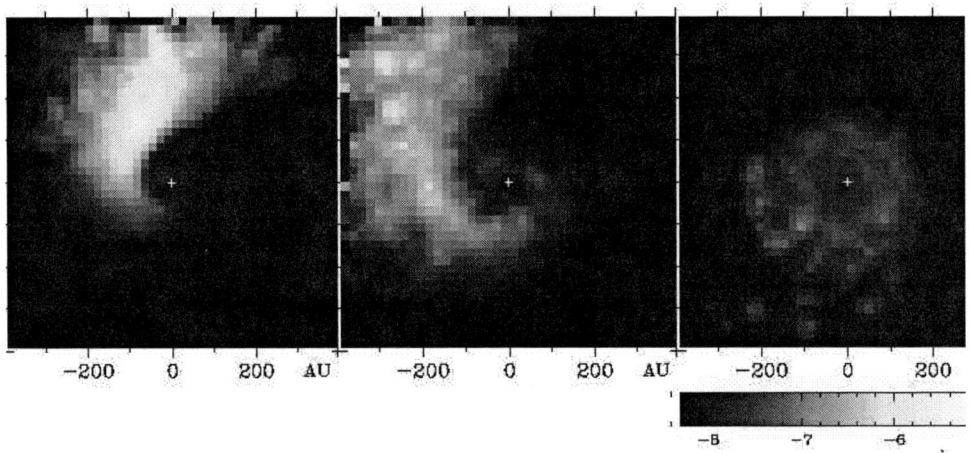

FIGURE 12. Three snapshots of a developing dust avalanche, growing in a β Pictoris-like disk. Disk particles are not shown. Brightness scale is logarithmic. (Grigorieva et al. 2006).

4. Conclusions

At the close of the previous millenium, we were fortunate to discover numerous planetary systems. Extrasolar planetary systems are fairly common, accompanying 10 to 20%

of all stars. These numbers will further climb in the future, as observational capability to see both planets and their accompanying disks increases. Uncharted terrain of super-Earths and Neptunes lies ahead in the radial velocity surveys. Giant planets, of which we seem to know already 188, are not arranged about their suns as ours are around the sun - and we need to know why.

Currently the most serious challenge in observations is to discover and study Earth-like planets, to understand how prevalent potentially life-supporting planets are. In theory of formation, there are likewise broad challenges: to understand how and why protoplanets migrate but do not die en masse during their extreme youth. Migration type III is but the newest item in our arsenal to confront the riddles of nature. It is a striking mechanism, which only very recently gained the support of the majority of dynamicists. Despite being so quick and so brief that we won't probably actually see it occurring, rapid migration has an interesting future.

Finally, the study of the origin of nonaxisymmetric structures in disks will be time well spent, if we are going in the future to go hunting for planets in the shifting sands of dusty disks. If we know enough, we might even succeed!

Acknowledgments

Contributions from many co-authors of the cited papers are incorporated in this overview. This work was supported by the NSERC research grant 5810-2005-312219. The author acknowledges the angelic patience and help from the editors of this volume. Some of the results reported here were obtained with a PPM hydrocode SVH partly based on the VH-1 program, genrously made public by J. Blondin.

REFERENCES

. Ardila, D. R., Lubow, S. H., Golimowski, D. A., Krist J. E. et al. 2005, ApJ, 627, 986
. Artymowicz P. 1993a, ApJ, 419, 155
. Artymowicz, P. 1993b, ApJ, 419, 166
. Artymowicz P. 2004, Astr. Soc. Pacific series, vol. 324, 39
. Artymowicz P. 1996, in Role of Dust in the Formation of Stars. Eds. HU Käufl & R Siebenmorgen (Berlin: Springer), 137
. Artymowicz, P. 1997, Ann. Rev. Earth Pl. Sci., 25, 175
. Artymowicz, P., Clampin, M. 1997. ApJ, 490, 863
. Artymowicz P., and Peplinski, A. 2006, in preparation
. Augereau, J. C., Lagrange, A. M., Mouillet, D., Ménard, F. 1999, A&A, 350, L51
. Augereau, J. C.; Lagrange, A. M.; Mouillet, D.; Papaloizou, J. C. B.; Grorod, P. A. 1999, A&A, 348, 557
. Aumann, H. H., Gillett, F. C., Beichman, C. A. et al. 1984, ApJ, 278, L23
. Backman D. E., Paresce F., eds. 1993. In Levy et al. (1993), p. 1253
. Boss A. 2000, ApJ, 536, L101
. Bryden G., Chen X., Lin D. N. C., Nelson R. P., and Papaloizou J. C. B. 1999, ApJ, 514, 344
. Charbonneau, D., Brown, T., Noyes R., Gilliland R. 2001, ApJ, 568, 377
. Charbonneau, D., Brown, T., Burrows, A., Laughlin, G. 2006, in Protostars and Planets V (Reipurth et al. 2006)
. Clampin, M., Krist, J. E., Golimowski, D. A., Ardila, D. R. et al. 2003, AJ, 126, 385
. Crida A., Morbidelli A., and Masset F. S. 2006, Icarus, in press; astro-ph/0511082

- D'Angelo G., Bate M., and Lubow S. 2005, MNRAS, 358, 316
- D'Angelo G., Henning T., and Kley W. 2003a, ApJ, 599, 548
- D'Angelo G., Kley W., and Henning T. 2003b, ApJ, 586, 540
- Decin, G., Dominik, C., Waters, L.B.F.M., Waelkens, C. 2003, 598, 636
- de Val Borro M., Edgar, R., Artymowicz, P., Ciecielag, P., Cresswell, P., et al. 2006, MNRAS, in print; cf. also http://www.astro.su.se/groups/planets/comparison/index.htm
- Dominik, C., Laureijs, R. J.; Jourdain de Muizon, M.; Habing, H. J. 1998, A&A, 329, L53
- Goldreich P., and Tremaine S. 1979, ApJ, 233, 857
- Goldreich, P., and Tremaine, S. 1980, ApJ, 241, 425
- Golimowski, D.,A., Ardila, D. R., Clampin, M., Krist, J. E., et al. 2006, ApJ, in print
- Grigorieva, A., Artymowicz, P., and Thebault, P. 2006, A&A, in print
- Heap, S. R., Linder, D. J., Lanz. T. M., Woodgate, B., Cornett, R., Hubeny, I., and Maran, S. P. 2000, ApJ, 539, 435
- Jang-Condell H., Sasselov D. D. 2005, ApJ, 619, 1123
- Krist, J. E., Ardila, D. R., Golimowski, D. A.; Clampin, M. et al. 2005, AJ, 129, 1008
- Lagrange A M., Backman, D., Artymowicz, P. 2000, in Mannings et al. (2000), p. 639
- Laughlin, G., Bodenheimer, P. 1994, ApJ, 436, 335
- Lin D. N. C. and Papaloizou J. C. B. 1986, ApJ, 309, 846
- Lin D. N. C. and Papaloizou J. C. B. 1993, in Protostars and Planets III, E. H. Levy and J. I. Lunine (Eds.), Univ. of Arizona, Tucson, p.749
- Lin D. N. C., Papaloizou J. C. B., Terquem C., Bryden G., and Ida S. 2000, in Mannings et al. (2000), p. 1111
- ubow S. H., Seibert M., and Artymowicz P. 1999, ApJ, 526, 1001
- Lissauer J.J. 1993. Ann. Rev. A&A, 31, 129
- Lissauer J.J., Griffith CA. 1989, ApJ, 340, 468
- Lubow, S. H., Seibert, M., Artymowicz, P. 1999, ApJ, 526, 1001
- Mannings, V., Boss A., Russell, S. (Eds.) 2000, Protostars and Planets IV, Tuscon: Univ. Arizona Press
- Marcy G. W., Butler R. P. 1998, Ann. Rev. A&A, 36, 57
- Mayor M., Queloz D. 1995. Nature, 378, 355
- Menou K. and Goodman J. 2004, ApJ, 606, 520
- Nelson A. F. and Benz W. 2003, ApJ, 589, 578
- Nelson R., and Papaloizou J.C.B. 2004, MNRAS, 350, 849
- Papaloizou J. C. B. and Larwood J. D. 2000, MNRAS, 315, 823
- Papaloizou J.C.B., Nelson, R. P., Kley, W., Masset, F. S., and Artymowicz, P. 2006, in Protostars and Planets V (Reipurth et al. 2006); astro-ph/0603196
- Papaloizou J.C.B., and Terquem, C. 2006, Rept. Prog. Phys. 69, 119
- Peplinski, A., and Artymowicz, P. 2006, in prep.
- Pierens A. and Huré J. M. 2005, A&A, 433, L37
- Rafikov R. 2005, ApJ, 621, L69
- Reipurth, Jewitt B. D., and Keil K. (Eds.) 2006, Protostars and Planets V, University of Arizona Press, Tucson; in print
- Schneider, G., Becklin, E., Smith, B. A., Weinberger A., et al. 2000, AJ, 121, 525
- Schneider, J., 2006, Extrasolar Planet Encyclopaedia on-line database at http://exoplanet.eu
- Smith B. A., Terrile R. J. 1984, Science, 226, 1421
- Stepinski, T., Valageas, P., 1997. A&A, 319, 1007
- Tanaka H., Takeuchi T., and Ward W. R. 2002, ApJ, 565, 1257
- Takeuchi T., and Artymowicz, P. 2001, ApJ, 557, 990
- Terquem C. 2003, MNRAS, 341, 1157
- Trilling, D., Brown, R. H. 1998, Nature, 395, 775
- Vidar-Madjar, A., Lecavelier des Etangs, A. and Ferlet, R. 1998, Pl. Sp. Sci., 46, 629
- Ward, W. R. 1986, Icarus, 67, 164
- Ward, W. R. 1997, ApJ, 482, 211
- Weinberger A. J. et al. 1999, ApJ, 525, L53
- Whitmire D.P., Matese J.J., Whitman P.G. 1992, ApJ, 388, 190
- Wolszczan, A., Frail D. A. 1992, Nature, 355, 145

CHAPTER 2

Globular Clusters
Raffaele G. Gratton

GLOBULAR CLUSTERS

Raffaele G. Gratton

INAF - Osservatorio Astronomico di Padova
Vicolo dell'Osservatorio, 5, 35142 Padova, Italy

Abstract.
Globular Clusters are among the most interesting objects in our own Galaxy. They have played a major role in our understanding of stellar evolution and dynamics of stellar systems in past decades. In the last few years, it is becoming clear that they are not so simple as originally thought. Their chemical evolution, although not as complex as that of a galaxy, is however not negligible. In globular clusters it seems possible to observe peculiar chemical abundances, due to the contribution to nucleosynthesis of groups of stars that are not usually well separated from the general enrichment of the interstellar medium in galaxies. This is stimulating new interesting investigations on stellar evolution, nucleosynthesis, and star formation.

Keywords: globular clusters: general, stars: abundances, horizontal branch, population II
PACS: 98.20.Gm; 97.20.Tr

1. INTRODUCTION AND GENERAL PROPERTIES

A significant fraction of the stars are grouped in clusters. Clusters are physically related groups of stars, including from tens up to millions of stars. There are two main classes of stellar clusters: the Open Clusters (OCs) and the Globular Clusters (GCs), characterized by very different properties (size, density, age, chemical composition, etc.). Stellar clusters play a major role in stellar astronomy, much more than simply due to the fraction of stars they include (which is of the order of a per cent of the total). The main reason is that clusters are the best examples we have of simple stellar populations: this is an idealized concept of a group of stars all having the same age and chemical composition but different masses, located at the same distance from us. Simple stellar populations are crucial in testing stellar models: for instance, the direct comparison between clusters colour magnitude diagrams and theoretical isochrones has been the basic test used in the development of reliable stellar models in the second half of the past century. Furthermore, distances and ages can be determined with accuracy for stellar clusters, while this is much more difficult for individual stars, although occasionally accurate ages can be derived for some wide binaries and nearby stars with good parallaxes and/or asteroseismic data. Accurate ages for very old objects like GCs allow to test cosmology in a way which is independent of assumptions about the Universe expansion. Ages for a large number of clusters also allow to strongly constrain galactic evolution.

GCs are large aggregations of stars of nearly spherical appearance, with a mass from 10^5 up to 10^6 $M_\odot$ (with a few objects out of this range), an integrated luminosity in the range $-5 < M_V < -10$, a half light radius of a few tens of pc, a central density of $\sim 10^5$ stars/cubic parsec, a metallicity in the range $-2.3 <$[Fe/H]< 0 [1], and an age larger than > 10 Gyr. There are about 150 GCs in the Milky Way; M31 has a population of GCs approximately twice as rich, while giant elliptical galaxies (like M87) may have thousands of them. In the Milky Way, GCs are clearly related to the oldest stellar populations (halo, thick disk, bulge), and are distinctly absent in the thin disk.

The colour-magnitude (c-m) diagrams of GCs are characterized by quite short Main Sequences (MS), with bluest (Turn Off, TO) points at an absolute magnitude of about $M_V \sim 4$ (indicating an old age), a well populated subgiant branch, a Red Giant Branch (RGB) extending up to a well defined upper luminosity ($M_I \sim -3$), and a distribution of stars along the so-called Horizontal Branch (HB), at an absolute magnitude of $M_V \sim 0.5$ over a broad range in colours. The HB is the most typical feature of GC c-m diagrams, not found in OCs. Other interesting features will be discussed later. Summarizing, this c-m diagram is typical of old stellar populations: a galactic GC is in fact a typical representative of Baade's population II, dominated by red stars.

OCs are much smaller systems including typically only $10^2 - 10^3$ stars. The integrated luminosity spans a wide range ($0 < M_V < -7$). The half light radius is typically of a few parsec. The central density is not very large (typically 10^2 stars/cubic parsec). They are almost invariably metal rich ([Fe/H]~ 0), and span a very large range in age (whatever value lower than 10 Gyr is possible, but most of them are only a few hundred million years old). There is a large number of OCs in the Milky Way (over 1000), and most of them are still to be discovered due to the small value of the overdensity and the fact they characteristically belong to the thin disk population and hence are located at low galactic latitudes.

The c-m diagram of OCs is more variable from object to object, as a function of the cluster age, than those of GCs. The oldest OCs have c-m diagrams similar to those of GCs, but with a very short red HB, usually simply a clump of stars very close to the RGB. Youngest clusters have much more extended MSs: for clusters younger than about 2 Gyr, there is no subgiant branch connecting the MS to the RGB (Hertzsprung gap), In the youngest clusters (age less than about 200 Myr), the RGB is replaced by a red supergiant sequence. In poor, young OCs, the red sequences may be absent. Summarizing, a (young) OC is a typical representative of Baade's population I, dominated by blue stars. Hereinafter in these lessons we will only speak of GCs.

Main parameters for 150 galactic GCs are listed by in Harris (1996) Catalogue (www.physics.mcmaster.ca/Globular.html). Using these data, we show in Figures 1, 2, and 3 the distribution of GCs in the Milky Way. As noticed by Zinn (1980), galactic GCs can be divided into two main groups: the Halo clusters; and the Disk clusters (thick disk or bulge), mainly on the basis of the metallicity distribution that shows two distinct peaks, at [Fe/H]~ -1.5 and [Fe/H]~ -0.8 (see Figure 4).

Considering in more detail the c-m diagram of GCs, a few important facts are to be considered:

- Since all cluster stars are assumed to be coeval, the age of a cluster can be derived

---

[1] Throughout these lessons, we will use to notations for metal abundances: $\log n(X)$ is the abundance of element X by number, on a scale where $\log n(H) = 12$; and [X/Y]$=\log n(X/Y) - \log n(X/Y_\odot)$.

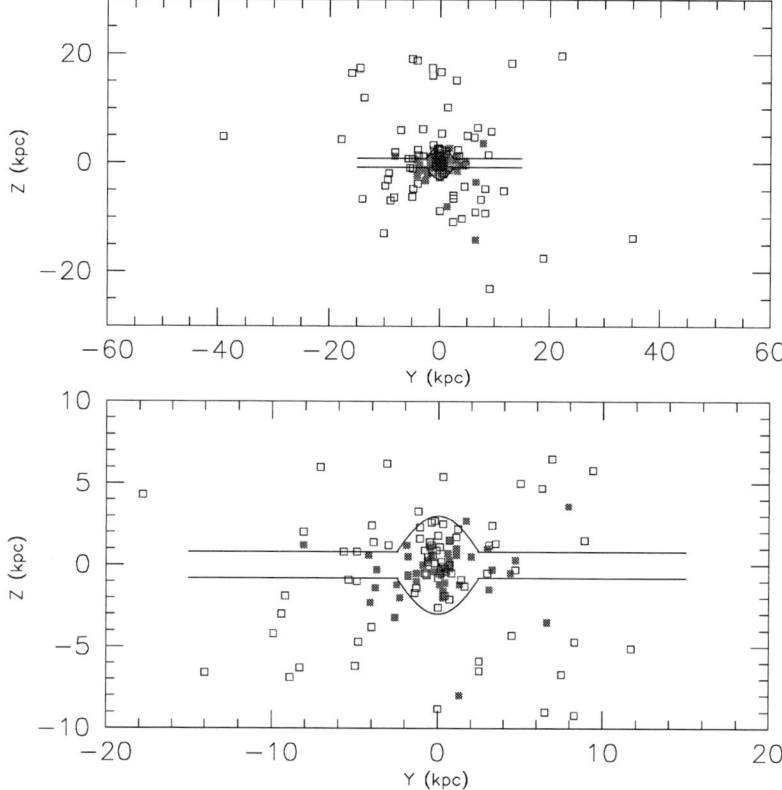

FIGURE 1. Galactic distribution of GCs along the YZ plane. Blue open symbols are halo clusters ([Fe/H]< −1.2); red filled symbols are Disk (or Bulge) clusters ([Fe/H]> −1.2). Notice the much greater concentration of Disk clusters toward the galactic center.

from the luminosity of the brightest stars burning H at their centers, that is from the TO magnitude.

- Due to the variation of opacity in the stellar envelope, the colour of the MS depends on metallicity. This is illustrated by Figure 5, that shows the colour of the MS at an absolute magnitude of $M_V = 6$ for several GCs. Lines overimposed are model predictions from Straniero et al. (1997).
- The presence of unresolved binaries broaden the MS. Sometimes the equal mass binary sequence may be observed[2]; this is expected to be ~ 0.7 mag brighter than

---

[2] The equal mass binary sequence is actually more prominent than expected simply from the fraction of binaries having really the same mass, because the presence of a fainter and cooler secondary reddens the colour of the primary.

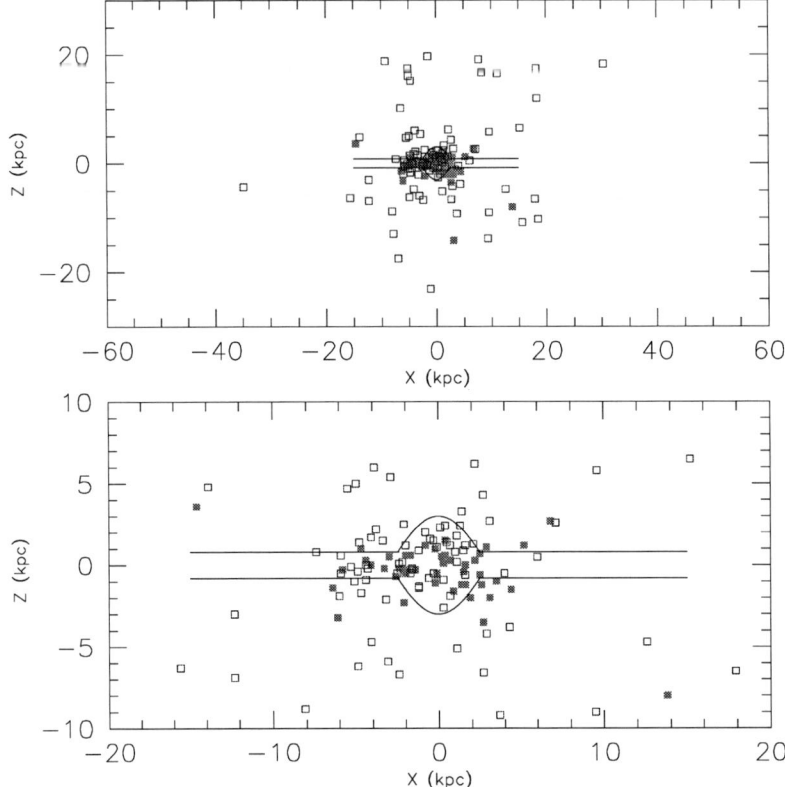

FIGURE 2. Galactic distribution of GCs along the XZ plane. Blue open symbols are halo clusters ([Fe/H]< −1.2); red filled symbols are Disk (or Bulge) clusters ([Fe/H]> −1.2). Notice the much greater concentration of Disk clusters toward the galactic center.

the single star MS.
- A few stars brighter (and bluer) then the TO are present in all GCs (the so-called Blue Stragglers; Sandage 1953; for a review, see Bailyn 1995; see also the recent survey by Piotto et al. 2004a). Blue Stragglers are explained by the evolution of binary systems. In general, it is then expected that the maximum mass of a blue straggler is about twice the TO mass. There are different creation channels for blue stragglers. (i) They may be formed by mass accretion in a (possible temporary) close binary system. The mass transfer may occur from an RGB star (this is the called McCrea Mechanism, McCrea 1964), or from an AGB star (this will generate Ba- and CH-stars: see McClure et al. 1980; McClure 1984). This channel is favoured in less dense environments, where in most cases the blue stragglers are produced by original binaries. (ii) In very dense environments, like the central regions of GCs, blue stragglers may be produced by direct collision of

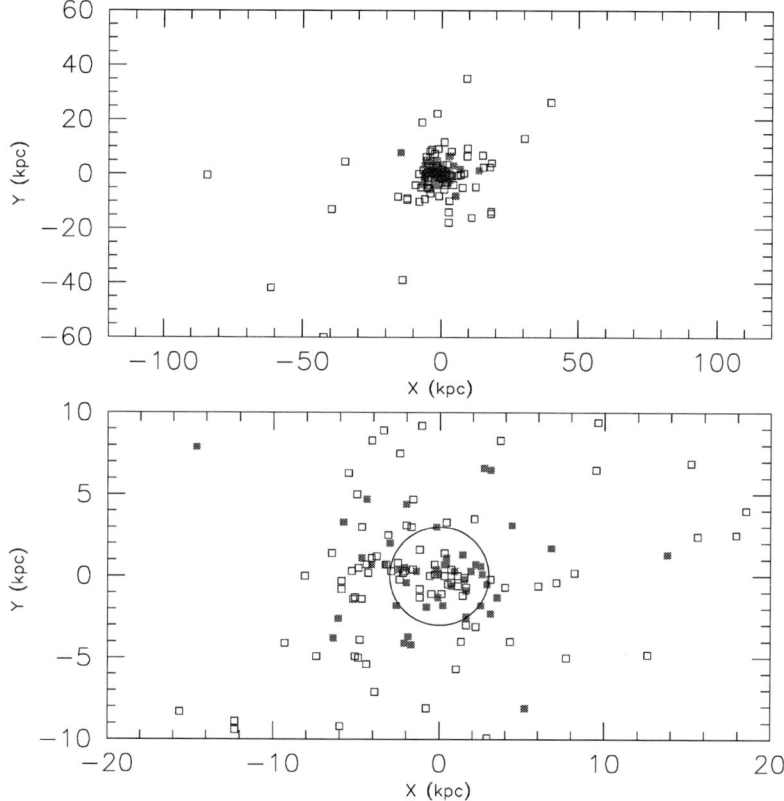

FIGURE 3. Galactic distribution of GCs along the XY plane. Blue open symbols are halo clusters ([Fe/H]< −1.2); red filled symbols are Disk (or Bulge) clusters ([Fe/H]> −1.2). Notice the much greater concentration center of Disk clusters toward the galactic.

two stars. While MS stars are much more frequent, efficient collision mechanisms require in this case the presence of a third body for energy and angular momentum conservation. Alternatively, one of the two stars may be a giant: in this case energy dissipation due to tides in the RGB star might be enough to allows capture of the second star. The properties of blue stragglers are then expected to be closely related to the dynamical evolution of a cluster (see Section 2).

- When stars evolve off the MS, the outer convective envelope penetrates inward, becoming very conspicuous and reaching its maximum extension (about half of the stellar mass) at the base of the RGB. The original material in the outer part of the star is diluted throughout the whole convective envelope, which also dredges up at the surface some material partially processed through the incomplete CN-cycle (first dredge-up: Iben 1964). This phenomenon creates a discontinuity in molecular weight (the so called μ-barrier) at this distance from the stellar centre that prevents

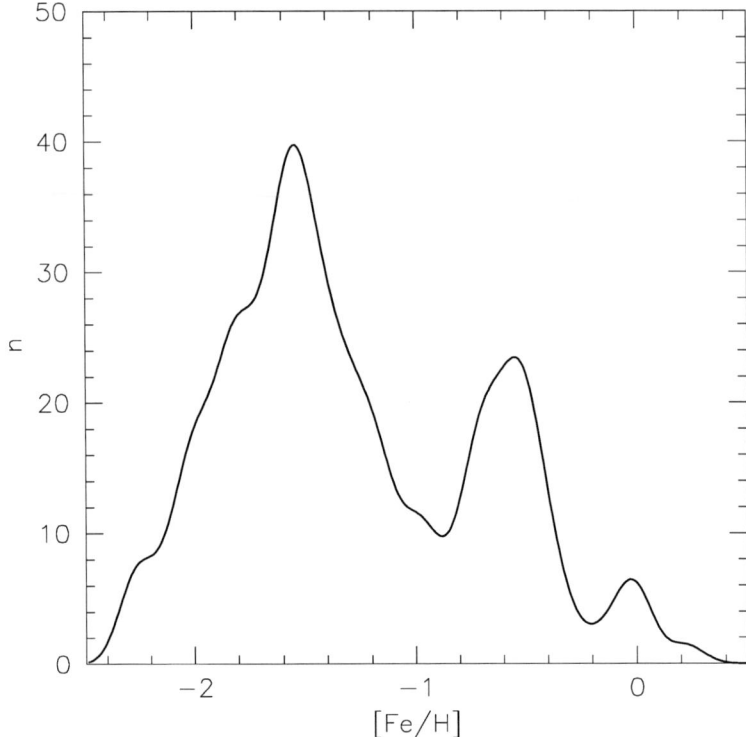

FIGURE 4. Metallicity distribution for galactic GCs. Note the presence of two distinct peaks, at [Fe/H]∼ −1.5 and [Fe/H]∼ −0.8 respectively. The first peak corresponds to the Halo, and the second to the Disk GCs, according to Zinn (1980).

further mixing, until the μ-barrier is cancelled by the outward expansion of the H-burning shell during the evolution along the RGB. When this occurs, fresh H can be available for H-burning, so that the stars stop their evolution along the RGB for some time. This produces a bump in the luminosity function, the so-called RGB bump (Sweigart & Mengel 1979; Charbonnel 1994, Charbonnel et al. 1998). The RGB bump is well observed in all globular clusters having accurate (and populous) enough c-m diagrams (see e.g. Bono et al. 2001). Stellar evolutionary models make clear predictions about the expected luminosity of the RGB bump: this is expected to depend on metallicity, the bump occurring later, that is at brighter luminosities, in more metal poor clusters. There is a good agreement between theoretical predictions and observations (see Riello et al. 2003)

- The HB (HB) is populated by stars in the core He-burning phase. The colour of stars along the HB can be described by the parameter HBR$= (n_{red} - n_{blue})/(n_{red} +$

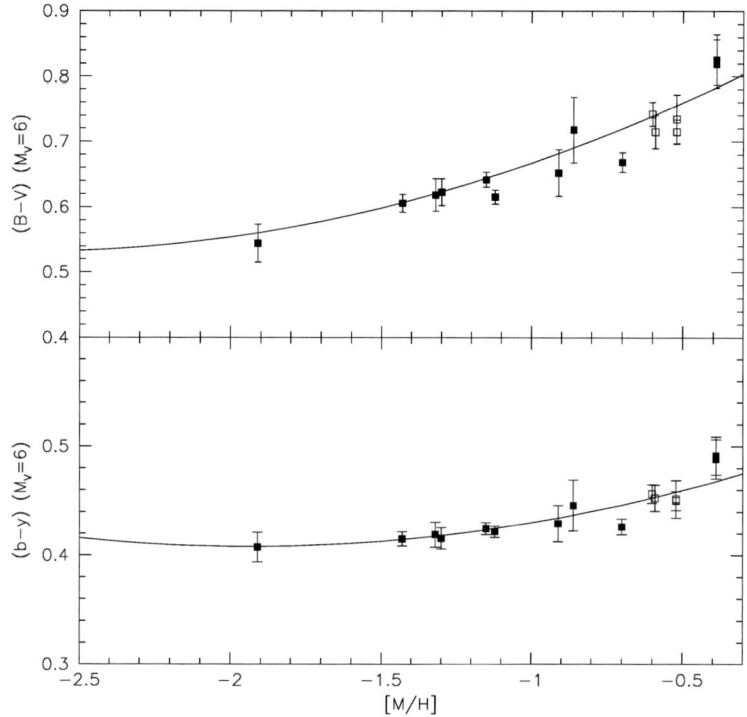

FIGURE 5. Colour of the MS at an absolute magnitude of $M_V = 6$ as a function of metallicity for several GCs. Lines overimposed are model predictions from Straniero et al. (1997).

$n_{RRLyrae} + n_{blue}$), where n_{red}, n_{blue}, and $n_{RRLyrae}$ are the number of HB stars on the red side, on the blue side, and within the RR Lyrae instability strip (see Section 3) respectively. It is expected that HBR is a function of the metallicity of the cluster. However, observations indicate that there are other parameters that are also important. This is the long-standing issue of the second parameter effect, discovered by Sandage & Wildey (1967) and Van den Bergh (1967). A classical example of second parameter is the couple M3-M13, which have nearly the same metallicity ([Fe/H]~ -1.4) and very different HB's. Zinn (1980) noticed that the galactocentric distance is a second parameter (see Figure 6). This might be related to age differences of about 2 Gyrs between inner and outer halo GCs. However, age is not the only second parameter, since there are cases of clusters with very similar ages but widely different HB's. Possible additional explanations for the second parameter include the helium content, mass loss, CNO abundances, and perhaps concentration. Most likely, there is more than one second parameter.

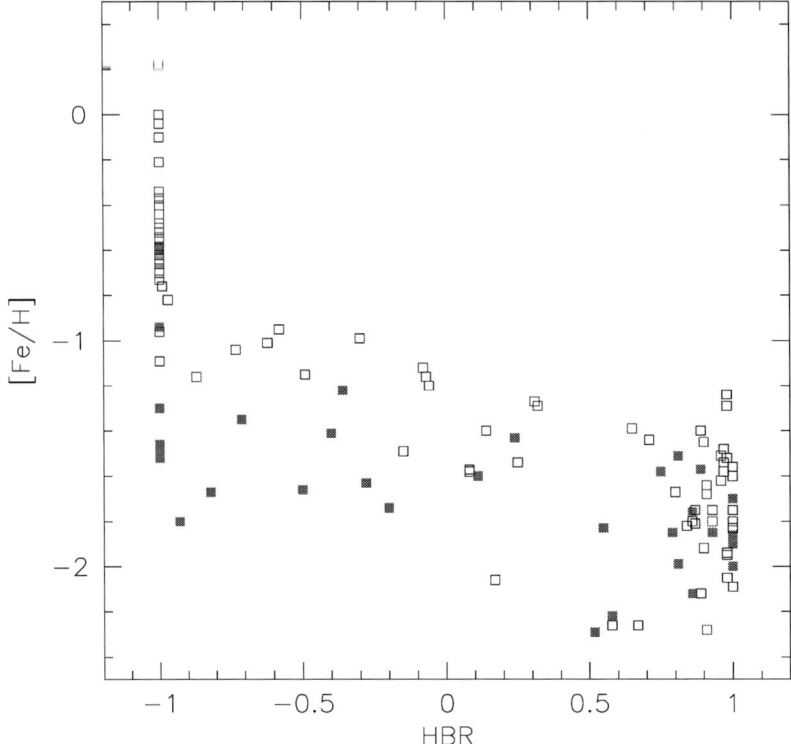

FIGURE 6. Metallicity of globular clusters [Fe/H] against the parameter HBR defining the colour of the HB. Blue open points are inner halo GCs (galactocentric distance < 20 kpc), red filled points are outer halo GCs (galactocentric distance > 20 kpc).

- In clusters with deep enough observational colour magnitude diagrams, the white dwarfs cooling sequence becomes prominent. At these faint magnitudes, contamination by background stars can be an issue. Proper motions can be used to clean the diagram (see e.g. the observations by of M4 Hansen et al. 2004). The white dwarf cooling sequence can be used to derive distances (by e.g. matching the sequence with that of nearby field stars) and ages, from the location of the peak of the luminosity function of the white dwarfs. This is set by the cooling time of the stars, which can be calibrated by models. At variance with the TO luminosities (that saturate at large ages), ages derived from the peak of WD luminosity function are only modestly sensitive to distances. Unluckily, current models of WD are still quite uncertain, so that different groups obtained very different age estimates using this technique (for opposite views, see Hansen et al. 2004 and De Marchi et al. 2004).

2. FORMATION SCENARIOS AND CLUSTER EVOLUTION

Scenarios for the formation of GCs have been discussed by several authors (Cayrel 1986; Brown et al. 1991, 1995; Murray & Lin 1993; Parmentier et al. 1999). In general, these scenarios start from a giant molecular cloud, where there is some early star formation while the cloud is still collapsing. Massive stars from this first generation explodes as SNe and generate a shock wave, which propagates through the cloud. Formation of a dense cluster in the densest regions of the cloud is then triggered. The original association might evaporate. An example of a massive cluster caught in the latest stages of this formation mechanism is 30 Dor (see e.g. Rubio et al. 1998). Note star formation on the NE filament, that suggests that a new generation of stars is triggered by the wind due to the massive OB stars of the center cluster, 30 Dor being too young for any supernova (SN) explosion being occurred within the cluster itself. It should be noted also that while it is among the most massive young clusters in the Local Group, 30 Dor (with a mass of a few 10^4 $M_\odot$) is however light in comparison with typical GCs.

Cluster self pollution should occur rather naturally in these scenarios, where the ISM from which stars form in a cluster is enriched in metals by a previous generation of stars born in the same giant molecular cloud. Surprisingly, there is little if any observational support to such self pollution for what concern those heavy elements produced by core collapse supernovae. A possible evidence in favour is given by the analysis of the chemical composition of very young stars observed by Cunha et al. (1998) in the Orion Nebula. In this case, stars with the higher O abundance tend to be concentrated in one area toward the southern part of the association. However the Orion Nebula is an extended association, where star formation is proceeding very slowly when compared to GCs. In most cases GCs have extraordinarily homogenous Fe content: a recent analysis of more than a hundred RGB stars in NGC6752 by Carretta et al. (2006b) shows a very small star-to-star scatter of only 0.026 dex, entirely justifiable by observational errors, leaving very little room for any intrinsic variation in the Fe content (similar results from smaller samples of stars in the same cluster were obtained by Yong et al, 2005, and Gratton et al., 2005). The extraordinary homogeneity in the abundances of Fe-peak elements is clearly a strong constraint for any model of cluster formation.

Once formed, cluster have a very interesting dynamical evolution (for reviews, see Weinberg 1993, Baylin 1995, Meylan & Heggie 1997, Hut et al. 2003). There are several competing mechanisms favouring cluster disruption. Some of these mechanisms are due to internal processes. The most classical is two-body relaxation, that leads to energy equipartition, mass segregation and slow evaporation of the stars from the cluster. Evaporation of stars is favoured by mass loss due to supernovae, planetary nebulae ejection and stellar winds, which reduces the potential well: during the first 10^8 yr a cluster looses a substantial fraction of its original mass, depending on its IMF. Loose clusters cannot survive this phase. Additionally, the presence of external gravitational fields (such as the galactic one) has important effects both due to tidal truncation and consequent loss of the stars in the outer part of the cluster, and to dynamical friction, which causes expansion of the cluster. A similar but much faster effect is caused by shock heating, that may occur during disk crossing. All these phenomena cause a loss of energy from the cluster (cooling); in order to support the cluster structure, the gradient of pressure should then increase, that is the core of the cluster should contract. The central density may become extremely large in advanced phases of the dynamical evolution of the cluster. Binaries also play an important role in the cluster evolution. A large fraction of the original binaries, mainly those with the smallest binding energy, are disrupted by close encounters with other cluster members. However, such encounters may also result in hardening of some systems; additionally, when densities become very large, three body encounters become frequent, favouring the formation of new binary systems. New binaries may also form through tidal capture by giants. Formation of new binary systems results in efficient heating, because the third object is ejected from the system at rather high velocities: this may halt and reverse core collapse, causing the so-called gravothermal oscillations. This complex behaviour can be easily understood when a GCs is considered as a gas of stars, like a star is a gas of particle. It contracts due to gravity unless some energy source is available to slow-down (or even reverse) the collapse. Usually, this is provided by the cluster gravitational energy; however the process is catastrophic. During the core collapse, the density in the central regions becomes so high that formation and disruption of binaries are very common. This releases large amounts of gravitational potential energy, that heats the gas composed of stars. The heated gas (that is the cluster core) then expands and cool adiabatically. Once the density has decreased enough, binary formation is inhibited and the core starts again to collapse (gravothermal oscillations, see e.g. Goodman, 1987).

The dynamical status of a cluster reflects into the mass density distribution, which may be mapped from the luminosity profile. The luminosity profiles for most GCs are well fitted by King (1962) profiles. These are obtained assuming a relaxed, tidally truncated system. King profiles are described by three parameters (central surface brightness, core radius, and concentration). These profiles have a central (isothermal) plateau and are truncated at the tidal radius (for some examples of these luminosity profiles, see Djorgovski & King 1986). For about 20% of the GCs the luminosity profile presents an approximate power-law dependence of surface brightness on radius. This is expected for violently relaxed system: it is generally assumed that GCs having this luminosity profile are in the post-core collapse phase. This is because the density profile of a cluster during the phase of gravothermal oscillations is quite different from a tidally truncated King profile. The release of energy in the central region due to formation and disruption of binaries, and its transport toward the outer regions, result in a very small or even absent central isothermal zone, and in a monotonic power-law decrease of density.

There should be correlations between the various dynamical parameters of GCs: for instance large clusters of low central concentration are easily destroyed by dynamical friction. Small mass clusters do not survive easily the mass loss phase, etc. An example of such correlations is shown in Figure 7, where we plotted central concentration against absolute magnitude of the cluster. The various disruption mechanisms generate a survival region in the parameter space. The important parameters are total mass (small mass clusters evaporates rapidly; very massive clusters are fragile to dynamical friction) and galactocentric distance (clusters closer to the center are tidally limited). Several authors have studied the survival region (see e.g. Vesperini, 1997). Dynamical friction also causes orbits decay: the clusters spiral toward the galactic center, where their dynamical evolution is faster (see e.g. Capriotti & Hawley 1996). Taking into account these effects the survival region may then be used to deduce original distribution of GCs from the properties of the observed population (see e.g. Fall & Rees 1977; Caputo & Castellani,

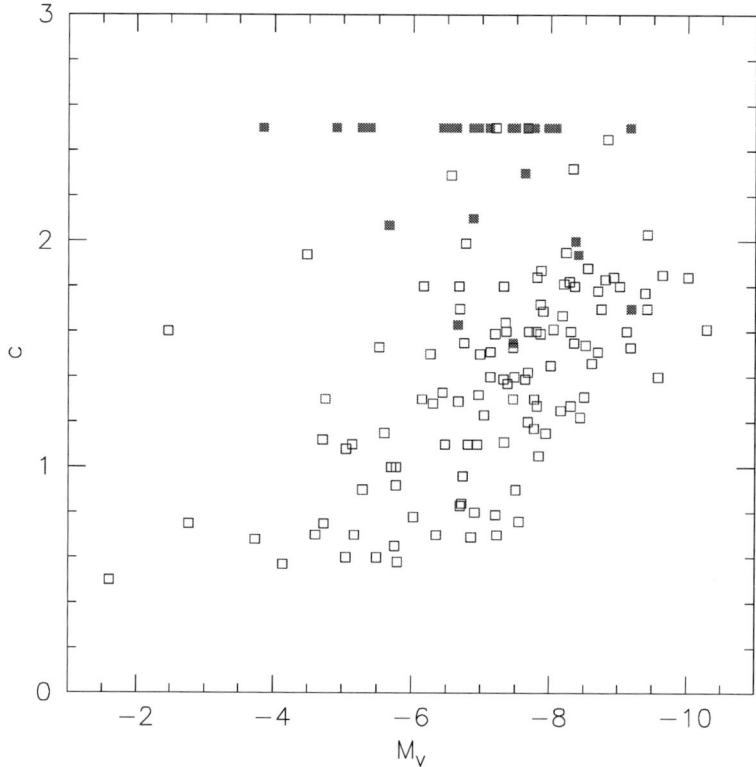

FIGURE 7. Plot of central concentration against absolute magnitude for clusters in the Harris (1996) catalogue. Blue open points are for clusters well fitted by King (1962) luminosity profiles, while red filled points mark clusters that are thought to be in the post-core collapse phase according to Djorgowski & King (1986).

1984).

Due to equipartition of kinetic energy for relaxed clusters, star loss is selective: small mass stars are lost much more rapidly than large mass ones. Very evolved clusters that have lost almost all their low mass stars then have very unusual luminosity function with almost complete lack of small mass stars. Examples of clusters with such unusual luminosity function are NGC6712 (De Marchi et al. 1999) and M12 (De Marchi et al. 2006).

Due to motion of the cluster around the Galaxy, stars lost from the clusters are not distributed isotropically. Rather, they are concentrated in narrow tails (both leading and trailing) along the cluster orbit. In a few cases such tidal tails have been clearly observed, the most famous case being that of Pal 5 (see e.g. Odenkirchen et al. 2003). Such tidal tails are well reproduced by N-body models (see e.g. Dehnen et al. 2004)

3. VARIABLE STARS IN GCS: THE RR LYRAE

The RR Lyrae are HB stars that fall into the instability strip caused by the second ionization of Helium. Hence they are radially pulsating stars in the core He-burning phase. RR Lyrae can be divided into three main groups (Bailey types): (i) ab-type RR Lyrae are fundamental pulsators: they have asymmetric light curves of rather large amplitudes (0.5-1 mag); (ii) c-type RR Lyrae are first harmonic pulsators: they have symmetric light curves of smaller amplitudes (< 0.5 mag); (iii) d-type RR Lyrae are double pulsators, pulsating both on the fundamental mode and on the first harmonic, generally the last mode having a larger amplitude.

Since RR Lyr are radial pulsators, the period of the fundamental mode is related to the stellar radius and to the average sound speed within the star: $P(\text{fundamental}) = R/<cs>$, where $<cs> \sim <cs>(\rho)$, where ρ is the average stellar density. Of course $\rho \sim M/R^3$, so that $P = P(R,M)$. Pulsational properties of the RR Lyrae (period and Amplitude (P and A) may then be used to derive luminosity and masses of the stars. While P may be derived from linear (adiabatic) theory, the derivation of A from models requires detailed treatment of the outer convective envelope using non-linear (non-adiabatic) models. Such models have been first developed by Stellingwerf (1982) and then by other authors. The mechanism of pulsation of RR Lyr is the same as for Cepheid, that is the $k-$mechanism activated by the region of second ionization of He (Eddington, Zhevakin). Like Cepheids, they obey a $P-L-A$ relation. However, since RR Lyrae are HB stars, all have quite similar luminosity, so that it is not possible to recognize readily a $P-L$ relation. The existence of a $P-L-A$ relation makes RR Lyr a precious distance indicator. In several applications, the amplitude A might be substituted by some measure of the asymmetry of the light curve (e.g. the variation of the phase at which the variable has the average luminosity). The $P-L-A$ relation is then usually used through the Period-shift technique, that is considering the variation of P at a given A or asymmetry of the light curve (see e.g. Sandage 1982).

The possibility to derive masses from pulsational models and to compare them with predictions from evolutionary models allow to derive severe tests on stellar evolution. These properties have been exploited by a number of authors (Sandage, Cox, Stellingwerf, Castellani, Caputo, Bono, Marconi, etc.). Note that the luminosity of the HB depends on several parameters (Metallicity, Helium Content, Core mass at He-flash, CNO abundances). The luminosity of the HB is also a function of the efficiency of the He-burning (nuclear cross sections), of the presence of WIMPS (massive neutrinos), etc. The temperature of HB stars (and then the fact that they are within the instability strip) depends also on their mass. It is then possible to compare evolutionary and pulsational masses.

RR Lyrae are frequent both in GCs and in the field. GC and Field RR Lyrae's are the same objects since they obey the same Period Shift-Metallicity Relation (Catelan 1998, Carretta et al. 2000a). Galactic GCs with RR Lyrae divide into two groups (Oosterhoff 1938): (i) Oosterhoff I clusters, where the mean period of ab-type RR Lyrae of ~ 0.55 d, and the c-type RR Lyrae are $\sim 1/5$ of the ab-type ones; and (ii) Oosterhoff II clusters, where mean period of ab-type RR Lyrae is of 0.65 d and c-type RR Lyrae are as common as ab-types. Clusters in other galaxies do not match this classification.

The instability strip for fundamental and first harmonic pulsators may be predicted by non-adiabatic pulsational models. There is a region of overlap where both modes are possible. The pulsating mode in this zone depends on the evolutionary path. In Oosterhoff I clusters the evolution is from red blueward: this corresponds to stars which are close to the ZAHB. In Oosterhoff II clusters the evolution is from blue redward: this corresponds to more evolved stars, that are brighter than the ZAHB. This hysteresis mechanism is at the base of the Oosterhoff dichotomy (Bono, Caputo & Marconi, 1995).

At variance with other type of stars, quite accurate metal abundances can be rather easily derived from low dispersion spectra of RR Lyrae exploiting the so-called ΔS method (Preston 1959). A modern version of this method has been recently applied to the analysis of several hundred RR Lyrae in local group galaxies by Gratton et al. (2004). This method starts with the definition of line indices (with reference to local 'continuum' regions), that were defined to describe the strength of the Ca II K line, and of Hydrogen lines ($<H>$ = average of Hβ, Hγ, Hδ). The strength of the Hydrogen lines is a temperature indicator, although it shows minor dependences on gravity and overall metal abundance, so that we may write $<H> = <H>(T, g, [Fe/H])$, but since RR Lyrae are on the HB, gravity is almost the same for all stars, so that we may write $<H> = <H>(T, [Fe/H])$. Note that since the star temperature changes along the cycle, also the Hydrogen line strength changes. The Ca II K line depends on temperature, on gravity and on metal abundance, so that we may write $K = K(T, g, [Fe/H])$; however, again gravity is almost constant for RR Lyrae, so that we may write $K = K(T, [Fe/H])$. We now notice that the dependence of $<H>$ on [Fe/H] is weak; then, a cluster will define a nearly monoparametric sequence in the $<H> - K$ plane, with the sequence of different clusters shifted according to metallicity. At a given strength of the H lines, the Ca K line is then a measure of metal abundance of the star. Metallicities can then be derived from the location of stars in the $<H> - K$ plane, provided that a suitable calibration sequence is available.

Abundances for RR Lyrae can of course be also derived with much more observational and analysis effort from analysis of high dispersion spectra (see e.g. Clementini et al. 1995, Lambert et al. 1996, Solano et al. 1997). These analysis provide detailed abundance patterns, and not simply an average metal abundance. They have shown that RR Lyrae and non variable metal-poor stars share the same abundance pattern (e.g. excess of the elements produced by α−captures, etc.).

Metal abundances are very useful to study various properties of RR Lyrae's. It has been found that e.g. the period of ab-variables is related to metallicity. Since the period is itself related to luminosity, there should be an absolute magnitude-metallicity relation. The slope of this relation have been studied in various environments. Among recent results, we may mention those obtained for M31 by Rich et al. (2005: 0.22 ± 0.09), for the Bar of the LMC by Clementini et al. (2003: 0.214 ± 0.047), and for the Sculptor Dwarf Spheroidal by Clementini et al. (2005 0.092 ± 0.027). While the two early results agree well each other, the third one is distinctly smaller. This suggests that there might be not an universal slope (perhaps due to a different proportion on stars still near the Zero Age HB and evolved objects), or that the slope is metallicity dependent (as suggested by several models for HB Stars: see e.g. Caputo et al. 2000). We finally notice that this relation can be used to measure distances (see e.g. Sandage 1982 and Clementini et al. 2003).

The mass of RR Lyrae's can be obtained by comparing pulsational properties with models. Double pulsators are particularly useful. For these objects, we may construct a diagram relating the period of the fundamental mode (P_0), with the ratio between the periods in the first harmonic and in the fundamental mode (P_1/P_0: Petersen diagram, Petersen 1973). The comparison of the location of stars in this diagram with predictions by stellar models convincingly show that RR Lyrae in Oosterhoff I cluster have a mass of $\sim 0.55\ M_\odot$, while those in Oosterhoff II clusters have larger masses of $\sim 0.7\ M_\odot$. This is $\sim 0.2\ M_\odot$ less then the mass of TO stars in the same clusters, showing that a significant mass loss should have occurred during the first ascent of the RGB.

Most RR Lyrae are single core-He burning stars near the ZAHB. However, not all RR Lyrae can be explained by this assumption. On this respect, it is interesting to compare the RR Lyrae frequency for different parent populations. Layden (1995) have estimated the ratios of RR Lyrae to the total number of HB stars. He found that while this ratio is quite high (1/25) among metal weak thick disk star, it is smaller (1/40) among thick disk stars with a metallicity [Fe/H]> -1, and very small (1/800) among old thin disk stars ([Fe/H]< -1). RR Lyrae are very rare in the Old Thin Disk, so that it may be assumed that the formation mechanism is likely different in this case: some special mechanism should have caused a substantial mass loss in order to bring an HB metal-rich stars within the instability strip.

In general, mass loss play an important role in the explanation of the age-metallicity relation for RR Lyrae. In Figure 8 we show a diagram we have constructed using GC relative ages from De Angeli et al. (2005) and metallicities from the Harris (1996) catalogue. In this diagram we plotted with different symbols GCs with different relative frequency of RR Lyrae (that is the number of RR Lyrae per unit luminosity), and with different mean colour of the HB. GCs rich in RR Lyrae define two clear sequences in this diagram, related to the two Oosterhoff's groups. Increasing rates of mass loss are expected to shift the sequences of the various clusters horizontally in this diagram. This diagram clearly shows that the RR Lyrae properties in Oosterhoff II clusters might be explained only by a very low mass loss. In general, this diagram favours a total mass lost during the RGB phase which is a function of metallicity, being almost negligible in the most metal poor GCs.

4. ABUNDANCES IN GCS

Derivations of chemical abundances in GCs play important roles in a number of issues (for a review, see Gratton et al., 2004b). This may be understood considering a few examples.

4.1 GC ages

Most estimates for GCs in the '90s gave very old ages for GCs, well in excess of 15 Gyrs. These were inconsistent with the cosmological models favoured at the epoch, that considered a flat universe with critical matter density. Depending on the Hubble constant the Universe age were thought to be ~ 10 Gyr. The problem is not any more as urgent, since on one hand the indication of an acceleration in the Universe expansion by type Ia SNe (Schmidt et al. 1998; Perlmutter et al. 1999) has made estimates of the Universe

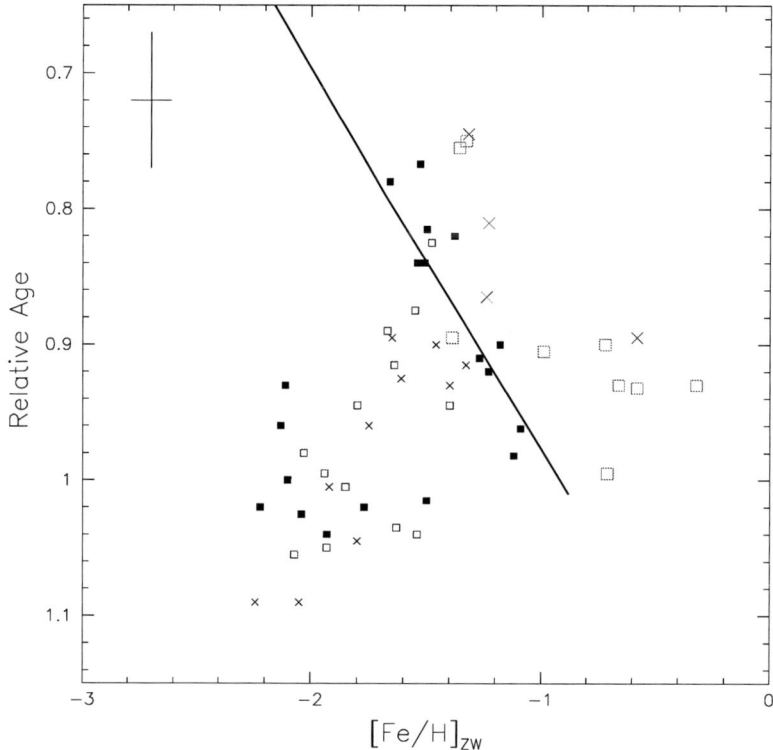

FIGURE 8. GC relative ages from De Angeli et al. (2005) against metallicities from the Harris (1996) catalogue. GCs with different relative frequency of RR Lyrae (that is the number of RR Lyrae per unit luminosity), and with different mean colour of the HB, are plotted with different symbols: crosses are clusters with very few RR Lyrae (relative frequency parameter less than 3); filled squares are clusters with many RR Lyrae (relative frequency parameter larger than 15); open squares are clusters with an intermediate number of RR Lyrae. Red/large symbols are for GCs with RHB< 0 (predominantly red HB's); blue/small symbols are for GCs with RHB> 0 (predominantly blue HB)'s. GCs rich in RR Lyrae define two clear sequences in this diagram, related to the two Oosterhoff's groups. The solid line represents a constant mass line (0.55 $M_\odot$), that fits well the location of Oosterhoff I GCs. Increasing rates of mass loss are expected to shift the sequences of the various clusters horizontally in this diagram. This diagram clearly shows that the RR Lyrae properties in Oosterhoff II clusters might be explained only by a very low mass loss.

age older, while on the other hand a number of factors (including the distance scale itself) have made our estimates of the ages of the oldest GCs younger (see e.g. Gratton et al. 2003). There is now a satisfactory agreement between these two quantities at an age of about 13-14 Gyr. However, the age of GCs is still telling a lot about the epoch of formation of GCs and the history of our own Galaxy in a cosmological context. Ages of GCs are then still a major issue.

It should be noticed that relative cluster-to-cluster ages can be derived with quite high accuracy even ignoring the distances, using the so called vertical and horizontal methods (Stetson et al. 1996); the vertical method exploits the magnitude differences between the HB and the TO point, a well known age indicator; the horizontal method exploits the colour difference between the TO and the base of the subgiant branch. Relative ages for a number of GCs have been derived using these two methods by various authors. The most recent determinations are those by De Angeli et al. (2005), that exploited large and homogeneous data sets gathered with HST and ground-based telescopes. However, these relative ages need to be calibrated using at least a few high quality absolute ages derived with other techniques, and these require accurate distances because they are derived from TO magnitudes, and as we have seen these magnitudes tend to saturate at old ages, those of interest in this context. Accurate distances must be derived in order absolute ages can be derived with enough accuracy: in general, an error of 0.07 mag in the distance modulus (3.5% in the distances) causes an error of about 1 Gyr in the absolute ages.

In perspective, distances accurate to about 2% will be obtained in the next few years by comparing the internal dispersion of radial velocities (obtained from large samples of stars observed with suitable multiobject spectrographs like FLAMES) with the internal scatter in proper motions derived from HST data (Piotto et al. 2004b). These distances are independent of stellar models, although high accuracy requires consideration of a number of factors including detailed dynamical modelling of the cluster, taking into account the effect of anisotropic velocity distribution and rotation; excision of spectroscopic binaries; consideration of systematic variations of the measured radial velocities with temperature and luminosity, etc.. Anyhow, such accurate dynamical distances are still to come.

Up to now, most distance estimates for GCs have been based on the HB, mainly on RR Lyrae. Up to a few years ago, these distance derivations have been plagued by uncertainties in the zero point of the absolute magnitudes of RR Lyrae, and the metallicity dependence of these zero points, so that two distance scales (the so called short and long distance scales) were obtained, and favoured by various authors. This had important impact on GC ages: the short distance scale, indicated for instance by the statistical parallaxes for RR Lyrae, implies very old ages for GCs, very difficult to reconcile with cosmological constraints (even with the current concordant model). The reasons for such inconsistencies are not entirely understood, although they might depend on the kinematical properties of the local RR Lyrae sample.

However, most accurate estimates of the GC distances, with typical accuracy of about 4% in the best cases, are provided by the fitting of the GC MS to that obtained from local subdwarfs, which is essentially a standard candle method. There are many subtleties in this method, that must be considered in order such high accuracies can be achieved. Before availability of high quality parallaxes for a number of local subdwarfs from the ESA HIPPARCOS satellite (ESA 1997), the limiting factor was the lack of well calibrated candles. After that big improvement, the error budget was dominated by other factors, independent of the parallaxes (which by themselves still contribute about 0.02 mag to the error in the distance moduli, that is 1% on the distances). These other factors are so much important essentially because of the (steep) slope of the MS in the colour-magnitude diagram: errors in colours of the order of 0.01 mag translates into errors in distances of the order of 0.07 mag. It is very difficult to control colours at this high accuracy: first of all we have to take into account that both the cluster and field sequences may be contaminated by the presence of unrecognized binaries. The impact of this effect can be estimated, and turns out to be about 0.02 mag on both sides. Much more important are the consequences of uncertainties in the photometric calibrations, of the adopted reddenings, and of the metallicities (in Section 1 we have seen that the colour of the MS is a function of metallicity, an effect that should be taken into account when comparing local sudwarfs and GCs). The impact of these effect can be estimated at 0.04, 0.07 and 0.08 mag respectively, even in the best calibration existing a few years ago (Carretta et al. 2000b): this implied total error bars of about 0.12 mag in the distance moduli (that is errors of about 6% in the distances, and of about 1.7 Gyrs in the ages). It should be noted that in the distance derivation, what matter are the relative displacements between the local subdwarf and the GC sequences. Most of these errors can then be eliminated by an homogeneous analysis of local subdwarfs and GC MS stars, based on a reddening free temperature indicator like the profile of the Balmer lines or the equilibrium of excitation for e.g. Fe I lines.

Such an analysis was one of the main subjects of an ESO Large Program, a total of 30 nights of observations with UVES at VLT2 (Gratton et al. 2001; Gratton et al. 2003). This program targeted at TO and subgiant stars in the three easiest GCs (NGC6397, NGC6752, and 47 Tuc). These three clusters well selected because they are close; they also have rather homogenous (and not large) interstellar reddening, and span a very large range in metal abundance ([Fe/H]=-2.0, -1.4, and -0.7 for NGC6397, NGC6752, and 47 Tuc respectively). In the same program, a number of local subdwarfs with accurate parallaxes were observed. The spectra covered a broad spectral range and have rather high S/N (between 20 and 100) and resolution ($R \sim 40,000$). Accurate EWs could be determined using an automatic procedure. Analysis procedure was kept strictly identical for field and cluster stars. The most critical parameter, the effective temperatures, were derived from the profile of Hα. Temperatures for the local subdwarfs agreed very well with those determined by Alonso et al. (1996) using the Infrared Flux Method, that is the most robust determination of temperatures from colours (i.e., affected by uncertainties in the interstellar reddening). The comparison between the colour-temperature relations for field and GC stars provided the value of the relative interstellar reddening (the absolute value, if the local subdwarfs are assumed to be unreddened, an excellent approximation in most, though not all, cases). Both broad band Johnson *BV* and intermediate band *by* Strömgren colours were used. Comparing results obtained for TO stars with those obtained for subgiants, and those obtained from different colours, typical errors in these reddenings were estimated to be about 0.005 mag. These errors are half those existing before in these quantities. Similarly, relative abundances between GC and field subdwarfs were set at an accuracy of about 0.04 dex, half the error bar of previous determinations. These achievements allowed to reduce to about half the error bar in the distance determinations, to about 0.08 mag (4%) for each cluster; the derived ages have then uncertainties of about 1.1 Gyr.

One of the interesting result of this analysis was that 47 Tuc (at an age of 11.1 ± 1.1 Gyr) turned out to be younger by about 2.5 Gyr than NGC6397 and NGC6752 (with ages of 13.8 ± 1.1 Gyr and 13.7 ± 1.1 Gyr). While this difference is only at about 2 σ level, it agrees perfectly with the completely independent relative ages based on both vertical and horizontal methods (Rosenberg et al. 1999; De Angeli et al. 2005). This indicates that the phase of formation of GCs lasted several Gyrs. Furthermore, from the cosmological point of view only the oldest GCs are of interest. The ages we determined for NGC6397 and NGC6752 is only slightly larger than that derived by WMAP group using the concordance model (13.4 ± 0.2 Gyr: Spergel et al. 2003), the difference being well within the error bars. This very old age implies that the oldest GCs of our own Galaxy formed very early, when the Universe was very young, less than about 1 Gyr. This would corresponds to a reddening of $z \gg 1$; while the youngest GCs formed later, at $z \sim 1$. The same data can be also used to set limits on Ω_M in a flat Universe, independent of the type Ia SNe results. This turns out to be $\Omega_M < 0.57$ at a 95% level of confidence.

4.2 Impact of microscopic diffusion on models of low mass stars

Data from the same ESO Large Program could be used to constrain other important aspects of stellar and cluster evolution. One of these concern the impact of microscopic diffusion. Microscopic diffusion is a basic physical mechanism, that should be included in stellar models. It causes sedimentation of heavy elements, mainly He; in low mass ($M \sim 0.8 M_\odot$), metal-poor ([Fe/H]< -2) stars near the TO, also O and Fe are expected to be depleted significantly. The net effects of sedimentation are: (i) derived ages are reduced by about 10%; and (ii) Li abundances may be significantly reduced with respect to the original value. This last feature is important in the context of primordial nucleosynthesis, having then cosmological implications. The ESO LP observations of TO and subgiants in NGC6397 (stars with a mass $M \sim 0.8\ M_\odot$ and [Fe/H]=-2.0) allow to constrain sedimentation effects, by comparing abundances in stars at the TO (where the effect of microscopic diffusion is expected to be the largest) with those in stars at the base of the subgiant branch (where the effect is expected to be cancelled by the deep inward penetration of the convective envelope). The result was that no difference in Fe abundance was observed between these two groups of stars, while most models predicted a factor of two difference. Models predict much larger sedimentation due to microscopic diffusion than actually observed. There should be some mechanism that prevents sedimentation. More sophisticated models presented by Richard et al. (2002) show that adding some turbulence at the base of the outer convective envelope greatly reduces the impact of sedimentation. This is a possible explanation for the ESO LP observations. Using this approach however, predictions about the impact on ages (Chaboyer et al. 2001) and Li abundances (Richard et al. 2002) are modified, both in the sense that variation with respect to standard models without diffusion are much more modest than previously thought.

4.3 Star-to-star chemical inhomogeneities: the Na-O anticorrelation

In Section 2 we have mentioned the extraordinary star-to-star homogeneity found in the abundances of Fe-peak elements in GCs. However, the same cannot be said for other elements. Large (anticorrelated) variations in the strength of CH and CN bands were noticed since early seventies (see e.g. Osborn 1971) from DDO photometry and spectroscopy. Bimodal distributions of the abundances of C and N were found along the RGB in various clusters (see e.g. Norris & Smith 1983) and even on the MS stars (in 47 Tuc: Briley et al. 1994). However, other elements were also found to vary from star-to-star. In the late eighties and early nineties, in a series of paper Kraft, Sneden and co-workers (see Kraft 1994 for a review of these results) have found that in most, perhaps all GCs there is an anticorrelation between the abundances of Oxygen and Sodium (and Magnesium and Aluminium), at least among RGB stars. It is was early acknowledged that these anticorrelations are due to the presence at the surfaces of a fraction of the GC stars of elements processed through the complete CNO-cycle. At these temperatures fresh Na can be produced by proton capture on ^{22}Ne (Denisenkov & Denisenkova 1990; Langer & Hoffman 1995; Cavallo et al. 1996). At slightly higher temperatures, a similar process on Mg isotopes can lead to the formation of ^{27}Al.

What was not clear at the epoch was where this hot CNO burning occurred. Initially most authors thought that it should occur in the same stars where it was observed (see Kraft 1994). The required mixing episodes were however not predicted by stellar models. In fact, according to models a first mixing episode occurs at the base of the RGB, due to the inward penetration of the outer convective envelope in regions where some H-burning (through incomplete CN-cycle) occurred during the latest phases of MS evolution (first dredge-up: Iben 1964). First dredge up causes only minor effect in metal-poor stars. At the same phases, dilution (by a factor of ~ 20) of the surface Li abundance occurs. As mentioned in the Introduction, the maximum inward penetration of the outer convective envelope at the base of the RGB creates a discontinuity in molecular weight (μ-barrier) that prevents further mixing, until is cancelled by the outward expansion of the H-burning shell (RGB clump) (Sweigart & Mengel 1979; Charbonnel 1994). Further mixing (due e.g. to meridional circulations activated by core rotation is possible only after the RGB clump.

Field stars conform well this theoretical paradigm (Gratton et al. 2000). However in field stars abundances of O and Na are not affected: mixing is not deep enough to reach regions where complete CNO cycle occurs. There is then a systematic difference between field and cluster stars. Furthermore, possible hints for a correlation between the 2nd parameter and the Na-O anticorrelation might exist (see e.g. Carretta & Gratton 1996). Summarizing, there were two competing scenarios: in the first one there are deep mixing episodes; such episodes may only occur along the RGB, after the bump (temperature is not large enough in TO-stars). In the second, stars might have accreted material processed in the interiors of other, now defunct, stars (probably massive AGB stars, see below). In this second scenario the O-Na anticorrelation should be present independent of the evolutionary phase. These two scenarios cannot be distinguished from observations of bright giants. Observations of stars fainter than the RGB bump were required.

Again, observations from the ESO LP provided the answer (Gratton et al. 2001), since it was found that the O-Na (and also Mg-Al and C-N) anticorrelations were clearly present (more or less in the same way as observed in RGB stars) also in stars at the TO and at the base of the subgiant branch in GCs. This clearly ruled out deep mixing as explanation for the O-Na anticorrelation. The sum of C+N abundances was found to be not constant: a substantial fraction of O is transformed into N. The sum of C+N+O was overabundant as in halo field stars.

The emerging scenario is then that in typical GCs there were two epochs of star formation. After the usual initial burst, a second generation of stars formed from CNO enriched material. In order to avoid these stars to have a different content of Fe-peak elements, this second generation of stars should not have been enriched by SNe: this set severe constraints on the type of stars that might have contributed. The most likely candidates are the most massive among the Intermediate Mass Stars (IMS) (the less massive IMS are excluded because there is no evidence for enrichment of C and s-process elements, that are the typical products of these stars). Massive IMS have hot bottom burning at the base of the outer convective envelope during the AGB phase: they may then loose in the ISM large amounts of material processed at the right temperature in order to produce the O-Na anticorrelation and related phenomena (see e.g. Ventura et al. 2001). There are however problems in producing the right amount of O, Na etc. (see e.g. Fenner et al. 2004), so that theoretical investigation are still in progress.

In this scenario, a correlation between the Na-O anticorrelation and the colour of stars on the HB is expected. In fact, complete CNO burning implies the production of He. As noticed by D'Antona & Caloi (2004), He-rich stars should have a faster evolution than normal-He ones, so that at present the TO masses should be smaller. For a difference $\Delta Y = 0.04$ (expected for the ejecta of the massive AGB stars), the difference in TO mass should be about 0.1 $M_\odot$. While such an He and mass difference will be almost unobservable during the evolution of stars on the MS and RGB, a very different location of the stars would be expected on the HB if they loose the same amount of mass. This may justify several properties of the HB, contributing a lot to the explanation of the second parameter effect. Statistical studies of Na-O anticorrelation and its relation to the HB are now in progress (Carretta et al. 2006): early results are very encouraging. The bimodal distributions of stars along the HB of some clusters like NGC2808 are easily explained in this context.

Are GCs (GCs) true example of Simple Stellar Population? Were the GCs able to sustain self-enrichment of metals? The Carretta et al. study intend to probe the first billion years in the life of GCs, to test: (a) if a second generation of stars born from the ejecta of intermediate mass stars does exist in GCs and (b) if any correlation exists between the cluster properties (in particular the extension of the HB) and the distribution of stars along the Na-O anticorrelation.

4.4 Lithium abundances in TO-stars and subgiants of GCs

Primordial Nucleosynthesis occurred when the Universe was only a few minutes old (Peebles 1966). Before this epoch, the Universe was too hot for atomic nuclei: it then consisted only of protons, neutrons, electrons, and photons, a general soup of subatomic particles and photons. As it expanded, it cooled off. Deuterium nuclei begins to form from fusion of neutrons and protons when the Universe was ~ 2 minutes old and the temperature had cooled to ~ 1 billion K. Leftover protons stay free as Hydrogen 'nuclei'. During this phase, deuterium fused to form ^{4}He nuclei. Other reactions make Li, Be, and B in very tiny quantities. By the time the Universe was ~ 4 minutes old, much of the Deuterium turned into ^{4}He. Further on, the Universe cooled so much that fusion stops and no heavy element get formed any more. The theoretical predictions about the aftermaths of this phase of primordial nucleosynthesis depend on the baryon density, the number of neutrino flavours, the neutron lifetime, and the cross sections of the relevant nuclear reactions. These predictions may then be compared with observation of D, He and Li abundances in objects with very low metal content, that we may assume are still formed mainly from material which has not been further processed e.g. in the stellar interiors.

Lithium abundances are of particular interest (see e.g. Suzuki et al. 2000). Li abundances in the warmest metal-poor dwarfs may give a clue to the original abundance of Li: they show a nearly constant value, the so called Spite's plateau (Spite & Spite 1982). The main concern in the interpretation of this datum for cosmology is that the surface Li might have been depleted due to sedimentation or to some mixing.

GCs are interesting because in this case we may compare abundances in TO and subgiants looking for constraints about sedimentation (see Subsection 4.2). Observations of Li in GCs in the nineties (Deliyannis et al. 1995; Pasquini & Molaro 1996, 1997; Castilho et al. 2000) showed the expected dilution effect between TO stars and subgiants, related to the expansion of convective envelope (the only region where Li was not burnt during the MS phase, and possible star-to-star variations in the Li content. Observations of TO stars in the ESO LP also provided Li abundances. The average Li abundance in NGC6397 resulted very close to the Spite Plateau value ($\log n(\text{Li}) = 2.34$, with a very small r.m.s scatter of 0.056 dex entirely justifiable by observational errors: Bonifacio et al. 2002). The maximum intrinsic scatter was only 0.035 dex. On the other hand, observations of the Li doublet in TO-stars of NGC6752 showed that there are clear star-to-star variations (Pasquini et al. 2005). These variations are strictly related to the O-Na anticorrelation issue. In fact there is a Na-Li anticorrelation for TO stars in NGC6752. This by itself was not surprising, since Li is expected to be destroyed at the high temperatures required for Na production by p-captures on Ne nuclei. What was more surprising was however that some Li is observed also in most Na-rich, O-poor stars, and that the stars of NGC6397 which exhibit nearly primordial values of Li abundances also are Na-rich and O-poor. How it is possible that some Li is observed also when products of complete CNO-burning are observed? This is possible in accretion scenarios since there are phases in which massive TP-AGB stars produce Li and other where they destroy Li (Ventura et al. 2001). This is of course a stringent constraint in models for these stars, since efficient Li production can obtained only upon peculiar conditions (activation of the so-called Cameron-Fowler mechanism, Cameron & Fowler 1971) which requires hot bottom burning in convective envelopes. Some fine tuning of models are required to produce just the correct amount of Li to compensate the previous losses during the RGB phases. This is quite disturbing, and it is one of the main concerns of the scenario called to explain the O-Na anticorrelation.

5. THE CASE OF ω CEN

ω Cen is the most luminous and massive ($M \sim 5 \times 10^6\ M_\odot$: Meylan et al. 1995) GC of the Milky Way. It has been suggested to have been the nucleus of a dwarf elliptical (see e.g. Zinnecker et al. 1988 and Freeman 1993). It is a low concentration, slightly elliptical object with some hint of rotation. The colour magnitude diagram displays evidences of multiple populations, differing in metal abundance and age (see e.g. Pancino et al. 2000). The metallicity distribution has been studied by Suntzeff & Kraft (1996). When compared with closed-box model of chemical evolution, it requires loss of some 90% of the original mass. This suggests that a strong wind generated by SNe cleaned the cluster.

Element-to-element ratios show evidences of contributions of core collapse SNe and Intermediate Mass Stars (s-process nucleosynthesis), but not of type Ia SNe (Smith et al. 2000). The O-Na, Mg-Al anticorrelation is present also among ω Cen stars. The excess of α-elements is a signature of contribution by only core collapse SNe to nucleosynthesis. The low Cu abundance is also a signature of the lack of contribution by type Ia SNe. There is a large excess of n-capture elements mostly manufactured through the s-process among the most metal-rich stars in ω Cen. This certifies the contribution by IMS. Note the very large overabundance of Rb, Ba and La, that are mainly, produced by the s-process. The correlation with Fe abundance is less evident for elements for which an important contribution come from the r-process (like Mo and Nd). Even more evident is the case of Eu, that is almost uniquely produced through the r-process. Since it seems likely that only the less massive (and long living) among core-collapse SNe contributed to the r-process, there is indication that these stars did not contribute to the chemical enrichment in ω Cen after this cluster formed. Abundances of n-capture elements like Rb may be reproduced by current models of IMS (with a mass of $< 2\ M_\odot$), with some limited tuning of the parameters.

These data suggested that the cluster was formed with the typical abundance pattern of halo objects. Likely due to its large mass, it was able to retain part of the ejecta of the earliest core collapse SNe, but not of those exploding at most later phases. Some of this metal-enriched gas accumulated within the cluster; this was further enriched in heavy elements by the low velocity winds from IMS (the most massive ones, for which hot bottom burning occurred, caused the O-Na anticorrelation; the less massive ones the overabundances of s-process elements), but not by the high velocity wind from type Ia SNe. Some stars formed from this metal enriched gas over a long period of time (> 1 Gyr), long enough for evolution of stars of $\sim 2\ M_\odot$.

However more recent data have much complicated this picture. The first data came from observation that ω Cen possess a double MS (from ACS HST data, Bedin et al. 2004). Rather surprisingly, the Blue Main Sequence (BMS) has about 1/4 of the stars of the Red MS (RMS), while the metal distribution of ω Cen is peaked toward lower metallicities. We would expect the BMS to be more populated than the RMS (see also Norris 2004). What is the metallicity of the two sequences? In order to answer this question, Piotto et al. (2005) have obtained 12 hr exposure time FLAMES spectra of 19 BMS and 19 RMS stars with $20 < V < 21$ at $R \sim 6000$ (spectral range 4000-4600 Å), likely the faintest stars with an abundance analysis so far. Summing the spectra a total of ~ 200 hrs effective exposure time was used to get $S/N \sim 25$ spectra of a template BMS star and of a template RMS star. The comparison of these spectra with synthesis indicated that RMS has a metallicity of [Fe/H]=-1.6 ± 0.2, and [C/Fe]=0.0; while the BMS has [Fe/H]=-1.2 ± 0.2, [C/Fe]=0.0, [N/Fe]< 1.5. While these results agree well with the abundance distribution obtained for RGB in the cluster, they imply the very surprising consequence that the BMS is more metal-rich than the RMS. In order to be bluer, it should then be more He-rich, with an incredibly large value of $Y \sim 0.40$. An alternative hypothesis is that there is a second further cluster on the same line of sight; this second cluster should be $\sim 2-3$ kpc farther away. However, this is unlikely because the mean radial velocity, proper motion and photocenters of the two clusters are the same. The probability that this might occur by chance are extremely low ($<< 10^{-5}$). Also the hypothesis that we are seeing a tidal tail is untenable. It is not clear how this well produce such a well defined sequence. Furthermore, tidal tails include only less than 1% of the cluster mass, while the BMS accounts for 25% of the cluster mass.

Where the He-rich population of ω Cen comes from? If we compare the composition of the BMS population with that of the RMS population we get an extraordinary value for $\Delta Y/\Delta Z > 100$. For comparison the normal value observed in typical galaxies is $\sim 2-3$. This calls for some selective production by only a limited group of stars. The He abundance of the BMS ($Y \sim 0.40$) is much larger than that required to explain the BHB of clusters in the D'Antona-Caloi scenario ($Y \sim 0.28$). Massive IMS simply do not produce enough He. The less massive IMS might perhaps produce large amounts of He, but they would produce a lot of C, which is not observed. Massive core collapse stars might perhaps produce a large $\Delta Y/\Delta Z$(Fe), but also large amounts of $\alpha-$elements, that are not observed. The less massive among core collapse SNe might be good candidates. Note that the mass of ω Cen is $2 \times 10^6\ M_\odot$. We have to produce $3 \times 10^5\ M_\odot$ of He to explain the BMS starting from the RMS. Such a selective element enrichment is difficult to conceive. Clearly, much is still to be expected from this extremely intriguing object.

REFERENCES

. Alonso, A., Arribas, S., & Martinez-Roger, C.. 1996, A&A, 313, 873
. Baylin, C.D. 1995, ARA&A, 33, 133
. Bedin, L.R. et al. 2004, ApJL, 605, 125
. Bonifacio, P. et al. 2002, A&A, 390, 91
. Bono, G., Caputo, F. & Marconi, M. 1995, AJ, 110, 2365
. Bono, G., Cassisi, S., Zoccali, M., & Piotto, G. 2001, ApJ, 546, L109
. Briley, M.M., Hesser, J.E., Bell, R.A., Bolte, M., & Smith, G.H. 1994, AJ, 108, 2183
. Brown, J.H., Burkert, A., & Truran, J.W. 1991, ApJ, 376, 115
. Brown, J.H., Burkert, A., & Truran, J.W. 1995, ApJ, 440, 666
. Cameron, A.G.W., & Fowler, W.A. 1971, ApJ, 164, 111
. Capriotti, E.R. & Hawley, S.L. 1996, ApJ, 464, 765
. Caputo, F. & Castellani, V. 1984, MNRAS, 207, 185
. Caputo, F., Castellani, V., Marconi, M., Ripepi, V, 2000, MNRAS, 316, 819
. Carretta, E., & Gratton, R.G., 1996, in Formation of the Galactic Halo...Inside and Out, ASP Conference Series, Vol. 92, 1996, H. Morrison & A. Sarajedini, eds., p. 359
. Carretta, E., Gratton, R.G., & Clementini, G., 2000a, MNRAS, 316, 721
. Carretta, E., Gratton, R.G., Clementini, G., & Fusi Pecci, F. 2000b, ApJ, 533, 215
. Carretta, E. 2006, A&A, in press (astro-ph/0511833)
. Castilho, B.V., Pasquini, L., Allen, D.M., Barbuy, B., & Molaro, P., 2000, A&A, 361, 92
. Catelan, M., 1998, ApJ, 495, 81
. Cavallo, R.M., Sweigart, A.V., & Bell, R.A. 1996, ApJ, 464, L79

- Cayrel, R. 1986, A&A, 168, 81
- Chaboyer, B., Fenton, W.H., Nelan, J.E., Patnaude, D.J., & Simon F.E. 2001, ApJ, 562, 521
- Charbonnel, C. 1994, A&A, 282, 811
- Charbonnel, C., Brown, J.A., & Wallerstein, G. 1998, A&A, 332, 204
- Clementini, G., et al. 1995, AJ, 110, 2319
- Clementini, G., et al. 2003, AJ, 125, 1309
- Clementini, G., et al. 2005, MNRAS, 363, 734
- Cunha, K., Smith, V.V., & Lambert, D.L. 1998, ApJ, 493, 195
- D'Antona, F., & Caloi, V. 2004, ApJ, 611, 871
- Dehnen, W., Odenkirchen, M., Grebel, E.V., & Rix, H.-W. 2004, AJ, 127, 2753
- De Angeli, F. et al. 2005, AJ, 130, 116
- De Marchi, G., Leibundgut, B., Paresce, F., & Pulone, L. 1999, A&A, 343, L9
- De Marchi, G., Paresce, F., Straniero, O., & Prada Moroni, P.G., 2004, A&A, 415, 971
- De Marchi, G., Pulone, L., & Paresce, F. 2006, A&A, in press (astro-ph/0512024)
- Deliyannis, C.P., Boesgaard, A.M., King, J.R. 1995, ApJ, 425, L13
- Denisenkov, P.A., & Denisenkova, S.N. 1990, SvAL, 16, 275
- Djorgovski, S. & King, I.R. 1986, ApJL, 305, L61
- ESA 1997, The Hipparcos and Tycho Catalogues, ESA SP-1200
- Fall, S.M. & Rees, M.J. 1977, MNRAS, 181, 37p
- Fenner, Y., Campbell, S., Karakas, A.I., Lattanzio, J.C., & Gibson, B.K. 2004, MNRAS, 353, 789
- Freeman, K.C. 1993, in IAU Symp. 153, Galacric Bulges, eds. H. Dejonghe & H.J. Habing (Dordrecht: Kluwer), p. 263
- Gratton, R.G., Sneden, C., Carretta, E., & Bragaglia, A. 2000, A&A, 354, 169
- Gratton, R.G., et al. 2001, A&A, 369, 87
- Gratton, R.G., et al. 2003, A&A, 408, 529
- Gratton, R.G., et al. 2004a, A&A, 421, 937
- Gratton, R.G., et al. 2004b, ARA&A, 42, 385
- Gratton, R.G., et al. 2005, A&A, 440, 901
- Goodman, J. 1987, ApJ 313, 576
- Hansen, B.M.S. et al. 2004, ApJS, 155, 551
- Harris, W.E. 1996, AJ, 112, 1487
- Hut, P., et al. 2003, New Astron., 8, 337
- Iben, I.Jr. 1964, AJ, 69, 545
- King, I. 1962, AJ, 67, 471
- Kraft, R.P. 1994, PASP, 106, 553
- Lambert, D.L., Heath, J.E., Lemke, M., & Drake, J. 1996, ApJS, 103, 183
- Langer, G.E., & Hoffman, R.D. 1995, PASP, 107, 1177
- Layden, A.C. 1995, AJ, 110, 2312
- McClure, R.D., Fletcher, J.M., & Nemec, J.M. 1980 ApJ, 238, 35
- McClure, R.D. 1984, ApJ, 280, L31
- McCrea, W.H., 1964, MNRAS, 128, 147
- Meylan, G., & Heggie, D.C. 1997, Astron. Astrophys. Rev., 8, 1
- Meylan, G., Mayor, M., Duquennoy, A., & Dubath, P. 1995, A&A, 393, 761
- Murray, S.D., & Lin, D.N.S. 1993, in The Globular Cluster-Galaxy Connection, Smith, G.H., & Brodie, J.P. eds. ASP. Conf. ser. 48, San Francisco, p. 738
- Norris, J.E. 2004, ApJ, 612, 25
- Norris, J.E. & Smith, G.H. 1983, ApJ, 275, 120
- Odenkirchen, M. et al. 2003, AJ, 126, 2385
- Oosterhoff, P.Th. 1938, BAN, 8, 277
- Osborn, W. 1971, Observatory, 91, 223
- Pancino, E., Ferraro, F., Bellazzini, M., Piotto, G. & Zoccali, M. 2000, ApJ, 534, L83
- Parmentier, G. et al. 1999, A&A, 352, 138
- Pasquini, L. & Molaro, P., 1996, A&A, 307, 761
- Pasquini, L. & Molaro, P., 1997, A&A, 322, 109
- Pasquini, L. et al. 2005, A&A, 441, 549
- Peebles, P.J.E. 1966, ApJ, 146, 542

- Perlmutter, S., 1999, ApJ, 517, 565
- Petersen, J.O. 1973, A&A, 27, 89
- Piotto, G., et al. 2004a, ApJ, 604, L109
- Piotto, G., et al. 2004b, MSAIt Supp., 5, 71
- Piotto, G., et al. 2005, ApJ, 621, 777
- Preston, G.W. 1959, ApJ, 130, 507
- Rich, R.M., et al. 2005, AJ, 129, 2670
- Richard, O. et al. 2002, ApJ, 568, 979
- Riello, M., et al. 2003, A&A, 410, 553
- Rosenberg, A., Saviane, I., Piotto, G., & Aparicio, A. 1999, AJ, 118, 2306
- Rubio, M., et al. 1998, AJ, 116, 1708
- Sandage, A.R., 1953, AJ, 58, 61
- Sandage, A.R., & Wildey, R. 1967, ApJ, 150, 469
- Sandage, A.R. 1982, ApJ, 252, 553
- Schmidt, B.P., 1998, ApJ, 507, 46
- Smith, V.V., et al. 2000, AJ, 119, 1239
- Spergel, D.N., et al. 2003, ApJS, 148, 175
- Spite, M., & Spite, F. 1982, A&A, 115, 357
- Solano, E., Garrido, R., Fernley, J., & Barnes, T.G. 1997, A&AS, 125, 321
- Stellingwerf, R.F., 1982, ApJ, 262, 330
- Stetson, P.B., Vandenberg, D.A., & Bolte, M., 1996, A&A, PASP, 108, 560
- Straniero, O., Chieffi, A., & Limongi, M. 1997, ApJ, 490, 425
- Suntzeff, N.B. & Kraft, R.P. 1996, AJ, 111, 191
- Suzuki, T.K., Yoshii, Y., & Beers, T.C. 2000, ApJ, 540, 99
- Sweigart, A.V. & Mengel, J.G. 1979, ApJ, 229, 624
- Van den Bergh, S. 1967, AJ, 72, 70
- Ventura, P., D'Antona, F., Mazzitelli, I., & Gratton, R.G. 2001, ApJ, 550, 65
- Vesperini, E. 1997, MNRAS, 287, 915
- Weinberg, M.D. 1993, ApJ, 410, 543
- Yong, D., Grundahl, F., Nissen, P.E., Jensen, H.R., & Lambert, D.L. 2005, A&A, 438, 875
- Zinn, R. 1980, ApJ, 241, 602
- Zinnecker, H., Keable, C.J., Dunlop, J.S., Cannon, R.D., & Griffiths, W.K. 1988, in IAU Symp. 126, GC Systems in Galaxies, eds. J.E. Grindlay & A.G.D. Philip (Dordrecht: Kluwer), p. 603

CHAPTER 3

The Evolution of Dwarf Galaxies
Evan D. Skillman

THE EVOLUTION OF DWARF GALAXIES

Evan D. Skillman

Astronomy Department
University of Minnesota
Minneapolis, MN 55455, USA
email: skillman@astro.umn.edu

Abstract.
Dwarf galaxies are important to study because they potentially provide a direct connection to the earliest epochs of galaxy formation. They also allow us to study the star formation process at relatively low abundances. Our understanding of the origins and evolution of dwarf galaxies has been changing very rapidly. New observations are giving better insight into the relationship between the two main families of dwarf galaxies, the dwarf ellipticals and the dwarf irregulars. Here I review a broad range of topics related to the formation and evolution of dwarf galaxies.

Keywords: galaxies: clusters, galaxies: dwarf, galaxies: evolution, galaxies: stellar content
PACS: 98.62.Ai; 98.52.Wz

1. DWARF GALAXIES – AN OVERVIEW

Quite often, when one reads an introduction to an article on dwarf galaxies, one encounters the phrase "these simple systems." I may be guilty of using that phrase myself. Usually the intent is to motivate the study of dwarf galaxies with the promise that if we can understand these simple systems, we will have learned vital clues which will help us in the study of the much more complex, more massive systems. I no longer believe this argument. The main reason is that I no longer believe that the smaller galaxies are the simple ones. Just as galaxies with cold gas are more complex than those without, low mass galaxies are more complex than their more massive brethren. The argument behind this is simple enough; the deeper the gravitational potential well, the more organized the system.

Nonetheless, I am a strong advocate of research of dwarf galaxies. My main argument is that of baseline. When one is studying the relative properties of galaxies, dwarf galaxies extend the baselines in mass, luminosity, gas mass fraction, dark matter fraction, and metallicity. If we are to understand the formation and evolution of galaxies, we will need to understand the formation and evolution of dwarf galaxies. It is often stated that since the smallest structures formed first (in cold dark matter dominated hierarchical structure formation) that the present day dwarf galaxies are a direct connection back to the earliest epoch of galaxy formation. It may be true that some of the nearest dwarf galaxies are truly "fossils" of star formation before the epoch of reionization [154].

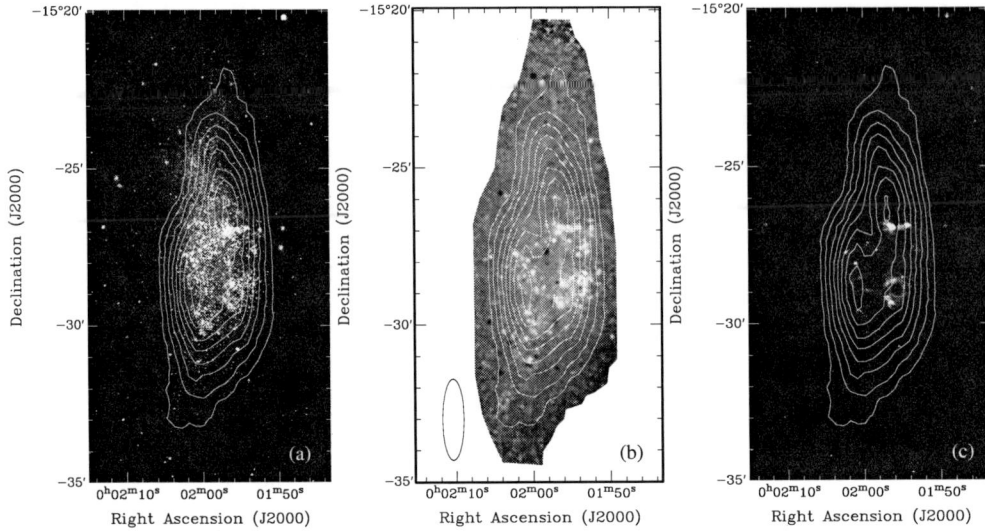

FIGURE 1. Three views of the Local Group dwarf irregular galaxy WLM. (a) Total HI intensity map of WLM superposed on the Local Group Survey [127] U image. Contours are from 25% to 95% of the peak column density (2.16×10^{21} cm^{-2}) in increments of 10%. (b) Same HI contours superposed on the U-B image. The image has been blanked against the first moment map to remove low signal-to-noise data. The synthesized beam size for the HI data is shown in the lower left corner. (c) Continuum-subtracted Hα image from the Local Group Survey, again with our HI contours superposed. Note the two HI peaks and their relationship to the bright stellar clusters and HII regions. (From [90])

1.1 Terminology

The history of astronomy is full of terrible mistakes in nomenclature. For example, we still use the term "planetary nebula." Dwarf galaxies provide several examples of similar misnomers. With some trepidation, I will attempt a brief overview of terminology.

The very word dwarf is problematic. While the word dwarf implies a small size, the most common use of the word when applied to galaxies is a measure of luminosity. Typically, a dwarf galaxy has an absolute magnitude greater than -16, -17, or even -18, depending on the author. For reference, the Large Magellanic Cloud, with an absolute magnitude of -17.7, should perhaps never be categorized as a dwarf, while the Small Magellanic Cloud, with an absolute magnitude of -16.4 lies near the border between dwarf and "normal" galaxies.

The word "irregular" in the term "dwarf irregular galaxy" is derived from the optical appearance of a typical dwarf galaxy with gas (and thus star formation). Since the star formation is not organized into a spiral pattern and appears to have a relatively random spatial distribution, the term irregular generally applies (see Figure 1 for an example). However, when the star formation appears more uniform (because it is depressed or widespread) this begs a new set of labels (e.g., "regular," "amorphous," etc.) which can lead to some fine distinctions and confusion. Also, if the current star formation

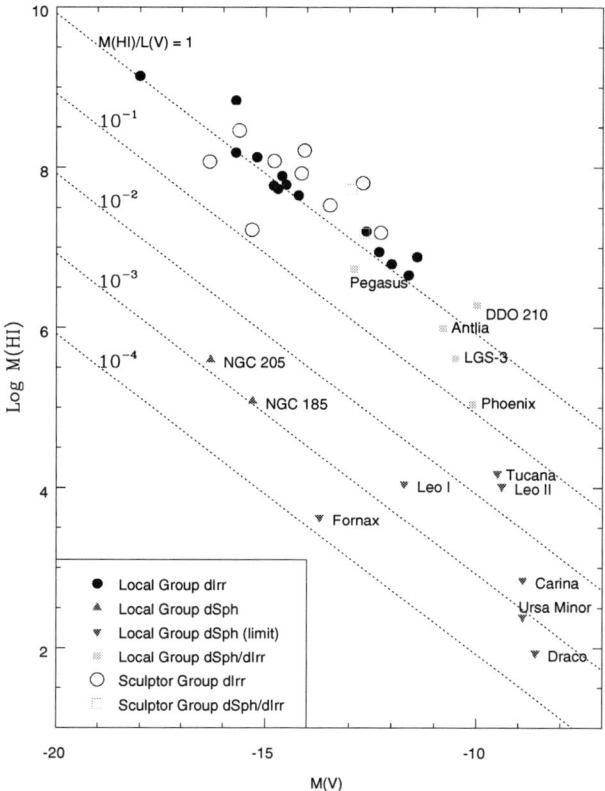

FIGURE 2. Plot of HI mass (in solar units) versus absolute V magnitude for Local Group dwarf galaxies compiled by [195]. The Sculptor group dIs from [32, 92] have been added for comparison.

occurs in a dominant burst this provokes a new set of labels ("blue compact galaxy," "HII galaxy") which all mean about the same thing. For most purposes these galaxies have many similar characteristics, and I will lump all of them together under the term dI, meaning a low luminosity galaxy with cold gas. Note that if reliable mass estimates were more easily obtainable, it would be preferable to place these galaxies on a mass scale instead of a luminosity scale (as mass is a more fundamental and stable characteristic; e.g., luminosities change with time simply as a function of normal evolution).

The other main family of dwarf galaxies is the dwarf ellipticals (dEs). Note that some choose to distinguish between the very low luminosity dwarf spheroidals (dSphs; $M_V \sim\leq -13$) which are found as companions to our Milky Way. Since the dSphs and the dEs appear to form a continuum in most properties, I do not distinguish between them. The dEs are similar to the dIs in many respects but have much lower HI masses and, on average, redder colors. Interesting early discussions of the relations between dEs and dIs can be found in [57, 106]. It is worthwhile to note the difference between low luminosity ellipticals (e.g., M 32) which follow the same trends in luminosity, size, and surface brightness as the elliptical galaxies and dEs, which closely follow the same trends in luminosity, size, and surface brightness as the dIs [106, 11].

Dwarf galaxies which have recent star formation and HI, but no HII regions (no current star formation) have been classified as dSph/dIrr galaxies [128] or "transition" galaxies. Whether these galaxies are actually transitioning from one class to the other, or if they are just caught between episodes of star formation is not yet clear; both may be true [166].

It is sometimes very useful to look at data graphically, and in Figure 2 I have plotted HI mass versus luminosity for a sample of nearby dwarf galaxies. I have taken the V magnitudes and distances from the compilation of [128] for the Local Group members, and calculated the HI masses and limits appropriately. I have also added the Sculptor dwarfs from [32] with new distances from [92]. Using different symbols, I have distinguished between dIs, dEs, and proposed transition type galaxies and also between detections and limits. In Figure 2, we see that the dIs tend to fall in a range of $0.1 - 10$ in M(HI)/L(V) in solar units, while most of the dEs are in the range of $10^{-5} - 10^{-2}$. The transition types appear in an intermediate range.

What is the origin of the gas in the dEs and transition types where HI is detected? That is, is it gas that is left over from normal star formation, or is it "recycled" gas – gas that is returned to the ISM from previous generations of star formation. One approach to this question is to determine how much gas can be attributed to the present stars. The return rate from a single-age population is a strong function of age (see [99]). However, after the first few billion years, the return fraction varies between roughly 1% Gyr^{-1} to 0.3% Gyr^{-1}. Assuming M/L ratios of roughly unity for the stellar populations in the the dEs, then one might easily account for all of the gas detected in NGC 205 and NGC 185 as recycled gas. In the transition cases, the larger M(HI)/L ratios are just barely consistent with the total gas return fractions ($0.26 - 0.46$ in 10 Gyr for different models [99]) and are probably more closely related to the dIs (since this would also require keeping star formation suppressed while all of this gas is returned to the ISM).

At some point early in its history, a galaxy which we observe to be a dE today was an actively star forming galaxy; thus, it had cold gas. Structurally, dE galaxies are quite similar to present day star forming dwarf galaxies (dIs, see next section). Thus, the defining moment of the creation of a dE is when it loses its cold gas. Since many dE galaxies show the presence of an intermediate age population, the origins of dE galaxies, as defined here, are not constrained to a single epoch. Some dEs are consistent with no intermediate age stars, and thus, were created quite early in the history of the Universe (e.g., Ursa Minor; [141]), while others show star formation up to very recent times (e.g., Leo I; [61]). Thus, the process or processes which convert actively star forming dwarf galaxies into dE galaxies have been taking place over the entire history of our Universe.

1.2. Similarities Between dEs and dIs

The primary distinction between dE and dI galaxies is the presence or absence of cold gas. This is usually measured through HI emission at 21 cm. The typical values of M(HI)/L for dIs range from 0.1 to 10, while most dEs are non-detections in HI or show ratios of 10^{-3} or less [163]. Otherwise, dE and dI galaxies have many similar properties. Most importantly, it has been known for a long time now that dEs and dIs have similar structures [57, 106, 19, 12].

When trying to understand the possible relationships between dE and dI galaxies, there are several observations to consider. Perhaps most important is the strong morphology – density relationships observed in both the group (e.g., [55]) and cluster (e.g., [13]) environments.

Because of their low masses, both are generally recognized as fragile systems (e.g., [33]). However, [107] have pointed out that the lowest mass galaxies have the highest central mass densities (a result of their early collapse redshift). For a long time, dEs were considered to be non-rotating systems, and lack of rotational support distinguished them from the dIs (e.g., [6]). Many dEs in the cluster environment have nuclei (e.g., [17]). In contrast, the typical dI does not show the presence of a nucleus, but centrally concentrated star formation is common (and defines the class of blue compact dwarf galaxies). Finally, almost by definition, dEs and dIs must have different star formation histories (as dEs have no current star formation and almost all dIs do). Although it has been known for quite a while that the Milky Way dSph companions show a great variety of star formation histories (e.g., [128]), it is now emerging that dIs may too (see section 2).

1.3. Recent Results: Rotation in dEs

One of the properties which was long thought to separate the dEs from the dIs was rotation. Bender and collaborators found very little evidence of rotation in the few systems that they observed (e.g., [6]). However, recent programs to observe dEs have discovered that a significant fraction of dEs show significant rotational support ([34, 35, 146, 65, 66, 198]). Interestingly, [198] find a Tully-Fisher relationship between luminosity and velocity width for the Virgo dEs which do show rotation (Figure 3). It is intriguing that the rotating and non-rotating dEs are not distinguished structurally (Figure 4).

2. GLOBAL STAR FORMATION HISTORIES OF DWARF GALAXIES

2.1 Dwarf Galaxies as Unique Cosmological Probes

The nearby dwarf galaxies of the Local Group are a unique probe of the chemical and structural evolution of the universe over its entire history. Interpretation of the fossil

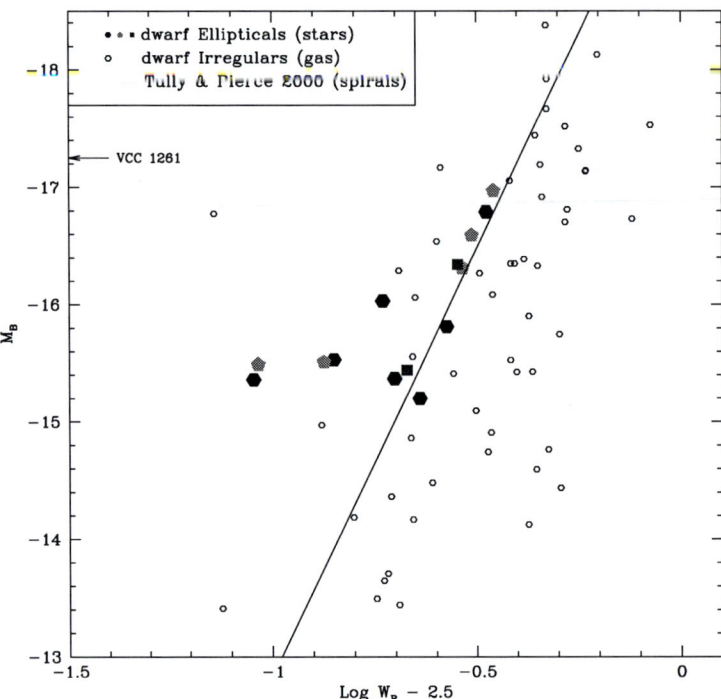

FIGURE 3. The luminosity-line width relation for dwarf elliptical galaxies (note that the values shown are the observed maximum linewidths, which are possible underestimates of the full rotation velocity; see [202] for a full discussion of possible correction factors to the observed widths). Dwarf ellipticals with blue cores (squares) and red cores (pentagons) follow the same relation as spiral galaxies (line; [194]) and dwarf irregular galaxies (open dots; [197]). (From [198])

evidence contained within these systems provides direct and quantitative constraints on their star formation histories (SFHs) and broader evolution (e.g., [128]). The number of systems for which these studies are possible is limited, and so far only the Milky Way (MW) subgroup has been analyzed in detail. However, dwarf galaxy evolution is dependent upon both local and cosmic environmental factors. It is therefore of tremendous importance to disentangle these effects for the nearby galaxies so that key results obtained locally can be correctly interpreted in a wider cosmological context.

In currently favored hierarchical structure formation models, density fluctuations on the scale of dwarf galaxies collapse early in the evolution of the universe and merge to form larger structures. The dwarf galaxies that we observe in the local universe are the potential surviving remnants of these original, primordial building blocks of larger galaxies. Indeed, the tidal disruption of the Sagittarius or Canis Major dwarf galaxies provide evidence of the ongoing hierarchical formation of our Galaxy [83, 125].

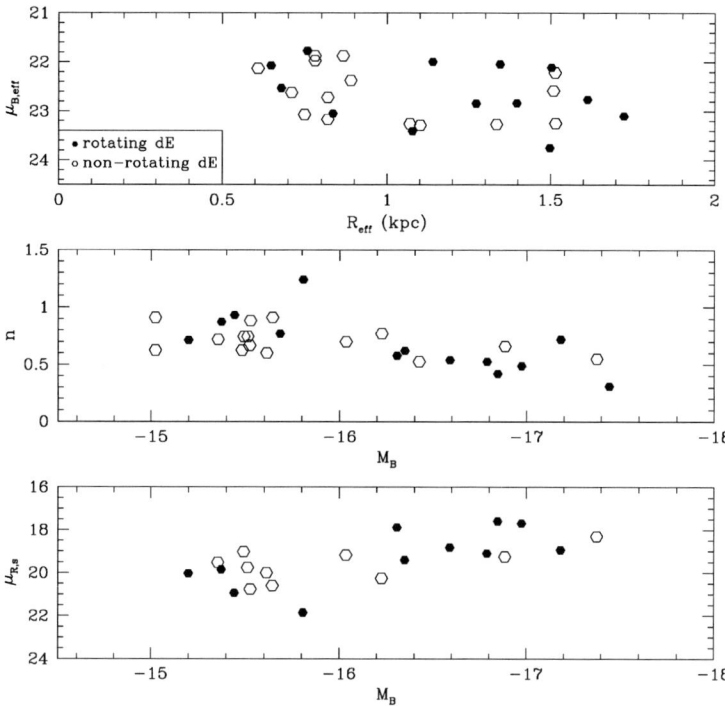

FIGURE 4. Structural parameters for Sérsic fits to dwarf elliptical galaxies in Virgo with measured kinematic properties ([146, 66, 198]); rotating (filled hexagons) and non-rotating (open hexagons) dE galaxies have similar structural properties. (a) Model independent parameters of half-light radius and effective surface brightness. (b) Absolute magnitude and Sérsic shape parameter. (c) Absolute magnitude and central surface brightness from a Sérsic fit to the R-band surface brightness profile. The non-rotating and rotating dwarf elliptical galaxies cannot be distinguished based on structural parameters. (From [198])

However, the accretion of gas and its subsequent retention to form the first generation of stars in dwarf galaxies is a controversial process. Cosmological simulations predict at least an order of magnitude more surviving dwarf galaxy-sized halos than are observed around the MW and M31 [95]. Its seems clear that not all these halos can accrete gas and form stars. Processes such as reionization [16] and feedback from the first generation of stars [33] are invoked to suppress star formation or remove the gas from some subset of dark matter halos. Crucially, such processes can leave their imprint in the stellar content of nearby systems.

Both local environmental factors and cosmological influences are expected to play an important role in dwarf galaxy evolution. Evidence for this comes from the position – morphology relation seen for the lowest-mass systems in the Local Group. The dSphs are preferentially found as satellites to the MW and M31, whereas the dIrrs are preferentially found in isolated locales (e.g., [195]). Additionally, the closest MW dSphs companions, like Draco and Ursa Minor [3, 27], have only an old stellar population with age ≥ 10 Gyr, whereas those at a distance of 100 kpc or greater, like Fornax or Leo I [179, 61, 62], have prominent young and intermediate-age stellar populations (cf., [196]).

Detailed dynamical modeling of the orbital evolution of dwarf satellites provides clues to the role of local environment in dwarf galaxy evolution [129, 130]. "Tidal stirring," which is a combination of tidal effects and disk shocking, can remove most of the gas from a dwarf galaxy and transform rotationally supported systems into pressure supported systems. Essentially, this will convert a dIrr galaxy into a dSph galaxy. The tidal stripping of satellites is also known to occur, and while this process alone is unlikely to change the morphology of a system from a dIrr to a dSph, it will still change the observable properties of the dwarf, as spectacularly demonstrated by the Sagittarius dwarf galaxy. Finally, there is some evidence for a link between tidal interactions and star formation, such that tides are able to trigger star formation. All of these effects suggest that the observed properties of dwarf galaxies should be a complex function of their spatial location and orbital properties within the group where they are observed.

Unfortunately, companions of our Milky Way are the only galaxies with robust derivations of their SFHs at *intermediate and old ages*. This accounts for a dozen or so systems (eight dSph satellites), out of the 40 or so which lie within ~ 1 Mpc. The significant variations between, and the general trends shown by the SFHs of the MW companions were only revealed through deep color-magnitude diagrams (CMDs) reaching below the old main sequence turnoff. Synthetic modeling of these CMDs provides the strongest possible constraint on the evolution of these galaxies over the entirety of cosmic time [63]. Considering the unique role of the MW companion dwarf galaxies as cosmological probes – the only such systems for which detailed information is available on their *full* star formation and chemical enrichment histories – it is vitally important that we understand if the early SFHs of these systems are representative of dwarf galaxies in the wider universe. Since environment has been shown to be important in dwarf galaxy evolution, and, since the evolutionary history, and therefore environment, of each large galaxy may be unique, it is possible that the MW dwarf companions may not be representative.

In the next section I will discuss a project to get a deep color-magnitude diagram of a nearby, isolated dI. Projects with the ACS on HST will allow us to expand our reach beyond the Milky Way satellites and into the Local Group. In this way, we can test the representative nature of the early SFHs of the MW dwarf galaxies.

2.2. The Star Formation History of the Local Group Dwarf Irregular IC 1613

Recently, my collaborators and I have published a star formation history for IC 1613, a Local Group dwarf irregular galaxy, based on relatively deep HST WFPC2 observations [174] (see Figure 5). Although detailed SFH studies exist for other dwarf irregular galaxies, no dwarf irregular galaxies at distances beyond the Magellanic Clouds have been observed to the depth of the present study of IC 1613 ($M_V \simeq +3.4$).

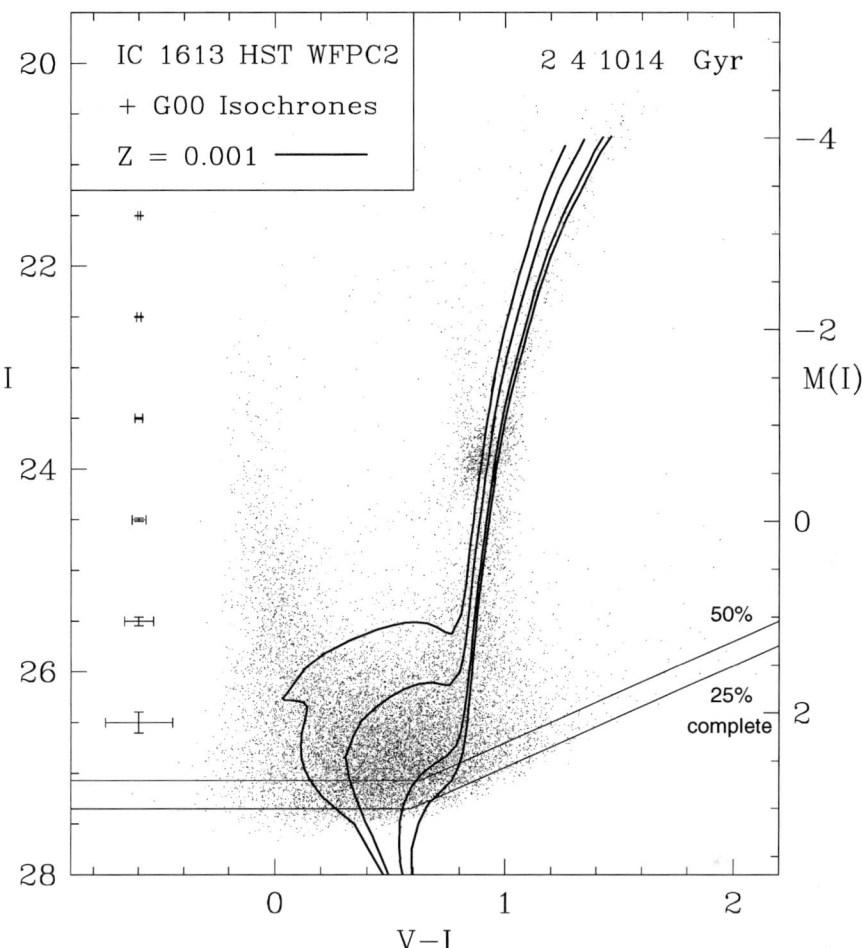

FIGURE 5. CMD of IC 1613 derived from HST WFPC2 observations. Isochrones for a metallicity of Z = 0.001 and ages of 2, 4, 10, and 14 Gyr from [67] have been added in order to show the limitations of the observations in terms of MS ages. MS turnoffs back to intermediate ages (~5 Gyr) are well represented in the observations, but the oldest MS turnoffs (~10 Gyr) fall below the 50% completeness limit and are not represented. Thus, constraints on the oldest populations will need to come from the evolved stars. (From [174])

The main feature seen in the SFH is an extended event from ~ 2 Gyr ago until $5-10$ Gyr ago (see Figure 6). While there has been star formation since that event (a significant amount coming 0.5 Gyr ago), the bulk of the stars in this region of IC 1613 come from the earlier age. Although [46] found RR Lyraes in this field, the ancient (≥ 10 Gyr) SFR was well below the lifetime average.

Note that one of the fundamental conclusions of this study, that star formation was relatively low at ages older than 7 Gyr compared to intermediate ages, is only possible with the present depth of photometry. In order to be able to determine whether this is a general feature of low mass dwarf irregular galaxies or particular to IC 1613, CMDs of similar depth are needed for a large sample of dwarf irregular galaxies. At present, this will only be possible with the HST for Local Group galaxies.

IC 1613 is not the first dwarf irregular galaxy for which it has been suggested that star formation has occurred predominantly at intermediate ages. The SMC is also known to have a SFH which is dominated by star formation at intermediate ages [47] (and references therein). From the study of a single field in the SMC, [47] find a slow rise in the SFR from the earliest ages to a peak at 7 Myr and then a steep decline to the present. This is very similar to that for IC 1613, with the exception of a higher SFR in the last Gyr for IC 1613. It is interesting that these two galaxies, with presumably very different evolutionary histories (IC 1613 evolving in isolation and the SMC being strongly influenced by both the LMC and the Galaxy), have very similar star formation and chemical enrichment histories. Note, however, that the changes in the SFR in the Magellanic Clouds are often associated with the tidal effects of a close encounter or close passage to the Milky Way galaxy (although the SMC and LMC have different SFHs, see discussions in [80, 142]).

There are also galaxies for which it has been suggested that most of the stars have been formed relatively recently. Our earlier study of Leo A [188] suggested that the majority of the star formation had occurred in the last 2 Gyr. [48] discovered RR Lyraes in Leo A, and thus the presence of very early star formation, but converting the number of RR Lyrae stars to an early SFR is very uncertain. Interestingly, a later study study of Leo A [161] concludes that the CMD is consistent with either similar SFRs at earliest and intermediate ages or decreasing SFR from earliest to intermediate ages, but not increasing SFR from earliest to intermediate ages as we see here for IC 1613. It would be interesting to model the newer HST Leo A observations with the techniques described in this paper to see if the same conclusion is derived. A similar SFH is found for Sextans A. From a relatively deep ($M_V \simeq +2.0$) CMD, [49] find that while there is evidence for very old stars in Sextans A, the SFR at intermediate ages (3 - 10 Gyr) was quite low, and the SFR has been the highest in the last 2 Gyr.

However, of those dwarf irregular and transition galaxies with relatively deep CMDs, the SFH history found in IC 1613 does not appear to be universal. In WLM, [43] finds a relatively high SFR at the earliest times, which is never reached again in the history of the galaxy. In LGS 3, [133] find a SFR which is highest in the first few Gyr, and then lower by at least a factor of 10 thereafter. In particular, the Phoenix dwarf galaxy shows a relatively high SFR in the earliest few Gyr followed by fluctuations but showing an overall decrease in SFH. These large differences in star formation histories probably point to different environmental influences, but identifying which environmental effects are dominant remains a challenge.

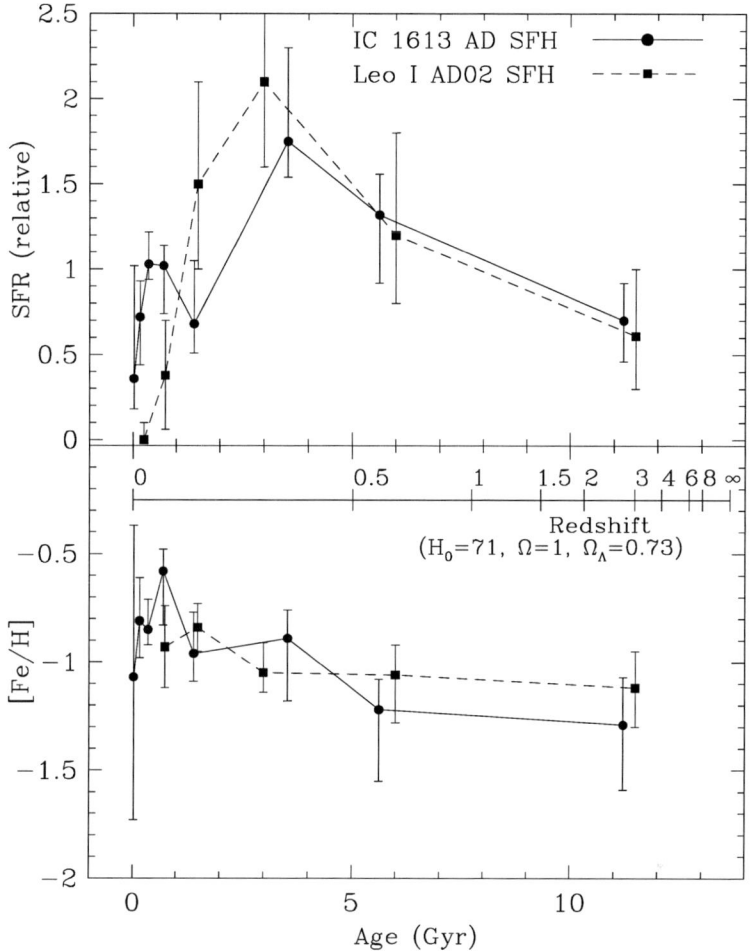

FIGURE 6. Comparison of SFHs and metal enrichment histories for IC 1613 and the dSph Leo I (both derived via the Dolphin method [44, 174]). Note that the two galaxies have nearly identical star formation and metal enrichment histories when analyzed in an identical fashion. A timeline comparing redshift to real time has been added for the noted cosmology for convenience. Note that the bulk of the star formation and chemical enrichment has occurred at $z < 1.0$. (From [174])

The currently favored ΛCDM models for galaxy formation afford a significant role for dwarf galaxies. Dwarf galaxies are assumed to trace early star formation in the Universe and galaxy evolution until the present. Due, in large part, to attempts to understand the possible evolutionary connections between the dwarfs with negligible or extremely low present SFRs (the dSph galaxies) and the dwarfs with obvious signs of present star formation (e.g., dIrrs, blue compact dwarfs, HII galaxies), many theorists are turning their attention to the problem of dwarf galaxy evolution. Environmental effects are turning out to be a key parameter (e.g., [195, 196, 102, 137, 70, 129, 130, 28]).

We have produced the deepest CMD of an isolated dwarf irregular galaxy. Given the density-morphology relationship in the Local Group, the dIrr galaxies are at much greater distances than the dSphs, and, thus, have correspondingly shallower CMDs. As a result, it has been difficult to make direct comparisons between the CMDs of dIrr galaxies and dSph galaxies. Even though our CMD for IC 1613 is still not as deep as the typical study of a dSph MW companion, we can now attempt such a comparison.

To first order, star formation in IC 1613 appears to have occurred predominantly at intermediate ages. This is also characteristic of several of the outer MW dSph satellites (specifically Carina, Fornax, Leo II and Leo I, see introduction). A particularly interesting comparison is between IC 1613 and Leo I; both appear to be dominated by star formation at the same intermediate ages [61, 44]. In Figure 6 we compare the Dolphin SFH and AMR solutions for IC 1613 with the Dolphin [44] solutions for Leo I. We also add the Gallart [61] solutions for Leo I. Figure 6 shows that the SFHs and AMRs for IC 1613 and Leo I, when derived via identical methodology, are nearly identical. Figure 6 also shows very good agreement between the SFHs derived by two different methods, even though the derived AMRs are quite different (the main difference most likely arising because the upper red giant branch, which is quite sensitive to metallicity, is not used in the methodology of [61]).

One possible interpretation of Figure 6 is that, absent the youngest stars, is it possible that there are no differences between the stellar populations of isolated dIrr and dSphs which are more distant from their parent galaxies. The implication is that dIrr and some dSph galaxies have similar progenitors, and that the differences which we see today are due to environmental influences during the lifetimes of the galaxies which allow one type of galaxy to retain its gas and form stars up the present and another not. Certainly the morphological census of the Local Group has evolved with time.

Do the similar SFHs and AMRs for IC 1613 and Leo I support the proposal by Lin & Faber [118] that dSphs can be formed by ram pressure stripping of dIrrs? At the time, Lin & Faber estimated that an ambient number density of 10^{-6} cm^{-3} would be required for stripping the gas from a dIrr over a Hubble time and inferred the presence of such gas through indirect arguments. Recently, FUSE and CHANDRA observations have provided evidence for extended coronal gas surrounding either the Milky Way galaxy or the Local Group with a density of $\sim 10^{-6}$ cm^{-3} [139, 140]. Additionally, [178] estimate surprisingly high densities of $\sim 10^{-4}$ cm^{-3} for the Galactic halo via observations of pressure confined clouds in the Magellanic Stream. Thus, there does appear to be material with the potential for stripping the gas from Local Group dwarf galaxies. Indeed, the HI cloud associated with the Phoenix dwarf ([209, 158, 86] may be direct evidence of a stripping event having occurred in the last 100 Myr [78].

The main problem with drawing a direct evolutionary link between IC 1613 and Leo I would appear to be the total number of stars. With an $M_V = -14.7$, IC 1613 is much more luminous than Leo I ($M_V = -11.9$). While small differences in luminosity could be explained by fading of the dSph after truncation of star formation, the nearly 3 magnitude difference would be difficult to account for. Although the V-band central surface brightnesses are comparable (22.8 ± 0.3 for IC 1613 versus 22.4 ± 0.3 for

Leo I, [128]), the optical scale lengths are significantly different (~ 700 pc for IC 1613 and ~ 130 pc for Leo I). Given that Leo I is a dark matter dominated system, it does not seem likely that ram pressure stripping of the HI gas would result in a significantly greater optical scale length. (Indeed, Faber & Lin calculated that IC 1613 was too large to evolve into a present day dSph.) A possible solution to this could be that only the central region of Leo I has a smaller scale length and that there is an underlying larger scale length stellar distribution (perhaps as suggested by [180].) In sum, the difference in luminosity between IC 1613 and Leo I is another manifestation of the bimodal nature of the metallicity-luminosity relationships for dwarf galaxies [128, 71], which remains as a key hurdle for the proposal of converting dSphs to dIrrs via ram pressure stripping.

2.3. Comparing Star Formation Histories of dIrr and dSph Galaxies

Figure 6 raises an interesting question. What is the best way to compare the star formation histories of galaxies? Certainly the uniformity of analysis is important. It is also important to concentrate on robust measures (Mario Mateo says that it is important to measure the climate, not the weather). As a result, it is important to keep things simple.

Jon Holtzman and Andy Dolphin have constructed an archive of all HST WFPC2 photometry in Local Group galaxies [77]. This is a wonderful resource, as all of the photometry has been compiled in a uniform way. Together with Dan Weisz (a graduate student at Minnesota), we are using this photometry database and Andy Dolphin's programs to produce star formation histories for all of these fields. In addition to taking a uniform approach, we are using only the most modern stellar evolution models, taking care to estimate systematic uncertainties in the isochrones, and quantifying random errors using Monte Carlo techniques. Through the use of well-defined statistical measures we hope to produce true comparisons of star formation histories. Preliminary results of this effort are reported in [50].

One of the diagnostic diagrams that we have come to favor is the plot of cumulative stars formed versus time. In this plot the y-axis spans from 0 to 1, so absolute star formation rates are normalized. Since Jon Holtzman advocated this diagram as meeting many of the criteria set forth above, we are now calling these "Holtzman" diagrams. Figure 7 shows a comparison of several Local Group dSphs in a single Holtzman diagram. Figure 8 shows a comparable Holtzman diagram for several Local Group dIrrs.

The surprising (to most people) aspect of Figures 7 and 8, is the similarity of the two plots. The large variety of the the SFHs for the Local Group dSphs is now well known. However, it appears that the Local Group dIrrs show a similar variety. Even though these two families of galaxies look very different, their star formation histories have much in common. Thus, the appearance of dwarf galaxies is affected disproportionately by their recent (~ 1 Gyr) star formation histories.

Admittedly, the HST field of view can be quite small compared to the angular size of some nearby Local Group galaxies, so it is possible that the HST fields are not truly representative of the whole galaxy. This is especially true since most of these galaxies are known to exhibit radial gradients in their stellar populations (e.g.,[49, 189]). Are the star formation histories dominated by local or global variations? Figure 9 addresses this

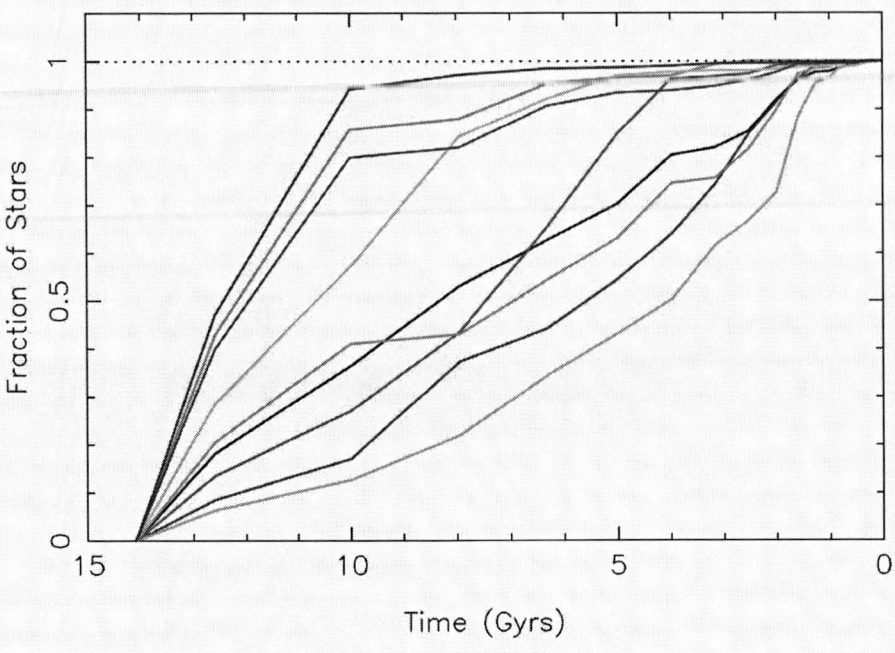

FIGURE 7. Comparison of cumulative SFHs for several Local Group dSphs.

question for the dIrr NGC 6822. Here we compare four fields in this galaxy. Although all four lines are not the same, evidence of rapid increases in the star formation rate happen at the same times in these four independent fields. It would appear from this one example that global influences may be more important than local ones.

Hopefully, with more observations of this type, analyzed in this way, we will begin to be able to identify the factors that are most important in determining the star formation histories of the dwarf galaxies. Most importantly, as proper motions and orbits become available, we can compare the star formation histories with their environmental influences to see to what degree interactions play a role in determining the star formation histories. Future HST ACS observations will be especially important in this regard as they will provide much tighter constraints on the star formation histories.

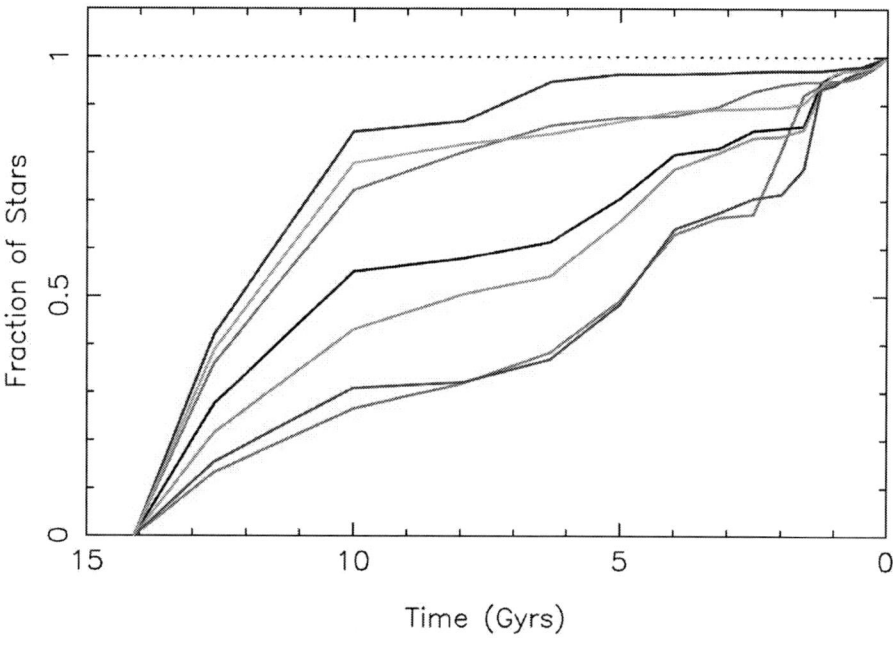

FIGURE 8. Comparison of cumulative SFHs for several Local Group dIrrs.

2.4. Evidence for Suppression of Early Star Formation by Photoionization?

An especially interesting question in this regard is the effect of reionization on the suppression of dwarf galaxy formation. Originally discussed within the context of explaining the absorbers responsible for the Ly-α forest [85, 152], later papers realized the potentially important effects of early heating of the ISM on the evolution of dwarf galaxies [53, 4, 29, 150, 185, 100, 5, 16]. With a rotation curve maximum of 25 km s^{-1}, IC 1613 is clearly in the regime of galaxies which should be susceptible to this effect. The model of Babul & Rees[4] specifically predicts a gap or a fallow period of star formation from the time of reionization ($z \geq 6$, [58]; or $z = 17 \pm 5$, [177]) to the time when the UV background dropped sufficiently for the gas in low mass haloes to cool (which they estimate to be about $z \sim 1$). A redshift timeline has been added to Figure 6 so that one can look at the SFH as a function of both real time and redshift. Although the time resolution is course, it appears that the heightened SFR in IC 1613 started between z of

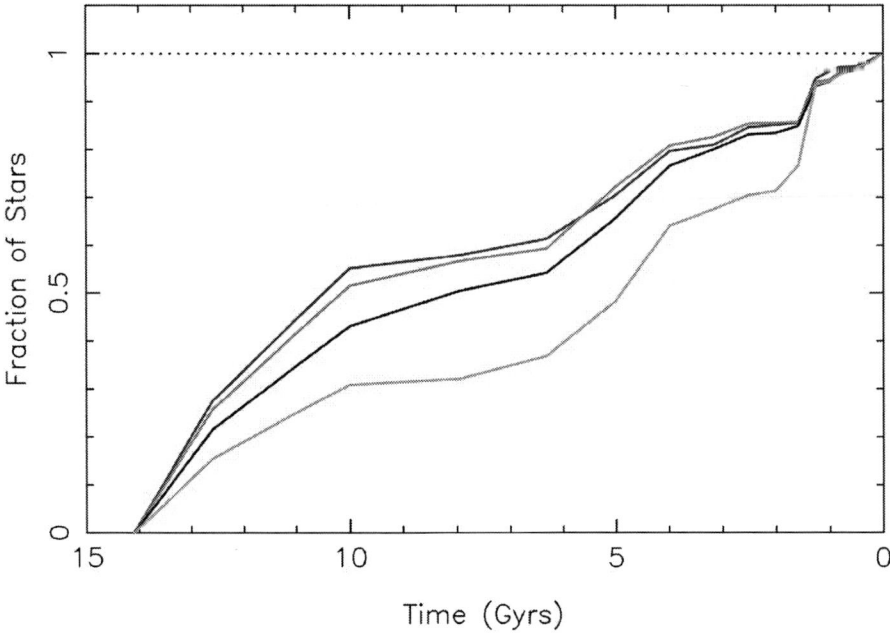

FIGURE 9. Comparison of cumulative SFHs for four different fields in the Local Group dIrr NGC 6822.

0.5 and 1. It could be argued that the SFH of IC 1613 is exactly what one expects from an isolated galaxy with roughly 10^9 $M_\odot$. It might have formed as a virialized structure sometime before reionization, and started to make stars then. After reionization, the high UV background prevented further infall and kept the gas within IC 1613 from cooling rapidly, so that it never formed too many stars until star formation in M31 and the Milky Way settled down enough to drop the UV background, at a redshift roughly between 1 and 2. It then took some time for that gas to cool, until finally at $z \approx 0.5$ the star-formation ramped up to a peak and slowly declined later. This is not "delayed galaxy formation," as we do see evidence for very old stars in IC 1613 (e.g., RR Lyrae stars), but formation of a dwarf in which much of the star formation was deferred.

Within the collapse and dissipation model of galaxy formation [206], the effects of reionization on the evolution of dwarf galaxies is twofold (see discussion in Benson et al. 2002a and references therein). The ionizing background heats the IGM which suppresses the collapse of low mass structures. The ionizing background can also heat the ISM in low mass haloes which have already formed and reduce the rate of radiative cooling by reducing the number of neutral atoms. The first effect has a strong influence on the low end of the galaxy luminosity function. The photoionizing background will reduce the fraction of gas which collapses with the dark matter especially in systems which are less massive than the "filtering mass" ([70]). Benson et al.[9] point out that the formation history is also an important parameter in determining the final gas content of a dark matter halo. In order to solve the perceived problem of the mismatch between the theoretically expected and observed low end of the galaxy luminosity function, much attention has been given to the effects of the suppression of the formation of dwarf galaxies (e.g., [16, 30, 175, 8, 9, 182]). However, these studies generally concentrate on the luminosity function and star formation histories of individual galaxies are not explored in depth.

The second effect is relevant to the question of suppressed star formation at intermediate ages. Can star formation in dwarf galaxies which have already formed before reionization be suppressed by the photoionizing background and then recommence at redshifts of 0.5 and lower? Babul & Rees [4] point to the fast decline in the UV background between $z = 2$ and the present and estimate that new star formation would precipitate in dwarfs at $z \leq 1$. Calculating a specific SFH depends strongly on the influence of both external (the photoionizing background) and internal (stellar feedback) variables [182]. The evidence of an environmental dependence of the low end of the galaxy luminosity function [193, 192] may imply a very large range of SFHs due simply to environmental differences on the effects of photoionization [9].

Could the low SFR in IC 1613 at early ages indicated by our CMD analysis be the signature of suppression of star formation by the photoionizing background? The effect could be environmentally dependent (i.e., for dwarf galaxies close to large galaxies, the effects of the UV radiation from the neighbor galaxies could be more important than the relatively uniform UV background from distant sources), so a statistically significant sample of SFHs for dwarf irregular galaxies will be needed for any definitive statements. However, it is interesting that the bulk of the star formation in IC 1613 occurs at intermediate ages, which may well be after much of the gas in the central parts of the galaxy has had time to recombine and cool. It is also interesting that the star formation and chemical enrichment histories for IC 1613 are similar to those of the SMC and Leo I. These three galaxies show very different morphologies, so why should their evolutionary characteristics be so similar? This would be possible if their evolution is driven by external forces and if these galaxies shared relatively similar environments. The extreme cases of Leo A [188] and Sextans A [49], in which it appears that star formation has been suppressed until $z \approx 0.2 - 0.3$, may present even stronger challenges. Note that while Sextans A is nearly identical to IC 1613 in terms of luminosity and rotation curve maximum [173] Leo A is an order of magnitude fainter and shows almost no rotation at all [208].

However, it should be noted that the evolutionary characteristics of IC 1613 are not universal. Early enhancements in SFR are detected in several of the dwarf galaxies in the Local Group. Our suggestion that we are able to detect the effects of reionization in the SFHs of the nearby dwarfs may raise as many questions as it answers. The UV background is just one of many factors which can influence the SFH of a dwarf galaxy, and it may be the dominant factor for only a fraction of dwarf galaxies. At this point it would be very useful for the galaxy evolution modelers to present compilations of the SFHs for the dwarf galaxies in their simulations. As the quality of the CMDs in the observational studies increases, and thus the time resolution improves, detailed comparisons between observational SFHs and theoretical simulations may prove to better constrain ideas about the relative importance of different effects on dwarf galaxy evolution.

3. MAPPING RECENT STAR FORMATION IN NEARBY DWARF GALAXIES: TESTING OUR KNOWLEDGE OF THE STAR FORMATION PROCESS

3.1. Resolved Studies of Star Formation in Nearby Dwarf Galaxies – An HST Forte

Due to its unprecedented angular resolution over a reasonably large field of view, the HST has revolutionized our knowledge of the stellar populations in nearby galaxies. The primary advances have come in two different areas, the *ancient* star formation histories (SFHs) of these galaxies (i.e., ages ≥ 1 Gyr) and the *recent* SFHs (i.e., ages ≤ 1 Gyr). Both studies are vital to our understanding of galaxy evolution. As shown in the last section, by measuring changes in star formation rate (SFR) over cosmological time scales, we measure the evolution directly. Second, by making detailed studies of the recent star formation, we understand the star formation process and its impact on the physical state of the galaxy.

Nearby dwarf galaxies have proven to be ideal laboratories to investigate how stars form out of gas and how, in turn, violent star formation shapes the ambient ISM. This is because dwarf galaxies are (mostly) solid body rotators, i.e., there is no shear, and they do not possess spiral density waves. The absence of these features (which destroy structures in more massive galaxies) allow us to recover a significant history of the star formation.

Understanding the evolution of dwarf galaxies is an important goal itself. Dwarf galaxies are now widely acknowledged to be the building blocks of today's massive galaxies. Today's dwarf galaxies, survivors of a much richer population, remain the most numerous type of galaxy. These intrinsically faint systems are believed to be a significant contributor to the high universal SFRs seen at intermediate redshift ($z\sim1$; e.g., [120]). Also, with metallicities of ~ 0.1 solar and less, dwarf galaxies are the closest counterparts to the early star–forming fragments. In–depth studies of nearby dwarf galaxies are the key to understanding the conditions in and evolution of galaxies in the early universe.

One particularly important question regards feedback: *"How does the impact of star formation ("feedback") change as a function of galaxy mass?"* We need a quantitative understanding of how one episode of star formation affects the surrounding ISM and the prospects for future star formation. In simplest terms, does an episode of star formation lead to another episode via compression of the cold ISM, or does it quench future star formation via heating of the ISM? While several aspects of feedback have

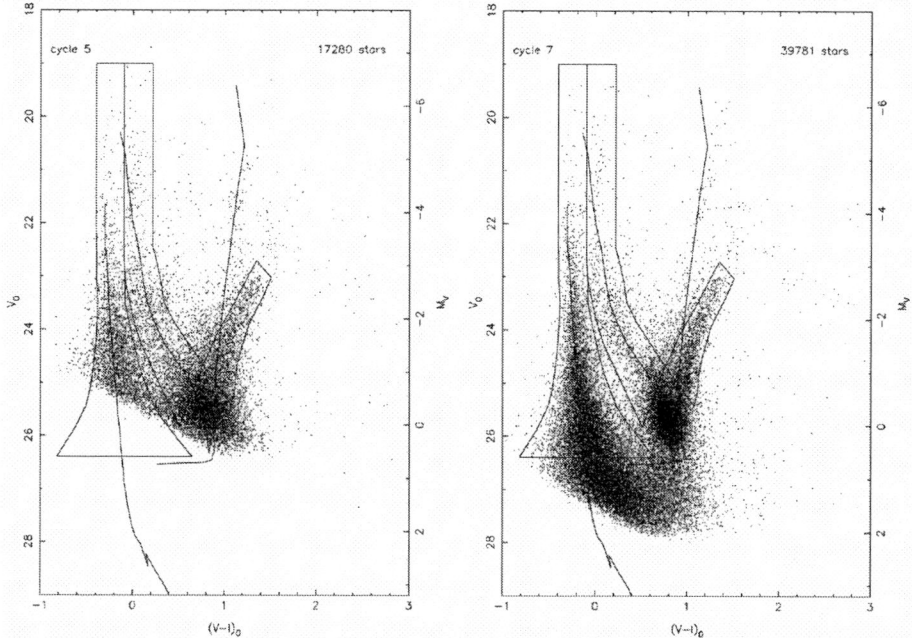

FIGURE 10. Color-magnitude diagrams for Sextans A [39]. The left panel shows Cycle 5 WFPC2 data (1 orbit each in V and I), and the right panel shows Cycle 7 data (8 orbits in V and 16 orbits in I). The increased photometric sensitivity of the Cycle 7 data reveals the entire sequence of BHeB stars merging into the red clump. The curves come from the stellar evolution models of Bertelli et al. [10] and indicate the main sequence, the blue edge of the He-burning loop, and the red edge of the He-burning loop. The polygonal regions indicate the selection regions for the MS, BHeB, and RGB. The agreement between the model curves and the data is excellent.

been well studied, in particular the effects on the warm and coronal gas phases in starbursts (e.g., [104, 124, 20] and references therein), the effect of feedback on future star formation remains an open question. This is a vital issue for modeling galaxy formation and evolution. Simple prescriptions for star formation and feedback are at the core of current galaxy evolution models (e.g., [95, 96]; however, these prescriptions often do not match our observations [97]. It is possible to answer this question by quantifying the recent SFHs of a large sample of galaxies covering a large range in mass. In the next section I will show how this is possible by showing the results from a handful of nearby galaxies.

3.2. Results from the HST with WFPC2

The first HST color magnitude diagram (CMD) of the stars in the nearby dwarf irregular (dI) galaxy Sextans A [36] revealed for the first time a clear separation between the brightest main sequence stars and the "blue loop" (or blue helium burning - BHeB) stars.

The separation of the main sequence stars and the BHeB stars was made possible by the high angular resolution of the HST (reducing photometric errors due to blends) and the low metallicity of Sextans A which leads to low differential reddening (Figure 10).

These BHeB stars afford a special opportunity to study the recent star formation histories (SFHs) of nearby galaxies. Because the position of a BHeB star in the CMD represents a unique age (as opposed to, for example, the main sequence or the red giant branch where a single position can correspond to a large range of ages), one can convert the BHeB luminosity function directly into a SFH (with the assumption of a universal initial mass function). The main limiting factor of this technique is that the position of the BHeB stars blends into the red clump at an age between 0.5 and 1 Gyr.

Translating the BHeB luminosity function into a SFH depends on the accuracy of the stellar evolution models. We have different lines of evidence that the stellar evolution models provide an excellent guide to this stage of evolution. The first evidence came from the early HST observations themselves. Although the position of the blueward extension of the stellar evolution tracks is a strong function of both metallicity and stellar mass, excellent agreement between observations and models was found by choosing the stellar evolution tracks for the metallicity determined from the HII region abundances for Sextans A. This is a very important point. There are no low metallicity, young stellar clusters in the Milky Way galaxy or the Magellanic Clouds which allow the stellar evolution modelers to calibrate their codes in this regime (the oxygen abundance in Sextans A is a factor 3 lower than in the Small Magellanic Cloud). When these stars are first observed in the extragalactic context, the agreement with models can be taken as confirmation of a prediction.

In recent studies, [39, 49] used deep HST photometry of Sextans A to compare recent SFHs recovered from both the main-sequence stars and the BHeB stars independently and collectively. The excellent agreement between these independent star formation rate (SFR) calculations is a confirmation for the legitimacy of using the BHeB stars to calculate the recent SFH. Additionally, [38] used the HST observations of Sextans A to compare the ratio of blue to red supergiants as a function of age, or, equivalently, mass. This ratio provides an observational constraint on the relative lifetimes of these two phases that is a sensitive test for convection, mass-loss, and rotation parameters. The functional form of the observed ratio matches the model extremely well.

Given these tests of reliability of the stellar models, we feel confident that using the BHeB stars to construct recent SFHs is well justified. [37] employed HST photometry of four nearby dIs (Sextans A, Leo A, Pegasus, and GR 8) and derived recent SFHs for these galaxies (Figure 11). At the time, the surprising result was the lack of bursts or episodes of enhanced star formation. With time bins of only 25 Myr for the last 500 Myr, with the possible exception of mildly enhanced SFRs in the last 50 Myr for Sextans A and Leo A, all four galaxies are best described as nearly constant SFRs. In retrospect, perhaps the lack of truly zero SFRs is as surprising as the lack of periods of enhanced star formation. These nearly constant, low level SFRs confirm the [79] picture for low surface brightness dIs as "down but not out," and the conclusion of Tosi and Greggio and their collaborators that the duration of truly quiescent phases must be very short compared to the active phase (e.g., [190]).

Because the BHeB star can be assigned a unique age, studying their spatial distribution allows the reconstruction of spatially resolved SFHs. Figure 12 demonstrates this

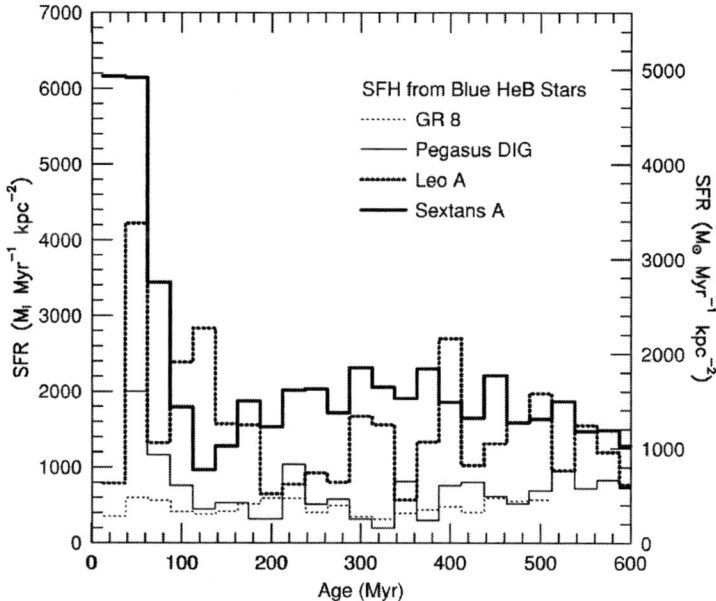

FIGURE 11. The recent SFHs of four nearby dI galaxies derived from the BHeB luminosity function [37]. Despite the relatively high time resolution which increases the sensitivity to variations, none of the galaxies show evidence for strong bursts of star formation, and there is little evidence for periods of no star formation.

for Sextans A. Note that three regions experience repeated episodes of star formation [39]. When compared to the present day HI distribution, two of these zones are associated with high column density neutral gas, while the third, and oldest, is not. Our interpretation of this pattern is that star formation begins on the edge of a gas cloud and progressively eats away at the cloud, breaking it up and inducing later star formation. Putting all of this together gives a picture of quasi-continuous star formation in present day dwarf galaxies, where bursts are the exception and not the rule.

The addition of the Advanced Camera for Surveys (ACS) to the HST has increased the volume in which this type of study is possible. Figure 13 shows a CMD obtained with the ACS on the HST of a galaxy at a distance of 3.6 Mpc. The clear separation of the main sequence from the blue helium burning stars indicates that we will be able to apply the same techniques to this more distance galaxy that we used on the Local Group dwarfs. This means that we will be able to increase our sample to a significant size so that meaningful comparisons can be made.

4. THE METAL POOR ISM OF DWARF GALAXIES

During the lectures, I spent some time covering the basics on how to derive chemical abundances from optical spectra of HII regions. Since much of this material is available

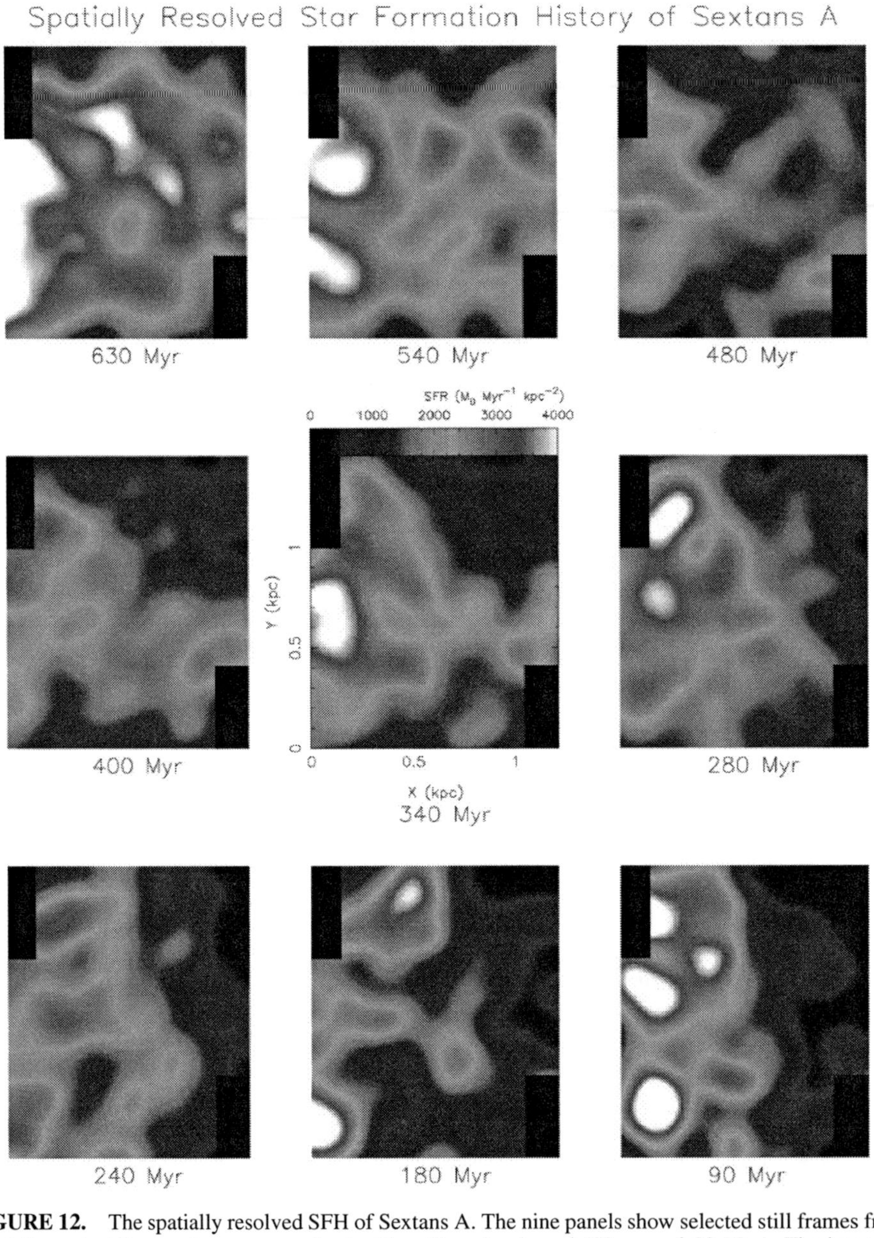

FIGURE 12. The spatially resolved SFH of Sextans A. The nine panels show selected still frames from the full movie. The movie was convolved with a Gaussian kernel (80 pc and 30 Myr). The intensity transfer function and spatial reference is labeled on the central frame. You can see this is color by going to the publication. The frames are not uniformly distributed in time; rather they were chosen to highlight peaks and valleys in the SFR. Most of the activity is found on the left side of the maps, and it is found in two primary zones: upper left and lower right. The lower right zone is associated with the highest column density neutral gas. (From [39]).

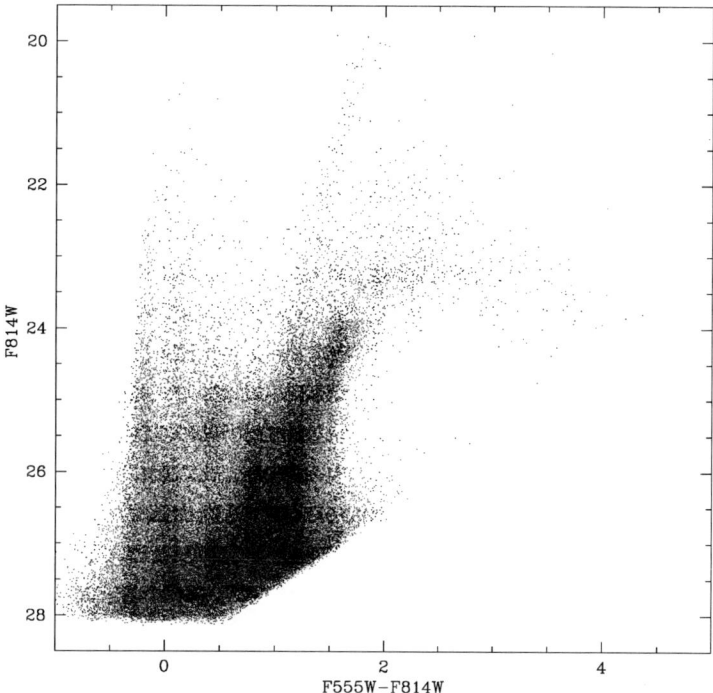

FIGURE 13. A CMD for the M81 group dI IC2574 from ACS observations (6400 s integration time in both V and I from our GO-program 9755, PI=Walter). Using Dolphot, over 200,000 stars were identified in the ACS field which is roughly 3.5 × 3.5 kpc. At a nominal distance of 3.6 Mpc and a metallicity of 1/6th of solar, the sequence of blue supergiants is clearly resolved from the main sequence. Thus, we can derive a spatially resolved SFH from these observations.

from textbooks [143] and my own personal take on it is available from another published set of lectures [164], I am going right to the results.

4.1. Absolute Abundances: The Dwarf Galaxy Metallicity–Luminosity Relationship

Since the nebular abundance studies of the Magellanic Clouds in the mid 1970's (e.g., [147, 148]), it has been suggested that there might be a correlation between galaxian mass and the metallicity of the interstellar medium. Surveys of the abundances in a number of H II regions in irregular galaxies by [117, 181, 101] all produced a clear correlation of oxygen abundance with both galaxy mass and luminosity. In the past, my collaborators and I have used this relationship to find very low metallicity objects for the

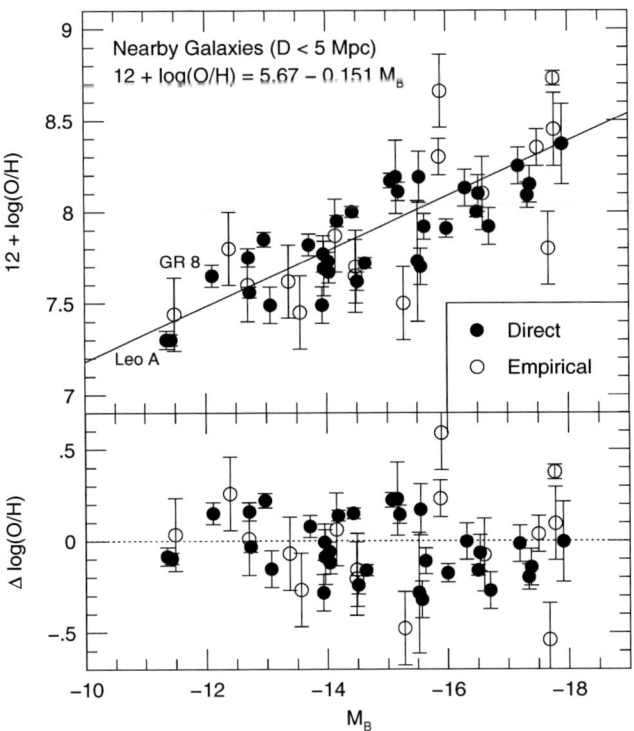

FIGURE 14. (Upper) The metallicity-luminosity relation for nearby (D < 5 Mpc) gas-rich galaxies fainter than M_B of -18. The new measurements of the oxygen abundances of Leo A and GR 8 provide valuable data at the low luminosity end of this relationship. Filled symbols indicate that the oxygen abundance was derived via a "direct" measurement, while open symbols indicate that the oxygen abundance was derived via the bright-line method. The solid line represents a weighted least squares fit to all the points. (Lower) Deviations from the average relationship between log(O/H) and M_B. Note that the dispersions are similar for the direct and bright-line abundances and for the low and high luminosity galaxies (see text). (From [203])

study of relative abundances [170, 172, 169, 171, 165].

In Figure 14, I present a very up-to-date version of the dwarf galaxy metallicity–luminosity relationship [203] for the local volume. Using the compilation of [93] to identify galaxies within the local 5 Mpc volume, van Zee et al. [203] compiled a list of all nearby low luminosity galaxies with known oxygen abundances. The 5 Mpc volume was chosen to include several of the nearest dwarf rich groups (e.g., Local Group, M81, Sculptor, and Centaurus). Of the 163 gas-rich galaxies (morphological type > 0) in this volume, 144 have $M_B > -18$. Of these, only 50 have measured oxygen abundances in the literature.

A weighted least squares fit to the data yields:

$$12 + \log(\text{O/H}) = 5.67 - 0.151 M_B \tag{1}$$

with an error in the slope and zeropoint of 0.014 and 0.21, respectively. This result is remarkably similar to that presented by [169]; the slight difference in the zero point (5.67 instead of 5.60) can easily be attributed to the slightly different distance scales used for the compilations. Similar results are also found by [155, 201, 113, 199].

Figure 14 gives the impression that the dispersion is larger for the empirically derived oxygen abundances relative to those derived via the direct method. Statistically, this is correct. For the 33 galaxies with direct oxygen abundances, the dispersion about the relationship is $\sigma = 0.17$ dex, and for the 16 galaxies with empirical oxygen abundances, the dispersion is $\sigma = 0.29$ dex. However, this could be misleading. Three of the galaxies in the compilation have empirical oxygen abundances based on relatively lower quality spectra (UGCA 86, DDO 168, NGC 5264). (Note that when [O III] $\lambda 4363$ is measured in a spectrum, it is, by definition, a higher quality spectrum.) When these three galaxies are removed from the empirical oxygen abundance sample, the dispersion decreases to $\sigma = 0.19$ dex – nearly identical to that of the direct abundance sample. This implies that the intrinsic scatter in the metallicity–luminosity relationship is at least of order the size of the uncertainty in the abundance measurements.

Not all dwarf galaxies comply with the metallicity – luminosity relationship shown in Figure 14. For example, many blue compact dwarf galaxies (BCDGs), which derive a significant fraction of their total luminosity from their high surface brightness, active star forming regions, lie to the left in Figure 14 (e.g., [156]). If the underlying correlation is between mass and metallicity, then this would be expected since the BCDGs are likely to have lower M/L ratios.

[155] found an increased scatter in the metallicity–luminosity relationship at lower luminosities, with an abrupt onset at $M_B = -15$. If we divide our data into a high luminosity sample ($M_B \leq -15$) and a low luminosity sample, for the 21 high luminosity galaxies we calculate a dispersion of $\sigma = 0.19$ dex and for the 25 low luminosity galaxies a dispersion of $\sigma = 0.16$ dex. Thus, we find no evidence for an increased dispersion at lower luminosities (see also [113]). This is surprising, as one expects that the lower luminosity galaxies should be susceptible to larger departures in both abundance and luminosity. Note that Leo A and GR 8 play a significant role in the differences between the two studies. Although the abundances for these two galaxies are nearly identical in the two studies, the distance to GR 8 is now known to be roughly double and the distance to Leo A is roughly half those used by [155].

On the other hand, the fundamental relationship may not be between mass and metallicity, but between surface density and metallicity. Mould, Kristian, & Da Costa [138] first discovered that dwarf elliptical galaxies also show a strong correlation between metallicity and luminosity, and Aaronson [1] showed that the metallicity vs. luminosity relationships for the two classes of galaxies are roughly identical in both slope and zero-point. Since low luminosity, high surface brightness, and relatively metal rich dwarf ellipticals have been observed, Bothun & Mould [15] suggested that surface density may be the fundamental parameter determining metallicity (see also Edmunds & Phillips [52]). The same may hold true for the dwarf irregulars, and is worth investigating observationally. To date, Van Zee [201] has found that her sample of low surface brightness dwarf galaxies obey the same metallicity – luminosity relationship, and note the result described by [18] for the dwarf galaxy F8D1 in the M81 group.

Additional measurements of dynamical masses and mass surface densities will hopefully clarify the situation. Because these type of measurements require HI synthesis imaging – to provide a gas distribution and a rotation curve, from which it is possible to derive the mass distribution – large surveys are quite expensive in terms of telescope time. Unlike the case for most spiral galaxies, a single dish line profile cannot be converted into a reliable total mass estimate because estimates of the appropriate inclination and radius from optical images can be specious. Since reliable mass estimates must be based on the more time consuming interferometric observations, results are lagging behind abundance measurements, but there is progress.

Finally, by moving from optical luminosities to infrared luminosities, one has a better chance to measure the stellar mass directly due to the smaller variations in the mass/light ratio in the infrared. Lee et al.[114] have used SPITZER observations at 4.5μ of 25 nearby dwarf irregular galaxies to construct an infrared luminosity–metallicity diagram. They find a very similar slope to the optical relationship, but a significantly smaller scatter. This is as expected if the true relationship is between the metallicity and the stellar mass. By using population synthesis models, they then convert the infrared luminosities to stellar masses, and a slightly smaller dispersion results. This dispersion of 0.12 dex is of order of the estimated uncertainties in the abundance measurements. Thus, it appears that the true underlying relationship is between metallicity and stellar mass.

4.2. Relative Abundances: N/O

Figure 15 shows the N/O abundances versus O/H for comparison samples of dIs and HII galaxies compiled by [203]. While the production of O in galaxies is dominated by nucleosynthesis in massive stars and relatively prompt return to the ISM via supernovae explosions, the dominant processes leading to the enrichment of N in galaxies is still not well understood. It seems clear that the secondary production of N from C and O in the CNO cycle in intermediate mass stars, with subsequent release into the ISM via red giant winds and planetary nebula, must play an important role. In the more massive spiral galaxies, at higher metallicities, N/O increases roughly linearly with O/H, as would be expected if this secondary production mechanism dominated N production [204].

In contrast, it has been known for some time that N/O is relatively constant over a large range in metallicity in the low metallicity stars in our galaxy [110, 24] and that the dwarf irregular galaxies also show relatively constant N/O (although with large scatter [64]) at low metallicity. A constant value of N/O over a large range in metallicity could be taken as evidence of primary production of N [145].

Two processes leading to primary N production have been suggested. Renzini & Voli [153] showed that increasing the convective scale length over the pressure scale length resulted in freshly synthesized ^{12}C being brought up to the convective envelope whereupon it can by converted to N via the CNO cycle. This "hot bottom burning"

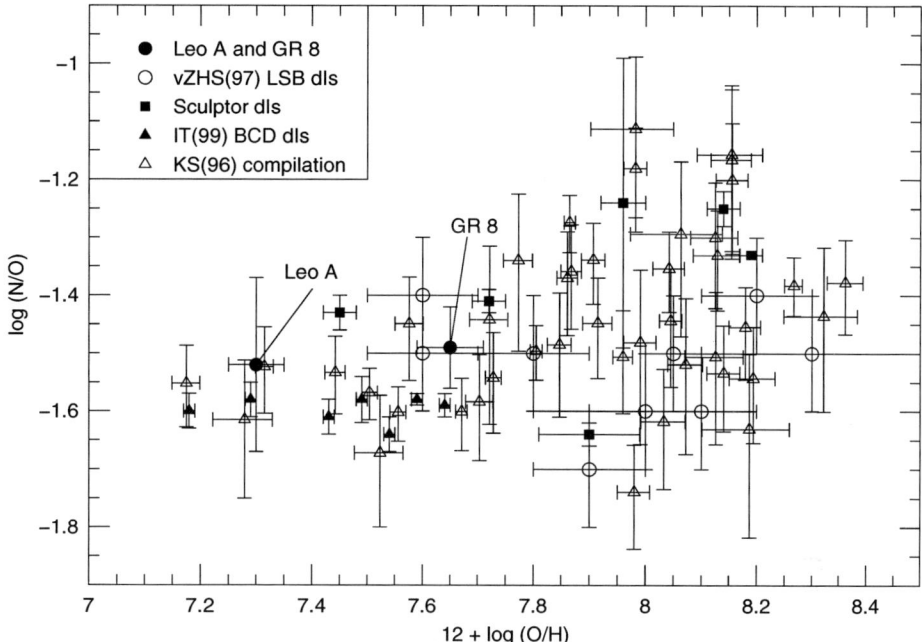

FIGURE 15. Comparison of the N/O and O/H in Leo A and GR 8 (filled circles) with other star forming dwarf galaxies from the literature. The empty circular symbols represent data for low surface brightness dwarf irregular galaxies from [200]. Four Sculptor dwarf irregular galaxies with direct abundance measurements are shown with filled squares [167]. The filled triangles represent the low metallicity blue compact dwarf galaxies from [88]. The collection of dwarf irregular galaxies and H II galaxies assembled by [103] are represented by open triangles. Only galaxies without WR emission features and errors in log (N/O) less than 0.2 have been plotted. (From [203])

mechanism [84] will be most effective in the mass range of 4 to 5 solar masses. Alternatively, it has been suggested [187, 207] that primary N might be produced in massive stars (heavier than 30 solar masses) of low metallicity. Again, if convection is enlarged beyond the standard models, a convective, helium burning shell penetrates into the hydrogen burning shell, and freshly synthesized C is converted into N.

These two primary N production processes would have substantially different delivery times. The primary N produced in hot bottom burning in intermediate mass stars would be returned to the ISM only after a few hundred million years. The primary N produced in the low metallicity, high mass stars would be returned in less than 10 million years. Note that the secondary N produced in intermediate mass stars would have the same delayed delivery as the primary N produced in intermediate mass stars.

Garnett [64] discussed the possibility that the spread in the values of N/O at a given O/H as measured in dwarf irregulars could be attributed to a delay between the delivery of O and N to the ISM [51]. If a dwarf galaxy experiences a dominant global burst of star formation, then the ISM O abundance will increase after roughly 10 million years, with a resulting decrease in N/O (as perhaps in the case of NGC 6822 [172]). Then, over the period of several hundred million years, the N/O abundance ratio will increase at constant O/H (given the absence of a subsequent burst of star formation in that time interval, as perhaps in the case of the Pegasus dwarf irregular galaxy [165]). Under these two assumptions (dominant bursts of star formation separated by quiescent periods and delayed N delivery to the ISM) the N/O ratio becomes a clock, measuring the time since the last major burst of star formation. Low values of N/O imply a very recent burst of star formation, while high values of N/O imply a long quiescent period.

4.3. The Homogeneity of ISM Abundance in Dwarf Galaxies

Kobulnicky conducted detailed studies of the nebular abundances in the dwarf galaxies NGC 4214 and NGC 1569 [103, 104]. Using long-slit optical spectra, he measured the N/O ratio at several positions throughout both galaxies. The N/O ratio is sensitive to abundance variations because it has a relatively low sensitivity to electron temperature and, in principle, can be sensitive to variations in either N or O (which are not thought to vary together).

NGC 4214 has numerous regions of recent star formation, some showing evidence of the presence of Wolf-Rayet stars, so one can sample a range in ages of HII regions. The presence and absence of Wolf-Rayet stars is important, as those regions where Wolf-Rayet stars are seen should be old enough that their most massive stars have had time to explode as SN II. NGC 1569 has been the site of a recent intense burst of star formation and appears to show evidence of gas outflows as a result. Thus, together, a range in environments was sampled. In both cases, there was no clear evidence of abundance variations. In some locations, small abundance variations were derived, but using the [O I]/[O III] vs. [O II]/[O III] line ratio diagram (e.g., [73]), these regions were determined to be contaminated by shock excitation. A recent study of NGC 6822 has shown a similar homogeneity of HII regions abundances [115].

It appears that the same phenomenon observed in giant HII regions [162, 157, 68] is repeated in the dwarf galaxies. In places where one expects that newly produced metals are being returned to the ISM, this "local pollution" is not detected in the warm phase of the ISM. Kobulnicky & Skillman [104] explore the various possible explanations for the uniformity of HII region abundances in dwarf galaxies and strongly favor the explanation that the newly synthesized metals are returned to the hot phase of the ISM, and that there is a significant time delay before these newly produced metals can be detected in the warm phase of the ISM. These results support the scenario promoted by [184, 31].

One relatively famous example of this homogeneity is found in the extremely low metallicity HII galaxy I Zw 18. Skillman & Kennicutt [168] demonstrated that the abundances in the two main HII regions were the same. This result has been reproduced several times now (e.g., [205]). Since the two HII regions are separated by more than 200 pc, and their stellar associations have very different ages [82], it seems quite unlikely that the metals in these regions have come from the current burst of star formation (e.g., [109]).

The one clear exception to this trend is found in the dwarf starburst galaxy NGC 5253. The brightest HII region in NGC 5253 has been known to have a high N abundance for some time. Kobulnicky et al.[105] used HST optical and ultraviolet spectra at three locations in the central HII complex and confirmed the enhanced nitrogen abundance seen in ground-based studies. However, 50 pc away, the N abundance is a factor 3 times lower and typical of metal-poor galaxies. Because no other elemental species shows spatial abundance fluctuations, including C, an N production mechanism that is decoupled from C and O production is required. Given the proximity of the N overabundance to a very young, heavily obscured star cluster, the N excess is likely due to recent "pollution" from massive stars. Plausible N enrichment scenarios involve O star winds, He-deficient W-R star winds, and/or ejection events from luminous blue variables. To date, this effect has not been observed in any other galaxy.

To what degree can the abundances of the different HII regions in dwarf galaxies be claimed to be uniform? Given that usually only a handful of HII regions are observable in a dI and that only a percentage of them have [O III] $\lambda 4363$ bright enough to be well measured, it is then problematic to seriously test the level of abundance variations. For example, in a recent study of NGC 625 [167], a dwarf starburst galaxy in the nearby Sculptor Group, we measured the oxygen abundance in several HII regions. We compared the results from "direct" measurements (using the [O III] $\lambda 4363$ line to determine the electron temperature), with empirical formulae derived by McGaugh [131] and Pilyugin [149]. Both the direct method and the empirical methods would indicate that there are abundance variations between the HII regions in NGC 625, but none of the methods are in agreement. Because the direct method is subject to several systematic uncertainties ($\lambda 4363$ is an inherently weak line and, at low velocities, is liable to possible contamination by terrestrial Hg emission; the assumption of a single temperature in the O^{++} zone is probably not correct; the assumption of a single relationship between the temperature in the O^{++} and O^+ zones is certainly only a first order assumption), a measurement of $\lambda 4363$ should not be taken as prima facie evidence of an accurate oxygen abundance. The disagreement between the two empirical methods indicates that small differences (≤ 0.2 dex) also cannot be trusted to be real differences. Given the interest in the problem of "self-pollution" and its role in the chemical evolution of dwarf galaxies (e.g., [116, 151]) a clearer view of the observational situation is probably warranted.

4.4. Implications for Chemical Evolution

Recently, Rob Kennicutt and I studied the H II regions in the low surface brightness dwarf irregular galaxy DDO 154 [98]. We confirmed the very low star formation rate and extremely long gas consumption times reported previously by van Zee, Haynes,

& Salzer [200]. Nonetheless, the low oxygen abundance of 0.055 ± 0.008 (O/H)$_\odot$ is in accordance with the metallicity-luminosity relationship for dwarf irregular galaxies. Although DDO 154 has been labeled "the dark galaxy" and is a prototype for low surface brightness galaxies with large H I content, its chemical abundances are consistent with an average, low-mass, dwarf irregular galaxy. Assuming that the neutral gas is chemically homogeneous, we derive an effective oxygen yield of roughly 50% of the solar value, a value that is close to the theoretically favored values for the true oxygen yield. Thus, it is possible that DDO 154 is evolving nearly as a closed system. On the other hand, if the abundances in the extended H I disk are lower than in the H II regions, the derived value of the effective yield has been artificially inflated, and DDO 154 may have experienced significant loss of metal-enriched gas.

What we really need to know is the metallicity in the large, extended cold gas disk of DDO 154 and similar dwarf irregular galaxies. Since the HII region abundances show no gradient, the normal assumption is that there is no metallicity gradient at all, but the HII regions only sample the inner parts of the disk. In all larger systems (i.e., spiral galaxies) metallicity gradients are detected. If one assumes that the extended HI disk of DDO 154 is more metal poor, then the effective yield plummets (since most of the gas is in the extended HI disk). Abundances for the extended disks of dwarf galaxies represent a crucial missing piece of information

4.5. The ISM at Low Metallicity

In low metallicity galaxies, gas temperatures are higher (less coolants), radiation fields are harder, and dust content is much reduced. Do this affect the star formation process? All of these things will be even more true in the early universe, so studying star formation at low metallicity may be quite helpful in understanding star formation in the early universe. Of course, the key connection between the ISM and star formation is the molecular gas. Comparing the recent star formation history to the molecular gas distribution is an obviously important line of inquiry. Unfortunately, this is more easily said than done.

H_2 is, by far, the major constituent of the molecular gas. However, H_2 has no dipole radiation, and therefore is not easily observed in emission. In the more metal rich spiral galaxies, CO is used quite successfully to trace the molecular gas. However, in low metallicity dwarfs, CO is not detected [183] (see Figurefig:tks).

Does the lack of CO detections in low metallicity dwarfs imply that they have no molecular gas? Note that most of these galaxies do have a lot of star formation, usually an indicator of molecular gas. Perhaps there is H_2 but no CO? This is possible as CO is easily dissociated while H_2 can effectively self-shield [121]. Note that recently a similar result has been revealed for PAH emission by SPITZER observations [56]. They note a sudden disappearance of 8μm PAH emission below an oxygen abundance of $12 + \log(O/H) = 8.0$. Recently, spatially resolved SPITZER infrared imaging has shown the same effect for nearby dwarf galaxies [91]. This all supports the conclusions of [176] that the character of the ISM is fundamentally different at low metallicities.

We're really just at the beginning on the problem of understanding molecular gas at

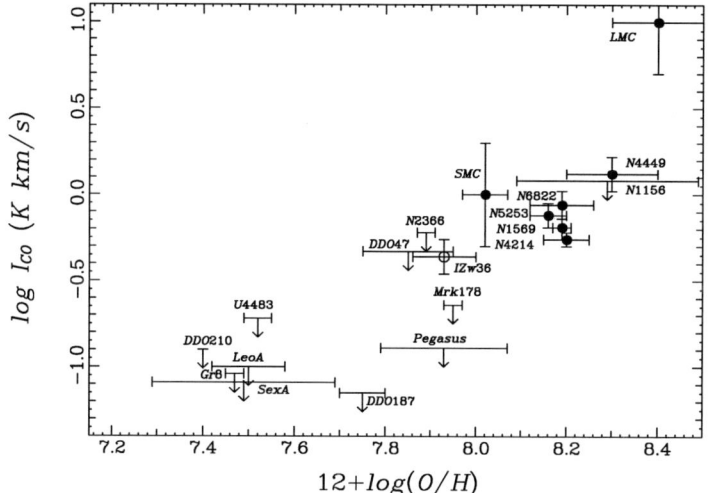

FIGURE 16. Log (I_{CO}) versus oxygen abundance, 12 + log(O/H), for all known dwarf (M > −18) galaxies within 10 Mpc which had CO observations and measured oxygen abundances (in 1998). Filled circles denote > 4σ detections. Positions of the SMC and LMC are mean values reported by [87]. For NGC 4214 and NGC 6822, only the locations of the peak CO surface brightness are plotted. The open circle represents a marginal (4σ) detection of I Zw 36 that has not been confirmed. All other systems have only upper limits, including some very low limits on extremely metal-poor systems reported in this work. It is striking that no galaxies with 12 + log(O/H) < 7.9 (Z < 0.1 Z$_\odot$) have been detected in CO, indicating that extremely metal-poor systems have much lower mean CO surface brightnesses. This data is consistent with a rise (perhaps sharply non-linear) in the $I_{CO}/M_{H_2} \equiv X_{CO}$ conversion factor at metallicities below 0.1 of the solar value. (From [183])

low metallicities. In principle, it is possible to detect H_2 directly through it's quadrupole emission of its pure rotational transitions at 28, 17, and 12μm. If the temperature in the low metallicity ISM is high enough, SPITZER will be able to detect this. By comparing H_2, CO, and HI observations of low metallicity galaxies we may be able to see if molecular clouds have a different mass spectrum as a function of metallicity. It may be that a phase change in the ISM is responsible for the differences above and below 12 + log(O/H) = 8.0. Finally, we would like to know if star formation histories are compared for low and intermediate metallicity galaxies, are there statistical differences?

5. STARBURSTS IN DWARF GALAXIES

5.1. Definition of a Starburst

The are many different definitions of a starburst galaxy. Usually they are based on (a) the amplitude of the current star formation rate, (b) the gas exhaustion time scale, (c) the fraction of a galaxy's light that is derived from the starburst, or some combination of the above. I adopt the definition of Heckman [74], where a starburst galaxy is any system that contains a spatially concentrated star formation region that dominates the overall luminosity of the galaxy, and that implies a gas depletion timescale much shorter than the age of the universe. Starbursts are thus a brief but important site for massive star formation locally ($\sim 25\%$ of massive star formation occurring therein [74]), and may have been even more important in previous epochs. They play an integral role in the evolution of galaxies through their interaction with the ISM. Furthermore, these galaxies represent a link between star formation and environment, as many are triggered by interactions, and some appear to vent metals into the IGM (e.g., NGC 1569 [124]).

5.2. Important Questions

5.2.1. A Shopping List

There are many outstanding questions concerning starbursts in dwarf galaxies:

- What triggers a starburst in a dwarf galaxy?
- What is the typical duration of a starburst?
- Can a starburst destroy or transform a dwarf galaxy?
- What happens to the new metals created by a starburst?
- Are starbursts in dwarf galaxies important cosmologically?
- Do some dwarf starbursts represent young galaxies?

In the next section I will discuss the second question in a bit more depth. You can take this as a representative exposition on one of the above questions. Following that, I will discuss a few prototype dwarf starburst galaxies, and touch on some of the above questions.

5.2.2. The Duration, A Fundamental Property of a Starburst

Starbursts are episodes of intense star formation that dominate the total luminosity of their host galaxies. Although, by definition, starbursts are short lived (by necessity due to limitations on fuel), actual measurements of the durations of starbursts in dwarf galaxies are scarce. Clearly the duration of the burst of star formation is an important parameter. Does feedback (stellar winds and super novae (SNe)) from the burst quench future star formation so that only short-duration bursts are possible [59]? Models of outflows from instantaneous bursts have different characteristics from those where the energy input is temporally extended (e.g., [119, 60]). Because both chemical yields and galaxy ages are functions of stellar mass, chemical enrichment scenarios depend on the duration of the burst. The successful modeling of the evolution of dwarf galaxies, and hence of a potentially important enrichment process of the inter galactic medium, depends fundamentally on this important parameter (e.g., [176]). Similarly, interpreting galaxy luminosity functions requires a detailed understanding of the burst durations, since this parameter directly affects the slope of the faint end of the distribution (e.g., [94, 76]).

The distinction between a short ($\sim$ 5 Myr) and long ($\sim$ 50 Myr) burst scenario is very important in dwarf galaxies. However, there is little agreement in the literature for an accepted value. For example, Krueger et al.[108] modeled only 5 Myr duration bursts when investigating the spectral energy distributions of blue compact dwarf (BCD) galaxies. Observational studies of the emission from Wolf-Rayet (WR) stars by [159, 126] find burst durations of $\sim$ 2 – 4 Myrs. However, contrasting results from studies of star clusters place a lower bound on burst durations at $\sim$ 40 – 50 Myrs [144]. Theoretical crossing time considerations are consistent with this longer burst scenario [132]. Longer duration bursts tend to "dampen" spectral features and lead to lower burst parameter strengths. Further, the degree of "burstiness" affects the detectability of low luminosity galaxies. Often, short duration bursts are assumed in such calculations, with the fiducial 10 Myr duration supported by the reasoning that at larger times the type II SNe produced by the burst will heat the interstellar medium, preventing any further star formation [59].

It is interesting to compare burst durations derived for the nearest BCD galaxies, where the age discrepancy between stellar clusters and nearby field stars is quite pronounced. In NGC 1569, Hunter et al.[81] find ages of most of the young star clusters to be less than 30 Myr (the two super-star clusters have ages of $\sim$ 7 Myr and 10-20 Myr), while Greggio et al.[72] find that the period of enhanced star formation in the field has lasted for $\sim$ 100 Myr. In NGC 5253, the ages of the central clusters range from 1 to 8 Myr, while the central field stars are consistent with ages up to 50 Myr[191]. These authors suggest that either the field stars are created without the uppermost initial mass function (IMF), or that clusters older than 10 Myr dissolve into the field. Since we are now observing starbursts where star formation has continued at an elevated rate for several tens of Myr, it would appear that such "self-quenching" is not necessarily a universal property of starbursts. Given the above theoretical and observational evidence, uniform measurements of the durations of nearby starbursts are necessary. In particular, it is important to provide detailed recent ($\sim$ 100-200 Myr) star formation histories (SFHs) of the young stellar populations in the starburst regions.

5.3. NGC 625 – A Case Study

NGC 625 is an intriguing nearby dwarf galaxy in the Sculptor Group (or South Polar Group), the nearest group of galaxies outside the Local Group ([92], and references therein). The spectroscopic studies of Marlowe et al. [122, 123] revealed strong starburst activity, with values of star formation rate and Hα equivalent width comparable to (but less than) those found in the prototypical local dwarf starbursts NGC 1705 and NGC 5253. The ROSAT discovery of faint x-ray emission [14] implied a large content of hot (T $\sim 10^6$ K) gas in the halo. Ground-based Hα imaging of [166] showed diffuse Hα emission is detected away from the disk and coincident with the soft x-ray emission. This leads to the interesting conclusion that this nearby galaxy is likely driving an outflow of hot gas from the major star formation region. As this low-mass galaxy presents a low-foreground reddening sightline to a nearby major star formation region, it serves as an ideal galaxy in which to study the starburst phenomenon in its own right.

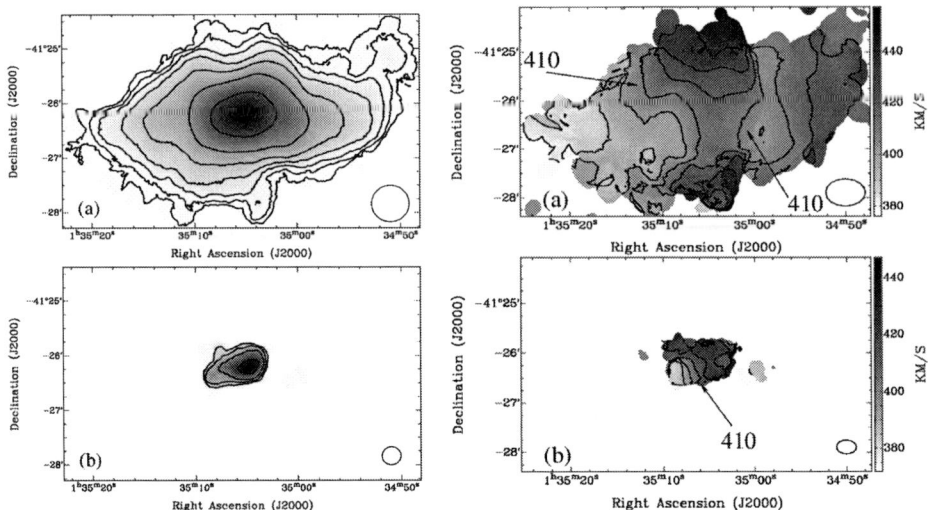

FIGURE 17. (Left) Velocity-integrated zeroth-moment images, representing total HI column density. (a) shows the low-resolution (45″ beam) image, while (b) shows the higher-resolution (22.5 ″ beam) image. Contours in (a) show levels of 1, 2, 4, 8, 16, 32 and 64% of the peak intensity (1178 K·km s^{-1}, or 2.15×10^{21} cm^{-2}), while the contours in (b) show levels of 10, 20, 40 and 80% of the peak intensity (1321 K·km s^{-1}, or 2.41×10^{21} cm^{-2}). The beam size and shape is shown at the bottom right of each image. (Right) Velocity-integrated first-moment images, representing radial velocity. (a) shows the low-resolution (45″ beam) velocity field, while (b) shows the higher-resolution (22.5 ″ beam) velocity field. The contours are spaced by 10 km s^{-1} intervals, ranging from 380 km s^{-1} to 440 km s^{-1} in (a) and from 380 km s^{-1} to 430 km s^{-1} in (b). The velocity field is highly disturbed, with components across the full velocity range within the disk, as well as components with steep velocity gradients. (From [22])

5.3.1. Evidence of an outflow in HI

Figure 17 presents the results of multi-configuration HI aperture synthesis imaging of NGC 625 obtained with the Australia Telescope Compact Array (Cannon et al. [22]). The left figure shows the total HI column density images at two different resolution. The HI gas is well-aligned with the optical major axis, and low-column density HI extends to > 6 optical scale lengths. The HI velocity field shown on the right, on the other hand, is highly disturbed, with neutral gas at nearly all detected velocities within the central region. Only by looking at position-velocity diagrams (shown in Figure 18) were we able to understand the velocity structure.

After considering various interpretations (simple rotating disk, blowout plus rotation, superposed or counter-rotating disks, infall, "ongoing assimilation", superposed anomalous-velocity clouds, ISM turbulence) we decided that a blowout scenario most accurately describes the data. A key feature in determining this model is seen in Figure 17. At high resolution, the central HI is shown to be participating in the normal rotation. It is only at lower resolution, when beam smearing combines the outflowing gas with the disk gas that the signature of rotation is lost from the central part of the galaxy. This is one of the clearest examples of HI outflow detected in a dwarf galaxy.

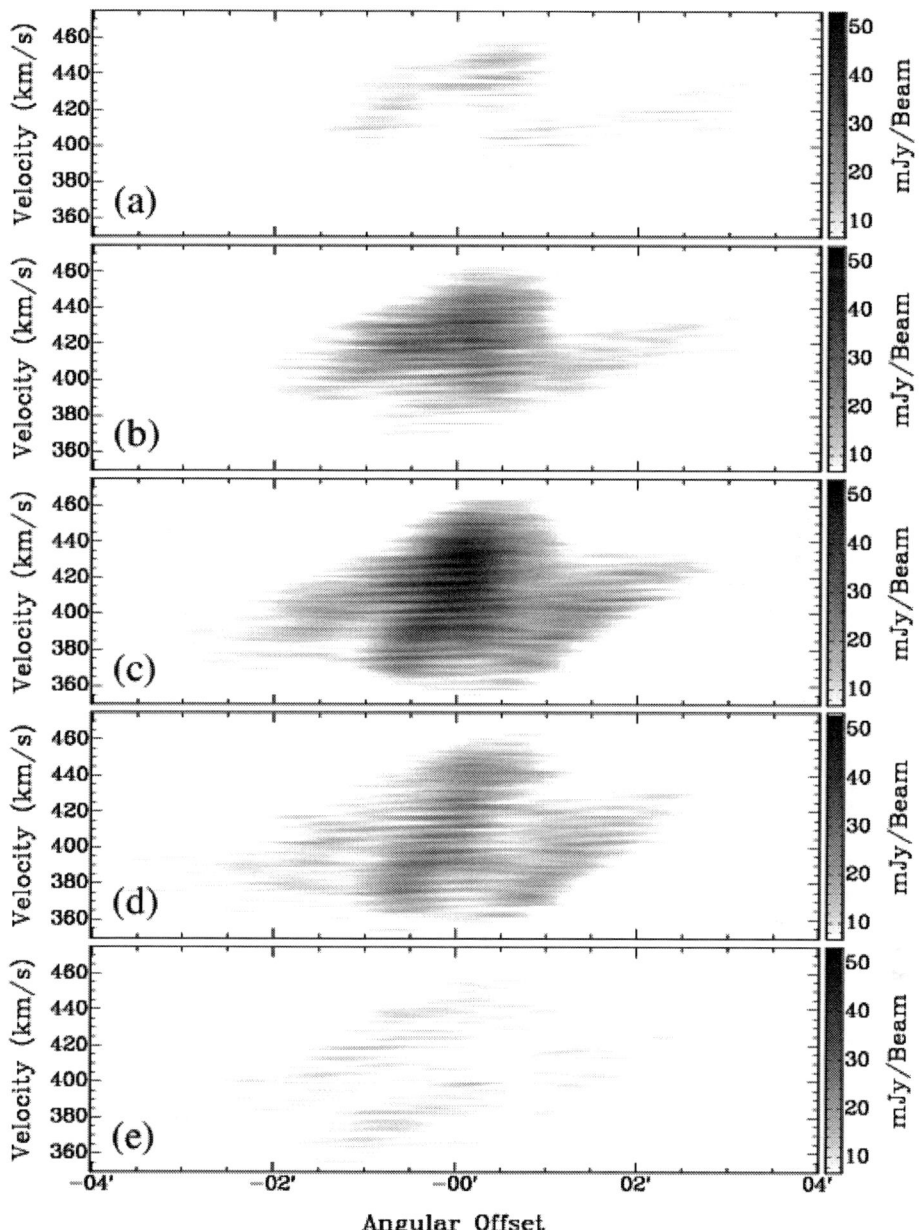

FIGURE 18. Five independent major-axis PV diagrams, taken at different distances from the central HI column density maximum. (a) is located 60″ N of the disk, (b) at 30″ N, (c) coincident with the HI peak, (d) at 30″ S, and (e) at 60″ S. The cuts are 8′ long, at a position angle of 90°. Near the disk, the kinematic signature of blowout dominates the HI velocity structure. (From [22])

We find no obvious external trigger (i.e., a tidal HI tail) for this extended star formation event.

5.3.2. The duration of the starburst in NGC 625

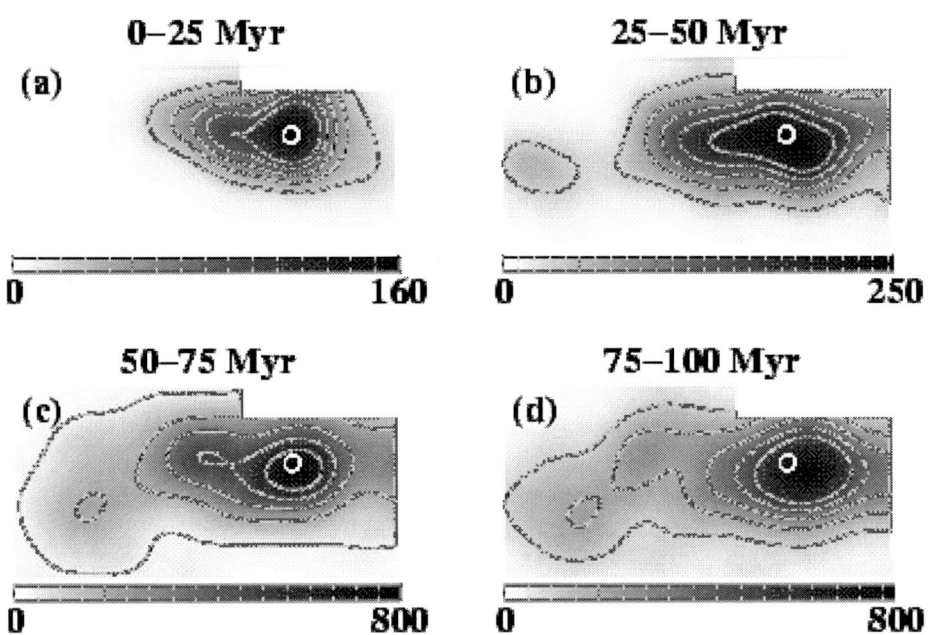

FIGURE 19. Spatial distribution of star formation over the last 100 Myr, as derived from the BHeB stars. In each plot, the number of BHeB stars · kpc^{-2} is plotted, with intensities indicated by the color bar under each image; the field of view is $\sim 1.7 \times 0.9$ kpc, with North up and East to the left. (a) shows the youngest stars, of age 0-25 Myr; note the concentrated star formation in the main giant HII region; (b) shows stars stars of age 25-50 Myr, and clearly demonstrates that star formation has been occurring in different regions of the galaxy during this epoch; (c) and (d) show older stars, of ages 50-100 Myr, and demonstrate that the star formation rate has been elevated for this entire 100 Myr period. The white circle in each plot is the highest contour for the young, 0-25 Myr population; comparing the location of this peak with past star formation peaks also shows that star formation has been moving throughout the disk over the last 100 Myr. The lowest contour in each plot demonstrates the extent of low-level star formation throughout these epochs. The contour levels (in number of stars · kpc^{-2}) in each image are: (a) 20, 40, 60, 80, 100; (b) 30, 70, 110, 150, 190; (c) 40, 200, 360, 520, 680; (d) 100, 205, 310, 415, 520. (From [21])

Figure 19 shows the reconstructed SFH for NGC 625 using the techniques discussed in section 3. Complication arises in NGC 625 in that there is sufficient dust so that the BHeB stars are not well separated from the MS stars in the CMD. Nonetheless, we found that the observations were sufficient to determine if the recent star formation is best described as an instantaneous burst as might be expected from the strong Wolf-Rayet (W-R) features in its optical spectrum [167], or alternatively, if the enhanced star formation is better described as long lived with a lifetime in excess of 10 Myr.

Additionally, the spatially resolved SFH allows us to determine whether the recent star formation been mainly confined to the very center of NGC 625 (or a single star forming region), or if it has been distributed throughout the central disk.

The BHeB stars were separated into four magnitude bins, which correspond to age regions based on the theoretical isochrones of [10]: 0-25 Myr, 25-50 Myr, 50-75 Myr, and 75-100 Myr. In Figure 19 we show the spatial distribution of the BHeB stars in these four magnitude bins. The clear separation into identifiable star forming regions in the youngest three epochs indicates that the coarse binning has overcome some of the "noise" introduced by the differential reddening. In particular, the brightest stellar association today (associated with the giant HII region) is seen to be relatively young, while the stellar association to the east appears to be roughly 20-40 Myr older. Furthermore, comparing the highest contour for the 0-25 Myr population (shown in white in Figure 19) with previous star formation peaks, it is clear that star formation has been moving throughout the disk during this time period. Taking these data at face value, it appears that a prior, stronger burst pervaded the disk 50-100 Myr ago.

Formally, analysis of the coarse BHeB luminosity function implies a large and declining star formation rate over the last 100 Myr. The relative star formation rates (originally in units of $M_\odot \, yr^{-1}$, then normalized to unit intensity) over the last 100 Myr are 1.0 ± 0.38 (0-25 Myr), 1.3 ± 0.38 (25-50 Myr), and 5.0 ± 1.3 (50-75 Myr) 5.0 ± 3.8 (75-100 Myr). Errors here reflect Poisson statistics on the number of stars detected in each age bin, as well as average contamination factors as derived from the simulations described below. We note that these star formation rates are lower limits, as there will undoubtedly be BHeB stars that suffer little or no differential extinction but undergo photometric errors carrying them blueward of the selection regions here; however, this effect should be independent of magnitude and hence will not drastically alter the *relative* star formation rates for each coarse age bin. We conclude that the average SFR from 100-50 Myr ago was a factor of ~ 5 higher than the average SFR from 50 Myr to the present epoch. This suggests that we may be witnessing the final stages of the extended star formation episode in NGC 625, and that this system may be rightly qualified as a "post-starburst" galaxy.

Such a scenario is consistent with the other observations of this system. In particular, [14] find diffuse soft (ROSAT 0.1 - 2.4 keV) x-ray emission above the northern side of the disk. The presence of this hot ($\sim 10^6$ K) gas at large distances from the current or recent star formation complexes (~ 1 kpc North and East of complex NGC 625 A) suggests that an active outflow has been at work in this system in recent times. For example, if an average outflow velocity of 100 km s^{-1} is assumed, only ~ 10 Myr would be needed; even if the average velocity is an order of magnitude smaller, the extended star formation event forwarded above could easily have expelled the gas to this distance.

The most important conclusion of this star formation history analysis is that NGC 625 appears to have sustained a heightened star formation rate for an extended period of time (i.e., ~ 10 Myr). With the aide of this modeling approach, we can easily discern between bursts of star formation that are of short (~ 5 Myr) or long (~ 50 Myr) duration. By comparing our data to various model realizations, we reject any model which does not sustain massive star formation long enough to populate the BHeB region of the CMD. From these tests we conclude that the star formation in NGC 625 is of extended duration compared with most models of starbursts (durations $\sim 3-6$ Myr), and that the presence of spectroscopic W-R features does not rule out a longer-duration star formation event.

5.3.3. NGC 625 with FUSE

We were able to use the FUSE observatory to obtain far ultra-violet spectroscopy of the starburst in NGC 625 [23]. The ultra-violet observations probe multiple phases of the interstellar medium, including the coronal, ionized, neutral and molecular gas. NGC 625 shows a clear detection of outflowing coronal gas as traced by O VI λ 1032 Å absorption. The centroid of the O VI profile is blueshifted with respect to the galaxy systemic velocity by $\sim$ 30 km s^{-1}, suggesting a low-velocity outflow. The implied O VI velocity extent is found to be 100 $\pm$ 20 km s^{-1}, which is fully consistent with the detected HI outflow velocity found in radio synthesis observations. We detect multiple lines of diffuse H_2 absorption from the ISM of NGC 625; this is one of only a few extragalactic systems with FUSE detections of H_2 lines in the Lyman and Werner bands.

Interestingly, we find a potential abundance offset between the neutral and nebular gas that exceeds the errors on the derived column densities. Our neutral gas oxygen abundance (taken at face value) is found to be lower by $\sim$ 0.9 dex, while the relative abundances between N and O are very similar. The offset between the neutral and nebular gas abundances may indicate that the outer regions of dwarf galaxies are less enriched in heavy elements compared to the inner, star-forming regions. However, the apparent offset may be due to saturation of the observed OI line, and higher S/N observations are required to resolve this issue.

Such abundance offsets between nebular and neutral gas are common in strongly star-forming dwarf galaxies studied to date with FUSE. Abundance differences of > 0.5 dex have been found in NGC 1705 [75], I Zw 18 [2] (but see also [112] for an alternative treatment), I Zw 36 [111], and Mrk 59 [186]. These abundance differences may be caused by FUSE sightlines sampling two different components of the ISM of dwarf galaxies: lower-abundance halo gas, and higher-abundance gas nearer to the active star formation regions.

If the absorption spectra of dwarf galaxies obtained by FUSE are indeed sampling a halo of neutral gas and are not primarily produced in the disks, then they provide a very important probe of a virtually unstudied component of the dwarf galaxy ISM. [98] have emphasized the importance of measuring abundances in the neutral gas in the outer parts of dwarf galaxies. In spiral galaxies, it is well known that there are chemical abundance gradients in the sense of lower abundances in the outer parts of the systems. However, in dwarf galaxies it is generally assumed that the entire HI disk has the same metallicity as measured in the HII regions, and this is a very uncertain assumption. The physical basis for this assumption is the general uniformity of HII region abundances in dwarf galaxies (e.g.,[104], and the inference that the whole HI disk is kept at a rather uniform chemical abundance by the rapid transportation of the metals in a hot phase of the ISM [31, 184]. However, the HII regions only sample the inner parts of the HI disk. In some dwarf galaxies, as much as 90% of the neutral hydrogen lies outside of the Holmberg radius (e.g., DDO 154 [25, 26]. If dwarf galaxies do have chemical abundance gradients, then assuming that the chemical abundances are constant overestimates the total metal content of the galaxy, and leads to a misinterpretation of their evolutionary status (e.g., artificially inflating the calculated effective yield). The edge-on orientation of NGC 625 implies that at least some of the absorption is occurring in the outer parts of the galaxy and thus providing a probe of this relatively unexplored ISM component.

The extended mission of FUSE offers an ideal opportunity to test for this important evolutionary scenario. One would ideally seek a sample of luminous, metal-poor ($\leq 10\%$ $Z_\odot$) dwarf systems that have low intrinsic HI foreground columns, low foreground and internal extinctions, along high-visibility sightlines not contaminated by intermediate- or high-velocity clouds. Deep integrations on such targets will provide sufficient S/N to allow inter-comparison of the columns derived from oxygen lines with different oscillator strengths throughout the FUSE spectral region. With the effects of line saturation eliminated, such a sample would allow the exploration of this potentially important ISM phase in dwarf galaxies.

5.4. NGC 1569 – An Extreme Case

In my lecture, I reviewed in considerable detail the CHANDRA observations of NGC 1569 by Martin, Kobulnicky, & Heckman [124]. These observations present exciting new insights into the current state of this galaxy. Because of the spatial resolution of Chandra, they are able to subtract out the x-ray point sources and conduct a detailed comparison of the distribution of the hot gas to the other components of the galaxy. *Absorption* spectra of the disk of the galaxy against the hot gas produce abundance measurements which are consistent with the abundance obtained from the HII regions. X-ray spectra of the hot gas yield a ratio of α-elements to Fe roughly 2-4 times the solar value. While the absolute abundances are not as strongly constrained, the best estimate of the metallicity in the hot gas is between solar and two times solar. Thus, their results provide the first direct evidence for metal-enriched winds from dwarf starburst galaxies. They also argue that the mass of interstellar gas entrained in the wind must be about 9 times the mass of stellar ejecta in the wind and that most of the oxygen carried by the wind comes from the stellar ejecta rather than entrained interstellar gas. Thus, the estimated mass of oxygen in the hot wind, 34,000 $M_\odot$, is similar to the oxygen yield of the current starburst. This implies that all of the metals produced by the starburst are in the hot phase, and if a wind carries this hot gas out of the galaxy, then the entire heavy element production of the starburst will be lost from the galaxy. Since the yield of this event would be zero, and since NGC 1569 is observed to be chemically evolved, this implies that much of the earlier star formation in NGC 1569 could not have been produced in this manner.

Note that the fate of this metal-rich hot phase is greatly debated. Many researchers estimate that this gas is destined to leave the galaxy to enrich the intergalactic medium. Others find that the galaxies can retain much of this gas for later chemical enrichment. This argument will not be solved soon, but the new observations presented by Martin et al. represent a giant step forward in this debate. Hopefully this is just a glimpse of things to come.

5.5. IZw18 and the Young Galaxy Hypothesis

Based on spectroscopic observations of HII regions in low-metallicity blue compact galaxies, [88] hypothesized that "galaxies with $12 + \log (O/H) < 7.6$ are now undergoing their first burst of star formation, and that they are therefore young, with ages not exceeding 40 Myr." This hypothesis is based on observations of nearly constant N/O and C/O ratios for their sample of galaxies. The reasoning holds that these galaxies have not had sufficient time for the intermediate mass stars to deliver their time-delayed production of N and C. IZw18 is a prototype because is has the lowest measured oxygen abundance and the stellar population appears to be completely dominated by young stars. Interestingly, in the Local Group, the dwarf irregular galaxy Leo A has an HII region oxygen abundance of $12 + \log (O/H) \leq 7.6$ and the value of $\log(N/O) = -1.53 \pm 0.09$, which is consistent with their remarkably narrow plateau of -1.60 ± 0.02. Thus, Leo A provides an excellent test case for the young galaxy hypothesis.

There is abundant evidence that Leo A is not a young galaxy. The Hubble Space Telescope color-magnitude diagram presented by [188] shows very well populated red giant branch and red clumps, indicative of intermediate and old age stars. Further, [48] discovered 8 RR Lyrae stars indicative of a ~ 10 Gyr old stellar population. Thus, although Leo A has not necessarily been forming stars at a constant rate over the lifetime of the Universe [188], it has clearly has stars with a wide variety of ages.

[136] come to a very similar conclusion in their study of Sag DIG. In fact, an ancient stellar population has been detected in all low metallicity dwarf galaxies with sufficiently deep observations of their resolved stellar populations [128]. The one possible exception has been I Zw 18; [89] claim an absence of any old stellar population based on new Hubble Space Telescope imaging. However, [136] have reanalyzed the same Hubble Space Telescope observations, and, based on photometry which reaches roughly one magnitude deeper than that of [89], find evidence consistent with the detection of a red giant branch tip corresponding to a distance of 15 Mpc. Although not noted, the extended red supergiant branch is also inconsistent with an age of less than 40 Myr for all of the resolved stars. Thus, it would appear that, to date, there is no evidence in support of dwarf galaxies being formed for the first time in the current epoch.

ACKNOWLEDGMENTS

I wish to thank Edu Telles for making this school a truly special experience. I am grateful to all members of the LOC (Simone Daflon, Jailson Alcaniz, Eduardo Telles, and Ramiro de la Reza) for helping to make my first visit to Rio a wonderful time. There is no possible way to give enough thanks to my students, postdocs, and collaborators for the great projects that we have carried out together. Finally, I thank NASA for financial support, especially two LTSARP grants, but also various HST, FUSE, CHANDRA, SPITZER etc, GO grants. The University of Minnesota has also provided key financial support. Finally, I wish to thank the Hertzburg Institute of Astrophysics in Victoria, BC, Canada for providing me with visiting worker status. Much of the preparation of these lectures was done there.

REFERENCES

1. Aaronson, M. 1986, In *Star Forming Dwarf Galaxies and Related Objects* (eds. D. Kunth, T.X. Thuan, and J.T.T. Van) Editions Frontieres, 125
2. Aloisi, A., Savaglio, S., Heckman, T. M., Hoopes, C. G., Leitherer, C., & Sembach, K. R. 2003, ApJ, 595, 760
3. Aparicio, A., Carrera, R., & Martínez-Delgado, D. 2001, AJ, 122, 2524
4. Babul, A. & Rees, M. J. 1992, MNRAS, 255, 346
5. Barkana, R., & Loeb, A. 1999, ApJ, 523, 54
6. Bender, R., Paquet, A., & Nieto, J.-L. 1991, A&A, 246, 349
7. Benson, A. J., Lacey, C. G., Baugh, C. M., Cole, S., & Frenk, C. S. 2002a, MNRAS, 333, 156
8. Benson, A. J., Frenk, C. S., Lacey, C. G., Baugh, C. M., & Cole, S. 2002b, MNRAS, 333, 177
9. Benson, A. J., Frenk, C. S., Baugh, C. M., Cole, S., & Lacey, C. G. 2003, MNRAS, 343, 679
10. Bertelli, G., Bressan, A., Chiosi, C., Fagotto, F., Nasi, E. 1994, A&AS, 106, 275
11. Binggeli, B. 1993, in Panchromatic View of Galaxies, eds. G. Hensler Ch. Theis, & J. Gallagher, 173
12. Binggeli, B., & Cameron, L. M. 1991, A&A, 252, 27
13. Binggeli, B., Tarenghi, M., & Sandage, A. 1990, A&A, 228, 42
14. Bomans, D. J. & Grant, M.-B. 1998, Astronomische Nachrichten, 319, 26
15. Bothun, G. D., & Mould, J. R. 1988, ApJ, 324, 123
16. Bullock, J.S., Kravtsov, A.V., & Weinberg, D.H. 2000, ApJ, 539, 517
17. Caldwell, N. 1983, AJ, 88, 804
18. Caldwell, N., Armandroff, T. E., Da Costa, G. S., & Seitzer, P. 1998, AJ, 115, 535
19. Caldwell, N., & Bothun, G. D. 1987, AJ, 94, 1126
20. Calzetti, D., Harris, J., Gallagher, J. S., Smith, D. A., Conselice, C. J., et al. 2004, AJ, 127, 1405
21. Cannon, J. M., Dohm-Palmer, R. C., Skillman, E. D., Bomans, D. J., Côté, S., & Miller, B. W. 2003, AJ, 126, 2806
22. Cannon, J. M., McClure-Griffiths, N. M., Skillman, E. D., & Côté, S. 2004, ApJ, 607, 274
23. Cannon, J. M., Skillman, E. D., Sembach, K. R., & Bomans, D. J. 2005, ApJ, 618, 247
24. Carbon, D. F., Barbuy, B., Kraft, R. P., Friel, E. D., & Suntzeff, N. B. 1987, PASP, 99, 335
25. Carignan, C. & Freeman, K. C. 1988, ApJL, 332, L33
26. Carignan, C. & Purton, C. 1998, ApJ, 506, 125
27. Carrera, R., Aparicio, A., Martínez-Delgado, D., & Alonso-García, J. 2002, AJ, 123, 3199
28. Carraro, G., Chiosi, C., Girardi, L., & Lia, C. 2001, MNRAS, 327, 69
29. Chiba, M. & Nath, B. B. 1994, ApJ, 436, 618
30. Chiu, W. A., Gnedin, N. Y., & Ostriker, J. P. 2001, ApJ, 563, 21
31. Clayton, D. D. & Pantelaki, I. 1993, Physics Reports, 227, 293
32. Côté, S. 1995, Ph.D. thesis, Australia National University
33. Dekel, A., & Silk, J. 1986, ApJ, 303, 39
34. De Rijcke, S., Dejonghe, H., Zeilinger, W. W., & Hau, G. K. T. 2001, ApJ, 559, L21
35. De Rijcke, S., Dejonghe, H., Zeilinger, W. W., & Hau, G. K. T. 2003, A&A, 400, 119
36. Dohm-Palmer, R. C. et al. 1997, AJ, 114, 2527
37. Dohm-Palmer, R. C. et al. 1998, AJ, 116, 1227
38. Dohm-Palmer, R. C. & Skillman, E. D. 2002, AJ, 123, 1433
39. Dohm-Palmer, R. C., Skillman, E. D., Mateo, M., Saha, A., Dolphin, A., Tolstoy, E., Gallagher, J. S., & Cole, A. A. 2002, AJ, 123, 813
40. Dolphin, A. E. 1997, New Astronomy, 2, 397
41. Dolphin, A. E. 2000a, PASP, 112, 1383
42. Dolphin, A. E. 2000b, PASP, 112, 1397
43. Dolphin, A. E. 2000c, ApJ, 531, 804
44. Dolphin, A. E. 2002, MNRAS, 332, 91
45. Dolphin, A. E. et al. 2001a, MNRAS, 324, 249
46. Dolphin, A.E., Saha, A., Skillman, E.D., Tolstoy, E., Cole, A. A., Dohm-Palmer, R. C., Gallagher, J.S., Mateo, M. & Hoessel, J.G. 2001b, ApJ, 550, 554
47. Dolphin, A. E., Walker, A. R., Hodge, P. W., Mateo, M., Olszewski, E. W., Schommer, R. A., & Suntzeff, N. B. 2001c, ApJ, 562, 303

48. Dolphin, A. E., et al. 2002, AJ, 123, 3154
49. Dolphin, A. E., et al. 2003, AJ, 126, 187
50. Dolphin, A. E., Weisz, D., Skillman, E.D., & Holtzman, J. A. 2006, astro-ph 0506430
51. Edmunds, M. G., & Pagel, B. E. J. 1978, MNRAS, 185, 77P
52. Edmunds, M. G., & Phillips, S. 1989, MNRAS, 241, 9p
53. Efstathiou, G. 1992, MNRAS, 256, 43P
54. Efstathiou, G. 2000, MNRAS, 317, 697
55. Einasto, J., Kaasik, A., & Saar, E. 1974, Nature, 250, 309
56. Engelbracht, C. W., Gordon, K. D., Rieke, G. H., Werner, M. W., Dale, D. A., & Latter, W. B. 2005, ApJL, 628, L29
57. Faber, S. M., & Lin, D. N. C. 1983, ApJ, 266, L17
58. Fan, X., Narayanan, V. K., Strauss, M. A., White, R. L., Becker, R. H., Pentericci, L., & Rix, H. 2002, AJ, 123, 1247
59. Ferguson, H. C., & Babul, A. 1998, MNRAS, 296, 585
60. Ferrara, A., & Tolstoy, E. 2000, MNRAS, 313, 291
61. Gallart, C., Freedman,W., Aparicio, A., Bertelli, G., & Chiosi, C. 1999, AJ, 118, 2245
62. Gallart, C., Freedman, W. L., Mateo, M., Chiosi, C., Thompson, I. B., Aparicio, A., Bertelli, G., Hodge, P. W., et al. Lee, M. G., Olszewski, E. W., Saha, A., Stetson, P. B., & Suntzeff, N. B. 1999, ApJ, 514, 665
63. Gallart, C., Zoccali, M., & Aparicio, A. 2005, ARA&A, 43, 387
64. Garnett, D. R. 1990, ApJ, 363, 142
65. Geha, M., Guhathakurta, P., & van der Marel, R. P. 2002, AJ, 124, 3073
66. Geha, M., Guhathakurta, P., & van der Marel, R. P. 2003, AJ, 126, 1794
67. Girardi, L., Bressan, A., Bertelli, G. & Chiosi, C. 2000, A&AS, 141, 371
68. Gonzalez-Delgado, R. M., et al. 1994, ApJ, 437, 239
69. Gnedin, N. 2000a, ApJ, 535, L75
70. Gnedin, N. Y. 2000b, ApJ, 542, 535
71. Grebel, E. K., Gallagher, J. S., & Harbeck, D. 2003, AJ, 125, 1926
72. Greggio, L., Tosi, M., Clampin, M., de Marchi, G., Leitherer, C., Nota, A., & Sirianni, M. 1998, ApJ, 504, 725
73. Heckman, T. M. 1980, A&A, 87, 152
74. Heckman, T. M. 1998, ASP Conf. Ser. 148: Origins, 127
75. Heckman, T. M., Sembach, K. R., Meurer, G. R., Strickland, D. K., Martin, C. L., Calzetti, D., & Leitherer, C. 2001, ApJ, 554, 1021
76. Hogg, D. W., & Phinney, E. S. 1997, ApJL, 488, L95
77. Holtzman, J. A., Alfonso, C., & Dolphin, A. 2006, ApJ, submitted
78. Holtzman, J. A., Smith, G. H., & Grillmair, C. 2000, AJ, 120, 3060
79. Hunter, D. A. & Gallagher, J. S. 1985, ApJS, 58, 533
80. Gardiner, L. T., & Hatzidimitriou, D. 1992, MNRAS, 257, 195
81. Hunter, D. A., O'Connell, R. W., Gallagher, J. S., & Smecker-Hane, T. A. 2000, AJ, 120, 2383
82. Hunter, D. A., & Thronson, H. A. 1995, ApJ, 452, 238
83. Ibata, R. A., Gilmore, G., & Irwin, M. J. 1994, Nature, 370, 194
84. Iben, I., & Renzini, A. 1983, ARA&A, 21, 271
85. Ikeuchi, S. 1986, ApSS, 118, 509
86. Irwin, M. & Tolstoy, E. 2002, MNRAS, 336, 643
87. Israel, F.P., Johansson, L. E. B., Lequeux, J., et al. 1993, A&A, 276, 25
88. Izotov, Y. I., & Thuan, T. X. 1999, ApJ, 511, 639
89. Izotov, Y. I., & Thuan, T. X. 2004, ApJ, 616, 768
90. Jackson, D. C., Skillman, E. D., Cannon, J. M., & Côté, S. 2004, AJ, 128, 1219
91. Jackson, D. C., Cannon, J. M., Skillman, E. D., Lee, H. Gehrz, R. D., Woodward, C., & Polomski, E., 2006, ApJ, in press
92. Karachentsev, I. D. et al. 2003, A&A, 404, 93
93. Karachentsev, I. D., Karachentsev, V. E., Huchtmeier, W. K., & Makarov, D. I. 2004, AJ, 127, 2031
94. Kauffmann, G., Guiderdoni, B., & White, S. D. M. 1994, MNRAS, 267, 981
95. Kauffmann, G., White, S. D. M., & Guiderdoni, B. 1993, MNRAS, 264, 201
96. Kauffmann, G., et al. 2003, MNRAS, 341, 33

97. Kennicutt, R. C. 1989, ApJ, 344, 685
98. Kennicutt, R. C. & Skillman, E. D. 2001, AJ, 121, 1461
99. Kennicutt, R. C. Jr., Tamblyn, P., & Congdon, C. W. 1994, ApJ, 435, 22
100. Kepner, J. V., Babul, A., & Spergel, D. N. 1997, ApJ, 487, 61
101. Kinman, T. D., & Davidson, K. 1981, ApJ, 243, 127
102. Klypin, A., Kravtsov, A. V., Valenzuela, O., & Prada, F. 1999, ApJ, 522, 82
103. Kobulnicky, H. A. & Skillman, E. D. 1996, ApJ, 471, 211
104. Kobulnicky, H. A. & Skillman, E. D. 1997, ApJ, 489, 636
105. Kobulnicky, H. A., Skillman, E. D., Roy, J., Walsh, J. R., & Rosa, M. R. 1997, ApJ, 477, 679
106. Kormendy, J. 1985, ApJ, 295, 73
107. Kormendy, J., & Freeman, K. C. 2004, IAU Symposium, 220, 377
108. Krueger, H., Fritze-v. Alvensleben, U., & Loose, H.-H. 1995, A&A, 303, 41
109. Kunth, D. & Sargent, W. L. W. 1986, ApJ, 300, 496
110. Laird, J. B. 1985, ApJ, 289, 556
111. Lebouteiller, V., Kunth, D., Lequeux, J., Lecavelier des Etangs, A., Désert, J.-M., Hébrard, G., & Vidal-Madjar, A. 2004, A&A, 415, 55
112. Lecavelier des Etangs, A., Désert, J.-M., Kunth, D., Vidal-Madjar, A., Callejo, G., Ferlet, R., Hébrard, G., & Lebouteiller, V. 2004, A&A, 413, 131
113. Lee, H., McCall, M. L., Kingsburgh, R. L., Ross, R., & Stevenson, C. C. 2003b, AJ, 125, 146
114. Lee, H., Skillman, E. D., Cannon, J. M., Jackson, D. C., Gehrz, R. D., Polomski, E. F., & Woodward, C. E. 2006, ApJ, submitted
115. Lee, H., Skillman, E. D., & Venn, K. A. 2006, ApJ, in press
116. Legrand, F., Tenorio-Tagle, G., Silich, S., Kunth, D., & Cerviño, M. 2001, ApJ, 560, 630
117. Lequeux, J., Peimbert, M., Rayo, J. M., Serrano, A., & Torres-Peimbert, S. 1979, A&A, 91, 269
118. Lin, D. N. C. & Faber, S. M. 1983, ApJL, 266, L21
119. Mac Low, M., & Ferrara, A. 1999, ApJ, 513, 142
120. Madau, P., Ferguson, H. C., Dickinson, M. E., Giavalisco, M., Steidel, C. C., & Fruchter, A. 1996, MNRAS, 283, 1388
121. Maloney, P., & Black, J. H. 1988, ApJ, 325, 389
122. Marlowe, A. T., Meurer, G. R., Heckman, T. M., & Schommer, R. 1997, ApJS, 112, 285
123. Marlowe, A. T., Meurer, G. R., & Heckman, T. M. 1999, ApJ, 522, 183
124. Martin, C. L., Kobulnicky, H. A., & Heckman, T. M. 2002, ApJ, 574, 663
125. Martin, N. F., Ibata, R. A., Bellazzini, M., Irwin, M. J., Lewis, G. F., & Dehnen, W. 2004, MNRAS, 348, 12
126. Mas-Hesse, J. M., & Kunth, D. 1999, A&A, 349, 765
127. Massey, P., Hodge, P. W., Holmes, S., Jacoby, G., King, N. L., Olsen, K., Saha, A., & Smith, C. 2001, BAAS, 33, 1496
128. Mateo, M. L. 1998, ARA&A, 36, 435
129. Mayer, L., Governato, F., Colpi, M., Moore, B., Quinn, T., Wadsley, J., Stadel, J., & Lake, G. 2001a, ApJ, 547, L123
130. Mayer, L., Governato, F., Colpi, M., Moore, B., Quinn, T., Wadsley, J., Stadel, J., & Lake, G. 2001b, ApJ, 559, 754
131. McGaugh, S. S. 1991, ApJ, 380, 140
132. Meurer, G. R. 2000, ASP Conf. Ser. 211: Massive Stellar Clusters, 211, 81
133. Miller, B. W., Dolphin, A. E., Lee, M. G., Kim, S. C., & Hodge, P. 2001, ApJ, 562, 713
134. Miller, B. W. 1996, AJ, 112, 991
135. Miller, B. W., & Hodge, P. 1996, ApJ, 458, 467
136. Momany, Y., et al. 2005, A&A, 439, 111
137. Moore, B., Ghigna, S., Governato, F., Lake, G., Quinn, T., Stadel, J., & Tozzi, P. 1999, ApJ, 524, L19
138. Mould, J. R., Kristian, J., and Da Costa, G. S. 1983, ApJ, 270, 471
139. Nicastro, F. et al. 2002, ApJ, 573, 157
140. Nicastro, F. et al. 2003, Nature, 421, 719
141. Olszewski, E. W., & Aaronson, M. 1985, AJ, 90, 2221
142. Olszewski, E. W., Suntzeff, N. B., & Mateo, M. 1996, ARA&A, 34, 511

143. Osterbrock, D. E. 1989, Astrophysics of Gaseous Nebulae and Active Galactic Nuclei, University Science Books
144. Östlin, G., Zackrisson, E., Bergvall, N., Roennback, J. 2003, A&A, 408, 887
145. Pagel, B. E. J. 1985, ESO Workshop on Production and Distribution of C,N,O Elements, Garching:ESO, 1985, eds. I.J. Danziger, F. Matteucci, and K. Kjär., 155
146. Pedraz, S., Gorgas, J., Cardiel, N., Sánchez-Blázquez, P., & Guzmán, R. 2002, MNRAS, 332, L59
147. Peimbert, M., & Torres-Peimbert, S. 1974, ApJ, 193, 327
148. Peimbert, M., & Torres-Peimbert, S. 1976, ApJ, 203, 581
149. Pilyugin, L. S. 2000, A&A, 362, 325
150. Quinn, T., Katz, N., & Efstathiou, G. 1996, MNRAS, 278, L49
151. Recchi, S., Matteucci, F., & D'Ercole, A. 2001, MNRAS, 322, 800
152. Rees, M. J. 1986, MNRAS, 218, 25P
153. Renzini, A., & Voli, M. 1981, A&A, 94, 175
154. Ricotti, M., & Gnedin, N. Y. 2005, ApJ, 629, 259
155. Richer, M. G., & McCall, M. L. 1995, ApJ, 445, 642
156. Roennback, J., & Bergvall, N. 1995, A&A, 302, 353
157. Rosa, M., & Mathis, J. S. 1987, ApJ, 317, 163
158. St-Germain, J., Carignan, C., Côte, S., & Oosterloo, T. 1999, AJ, 118, 1235
159. Schaerer, D., Contini, T., & Kunth, D. 1999, A&A, 341, 399
160. Schulte-Ladbeck, R. E., Crone, M. M., & Hopp, U. 1998, ApJL, 493, L23
161. Schulte-Ladbeck, R. E., Hopp, U., Drozdovsky, I. O., Greggio, L., & Crone, M. M. 2002, AJ, 124, 896
162. Skillman, E. D. 1985, ApJ, 290, 449
163. Skillman, E. D. 1996, ASP Conf. Ser. 106: The Minnesota Lectures on Extragalactic Neutral Hydrogen, 106, 208
164. Skillman, E. D. 1998, in Stellar Astrophysics for the Local Group: VIII Canary Islands Winter School of Astrophysics, eds., A. Aparicio, A. Herrero, & F. Sanchez, Cambridge University Press, 457
165. Skillman, E. D., Bomans, D. J., & Kobulnicky, H. A. 1997, ApJ, 474, 205
166. Skillman, E. D., Côté, S., & Miller, B. W. 2003a, AJ, 125, 593
167. Skillman, E. D., Côté, S., & Miller, B. W. 2003b, AJ, 125, 610
168. Skillman, E. D., & Kennicutt, R. C., Jr. 1993, ApJ, 411, 655
169. Skillman, E. D., Kennicutt, R. C., & Hodge, P. W. 1989b, ApJ, 347, 875
170. Skillman, E. D., Melnick, J., Terlevich, R., & Moles, M. 1988a, A&A, 196, 31
171. Skillman, E. D., Terlevich, R. J., Kennicutt, R. C., Garnett, D. R., & Terlevich, E. 1994, ApJ, 431, 172
172. Skillman, E. D., Terlevich, R., and Melnick, J. 1989a, MNRAS, 240, 563
173. Skillman, E. D., Terlevich, R., Teuben, P. J., & van Woerden, H. 1988, A&A, 198, 33
174. Skillman, E. D., Tolstoy, E., Cole, A. A., Dolphin, A. E., Saha, A., Gallagher, J. S., Dohm-Palmer, R. C., & Mateo, M. 2003, ApJ, 596, 253
175. Somerville, R. S. 2002, ApJL, 572, L23
176. Spaans, M., & Norman, C. A. 1997, ApJ, 483, 87
177. Spergel, D. N., et al. 2003, ApJS, 148, 175
178. Stanimirović, S., Dickey, J. M., Krčo, M., & Brooks, A. M. 2002, ApJ, 576, 773
179. Stetson, P. B., Hesser, J. E., & Smecker-Hane, T. A. 1998, PASP, 110, 533
180. Stoehr, F., White, S. D. M., Tormen, G., & Springel, V. 2002, MNRAS, 335, L84
181. Talent, D. L. 1980, Ph.D. Thesis, Rice University
182. Tassis, K., Abel, T., Bryan, G. L., & Norman, M. L. 2003, ApJ, 587, 13
183. Taylor, C. L., Kobulnicky, H. A., & Skillman, E. D. 1998, AJ, 116, 2746
184. Tenorio-Tagle, G. 1996, AJ, 111, 1641
185. Thoul, A. A. & Weinberg, D. H. 1996, ApJ, 465, 608
186. Thuan, T. X., Lecavelier des Etangs, A., & Izotov, Y. I. 2002, ApJ, 565, 941
187. Timmes, F. X., Woosley, S. E., & Weaver, T. A. 1995, ApJS, 98, 617
188. Tolstoy, E., et al. 1998, AJ, 116, 1244
189. Tolstoy, E., et al. 2004, ApJL, 617, L119
190. Tosi, M., Greggio, L., Marconi, G., & Focardi, P. 1991, AJ, 102, 951

191. Tremonti, C. A., Calzetti, D., Leitherer, C., & Heckman, T. M. 2001, ApJ, 555, 322
192. Trentham, N. & Hodgkin, S. 2002, MNRAS, 333, 423
193. Tully, R. B., Somerville, R. S., Trentham, N., & Verheijen, M. A. W. 2002, ApJ, 569, 573
194. Tully, R. B., & Pierce, M. J. 2000, ApJ, 533, 744
195. van den Bergh, S. 1994a, AJ, 107, 1328
196. van den Bergh, S. 1994b, ApJ, 428, 617
197. van Zee, L. 2001, AJ, 121, 2003
198. van Zee, L., Barton, E. J., & Skillman, E. D. 2004b, AJ, 128, 2797
199. van Zee, L., & Haynes, M. P. 2006, ApJ, 636, 214
200. van Zee, L., Haynes, M. P., & Salzer, J. J. 1997a, AJ, 114, 2479
201. van Zee, L., Haynes, M. P., & Salzer, J. J. 1997b, AJ, 114, 2497
202. van Zee, L., Skillman, E. D., & Haynes, M. P. 2004a, AJ, 128, 121
203. van Zee, L., Skillman, E. D., & Haynes, M. P. 2006, ApJ, 637, 269
204. Vila Costas, M. B., & Edmunds, M. G. 1993, MNRAS, 265, 199
205. Vílchez, J. M., & Iglesias-Páramo, J. 1998, ApJ, 508, 248
206. White, S. D. M. & Rees, M. J. 1978, MNRAS, 183, 341
207. Woosley, S. E., & Weaver, T. A. 1995, ApJS, 101, 181
208. Young, L. M. & Lo, K. Y. 1996, ApJ, 462, 203
209. Young, L. M. & Lo, K. Y. 1997, ApJ, 490, 710

CHAPTER 4

Advanced Topics in Cosmology: A Pedagogical Introduction
T. Padmanabhan

ADVANCED TOPICS IN COSMOLOGY: A PEDAGOGICAL INTRODUCTION

T. Padmanabhan

IUCAA,
Pune University Campus, Ganeshkhind,
Pune 411 007, INDIA.
email: nabhan@iucaa.ernet.in

Abstract. These lecture notes provide a concise, rapid and pedagogical introduction to several advanced topics in contemporary cosmology. The discussion of thermal history of the universe, linear perturbation theory, theory of CMBR temperature anisotropies and the inflationary generation of perturbation are presented in a manner accessible to someone who has done a first course in cosmology. The discussion of dark energy is more research oriented and reflects the personal bias of the author. Contents: (I) The cosmological paradigm and Friedmann model; (II) Thermal history of the universe; (III) Structure formation and linear perturbation theories; (IV) Perturbations in dark matter and radiation; (V) Transfer function for matter perturbations; (VI) Temperature anisotropies of CMBR; (VII) Generation of initial perturbations from inflation; (VIII) The dark energy.

Keywords: Cosmology: theory, dark energy, distance scale, large-scale structure
PACS: 98.80.-k; 98.80.Es; 95.36.+x; 98.65.Dx

1. THE COSMOLOGICAL PARADIGM AND FRIEDMANN MODEL

Observations show that the universe is fairly homogeneous and isotropic at scales larger than about $150h^{-1}$ Mpc where 1 Mpc $\simeq 3 \times 10^{24}$ cm and $h \approx 0.7$ is a parameter related to the expansion rate of the universe. The conventional — and highly successful — approach to cosmology separates the study of large scale ($l \gtrsim 150h^{-1}$ Mpc) dynamics of the universe from the issue of structure formation at smaller scales. The former is modeled by a homogeneous and isotropic distribution of energy density; the latter issue is addressed in terms of gravitational instability which will amplify the small perturbations in the energy density, leading to the formation of structures like galaxies. In such an approach, the expansion of the background universe is described by the metric (We shall use units with with $c = 1$ throughout, unless otherwise specified):

$$ds^2 \equiv dt^2 - a^2 d\mathbf{x}^2 \equiv dt^2 - a^2(t)\left[d\chi^2 + S_k^2(\chi)\left(d\theta^2 + \sin^2\theta d\phi^2\right)\right] \quad (1)$$

with $S_k(\chi) = (\sin\chi, \chi, \sinh\chi)$ for the three values of the label $k = (1, 0, -1)$. The function $a(t)$ is governed by the equations:

$$\frac{\dot{a}^2 + k}{a^2} = \frac{8\pi G \rho}{3}; \quad d(\rho a^3) = -p\,da^3 \quad (2)$$

The first one relates expansion rate of the universe to the energy density ρ and $k = 0, \pm 1$ is a parameter which characterizes the spatial curvature of the universe. The second equation, when coupled with the equation of state $p = p(\rho)$ which relates the pressure p to the energy density, determines the evolution of energy density $\rho = \rho(a)$ in terms of the expansion factor of the universe. In particular if $p = w\rho$ with (at least, approximately) constant w then, $\rho \propto a^{-3(1+w)}$ and (if we further assume $k = 0$, which is strongly favoured by observations) the first equation in Eq.(2) gives $a \propto t^{2/[3(1+w)]}$. We will also often use the redshift $z(t)$, defined as $(1+z) = a_0/a(t)$ where the subscript zero denotes quantities evaluated at the present moment. in a $k = 0$ universe, we can set $a_0 = 1$ by rescaling the spatial coordinates.

It is convenient to measure the energy densities of different components in terms of a *critical energy density* (ρ_c) required to make $k = 0$ at the present epoch. (Of course, since k is a constant, it will remain zero at all epochs if it is zero at any given moment of time.) From Eq.(2), it is clear that $\rho_c = 3H_0^2/8\pi G$ where $H_0 \equiv (\dot{a}/a)_0$ — called the Hubble constant — is the rate of expansion of the universe at present. Numerically

$$\rho_c = \frac{3H_0^2}{8\pi G} = 1.88h^2 \times 10^{-29} \text{ gm cm}^{-3} = 2.8 \times 10^{11} h^2 M_\odot \text{ Mpc}^{-3}$$
$$= 1.1 \times 10^4 h^2 \text{ eV cm}^{-3} = 1.1 \times 10^{-5} h^2 \text{ protons cm}^{-3} \quad (3)$$

The variables $\Omega_i \equiv \rho_i/\rho_c$ will give the fractional contribution of different components of the universe (i denoting baryons, dark matter, radiation, etc.) to the critical density. Observations then lead to the following results:

(1) Our universe has $0.98 \lesssim \Omega_{tot} \lesssim 1.08$. The value of Ω_{tot} can be determined from the angular anisotropy spectrum of the cosmic microwave background radiation (CMBR; see Section) and these observations (combined with the reasonable assumption that $h > 0.5$) show[1] that we live in a universe with critical density, so that $k = 0$.

(2) Observations of primordial deuterium produced in big bang nucleosynthesis (which took place when the universe was about few minutes in age) as well as the CMBR observations show[2] that the *total* amount of baryons in the universe contributes about $\Omega_B = (0.024 \pm 0.0012)h^{-2}$. Given the independent observations[3] which fix $h = 0.72 \pm 0.07$, we conclude that $\Omega_B \cong 0.04 - 0.06$. These observations take into account all baryons which exist in the universe today irrespective of whether they are luminous or not. *Combined with previous item we conclude that most of the universe is non-baryonic.*

(3) Host of observations related to large scale structure and dynamics (rotation curves of galaxies, estimate of cluster masses, gravitational lensing, galaxy surveys ..) all suggest[4] that the universe is populated by a non-luminous component of matter (dark matter; DM hereafter) made of weakly interacting massive particles which *does* cluster at galactic scales. This component contributes about $\Omega_{DM} \cong 0.20 - 0.35$ and has the simple equation of state $p_{DM} \approx 0$. The second equation in Eq.(2), then gives $\rho_{DM} \propto a^{-3}$ as the universe expands which arises from the evolution of number density of particles: $\rho = nmc^2 \propto n \propto a^{-3}$.

(4) Combining the last observation with the first we conclude that there must be (at least) one more component to the energy density of the universe contributing about 70% of critical density. Early analysis of several observations[5] indicated that this component is unclustered and has negative pressure. This is confirmed dramatically by the supernova observations (see Ref. [6]; for a critical look at the current data, see

Ref. [7]). The observations suggest that the missing component has $w = p/\rho \lesssim -0.78$ and contributes $\Omega_{DE} \cong 0.60 - 0.75$. The simplest choice for such *dark energy* with negative pressure is the cosmological constant which is a term that can be added to Einstein's equations. This term acts like a fluid with an equation of state $p_{DE} = -\rho_{DE}$; the second equation in Eq.(2), then gives $\rho_{DE} =$ constant as universe expands.

(5) The universe also contains radiation contributing an energy density $\Omega_R h^2 = 2.56 \times 10^{-5}$ today most of which is due to photons in the CMBR. The equation of state is $p_R = (1/3)\rho_R$; the second equation in Eq.(2), then gives $\rho_R \propto a^{-4}$. Combining it with the result $\rho_R \propto T^4$ for thermal radiation, it follows that $T \propto a^{-1}$. Radiation is dynamically irrelevant today but since $(\rho_R/\rho_{DM}) \propto a^{-1}$ it would have been the dominant component when the universe was smaller by a factor larger than $\Omega_{DM}/\Omega_R \simeq 4 \times 10^4 \Omega_{DM} h^2$.

(6) Taking all the above observations together, we conclude that our universe has (approximately) $\Omega_{DE} \simeq 0.7, \Omega_{DM} \simeq 0.26, \Omega_B \simeq 0.04, \Omega_R \simeq 5 \times 10^{-5}$. All known observations are consistent with such an — admittedly weird — composition for the universe.

Using $\rho_{NR} \propto a^{-3}, \rho_R \propto a^{-4}$ and ρ_{DE}=constant we can write Eq.(2) in a convenient dimensionless form as

$$\frac{1}{2}\left(\frac{dq}{d\tau}\right)^2 + V(q) = E \tag{4}$$

where $\tau = H_0 t, a = a_0 q(\tau), \Omega_{NR} = \Omega_B + \Omega_{DM}$ and

$$V(q) = -\frac{1}{2}\left[\frac{\Omega_R}{q^2} + \frac{\Omega_{NR}}{q} + \Omega_{DE} q^2\right]; \quad E = \frac{1}{2}(1 - \Omega_{tot}). \tag{5}$$

This equation has the structure of the first integral for motion of a particle with energy E in a potential $V(q)$. For models with $\Omega = \Omega_{NR} + \Omega_{DE} = 1$, we can take $E = 0$ so that $(dq/d\tau) = \sqrt{V(q)}$. Based on the observed composition of the universe, we can identify three distinct phases in the evolution of the universe when the temperature is less than about 100 GeV. At high redshifts (small q) the universe is radiation dominated and $\dot{q}$ is independent of the other cosmological parameters. Then Eq.(4) can be easily integrated to give $a(t) \propto t^{1/2}$ and the temperature of the universe decreases as $T \propto t^{-1/2}$. As the universe expands, a time will come when ($t = t_{eq}$, $a = a_{eq}$ and $z = z_{eq}$, say) the matter energy density will be comparable to radiation energy density. For the parameters described above, $(1 + z_{eq}) = \Omega_{NR}/\Omega_R \simeq 4 \times 10^4 \Omega_{DM} h^2$. At lower redshifts, matter will dominate over radiation and we will have $a \propto t^{2/3}$ until fairly late when the dark energy density will dominate over non relativistic matter. This occurs at a redshift of z_{DE} where $(1 + z_{DE}) = (\Omega_{DE}/\Omega_{NR})^{1/3}$. For $\Omega_{DE} \approx 0.7, \Omega_{NR} \approx 0.3$, this occurs at $z_{DE} \approx 0.33$. In this phase, the velocity $\dot{q}$ changes from being a decreasing function to an increasing function leading to an accelerating universe. In addition to these, we believe that the universe probably went through a rapidly expanding, inflationary, phase very early when $T \approx 10^{14}$ GeV; we will say more about this in Section . (For a textbook description of these and related issues, see e.g. Ref. [8].)

Before we conclude this section, we will briefly mention some key aspects of the background cosmology described by a Friedmann model.

(a) The metric in Eq.(1) can be rewritten using the expansion parameter a or the redshift $z = (a_0/a)^{-1} - 1$ as the time coordinate in the form

$$ds^2 = H^{-2}(a)\left(\frac{da}{a}\right)^2 a^2 dx^2 - \frac{1}{(1+z)^2}\left[\Pi^{-2}(z)dz^2 - dx^2\right] \tag{6}$$

This form clearly shows that the only dynamical content of the metric is encoded in the function $H(a) = (\dot{a}/a)$. An immediate consequence is that any observation which is capable of determining the geometry of the universe can only provide — at best — information about this function.

(b) Since cosmological observations usually use radiation received from distant sources, it is worth reviewing briefly the propagation of radiation in the universe. The radial light rays follow a trajectory given by

$$r_{em}(z) = S_k(\alpha); \qquad \alpha \equiv \frac{1}{a_0}\int_0^z H^{-1}(z)dz \tag{7}$$

if the photon is emitted at r_{em} at the redshift z and received here today. Two other quantities closely related to $r_{em}(z)$ are the luminosity distance, d_L, and the angular diameter distance d_A. If we receive a flux F from a source of luminosity L, then the luminosity distance is defined via the relation $F \equiv L/4\pi d_L^2(z)$. If an object of transverse length l subtends a small angle θ, the angular diameter distance is defined via ($l = \theta d_A$). Simple calculation shows that:

$$d_L(z) = a_0 r_{em}(z)(1+z) = a_0(1+z)S_k(\alpha); \qquad d_A(z) = a_0 r_{em}(z)(1+z)^{-1} \tag{8}$$

(c) As an example of determining the spacetime geometry of the universe from observations, let us consider how one can determine $a(t)$ from the observations of the luminosity distance. It is clear from the first equation in Eq. (8) that

$$H^{-1}(z) = \left[1 - \frac{kd_L^2(z)}{a_0^2(1+z)^2}\right]^{-1/2}\frac{d}{dz}\left[\frac{d_L(z)}{1+z}\right] \to \frac{d}{dz}\left[\frac{d_L(z)}{1+z}\right] \tag{9}$$

where the last form is valid for a $k = 0$ universe. If we determine the form of $d_L(z)$ from observations — which can be done if we can measure the flux F from a class of sources with known value for luminosity L — then we can use this relation to determine the evolutionary history of the universe and thus the dynamics.

2. THERMAL HISTORY OF THE UNIVERSE

Let us next consider some key events in the evolutionary history of our universe [8]. The most well understood phase of the universe occurs when the temperature is less than about 10^{12} K. Above this temperature, thermal production of baryons and their strong interaction is significant and somewhat difficult to model. We can ignore such complications at lower temperatures and — as we shall see — several interesting physical phenomena did take place during the later epochs with $T \lesssim 10^{12}$.

The first thing we need to do is to determine the composition of the universe when $T \approx 10^{12}$ K. We will certainly have, at this time, copious amount of photons and all species of neutrinos and antineutrinos. In addition, neutrons and protons must exist at this time since there is no way they could be produced later on. (This implies that phenomena which took place at higher temperatures should have left a small excess of baryons over anti baryons; we do not quite understand how this happened and will just take it as an initial condition.) Since the rest mass of electrons correspond to a much lower temperature (about 0.5×10^{10} K), there will be large number of electrons and positrons at this temperature but in order to maintain charge neutrality, we need to have a slight excess of electrons over positrons (by about 1 part in 10^9) with the net negative charge compensating the positive charge contributed by protons.

An elementary calculation using the known interaction rates show that all these particles are in thermal equilibrium at this epoch. Hence standard rules of statistical mechanics allows us to determine the number density (n), energy density (ρ) and the pressure (p) in terms of the distribution function f:

$$n = \int f(\mathbf{k}) d^3 \mathbf{k} = \frac{g}{2\pi^2} \int_m^\infty \frac{(E^2 - m^2)^{1/2} E dE}{\exp[(E-\mu)/T] \pm 1} \tag{10}$$

$$\rho = \int E f(\mathbf{k}) d^3 \mathbf{k} = \frac{g}{2\pi^2} \int_m^\infty \frac{(E^2 - m^2)^{1/2} E^2 dE}{\exp[(E-\mu)/T] \pm 1} \tag{11}$$

$$p = \frac{1}{3} \int d^3\mathbf{k} f(\mathbf{k}) k v(\mathbf{k}) = \int \frac{1}{3} \frac{|\mathbf{k}|^2}{E} f(\mathbf{k}) d^3\mathbf{k} = \frac{g}{6\pi^2} \int_m^\infty \frac{(E^2 - m^2)^{3/2} dE}{e^{[(E-\mu)/T]} \pm 1} \tag{12}$$

Next, we can argue that the chemical potentials for electrons, positrons and neutrinos can be taken to be zero. For example, conservation of chemical potential in the reaction $e^+ e^- \to 2\gamma$ implies that the chemical potentials of electrons and positrons must differ in a sign. But since the number densities of electrons and positrons, which are determined by the chemical potential, are very close to each other, the chemical potentials of electrons and positrons must be (very closely) equal to each other. Hence both must be (very close to) zero. Similar reasoning based on lepton number shows that neutrinos should also have zero chemical potential. Given this, one can evaluate the integrals for all the relativistic species and we obtain for the total energy density

$$\rho_{\text{total}} = \sum_{i=\text{boson}} g_i \left(\frac{\pi^2}{30}\right) T_i^4 + \sum_{i=\text{fermion}} \frac{7}{8} g_i \left(\frac{\pi^2}{30}\right) T_i^4 = g_{\text{total}} \left(\frac{\pi^2}{30}\right) T^4 \tag{13}$$

where

$$g_{\text{total}} \equiv \sum_{\text{boson}} g_B + \sum_{\text{fermion}} \frac{7}{8} g_F. \tag{14}$$

The corresponding entropy density is given by

$$s \cong \frac{1}{T}(\rho + p) = \frac{2\pi^2}{45} q T^3; \quad q \equiv q_{\text{total}} = \sum_{\text{boson}} g_B + \frac{7}{8} \sum_{\text{fermion}} g_F. \tag{15}$$

115

2.1 Neutrino background

As a simple application of the above result, let us consider the fate of neutrinos in the expanding universe. From the standard weak interaction theory, one can compute the reaction rate Γ of the neutrinos with the rest of the species. When this reaction rate fall below the expansion rate H of the universe, the reactions cannot keep the neutrinos coupled to the rest of the matter. A simple calculation [8] shows that the relevant ratio is given by

$$\frac{\Gamma}{H} \simeq \left(\frac{T}{1.4\text{MeV}}\right)^3 = \left(\frac{T}{1.6 \times 10^{10}\text{K}}\right)^3 \qquad (16)$$

Thus, for $T \lesssim 1.6 \times 10^{10}$ K, the neutrinos decouple from matter. At slightly lower temperature, the electrons and positrons annihilate increasing the number density of photons. Neutrinos do not get any share of this energy since they have already decoupled from the rest of the matter. As a result, the photon temperature goes up with respect to the neutrino temperature once the e^+e^- annihilation is complete. This increase in the temperature is easy to calculate. As far as the photons are concerned, the increase in the temperature is essentially due to the change in the degrees of freedom g and is given by:

$$\frac{(aT_\gamma)^3_{\text{after}}}{(aT_\gamma)^3_{\text{before}}} = \frac{g_{\text{before}}}{g_{\text{after}}} = \frac{\frac{7}{8}(2+2)+2}{2} = \frac{11}{4}. \qquad (17)$$

(In the numerator, one 2 is for electron; one 2 is for positron; the 7/8 factor arises because these are fermions. The final 2 is for photons. In the denominator, there are only photons to take care of.) Therefore

$$\begin{aligned}(aT_\gamma)_{\text{after}} &= \left(\frac{11}{4}\right)^{1/3}(aT_\gamma)_{\text{before}} = \left(\frac{11}{4}\right)^{1/3}(aT_\nu)_{\text{before}} \\ &= \left(\frac{11}{4}\right)^{1/3}(aT_\nu)_{\text{after}} \simeq 1.4(aT_\nu)_{\text{after}}.\end{aligned} \qquad (18)$$

The first equality is from Eq. (17); the second arises because the photons and neutrinos had the same temperature originally; the third equality is from the fact that for decoupled neutrinos aT_ν is a constant. This result leads to the prediction that, at present, the universe will contain a bath of neutrinos which has temperature that is (predictably) lower than that of CMBR. The future detection of such a cosmic neutrino background will allow us to probe the universe at its earliest epochs.

2.2 Primordial Nucleosynthesis

When the temperature of the universe is higher than the binding energy of the nuclei ($\sim$ MeV), none of the heavy elements (helium and the metals) could have existed in the universe. The binding energies of the first four light nuclei, ^2H, ^3H, ^3He and ^4He are 2.22 MeV, 6.92 MeV, 7.72 MeV and 28.3 MeV respectively. This would suggest that these nuclei could be formed when the temperature of the universe is in the range of $(1-30)$ MeV. The actual synthesis takes place only at a much lower temperature, $T_{\text{nuc}} = T_n \simeq 0.1$ MeV. The main reason for this delay is the 'high entropy' of our universe, i.e., the high value for the photon-to-baryon ratio, η^{-1}. Numerically,

$$\eta = \frac{n_B}{n_\gamma} = 5.5 \times 10^{-10} \left(\frac{\Omega_B h^2}{0.02}\right); \quad \Omega_B h^2 = 3.65 \times 10^{-3} \left(\frac{T_0}{2.73 \text{ K}}\right)^3 \eta_{10} \qquad (19)$$

To see this, let us assume, for a moment, that the nuclear (and other) reactions are fast enough to maintain thermal equilibrium between various species of particles and nuclei. In thermal equilibrium, the number density of a nuclear species $^A N_Z$ with atomic mass A and charge Z will be

$$n_A = g_A \left(\frac{m_A T}{2\pi}\right)^{3/2} \exp\left[-\left(\frac{m_A - \mu_A}{T}\right)\right]. \qquad (20)$$

From this one can obtain the equation for the temperature T_A at which the mass fraction of a particular species-A will be of order unity ($X_A \simeq 1$). We find that

$$T_A \simeq \frac{B_A/(A-1)}{\ln(\eta^{-1}) + 1.5 \ln(m_B/T)} \qquad (21)$$

where B_A is the binding energy of the species. This temperature will be fairly lower than B_A because of the large value of η^{-1}. For ^2H, ^3He and ^4He the value of T_A is 0.07 MeV, 0.11 MeV and 0.28 MeV respectively. Comparison with the binding energy of these nuclei shows that these values are lower than the corresponding binding energies B_A by a factor of about 10, at least.

Thus, even when the thermal equilibrium is maintained, significant synthesis of nuclei can occur only at $T \lesssim 0.3$ MeV and not at higher temperatures. If such is the case, then we would expect significant production ($X_A \lesssim 1$) of nuclear species-A at temperatures $T \lesssim T_A$. It turns out, however, that the rate of nuclear reactions is *not* high enough to maintain thermal equilibrium between various species. We have to determine the temperatures up to which thermal equilibrium can be maintained and redo the calculations to find non-equilibrium mass fractions. The general procedure for studying non equilibrium abundances in an expanding universe is based on *rate equations*. Since we will require this formalism again in Section (for the study of recombination), we will develop it in a somewhat general context.

Consider a reaction in which two particles 1 and 2 interact to form two other particles 3 and 4. For example, $n + \nu_e \rightleftharpoons p + e$ constitutes one such reaction which converts neutrons into protons in the forward direction and protons into neutrons in the reverse direction; another example we will come across in the next section is $p + e \rightleftharpoons H + \gamma$ where the forward reaction describes recombination of electron and proton forming a neutral hydrogen atom (with the emission of a photon), while the reverse reaction is the photoionisation of a hydrogen atom. In general, we are interested in how the number density n_1 of particle species 1, say, changes due to a reaction of the form $1+2 \rightleftharpoons 3+4$.

We first note that even if there is no reaction, the number density will change as $n_1 \propto a^{-3}$ due to the expansion of the universe; so what we are really after is the change in $n_1 a^3$. Further, the forward reaction will be proportional to the product of the number densities $n_1 n_2$ while the reverse reaction will be proportional to $n_3 n_4$. Hence we can write an equation for the rate of change of particle species n_1 as

$$\frac{1}{a^3}\frac{d(n_1 a^3)}{dt} = \mu(A n_3 n_4 - n_1 n_2). \tag{22}$$

The left hand side is the relevant rate of change over and above that due to the expansion of the universe; on the right hand side, the two proportionality constants have been written as μ and $(A\mu)$, both of which, of course, will be functions of time. (The quantity μ has the dimensions of cm^{3}s^{-1}, so that $n\mu$ has the dimensions of s^{-1}; usually $\mu \simeq \sigma v$ where σ is the cross-section for the relevant process and v is the relative velocity.) The left hand side has to vanish when the system is in thermal equilibrium with $n_i = n_i^{eq}$, where the superscript 'eq' denotes the equilibrium densities for the different species labeled by $i = 1-4$. This condition allows us to rewrite A as $A = n_1^{eq} n_2^{eq}/(n_3^{eq} n_4^{eq})$. Hence the rate equation becomes

$$\frac{1}{a^3}\frac{d(n_1 a^3)}{dt} = \mu n_1^{eq} n_2^{eq}\left(\frac{n_3 n_4}{n_3^{eq} n_4^{eq}} - \frac{n_1 n_2}{n_1^{eq} n_2^{eq}}\right). \tag{23}$$

In the left hand side, one can write $(d/dt) = Ha(d/da)$ which shows that the relevant time scale governing the process is H^{-1}. Clearly, when $H/n\mu \gg 1$ the right hand side becomes ineffective because of the (μ/H) factor and the number of particles of species 1 does not change. We see that when the expansion rate of the universe is large compared to the reaction rate, the given reaction is ineffective in changing the number of particles. This certainly does *not* mean that the reactions have reached thermal equilibrium and $n_i = n_i^{eq}$; in fact, it means exactly the opposite: The reactions are not fast enough to drive the number densities towards equilibrium densities and the number densities "freeze out" at non equilibrium values. Of course, the right hand side will also vanish when $n_i = n_i^{eq}$ which is the other extreme limit of thermal equilibrium.

Having taken care of the general formalism, let us now apply it to the process of nucleosynthesis which requires protons and neutrons combining together to form bound nuclei of heavier elements like deuterium, helium etc.. The abundance of these elements are going to be determined by the relative abundance of neutrons and protons in the universe. Therefore, we need to first worry about the maintenance of thermal equilibrium between protons and the neutrons in the early universe. As long as the inter-conversion between n and p through the weak interaction processes $(v + n \leftrightarrow p + e)$, $(\bar{e} + n \leftrightarrow p + \bar{v})$ and the 'decay' $(n \leftrightarrow p + e + \bar{v})$, is rapid (compared to the expansion rate of the universe), thermal equilibrium will be maintained. Then the equilibrium (n/p) ratio will be

$$\left(\frac{n_n}{n_p}\right) = \frac{X_n}{X_p} = \exp(-Q/T), \tag{24}$$

where $Q = m_n - m_p = 1.293$ MeV. At high $(T \gg Q)$ temperatures, there will be equal number of neutrons and protons but as the temperature drops below about 1.3 MeV, the neutron fraction will start dropping exponentially provided thermal equilibrium is still maintained. To check whether thermal equilibrium is indeed maintained, we need to compare the expansion rate with the reaction rate. The expansion rate is given by $H = (8\pi G\rho/3)^{1/2}$ where $\rho = (\pi^2/30)gT^4$ with $g \approx 10.75$ representing the effective relativistic degrees of freedom present at these temperatures. At $T = Q$, this gives $H \approx 1.1$ s^{-1}. The reaction rate needs to be computed from weak interaction theory. The neutron to proton conversion rate, for example, is well approximated by

$$\lambda_{np} \approx 0.29 \text{ s}^{-1} \left(\frac{T}{Q}\right)^5 \left[\left(\frac{Q}{T}\right)^2 + 6\left(\frac{Q}{T}\right) + 12\right]. \tag{25}$$

At $T = Q$, this gives $\lambda \approx 5$ s^{-1}, slightly more rapid than the expansion rate. But as T drops below Q, this decreases rapidly and the reaction ceases to be fast enough to maintain thermal equilibrium. Hence we need to work out the neutron abundance by using Eq. (23).

Using $n_1 = n_n, n_3 = n_p$ and $n_2, n_4 = n_l$ where the subscript l stands for the leptons, Eq. (23) becomes

$$\frac{1}{a^3}\frac{d(n_n a^3)}{dt} = \mu n_l^{eq}\left(\frac{n_p n_n^{eq}}{n_p^{eq}} - n_n\right). \tag{26}$$

We now use Eq. (24), write $(n_l^{eq}\mu) = \lambda_{np}$ which is the rate for neutron to proton conversion and introduce the fractional abundance $X_n = n_n/(n_n + n_p)$. Simple manipulation then leads to the equation

$$\frac{dX_n}{dt} = \lambda_{np}\left((1 - X_n)e^{-Q/T} - X_n\right). \tag{27}$$

Converting from the variable t to the variable $s = (Q/T)$ and using $(d/dt) = -HT(d/dT)$, the equations we need to solve reduce to

$$-Hs\frac{dX_n}{ds} = \lambda_{np}\left((1 - X_n)e^{-s} - X_n\right);$$

$$H = (1.1 \text{ sec}^{-1}) s^{-4}; \quad \lambda_{np} = \frac{0.29 \text{ s}^{-1}}{s^5}\left[s^2 + 6s + 12\right]. \tag{28}$$

It is now straightforward to integrate these equations numerically and determine how the neutron abundance changes with time. The neutron fraction falls out of equilibrium when temperatures drop below 1 MeV and it freezes to about 0.15 at temperatures below 0.5 MeV.

As the temperature decreases further, the neutron decay with a half life of $\tau_n \approx 886.7$ sec (which is *not* included in the above analysis) becomes important and starts depleting the neutron number density. The only way neutrons can survive is through the synthesis of light elements. As the temperature falls further to $T = T_{He} \simeq 0.28$MeV, significant amount of He could have been produced if the nuclear reaction rates were high enough. The possible reactions which produces ^{4}He are [$D(D,n)\ ^3He(D,p)\ ^4He$, $D(D,p)\ ^3H(D,n)\ ^4He, D(D,\gamma)\ ^4He$]. These are all based on D, ^3He and ^3H and do not occur rapidly enough because the mass fraction of D, ^3He and ^3H are still quite small [$10^{-12}, 10^{-19}$ and 5×10^{-19} respectively] at $T \simeq 0.3$MeV. The reactions $n + p \rightleftharpoons d + \gamma$

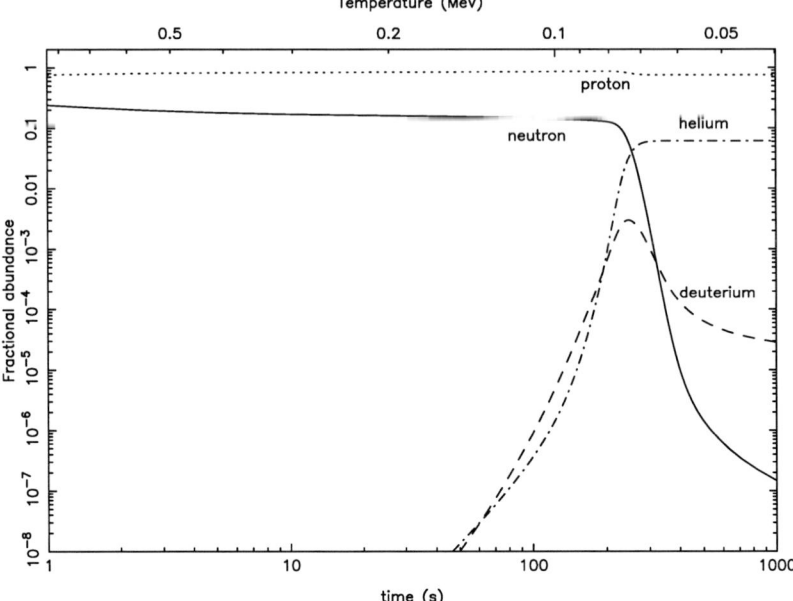

FIGURE 1. The evolution of mass fraction of different species during nucleosynthesis

will lead to an equilibrium abundance ratio of deuterium given by

$$\frac{n_p n_n}{n_d n} = \frac{4}{3}\left(\frac{m_p m_n}{m_d}\right)^{3/2} \frac{(2\pi k_B T)^{3/2}}{(2\pi \hbar)^3 n} e^{-B/k_B T} = \exp\left[25.82 - \ln \Omega_B h^2 T_{10}^{3/2} - \left(\frac{2.58}{T_{10}}\right)\right]. \quad (29)$$

The equilibrium deuterium abundance passes through unity (for $\Omega_B h^2 = 0.02$) at the temperature of about 0.07 MeV which is when the nucleosynthesis can really begin.

So we need to determine the neutron fraction at $T = 0.07$ MeV given that it was about 0.15 at 0.5 MeV. During this epoch, the time-temperature relationship is given by $t = 130$ sec $(T/0.1 \text{ MeV})^{-2}$. The neutron decay factor is $\exp(-t/\tau_n) \approx 0.74$ for $T = 0.07$ MeV. This decreases the neutron fraction to $0.15 \times 0.74 = 0.11$ at the time of nucleosynthesis. When the temperature becomes $T \lesssim 0.07$MeV, the abundance of D and ^3H builds up and these elements further react to form ^4He. A good fraction of D and ^3H is converted to ^4He (See Fig.1 which shows the growth of deuterium and its subsequent fall when helium is built up). The resultant abundance of ^4He can be easily calculated by assuming that almost all neutrons end up in ^4He. Since each ^4He nucleus has two neutrons, $(n_n/2)$ helium nuclei can be formed (per unit volume) if the number density of neutrons is n_n. Thus the mass fraction of ^4He will be

$$Y = \frac{4(n_n/2)}{n_n + n_p} = \frac{2(n/p)}{1 + (n/p)} = 2x_c \quad (30)$$

where $x_c = n/(n+p)$ is the neutron abundance at the time of production of deuterium.

For $\Omega_B h^2 = 0.02$, $x_c \approx 0.11$ giving $Y \approx 0.22$. Increasing baryon density to $\Omega_B h^2 = 1$ will make $Y \approx 0.25$. An accurate fitting formula for the dependence of helium abundance on various parameters is given by

$$Y = 0.226 + 0.025 \log \eta_{10} + 0.0075(g_* - 10.75) + 0.014(\tau_{1/2}(n) - 10.3 \text{ min}) \quad (31)$$

where η_{10} measures the baryon-photon ratio today via Eq. (19) and g_* is the effective number of relativistic degrees of freedom contributing to the energy density and $\tau_{1/2}(n)$ is the neutron half life. The results (of a more exact treatment) are shown in Fig. 1.

As the reactions converting D and ^3H to ^4He proceed, the number density of D and ^3H is depleted and the reaction rates - which are proportional to $\Gamma \propto X_A(\eta n_\gamma) <\sigma v>$ - become small. These reactions soon freeze-out leaving a residual fraction of D and ^3H (a fraction of about 10^{-5} to 10^{-4}). Since $\Gamma \propto \eta$ it is clear that the fraction of $(D,^3H)$ left unreacted will decrease with η. In contrast, the ^4He synthesis - which is not limited by any reaction rate - is fairly independent of η and depends only on the (n/p) ratio at $T \simeq 0.1 \text{MeV}$. The best fits, with typical errors, to deuterium abundance calculated from the theory, for the range $\eta = (10^{-10} - 10^{-9})$ is given by

$$Y_2 \equiv \left(\frac{D}{H}\right)_p = 3.6 \times 10^{-5 \pm 0.06} \left(\frac{\eta}{5 \times 10^{-10}}\right)^{-1.6}. \quad (32)$$

The production of still heavier elements - even those like ^{16}C, ^{16}O which have *higher* binding energies than ^4He - is suppressed in the early universe. Two factors are responsible for this suppression: (1) For nuclear reactions to proceed, the participating nuclei must overcome their Coulomb repulsion. The probability to tunnel through the Coulomb barrier is governed by the factor $F = \exp[-2A^{1/3}(Z_1 Z_2)^{2/3}(T/1\text{MeV})^{-1/3}]$ where $A^{-1} = A_1^{-1} + A_2^{-1}$. For heavier nuclei (with larger Z), this factor suppresses the reaction rate. (2) Reaction between helium and proton would have led to an element with atomic mass 5 while the reaction of two helium nuclei would have led to an element with atomic mass 8. However, there are no stable elements in the periodic table with the atomic mass of 5 or 8! The ^8Be, for example, has a half life of only 10^{-16} seconds. One can combine ^4He with ^8Be to produce ^{12}C but this can occur at significant rate only if it is a resonance reaction. That is, there should exist an excited state ^{12}C nuclei which has an energy close to the interaction energy of $^4He + ^8Be$. Stars, incidentally, use this route to synthesize heavier elements. It is this triple-alpha reaction which allows the synthesis of heavier elements in stars but it is not fast enough in the early universe. (You must thank your stars that there is *no* such resonance in ^{16}O or in ^{20}Ne — which is equally important for the survival of carbon and oxygen.)

The current observations indicate, with reasonable certainty that: (i) $(D/H) \gtrsim 1 \times 10^{-5}$. (ii) $[(D+^3He)/H] \simeq (1-8) \times 10^{-5}$ and (iii) $0.236 < (^4He/H) < 0.254$. These observations are consistent with the predictions if $10.3 \text{ min} \lesssim \tau \lesssim 10.7 \text{ min}$, and $\eta = (3-10) \times 10^{-10}$. Using $\eta = 2.68 \times 10^{-8} \Omega_B h^2$, this leads to the important conclusion: $0.011 \leq \Omega_B h^2 \leq 0.037$. When combined with the broad bounds on h, $0.6 \lesssim h \lesssim 0.8$, say, we can constrain the baryonic density of the universe to be: $0.01 \lesssim \Omega_B \lesssim 0.06$. These are the typical bounds on Ω_B available today. It shows that, if $\Omega_{\text{total}} \simeq 1$ then most of the matter in the universe must be non baryonic.

Since the ^4He production depends on g, the observed value of ^4He restricts the total energy density present at the time of nucleosynthesis. In particular, it constrains the number (N_v) of light neutrinos (that is, neutrinos with $m_v \lesssim 1\text{MeV}$ which would have been relativistic at $T \simeq 1\text{MeV}$). The observed abundance is best explained by $N_v = 3$, is barely consistent with $N_v = 4$ and rules out $N_v > 4$. The laboratory bound on the total number of particles including neutrinos, which couples to the Z^0 boson is determined by measuring the decay width of the particle Z^0; each particle with mass less than $(m_z/2) \simeq 46$ GeV contributes about 180 MeV to this decay width. This bound is $N_v = 2.79 \pm 0.63$ which is consistent with the cosmological observations.

2.3 Decoupling of matter and radiation

In the early hot phase, the radiation will be in thermal equilibrium with matter; as the universe cools below $k_B T \simeq (\varepsilon_a/10)$ where ε_a is the binding energy of atoms, the electrons and ions will combine to form neutral atoms and radiation will decouple from matter. This occurs at $T_{\text{dec}} \simeq 3 \times 10^3$ K. As the universe expands further, these photons will continue to exist without any further interaction. It will retain thermal spectrum since the redshift of the frequency $v \propto a^{-1}$ is equivalent to changing the temperature in the spectrum by the scaling $T \propto (1/a)$. It turns out that the major component of the extragalactic background light (EBL) which exists today is in the microwave band and can be fitted very accurately by a thermal spectrum at a temperature of about 2.73 K. It seems reasonable to interpret this radiation as a relic arising from the early, hot, phase of the evolving universe. This relic radiation, called *cosmic microwave background radiation*, turns out to be a gold mine of cosmological information and is extensively investigated in recent times. We shall now discuss some details related to the formation of neutral atoms and the decoupling of photons.

The relevant reaction is, of course, $e + p \rightleftharpoons H + \gamma$ and if the rate of this reaction is faster than the expansion rate, then one can calculate the neutral fraction using Saha's equation. Introducing the fractional ionisation, X_i, for each of the particle species and using the facts $n_p = n_e$ and $n_p + n_H = n_B$, it follows that $X_p = X_e$ and $X_H = (n_H/n_B) = 1 - X_e$. Saha's equation now gives

$$\frac{1-X_e}{X_e^2} \cong 3.84\eta (T/m_e)^{3/2} \exp(B/T) \tag{33}$$

where $\eta = 2.68 \times 10^{-8}(\Omega_B h^2)$ is the baryon-to-photon ratio. We may define T_{atom} as the temperature at which 90 percent of the electrons, say, have combined with protons: i.e. when $X_e = 0.1$. This leads to the condition:

$$(\Omega_B h^2)^{-1} \tau^{-\frac{3}{2}} \exp\left[-13.6\tau^{-1}\right] = 3.13 \times 10^{-18} \tag{34}$$

where $\tau = (T/1\text{eV})$. For a given value of $(\Omega_B h^2)$, this equation can be easily solved by iteration. Taking logarithms and iterating once we find $\tau^{-1} \cong 3.084 - 0.0735 \ln(\Omega_B h^2)$ with the corresponding redshift $(1+z) = (T/T_0)$ given by

$$(1+z) = 1367[1 - 0.024\ln(\Omega_B h^2)]^{-1}. \tag{35}$$

For $\Omega_B h^2 = 1, 0.1, 0.01$ we get $T_{\text{atom}} \cong 0.324\text{eV}, 0.307\text{eV}, 0.292\text{eV}$ respectively. These values correspond to the redshifts of $1367, 1296$ and 1232.

Because the preceding analysis was based on equilibrium densities, it is important to check that the rate of the reactions $p + e \leftrightarrow H + \gamma$ is fast enough to maintain equilibrium. For $\Omega_B h^2 \approx 0.02$, the equilibrium condition is only marginally satisfied, making this analysis suspect. More importantly, the direct recombination to the ground state of the hydrogen atom — which was used in deriving the Saha's equation — is not very effective in producing neutral hydrogen in the early universe. The problem is that each such recombination releases a photon of energy 13.6 eV which will end up ionizing another neutral hydrogen atom which has been formed earlier. As a result, the direct recombination to the ground state does not change the neutral hydrogen fraction at the lowest order. Recombination through the excited states of hydrogen is more effective since such a recombination ends up emitting more than one photon each of which has an energy less than 13.6 eV. Given these facts, it is necessary to once again use the rate equation developed in the previous section to track the evolution of ionisation fraction.

A simple procedure for doing this, which captures the essential physics, is as follows: We again begin with Eq. (23) and repeating the analysis done in the last section, now with $n_1 = n_e, n_2 = n_p, n_3 = n_H$ and $n_4 = n_\gamma$, and defining $X_e = n_e/(n_e + n_H) = n_p/n_H$ one can easily derive the rate equation for this case:

$$\frac{dX_e}{dt} = [\beta(1 - X_e) - \alpha n_b X_e^2] = \alpha \left(\frac{\beta}{\alpha}(1 - X_e) - n_b X_e^2 \right). \tag{36}$$

This equation is analogous to Eq. (27); the first term gives the photoionisation rate which produces the free electrons and the second term is the recombination rate which converts free electrons into hydrogen atom and we have used the fact $n_e = n_b X_e$ etc.. Since we know that direct recombination to the ground state is not effective, the recombination rate α is the rate for capture of electron by a proton forming an excited state of hydrogen. To a good approximation, this rate is given by

$$\alpha = 9.78 r_0^2 c \left(\frac{B}{T} \right)^{1/2} \ln \left(\frac{B}{T} \right) \tag{37}$$

where $r_0 = e^2/m_e c^2$ is the classical electron radius. To integrate Eq. (36) we also need to know β/α. This is easy because in thermal equilibrium the right hand side of Eq. (36) should vanish and Saha's equation tells us the value of X_e in thermal equilibrium. On using Eq. (33), this gives

$$\frac{\beta}{\alpha} = \left(\frac{m_e T}{2\pi} \right)^{3/2} \exp[-(B/T)]. \tag{38}$$

We can now integrate Eq. (36) using the variable B/T just as we used the variable Q/T in solving Eq. (27). The result shows that the actual recombination proceeds more slowly compared to that predicted by the Saha's equation. The actual fractional ionisation is higher than the value predicted by Saha's equation at temperatures below about 1300. For example, at $z = 1300$, these values differ by a factor 3; at $z \simeq 900$, they differ by a factor of 200. The value of T_{atom}, however, does not change significantly. A more rigorous analysis shows that, in the redshift range of $800 < z < 1200$, the fractional ionisation varies rapidly and is given (approximately) by the formula,

$$X_e = 2.4 \times 10^{-3} \frac{(\Omega_{\text{NR}}h^2)^{1/2}}{(\Omega_B h^2)} \left(\frac{z}{1000}\right)^{12.75}. \tag{39}$$

This is obtained by fitting a curve to the numerical solution.

The formation of neutral atoms makes the photons decouple from the matter. The redshift for decoupling can be determined as the epoch at which the optical depth for photons is unity. Using Eq. (39), we can compute the optical depth for photons to be

$$\tau = \int_0^t n(t) X_e(t) \sigma_T dt = \int_0^z n(z) X_e(z) \sigma_T \left(\frac{dt}{dz}\right) dz \simeq 0.37 \left(\frac{z}{1000}\right)^{14.25} \tag{40}$$

where we have used the relation $H_0 dt \cong -\Omega_{\text{NR}}^{-1/2} z^{-5/2} dz$ which is valid for $z \gg 1$. This optical depth is unity at $z_{\text{dec}} = 1072$. From the optical depth, we can also compute the probability that the photon was last scattered in the interval $(z, z+dz)$. This is given by $(\exp-\tau)(d\tau/dz)$ which can be expressed as

$$P(z) = e^{-\tau}\frac{d\tau}{dz} = 5.26 \times 10^{-3} \left(\frac{z}{1000}\right)^{13.25} \exp\left[-0.37\left(\frac{z}{1000}\right)^{14.25}\right]. \tag{41}$$

This $P(z)$ has a sharp maximum at $z \simeq 1067$ and a width of about $\Delta z \cong 80$. It is therefore reasonable to assume that decoupling occurred at $z \simeq 1070$ in an interval of about $\Delta z \simeq 80$. We shall see later that the finite thickness of the surface of last scattering has important observational consequences.

3. STRUCTURE FORMATION AND LINEAR PERTURBATION THEORY

Having discussed the evolution of the background universe, we now turn to the study of structure formation. Before discussing the details, let us briefly summarise the broad picture and give references to some of the topics that we will *not* discuss. The key idea is that if there existed small fluctuations in the energy density in the early universe, then gravitational instability can amplify them in a well-understood manner leading to structures like galaxies etc. today. The most popular model for generating these fluctuations is based on the idea that if the very early universe went through an inflationary phase [9], then the quantum fluctuations of the field driving the inflation can lead to energy density fluctuations[10, 11]. It is possible to construct models of inflation such that these fluctuations are described by a Gaussian random field and are characterized by a power spectrum of the form $P(k) = Ak^n$ with $n \simeq 1$ (see Sec.). The models cannot predict the value of the amplitude A in an unambiguous manner but it can be determined from CMBR observations. The CMBR observations are consistent with the inflationary model for the generation of perturbations and gives $A \simeq (28.3h^{-1}Mpc)^4$ and $n = 0.97 \pm 0.023$

(The first results were from COBE [12] and WMAP has reconfirmed them with far greater accuracy). When the perturbation is small, one can use well defined linear perturbation theory to study its growth. But when $\delta \approx (\delta\rho/\rho)$ is comparable to unity the perturbation theory breaks down. Since there is more power at small scales, smaller scales go non-linear first and structure forms hierarchically. The non linear evolution of the *dark matter halos* (which is an example of statistical mechanics of self gravitating systems; see e.g.[13]) can be understood by simulations as well as theoretical models based on approximate ansatz [14] and nonlinear scaling relations [15]. The baryons in the halo will cool and undergo collapse in a fairly complex manner because of gas dynamical processes. It seems unlikely that the baryonic collapse and galaxy formation can be understood by analytic approximations; one needs to do high resolution computer simulations to make any progress [16]. All these results are broadly consistent with observations.

As long as these fluctuations are small, one can study their evolution by linear perturbation theory, which is what we will start with [17]. The basic idea of linear perturbation theory is well defined and simple. We perturb the background FRW metric by $g_{ik}^{FRW} \to g_{ik}^{FRW} + h_{ik}$ and also perturb the source energy momentum tensor by $T_{ik}^{FRW} \to T_{ik}^{FRW} + \delta T_{ik}$. Linearising the Einstein's equations, one can relate the perturbed quantities by a relation of the form $\mathscr{L}(g_{ik}^{FRW})h_{ik} = \delta T_{ik}$ where $\mathscr{L}$ is second order linear differential operator depending on the back ground metric g_{ik}^{FRW}. Since the background is maximally symmetric, one can separate out time and space; for e.g, if $k = 0$, simple Fourier modes can be used for this purpose and we can write down the equation for any given mode, labelled by a wave vector $\mathbf{k}$ as:

$$\mathscr{L}(a(t),\mathbf{k})h_{ab}(t,\mathbf{k}) = \delta T_{ab}(t,\mathbf{k}) \quad (42)$$

To every mode we can associate a wavelength normalized to today's value: $\lambda(t) = (2\pi/k)(1+z)^{-1}$ and a corresponding mass scale which is invariant under expansion:

$$M = \frac{4\pi\rho(t)}{3}\left[\frac{\lambda(t)}{2}\right]^3 = \frac{4\pi\rho_0}{3}\left(\frac{\lambda_0}{2}\right)^3 = 1.5 \times 10^{11} M_\odot (\Omega_m h^2) \left(\frac{\lambda_0}{1\,\text{Mpc}}\right)^3. \quad (43)$$

The behaviour of the mode depends on the relative value of $\lambda(t)$ as compared to the Hubble radius $d_H(t) \equiv (\dot{a}/a)^{-1}$. Since the Hubble radius: $d_H(t) \propto t$ while the wavelength of the mode: $\lambda(t) \propto a(t) \propto (t^{1/2}, t^{2/3})$ in the radiation dominated and matter dominated phases it follows that $\lambda(t) > d_H(t)$ at sufficiently early times. When $\lambda(t) = d_H(t)$, we say that the mode is entering the Hubble radius. Since the Hubble radius at $z = z_{eq}$ is

$$\lambda_{eq} \cong \left(\frac{H_0^{-1}}{\sqrt{2}}\right)\left(\frac{\Omega_R^{1/2}}{\Omega_{NR}}\right) \cong 14\,\text{Mpc}(\Omega_{NR}h^2)^{-1} \quad (44)$$

it follows that modes with $\lambda_0 > \lambda_{eq}$ enter Hubble radius in MD phase while the more relevant modes with $\lambda < \lambda_{eq}$ enter in the RD phase. Thus, for a given mode we can identify three distinct phases: First, very early on, when $\lambda > d_H, z > z_{eq}$ the dynamics is described by general relativity. In this stage, the universe is radiation dominated, gravity is the only relevant force and the perturbations are linear. Next, when $\lambda < d_H$ and $z > z_{eq}$ one can describe the dynamics by Newtonian considerations. The perturbations are still linear and the universe is radiation dominated. Finally, when $\lambda < d_H, z < z_{eq}$ we have a matter dominated universe in which we can use the Newtonian formalism; but at this stage — when most astrophysical structures form — we need to grapple with nonlinear astrophysical processes.

Let us now consider the metric perturbation in greater detail. When the metric is perturbed to the form: $g_{ab} \to g_{ab} + h_{ab}$ the perturbation can be split as $h_{ab} - (h_{00}, h_{0\alpha} \equiv w_\alpha, h_{\alpha\beta})$. We also know that any 3-vector $\mathbf{w}(\mathbf{x})$ can be split as $\mathbf{w} = \mathbf{w}^\perp + \mathbf{w}^\parallel$ in which $\mathbf{w}^\parallel = \nabla \Phi^\parallel$ is curl-free (and carries one degree of freedom) while $\mathbf{w}^\perp$ is divergence-free (and has 2 degrees of freedom). This result is obvious in $\mathbf{k}$–space since we can write any vector $\mathbf{w}(\mathbf{k})$ as a sum of two terms, one along $\mathbf{k}$ and one transverse to $\mathbf{k}$:

$$\mathbf{w}(\mathbf{k}) = \mathbf{w}^\parallel(\mathbf{k}) + \mathbf{w}^\perp(\mathbf{k}) = \underbrace{\mathbf{k}\left(\frac{\mathbf{w}(\mathbf{k}) \cdot \mathbf{k}}{k^2}\right)}_{\text{along } \mathbf{k}} + \underbrace{\left[\mathbf{w}(\mathbf{k}) - \mathbf{k}\left(\frac{\mathbf{k} \cdot \mathbf{w}(\mathbf{k})}{k^2}\right)\right]}_{\text{transverse to } \mathbf{k}};$$

$$\mathbf{k} \times \mathbf{w}^\parallel = 0; \qquad \mathbf{k} \cdot \mathbf{w}^\perp = 0 \tag{45}$$

Fourier transforming back, we can split $\mathbf{w}$ into a curl-free and divergence-free parts. Similar decomposition works for $h_{\alpha\beta}$ by essentially repeating the above analysis on each index. We can write:

$$h_{\alpha\beta} = \underbrace{\psi \delta_{\alpha\beta}}_{\text{trace}} + \underbrace{\left(\nabla_\alpha u_\beta^\perp + \nabla_\beta u_\alpha^\perp\right)}_{\text{traceless from vector}} + \underbrace{\left(\nabla_\alpha \nabla_\beta - \frac{1}{3}\delta_{\alpha\beta}\nabla^2\right)\Phi_1}_{\text{traceless from scalar}} + h_{\alpha\beta}^{\perp\perp} \Rightarrow 1 + 2 + 1 + 2 = 6$$
(46)

The $u_\alpha^\perp$ is divergence free and $h_{\alpha\beta}^{\perp\perp}$ is traceless and divergence free. Thus the most general perturbation h_{ab} (ten degrees of freedom) can be built out of

$$h_{ab} = (h_{00}, h_{0\alpha} \equiv w_\alpha, h_{\alpha\beta}) = [h_{00}, (\Phi^\parallel, \mathbf{w}^\perp), (\psi, \Phi_1, u_\alpha^\perp, h_{\alpha\beta}^{\perp\perp})] \Rightarrow [1, (1,2), (1,1,2,2)]$$
(47)

We now use the freedom available in the choice of four coordinate transformations to set four conditions: $\Phi^\parallel = \Phi_1 = 0$ and $u_\alpha^\perp = 0$ thereby leaving six degrees of freedom in $(h_{00} \equiv 2\Phi, \psi, \mathbf{w}^\perp, h_{\alpha\beta}^{\perp\perp})$ as nonzero. Then the perturbed line element takes the form:

$$ds^2 = a^2(\eta) \left[\{1 + 2\Phi(\mathbf{x}, \eta)\} d\eta^2 - 2w_\alpha^\perp(\mathbf{x}, \eta) d\eta dx^\alpha \right.$$
$$\left. - \{(1 - 2\psi(\mathbf{x}, \eta))\delta_{\alpha\beta} + 2h_{\alpha\beta}^{\perp\perp}(\mathbf{x}, \eta)\} dx^\alpha dx^\beta\right] \tag{48}$$

To make further simplification we need to use two facts from Einstein's equations. It turns out that the Einstein's equations for $\mathbf{w}^\perp$ and $h_{\alpha\beta}^{\perp\perp}$ decouple from those for (Φ, ψ). Further, in the absence of anisotropic stress, one of the equations give $\psi = \Phi$. If we use these two facts, we can simplify the structure of perturbed metric drastically. As far as the growth of matter perturbations are concerned, we can ignore $w_\alpha^\perp$ and $h_{\alpha\beta}^{\perp\perp}$ and work with a simple metric:

$$ds^2 = a^2(\eta)[(1 + 2\Phi)d\eta^2 - (1 - 2\Phi)\delta_{\alpha\beta}dx^\alpha dx^\beta] \tag{49}$$

with just one perturbed scalar degree of freedom in Φ. This is what we will study.

Having decided on the gauge, let us consider the evolution equations for the perturbations. While one can directly work with the Einstein's equations, it turns out to be convenient to use the equations of motion for matter variables, since we are eventually interested in the matter perturbations. In what follows, we will use the over-dot to denote $(d/d\eta)$ so that the standard Hubble parameter is $H = (1/a)(da/dt) = \dot{a}/a^2$. With this notation, the continuity equation becomes:

$$\dot{\rho} + 3\left(aH - \dot{\Phi}\right)(\rho + p) = -\nabla_\alpha[(\rho + p)v^\alpha] \tag{50}$$

Since the momentum flux in the relativistic case is $(\rho + p)v^\alpha$, all the terms in the above equation are intuitively obvious, except probably the $\dot{\Phi}$ term. To see the physical origin of this term, note that the perturbation in Eq. (49) changes the factor in front of the spatial metric from a^2 to $a^2(1 - 2\Phi)$ so that $\ln a \to \ln a - \Phi$; hence the effective Hubble parameter from $(\dot{a}/a)$ to $(\dot{a}/a) - \dot{\Phi}$ which explains the extra $\dot{\Phi}$ term. This is, of course, the exact equation for matter variables in the perturbed metric given by Eq. (49); but we only need terms which are of linear order. Writing the curl-free velocity part as $v^\alpha = \nabla^\alpha v$, the *linearised* equations, for dark matter (with $p = 0$) and radiation (with $p = (1/3)\rho$) perturbations are given by:

$$\dot{\delta}_m = \frac{d}{d\eta}\left(\frac{\delta n_m}{n_m}\right) = \nabla^2 v_m + 3\dot{\Phi}; \quad \frac{3}{4}\dot{\delta}_R = \frac{d}{d\eta}\left(\frac{\delta n_R}{n_R}\right) = \nabla^2 v_R + 3\dot{\Phi} \tag{51}$$

where n_m and n_R are the number densities of dark matter particles and radiation. The same equations in Fourier space [using the same symbols for, say, $\delta(t, \mathbf{x})$ or $\delta(t, \mathbf{k})$] are simpler to handle:

$$\dot{\delta}_m = \frac{d}{d\eta}\left(\frac{\delta n_m}{n_m}\right) = -k^2 v_m + 3\dot{\Phi}; \quad \frac{3}{4}\dot{\delta}_R = \frac{d}{d\eta}\left(\frac{\delta n_R}{n_R}\right) = -k^2 v_R + 3\dot{\Phi} \tag{52}$$

Note that these equations imply

$$\frac{d}{d\eta}\left[\frac{\delta n_R}{n_R} - \frac{\delta n_m}{n_m}\right] = \frac{d}{d\eta}\left[\delta \ln\left(\frac{n_R}{n_m}\right)\right] = \frac{d}{d\eta}\left[\delta\left(\ln\left(\frac{s}{n_m}\right)\right)\right] = -k^2(v_R - v_m) \tag{53}$$

For long wavelength perturbations (in the limit of $k \to 0$), this will lead to the conservation of perturbation $\delta(s/n_m)$ in the entropy per particle.

Let us next consider the Euler equation which has the general form:

$$\partial_\eta[(\rho + p)v^\alpha] = -(\rho + p)\nabla^\alpha\Phi - \nabla^\alpha p - 4aH(\rho + p)v^\alpha \tag{54}$$

Once again each of the terms is simple to interpret. The $(\rho + p)$ arises because the pressure also contributes to inertia in a relativistic theory and the factor 4 in the last term on the right hand side arises because the term $v^\alpha \partial_\eta(\rho + p)$ on the left hand side needs to be compensated. Taking the linearised limit of this equation, for dark matter and radiation, we get:

$$\dot{v}_m = \Phi - aHv_m; \quad \dot{v}_R = \Phi + \frac{1}{4}\delta_R \tag{55}$$

Thus we now have four equations in Eqs. (52), (55) for the five variables $(\delta_m, \delta_R, v_m, v_R, \Phi)$. All we need to do is to pick one more from Einstein's equations to complete the set. The Einstein's equations for our perturbed metric are:

$$\substack{0 \\ 0} \text{ component}: \quad k^2\Phi + 3\frac{\dot{a}}{a}\left(\dot{\Phi} + \frac{\dot{a}}{a}\Phi\right) = -4\pi G a^2 \sum_A \rho_A \delta_A = -4\pi G a^2 \rho_{bg} \delta_{total} \quad (56)$$

$$\substack{0 \\ \alpha} \text{ component}: \quad \dot{\Phi} + \frac{\dot{a}}{a}\Phi = -4\pi G a^2 \sum_A (\rho + p)_A v_A; \quad \mathbf{v} = \nabla v \quad (57)$$

$$\substack{\alpha \\ \alpha} \text{ component}: \quad 3\frac{\dot{a}}{a}\dot{\Phi} + 2\frac{\ddot{a}}{a}\Phi - \frac{\dot{a}^2}{a^2}\Phi + \ddot{\Phi} = 4\pi G a^2 \delta p \quad (58)$$

where A denotes different components like dark matter, radiation etc. Using Eq. (57) in Eq. (56) we can get a modified Poisson equation which is purely algebraic:

$$-k^2\Phi = 4\pi G a^2 \sum_A \left(\rho_A \delta_A - 3\left(\frac{\dot{a}}{a}\right)(\rho_A + p_A)v_A\right) \quad (59)$$

which once again emphasizes the fact that in the relativistic theory, both pressure and density act as source of gravity.

To get a feel for the solutions let us consider a flat universe dominated by a single component of matter with the equation of state $p = w\rho$. (A purely radiation dominated universe, for example, will have $w = 1/3$.) In this case the Friedmann background equation gives $\rho \propto a^{-3(1+w)}$ and

$$\frac{\dot{a}}{a} = \frac{2}{(1+3w)\eta}; \quad \frac{\ddot{a}}{a} = \frac{2(1-3w)}{(1+3w)^2\eta^2} \quad (60)$$

The equation for the potential Φ can be reduced to the form:

$$\ddot{\Phi} + \frac{6(1+w)}{1+3w}\frac{\dot{\Phi}}{\eta} + k^2 w \Phi = 0 \quad (61)$$

The second term is the damping due to the expansion while last term is the pressure support that will lead to oscillations. Clearly, the factor $k\eta$ determines which of these two terms dominates. When the pressure term dominates ($k\eta \gg 1$), we expect oscillatory behaviour while when the background expansion dominates ($k\eta \ll 1$), we expect the growth to be suppressed. This is precisely what happens. The exact solution is given in terms of the Bessel functions

$$\Phi(\eta) = \frac{C_1(\mathbf{k})J_{v/2}(\sqrt{w}k\eta) + C_2(\mathbf{k})Y_{v/2}(\sqrt{w}k\eta)}{\eta^{v/2}}; \quad v = \frac{5+3w}{1+3w} \quad (62)$$

From the theory of Bessel functions, we know that:

$$\lim_{x \to 0} J_{v/2}(x) \simeq \frac{x^{v/2}}{2^{v/2}\Gamma(v/2+1)}; \quad \lim_{x \to 0} Y_{v/2}(x) \propto -\frac{1}{x^{v/2}} \quad (63)$$

This shows that if we want a finite value for Φ as $\eta \to 0$, we can set $C_2 = 0$. This gives the gravitational potential to be

$$\Phi(\eta) = \frac{C_1(\mathbf{k}) J_{\nu/2}(\sqrt{w}k\eta)}{\eta^{\nu/2}}; \quad \nu = \frac{5+3w}{1+3w} \tag{64}$$

The corresponding density perturbation will be:

$$\delta = -2\Phi - \frac{(1+3w)^2 k^2 \eta^2}{6} \frac{C_1(\mathbf{k}) J_{\nu/2}(\sqrt{w}k\eta)}{\eta^{\nu/2}} + (1+3w)\sqrt{w}k\eta \frac{C_1(\mathbf{k}) J_{(\nu/2)+1}(\sqrt{w}k\eta)}{\eta^{\nu/2}} \tag{65}$$

To understand the nature of the solution, note that $d_H = (\dot{a}/a)^{-1} \propto \eta$ and $kd_H \simeq d_H/\lambda \propto k\eta$. So the argument of the Bessel function is just the ratio (d_H/λ). From the theory of Bessel functions, we know that for small values of the argument $J_\nu(x) \propto x^\nu$ is a power law while for large values of the argument it oscillates with a decaying amplitude:

$$\lim_{x\to\infty} J_{\nu/2}(x) \sim \frac{\cos[x-(\nu-1)\pi/4]}{\sqrt{x}}; \tag{66}$$

Hence, for modes which are still outside the Hubble radius ($k \ll \eta^{-1}$), we have a constant amplitude for the potential and density contrast:

$$\Phi \approx \Phi_i(\mathbf{k}); \quad \delta \approx -2\Phi_i(\mathbf{k}) \tag{67}$$

That is, the perturbation is frozen (except for a decaying mode) at a constant value. On the other hand, for modes which are inside the Hubble radius ($k \gg \eta^{-1}$), the perturbation is rapidly oscillatory (if $w \neq 0$). That is the pressure is effective at small scales and leads to acoustic oscillations in the medium.

A special case of the above is the flat, matter-dominated universe with $w = 0$. In this case, we need to take the $w \to 0$ limit and the general solution is indeed a constant $\Phi = \Phi_i(\mathbf{k})$ (plus a decaying mode $\Phi_{decay} \propto \eta^{-5}$ which diverges as $\eta \to 0$). The corresponding density perturbations is:

$$\delta = -(2 + \frac{k^2\eta^2}{6})\Phi_i(\mathbf{k}) \tag{68}$$

which shows that density perturbation is "frozen" at large scales but grows at small scales:

$$\delta = \begin{cases} -2\Phi_i(\mathbf{k}) = \text{constant} & (k\eta \ll 1) \\ -\frac{1}{6}k^2\eta^2\Phi_i(\mathbf{k}) \propto \eta^2 \propto a & (k\eta \gg 1) \end{cases} \tag{69}$$

We will use these results later on.

4. PERTURBATIONS IN DARK MATTER AND RADIATION

We shall now move on to the more realistic case of a multi-component universe consisting of radiation and collisionless dark matter. (For the moment we are ignoring the baryons, which we will study in Sec.). It is convenient to use $y = a/a_{eq}$ as independent variable rather than the time coordinate. The background expansion of the universe described by the function $a(t)$ can be equivalently expressed (in terms of the conformal time η) as

$$y \equiv \frac{\rho_M}{\rho_R} = \frac{a}{a_{eq}} = x^2 + 2x, \qquad x \equiv \left(\frac{\Omega_M}{4a_{eq}}\right)^{1/2} H_0 \eta \qquad (70)$$

It is also useful to define a critical wave number k_c by:

$$k_c^2 = \frac{H_0^2 \Omega_m}{a_{eq}} = 4(\sqrt{2}-1)^2 \eta_{eq}^{-2} = 4(\sqrt{2}-1)^2 k_{eq}^2; \qquad k_c^{-1} = 19(\Omega_m h^2)^{-1} Mpc \qquad (71)$$

which essentially sets the comoving scale corresponding to matter-radiation equality. Note that $2x = k_c \eta$ and $y \approx k_c \eta$ in the radiation dominated phase while $y = (1/4)(k_c \eta)^2$ in the matter dominated phase.

We now manipulate Eqs. (52), (55), (56), (57) governing the growth of perturbations by essentially eliminating the velocity. This leads to the three equations

$$y\Phi' + \Phi + \frac{1}{3}\frac{k^2}{k_c^2}\frac{y^2}{1+y}\Phi = -\frac{1}{2}\frac{y}{1+y}\left(\delta_m + \frac{1}{y}\delta_R\right) \qquad (72)$$

$$(1+y)\delta_m'' + \frac{2+3y}{2y}\delta_m' = 3(1+y)\Phi'' + \frac{3(2+3y)}{2y}\Phi' - \frac{k^2}{k_c^2}\Phi \qquad (73)$$

$$(1+y)\delta_R'' + \frac{1}{2}\delta_R' + \frac{1}{3}\frac{k^2}{k_c^2}\delta_R = 4(1+y)\Phi'' + 2\Phi' - \frac{4}{3}\frac{k^2}{k_c^2}\Phi \qquad (74)$$

for the three unknowns Φ, δ_m, δ_R. Given suitable initial conditions we can solve these equations to determine the growth of perturbations. The initial conditions need to imposed very early on when the modes are much bigger than the Hubble radius which corresponds to the $y \ll 1, k \to 0$ limit. In this limit, the equations become:

$$y\Phi' + \Phi \approx -\frac{1}{2}\delta_R; \qquad \delta_m'' + \frac{1}{y}\delta_m' \approx 3\Phi'' + \frac{3}{y}\Phi'; \qquad \delta_R'' + \frac{1}{2}\delta_R' \approx 4\Phi'' + 2\Phi' \qquad (75)$$

We will take $\Phi(y_i, k) = \Phi_i(k)$ as given value, to be determined by the processes that generate the initial perturbations. First equation in Eq. (75) shows that we can take $\delta_R = -2\Phi_i$ for $y_i \to 0$. Further Eq. (53) shows that adiabaticity is respected at these scales and we can take $\delta_m = (3/4)\delta_R = -(3/2)\Phi_i$;. The exact equation Eq. (72) determines Φ' if $(\Phi, \delta_m, \delta_R)$ are given. Finally we use the last two equations to set $\delta'_m = 3\Phi', \delta'_R = 4\Phi'$, Thus we take the initial conditions at some $y = y_i \ll 1$ to be:

$$\Phi(y_i, k) = \Phi_i(k); \qquad \delta_R(y_i, k) = -2\Phi_i(k); \qquad \delta_m(y_i, k) = -(3/2)\Phi_i(k) \qquad (76)$$

with $\delta'_m(y_i, k) = 3\Phi'(y_i, k); \delta'_R(y_i, k) = 4\Phi'(y_i, k)$.

Given these initial conditions, it is fairly easy to integrate the equations forward in time and the numerical results are shown in Figs 2, 3, 4, 5. (In the figures k_{eq} is taken to be $a_{eq} H_{eq}$.) To understand the nature of the evolution, it is, however, useful to try out a few analytic approximations to Eqs. (72) – (74) which is what we will do now.

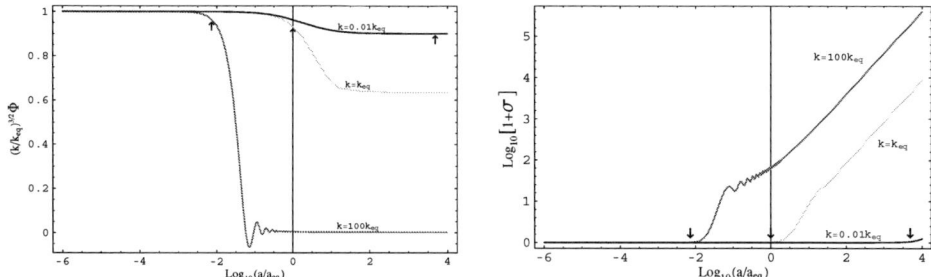

FIGURE 2. Left Panel: The evolution of gravitational potential Φ for 3 different modes. The wavenumber is indicated by the label and the epoch at which the mode enters the Hubble radius is indicated by a small arrow. The top most curve is for a mode which stays outside the Hubble radius for most of its evolution and is well described by Eq. (78). The other two modes show the decay of Φ after the mode has entered the Hubble radius in the radiation dominated epoch as described by Eq. (79). Right Panel: Evolution of entropy perturbation (see Eq. (87) for the definition). The entropy perturbation is essentially zero till the mode enters Hubble radius and grows afterwards tracking the dominant energy density perturbation.

4.1 Evolution for $\lambda \gg d_H$

Let us begin by considering very large wavelength modes corresponding to the $k\eta \to 0$ limit. In this case adiabaticity is respected and we can set $\delta_R \approx (4/3)\delta_m$. Then Eqs. (72), (73) become

$$y\Phi' + \Phi \approx -\frac{3y+4}{8(1+y)}\delta_R; \quad \delta_R' \approx 4\Phi' \qquad (77)$$

Differentiating the first equation and using the second to eliminate δ_m, we get a second order equation for Φ. Fortunately, this equation has an exact solution

$$\Phi = \Phi_i \frac{1}{10y^3}\left[16\sqrt{(1+y)} + 9y^3 + 2y^2 - 8y - 16\right]; \quad \delta_R \approx 4\Phi - 6\Phi_i \qquad (78)$$

[There is simple way of determining such an exact solution, which we will describe in Sec. .]. The initial condition on δ_R is chosen such that it goes to $-2\Phi_i$ initially. The solution shows that, as long as the mode is bigger than the Hubble radius, the potential changes very little; it is constant initially as well as in the final matter dominated phase. At late times ($y \gg 1$) we see that $\Phi \approx (9/10)\Phi_i$ so that Φ decreases only by a factor (9/10) during the entire evolution if $k \to 0$ is a valid approximation.

4.2 Evolution for $\lambda \ll d_H$ in the radiation dominated phase

When the mode enters Hubble radius in the radiation dominated phase, we can no longer ignore the pressure terms. The pressure makes radiation density contrast oscillate and the gravitational potential, driven by this, also oscillates with a decay in the overall amplitude. An approximate procedure to describe this phase is to solve the coupled

$\delta_R - \Phi$ system, ignoring δ_m which is sub-dominant and *then* determine δ_m using the form of Φ.

When δ_m is ignored, the problem reduces to the one solved earlier in Eqs (64), (65) with $w = 1/3$ giving $v = 3$. Since $J_{3/2}$ can be expressed in terms of trigonometric functions, the solution given by Eq. (64) with $v = 3$, simplifies to

$$\Phi = \Phi_i \frac{3}{l^3 y^3} [\sin(ly) - ly \cos(ly)]; \quad l^2 = \frac{k^2}{3k_c^2} \tag{79}$$

Note that as $y \to 0$, we have $\Phi = \Phi_i, \Phi' = 0$. This solution shows that once the mode enters the Hubble radius, the potential decays in an oscillatory manner. For $ly \gg 1$, the potential becomes $\Phi \approx -3\Phi_i(ly)^{-2} \cos(ly)$. In the same limit, we get from Eq. (65) that

$$\delta_R \approx -\frac{2}{3} k^2 \eta^2 \Phi \approx -2l^2 y^2 \Phi \approx 6\Phi_i \cos(ly) \tag{80}$$

(This is analogous to Eq. (68) for the radiation dominated case.) This oscillation is seen clearly in Fig 3 and Fig.4 (left panel). The amplitude of oscillations is accurately captured by Eq. (80) for $k = 100k_{eq}$ mode but not for $k = k_{eq}$; this is to be expected since the mode is not entering in the radiation dominated phase.

Let us next consider matter perturbations during this phase. They grow, driven by the gravitational potential determined above. When $y \ll 1$, Eq.(73) becomes:

$$\delta_m'' + \frac{1}{y} \delta_m' = 3\Phi'' + \frac{3}{y}\Phi' - \frac{k^2}{k_c^2}\Phi \tag{81}$$

The Φ is essentially determined by radiation and satisfies Eq. (61); using this, we can rewrite Eq. (81) as

$$\frac{d}{dy}(y\delta_m') = -9(\Phi' + \frac{2}{3}l^2 y\Phi) \tag{82}$$

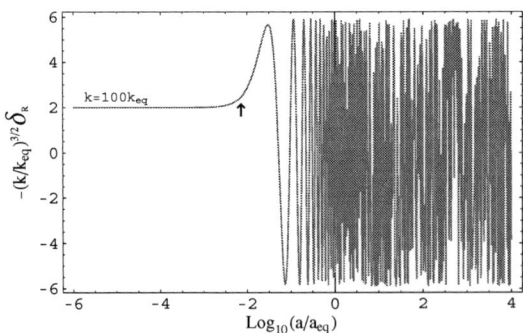

FIGURE 3. Evolution of δ_R for a mode with $k = 100k_{eq}$. The mode remains frozen outside the Hubble radius at $(k/k_{eq})^{3/2}(-\delta_R) \approx (k/k_{eq})^{3/2} 2\Phi = 2$ (in the normalisation used in Fig. 2) and oscillates when it enters the Hubble radius. The oscillations are well described by Eq. (80) with an amplitude of 6.

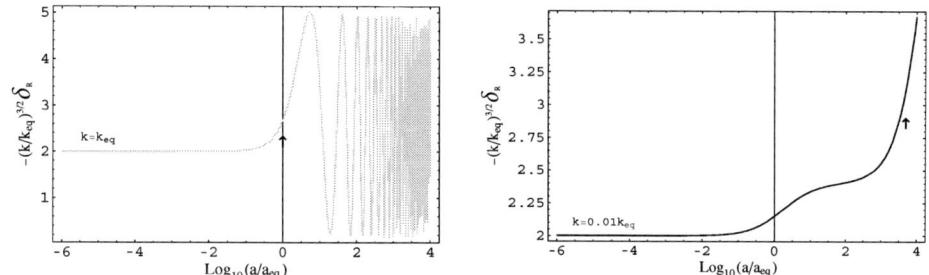

FIGURE 4. Evolution of δ_R for two modes $k = k_{eq}$ and $k = 0.01 k_{eq}$. The modes remain frozen outside the Hubble radius at $(-\delta_R) \approx 2$ and oscillates when it enters the Hubble radius. The mode in the right panel stays outside the Hubble radius for most part of its evolution and hence changes very little.

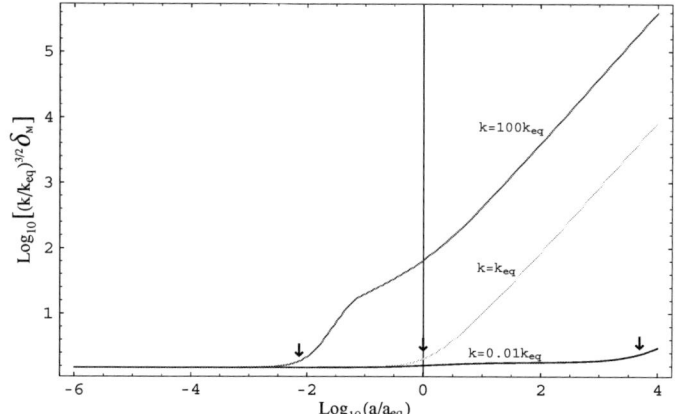

FIGURE 5. Evolution of $|\delta_m|$ for 3 different modes. The modes are labelled by their wave numbers and the epochs at which they enter the Hubble radius are shown by small arrows. All the modes remain frozen when they are outside the Hubble radius and grow linearly in the matter dominated phase once they are inside the Hubble radius. The mode that enters the Hubble radius in the radiation dominated phase grows logarithmically until $y = y_{eq}$. These features are well approximated by Eqs. (83), (85).

The general solution to the homogeneous part of Eq. (82) (obtained by ignoring the right hand side) is $(c_1 + c_2 \ln y)$; hence the general solution to this equation is

$$\delta_m = (c_1 + c_2 \ln y) - 9 \int \frac{dy}{y} \int^y dy_1 [\Phi'(y_1) + \frac{2}{3} l^2 y_1 \Phi(y_1)] \tag{83}$$

For $y \ll 1$ the growing mode varies as $\ln y$ and dominates over the rest; hence we conclude that, matter, driven by Φ, grows logarithmically during the radiation dominated phase for modes which are inside the Hubble radius.

4.3 Evolution in the matter dominated phase

Finally let us consider the matter dominated phase, in which we can ignore the radiation and concentrate on Eq (72) and Eq. (73). When $y \gg 1$ these equations become:

$$y\Phi' + \Phi \approx -\frac{1}{2}\delta_m - \frac{k^2 y}{3k_c^2}\Phi; \qquad y\delta_m'' + \frac{3}{2}\delta_m' = -\frac{k^2}{k_c^2}\Phi \qquad (84)$$

These have a simple solution which we found earlier (see Eq. (69)):

$$\Phi = \Phi_\infty = \text{const.}; \qquad \delta_m = -2\Phi_\infty - \frac{2k^2}{3k_c^2}\Phi_\infty y \sim y \qquad (85)$$

In this limit, the matter perturbations grow linearly with expansion: $\delta_m \propto y \propto a$. In fact this is the most dominant growth mode in the linear perturbation theory.

4.4 An alternative description of matter-radiation system

Before proceeding further, we will describe an alternative procedure for discussing the perturbations in dark matter and radiation, which has some advantages. In the formalism we used above, we used perturbations in the energy density of radiation (δ_R) and matter (δ_m) as the dependent variables. Instead, we now use perturbations in the *total* energy density, δ and the perturbations in the entropy per particle, σ as the new dependent variables. In terms of δ_R, δ_m, these variables are defined as:

$$\delta \equiv \frac{\delta \rho_{\text{total}}}{\rho_{\text{total}}} = \frac{\rho_R \delta_R + \rho_m \delta_m}{\rho_R + \rho_m} = \frac{\delta_R + y\delta_m}{1+y}; \qquad y = \frac{\rho_m}{\rho_R} = \frac{a}{a_{\text{eq}}} \qquad (86)$$

$$\sigma \equiv \left(\frac{\delta s}{s}\right) = \frac{3\delta T_R}{T_R} - \frac{\delta \rho_m}{\rho_m} = \frac{3}{4}\delta_R - \delta_m = \frac{\delta n_R}{n_R} - \frac{\delta n_m}{n_m} \qquad (87)$$

Given the equations for δ_R, δ_m, one can obtain the corresponding equations for the new variables (δ, σ) by straight forward algebra. It is convenient to express them as two coupled equations for Φ and σ. After some direct but a bit tedious algebra, we get:

$$y\Phi'' + \frac{y\Phi'}{2(1+y)} + 3(1+c_s^2)\Phi' + \frac{3c_s^2 \Phi}{4(1+y)} + c_s^2\frac{k^2}{k_c^2}\frac{y}{1+y}\Phi = \frac{3c_s^2 \sigma}{2(1+y)} \qquad (88)$$

$$y\sigma'' + \frac{y\sigma'}{2(1+y)} + 3c_s^2 \sigma' + \frac{3c_s^2 y^2}{4(1+y)}\frac{k^2}{k_c^2}\sigma = \frac{c_s^2 y^3}{2(1+y)}\left(\frac{k}{k_c}\right)^4 \Phi \qquad (89)$$

where we have defined

$$c_s^2 = \frac{(4/3)\rho_R}{4\rho_R + 3\rho_m} = \frac{1}{3}\left(1 + \frac{3}{4}\frac{\rho_m}{\rho_R}\right)^{-1} = \frac{1}{3}\left(1 + \frac{3}{4}y\right)^{-1} \qquad (90)$$

These equations show that the entropy perturbations and gravitational potential (which is directly related to total energy density perturbations) act as sources for each other. The coupling between the two arises through the right hand sides of Eq. (88) and Eq. (89). We also see that if we set $\sigma = 0$ as an initial condition, this is preserved to $\mathcal{O}(k^4)$ and — for long wave length modes — the Φ evolves independent of σ. The solutions to the coupled equations obtained by numerical integration is shown in Fig.(2) right panel. The entropy perturbation $\sigma \approx 0$ till the mode enters Hubble radius and grows afterwards tracking either δ_R or δ_m whichever is the dominant energy density perturbation. To illustrate the behaviour of Φ, let us consider the adiabatic perturbations at large scales with $\sigma \approx 0, k \to 0$; then the gravitational potential satisfies the equation:

$$y\Phi'' + \frac{y\Phi'}{2(1+y)} + 3(1+c_s^2)\Phi' + \frac{3c_s^2\Phi}{4(1+y)} = \frac{3c_s^2\sigma}{2(1+y)} \approx 0 \tag{91}$$

which has the two independent solutions:

$$f_1(y) = 1 + \frac{2}{9y} - \frac{8}{9y^2} - \frac{16}{9y^3}, \quad f_2(y) = \frac{\sqrt{1+y}}{y^2} \tag{92}$$

both of which diverge as $y \to 0$. We need to combine these two solutions to find the general solution, keeping in mind that the general solution should be nonsingular and become a constant (say, unity) as $y \to 0$. This fixes the linear combination uniquely:

$$f(y) = \frac{9}{10}f_1 + \frac{8}{5}f_2 = \frac{1}{10y^3}\left[16\sqrt{(1+y)} + 9y^3 + 2y^2 - 8y - 16\right] \tag{93}$$

Multiplying by Φ_i we get the solution that was found earlier (see Eq. (78)). Given the form of Φ and $\sigma \simeq 0$ we can determine all other quantities. In particular, we get:

$$\delta_R = \frac{-2(1+y)d(y\Phi)/dy + y\sigma}{1+(3/4)y} \simeq -\frac{2(1+y)}{1+(3/4)y}\frac{d}{dy}(y\Phi) \tag{94}$$

The corresponding velocity field, which we quote for future reference, is given by:

$$v_\alpha = -\frac{3c_s^2}{2(\dot{a}/a)}(1+y)\nabla_\alpha \frac{d(y\Phi)}{dy} \tag{95}$$

We conclude this section by mentioning another useful result related to Eq. (88). When $\sigma \approx 0$, the equation for Φ can be re-expressed as

$$a\frac{d\zeta}{da} = -\frac{2c_s^2 k^2/a^2}{3}\frac{\rho}{H^2}\frac{\rho}{\rho+p}\Phi \approx 0 \quad \text{(for } \frac{k}{aH} \ll 1\text{)} \tag{96}$$

where we have defined:

$$\zeta = \frac{2}{3}\frac{\rho}{\rho+p}\frac{a}{\dot{a}}\left(\dot{\Phi} + \frac{\dot{a}}{a}\Phi\right) + \Phi = \frac{H}{\rho+p}\frac{ik^\alpha}{k^2}\delta T_\alpha^0 + \Phi \tag{97}$$

(The i factor arises because of converting a gradient to the **k** space; of course, when everything is done correctly, all physical quantities will be real.) Other equivalent alternative forms for ζ, which are useful are:

$$\zeta = \frac{2}{3[1+w(a)]} \frac{d}{da}(a\Phi) + \Phi = \frac{H^2}{a(\rho+p)} \frac{d}{dt}\left(\frac{a\Phi}{H}\right) \qquad (98)$$

For modes which are bigger than the Hubble radius, Eq. (96) shows that ζ is conserved. When ζ=constant, we can integrate Eq. (98) easily to obtain:

$$\Phi = c_1 \frac{H}{a} + c_2 \left[1 - \frac{H}{a}\int_0^a \frac{da'}{H(a')}\right] \qquad (99)$$

This is the easiest way to obtain the solution in Eq. (78).

The conservation law for ζ also allows us to understand in a simple manner our previous result that Φ only deceases by a factor $(9/10)$ when the mode remains bigger than Hubble radius as we evolve the equations from $y \ll 1$ to $y \gg 1$. Let us compare the values of ζ early in the radiation dominated phase and late in the matter dominated phase. From the first equation in Eq. (98), [using $\Phi' \approx 0$] we find that, in the radiation dominated phase, $\zeta \approx (1/2)\Phi_i + \Phi_i = (3/2)\Phi_i$; late in the matter dominated phase, $\zeta \approx (2/3)\Phi_f + \Phi_f = (5/3)\Phi_f$. Hence the conservation of ζ gives $\Phi_f = (3/5)(3/2)\Phi_i = (9/10)\Phi_i$ which was the result obtained earlier. The expression in Eq. (99) also works at late times in the Λ dominated or curvature dominated universe.

One key feature which should be noted in the study of linear perturbation theory is the different amount of growths for Φ, δ_R and δ_m. The Φ either changes very little or decays; the δ_R grows in amplitude only by a factor of few. The physical reason, of course, is that the amplitude is frozen at super-Hubble scales and the pressure prevents the growth at sub-Hubble scales. In contrast, δ_m, which is pressureless, grows logarithmically in the radiation dominated era and linearly during the matter dominated era. Since the later phase lasts for a factor of 10^4 in expansion, we get a fair amount of growth in δ_m.

5. TRANSFER FUNCTION FOR MATTER PERTURBATIONS

We now have all the ingredients to evolve the matter perturbation from an initial value $\delta = \delta_i$ at $y = y_i \ll 1$ to the current epoch $y = y_0 = a_{eq}^{-1}$ in the matter dominated phase at $y \gg 1$. Initially, the wavelength of the perturbation will be bigger than the Hubble radius and the perturbation will essentially remain frozen. When it enters the Hubble radius in the radiation dominated phase, it begins to grow but only logarithmically (see section) until the universe becomes matter dominated. In the final matter dominated phase, the perturbation grows linearly with expansion factor. The relation between final and initial perturbation can be obtained by combining these results.

Usually, one is more interested in the power spectrum $P_k(t)$ and the power per logarithmic band in k-space $\Delta_k(t)$. These quantities are defined in terms of $\delta_k(t)$ through the equations:

$$P_k(t) \equiv |\delta_k(t)|^2; \quad \Delta_k^2(t) \equiv \frac{k^3 P_k(t)}{2\pi^2} \qquad (100)$$

It is therefore convenient to study the evolution of $k^{3/2}\delta_k$ since its square will immediately give the power per logarithmic band Δ_k^2 in k-space.

Let us first consider a mode which enters the Hubble radius in the radiation dominated phase at the epoch a_{enter}. From the scaling relation, $a_{ent}/k \propto t_{ent} \propto a_{ent}^2$ we find that $y_{ent} = (k_{eq}/k)$. Hence

$$k^{3/2}\delta_m(k, a=1) = \underbrace{\frac{1}{a_{eq}} \ln\left(\frac{a_{eq}}{a_{ent}}\right)}_{\text{MD} \quad \text{RD}} \underbrace{\left[k^{3/2}\delta_{ent}(k)\right]}_{\text{at entry}} \propto \ln\left(\frac{k}{k_{eq}}\right) [k^{3/2}\delta_{ent}(k)] \quad (101)$$

where two factors — as indicated — gives the growth in radiation (RD) and matter dominated (MD) phases. Let us next consider the modes that enter in the matter dominated phase. In this case, $a_{ent}/k \propto t_{ent} \propto a_{ent}^{3/2}$ so that $y_{ent} = (k_{eq}/k)^2$. Hence

$$k^{3/2}\delta_m(k, a=1) = \underbrace{\frac{1}{a_{ent}}}_{\text{MD}} \underbrace{\left[k^{3/2}\delta_{ent}(k)\right]}_{\text{at entry}} \propto k^2 [k^{3/2}\delta_{ent}(k)] \quad (102)$$

To proceed further, we need to know the k-dependence of the perturbation when it enters the Hubble radius which, of course, is related to the mechanism that generates the initial power spectrum. The most natural choice will be that all the modes enter the Hubble radius with a constant amplitude at the time of entry. This would imply that the physical perturbations are scale invariant at the time of entering the Hubble radius, a possibility that was suggested by Zeldovich and Harrison [18] (years before inflation was invented!). We will see later that this is also true for perturbations generated by inflation and thus is a reasonable assumption at least in such models. Hence we shall assume

$$k^3|\delta_{ent}(k)|^2 = k^3 P_{ent}(k) = C = \text{constant}, \quad (103)$$

Using this we find that the current value of perturbation is given by

$$P(k, a=1) \propto \left|\delta_m(k, a=1)\right|^2 \propto \begin{cases} k & (\text{for } k \ll k_{eq}) \\ k^{-3}(\ln k)^2 & (\text{for } k \gg k_{eq}) \end{cases} \quad (104)$$

The corresponding power per logarithmic band is

$$\Delta^2(k, a=1) \propto k^3 \left|\delta_m(k, a=1)\right|^2 \propto \begin{cases} k^4 & (\text{for } k \ll k_{eq}) \\ (\ln k)^2 & (\text{for } k \gg k_{eq}) \end{cases} \quad (105)$$

The form for $P(k)$ shows that the evolution imprints the scale k_{eq} on the power spectrum even though the initial power spectrum is scale invariant. For $k < k_{eq}$ (for large spatial scales), the primordial form of the spectrum is preserved and the evolution only increases the amplitude preserving the shape. For $k > k_{eq}$ (for small spatial scales), the shape is distorted and in general the power is suppressed in comparison with larger spatial scales. This arises because modes with small wavelengths enter the Hubble radius early on and have to wait till the universe becomes matter dominated in order to grow in amplitude.

This is in contrast to modes with large wavelengths which continue to grow. It is this effect which suppresses the power at small wavelengths (for $k > k_{eq}$) relative to power at larger wavelengths.

6. TEMPERATURE ANISOTROPIES OF CMBR

We shall now apply the formalism we have developed to understand the temperature anisotropies in the cosmic microwave background radiation which is probably the most useful application of *linear* perturbation theory. We shall begin by developing the general formulation and the terminology which is used to describe the temperature anisotropies.

Towards every direction in the sky, $\mathbf{n} = (\theta, \psi)$ we can define a fractional temperature fluctuation $\Delta(\mathbf{n}) \equiv (\Delta T/T)(\theta, \psi)$. Expanding this quantity in spherical harmonics on the sky plane as well as in terms of the spatial Fourier modes, we get the two relations:

$$\Delta(\mathbf{n}) \equiv \frac{\Delta T}{T}(\theta,\psi) = \sum_{l,m} a_{lm} Y_{lm}(\theta,\psi) = \int \frac{d^3k}{(2\pi)^3} \Delta(\mathbf{k}) e^{i\mathbf{k}\cdot\mathbf{n}L} \quad (106)$$

where $L = \eta_0 - \eta_{\mathrm{LSS}}$ is the distance to the last scattering surface (LSS) from which we are receiving the radiation. The last equality allows us to define the expansion coefficients a_{lm} in terms of the temperature fluctuation in the Fourier space $\Delta(\mathbf{k})$. Standard identities of mathematical physics now give

$$a_{lm} = \int \frac{d^3k}{(2\pi)^3} (4\pi) \, i^l \, \Delta(\mathbf{k}) \, j_l(kL) \, Y_{lm}(\hat{\mathbf{k}}) \quad (107)$$

Next, let us consider the angular correlation function of temperature anisotropy, which is given by:

$$\mathscr{C}(\alpha) = \langle \Delta(\mathbf{n})\Delta(\mathbf{m}) \rangle = \sum\sum \langle a_{lm} a^*_{l'm'} \rangle Y_{lm}(\mathbf{n}) Y^*_{l'm'}(\mathbf{m}). \quad (108)$$

where the wedges denote an ensemble average. For a Gaussian random field of fluctuations we can express the ensemble average as $\langle a_{lm} a^*_{l'm'} \rangle = C_l \delta_{ll'} \delta_{mm'}$. Using Eq. (107), we get a relation between C_l and $\Delta(k)$. Given $\Delta(k)$, the C_l's are given by:

$$C_l = \frac{2}{\pi} \int_0^\infty k^2 dk \, |\Delta(k)|^2 \, j_l^2(kL) \quad (109)$$

Further, Eq. (108) now becomes:

$$\mathscr{C}(\alpha) = \sum_l \frac{(2l+1)}{4\pi} C_l P_l(\cos\alpha) \quad (110)$$

Equation (110) shows that the mean-square value of temperature fluctuations and the quadrupole anisotropy corresponding to $l = 2$ are given by

$$\left(\frac{\Delta T}{T}\right)^2_{\mathrm{rms}} = \mathscr{C}(0) = \frac{1}{4\pi} \sum_{l=2}^\infty (2l+1) C_l, \quad \left(\frac{\Delta T}{T}\right)^2_Q = \frac{5}{4\pi} C_2. \quad (111)$$

These can be explicitly computed if we know $\Delta(k)$ from the perturbation theory. (The motion of our local group through the CMBR leads to a large $l = 1$ dipole contribution in the temperature anisotropy. In the analysis of CMBR anisotropies, this is usually subtracted out. Hence the leading term is the quadrupole with $l = 2$.)

It should be noted that, for a given l, the C_l is the average over all $m = -l, \ldots -1, 0, 1, \ldots l$. For a Gaussian random field, one can also compute the variance around this mean value. It can be shown that this variance in C_l is $2C_l^2/(2l+1)$. In other words, there is an intrinsic root-mean-square fluctuation in the observed, mean value of C_l's which is of the order of $\Delta C_l/C_l \approx (2l+1)^{-1/2}$. It is not possible for any CMBR observations which measures the C_l's to reduce its uncertainty below this intrinsic variance — usually called the "cosmic variance". For large values of l, the cosmic variance is usually sub-dominant to other observational errors but for low l this is the dominant source of uncertainty in the measurement of C_l's. Current WMAP observations are indeed only limited by cosmic variance at low-l.

As an illustration of the formalism developed above, let us compute the C_l's for low l which will be contributed essentially by fluctuations at large spatial scales. Since these fluctuations will be dominated by gravitational effects, we can ignore the complications arising from baryonic physics and compute these using the formalism we have developed earlier.

We begin by noting that the redshift law of photons in the unperturbed Friedmann universe, $v_0 = v(a)/a$, gets modified to the form $v_0 = v(a)/[a(1+\Phi)]$ in a perturbed FRW universe. The argument of the Planck spectrum will thus scale as

$$\frac{v_0}{T_0} = \frac{v(a)}{aT_0(1+\Phi)} = \frac{v(a)}{a\langle T_0\rangle[1+(\delta_R/4)](1+\Phi)} \simeq \frac{v(a)}{a\langle T_0\rangle[1+\Phi+(\delta_R/4)]} \tag{112}$$

This is equivalent to a temperature fluctuation of the amount

$$\left(\frac{\Delta T}{T}\right)_{obs} = \frac{1}{4}\delta_R + \Phi \tag{113}$$

at large scales. (Note that the observed $\Delta T/T$ is not just $(\delta_R/4)$ as one might have naively imagined.) To proceed further, we recall our large scale solution (see Eq. (78)) for the gravitational potential:

$$\Phi = \Phi_i \frac{1}{10y^3}\left[16\sqrt{(1+y)}+9y^3+2y^2-8y-16\right]; \quad \delta_R = 4\Phi - 6\Phi_i \tag{114}$$

At $y = y_{dec}$ we can take the asymptotic solution $\Phi_{dec} \approx (9/10)\Phi_i$. Hence we get

$$\left(\frac{\Delta T}{T}\right)_{obs} = \left[\frac{1}{4}\delta_R+\Phi\right]_{dec} = 2\Phi_{dec}-\frac{3}{2}\Phi_i \approx 2\Phi_{dec}-\frac{3}{2}\frac{10}{9}\Phi_{dec} = \frac{1}{3}\Phi_{dec} \tag{115}$$

We thus obtain the nice result that the observed temperature fluctuations at very large scales is simply related to the fluctuations of the gravitational potential at these scales. (For a discussion of the $1/3$ factor, see [19]). Fourier transforming this result we get $\Delta(\mathbf{k}) = (1/3)\Phi(\mathbf{k},\eta_{LSS})$ where η_{LSS} is the conformal time at the last scattering surface.

(This contribution is called Sachs-Wolfe effect.) It follows from Eq. (109) that the contribution to C_l from the gravitational potential is

$$C_l = \frac{2}{\pi} \int k^2 dk |\Delta(k)|^2 j_l^2(kL) = \frac{2}{\pi} \int_0^\infty \frac{dk}{k} \frac{k^3 |\Phi_k|^2}{9} j_l^2(kL) \qquad (116)$$

with

$$L = \eta_0 - \eta_{LSS} \approx \eta_0 \approx 2(\Omega_m H_0^2)^{-1/2} \approx 6000 \, \Omega_m^{-1/2} \, h^{-1} \text{ Mpc} \qquad (117)$$

For a scale invariant spectrum, $k^3|\Phi_k|^2$ is a constant independent of k. (Earlier on, in Eq. (103) we said that scale invariant spectrum has $k^3|\delta_k|^2 = $ constant. These statements are equivalent since $\delta \approx -2\Phi$ at the large scales because of Eq. (85) with the extra correction term in Eq. (85) being about 3×10^{-4} for $k \approx L^{-1}, y = y_{dec}$.) As we shall see later, inflation generates such a perturbation. In this case, it is conventional to introduce a constant amplitude A and write:

$$\Delta_\Phi^2 \equiv \frac{k^3|\Phi_k|^2}{2\pi^2} = A^2 = \text{constant} \qquad (118)$$

Substituting this form into Eq. (116) and evaluating the integral, we find that

$$\frac{l(l+1)C_l}{2\pi} = \left(\frac{A}{3}\right)^2 \qquad (119)$$

As an application of this result, let us consider the observations of COBE which measured the temperature fluctuations for the first time in 1992. This satellite obtained the RMS fluctuations and the quadrupole after smoothing over an angular scale of about $\theta_c \approx 10°$. Hence the observed values are slightly different from those in Eq. (111). We have, instead,

$$\left(\frac{\Delta T}{T}\right)_{rms}^2 = \frac{1}{4\pi} \sum_{l=2}^{\infty} (2l+1) C_l \exp\left(-\frac{l^2 \theta_c^2}{2}\right); \quad \left(\frac{\Delta T}{T}\right)_Q^2 = \frac{5}{4\pi} C_2 e^{-2\theta_c^2}. \qquad (120)$$

Using Eqs. (118), (119) we find that

$$\left(\frac{\Delta T}{T}\right)_Q \cong 0.22A; \quad \left(\frac{\Delta T}{T}\right)_{rms} \cong 0.51A. \qquad (121)$$

Given these two measurements, one can verify that the fluctuations are consistent with the scale invariant spectrum by checking their ratio. Further, the numerical value of the observed $(\Delta T/T)$ can be used to determine the amplitude A. One finds that $A \approx 3 \times 10^{-5}$ which sets the scale of fluctuations in the gravitational potential at the time when the perturbation enters the Hubble radius.

Incidentally, note that the solution $\delta_R = 4\Phi - 6\Phi_i$ corresponds to $\delta_m = (3/4)\delta_R = 3\Phi - (9/2)\Phi_i$. At $y = y_{dec}$, taking $\Phi_{dec} = (9/10)\Phi_i$, we get $\delta_m = 3\Phi_{dec} - (9/2)(10/9)\Phi_{dec} = -2\Phi_{dec}$. Since $(\Delta T/T)_{obs} = (1/3)\Phi_{dec}$ we get $\delta_m = -6(\Delta T/T)_{obs}$. This shows that the amplitude of matter perturbations is a factor six larger that the amplitude of temperature anisotropy for our adiabatic initial conditions. In several other models, one gets $\delta_m = \mathcal{O}(1)(\Delta T/T)_{obs}$. So, to reach a given level of nonlinearity in the matter distribution at later times, these models will require higher values of $(\Delta T/T)_{obs}$ at decoupling. This is one reason for such models to be observationally ruled out.

There is another useful result which we can obtain from Eq. (109) along the same lines as we derived the Sachs-Wolfe effect. Whenever $k^3|\Delta(k)|^2$ is a slowly varying function of k, we can pull out this factor out of the integral and evaluate the integral over j_l^2. This will give the result for any slowly varying $k^3|\Delta(k)|^2$

$$\frac{l(l+1)C_l}{2\pi} \approx \left(\frac{k^3|\Delta(k)|^2}{2\pi^2}\right)_{kL\approx l} \tag{122}$$

This is applicable even when different processes contribute to temperature anisotropies as long as they add in quadrature. While far from accurate, it allows one to estimate the effects rapidly.

6.1 CMBR Temperature Anisotropy: More detailed theory

We shall now work out a more detailed theory of temperature anisotropies of CMBR so that one can understand the effects at small scales as well. A convenient starting point is the distribution function for photons with perturbed Planckian distribution, which we can write as:

$$f(x^\alpha, \eta, E, n^\alpha) = \frac{I_\nu}{2\pi\nu^3} = f_P\left(\frac{aE}{1+\Delta}\right); \qquad f_P(\varepsilon) \equiv 2[\exp(\varepsilon/T_0) - 1]^{-1} \tag{123}$$

The $f_P(\varepsilon)$ is the standard Planck spectrum for energy ε and we take $\varepsilon = aE(1+\Delta)^{-1}$ to take care of the perturbations. In the absence of collisions, the distribution function is conserved along the trajectories of photons so that $df/d\eta = 0$. So, in the presence of collisions, we can write the time evolution of the distribution function as

$$\frac{df}{d\eta} = \left(\frac{aE}{1+\Delta}\right) f'_P\left(\frac{aE}{1+\Delta}\right) \left[\frac{d\ln(aE)}{d\eta} - \frac{d\Delta}{d\eta}\right] = \left(\frac{df}{d\eta}\right)_{coll} \tag{124}$$

where the right hand side gives the contribution due to collisional terms. Equivalently, in terms of Δ, the same equation takes the form:

$$\frac{d\Delta}{d\eta} - \frac{d\ln(aE)}{d\eta} = -\left(\frac{1+\Delta}{aE}\right) [f'_P]^{-1} \left(\frac{df}{d\eta}\right)_{coll} \equiv \left(\frac{d\Delta}{d\eta}\right)_{coll} \tag{125}$$

To proceed further, we need the expressions for the two terms on the left hand side. First term, on using the standard expansion for total derivative, gives:

$$\frac{d\Delta}{d\eta} = \frac{\partial\Delta}{\partial\eta} + \frac{\partial\Delta}{\partial x^\alpha} \underbrace{\frac{dx^\alpha}{d\eta}}_{n^\alpha} + \underbrace{\frac{\partial\Delta}{\partial E}\frac{dE}{d\eta}}_{\text{zero}} + \underbrace{\frac{\partial\Delta}{\partial n^\alpha}\frac{dn^\alpha}{d\eta}}_{\mathcal{O}(\Delta^2)=0} \cong \partial_\eta\Delta + n^\alpha\partial_\alpha\Delta \tag{126}$$

(Note that we are assuming $\partial \Delta/\partial E = 0$ so that the perturbations do not depend on the frequency of the photon.) To determine the second term, we note that it vanishes in the unperturbed Friedmann universe and arises essentially due to the variation of Φ. Both the intrinsic time variation of Φ as well as its variation along the photon path will contribute, giving:

$$\frac{d\ln(aE)}{d\eta} = -n^\alpha \partial_\alpha \Phi + \partial_\eta \Phi \qquad (127)$$

(The minus sign arises from the fact that the we have $(1+2\Phi)$ in g_{00} but $(1-2\Phi)$ in the spatial perturbations.) Putting all these together, we can bring the evolution equation Eq. (125) to the form:

$$\frac{d\Delta}{d\eta} = -n^\alpha \partial_\alpha \Phi + \partial_\eta \Phi + \left(\frac{d\Delta}{d\eta}\right)_{coll} \qquad (128)$$

Let us next consider the collision term, which can be expressed in the form:

$$\left(\frac{d\Delta}{ad\eta}\right)_{coll} = -N_e \sigma_T \Delta + N_e \sigma_T \left(\frac{1}{4}\delta_R\right) + N_e \sigma_T (\mathbf{v}\cdot\mathbf{n})$$

$$= N_e \sigma_T \left(-\Delta + \frac{1}{4}\delta_R + \mathbf{v}\cdot\mathbf{n}\right) \qquad (129)$$

Each of the terms in the right hand side of the first line has a simple interpretation. The first term describes the removal of photons from the beam due to Thomson scattering with the electrons while the second term gives the scattering contribution into the beam. In a static universe, we expect these two terms to cancel if $\Delta = (1/4)\delta_R$ which fixes the relative coefficients of these two terms. The third term is a correction due to the fact that the electrons which are scattering the photons are not at rest relative to the cosmic frame. This leads to a Doppler shift which is accounted for by the third term. (We denote electron number *density* by N_e rather than n_e to avoid notational conflict with n^α.)

Formally, Eq. (128) is a first order linear differential equation for Δ. To eliminate the $-N_e\sigma_T\Delta$ term which is linear in Δ in the right hand side, we use the standard integrating factor $\exp(-\tau)$ where

$$\tau(\chi) \equiv \int_0^\chi d\eta\, (aN_e\sigma_T) \qquad (130)$$

We can then formally integrate Eq. (128) to get:

$$\Delta(\mathbf{n}) = \int_0^{\eta_0} d\chi\, e^{-\tau(\chi)} \left[-n^\alpha \partial_\alpha \Phi + \partial_\eta \Phi + aN_e\sigma_T\left(\frac{1}{4}\delta_R + \mathbf{v}\cdot\mathbf{n}\right)\right] \qquad (131)$$

We can write

$$e^{-\tau}(-n^\alpha\partial_\alpha\Phi) = -\left(\frac{d\Phi}{d\eta}\right)e^{-\tau} + (\partial_\eta\Phi)e^{-\tau} = -\frac{d}{d\eta}(\Phi e^{-\tau}) + (aN_e\sigma_T\Phi)e^{-\tau} + (\partial_\eta\Phi)e^{-\tau} \qquad (132)$$

On integration, the first term gives zero at the lower limit and an unimportant constant (which does not depend on **n**). Using the rest of the terms, we can write Eq. (131) in the form:

$$\Delta(\mathbf{n}) = \int_0^{\eta_0} d\chi\, e^{-\tau} \left[2\partial_\eta \Phi + aN_e \sigma_T \left(\Phi + \frac{1}{4}\delta_R + \mathbf{v}\cdot\mathbf{n} \right) \right]$$

$$= \int_0^{\eta_0} d\chi\, e^{-\tau} [2\partial_\eta \Phi] + \int_0^{\eta_0} d\chi\, (e^{-\tau} aN_e \sigma_T) \left(\Phi + \frac{1}{4}\delta_R + \mathbf{v}\cdot\mathbf{n} \right) \quad (133)$$

The first term gives the contribution due to the intrinsic time variation of the gravitational potential along the path of the photon and is called the integrated Sachs-Wolfe effect. In the second term one can make further simplifications. Note that $e^{-\tau}$ is essentially unity (optically thin) for $z < z_{\text{rec}}$ and zero (optically thick) for $z > z_{\text{rec}}$; on the other hand, $N_e \sigma_T$ is zero for $z < z_{\text{rec}}$ (all the free electrons have disappeared) and is large for $z > z_{\text{rec}}$. Hence the product $(aN_e e^{-\tau})$ is sharply peaked at $\chi = \chi_{\text{rec}}$ (i.e. at $z \simeq 10^3$ with $\Delta z \simeq 80$). Treating this sharply peaked quantity as essentially a Dirac delta function (usually called the instantaneous recombination approximation) we can approximate the second term in Eq. (133) as a contribution occurring just on the LSS:

$$\Delta(\mathbf{n}) = \left(\frac{1}{4}\delta_R + \mathbf{v}\cdot\mathbf{n} + \Phi \right)_{\text{LSS}} + 2\int_{\eta_{\text{LSS}}}^{\eta_0} d\chi\, \partial_\eta \Phi \quad (134)$$

In the second term we have put $\tau = \infty$ for $\eta < \eta_{\text{LSS}}$ and $\tau = 0$ for $\eta > \eta_{\text{LSS}}$.

Once we know δ_R, Φ and $\mathbf{v}$ on the LSS from perturbation theory, we can take a Fourier transform of this result to obtain $\Delta(k)$ and use Eq. (109) to compute C_l. At very large scales the velocity term is sub-dominant and we get back the Sachs-Wolfe effect derived earlier in Eq. (118). For understanding the small scale effects, we need to introduce baryons into the picture which is our next task.

6.2 Description of photon-baryon fluid

To study the interaction of photons and baryons in the fluid limit, we need to again start from the continuity equation and Euler equation. In Fourier space, the continuity equation is same as the one we had before (see Eq. (52)):

$$\left(\frac{3}{4}\right)\dot{\delta}_R = -k^2 v_R + 3\dot{\Phi}; \qquad \dot{\delta}_B = -k^2 v_B + 3\dot{\Phi} \quad (135)$$

The Euler equations, however, gets modified; for photons, it becomes:

$$\dot{v}_R = \left(\frac{1}{4}\delta_R + \Phi\right) - \dot{\tau}(v_R - v_B); \qquad \dot{\tau} = N_e \sigma_T a \quad (136)$$

The first two terms in the right hand side are exactly the same as the ones in Eq. (55). The last term is analogous to a viscous drag force between the photons and baryons which arises because of the non zero relative velocity between the two fluids. The coupling is essentially due to Thomson scattering which leads to the factor $\dot{\tau}$. (The notation, and the physics, is the same as in Eq. (130)). The corresponding Euler equation for the baryons is:

$$\dot{v}_B = -\frac{\dot{a}}{a}v_B + \Phi + \frac{\dot{\tau}(v_R - v_B)}{R} \qquad (137)$$

where

$$R \equiv \frac{p_B + \rho_B}{p_R + \rho_R} \simeq \frac{3\rho_B}{4\rho_R} \approx 30\,\Omega_B h^2 \left(\frac{a}{10^{-3}}\right) \qquad (138)$$

Again, the first two terms in the right hand side of Eq. (137) are the same as what we had before in Eq. (55). The last term has the same interpretation as in the case of Euler equation Eq. (136) for photons, except for the factor R. This quantity essentially takes care of the inertia of baryons relative to photons. Note that the the conserved momentum density of photon-baryon fluid has the form

$$(\rho_R + p_R)v_R + (\rho_B + p_B)v_B \approx (1+R)(\rho_R + p_R)v_R \qquad (139)$$

which accounts for the extra factor R in Eq. (137).

We can now combine the Eqs. (135), (136), (137) to obtain, to lowest order in $(k/\dot{\tau})$ the equation:

$$\ddot{\delta}_R + \frac{\dot{R}}{(1+R)}\dot{\delta}_R + k^2 c_s^2 \delta_R = F \qquad (140)$$

with

$$F = 4\left[\ddot{\Phi} + \frac{\dot{R}}{(1+R)}\dot{\Phi} - \frac{1}{3}k^2\Phi\right]; \quad c_s^2 = \frac{1}{3(1+R)} \qquad (141)$$

An exact solution to this equation is difficult to obtain. However, we can try to understand several features by an approximate method in which we treat the time variation of R to be small. In that case, we can drop the $\dot{R}$ terms on both sides of the equation. Since we know that the physically relevant temperature fluctuation is $\Delta = (1/4)\delta_R + \Phi$, we can recast the above equation for Δ as:

$$\ddot{\Delta} + k^2 c_s^2 \Delta \approx -k^2 c_s^2 R\Phi + 2\ddot{\Phi} \qquad (142)$$

Let us further ignore the time variation of all terms (especially $\ddot{\Phi}$ on the right hand side). Then, the solution is just $\Delta = -R\Phi + A\cos(kc_s\eta_{\rm LSS}) + B\sin(kc_s\eta_{\rm LSS})$. To fix the initial conditions which determine A and B, we recall that early on ($\eta \to 0$), we have $\Delta \to \Phi/3$ (see Eq. (115)) and corresponding velocity should vanish. This gives the solution:

$$\frac{1}{4}\delta_R + \Phi = \frac{\Phi_i}{3}(1+3R)\cos(kc_s\eta_{\rm LSS}) - \Phi_i R; \quad v = -\Phi_i(1+3R)c_s\sin(kc_s\eta_{\rm LSS}) \qquad (143)$$

(One can do a little better by using WKB approximation in which $(kc_s\eta_{\rm LSS})$ can be replaced by the integral of kc_s over η but it is not very important.) Given this solution, one can proceed as before and compute the C_l's. Adding the effects of $[\Phi + (1/4)\delta_R]$ and that of $[\mathbf{v}\cdot\mathbf{n}]$ in quadrature and noticing that the angular average of $\langle(\mathbf{v}\cdot\mathbf{n})^2\rangle = (1/3)v^2$

we can estimate the C_l for scale invariant ($k^3|\Phi_k|^2 = 2\pi^2 A^2$) spectrum to be:

$$l(l+1)C_l = 2\pi^2 A^2 \left\{ \left[\frac{(1+3R)}{3} \cos(k^* c_s \eta_{\text{LSS}}) - R \right]^2 + \frac{(1+3R)^2}{3} c_s^2 \sin^2(k^* c_s \eta_{\text{LSS}}) \right\} \tag{144}$$

with $k^* L \approx l$ with $L = \eta_0 - \eta_{\text{LSS}} \simeq \eta_0$. The key feature is, of course, the maxima and minima which arises from the trigonometric functions. The peaks of C_l are determined by the condition $k^* c_s \eta_{\text{LSS}} = l c_s \eta_{\text{LSS}}/\eta_0 = n\pi$; that is

$$l_{\text{peak}} = \frac{n\pi}{c_s} \left(\frac{\eta_0}{\eta_{\text{LSS}}} \right) = n\pi\sqrt{3}(1+z_{\text{dec}})^{1/2} \approx 172n \tag{145}$$

More precise work gives the first peak at $l_{\text{peak}} \simeq 200$. It is also clear that because of non zero R the peaks are larger when the cosine term is negative; that is, the odd peaks corresponding to $n = 1, 3, \ldots$ have larger amplitudes than the even peaks with $n = 2, 4, \ldots$.

Incidentally, the above approximation is not very good for modes which enter the Hubble radius during the radiation dominated phase since Φ does evolve with time (and decays) in the radiation dominated phase. We saw that $\Phi \approx -3\Phi_i (ly)^{-2} \cos(ly)$ asymptotically in this phase (see Eq. (80)). From Eq. (80) we find that during this phase, for modes which are inside the Hubble radius, we can take $\delta_R \approx 6\Phi_i \cos(ly)$, so that $\Delta \approx \delta_R/4 \approx (3/2)\Phi_i \cos(ly)$. On the other hand, at very large scale, the amplitude was $\Delta = \Phi/3 = (1/3)(9/10)\Phi_i = (3/10)\Phi_i$. Hence the amplitude of the modes that enter the horizon during the radiation dominated phase is enhanced by a factor $(3/2)(10/9) = 5$, relative to the large scale amplitude contributed by modes which enter during matter dominated phase. This is essentially due to the driving term $\ddot{\Phi}$ which is nonzero in the radiation dominated phase but zero in the matter dominated phase. (In reality, the enhancement is smaller because the relevant modes have $k \gtrsim k_{\text{eq}}$ rather than $k \gg k_{\text{eq}}$; see Figs. 3 and 4.)

If this were the whole story, we will see a series of peaks and troughs in the temperature anisotropies as a function of angular scale. In reality, however, there are processes which damp out the anisotropies at small angular scales (large -l) so that only the first few peaks and troughs are really relevant. We will now discuss two key damping mechanisms which are responsible for this.

The first one is the finite width of the last scattering surface which makes it uncertain from which event we are receiving the photons. In general, if $\mathscr{P}(z)$ is the probability that the photon was last scattered at redshift z, then we can write:

$$\left(\frac{\Delta T}{T} \right)_{\text{obs}} = \int dz \left\{ \begin{array}{c} (\Delta T/T) \text{ if the last} \\ \text{scattering was at } z \end{array} \right\} \times \mathscr{P}(z). \tag{146}$$

From Eq. (41) we know that $\mathscr{P}(z)$ is a Gaussian with width $\Delta z = 80$. This corresponds to a length scale

$$\Delta l = c \left(\frac{dt}{dz} \right) \Delta z \cdot (1+z_{\text{dec}}) \approx H_0^{-1} \frac{\Delta z}{\Omega^{1/2} z_{\text{dec}}^{3/2}} \approx 8 \left(\Omega h^2 \right)^{-1/2} \text{Mpc}. \tag{147}$$

over which the temperature fluctuations will be smoothed out.

It turns out that there is another effect, which is slightly more important. This arises from the fact that the photon-baryon fluid is not tightly coupled and the photons can diffuse through the fluid. This diffusion can be modeled as a random walk and the root mean square distance traveled by the photon during this diffusion process will smear the temperature anisotropies over that length scale. This photon diffusion length scale can be estimated as follows:

$$(\Delta x)^2 = \underbrace{N}_{\text{number of collisions}} \times \underbrace{\left(\frac{q}{a}\right)^2}_{\text{comoving meanfree path}} = \frac{\Delta t}{q(t)} \frac{q^2}{a^2} = \frac{\Delta t}{a^2} q(t) \qquad (148)$$

Integrating, we find the mean square distance traveled by the photon to be

$$x^2 \equiv \int_0^{t_{\text{dec}}} \frac{dt}{a^2(t)} q(t) = \frac{3}{5} \frac{t_{\text{dec}} q(t_{\text{dec}})}{a^2(t_{\text{dec}})} \qquad (149)$$

The corresponding proper length scale below which photon diffusion will wipe out temperature anisotropies is:

$$q_{\text{diff}} = a(t_{\text{dec}}) x = \left[\frac{3}{5} t_{\text{dec}} q(t_{\text{dec}})\right]^{\frac{1}{2}} \simeq 35 \text{ Mpc} \left(\frac{\Omega_B h^2}{0.02}\right)^{-\frac{1}{2}} (\Omega h_{50}^2)^{-\frac{1}{4}}. \qquad (150)$$

It turns out that this is the dominant sources of damping of temperature anisotropies at large $l \approx 10^3$.

7. GENERATION OF INITIAL PERTURBATIONS FROM INFLATION

In the description of linear perturbation theory given above, we assumed that some small perturbations existed in the early universe which are amplified through gravitational instability. To provide a complete picture we need a mechanism for generation of these initial perturbations. One such mechanism is provided by inflationary scenario which allows for the quantum fluctuations in the field driving the inflation to provide classical energy density perturbations at a late epoch. (Originally inflationary scenarios were suggested as pseudo-solutions to certain pseudo-problems; that is only of historical interest today and the only reason to take the possibility of an inflationary phase in the early universe seriously is because it provides a mechanism for generating these perturbations.) We shall now discuss how this can come about.

The basic assumption in inflationary scenario is that the universe underwent a rapid — nearly exponential — expansion for a brief period of time in very early universe. The simplest way of realizing such a phase is to postulate the existence of a scalar field with a nearly flat potential. The dynamics of the universe, driven by a scalar field source, is described by:

$$\frac{1}{a^2}\left(\frac{da}{dt}\right)^2 = H^2(t) = \frac{1}{3M_{\text{Pl}}^2}\left[V(\phi) + \frac{1}{2}\left(\frac{d\phi}{dt}\right)^2\right]; \quad \frac{d^2\phi}{dt^2} + 3H\frac{d\phi}{dt} = -\frac{dV}{d\phi} \qquad (151)$$

where $M_{pl} = (8\pi G)^{-1/2}$. If the potential is nearly flat for certain range of ϕ, we can introduce the "slow roll-over" approximation, under which these equations become:

$$H^2 \simeq \frac{V(\phi)}{3M_{\text{Pl}}^2}; \qquad 3H\frac{d\phi}{dt} \simeq -V'(\phi) \qquad (152)$$

For this slow roll-over to last for reasonable length of time, we need to assume that the terms ignored in the Eq. (151) are indeed small. This can be quantified in terms of the parameters:

$$\varepsilon(\phi) = \frac{M_{\text{Pl}}^2}{2}\left(\frac{V'}{V}\right)^2; \qquad \eta(\phi) = M_{\text{Pl}}^2\frac{V''}{V} \qquad (153)$$

which are taken to be small. Typically the inflation ends when this assumption breaks down. If such an inflationary phase lasts up to some time t_{end} then the universe would have undergone an expansion by a factor $\exp N(t)$ during the interval (t, t_{end}) where

$$N \equiv \ln\frac{a(t_{\text{end}})}{a(t)} = \int_t^{t_{\text{end}}} H\, dt \simeq \frac{1}{M_{\text{Pl}}^2}\int_{\phi_{\text{end}}}^{\phi} \frac{V}{V'} d\phi \qquad (154)$$

One usually takes $N \simeq 65$ or so.

Before proceeding further, we would like to make couple of comments regarding such an inflationary phase. To begin with, it is not difficult to obtain *exact* solutions for $a(t)$ with rapid expansion by tailoring the potential for the scalar field. In fact, given any $a(t)$ and thus a $H(t) = (\dot{a}/a)$, one can determine a potential $V(\phi)$ for a scalar field such that Eq. (151) are satisfied (see the first reference in [27]). One can verify that, this is done by the choice:

$$V(t) = \frac{1}{16\pi G}H\left[6H + \frac{2}{H}\frac{dH}{dt}\right]; \qquad \phi(t) = \int dt \left[\frac{-2}{8\pi G}\frac{dH}{dt}\right]^{1/2} \qquad (155)$$

Given any $H(t)$, these equations give $(\phi(t), V(t))$ and thus implicitly determine the necessary $V(\phi)$. As an example, note that a power law inflation, $a(t) = a_0 t^p$ (with $p \gg 1$) is generated by:

$$V(\phi) = V_0 \exp\left(-\sqrt{\frac{2}{p}}\frac{\phi}{M_{\text{Pl}}}\right) \qquad (156)$$

while an exponential of power law

$$a(t) \propto \exp(At^f), \qquad f = \frac{\beta}{4+\beta}, \qquad 0 < f < 1, \qquad A > 0 \qquad (157)$$

can arise from

$$V(\phi) \propto \left(\frac{\phi}{M_{\text{Pl}}}\right)^{-\beta}\left(1 - \frac{\beta^2}{6}\frac{M_{\text{Pl}}^2}{\phi^2}\right) \qquad (158)$$

Thus generating a rapid expansion in the early universe is trivial if we are willing to postulate scalar fields with tailor made potentials. This is often done in the literature.

The second point to note regarding any inflationary scenarios is that the modes with reasonable size today originated from sub-Planck length scales early on. A scale λ_0 today will be

$$\lambda_{end} = \lambda_0 \frac{a_{end}}{a_0} = \lambda_0 \frac{T_0}{T_{end}} \approx \lambda_0 \times 10^{-28} \tag{159}$$

at the end of inflation (if inflation took place at GUT scales) and

$$\lambda_{begin} = \lambda_{end} A^{-1} \approx \lambda_0 \times 10^{-58} (A/10^{30})^{-1} \tag{160}$$

at the beginning of inflation if the inflation changed the scale factor by $A \simeq 10^{30}$. Note that $\lambda_{begin} < L_P$ for $\lambda_0 < 3$ Mpc!! Most structures in the universe today correspond to transplanckian scales at the start of the inflation. It is not clear whether we can trust standard physics at early stages of inflation or whether transplanckian effects will lead to observable effects [20, 21].

Let us get back to conventional wisdom and consider the evolution of perturbations in a universe which underwent exponential inflation. During the inflationary phase the $a(t)$ grows exponentially and hence the wavelength of any perturbation will also grow with it. The Hubble radius, on the other hand, will remain constant. It follows that, one can have situation in which a given mode has wavelength smaller than the Hubble radius at the beginning of the inflation but grows and becomes bigger than the Hubble radius as inflation proceeds. It is conventional to say that a perturbation of comoving wavelength λ_0 "leaves the Hubble radius" when $\lambda_0 a = d_H$ at some time $t = t_{exit}(\lambda_0)$. For $t > t_{exit}$ the wavelength of the perturbation is bigger than the Hubble radius. Eventually the inflation ends and the universe becomes radiation dominated. Then the wavelength will grow ($\propto t^{1/2}$) slower than the Hubble radius ($\propto t$) and will enter the Hubble radius again during $t = t_{enter}(\lambda_0)$. Our first task is to relate the amplitude of the perturbation at $t = t_{exit}(\lambda_0)$ with the perturbation at $t = t_{enter}(\lambda_0)$.

We know that for modes bigger than Hubble radius, we have the conserved quantity (see Eq. (97))

$$\zeta = \frac{2}{3} \frac{\rho}{\rho+p} \frac{a}{\dot{a}} \left(\dot{\Phi} + \frac{\dot{a}}{a} \Phi \right) + \Phi = \frac{H}{\rho+p} \frac{ik^\alpha}{k^2} \delta T_\alpha^0 + \Phi \tag{161}$$

At the time of re-entry, the universe is radiation dominated and $\zeta_{entry} \approx (2/3)\Phi$. On the other hand, during inflation, we can write the scalar field as a dominant homogeneous part plus a small, spatially varying fluctuation: $\phi(t,\mathbf{x}) = \phi_0(t) + f(t,\mathbf{x})$. Perturbing the equation in Eq. (151) for the scalar field, we find that the homogeneous mode ϕ_0 satisfies Eq. (151) while the perturbation, in Fourier space satisfies:

$$\frac{d^2 f_k}{dt^2} + 3H \frac{df_k}{dt} + \frac{k^2}{a^2} f_k = 0 \tag{162}$$

Further, the energy momentum tensor for the scalar field gives [with the "dot" denoting $(d/d\eta) = a(d/dt)$]:

$$\rho = \frac{\dot{\phi}_0^2}{2a^2} + V; \quad p = \frac{\dot{\phi}_0^2}{2a^2} - V; \quad \delta T_0^\alpha = \frac{ik^\alpha}{a} \dot{\phi}_0 f \tag{163}$$

It is easy to see that Φ is negligible at $t = t_{\text{exit}}$ since

$$\Phi \sim \frac{4\pi G a^2}{k^2} \sim \frac{4\pi G}{H^2} \delta\rho \sim \frac{\delta\rho}{\rho} \sim \left(\frac{\rho+p}{\rho}\right)\left(\frac{\delta\rho}{\rho+p}\right) \ll \frac{H}{(\rho+p)}\frac{\dot{\phi}_0}{a} f_k \quad (164)$$

Therefore,

$$\zeta_{\text{exit}} \approx \frac{H}{(\dot{\phi}_0^2/a^2)}\left[-\frac{\dot{\phi}_0 f_k}{a}\right] = -aH \frac{f_k}{\dot{\phi}_0} \approx \frac{3H^2}{V'} f_k \quad (165)$$

Using the conservation law $\zeta_{\text{exit}} = \zeta_{\text{entry}}$, we get

$$\Phi_k\bigg|_{\text{entry}} = \frac{9H^2}{2V'} f_k\bigg|_{\text{exit}} \quad (166)$$

Thus, given a perturbation of the scalar field f_k during inflation, we can compute its value at the time of re-entry, which — in turn — can be used to compare with observations.

Equation (166) connects a *classical* energy density perturbation f_k at the time of exit with the corresponding quantity Φ_k at the time of re-entry. The next important — and conceptually difficult — question is how we can obtain a *c-number* field f_k from a quantum scalar field. There is no simple answer to this question and one possible way of doing it is as follows: Let us start with the quantum operator for a scalar field decomposed into the Fourier modes with $\hat{q}_{\mathbf{k}}(t)$ denoting an infinite set of operators:

$$\hat{\phi}(t,\mathbf{x}) = \int \frac{d^3\mathbf{k}}{(2\pi)^3} \hat{q}_{\mathbf{k}}(t) e^{i\mathbf{k}\cdot\mathbf{x}}. \quad (167)$$

We choose a quantum state $|\psi>$ such the expectation value of $\hat{q}_{\mathbf{k}}(t)$ vanishes for all non-zero $\mathbf{k}$ so that the expectation value of $\hat{\phi}(t,\mathbf{x})$ gives the homogeneous mode that drives the inflation. The quantum fluctuation around this homogeneous part in a quantum state $|\psi>$ is given by

$$\sigma_{\mathbf{k}}^2(t) = <\psi|\hat{q}_{\mathbf{k}}^2(t)|\psi> - <\psi|\hat{q}_{\mathbf{k}}(t)|\psi>^2 = <\psi|\hat{q}_{\mathbf{k}}^2(t)|\psi> \quad (168)$$

It is easy to verify that this fluctuation is just the Fourier transform of the two-point function in this state:

$$\sigma_{\mathbf{k}}^2(t) = \int d^3\mathbf{x} <\psi|\hat{\phi}(t,\mathbf{x}+\mathbf{y})\hat{\phi}(t,\mathbf{y})|\psi> e^{i\mathbf{k}\cdot\mathbf{x}}. \quad (169)$$

Since $\sigma_{\mathbf{k}}$ characterises the quantum fluctuations, it seems reasonable to introduce a c-number field $f(t,\mathbf{x})$ by the definition:

$$f(t,\mathbf{x}) \equiv \int \frac{d^3\mathbf{k}}{(2\pi)^3} \sigma_{\mathbf{k}}(t) e^{i\mathbf{k}\cdot\mathbf{x}} \quad (170)$$

This c-number field will have same *c-number power spectrum* as the *quantum* fluctuations. Hence we may take this as our definition of an equivalent classical perturbation.

(There are more sophisticated ways of getting this result but none of them are fundamentally more sound that the elementary definition given above. There is a large literature on the subject of quantum to classical transition, especially in the context of gravity, see e.g.[22]) We now have all the ingredients in place. Given the quantum state $|\psi>$, one can explicitly compute σ_k and then — using Eq. (166) with $f_k = \sigma_k$ — obtain the density perturbations at the time of re-entry.

The next question we need to address is what is $|\psi>$. The free quantum field theory in the Friedmann background is identical to the quantum mechanics of a bunch of time dependent harmonic oscillators, each labelled by a wave vector $\mathbf{k}$. The action for a free scalar field in the Friedmann background

$$A = \frac{1}{2}\int d^4x \sqrt{-g}\,\partial_a\phi\partial^a\phi = \frac{1}{2}\int dt\,d^3x\,a^3\left[\left(\frac{\partial\phi}{\partial t}\right)^2 - \frac{1}{a^2}(\nabla\phi)^2\right]$$

$$\to \frac{1}{2}\int dt\,d^3k\,a^3\left[\left(\frac{dq_k}{dt}\right)^2 - \frac{k^2}{a^2}q_k^2\right] \quad (171)$$

can be thought of as the sum over the actions for an infinite set of harmonic oscillators with mass $m = a^3$ and frequency $\omega_k^2 = k^2/a^2$. (To be precise, one needs to treat the real and imaginary parts of the Fourier transform as independent oscillators and restrict the range of $\mathbf{k}$; just pretending that q_k is real amounts the same thing.) The quantum state of the field is just an infinite product of the quantum state $\psi_k[q_k,t]$ for each of the harmonic oscillators and satisfies the Schrodinger equation

$$i\frac{\partial \psi_k}{\partial t} = -\frac{1}{2a^3}\frac{\partial^2 \psi_k}{\partial q_k^2} + \frac{1}{2}ak^2\psi_k \quad (172)$$

If the quantum state $\psi_k[q_k,t']$ of any given oscillator, labelled by $\mathbf{k}$, is given at some initial time, t', we can evolve it to final time:

$$\psi[q_k,t] = \int dq'_k\, K[q_k,t;q'_k,t']\psi[q'_k,t'] \quad (173)$$

where K is known in terms of the solutions to the classical equations of motion and $\psi[q'_k,t']$ is the initial state. There is nothing non-trivial in the mathematics, but the physics is completely unknown. The real problem is that unfortunately — in spite of confident assertions in the literature occasionally — we have no clue what $\psi[q'_k,t']$ is. So we need to make more assumptions to proceed further.

One natural choice is the following: It turns out that, Gaussian states of the form

$$\psi_k = A_k(t)\exp[-B_k(t)q_k^2] \quad (174)$$

preserve their form under evolution governed by the Schrodinger equation in Eq. (172). Substituting Eq. (174) in Eq. (172) we can determine the ordinary differential equation which governs $B_k(t)$. (The $A_k(t)$ is trivially fixed by normalization.) Simple algebra shows that $B_k(t)$ can be expressed in the form

$$B_k = -\frac{i}{2}a^3\left(\frac{1}{f_k}\frac{df_k}{dt}\right) \quad (175)$$

where f_k is the solution to the classical equation of motion:

$$\frac{d^2 f_k}{dt^2} + 3H\frac{df_k}{dt} + \frac{k^2}{a^2}f_k = 0 \tag{176}$$

For the quantum state in Eq. (174), the fluctuations are characterized by

$$\sigma_k^2 = \frac{1}{2}(\text{Re } B_k)^{-1} = |f_k|^2 \tag{177}$$

Since one can take different choices for the solutions of Eq. (176) one get different values for σ_k and different spectra for perturbations. Any prediction one makes depends on the choice of mode functions. One possibility is to choose the modes so that ψ_k represents the instantaneous vacuum state of the oscillators at some time $t = t_i$. (That is Re $B_k(t_i) = (1/2)\omega_k^2(t_i)$, say). The final result will then depend on the choice for t_i. One can further make an assumption that we are interested in the limit of $t_i \to -\infty$; that is the quantum state is an instantaneous ground state in the infinite past. It is easy to show that this corresponds to choosing the following solution to Eq. (176):

$$f_k = \frac{1}{a\sqrt{2k}}(1+ix)e^{ix}; \qquad x = \frac{k}{Ha} \tag{178}$$

which is usually called the Bunch-Davies vacuum. For this choice,

$$|f_k|^2 = \frac{1}{2ka^2}\left(1 + \frac{k^2}{a^2 H^2}\right); \quad |f_k|^2|_{k=aH} \approx \frac{H^2}{k^3} \tag{179}$$

where the second result is at $t = t_{\text{exit}}$ which is what we need to use in Eq. (166), (Numerical factors of order unity cannot be trusted in this computation). We can now determine the amplitude of the perturbation when it re-enters the Hubble radius. Eq. (166) gives:

$$|\Phi_k|^2_{entry} = \left(\frac{9H^2}{2V'}\right)^2 |f_k|^2 = \frac{1}{k^3}\frac{9H^6}{4V'^2}; \quad k^3|\Phi_k|^2_{entry} \simeq \left(\frac{H^3}{V'}\right)^2_{\text{exit}} \tag{180}$$

One sees that the result is scale invariant in the sense that $k^3|\Phi_k|^2_{entry}$ is independent of k.

It is sometimes claimed in the literature that scale invariant spectrum is a prediction of inflation. *This is simply wrong.* One has to make several *other* assumptions including an all important choice for the quantum state (about which we know nothing) to obtain scale invariant spectrum. In fact, one can prove that, given any power spectrum $\Phi(k)$, one can find a quantum state such that this power spectrum is generated (for an explicit construction, see the last reference in [20]). So whatever results are obtained by observations can be reconciled with inflationary generation of perturbations.

To conclude the discussion, let us work out the perturbations for one specific case. Let us consider the case of the $\lambda \phi^4$ model for which

$$\frac{d^2\phi}{dt^2} + 3H\frac{d\phi}{dt} + V'(\phi) = 0; \quad V(\phi) \approx V_0 - \frac{\lambda}{4}\phi^4 \tag{181}$$

Using

$$N \cong 8\pi G \int_{\phi}^{\phi_f} \frac{V_0}{[-V']} d\phi = \frac{3H^2}{2\lambda}\left(\frac{1}{\phi^2} - \frac{1}{\phi_f^2}\right) \approx \frac{3H^2}{2\lambda\psi^2} \qquad (182)$$

we can write

$$-V'(\phi) = \lambda \phi^3 \simeq \frac{H^3}{\lambda^{1/2} N^{3/2}}. \qquad (183)$$

so that the result in Eq. (180) becomes:

$$k^{3/2}\Phi_k \simeq H^3 \frac{\lambda^{1/2} N^{3/2}}{H^3} \approx \lambda^{1/2} N^{3/2}. \qquad (184)$$

We do get scale invariant spectrum but the amplitude has a serious problem. If we take $N \gtrsim 50$ and note that observations require $k^{3/2}\Phi_k \sim 10^{-4}$ we need to take $\lambda \lesssim 10^{-15}$ for getting consistent values. Such a fine tuning of a dimensionless coupling constant is fairly ridiculous; but over years inflationists have learnt to successfully forget this embarrassment.

Our formalism can also be used to estimate the deviation of the power spectrum from the scale invariant form. To the lowest order we have

$$\Delta_\Phi^2 \sim k^3 |\Phi_k|^2 \sim \frac{H^6}{(V')^2} \sim \left(\frac{V^3}{m_P^6 V'^2}\right) \qquad (185)$$

Let us define the deviation from the scale invariant index by $(n-1) = (d \ln \Delta_\phi^2 / d \ln k)$. Using

$$\frac{d}{d \ln k} = a\frac{d}{da} = \frac{\dot\phi}{H}\frac{d}{d\phi} = -\frac{m_P^2 V'}{8\pi V}\frac{d}{d\phi} \qquad (186)$$

one finds that

$$1 - n = 6\varepsilon - 2\eta \qquad (187)$$

Thus, as long as ε and η are small we do have $n \approx 1$; what is more, given a potential one can estimate ε and η and thus the deviation $(n-1)$.

Finally, note that the same process can also generate spin-2 perturbations. If we take the normalised gravity wave amplitude as $h_{ab} = \sqrt{16\pi G} e_{ab}\phi$, the mode function ϕ behaves like a scalar field. (The normalisation is dictated by the fact that the action for the perturbation should reduce to that of a spin-2 field.) The corresponding power spectrum of gravity waves is

$$P_{\text{grav}}(k) \cong \frac{k^3 |h_k|^2}{2\pi^2} = \frac{4}{\pi}\left(\frac{H}{m_P}\right)^2, \quad \Omega_{\text{grav}}(k)h^2 \simeq 10^{-5}\left(\frac{M}{m_P}\right)^3 \qquad (188)$$

Comparing the two results

$$\Delta_{\text{scalar}}^2 \sim \frac{H^6}{(V')^2} \sim \left(\frac{V^3}{m_P^6 V'^2}\right); \quad \Delta_{\text{tensor}}^2 \sim \left(\frac{H^2}{m_P^2}\right) \sim \left(\frac{V}{m_P^4}\right) \qquad (189)$$

we get $(\Delta_{\text{tensor}}/\Delta_{\text{scalar}})^2 \approx 16\pi\varepsilon \ll 1$. Further, if $(1-n) \approx 4\varepsilon$ (see Eq. (187) with $\varepsilon \sim \eta$) we have the relation $(\Delta_{\text{tensor}}/\Delta_{\text{scalar}})^2 \approx \mathcal{O}(3)(1-n)$ which connects three quantities, all of which are independently observable in principle. If these are actually measured in future it could act as a consistency check of the inflationary paradigm.

8. THE DARK ENERGY

It is rather frustrating that the only component of the universe which we understand theoretically is the radiation! While understanding the baryonic and dark matter components [in particular the values of Ω_B and Ω_{DM}] is by no means trivial, the issue of dark energy is lot more perplexing, thereby justifying the attention it has received recently. In this section we will discuss several aspects of the dark energy problem.

The key observational feature of dark energy is that — treated as a fluid with a stress tensor $T_b^a = \text{dia}(\rho, -p, -p, -p)$ — it has an equation state $p = w\rho$ with $w \lesssim -0.8$ at the present epoch. The spatial part $\mathbf{g}$ of the geodesic acceleration (which measures the relative acceleration of two geodesics in the spacetime) satisfies an *exact* equation in general relativity given by:

$$\nabla \cdot \mathbf{g} = -4\pi G(\rho + 3p) \tag{190}$$

This shows that the source of geodesic acceleration is $(\rho + 3p)$ and not ρ. As long as $(\rho + 3p) > 0$, gravity remains attractive while $(\rho + 3p) < 0$ can lead to repulsive gravitational effects. In other words, dark energy with sufficiently negative pressure will accelerate the expansion of the universe, once it starts dominating over the normal matter. This is precisely what is established from the study of high redshift supernova, which can be used to determine the expansion rate of the universe in the past [6].

The simplest model for a fluid with negative pressure is the cosmological constant (for some recent reviews, see [23]) with $w = -1, \rho = -p = $ constant. If the dark energy is indeed a cosmological constant, then it introduces a fundamental length scale in the theory $L_\Lambda \equiv H_\Lambda^{-1}$, related to the constant dark energy density ρ_{DE} by $H_\Lambda^2 \equiv (8\pi G \rho_{\text{DE}}/3)$. In classical general relativity, based on the constants G, c and L_Λ, it is not possible to construct any dimensionless combination from these constants. But when one introduces the Planck constant, $\hbar$, it is possible to form the dimensionless combination $H_\Lambda^2(G\hbar/c^3) \equiv (L_P^2/L_\Lambda^2)$. Observations then require $(L_P^2/L_\Lambda^2) \lesssim 10^{-123}$. As has been mentioned several times in literature, this will require enormous fine tuning. What is more, in the past, the energy density of normal matter and radiation would have been higher while the energy density contributed by the cosmological constant does not change. Hence we need to adjust the energy densities of normal matter and cosmological constant in the early epoch very carefully so that $\rho_\Lambda \gtrsim \rho_{\text{NR}}$ around the current epoch. This raises the second of the two cosmological constant problems: Why is it that $(\rho_\Lambda/\rho_{\text{NR}}) = \mathcal{O}(1)$ at the *current* phase of the universe ?

Because of these conceptual problems associated with the cosmological constant, people have explored a large variety of alternative possibilities. The most popular among them uses a scalar field ϕ with a suitably chosen potential $V(\phi)$ so as to make the vacuum energy vary with time. The hope then is that, one can find a model in which the current value can be explained naturally without any fine tuning. A simple form of the source with variable w are scalar fields with Lagrangians of different forms, of which we will discuss two possibilities:

$$L_{\text{quin}} = \frac{1}{2}\partial_a\phi\partial^a\phi - V(\phi); \quad L_{\text{tach}} = -V(\phi)[1 - \partial_a\phi\partial^a\phi]^{1/2} \quad (191)$$

Both these Lagrangians involve one arbitrary function $V(\phi)$. The first one, L_{quin}, which is a natural generalization of the Lagrangian for a non-relativistic particle, $L = (1/2)\dot{q}^2 - V(q)$, is usually called quintessence (for a small sample of models, see [24]; there is an extensive and growing literature on scalar field models and more references can be found in the reviews in ref.[23]). When it acts as a source in Friedmann universe, it is characterized by a time dependent $w(t)$ with

$$\rho_q(t) = \frac{1}{2}\dot{\phi}^2 + V; \quad p_q(t) = \frac{1}{2}\dot{\phi}^2 - V; \quad w_q = \frac{1 - (2V/\dot{\phi}^2)}{1 + (2V/\dot{\phi}^2)} \quad (192)$$

The structure of the second Lagrangian (which arise in string theory [25]) in Eq. (191) can be understood by a simple analogy from special relativity. A relativistic particle with (one dimensional) position $q(t)$ and mass m is described by the Lagrangian $L = -m\sqrt{1-\dot{q}^2}$. It has the energy $E = m/\sqrt{1-\dot{q}^2}$ and momentum $k = m\dot{q}/\sqrt{1-\dot{q}^2}$ which are related by $E^2 = k^2 + m^2$. As is well known, this allows the possibility of having *massless* particles with finite energy for which $E^2 = k^2$. This is achieved by taking the limit of $m \to 0$ and $\dot{q} \to 1$, while keeping the ratio in $E = m/\sqrt{1-\dot{q}^2}$ finite. The momentum acquires a life of its own, unconnected with the velocity $\dot{q}$, and the energy is expressed in terms of the momentum (rather than in terms of $\dot{q}$) in the Hamiltonian formulation. We can now construct a field theory by upgrading $q(t)$ to a field ϕ. Relativistic invariance now requires ϕ to depend on both space and time [$\phi = \phi(t,\mathbf{x})$] and $\dot{q}^2$ to be replaced by $\partial_i\phi\partial^i\phi$. It is also possible now to treat the mass parameter m as a function of ϕ, say, $V(\phi)$ thereby obtaining a field theoretic Lagrangian $L = -V(\phi)\sqrt{1 - \partial^i\phi\partial_i\phi}$. The Hamiltonian structure of this theory is algebraically very similar to the special relativistic example we started with. In particular, the theory allows solutions in which $V \to 0$, $\partial_i\phi\partial^i\phi \to 1$ simultaneously, keeping the energy (density) finite. Such solutions will have finite momentum density (analogous to a massless particle with finite momentum k) and energy density. Since the solutions can now depend on both space and time (unlike the special relativistic example in which q depended only on time), the momentum density can be an arbitrary function of the spatial coordinate. The structure of this Lagrangian is similar to those analyzed in a wide class of models called K-essence [26] and provides a rich gamut of possibilities in the context of cosmology [27, 28].

Since the quintessence field (or the tachyonic field) has an undetermined free function $V(\phi)$, it is possible to choose this function in order to produce a given $H(a)$. To see this explicitly, let us assume that the universe has two forms of energy density with $\rho(a) = \rho_{\text{known}}(a) + \rho_\phi(a)$ where $\rho_{\text{known}}(a)$ arises from any known forms of source (matter, radiation, ...) and $\rho_\phi(a)$ is due to a scalar field. Let us first consider quintessence.

Here, the potential is given implicitly by the form [29, 27].

$$V(a) = \frac{1}{16\pi G} H(1-Q) \left[6H + 2aH' - \frac{aHQ'}{1-Q} \right];$$

$$\phi(a) = \left[\frac{1}{8\pi G} \right]^{1/2} \int \frac{da}{a} \left[aQ' - (1-Q) \frac{d\ln H^2}{d\ln a} \right]^{1/2} \quad (193)$$

where $Q(a) \equiv [8\pi G \rho_{\text{known}}(a)/3H^2(a)]$ and prime denotes differentiation with respect to a. (The result used in Eq. (155) is just a special case of this when $Q = 0$) Given any $H(a), Q(a)$, these equations determine $V(a)$ and $\phi(a)$ and thus the potential $V(\phi)$. *Every quintessence model studied in the literature can be obtained from these equations.*

Similar results exists for the tachyonic scalar field as well [27]. For example, given any $H(a)$, one can construct a tachyonic potential $V(\phi)$ so that the scalar field is the source for the cosmology. The equations determining $V(\phi)$ are now given by:

$$\phi(a) = \int \frac{da}{aH} \left(\frac{aQ'}{3(1-Q)} - \frac{2}{3} \frac{aH'}{H} \right)^{1/2}; \quad V = \frac{3H^2}{8\pi G}(1-Q)\left(1 + \frac{2}{3}\frac{aH'}{H} - \frac{aQ'}{3(1-Q)}\right)^{1/2} \quad (194)$$

Equations (194) completely solve the problem. Given any $H(a)$, these equations determine $V(a)$ and $\phi(a)$ and thus the potential $V(\phi)$. A wide variety of phenomenological models with time dependent cosmological constant have been considered in the literature all of which can be mapped to a scalar field model with a suitable $V(\phi)$.

While the scalar field models enjoy considerable popularity (one reason being they are easy to construct!) it is very doubtful whether they have helped us to understand the nature of the dark energy at any deeper level. These models, viewed objectively, suffer from several shortcomings:

- They completely lack predictive power. As explicitly demonstrated above, virtually every form of $a(t)$ can be modeled by a suitable "designer" $V(\phi)$.
- These models are degenerate in another sense. The previous discussion illustrates that even when $w(a)$ is known/specified, it is not possible to proceed further and determine the nature of the scalar field Lagrangian. The explicit examples given above show that there are *at least* two different forms of scalar field Lagrangians (corresponding to the quintessence or the tachyonic field) which could lead to the same $w(a)$. (See the second paper in ref.[7] for an explicit example of such a construction.)
- All the scalar field potentials require fine tuning of the parameters in order to be viable. This is obvious in the quintessence models in which adding a constant to the potential is the same as invoking a cosmological constant. So to make the quintessence models work, *we first need to assume the cosmological constant is zero*. These models, therefore, merely push the cosmological constant problem to another level, making it somebody else's problem!.
- By and large, the potentials used in the literature have no natural field theoretical justification. All of them are non-renormalisable in the conventional sense and have to be interpreted as a low energy effective potential in an ad hoc manner.

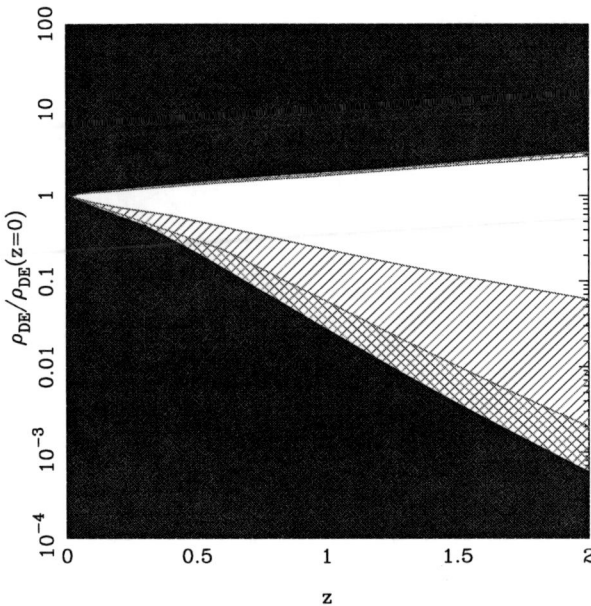

FIGURE 6. The observational constraints on the variation of dark energy density as a function of redshift from WMAP and SNLS data (see [30]). The green/hatched region is excluded at 68% confidence limit, red/cross-hatched region at 95% confidence level and the blue/solid region at 99% confidence limit. The white region shows the allowed range of variation of dark energy at 68% confidence limit.

- One key difference between cosmological constant and scalar field models is that the latter lead to a $w(a)$ which varies with time. If observations have demanded this, or even if observations have ruled out $w = -1$ at the present epoch, then one would have been forced to take alternative models seriously. However, all available observations are consistent with cosmological constant ($w = -1$) and — in fact — the possible variation of w is strongly constrained [30] as shown in Figure 6.
- While on the topic of observational constraints on $w(t)$, it must be stressed that: (a) There is fair amount of tension between WMAP and SN data and one should be very careful about the priors used in these analysis. (b) There is no observational evidence for $w < -1$. (c) It is likely that more homogeneous, future, data sets of SN might show better agreement with WMAP results. (For more details related to these issues, see the last reference in [30].)

The observational and theoretical features described above suggests that one should consider cosmological constant as the most natural candidate for dark energy. Though it leads to well know fine tuning problems, it also has certain attractive features that need to kept in mind.

- Cosmological constant is the most economical [just one number] and simplest explanation for all the observations. We stress that there is absolutely *no* evidence for variation of dark energy density with redshift, which is consistent with the

assumption of cosmological constant .
- Once we invoke the cosmological constant classical gravity will be described by the three constants G, c and $\Lambda \equiv L_\Lambda^{-2}$. It is *not* possible to obtain a dimensionless quantity from these; so, within classical theory, there is no fine tuning issue. Since $\Lambda(G\hbar/c^3) \equiv (L_P/L_\Lambda)^2 \approx 10^{-123}$, it is obvious that the cosmological constant is telling us something regarding *quantum gravity*, indicated by the combination $G\hbar$. *An acid test for any quantum gravity model will be its ability to explain this value;* needless to say, all the currently available models — strings, loops etc. — flunk this test.
- So, if dark energy is indeed cosmological constant this will be the greatest contribution from cosmology to fundamental physics. It will be unfortunate if we miss this chance by invoking some scalar field epicycles!

In this context, it is worth stressing another peculiar feature of cosmological constant when it is treated as a clue to quantum gravity. It is well known that, based on energy scales, the cosmological constant problem is an infra red problem *par excellence*. At the same time, it is a relic of a quantum gravitational effect or principle of unknown nature. An analogy [31] will be helpful to illustrate this point. Suppose one solves the Schrodinger equation for the Helium atom for the quantum states of the two electrons $\psi(x_1,x_2)$. When the result is compared with observations, one will find that only half the states — those in which $\psi(x_1,x_2)$ is antisymmetric under $x_1 \longleftrightarrow x_2$ interchange — are realized in nature. But the low energy Hamiltonian for electrons in the Helium atom has no information about this effect! Here is low energy (IR) effect which is a relic of relativistic quantum field theory (spin-statistics theorem) that is totally non perturbative, in the sense that writing corrections to the Helium atom Hamiltonian in some $(1/c)$ expansion will *not* reproduce this result. The current value of cosmological constant could very well be related to quantum gravity in a similar way. There must exist a deep principle in quantum gravity which leaves its non perturbative trace even in the low energy limit that appears as the cosmological constant .

Let us now turn our attention to few of the many attempts to understand the cosmological constant. The choice is, of course, dictated by personal bias and is definitely a non-representative sample. A host of other approaches exist in literature, some of which can be found in [32].

8.1 Gravitational Holography

One possible way of addressing this issue is to simply eliminate from the gravitational theory those modes which couple to cosmological constant. If, for example, we have a theory in which the source of gravity is $(\rho + p)$ rather than $(\rho + 3p)$ in Eq. (190), then cosmological constant will not couple to gravity at all. (The non linear coupling of matter with gravity has several subtleties; see eg. [33].) Unfortunately it is not possible to develop a covariant theory of gravity using $(\rho + p)$ as the source. But we can probably gain some insight from the following considerations. Any metric g_{ab} can be expressed in the form $g_{ab} = f^2(x) q_{ab}$ such that $\det q = 1$ so that $\det g = f^4$. From the action functional for gravity

$$A = \frac{1}{16\pi G}\int d^4x (R-2\Lambda)\sqrt{-g} = \frac{1}{16\pi G}\int d^4x R\sqrt{-g} - \frac{\Lambda}{8\pi G}\int d^4x f^4(x) \quad (195)$$

it is obvious that the cosmological constant couples *only* to the conformal factor f. So if we consider a theory of gravity in which $f^4 = \sqrt{-g}$ is kept constant and only q_{ab} is varied, then such a model will be oblivious of direct coupling to cosmological constant. If the action (without the Λ term) is varied, keeping $\det g = -1$, say, then one is lead to a *unimodular theory of gravity* that has the equations of motion $R_{ab} - (1/4)g_{ab}R = \kappa(T_{ab} - (1/4)g_{ab}T)$ with zero trace on both sides. Using the Bianchi identity, it is now easy to show that this is equivalent to the usual theory with an *arbitrary* cosmological constant. That is, cosmological constant arises as an undetermined integration constant in this model [34].

The same result arises in another, completely different approach to gravity. In the standard approach to gravity one uses the Einstein-Hilbert Lagrangian $L_{EH} \propto R$ which has a formal structure $L_{EH} \sim R \sim (\partial g)^2 + \partial^2 g$. If the surface term obtained by integrating $L_{sur} \propto \partial^2 g$ is ignored (or, more formally, canceled by an extrinsic curvature term) then the Einstein's equations arise from the variation of the bulk term $L_{bulk} \propto (\partial g)^2$ which is the non-covariant Γ^2 Lagrangian. There is, however, a remarkable relation between L_{bulk} and L_{sur}:

$$\sqrt{-g}L_{sur} = -\partial_a\left(g_{ij}\frac{\partial\sqrt{-g}L_{bulk}}{\partial(\partial_a g_{ij})}\right) \quad (196)$$

which allows a dual description of gravity using either L_{bulk} or L_{sur}! It is possible to obtain the dynamics of gravity [35] from an approach which uses *only* the surface term of the Hilbert action; *we do not need the bulk term at all!*. This suggests that *the true degrees of freedom of gravity for a volume $\mathcal{V}$ reside in its boundary $\partial\mathcal{V}$* — a point of view that is strongly supported by the study of horizon entropy, which shows that the degrees of freedom hidden by a horizon scales as the area and not as the volume. The resulting equations can be cast in a thermodynamic form $TdS = dE + PdV$ and the continuum spacetime is like an elastic solid (see e.g. [36]) with Einstein's equations providing the macroscopic description. Interestingly, the *cosmological constant arises again in this approach as a undetermined integration constant* but closely related to the 'bulk expansion' of the solid.

While this is all very interesting, we still need an extra physical principle to fix the value (even the sign) of cosmological constant. One possible way of doing this is to interpret the Λ term in the action as a Lagrange multiplier for the proper volume of the spacetime. Then it is reasonable to choose the cosmological constant such that the total proper volume of the universe is equal to a specified number. While this will lead to a cosmological constant which has the correct order of magnitude, it has several obvious problems. First, the proper four volume of the universe is infinite unless we make the spatial sections compact and restrict the range of time integration. Second, this will lead to a dark energy density which varies as t^{-2} (corresponding to $w = -1/3$) which is ruled out by observations.

8.2 Cosmic Lenz law

Another possibility which has been attempted in the literature tries to "cancel out" the cosmological constant by some process, usually quantum mechanical in origin. One of the simplest ideas will be to ask whether switching on a cosmological constant will lead to a vacuum polarization with an effective energy momentum tensor that will tend to cancel out the cosmological constant. A less subtle way of doing this is to invoke another scalar field (here we go again!) such that it can couple to cosmological constant and reduce its effective value [37]. Unfortunately, none of this could be made to work properly. By and large, these approaches lead to an energy density which is either $\rho_{UV} \propto L_P^{-4}$ (where L_P is the Planck length) or to $\rho_{IR} \propto L_\Lambda^{-4}$ (where $L_\Lambda = H_\Lambda^{-1}$ is the Hubble radius associated with the cosmological constant). The first one is too large while the second one is too small!

8.3 Geometrical Duality in our Universe

While the above ideas do not work, it gives us a clue. A universe with two length scales L_Λ and L_P will be asymptotically De Sitter with $a(t) \propto \exp(t/L_\Lambda)$ at late times. There are some curious features in such a universe which we will now describe. Given the two length scales L_P and L_Λ, one can construct two energy scales $\rho_{UV} = 1/L_P^4$ and $\rho_{IR} = 1/L_\Lambda^4$ in natural units ($c = \hbar = 1$). There is sufficient amount of justification from different theoretical perspectives to treat L_P as the zero point length of spacetime [38], giving a natural interpretation to ρ_{UV}. The second one, ρ_{IR} also has a natural interpretation. The universe which is asymptotically De Sitter has a horizon and associated thermodynamics [39] with a temperature $T = H_\Lambda/2\pi$ and the corresponding thermal energy density $\rho_{thermal} \propto T^4 \propto 1/L_\Lambda^4 = \rho_{IR}$. Thus L_P determines the *highest* possible energy density in the universe while L_Λ determines the *lowest* possible energy density in this universe. As the energy density of normal matter drops below this value, the thermal ambience of the De Sitter phase will remain constant and provide the irreducible 'vacuum noise'. Note that the dark energy density is the the geometric mean $\rho_{DE} = \sqrt{\rho_{IR}\rho_{UV}}$ between the two energy densities. If we define a dark energy length scale L_{DE} such that $\rho_{DE} = 1/L_{DE}^4$ then $L_{DE} = \sqrt{L_P L_\Lambda}$ is the geometric mean of the two length scales in the universe. (Incidentally, $L_{DE} \approx 0.04$ mm is macroscopic; it is also pretty close to the length scale associated with a neutrino mass of 10^{-2} eV; another intriguing coincidence ?!)

Using the characteristic length scale of expansion, the Hubble radius $d_H \equiv (\dot{a}/a)^{-1}$, we can distinguish between three different phases of such a universe. The first phase is when the universe went through a inflationary expansion with $d_H =$ constant; the second phase is the radiation/matter dominated phase in which most of the standard cosmology operates and d_H increases monotonically; the third phase is that of re-inflation (or accelerated expansion) governed by the cosmological constant in which d_H is again a constant. The first and last phases are time translation invariant; that is, $t \to t+$ constant is an (approximate) invariance for the universe in these two phases. The universe satisfies the perfect cosmological principle and is in steady state during these phases!

In fact, one can easily imagine a scenario in which the two De Sitter phases (first and last) are of arbitrarily long duration [40]. If $\Omega_\Lambda \approx 0.7, \Omega_{DM} \approx 0.3$ the final De Sitter phase *does* last forever; as regards the inflationary phase, nothing prevents it from lasting for arbitrarily long duration. Viewed from this perspective, the in between phase — in which most of the 'interesting' cosmological phenomena occur — is of negligible measure in the span of time. It merely connects two steady state phases of the universe.

While the two De Sitter phases can last forever in principle, there is a natural cut off length scale in both of them which makes the region of physical relevance to be finite [40]. Let us first discuss the case of re-inflation in the late universe. As the universe grows exponentially in the phase 3, the wavelength of CMBR photons are being redshifted rapidly. When the temperature of the CMBR radiation drops below the De Sitter temperature (which happens when the wavelength of the typical CMBR photon is stretched to the L_Λ.) the universe will be essentially dominated by the vacuum thermal noise [39] due to the horizon in the De Sitter phase. This happens when the expansion factor is $a = a_F$ determined by the equation $T_0(a_0/a_F) = (1/2\pi L_\Lambda)$. Let $a = a_\Lambda$ be the epoch at which cosmological constant started dominating over matter, so that $(a_\Lambda/a_0)^3 = (\Omega_{DM}/\Omega_\Lambda)$. Then we find that the dynamic range of the phase 3 is

$$\frac{a_F}{a_\Lambda} = 2\pi T_0 L_\Lambda \left(\frac{\Omega_\Lambda}{\Omega_{DM}}\right)^{1/3} \approx 3 \times 10^{30} \quad (197)$$

Interestingly enough, one can also impose a similar bound on the physically relevant duration of inflation. We know that the quantum fluctuations, generated during this inflationary phase, could act as seeds of structure formation in the universe. Consider a perturbation at some given wavelength scale which is stretched with the expansion of the universe as $\lambda \propto a(t)$. During the inflationary phase, the Hubble radius remains constant while the wavelength increases, so that the perturbation will 'exit' the Hubble radius at some time. In the radiation dominated phase, the Hubble radius $d_H \propto t \propto a^2$ grows faster than the wavelength $\lambda \propto a(t)$. Hence, normally, the perturbation will 're-enter' the Hubble radius at some time. If there was no re-inflation, *all* wavelengths will re-enter the Hubble radius sooner or later. But if the universe undergoes re-inflation, then the Hubble radius 'flattens out' at late times and some of the perturbations will *never* reenter the Hubble radius ! If we use the criterion that we need the perturbation to reenter the Hubble radius, we get a natural bound on the duration of inflation which is of direct astrophysical relevance. Consider a perturbation which leaves the Hubble radius (H_{in}^{-1}) during the inflationary epoch at $a = a_i$. It will grow to the size $H_{in}^{-1}(a/a_i)$ at a later epoch. We want to determine a_i such that this length scale grows to L_Λ just when the dark energy starts dominating over matter; that is at the epoch $a = a_\Lambda = a_0(\Omega_{DM}/\Omega_\Lambda)^{1/3}$. This gives $H_{in}^{-1}(a_\Lambda/a_i) = L_\Lambda$ so that $a_i = (H_{in}^{-1}/L_\Lambda)(\Omega_{DM}/\Omega_\Lambda)^{1/3}a_0$. On the other hand, the inflation ends at $a = a_{end}$ where $a_{end}/a_0 = T_0/T_{reheat}$ where T_{reheat} is the temperature to which the universe has been reheated at the end of inflation. Using these two results we can determine the dynamic range of this phase 1 to be

$$\frac{a_{end}}{a_i} = \left(\frac{T_0 L_\Lambda}{T_{reheat} H_{in}^{-1}}\right)\left(\frac{\Omega_\Lambda}{\Omega_{DM}}\right)^{1/3} = \frac{(a_F/a_\Lambda)}{2\pi T_{reheat} H_{in}^{-1}} \cong 10^{25} \quad (198)$$

where we have used the fact that, for a GUTs scale inflation with $E_{GUT} = 10^{14} GeV$, $T_{reheat} = E_{GUT}$, $\rho_{in} = E_{GUT}^4$ we have $2\pi H_{in}^{-1} T_{reheat} = (3\pi/2)^{1/2}(E_P/E_{GUT}) \approx 10^5$. If we consider a quantum gravitational, Planck scale, inflation with $2\pi H_{in}^{-1} T_{reheat} = \mathcal{O}(1)$, the ranges in Eq. (197) and Eq. (198) are approximately equal.

This fact is definitely telling us something regarding the duality between Planck scale and Hubble scale or between the infrared and ultraviolet limits of the theory. The mystery is compounded by the fact the asymptotic De Sitter phase has an observer dependent horizon and related thermal properties [39]. Recently, it has been shown — in a series of papers, see ref.[35] — that it is possible to obtain classical relativity from purely thermodynamic considerations. It is difficult to imagine that these features are unconnected and accidental; at the same time, it is difficult to prove a definite connection between these ideas and the cosmological constant.

8.4 Gravity as detector of the vacuum energy

Finally, we will describe an idea which *does* lead to the correct value of cosmological constant. The conventional discussion of the relation between cosmological constant and vacuum energy density is based on evaluating the zero point energy of quantum fields with an ultraviolet cutoff and using the result as a source of gravity. Any reasonable cutoff will lead to a vacuum energy density ρ_{vac} which is unacceptably high. This argument, however, is too simplistic since the zero point energy — obtained by summing over the $(1/2)\hbar\omega_k$ — has no observable consequence in any other phenomena and can be subtracted out by redefining the Hamiltonian. The observed non trivial features of the vacuum state of QED, for example, arise from the *fluctuations* (or modifications) of this vacuum energy rather than the vacuum energy itself. This was, in fact, known fairly early in the history of cosmological constant problem and is stressed by Zeldovich [41] who explicitly calculated one possible contribution to *fluctuations* after subtracting away the mean value. This suggests that we should consider the fluctuations in the vacuum energy density in addressing the cosmological constant problem.

If the vacuum probed by the gravity can readjust to take away the bulk energy density $\rho_{UV} \simeq L_P^{-4}$, quantum *fluctuations* can generate the observed value ρ_{DE}. One of the simplest models [42] which achieves this uses the fact that, in the semi-classical limit, the wave function describing the universe of proper four-volume $\mathcal{V}$ will vary as $\Psi \propto \exp(-iA_0) \propto \exp[-i(\Lambda_{eff}\mathcal{V}/L_P^2)]$. If we treat $(\Lambda/L_P^2, \mathcal{V})$ as conjugate variables then uncertainty principle suggests $\Delta\Lambda \approx L_P^2/\Delta\mathcal{V}$. If the four volume is built out of Planck scale substructures, giving $\mathcal{V} = NL_P^4$, then the Poisson fluctuations will lead to $\Delta\mathcal{V} \approx \sqrt{\mathcal{V}}L_P^2$ giving $\Delta\Lambda = L_P^2/\Delta\mathcal{V} \approx 1/\sqrt{\mathcal{V}} \approx H_0^2$. (This idea can be a more quantitative; see [42]).

Similar viewpoint arises, more rigorously, when we study the question of *detecting* the energy density using gravitational field as a probe. Recall that an Unruh-DeWitt detector with a local coupling $L_I = M(\tau)\phi[x(\tau)]$ to the *field* ϕ actually responds to $\langle 0|\phi(x)\phi(y)|0\rangle$ rather than to the field itself [43]. Similarly, one can use the gravitational field as a natural "detector" of energy momentum tensor T_{ab} with the standard coupling $L = \kappa h_{ab}T^{ab}$. Such a model was analysed in detail in ref. [44] and it was shown that the gravitational field responds to the two point function $\langle 0|T_{ab}(x)T_{cd}(y)|0\rangle$. In fact, it is essentially this fluctuations in the energy density which is computed in the inflationary models (see Eq. (170)) as the seed *source* for gravitational field, as stressed in ref [11]. All these suggest treating the energy fluctuations as the physical quantity "detected" by gravity, when one needs to incorporate quantum effects. If the cosmological constant arises due to the energy density of the vacuum, then one needs to understand the structure of the quantum vacuum at cosmological scales. Quantum theory, especially the paradigm of renormalization group has taught us that the energy density — and even the concept of the vacuum state — depends on the scale at which it is probed. The vacuum state which we use to study the lattice vibrations in a solid, say, is not the same as vacuum state of the QED.

In fact, it seems *inevitable* that in a universe with two length scale L_Λ, L_P, the vacuum fluctuations will contribute an energy density of the correct order of magnitude $\rho_{DE} = \sqrt{\rho_{IR}\rho_{UV}}$. The hierarchy of energy scales in such a universe, as detected by the gravitational field has [40, 45] the pattern

$$\rho_{\rm vac} = \frac{1}{L_P^4} + \frac{1}{L_P^4}\left(\frac{L_P}{L_\Lambda}\right)^2 + \frac{1}{L_P^4}\left(\frac{L_P}{L_\Lambda}\right)^4 + \cdots \qquad (199)$$

The first term is the bulk energy density which needs to be renormalized away (by a process which we do not understand at present); the third term is just the thermal energy density of the De Sitter vacuum state; what is interesting is that quantum fluctuations in the matter fields *inevitably generate* the second term.

The key new ingredient arises from the fact that the properties of the vacuum state depends on the scale at which it is probed and it is not appropriate to ask questions without specifying this scale. If the spacetime has a cosmological horizon which blocks information, the natural scale is provided by the size of the horizon, L_Λ, and we should use observables defined within the accessible region. The operator $H(<L_\Lambda)$, corresponding to the total energy inside a region bounded by a cosmological horizon, will exhibit fluctuations ΔE since vacuum state is not an eigenstate of *this* operator. The corresponding fluctuations in the energy density, $\Delta\rho \propto (\Delta E)/L_\Lambda^3 = f(L_P, L_\Lambda)$ will now depend on both the ultraviolet cutoff L_P as well as L_Λ. To obtain $\Delta\rho_{\rm vac} \propto \Delta E/L_\Lambda^3$ which scales as $(L_P L_\Lambda)^{-2}$ we need to have $(\Delta E)^2 \propto L_P^{-4}L_\Lambda^2$; that is, the square of the energy fluctuations should scale as the surface area of the bounding surface which is provided by the cosmic horizon. Remarkably enough, a rigorous calculation [45] of the dispersion in the energy shows that for $L_\Lambda \gg L_P$, the final result indeed has the scaling

$$(\Delta E)^2 = c_1 \frac{L_\Lambda^2}{L_P^4} \qquad (200)$$

where the constant c_1 depends on the manner in which ultra violet cutoff is imposed. Similar calculations have been done (with a completely different motivation, in the context of entanglement entropy) by several people and it is known that the area scaling found in Eq. (200), proportional to L_Λ^2, is a generic feature [46]. For a simple exponential UV-cutoff, $c_1 = (1/30\pi^2)$ but cannot be computed reliably without knowing the full theory. We thus find that the fluctuations in the energy density of the vacuum in a sphere of radius L_Λ is given by

$$\Delta\rho_{\text{vac}} = \frac{\Delta E}{L_\Lambda^3} \propto L_P^{-2} L_\Lambda^{-2} \propto \frac{H_\Lambda^2}{G} \tag{201}$$

The numerical coefficient will depend on c_1 as well as the precise nature of infrared cutoff radius (like whether it is L_Λ or $L_\Lambda/2\pi$ etc.). It would be pretentious to cook up the factors to obtain the observed value for dark energy density. But it is a fact of life that a fluctuation of magnitude $\Delta\rho_{vac} \simeq H_\Lambda^2/G$ will exist in the energy density inside a sphere of radius H_Λ^{-1} if Planck length is the UV cut off. *One cannot get away from it.* On the other hand, observations suggest that there is a ρ_{vac} of similar magnitude in the universe. It seems natural to identify the two, after subtracting out the mean value by hand. Our approach explains why there is a *surviving* cosmological constant which satisfies $\rho_{\text{DE}} = \sqrt{\rho_{\text{IR}}\rho_{\text{UV}}}$ which — in our opinion — is *the* problem.

ACKNOWLEDGEMENT

I thank J. Alcaniz for his friendship and warm hospitality during the X Special Courses at Observatorio Nacional, Rio de Janeiro, Brazil and for persuading me to write up my lecture notes. I am grateful to Gaurang Mahajan for help in generating the figures.

REFERENCES

1. P. de Bernardis et al., *Nature* **404**, 955 (2000); A. Balbi et al., *Ap.J.* **545**, L1 (2000); S. Hanany et al., *Ap.J.* **545**, L5 (2000); T.J. Pearson et al., *Ap.J.* **591**, 556 (2003); C.L. Bennett et al, *Ap. J. Suppl.* **148**, 1 (2003); D. N. Spergel et al., *Ap.J.Suppl.* **148**, 175 (2003); B. S. Mason et al., *Ap.J.* **591**, 540 (2003). For a summary, see e.g., L. A. Page, astro-ph/0402547.
2. For a review of Big Bang Nucleosynthesis (BBN), see S.Sarkar, *Rept.Prog.Phys.*, **59**, 1493 (1996); G.Steigman, astro-ph/0501591. The consistency between CMBR observations and BBN is gratifying since the initial MAXIMA-BOOMERANG data gave too high a value as stressed by T. Padmanabhan and Shiv Sethi, *Ap. J.* **555**, 125 (2001), [astro-ph/0010309].
3. W. Freedman et al., *Ap.J.* **553**, 47 (2001); J.R. Mould et al.,*Ap.J.* **529**, 786 (2000).
4. For a discussion of the evidence, see P.J.E. Peebles, astro-ph/0410284.
5. G. Efstathiou et al., *Nature* **348**, 705 (1990); J. P. Ostriker, P. J. Steinhardt, *Nature* **377**, 600 (1995); J. S. Bagla et al., *Comments on Astrophysics* **18**, 275 (1996), [astro-ph/9511102].
6. S.J. Perlmutter et al., *Astrophys. J.* **517**, 565 (1999); A.G. Reiss et al., *Astron. J.* **116**, 1009 (1998); J. L. Tonry et al., *ApJ* **594**, 1 (2003); B. J. Barris,*Astrophys.J.* **602**, 571 (2004); A. G.Reiss et al., *Astrophys.J.* **607**, 665(2004).
7. T. Roy Choudhury, T. Padmanabhan, *Astron.Astrophys.* **429**, 807 (2005), [astro-ph/0311622]; T. Padmanabhan,T. Roy Choudhury, *MNRAS* **344**, 823 (2003) [astro-ph/0212573]. H.K.Jassal et al., *Phys.Rev.* **D 72**, 103503 (2005) [astro-ph/0506748].
8. T. Padmanabhan, *Structure Formation in the Universe*, (Cambridge University Press, Cambridge, 1993); T. Padmanabhan, *Theoretical Astrophysics, Volume III: Galaxies and Cosmology*, (Cambridge University Press, Cambridge, 2002); J.A. Peacock, *Cosmological Physics*, (Cambridge University Press, Cambridge, 1999); S. Dodelson, *Modern Cosmology*, (Academic Press, 2003); J. Bernstein, *Kinetic Theory in the Expanding Universe* (Cambridge University Press, Cambridge, 1988).
9. D. Kazanas, *Ap. J. Letts.* **241**, 59 (1980); A. A. Starobinsky, *JETP Lett.* **30**, 682 (1979); *Phys. Lett.* **B 91**, 99 (1980); A. H. Guth, *Phys. Rev.* **D 23**, 347 (1981); A. D. Linde, *Phys. Lett.* **B 108**, 389 (1982); A. Albrecht, P. J. Steinhardt, *Phys. Rev. Lett.* **48**, 1220 (1982); for a review, see e.g.,J. V. Narlikar and T. Padmanabhan, *Ann. Rev. Astron. Astrophys.* **29**, 325 (1991).

10. S. W. Hawking, *Phys. Lett.* **B 115**, 295 (1982); A. A. Starobinsky, *Phys. Lett.* **B 117**, 175 (1982); A. H. Guth, S.-Y. Pi, *Phys. Rev. Lett.* **49**, 1110 (1982); J. M. Bardeen et al., *Phys. Rev.* **D 28**, 679 (1983); L. F. Abbott, M. B. Wise, *Nucl. Phys.* **B 244**, 541 (1984).
11. T. Padmanabhan, *Phys. Rev. Letts.*, (1988), **60**, 2229; T. Padmanabhan, T.R. Seshadri and T.P. Singh, *Phys.Rev* **D 39**, 2100 (1989).
12. G.F. Smoot. et al., *Ap.J.* **396**, L1 (1992); T. Padmanabhan, D. Narasimha, *MNRAS* **259**, 41P (1992); G. Efstathiou et al., *MNRAS*, **258**, 1 (1992).
13. For a review, see T.Padmanabhan, *Phys. Rept.* **188**, 285 (1990); *Astrophys. Jour. Supp.*, **71**, 651 (1989); astro-ph/0206131.
14. Ya.B. Zeldovich, *Astron.Astrophys.* **5**, 84 (1970); Gurbatov, S. N. et al, *MNRAS* **236**, 385 (1989); T.G. Brainerd et al., *Astrophys.J.* **418**, 570 (1993); J.S. Bagla, T.Padmanabhan, *MNRAS* **266**, 227 (1994), [gr-qc/9304021]; *MNRAS*, **286**, 1023 (1997), [astro-ph/9605202]; T.Padmanabhan, S.Engineer, *Ap. J.* **493**, 509 (1998), [astro-ph/9704224]; S. Engineer et.al., *MNRAS* **314**, 279 (2000), [astro-ph/9812452]; for a recent review, see T.Tatekawa, [astro-ph/0412025].
15. A. J. S. Hamilton et al., *Ap. J.* **374**, L1 (1991); R. Nityananda, T. Padmanabhan, *MNRAS* **271**, 976 (1994), [gr-qc/9304022]; T. Padmanabhan, *MNRAS* **278**, L29 (1996), [astro-ph/9508124]. T.Padmanabhan et al., *Ap. J.* **466**, 604 (1996), [astro-ph/9506051]; D. Munshi et al., *MNRAS*, **290**, 193 (1997), [astro-ph/9606170]; J. S. Bagla, et.al., *Ap.J.* **495**, 25 (1998), [astro-ph/9707330]; N.Kanekar et al., *MNRAS*, **324**, 988 (2001), [astro-ph/0101562].
16. For a pedagogical description, see J.S. Bagla, astro-ph/0411043; J.S. Bagla, T. Padmanabhan, *Pramana* **49**, 161-192 (1997), [astro-ph/0411730].
17. There is extensive literature on linear perturbation theory as well as generation of perturbations from inflation. I am not giving original references while discussing these topics. In addition to the textbooks mentioned in [8], the following review articles will be useful: V.F. Mukhanov et al., *Physics Reports* **215**, 203 (1992); D. H. Lyth and A. Riotto, *Physics Reports* **314**, 1 (1999); A. R. Liddle and D. H. Lyth, *Physics Reports* **231**, 1 (1993); H. Kodama and M. Sasaki, *Prog. Theor. Phys. Suppl.* **78**, 1 (1984).
18. E.R. Harrison, *Phys. Rev.* **D1**, 2726 (1970); Zeldovich Ya B. *MNRAS* **160**, 1p (1972).
19. J. Hwang et al., *Phys. Rev.* **D65**, 043005 (2002) [astro-ph/0107307].
20. One of the earliest attempts to include transplanckian effects in inflation is in [11]. A sample of more recent papers are J.Martin, R.H. Brandenberger, *Phys.Rev.* **D 63**, 123501 (2001); A. Kempf, *Phys.Rev.* **D 63**, 083514 (2001); U.H. Danielsson, *Phys.Rev.* **D 66**, 023511 (2002); A. Ashoorioon et al., *Phys.Rev.* **D 71** 023503 (2005); R. Easther, astro-ph/0412613; for a more extensive set of references, see L. Sriramkumar et al., *Phys. Rev.*, **D 71**, 103512 (2005) [gr-qc/0408034].
21. S. Corley, T. Jacobson, *Phys.Rev.* **D 54**, 1568 (1996); T. Padmanabhan, *Phys.Rev.Lett.* **81**, 4297 (1998), [hep-th/9801015]; *Phys.Rev.* **D 59** 124012 (1999), [hep-th/9801138]; A.A. Starobinsky, *JETP Lett.* **73** 371-374 (2001); J.C. Niemeyer, R. Parentani, *Phys.Rev.* **D 64** 101301 (2001); J. Kowalski-Glikman, *Phys.Lett.* **B 499** 1 (2001); G.Amelino-Camelia, *Int.J.Mod.Phys.* **D 11** 35 (2002).
22. V.G. Lapchinsky, V.A. Rubakov, *Acta Phys.Polon.* **B 10**, 1041 (1979); J. B. Hartle, *Phys. Rev.* **D 37**, 2818 (1988); **D 38**, 2985 (1988); T.Padmanabhan, *Class. Quan. Grav.* **6**, 533 (1989); T.P. Singh, T. Padmanabhan, *Annals Phys.* **196**, 296(1989). T. Padmanabhan, *Phys.Rev.* **D 39**, 2924 (1989); T.Padmanabhan and T.P. Singh, Class. Quan. Grav.. **7**, 441 (1990); J.J. Hallwell, *Phys.Rev.* **D 39**, 2912 (1989).
23. L. Perivolaropoulos, astro-ph/0601014; S. Hannestad, astro-ph/0509320; P. J. E. Peebles and B. Ratra, *Rev. Mod. Phys.* **75**, 559 (2003); T. Padmanabhan, *Phys. Rept.* **380**, 235 (2003) [hep-th/0212290]; *Current Science*, **88**,1057, (2005) [astro-ph/0411044]; gr-qc/0503107; J. R. Ellis, *Phil. Trans. Roy. Soc. Lond.* **A 361**, 2607 (2003).
24. A small sample of papers covering varied aspects are: S. Nojiri, S.D. Odintsov. hep-th/0601213; Mian Wang. hep-th/0601189; Hao Wei et al., *Phys.Rev.* **D 72**, 123507 (2005); S. Capozziello, astro-ph/0508350; D. Polarski, A. Ranquet, *Phys.Lett.* **B 627**, 1 (2005); A. A. Andrianov et al., *Phys.Rev.* **D 72**, 043531 (2005); H.Stefancic, astro-ph/0504518; Martin Sahlen et al., astro-ph/0506696; Zhuo-Yi Huang et al., astro-ph/0511745; Z. K. Guo, N. Ohta and Y. Z. Zhang, astro-ph/0505253; Shin'ichi Nojiri, S. D. Odintsov, hep-th/0506212; hep-th/0408170; W. Godlowski et al.,astro-ph/0309569; V. F. Cardone et al., Phys.Rev. **D69**, (2004), 083517; I.P. Neupane, *Class.Quant.Grav.* **21**, 4383 (2004); M.C. Bento et al.,, astro-ph/0407239; A. DeBenedictis et al., gr-qc/0402047; M.

Axenides and K.Dimopoulos, hep-ph/0401238; M. D. Maia et al., astro-ph/0403072; J. A. S. Lima, J. S. Alcaniz, *Phys.Lett.* **B 600** 191 (2004); J. S. Alcaniz, astro-ph/0312424; Xin-Zhou Li et al., *Int.J.Mod.Phys.* **A18**, 5921 (2003); P. J. Steinhardt, *Phil. Trans. Roy. Soc. Lond.* **A 361**, 2497 (2003); S. Sen and T. R. Seshadri, *Int. J. Mod. Phys.* **D 12**, 445 (2003); C. Rubano and P. Scudellaro, *Gen. Rel. Grav.* **34**, 307 (2002); S. A. Bludman and M. Roos, *Phys. Rev.* **D 65**, 043503 (2002); R. de Ritis and A. A. Marino, *Phys. Rev.* **D 64**, 083509 (2001); A. de la Macorra and G. Piccinelli, *Phys. Rev.* **D 61**, 123503 (2000); L. A. Urena-Lopez and T. Matos, *Phys. Rev.* **D 62**, 081302 (2000); P. F. Gonzalez-Diaz, *Phys. Rev.* **D 62**, 023513 (2000); *Phys. Lett.* B **562**, 1 (2003); T. Barreiro, E. J. Copeland and N. J. Nunes, *Phys. Rev.* **D 61**, 127301 (2000). B. Ratra, P.J.E. Peebles, *Phys.Rev.* **D 37**, 3406 (1988).

25. A. Sen, *JHEP* **0204** 048 (2002), [hep-th/0203211].
26. A small sample of papers are Hui Li et al., astro-ph/0601007; L. P. Chimento and A. Feinstein, *Mod. Phys. Lett.* **A 19**, 761 (2004); R. J. Scherrer, *Phys. Rev. Lett.* 93) 011301 (2004; P. F. Gonzalez-Diaz,hep-th/0408225; L. P. Chimento, *Phys.Rev.* **D69**, 123517, (2004); O.Bertolami, astro-ph/0403310; R.Lazkoz, gr-qc/0410019; J.S. Alcaniz, J.A.S. Lima, astro-ph/0308465; M. Malquarti et al., *Phys. Rev.* **D 67**, 123503 (2003); T. Chiba, *Phys. Rev.* **D 66**, 063514 (2002); C. Armendariz-Picon et al., *Phys. Rev.* **D 63**, 103510 (2001).
27. T. Padmanabhan, *Phys. Rev.* **D 66**, 021301 (2002), [hep-th/0204150]; T. Padmanabhan and T. R. Choudhury, *Phys. Rev.* **D 66**, 081301 (2002) [hep-th/0205055]; J. S. Bagla, et al., *Phys. Rev.* **D 67**, 063504 (2003) [astro-ph/0212198].
28. For a varied sample, see H. Singh, hep-th/0505012; hep-th/0508101; Anupam Das et al., *Phys.Rev.* **D 72**, 043528 (2005); I.Ya. Aref'eva et al., astro-ph/0505605; astro-ph/0410443; J. M. Aguirregabiria and R. Lazkoz, hep-th/0402190; C. Kim et al., hep-th/0404242; R. Herrera et al.,astro-ph/0404086; A. Ghodsi and A.E.Mosaffa,hep-th/0408015; D.J. Liu and X.Z.Li, astro-ph/0402063; V. Gorini et al., *Phys.Rev.* **D 69** 123512 (2004); M. Sami et al., *Pramana* **62**, 765 (2004); D.A. Steer, *Phys.Rev.* **D70**, 043527 (2004); L.Raul W. Abramo, Fabio Finelli, *Phys.Lett.* **B 575**, 165 (2003); L. Frederic, A. W. Peet, *JHEP* **0304**, 048 (2003); M. Sami, *Mod.Phys.Lett.* **A 18**, 691 (2003); G. W. Gibbons, *Class. Quant Grav.* **20**, S321 (2003); C. J. Kim et al., *Phys. Lett.* **B 552**, 111 (2003); G. Shiu and I. Wasserman, *Phys. Lett.* **B 541**, 6 (2002); D. Choudhury et al., *Phys. Lett.* **B 544**, 231 (2002); A. V. Frolov, et al., *Phys. Lett.* **B 545**, 8 (2002); G. W. Gibbons, *Phys. Lett.* **B 537**, 1 (2002).
29. G.F.R. Ellis and M.S.Madsen, *Class.Quan.Grav.* **8**, 667 (1991).
30. H.K. Jassal et al., *MNRAS* **356**, L11-L16 (2005), [astro-ph/0404378]; [astro-ph/0601389].
31. T. Padmanabhan and T. Roy Choudhury, *Mod. Phys. Lett.* **A 15**, 1813 (2000), [gr-qc/0006018].
32. There is extensive literature on different paradigms for solving the cosmological constant problem, like e.g., those based on QFT in CST: E. Mottola, *Phys.Rev.* **D 31**, 754 (1985); N.C. Tsamis,R.P. Woodard, *Phys.Lett.* **B301**, 351 (1993); E. Elizalde and S.D. Odintsov, *Phys.Lett.* **B 321** 199 (1994); **B 333** 331 (1994); J.V. Lindesay, H.P. Noyes, astro-ph/0508450; Shi Qi, hep-th/0505109. Non-ideal fluids mimicking cosmological constant, like e.g., E. Baum, *Phys. Letts.* **B 133**, 185 (1983); T. Padmanabhan, *Phys. Letts.*, **A104**, 196 (1984); S.W. Hawking, *Phys. Letts.* **B 134**, 403 (1984); T.Padmanabhan and S.M. Chitre, *Phys. Letts.* **A 120**, 433 (1987); S. Coleman, *Nucl. Phys.* **B 310** 643 (1988); Quantum cosmological considerations: T. Mongan, *Gen. Rel. Grav.*, **33** 1415 (2001) [gr-qc/0103021]; *Gen.Rel.Grav.* **35** 685 (2003). Holographic dark energy: Yungui Gong, Yuan-Zhong Zhang, hep-th/0505175; astro-ph/0502262; hep-th/0412218; Xin Zhang, Feng-Quan Wu, astro-ph/0506310; M.G.Hu, Xin-He Meng, astro-ph/0511615. Those based on renormalization group, running coupling constants and more general time dependent decay schemes: I.L. Shapiro, *Phys.Lett.* **B 329**, 181 (1994); I.L. Shapiro and J. Sola, *Phys.Lett.* **B475**, 236 (2000); hep-ph/0305279; astro-ph/0401015; I.L. Shapiro et al., hep-ph/0410095; Cristina Espana-Bonet, et.al., *Phys.Lett.* **B 574** 149 (2003); *JCAP* **0402**, 006 (2004); F.Bauer, gr-qc/0501078; gr-qc/0512007; I. L. Shapiro, J. Sola, *JHEP*, **0202** 006 (2002), hep-ph/0012227; J.Sola and H.Stefancic, astro-ph/0505133; astro-ph/0507110; J. S. Alcaniz, J. A. S. Lima, *Phys.Rev.* **D 72** 063516 (2005), [astro-ph/0507372]; J. S. Alcaniz , J. M. F. Maia, *Phys.Rev.* **D 67** 043502 (2003); F. Bauer, *Class.Quant.Grav.*, **22**, 3533 (2005) and many more.
33. T. Padmanabhan (2004) [gr-qc/0409089]; R. R. Caldwell, astro-ph/0209312; T.Padmanabhan, *Int.Jour. Mod.Phys.* **A 4**, 4735 (1989), Sec.6.1.
34. A. Einstein, *Siz. Preuss. Acad. Scis.* (1919), translated as "Do Gravitational Fields Play an essential

Role in the Structure of Elementary Particles of Matter," in The *Principle of Relativity*, by edited by A. Einstein et al. (Dover, New York, 1952); J. J. van der Bij et al., *Physica* **A 116**, 307 (1982); F. Wilczek, *Phys. Rep.* **104**, 111 (1984); A. Zee, in *High Energy Physics*, proceedings of the 20th Annual Orbis Scientiae, Coral Gables, (1983), edited by B. Kursunoglu, S. C. Mintz, and A. Perlmutter (Plenum, New York, 1985); W. Buchmuller and N. Dragon, *Phys.Lett.* **B 207**, 292, (1988); W.G. Unruh, *Phys.Rev.* **D 40** 1048 (1989).

35. T. Padmanabhan, *Int.Jour.Mod.Phys* **D** (in press)[gr-qc/0510015]; *Brazilian Jour.Phys.* (Special Issue) **35**, 362 (2005) [gr-qc/0412068]; *Class. Quan. Grav.*, **21**, L1 (2004) [gr-qc/0310027]; *Gen.Rel.Grav.*, **35**, 2097 (2003); *ibid.*, **34** 2029 (2002) [gr-qc/0205090].

36. A. D. Sakharov, *Sov. Phys. Dokl.*, **12**, 1040 (1968); T. Jacobson, *Phys. Rev. Lett.* **75**, 1260 (1995); T. Padmanabhan, *Mod. Phys. Lett.* **A 17**, 1147 (2002) [hep-th/0205278]; **18**, 2903 (2003) [hep-th/0302068]; *Class.Quan.Grav.*, **21**, 4485 (2004) [gr-qc/0308070]; G.E. Volovik, *Phys.Rept.*, **351**, 195 (2001); T. Padmanabhan, *Int.Jour.Mod.Phys.* **D 13**, 2293-2298 (2004), [gr-qc/0408051]; G. E. Volovik, *The universe in a helium droplet*, (Oxford University Press, 2003); B.L. Hu, gr-qc/0503067 and references therein.

37. A.D. Dolgov, in *The very early universe: Proceeding of the 1982 Nuffield Workshop at Cambridge*, ed. G.W. Gibbons, S.W. Hawking and S.T.C. Sikkos (Cambridge University Press), (1982), p. 449; S.M. Barr, *Phys. Rev.* **D 36**, 1691 (1987); Ford, L.H., *Phys. Rev.* **D 35**, 2339 (1987); A. Hebecker and C. Wetterich, *Phy. Rev. Lett.*, **85** 3339 (2000); A. Hebecker hep-ph/0105315; T.P. Singh, T. Padmanabhan, *Int. Jour. Mod. Phys.* **A 3**, (1988), 1593; M. Sami, T. Padmanabhan, (2003) *Phys. Rev.* **D 67**, 083509 [hep-th/0212317].

38. H. S. Snyder *Phys. Rev.*, **71**, 38 (1947); B. S. DeWitt, *Phys. Rev. Lett.*, **13**, 114 (1964); T. Yoneya *Prog. Theor. Phys.*, **56**, 1310 (1976); T. Padmanabhan *Ann. Phys.* (N.Y.), **165**, 38 (1985); *Class. Quantum Grav.* **4**, L107 (1987); A. Ashtekar et al., *Phys. Rev. Lett.*, **69**, 237 (1992); T. Padmanabhan *Phys. Rev. Lett.* **78**, 1854 (1997) [hep-th/9608182]; *Phys. Rev.* **D 57**, 6206 (1998); K.Srinivasan et al., *Phys. Rev.* **D 58** 044009 (1998) [gr-qc/9710104]; M. Fontanini et al. *Phys.Lett.* **B 633**, 627 (2006) hep-th/0509090. For a review, see L.J. Garay, *Int. J. Mod. Phys.* **A10**, 145 (1995).

39. G. W. Gibbons and S.W. Hawking, *Phys. Rev.* **D 15**, 2738 (1977); T.Padmanabhan, *Mod.Phys.Letts.*, **A 17**, 923 (2002) [gr-qc/0202078]; *Class. Quant. Grav.*, **19**, 5387 (2002) [gr-qc/0204019]; *Mod.Phys.Letts.* **A 19**, 2637 (2004) [gr-qc/0405072]; For a recent review see e.g., T. Padmanabhan, *Phys. Reports,* **406**, 49 (2005) [gr-qc/0311036].

40. T.Padmanabhan Lecture given at the *Plumian 300 - The Quest for a Concordance Cosmology and Beyond* meeting at Institute of Astronomy, Cambridge, July 2004; [astro-ph/0510492].

41. Y.B. Zel'dovich, *JETP letters* **6**, 316 (1967); *Soviet Physics Uspekhi* **11**, 381 (1968).

42. T. Padmanabhan, *Class.Quan.Grav.* **19**, L167 (2002), [gr-qc/0204020]; for an earlier attempt, see D. Sorkin, *Int.J.Theor.Phys.* **36**, 2759 (1997); for related ideas, see Volovik, G. E., gr-qc/0405012; J. V. Lindesay et al., astro-ph/0412477; Yun Soo Myung, hep-th/0412224; E.Elizalde et al., hep-th/0502082.

43. S. A. Fulling, *Phys. Rev.* **D7** 2850 (1973); W.G. Unruh, *Phys. Rev.* **D14**, 870 (1976); K. Srinivasan et al., *Phys. Rev.* **D 60**, 24007 (1999) [gr-qc-9812028]; L. Sriramkumar et al., *Int. Jour. Mod. Phys.* **D 11**,1 (2002) [gr-qc/9903054].

44. T. Padmanabhan and T.P. Singh, *Class. Quan. Grav.*, (1987), **4** , 1397.

45. T. Padmanabhan, *Class.Quan.Grav.*, **22**, L107, (2005) [hep-th/0406060].

46. L. Bombelli et al., *Phys. Rev.* **D34**, 373 (1986); M. Srednicki, *Phys. Rev. Lett.* **71**, 666 (1993); R. Brustein et al., *Phys. Rev.* **D65**, 105013 (2002); A. Yarom, R. Brustein, hep-th/0401081. This result can also be obtained from those in ref. [44].

LIST OF PARTICIPANTS

Alexandre Pedro Botelho de Melo (UFRRJ) — ph.lodo@uol.com.br
Alvaro Augusto Alvarez Candal (ON) — alvarez@on.br
Ana Beatriz de Mello (ON) — bellatx@terra.com.br
Ana Helena Fernandes Guimarães (UNESP) — anah@feg.unesp.br
Andrea Verónica Ahumada (UNCOR-Argentina) — andrea@oac.uncor.edu
Ariel G. Sánchez-Vendramini (UNCOR-Argentina) — arielsan@oac.uncor.edu
Armando Bernui (INPE) — bernui@das.inpe.br
Beatriz Henriques Ferreira Ramos (UFRJ) — ramos@if.ufrj.br
Carlos Saffe (UNCOR-Argentina) — saffe@oac.uncor.edu
Carolina Andrea Chavero (ON) — carolina@on.br
Cássio Bruno Magalhães Pigozzo (UFBA) — cpigozzo@ufba.br
Cintia Quireza Campos (ON) — quireza@on.br
Daniel Nicolato Epitácio Pereira (ON) — danielnep@gmail.com
Daniel Costa Mello (ON) — drcmello@yahoo.com.br
Daniela Borges Pavani (UFRGS) — dpavani@if.ufrgs.br
Diana Paula A. P. G. de Oliveira (UFRJ) — astronoma.diana@gmail.com
Eder Martioli (INPE) — eder@das.inpe.br
Eduardo Fernandez del Peloso (ON) — epeloso@on.br
Erica Cristina Nogueira (UFRJ) — erica@if.ufrj.br
Erik Gregorio Meza Quispe (UNI-Peru) — erickmeza@uni.edu.pe
Fernando Virgilio Roig (ON) — froig@on.br
Francisco Ernandes M. Costa (ON) — ernandes@on.br
German Racca (ON) — racca@on.br
Gustavo F. Porto de Mello (UFRJ) — gustavo@ov.ufrj.br
Hidalyn Theodory C. M. de Souza (UFRN) — hidalyn@yahoo.com.br
Humberto Borges (UFBA) — humberto@ufba.br
Jackson Max Fortunato Maia (CNPq) — jmaia@cnpq.br
Jairo Cavalcanti Amaral (UFPE) — jairo.amaral@uol.com.br
Javier Adrián Rodón (UNCOR-Argentina) — javier.rodon@gmail.com
José Ademir Sales de Lima (IAG/USP) — limajas@astro.iag.usp.br
Julio César Tello Gálvez (INPE) — julio@das.inpe.br
Karla de Souza Torres (INPE) — karlche79@hotmail.com
Lucas Saldanha Werneck (UFRJ) — lucas.astronomo@gmail.com
Luciana Verónica Gramajo (UNCOR-Argentina) — luciana@mail.oac.uncor.edu
Luis Gustavo Almeida (CBPF) — lgalmeida@cbpf.br
Maria Aldinêz Dantas (ON) — aldinez@on.br
Maria Celeste Parisi (UNCOR-Argentina) — celeste@oac.uncor.edu

María Isela Zevallos Herencia (ON) — mzevallos@on.br
Martín Makler (CBPF) — martin@cbpf.br
Maurício Ferraresi Junior (UFRJ) — mauricio@ov.ufrj.br
Maximiliano Pivato (UNCOR-Argentina) — maxip@mail.oac.uncor.edu
Myriam V Pajuelo Cubillas (PUCP-Peru) — mpajuelo@fisica.pucp.edu.pe
Nobar Baella Pajuelo (ON) — baella@on.br
Othon Cabo Winter (UNESP) — ocwinter@feg.uncsp.br
Patricio Andres Lagos Lizana (ON) — plagosl@on.br
Rafael Sfair de Oliveira (UNESP) — rsfair@feg.unesp.br
Raimundo Silva Jr. (ON) — rsilva@on.br
Renato Neves Cabral (ON) — renato@on.br
Ribamar Rondon de Rezende dos Reis (UFRJ) — ribamar@if.ufrj.br
Ricardo L. C. Ogando (UFRJ) — ogando@if.ufrj.br
Rita de Cássia Domingos (UNESP) — rcassia@feg.unesp.br
Rodolfo Henrique Silva Smiljanic (IAG/USP) — rodolfo@astro.iag.usp.br
Rodolfo Valentim da Costa Lima (IAG/USP) — valentim@astro.iag.usp.br
Rosicler S Neves (UFRJ) — rosiclerneves@oi.com.br
Thierry Gregory Gil Chanut (UNESP) — madamechanut@terra.com.br
Tibério Borges Vale (UFRGS) — tiberio@if.ufrgs.br
Vinicius Bordalo S. Marques (ON) — bordalo@on.br
Ximena Mazzalay (UNCOR-Argentina) — ximena@mail.oac.uncor.edu

MAY 19 2005

WITHDRAWN

ELKHART PUBLIC LIBRARY

Elkhart, Indiana

dog of a reason bit my ass or fate jumped the curb and knocked me down an unknown road.

A thought of Leeli twinged my heart. Appeared I'd cared about that old girl somewhat deeper than I knew.

The air-horn of an eighteen-wheeler bawled out on the highway, something huge going crazy, and trailing behind it, almost lost in the roar of tires and engine, a siren corkscrewed through the night.

Rickey spat up more blood.

Like they say, shit happens.

I figure that about tells it.

HANDS UP! WHO WANTS TO DIE?

He'd moved to the steps and was sitting on the bottom one, the sawed-off angled across his knees.

—Hands up! Who wants to die? he said. How you like them apples, huh?

A queer little road of moonlight slithered off along the water into the east. I wished I could follow it. I wished there was a tree with hundred dollar bills for leaves growing out behind the lodge, and that Rickey was too weak and sore to pull off both barrels before I could reach him, and that the end of this world was the beginning of the next, and I wished I'd had more time with Leeli.

—I feel them police dogs panting, Rickey said, stretching out his legs and getting comfortable. I feel that heat humming out along the road.

It come to seem all like a painting, then. One you'd see in a museum with a brass plate on a frame enclosing a night on the marshlands south of South Daytona, a night wild with stars and a wicked moon hanging like a bone grin among the remains of the running clouds, a gray tumbledown lodge with a stove-in roof and a lumpy, bloody man sitting on the steps, aiming a chest-buster at another man sitting in the grass, and a corpse lying near the water's edge, gone pale and strange. It would look awful pretty and have the feeling of something going on behind the scenes. Like silver nooses were hanging from the stars and important shapes were hiding back of the clouds, big ones with the heads of beasts, showing a shade darker than the blue darkness of the sky. It was that rich, dark blue give the picture a soul. The rest of it was up to you. You could study it and arrive at all sorts of erroneous conclusions.

—Damn if I don't believe I can smell 'em, Rickey said. Y'know the smell I'm talking about? That oiled-up leather and aftershave smell them state pigs have? He spat again. You shouldn't go fucking over your friends, man. It just don't seem to never work out.

I took another stab at explaining things to myself. Witches and spacemen and scum of the earth. Somewhere in all that slop of life was a true thing. I knew in my gut it was an amazing thing, unlike any you'd expect to meet up with on your way through hell, and I believed if I was to chew on it a time, jot down a list of what I saw and what I thought, I might understand who Ava and Carl and Squire were. But I'd always been bound for this patch of chilly ground. It wasn't worth pursuing how I got there, whether it was some old so when I tried to fit Squire cooling out at my feet and the bossy way he'd acted in with Ava's stories, it only made a deeper puzzle, one I knew I'd never get straight.

I kept the gun aimed at him, hoping he'd sit up, halfway hoping he would just so I could shoot his ass again. Anger seeped out of my skin, leaving me shaky. The painted eye on Squire's chest smouldered. I had an urge to throw the gun into the marsh, but I didn't have enough fire in me to follow through and I dropped it on the ground. Thing to do, I realized, was to gather food and whatever else I could use from the lodge and hightail it into the marsh. I'd need the gun. My chest felt scraped hollow and filled with cold gas. It cost me some effort to reach for the gun. I bent over halfway, put my hands on my knees, and stalled there. A black rope was being pulled through my head, scouring out the positive thoughts.

—Stand up straight, motherfucker!

Rickey was leaning against the side of the porch, holding a sawed-off 12 guage with a taped grip. Didn't appear he could see out of one eye, but the other was working good and pinned on me.

—Come thisaway! he said.

I walked a few steps toward him. He gestured with the sawed-off and told me to sit.

—You a cocksure son-of-a-bitch, leaving me alive. Rickey spat a dark wad of blood and saliva.

The wet soaked through the seat of my pants. Rickey started toward me, weaving a little, then thought better of it and leaned back against the porch. His face was all lumped and discolored, like an atomic war radiation victim.

—I saw you kill that boy, he said. Kill him how you'd do a sick dog. You didn't useta be that cold, man. Something happen in Raiford make you that way?

I didn't have no answers for him.

—You liked to kill me, but I don't kill so easy. Rickey fumbled in his pocket and fetched out a cell phone. One fine morning a few years from now, they be strapping you down and fixing to kill you. You remember me on that day, Maceo.

He thumbed three numbers, gave a show of doing it so I'd know he was calling 911. I drew up my knees and rested my head on my arms. Rickey talked for a minute, too low for me to hear.

—Hey, Maceo!

HANDS UP! WHO WANTS TO DIE?

—It don't bother you, you set there and watched Ava and them roll off into the fucking sunset, but this here—he punched at me again—that bothers you?

A thready strip of cloud spooled out across the moon, a golden bridge unraveling.

—You are hillbilly shit piled high, y'know that? Squire said. I heard him kick at the ground and then his voice came from a distance away: Guess you must like the idea of ol' Ava licking your girlfriend's pussy.

I turned on him, seeing only those two ugly round faces, one atop the other mutant-style, and I lifted my right hand. I was kind of surprised to see the gun—guess I'd forgotten I was holding it—and maybe it was surprise twitched my trigger finger, or maybe another flickering snake tongue of anger. Or maybe I just wanted to kill him, though I had the notion somewhere in the back of my mind that he was not a man, he'd eat the bullet, lie there a while, then sit up all of a sudden the way he'd done back in Ocala. The shot punched out the left eye of his lower face. He gave a melancholy grunt, like a hog disappointed by its supper, and went spinning to the ground. Heart's blood came from his chest in such a hurry, it might've had somewhere more important to go. Speckles of wet dirt clung to his cheek. His one true eye was open blind and the other was pressed into the earth. I thought I heard a voice of wind and rustling grass say my name in welcome.

* * *

You might not understand, but then again you might, how when you reach the end of the road and still find yourself breathing, the unraveled threads that tied you to your life resemble a puzzle you could easily have solved if you'd been one ounce smarter or one inch less crazy, and you think now that you've gained a perspective, you can probably develop some sort of reasonable explanation for all the crap you hadn't understood, but when you gather those threads up they hang limp from your fist and don't none of the frayed ends match, and you realize they weren't really connected, they had no more connection to each other than stalks of dead grass floating on marsh water, and everything you depended on being true was just a tricky kind of emptiness that looked like something real, and

—Aw, Jesus! He wheeled away from me and looked to the sky. Thank you for sticking me with this ignorant fucking hillbilly!

I refitted my eyes to the marsh, the stirring grasses and the moon-licked water to the east.

—Goddamn it! Squire said. You'n me, we need to work together. I can find 'em!

It struck me that he was speaking with more authority than he'd previously displayed, but I didn't concern myself with this. Wasn't that it didn't tweak my interest, just I was more interested in the way my head was emptying out, like a car engine giving little ticks as it cools.

Squire went to hammering at me, trying to rouse me to action, and finally I said, What you want me to do, asshole? Drive you around in a stolen van 'til we get popped?

—We don't hafta go far. Won't be on the road more'n a few minutes.

—They been gone an hour…maybe more. You think they just circling out there?

—Trust me, man. I know what I'm talking about.

—Trust you? I said. Fuck you! Now I told you, leave me be.

I stepped away along the shore and stopped at the very edge of the water, my shoes sinking into the muck, wanting to restore the glum yet comforting acceptance into which my thoughts had been sinking. Squire followed me, giving orders, pleading, working every angle. Didn't matter what he said, it was all the same to my ears, a yammering that bored holes in my skull and poured itself in hot and heavy like lead into a mold. I told him to shut up. He kept at it. I told him again to shut up and it didn't even put a hitch in his delivery. I was acting like I had shit for brains, he said. Behaving like a child. Didn't matter what he said. Every word hardened into a white-hot ingot, stacks of them crowding the space between my ears. I tried to see past him, past the heat growing inside me, looking to cool my eyes in the lavender cave of sky among the last clouds where the moon floated. It wasn't a help.

—What do I gotta do, spell it out for your sorry ass? Squire said. What the fuck's it gonna take to get through?

He punched at my shoulder with the heel of his hand.

—Don't be doing that, I said.

HANDS UP! WHO WANTS TO DIE?

recognition stole over me not just of how fucked I was at the moment, but how fucked the normal weather was in Maceo's world. Everything was returning to normal. The frogs squelched up their bleepy cries. Cicadas established a drone. A fish jumping for a bug out in the marsh made a squishy plop and I could have sworn it was my own heart's sound. Squire came out onto the porch steps, rubbing his stubbly scalp, sleepy as a tick full of juice, and asked, Where they all at?

—Went to charter a plane.

He gaped at me. They gone? Ava and everybody?

—Yeah.

—We gotta go find 'em! He tripped on the bottom step and reeled out sideways into the yard, catching a furl of the rusted screen to right himself. He was wearing jeans that still had creases in the legs and that stupid T-shirt with his face spraypainted on it Ava had bought him in Silver Springs. Move it! he said. We gotta find 'em now!

He got to scooting around the yard, little dashes this way and that, like a dog with the runs in a hurry to locate a good place to do his business. Which way they go? he asked.

—I told you. They went to charter a plane somewheres 'round New Smyrna.

—They ain't gone to New Smyrna! Dumb motherfucker! They ain't going nowhere near New Smyrna!

Usually somebody calls me a dumb motherfucker, I don't have much of an argument. It's not much different from saying that there grass is pretty green or the water looks wet. But Squire irked me with his agitated movement and his two round faces, the one on his chest smiling, the other scowling, both of them staring at me.

—Leave me be! I walked off a few paces and gazed out into the marsh. With the passage of the storm, heat was coming back into the world. A drop of sweat trickled down my side. The air was slow and thick and humid. Something with curved black wings scythed across the low-hanging moon. A dullness swept over my thoughts, an oppressive, clammy feeling like the first sign of a fever.

—You just gonna stand there? Squire grabbed onto my shoulder and spun me about. We gotta get us a move on!

—Don't put your hands on me, I said.

found nothing. No bulge, no envelope sticking out. I patted my other pockets and looked on the ground close by. Since I'd come out from the porch to watch them drive away, I hadn't hardly moved a step, but there was no sign of the envelope. I told myself the wind must have took it. I searched along the edge of the water, near the porch, and as I was poking around in the grass, kicking scrap wood and fallen shingles aside, growing more desperate every second, because with or without Leeli I needed that money to get clear of Volusia County, it occurred to me there might never have been an envelope. Maybe Ava was that much of a witch. Maybe she'd handed me a parlor trick, an illusion, and made Leeli and me see what she wanted. Maybe Leeli had been in on the hustle and just pretended to be worried about the money. It was her, wasn't it, led me to Ava in the first place? The missing envelope and the green flash and the stories Ava told, they all washed together into a stew of possibilities. I couldn't separate out anything from it that sounded more than half true.

I stopped my searching and stood by the water. The clouds had slid off to the north, except for a wedge that was convoying the rising moon. The stars were thick. It was as if there had been no storm, just a gentle rain that smeared the vegetable smells around into a sickly green sweetness. I told myself I must be wrong about everything. Before long they'd be pulling into the driveway, talking about our plane ride. But fool though I was, I wasn't that big of a fool. I could mumble all the pretty wishes I wanted to, but gone was still the impression I got.

* * *

I felt like a baby trapped under a bear rug, unable to crawl, too smothered to cry, and I must've stood by the water damn near an hour, trying to poke holes in the weighty thing that held me down. I was flummoxed by a question I wasn't even sure had been asked, stumped and dumb, unable to work out a plan or think of a direction to travel in. I didn't know what to do. Hitchhike out of there? Drive away in a van every cop in Central Florida was probably on the look-out for? Heading into the marsh and living off mullet and gator tail was about my only option. The skeeters began to trouble me. Mostly I let them have my blood, but I spanked a few dead. Seemed like I'd been living with my brain switched off and now a ing buddha in my mind, scrunched up and angry from having me in his sight. It seemed I could feel the wickedness of that place and time, the mortal separation from the flow of life that wickedness enforces. I was flying, stranded on a scrap of soggy marsh that had been chewed off from the planet and set to spinning loose in the void. The rain needled my cheeks and brow, spitting alternately dark and silver. The lodge looked to be changing shape, crouching like a beast one second, the next blurring into an emblem of negativity, a symbol on a rippling banner, then collapsing back into the ruinous thing it pretended to be. I had the idea this was my night, my big moment, that I was being showed a reflection of everything I'd said and thought and done, the chaos of my life given larger, windier form, and this was the only celebration of my useless days I'd likely get, this storm too small to have a name but big enough to damage the unprepared, the tore-down spaces, the vacant properties of the world. Then I glanced south to where Ava and Carl and Leeli had gone and saw a flash of green. Not a dazzling seam and not the dull flicker of heat lightning, but a dynamic burst of bright neon color like an enormous bug zapper taking a hit. The color hung in the air, draping its afterimages around the palm crowns, and I recalled Ava's story about the green light coming from the UFO. I tried to think of something else it could have been. I expect there must have been a hundred possibilities, but I couldn't come up with one. The rain slowed to a drizzle and as if the green flash had been a cue, the storm began to fade, flaring up now and again with a grumble and a distant snip of fire, then fading even more, its battery running low. Drips and plops succeeded the fury of the wind. Through scudding clouds you could glimpse a freckling of stars, and soon a slice of moon surfaced from the horizon. I knew Carl and Ava and Leeli were gone. It wasn't the flash that told me so. Too many thoughts were flapping around inmy attic for me to work that part of it out. The alignment of the world, the wrecked lodge and foundered cabins, the swaying grasses and the dark water slurping at the mucky bank, the stars and all the rest—it was like a sign saying Gone had been struck through every layer of creation.

Naturally I didn't entirely believe this sign. Despite Ava's anything-goes attitude toward screwing, I figured Squire must do something special for her, and I just knew Leeli wasn't about to leave that money on the table. I patted my hip pocket again and this time I lottery can be won, great prizes are within your grasp, and though the only winning ticket ever came your parents' way was an error in their favor made by a bartender or a grocery clerk, though you understand you're their homemade fool, you just can't accept that the rules of their life apply to you. That golden ticket is a guarantee all right, a twenty-four karat guaranteed loser. You know this in your heart, but you hang onto the bitch like it was a pass through the Gates of Glory or a voucher for all-expense-paid weekend at Casino World on the Redneck Riviera, whichever premium you prefer.

Thoughts such as these slammed my head as I dug through Rickey's pockets, hunting for his keys. He was still unconscious, his face swollen from the beating I'd supplied him. Looked like he'd pissed off a swarm of bees. The keys were in the bib pocket of his overalls. I stood jingling them in my hand, holding a last debate over the wisdom of giving them to Ava. An old movie was playing on the TV. Japanese men in moonsuits were gazing awestruck at a fleet of flying saucers that soon began incinerating them with fiery beams. Watching them turn into bright wavering silhouettes and vanish somehow made my decision for me.

Things moved right smartly after that. Ava and Carl went for the car, Leeli gave me a pert little kiss and said, Be back soon, and ran off after them. I patted my hip pocket to make certain the money was still there. A minute later I was standing on the porch steps, watching a pair of red tailights, one patched with duct tape, jouncing along over the uneven ground toward the highway, shining up tracers of rain. I had a moment of dissatisfaction with my decision and I pulled Ava's gun from the waist of my jeans with half a thought of shooting out a tire. The car stopped at the end of the drive. There wasn't any traffic I could see and I wondered what was going on. A creep of paranoia stirred me from the steps and out in the rain. I imagined Ava and Leeli arguing over whether or not to betray me. Thunder mauled the sky. The car swung out onto the highway. I felt like six kinds of fool, with the rain running down my neck, alone as ever was, the gun cold and weighty in my hand.

The night grew wilder yet, the thunder continuous. A ring of fiery stick men a thousand feet tall jabbed and flashed on the horizons, penning me into their magic circle. There was such a confusion of light and sound, it rooted me to the spot. Behind the lodge a clump of palms bulked up solid, taking the shape of a black frown-

HANDS UP! WHO WANTS TO DIE?

—All those country roads. Leeli put a hand to her brow like a mentalist trying to make contact. I can show her, but I don't know I can tell her.

Rain drove in through the screen and we all moved back from it except for Carl, who just sat there rocking.

—I don't trust you no more'n you trust me, I said to Ava. We gonna have to work something else out.

Another lightning flash brought leached colors to the porch and fitted a long shadow beneath every object. Things looked to be tilted, as if the wind had knocked the lodge askew.

—Hang on, Ava said, and went off toward her bedroom.

Leeli caught my hand and said something I didn't catch, but had the sound of an assurance, and then Ava came back out onto the porch and handed me a thick envelope.

—Fuck's this? I asked.

—The rest of the money I promised Leeli. You can hold it while we're gone.

Leeli's eyes got stuck on the envelope as I inspected the contents. Hundred dollar bills and plenty of them.

—That guarantee enough for ya? Ava asked. 'Tween Squire and the money, it's 'bout the best I can do.

I stuffed the envelope into my hip pocket. Leeli unstuck her eyes. I could see it was a strain for her and that she didn't love the idea of leaving the envelope behind. All right, I said. I started to deliver a warning, to pose consequences, but there didn't seem much point to it. We all knew the lay of the land.

All right, I repeated. Let's get it rolling.

* * *

You know how it goes. Sometimes you're so deep in the world, so mired in its trouble, you forget that you were born, you forget you were raised to be a dead man, you think you got where you're standing all on your own and that you're holding destiny in your hands, and when somebody passes you a golden ticket that's stamped Freedom or Foreverafter, you don't check to see if the ink's dry or if there's printing on the back, because you're walking the road your daddy cut for you and stepping along in clothes your mama sewed, because it's the tendency of your kind to believe the standard model. Everything considered, it was a goddamn miracle I'd come this far in life.

* * *

The storm lived around us. Seemed the lodge was a battery discharging thunder cracks and splintered lightning that made stretches of churning marsh grass bloom for unholy seconds against the dark gulf of land and sky. I told Leeli about Rickey and the reverend and the cops and tried once again to persuade her to leave with me. She wouldn't budge. Mexico, she kept saying, was the way to go. I didn't put up all that much of an argument, having no better choice to offer. We brought Ava and Carl into the conversation, leaving Squire asleep, and stood on the porch in the flickering light and hashed things out. The storm appeared to frighten Carl. He sat in one of the rotted porch chairs, his hands to his ears, rocking his upper body.

Leeli said she knew of a little rural airport west of New Smyrna where we could charter a plane, no questions, and Ava said she and Carl and Leeli would use Rickey's car and take care of it right away.

—Like hell! I said. We'll go together.

—You crazy? You know how it is when there's a big storm, Ava said. Accidents and drownings. Cops'll be all over the highway. There'll be roadblocks. They see you, we're finished.

—That's right! Leeli said. They gonna be too busy to worry 'bout looking for us now.

—I'll be damned I'm gonna let you run off without me, I said.

—We can't run off! Won't nothing be flying 'til the storm blows out. But we set things up, we can fly soon as it does.

—Just you go then, I said to Ava.

—I can't leave Carl. You see how he is. And I need Leeli to point the way.

A pitchfork of lightning ripped away the dark and the thunder had a metallic sound, like somebody was pounding out a dent in the sky. Wind shivered the lodge and slammed loose boards.

—Naw, I said. Leeli can give you directions.

—What if I get 'em wrong? You got Squire here. Ain't that enough of a guarantee?

I couldn't see Ava's face in that moment, but I thought I felt slyness steaming off of her. Tell her the directions, Leeli, I said.

did it myself. The reverend shook his head mournfully and said, There was so much confusion, I don't know which one actually fired. It was the skinny one I saw holding the gun, but that's after the shooting. All I can tell you for certain is I heard somebody shout, Hands up! Who wants to die? And then I heard the shots.

—Hands up! Who wants to die? The blonde reporter acquired a serious look as the camera went to a close-up on her. Vikay Choudhoury responded to that challenge with a hero's answer and now he lies dead. She paused for effect and said, This is Gloria Renard. Channel Twelve...

I thumbed the mute button. There was a cold spread of panic inside me, like I was standing on the edge of a cliff and had just lost my balance.

—You get on outa here, Maceo! Rickey stared at me through the straggles of his hair. I mean right fucking now!

—I didn't kill nobody, I said.

—I don't care you did or you didn't. Every damn cop in Volusia knows who it is says that dumb fucking hands-up-who-wants-to-die bullshit. You think they won't be snooping 'round here? Wonder is, they ain't here already.

—We can't leave now. They be on us 'fore we get clear the driveway.

Rickey reached down beside his hip and produced his pistol. I'll shoot you my own self, you don't get on out.

Anger was a cold snake snapping out of me. I ripped the gun from his hand, then I stood and began punching him. He tried to block the first couple with his forearms, but each one was a lesson I'd been taught to deliver, a preachment of old pain. The blows drove him lower in the chair until his butt was hanging half off the seat and his head was jammed into the join of the cushions and there was blood in his eyes. I couldn't have said why, but the sight of him unconscious jabbed another red-hot stick into my brain. I smashed the pistol against the wall again and again. The trigger guard fell off and the cylinder popped out from the housing and I threw the rest to the floor. I knew Rickey was right about the cops. Maybe that was what set me off. That and recognizing how good a look at my face I'd given everybody in the HoJos. When God invented the notion of crazy trumping common sense, He must've had me in mind for the playing in Rickey's room. I figured Ava must have kicked him to the curb.

I returned to the bedroom and drifted beside Leeli. My flesh felt light and insubstantial and everything had the sharpness of an important memory, how you feel the thing remembered before you see and smell and taste it. It was like the world itself was forming a memory that used me how a pearl uses a sore spot, sealing me in so I could be dug out at some later date to be admired. The rain blew slanty, then straightened out, then it blew sideways and the lightning moved closer. The air darkened to an ashy color. Things bumped and clanked against some section of the lodge. You'd have thought the rain had turned to chains. The marsh grass rippled with pantherish fury, twisting and flowing in every direction. The storm smell was ozone and dank trouble.

Sleep wouldn't take me. I got dressed and padded down the hall to visit Rickey. He was in his chair, scratching himself, watching the local news with the sound low. He gave a disinterested, Hey, and paid me no mind as I drew up a chair.

— You get laid? I asked.

— Damn! Did I! That woman's got some evil fucking ways!

Rickey didn't look much different for the experience and I thought the last shriveled-up scrap of soul must have been sucked out before Ava got to him.

He craned his neck to see me. How long y'all staying?

— Day or two. Why, you wanna go again with her?

— She promises not to kill me.

— Better ask for the pony ride next time.

Rickey coughed out a laugh and spat into the garbage alongside his chair. He spaced out on the TV and I couldn't think of anything more to say. Rickey wasn't much of a talker but he enjoyed people with him when he watched his programs. I knew if I didn't hang out a while, he'd feel he wasn't being respected, so I sat there dead-headed, peering at his mess. Must have been every kind of candy wrapper in the world scattered around that floor. It was like investigating a cave where some sick animal had puked up a month of bad meals. The next time I glanced toward the TV, I saw a blonde woman in a pants suit with her microphone stuck in the face of the gray-haired reverend I'd manhandled back in Ocala. I told Rickey to hit the volume, and when he was slow to act, I grabbed the remote and

HANDS UP! WHO WANTS TO DIE?

lar folks who could do the same sort of job on you and I said as much to Leeli.

—Naw, un-uh, it's more'n that. It's what you were saying. She pulls at you, but she's not playing you. It's who she is, know what I mean? It's like that's all she is...this force.

A lightning crack ran violet down the eastern sky, like we were inside a gray egg that was cracking open in the middle of hell. The thunder came a few seconds later.

—You pull at me, too, I said. Know that? You been pulling at me since New Smyrna.

Leeli's face went little girl serious and big-eyed.

I eased down beside her, laid a hand on her hip.

—I'm scared, she said. Ava wants to go to Mexico. I can't think what to do.

—Let's leave tonight. Let's just go.

—Where? Where can we go?

—This old boy I got to know in Raiford runs with some bikers got land over 'round Palatka. Cops never come near their place. We could stay 'long as we want.

—Maybe you'd be comfortable with a buncha bikers, but I wouldn't. She snuggled in closer. Maybe we should go with Ava and the second we get to Mexico, that's it. Money or not.

—I don't like the idea of traveling more miles with her.

—It's the safest way. Won't be no security to pass through with a charter. Leeli picked up my hand from her hip and moved it around so I was holding her. 'Less you got something better'n bikers.

I considered Lauderdale, but Lauderdale was a hell of a drive and we couldn't stay for long at my friend's house.

—Ain't you scared? Leeli asked. I can't tell if you are or not.

—I'm past scared, I'm on into survive. That's why I say get shut of 'em now.

We left it hanging that way and closed the door and got foolish on the bed. Desperate straits and the desire to forget them lit up our nerves and made us better lovers. Leeli like to have died in my arms and my heart was sprained and limping my chest, I worked it so long and furious. I left her drowsing and went into the kitchen and had another burger and a purple milk shake that tasted like nothing purple and puddled like melted plastic in my stomach. The TV was eye wide and the other narrowed. I figured Leeli and that Seminole had about the same ambition toward me.

I finished the burger and Leeli stomped over, snatched the bag and switched past me into the lodge. Don't you come after me! she said. I'm not talking to you.

—I hear you, sugar, I said. I'll be right in.

* * *

With her belly full, Leeli's mood improved. She was near to purring, curled up on the bed and looking out at the rain, but still it took me a few tries to drag her into a conversation. I was just sitting there, I said, when they started going at it. What you expect me to do?

—Leave, she said. I know how Ava and Squire get. You had plenty of warning.

—That mean you watched 'em?

—She wants me to!

—Then why go beating on me about it?

She clammed up, so I worked another angle, and when that didn't satisfy her, I said, 'Member what you told me 'bout how you felt sometimes Ava was drowning you? I think I got a taste of what you were talking about.

A little something tweaked behind Leeli's face, but she didn't let it out.

—Yeah, it was strange, I said. It was like she was pulling on me. Maybe that's why I kept setting there.

—She's a witch, Leeli said. I swear she is.

—I don't 'bout know that,

—That's right! You don't know fuck all! I'm telling you she's got this power...it just eats away at you 'til you're nothing. 'Til you're like Carl or Squire.

I spun this around and then said, That's how come you think Carl and Squire are slow?

—Sometimes I think that. Leeli picked at a fray on the pillowcase. Sometimes I think she just wore 'em away.

The witchy woman had tried to draw me close and drown me in her power. This seemed crazier than what Ava had told me, but only a little. Thinking about Ava as someone who left you hollow inside but still walking around wasn't that tough a chore. I'd known regu-

HANDS UP! WHO WANTS TO DIE?

This inspired Carl to point at me and say, Hands up! Who wants to die?

Rickey pricked up his ears at that, but again gave no response. Squire had climbed on board the Ava train and was making tracks for the station, giving out with chuffing noises. The springs backed him up with a jangly, crunchy rhythm and the rain kept drumming and Ava sang a lyric with a single breathy word. Carl nodded, smiled. Rickey's eyes cut toward me—I expect he was wanting a sign it would be okay for him to mix in.

The floorboards creaked. Leeli had crept in and was nailing me with a .45 caliber stare. She said, You asshole!, and ducked back out. Catching a last glimpse of Ava's heels and Squire's pimply backside, I wheeled up from the chair and after her. I checked the porch and saw Leeli standing with her arms folded out in the rain. I didn't think she was crying or nothing, just had a mad on. Rickey came up at my shoulder and said, Hey, man! Is that Ava, she doing everybody?

—Don't be shy, boy. Ask her.

—You serious?

—She ain't gonna screech and hold her knees together if you do. She'll just tell you yes or no.

—Cool.

—You might wanna wait to ask 'til Squire's finished, I said as he turned away.

—Oh...yeah. Okay.

—But you better go back on in now. You wanna be there so you can get next.

He set off again and I called to him, asked where the food was.

—Kitchen, he said and slipped into Ava's room.

Eight Burger King take-out sacks were resting on the kitchen table. I found one full of double cheeseburgers and carried it onto the porch. Leeli! I shouted, and waggled the sack out through the hole in the screen door. I got burgers!

Her head twitched, but she didn't turn. I sat on the porch steps under the porch overhang and unwrapped a cheeeburger and had a bite. Soaked through, Leeli's yellowy white hair had the look of the down on a baby chick. She glared at me similar to how this drunk Seminole boy I'd met in the Panama Beach lock-up one fine morning had glared: sideways, his shoulders rolled forward, with his close turn from watching Squire and Ava. The rainy noise seemed to be tightening the space around us, compressing and heating the air. I told myself the minute Squire started taking off his clothes, I was gone, but there was something mesmerizing about Ava, about the lush, lazy strain of her belly, the slow surges of her hips, and the way her eyes would graze me every so often. I felt the cold pull of her. The sexy warmth of her surface was a dream and beneath lay an undertow that sucked in all the swimmers who'd strayed out past the bar into whatever deep lightless place her story really sprung from. I had a glimmering of how it would be to go with the flow, to stroke hard and arrow down into her dark, to reach the great secret at the bottom, whether toothy maw or golden kingdom, it wasn't much important, because you were bound to be part of it, and as Squire's fingers traipsed between her thighs and her hips lifted, I thought what I was feeling now was closer to the truth than anything she'd said, and knew that she was willful and careless and irresistably strong. The instant I understood this, however, I declared bullshit on it. I was watching a dirty movie, I told myself, and not falling down no rabbit hole.

—Fuck y'all doing? Rickey had popped his head in and was gawking at the bed, where Squire and Ava hadn't missed a beat.

—Notice how the entire school turns as one, Carl said happily.

—Hallelujah! I said. The single mind's directing.

Rickey slid himself in past the stuck door. I could see he was hopng to get in on the act, but was all puffed up and ready to be outraged in case he couldn't. Goddamn it! he said, and stepped over to the window, getting a side angle on the center ring, I don't want no weird shit going on in my house!

—God, no! I said. There's never been no weird shit like people fucking and people watching going on out here. Not in this holy temple.

Rickey might have said something back, but his mouth stopped working, because right then Ava opened her legs and Squire started wrestling off his jeans.

—That's Ava there showing her rosy, I said to Rickey. Squire, he's the boy 'bout to have some fun. Down there in the front row, that's Carl.

—In concert, said Carl. In simple harmony and balance.

—Carl's got this kinda religious thing going, I told Rickey.

HANDS UP! WHO WANTS TO DIE?

—Uh-huh. I was thinking I'd charter a plane and we'd lay low for a few and then jump on over. After Leeli finishes her time with me, the two of you can skedaddle. Twenty thousand'll go a long way in Mexico.

—Whyn't you just call your bigwig friends to haul your ass outa this?

—Maybe I will, things don't go well. But you know how it is, Maceo. You got a favor in the bank, you want to hold back from using it long as you can.

My thoughts skipped back and forth from story to story. I didn't believe any of them, but I kind of believed them all. I suspected there was a spoonful of truth in each, or that each was a stand-in double for a truth she hadn't spoken.

—It don't matter who I am, who Carl and Squire are, she said. We still hafta deal with the problem.

Trying to decide what to believe and what to do about it tied knots in my thought strings. Ava lay grinning at me, looking from the neck down like a dessert tray. I gave myself a nudge toward the bed, pretending to buy the proposition that if I tore one off with her, I'd have a better feel for the situation. Old hayseed philosophers gathered in the boiler room of my brain, swapped round a bottle, and spewed dipshit wisdoms: You can't say how a peach tastes 'til the juice runs down your chin. Staring at the groceries don't tell you who the cook is. Video footage of a naked, sucked-dry corpse, its mouth wrenched open in a final agony, was playing in the den, with graphics reading ALIEN EMBRACE KILLS REDNECK LOVER. I stayed where I was, speculating pro and con upon what I might be missing.

The door shrieked as someone shoved against it. Squire squeezed on in, followed by Carl. Squire glared at Ava, at me, and Carl beamed. His bandage was soaking wet, smudged with dirty finger marks.

—Hi, honey, Ava said.

—That man went for food's coming down the drive, Squire said.

—That's nice. Soon we can have us a feast! She patted the bed, an invitation, and Squire, good dog that he was, laid down beside her. Carl gazed at the chair I was on for a second, then plunked himself down on the floor next to the bed. Squire began toying with Ava's nipples, kissing her neck. The rain swept back in. I heard a clattering from the front of the lodge, a door slamming, but I didn't

—You're not a believer, Ava said. You're a doubter. Don't matter what I say, you're gonna pick at it.

The rain had ceased and you could hear everything dripping. A bluejay began jattering and a dog started going crazy at the sound. Four-legged somethings, probably squirrels, skittered across the roof. All those noises, it was like the world was surfacing to snatch a breath before the rain went to downing it again.

—Carl's my son, Ava said. He's the spitting image of his daddy. He's dead…Carl Senior. He was killed in a car wreck right before we was about to marry. I was already pregnant. Carl was born retarded and he's got lotta other problems. There's this disease makes his nerves not work right. He can't hardly feel a thing. It's killing him. I don't know how much longer he's got. Not long, I expect. Squire, he's just this fella I met in a bar over in Boynton Beach. He keeps me happy and he's simple enough to relate to Carl. Carl Senior's daddy worked for NASA. One of the directors. Even though I never married his son, he was kind to us. When he died he left a trust for me and Carl. The house where you met us? He had it built for us. Pulled some strings so we could have access. The government don't care about the land no more and his friends make sure people leave us be when we're there. Ava crossed her legs and clasped her hands behind her head. That fly any higher for you?

—You're a piece of fucking work, I'll give you that, I said.

Ava grinned. You'll never know 'til you cut you a slice.

—What the hell you hanging around with us for, you got all this money?

—I like Leeli. I like you, too. Different, though. I was enjoying myself with y'all until yesterday.

—The thing gets me, I said after studying on things a patch, is how come you don't seem so worried about your son or your old boyfriend or your experimental subject, whichever he is…about him committing murder.

—Oh we'll be all right. I got confidence in you.

—Now that's a lie.

—You got us outa Ocala, didn't you? With your experience in these matters and my money, we're gonna do fine. I was thinking about Mexico.

—Mexico?

to think coolness ran deep in her, that instead of a heart, a little refrigeration unit was humming in her chest, pumping out frosty air. She seemed like a lot a women I'd known who'd survived bar fights that passed for marriages. Women who felt you couldn't do nothing more to them than had been done already. Yet I didn't accept that picture of her. She was too steady, too unconcerned. I had a notion that her steadiness came from a perception of my weaknesses. Like she was X-raying me, reading all my flaws.

—You'd like me to tell you a story, she said. Is that it?

—A true story. I don't want no fairy tales.

—All right.

She proceeded to whip one off about how she and Carl had been dating back in the 60s while she was in high school and he was in college, and they had gone down to State Road 44 to look at the flying saucers and have sex, and a saucer had abducted them, worked some weird change on them both, and set them back on earth for God knows what purpose, maybe just as test subjects, and they were prodded this way and that by alien agencies—powerful ones that penetrated every layer of society, even the FBI—and they were always being put in strange situations, and this was why they had been at the house in the dunes when Leeli and I showed up.

I was about to ask if Squire was an alien agent, one who was doing the prodding, when she launched into a second story, saying Carl and Squire had been hybrid clone babies, grown from human eggs and alien juice extracted from a dead UFO pilot, and she'd been in charge of them when the government decided the experiment wasn't producing any valuable result and decided to kill the two boys, so Ava, with the help of highly placed friends, had run off with them, and they'd been pursued for a time, but then the government changed their minds and thought the thing to do was let the boys run, acquire life experiences, and see if they developed into a crop worth harvesting. They lived in constant fear of judgment, she said. Never knowing if the government would change their minds again. She was worried that Carl shooting the HoJo's manager might be the last straw and the government would send their killers.

I wondered if she could've tapped into my thoughts of the night before and devised these stories to suit my tabloid fantasies. Why'd you tell two stories? I asked. You told me just the one, I might've believed it.

—In a way.

She crossed to the bed with a three-step stroll and laid herself out, back against the headboard, arms spread on the pillows. Her pubic hair was trimmed to neat strip and she had a long waist to go with her trophy chest. She reminded me of this naked woman in a painting one of my high school teachers had prattled on about, some rich horny bitch from another century lying on a couch and looking at you with a similar scornful, seductive attitude.

—If you want to come over here with me, it's all right, she said.

—I'm fine where I am.

—Leeli won't mind, that's what's worrying you.

—You don't know nothing about that, believe me.

She shrugged, smiled.

—Why would you even want me to come over there? I asked. We ain't got nothing going on.

—I like sex.

—So do I, but...

—Oh I see! You have to like the girl first. You require an emotional attachment.

I didn't care for her mocking me and I was tempted to fuck her knock-kneed, but that would have been playing with her deck. I don't have to like her all that much, I said. Helps if I like her some, though.

Her smile cut itself a wider curve. You don't like me a tiny bit?

—I ain't even sure what the fuck you are. Whyn't you clear that up for me?

The rain came harder, spitting through the window screen, drops darkening a wedge of floor beneath it. Some giant's stomach grumbled and the light dimmed.

—You gonna shoot me if I don't tell you?

—That wasn't my intention.

—No? Yet you come in here with my gun on display.

—Just making a point.

—The point being, you might be prepared to shoot me.

—You want me to shoot you? You keep pissing me off, maybe I will. Don't seem like it would affect you that much, anyway. Or is it just the boys who's good at taking bullets?

This was the first real conversation I'd had with Ava. I'd seen that on the outside she was a cool, collected sort. Now I was coming which the Founding Fathers sacrificed their lives, and I'd be called upon to uphold its sacred honor.

It was an uncommon hard and lasting rain. A drizzle started about ten o'clock and five minutes later it was like a billion hailstones were bouncing off the roof, filling the house with a roar. A weird slivery darkness ensued. The cloud bellies passing over us were black as Satan's boot soles and the wind flattened the marsh grasses with a constant rush. The rain slacked off many times during the day; a couple of times it stopped altogether and the land yielded up a sodden, animal smell, but it kept returning in strength. Rickey drove off to buy food. Carl and Squire sat on the porch playing a hand-held game of some kind. Leeli got a little closer to her new best friend, Mr. Dilaudid, and fell asleep. I wedged the Colt in my waist and paid a visit to Ava.

Her door was open a foot and I stuck my head in without knocking. She was standing at the window, stark naked, arms folded beneath her breasts and hair loose about her shoulders, gazing out at the rain. She must have felt me there, because she turned her head and delivered me a flat, unsurprised stare. What do you want? she asked.

— A few words would be good.
— I guess it's inevitable.
— I'll wait out here while you throw something on.
— No need. We're like family now.

Ava went back to watching the weather and I let my eyes out for a run. Though her face was hagging out, her body belonged to a woman in her prime. She wanted to give me a show, it didn't bother me none. The door proved to be stuck open. I eased in and perched on a straight chair set next to a dresser with its drawers stove-in. Her room was shabbier than ours. Rat turds speckled the boards along the molding and spiderwebs spanned the corners. The bed was so swaybacked, some of the springs were flush to the floor.

— I sneaked a look at your photograph album last night, I said,
— Oh? What did you think?
— I think you're damn sexy for a woman's gotta be in her fifties.
— Sixty-one, she said. I'm sixty-one.
— Okay. A woman in her sixties. And Carl, how old is he?
— Carl. Her smile had a fond quality. Carl's ageless.
— Squire, too. He ageless?

looking extra fine with her breasts gathered above her arm and her ass sticking out from the sheet.

—Hey, Leeli. Get your tail over here, I said. This here's my ol' pal Rickey.

I tried to move Rickey on out of there before he could get paranoid again, but his eyes were leaving tracks all over Leeli, even after she covered everything up, and he kept hanging around. He began asking why we needed to hide and such. I told him some lies and when that didn't stop his questions, I said I wanted to borrow his car so we could buy food and stuff. The best way to derail Rickey's suspicions always was to beg a favor. If he could deny you something, he'd start feeling masterful and forget whatever was bothering him. I argued and pleaded, but he was resolute. Nobody drives my car but me, he said. Like everyone in the world was dying to park their behinds in his funky-smelling shitbox so they could race off to Monaco and display this automotive jewel before graceful society. It ended with Rickey agreeing to bring us food himself and stalking off to search for his missing Dilaudid with head held high.

—That was sly, way you managed that, Leeli said, giving me a smooch. You're pretty smart for white trash.

—Guess what that makes me in the real world, I said.

* * *

Rain and guns. I think it must've been raining when the first gun was drawn hot from its tempering fire, because when it comes rain, I get a itch to handle a gun if I've got one. Which is a roundabout way of saying it rained and Rickey went for food, Leeli hunkered beside me on the bed fixing her nails, while I sat turning Ava's Colt in my hands, picking at the plaque on the grip, rubbing a little raised, rough patch alongside the chamber, thinking gun thoughts, testing its heft and balance, knowing that if I was really pretty smart I would walk down to the water's edge and toss it on in. Having a gun was not in my best interests. Without one, if I was at a beach party, let's say, and some worthless drunken individual tipped over my beer and said diddley dog about it, the worst could happen was busted knuckles and a hospital trip—but I had a gun, God knows, that beer might seem like the very selfsame beer for me a close-up of the dark sour-smelling rathole they opened into. It was like the little room he lived in was inside him, too. Straggles of hair curtained off his face, but did nothing to filter his rotten breath.

—Motherfucker, you stole my dope! he said.

Leeli gave a squeak and rolled off the bed, covering herself with the sheet.

—Where the fuck is it? Rickey asked.

—I took four goddamn tabs! I said. You want 'em back, you gonna have to scrape out my nose!

—Don't think I won't! He screwed the barrel down hard against my cheek. I'm missing a bottle.

—He didn't take nothing! Leeli said. I promise!

—You check around by your chair? I asked. Jesus, you could hide a Volkswagon under all the crap you got on your floor.

His face lost some intensity.

—I guess you were so clearheaded last night, you couldn't have set it down somewheres and forgot, I said. You wouldn't know if you give it a kick accidental when you got up to piss or something.

Thought confused his expression. He backed away from the bed, the pistol angled toward the side.

—Jesus Christ! I sat up and swung my legs onto the floor. Fuck you so crazy about, anyway? You said you had a good goddamn supply.

—It's gotta last the weekend, he said sullenly.

—You run out, I know you'll get you some more. I pulled on my undershorts. What's wrong with you, man? Busting in here like that. I ever cheat you before? I ever treat you anything but righteous?

Rickey puzzled over that. The words came slow from his mouth, like slobber off a bull's lip. I can't recall.

—Well, you'd remember if I did, wouldn't you?

—I s'pose so. Yeah. He lowered the pistol and let out a soggy, rueful snort of laughter. Fuck, man. Y'know, I...just people been fucking me around a lot lately.

—If you can't find it, don't come back in here busting on me about it. You know you gonna find it sooner or later in that mess. Someday you run out, you gonna be stumbling around and it'll turn up under your big toe. Be like finding a diamond in a cornfield.

This fairly brightened Rickey—he nodded energetically, seeing a vision of that glorious day. I noticed Leeli cowering in the corner,

LUCIUS SHEPARD

His face was a blur of sunlight, but going by his round head, I guessed this to be Squire. Both Ava and Carl were grinning and pointing at a shield-shaped sign on the shoulder of the road. The sign was also blurred, but readable: State Road 44.

Several of the remaining pictures were shots of Carl, some of Ava and Carl. A few recent ones showed them with Squire. None of these said much to me, not like the first. Seeing that Ava had aged, though not so much as she should have, and Carl hadn't aged a day, this gave rise to Star Trek movies in my head. Space aliens, UFOs, abductions. secret government projects, intelligent robots, all kinds of happy horseshit. A couple of times I thought I'd figured out who they must be, but if they were aliens or whatever on the run from the government, what the hell were they doing on government property? If they were working with the government, why were they hanging out with the likes of Leeli and me? And what was that house doing in the dunes near the Cape? A trap for lowlifes such as myself, I decided. That was it. Damn straight. Alien creatures from beyond the stars were studying the pork rind set. Government superclones were learning how to mimick the scum of the earth so they would be in place to assasinate the redneck Jesus, who'd be coming to a womb in Kissimmee any day now. Or could be robot killers who did the evil bidding of the Bush administration were given vacations during which they hung out with real folks and fucked them up every whichaway. Or Squire and Carl were aliens who'd suffered brain damage in the Roswell crash and Ava was their rehab nurse, training them in the ways of society, and their vibrations were keeping her young. I got somewhat insane behind all this, creating tabloid headlines, picturing me and Leeli on the talk shows, discussing her alien lesbian lover with Jerry and Jay and David and the rest, going out to Hollywood to attend the premiere of the movie about our life story. Gradually I calmed down. There was bound to be a logical explanation for the photo and Carl's recuperative powers and everything else. I told myself I'd get to the bottom of it eventually.

* * *

I woke the following morning with a pistol barrel poking my nose and Rickey's hand on my throat and his burnt out eyes giving parting around it, and the grasses gave forth with an approving chorus, like the sound Leeli made when the Dilaudid rushed upon her, only louder by a million throats, seeming to appreciate the architecture of dust and reflected fire in the sky, the hosanna clouds, the lacquered moon-colored water, the grasses tipped in silver, the black cut-outs of the palm islands like left-over pieces of Africa. I had that feeling of small nobility and pure solitude the world wants you to feel when it reveals this side of itself, so you'll believe nature was this awesome beautiful peaceful rock concert deal before man come along and doggy-fucked it full of disease, and not the bloody, biting, eat-your-meat-while-its-alive horror show it truly is. That night I was okay about feeling this way and I walked along the shore, sucking in the odors of fish and frogs and the millions of unrecorded deaths that had accompanied the HoJo manager's as if they were the latest Paris perfumes.

I thought I was out there on my lonesome, just me and a scrap of wilderness and Dilaudid, but when I climbed a hummock to avoid wading through the marsh, I spied Ava, Carl, and Squire standing at the tip of a grassy point about sixty feet farther along. Ava was gesturing at the sky like she was naming stars or teaching about the weather or something. Squire and Carl, whose jaw was bandaged, were gazing upward. I was too fogged to jam their nature walk in with all the other nothing junk I knew concerning them and make any sense of it, but when they strolled off still farther from the lodge, I realized this was my opportunity to take a peek at Ava's personals and maybe scoop up some cash. I hustled back as fast I could, which was not real fast, and located the room where she was bunking. Her tote bag was stuffed under a pillow. I found no money, but among the keys and Keenex and cosmetics and all was a badge holder holding a photo ID. Official evidence that Ava was affiliated with the FBI. A fake, I thought, but then remembered where I'd met up with her and wasn't so sure. At the bottom of the bag was a leatherette photo album. The first picture was an overexposed black and white shot of Ava and Carl leaning against a vintage Chevy Impala. The 'sixty-two convertible. She appeared to be around seventeen, eighteen, and wore whte socks and buckle shoes and a print dress with a belling skirt that covered her legs to the mid-calves. Carl had on jeans and a sport shirt with its tail hanging out. He looked no younger than he did now. Another guy sat behind the wheel of the Impala.

—Oooh, she said, sliding down in the bed, closing her eyes.
—What I tell ya?

I did more than Leeli, enough so the world fitted around me like a warm liquid glove and there were little sparkles at the corners of my sight and when I moved my hand I felt the exact curve of my shoulder and the muscles playing sweetly in my arm. I lay back next to Leeli. The ceiling was bare gray boards and beams with black grainy patterns and sparkles pricking the gaps that were probably stars. It looked distant and enormous, part of some ancient building that was proud of itself, a church where saints and great soldiers were buried, and terrible instruction was regularly given to the faithful, lots of Go-thous and Verily-thee-must-hastens that resulted in dungeons filled with bones and chained apes with blood on their teeth and crestfallen martyrs, but it didn't have no message for me. My eyelids were trying to droop and my mind drooped too, blissfully trivial, noticing stuff about the high, the tremor in my leg, a pincushion sensation in my left foot, a nerve jigging in my chest. Something landed softly on my stomach, its warmth spreading like a melting pat of butter. Leeli's palm. Feel up to having some fun? she asked. Her hand slipped lower and she flicked my zipper.

—I ain't never gonna say no, but I'm pretty damn wasted.
—Me, too. I don't really need to or nothing. I just want to see what it's like…when I'm like this, y'know. Okay?

We fucked like space babies in no gravity, coming together at goofy angles, forgetting for long moments what we were doing, our minds scatting on some loopy riff, reawakened by the touch of lips, a breast, something that got us all juicy and eager for a time, speeding it up and lapsing again into slow motion, into stillness. It took Leeli damn near an hour to come and once she started it took her almost the same to stop. She curled up into me after like a dazed, sleek bug that had eaten too much of a leaf and said, Sweet Jesus. That was amazing! I was too gassed to respond. If we'd been a pair of spiders, she could have gnawed off my legs and laid eggs in my belly and I wouldn't have argued the matter.

Leeli had some trouble sleeping due to the itching that goes with the Dilaudid wearing off, but finally her breathing grew even and deep. I did a few more hits, pulled on my pants and went onto the porch. A wind had sprung up, driving away the skeeters and quieting the frogs. Clouds edged with milky light were racing the moon,

HANDS UP! WHO WANTS TO DIE?

—'Member that little honey you's fucking, one with the blue streak in her hair?

—Twila, I said.

—Yeah, her. She got the virus. He said this with the sort of cheerful expectancy you might use to announce the birth of twins. 'Spect some of them NASCAR boys better get theyselves checked, he went on. Last I heard, she was passing out blowjobs at Mac's Famous Bar like they was dollar kisses.

—She musta knew what she was doing. Twila didn't give a shit. My feet crunched the litter ocean as I stepped toward the door.

—Maceo?

—What?

—You wanna bring me something from the 'frigerator? I got pizza in there and I'm too fucked-up to walk.

—I'll do 'er in a while.

The corridor had gone dark. I stood a moment, getting my bearings, and heard Rickey quietly say, Oh, God...God! Maybe he was hurting, maybe the veil of the future had lifted and he saw a shadow stealing toward him. Or maybe it was the Gators done something stupid.

* * *

Leeli had spread sheets on the bed in a room off the kitchen, and sealed a hole in the window screen with a stuffed rag, and secured a lamp for the bedside table. She was sitting on the bed, her knees tucked to her chin, tanned legs agleam in the tallowy light.

—What we gonna do? she asked.

—I told you what I wanted to do back in Ocala.

She hid her face, resting her forehead on her knees. It's not back in Ocala now. We gotta figure something to do.

—Don't know about you, but I'm getting high. I showed her the pills.

—What is it?

—Dilaudid.

—Is it something good?

—It's evil. You gonna fucking adore it.

I powdered a handful of pills in the bottom of a teacup and let Leeli feed her nose from the tip of a knife blade.

touching a settlement of pill bottles on the floor. He was watching football. The Gators and somebody. I asked who was winning and he tipped back his head, trying to find me, but not in an awful hurry about it.

—Shit! The word leaked out of him like a last gasp. He gave a blitzed laugh, two grunts and a hiccup. That you, man?

I picked a straight chair from beside a sheetless mattress in the corner and sat so he could watch me and the TV both.

—Maceo. He made a fumbly gesture, patting an invisible dog by his knee. Crazy motherfucker. Where you been?

—Raiford. New Smyrna for a while after.

—Oh, yeah…right. Rickey's face was gaunt, greasy with sweat, ready to crack and sag. The bridge of his nose was swollen and had a ragged cut across it that wasn't healing too good.

I asked what he was up to and he said, Dilaudid. Crystal meth. Mostly dilaudid lately. You want some? I got a shitload.

—There's people with me. We need to hide out here a couple or three days.

He blinked rapidly. It was like part of his brain was attempting to semaphore another part that trouble was at hand, but the message didn't come through. Yeah…okay, he said feebly. Wherever you want, y'know. There's rooms. His eyes, charcoal smudges, returned to the TV. A faint cheer mounted as a tiny guy in blue-and-orange scampered down the sideline. The Gators were kicking ass. Rickey made a grinding, choking noise in the back of his throat. I knew that paved-over feeling in the esophagus, the warm dry space that kept him safe from the guttering of his own life, the valueless thoughts featherdusting the inside of his skull. Like a perfect fever.

—I'll take a few of them Dilaudid, you don't mind, I said.

—I told you go ahead. His fingernail ticked one of the bottle caps. I got a whole shitload.

I kneeled by the chair, palmed one of the bottles and shook four white tabs out of another.

—You get settled, come on back you wanna talk. Rickey wriggled his ass around as if he had an itch.

—Yeah, maybe. We're kinda wore down.

—Hey, Maceo!

I could see him looking for a way to hold me there. I guess I'd reminded him he was lonely.

dinosaurs, and its teeth had busted from its mouth or it had laid a number of curious square white eggs before passing.

We hid the van behind a shed and straggled toward the main lodge. Lodge was a hundred dollar name for a structure that was the house equivalent of a crooked old beekeeper who had stroked out in his sleep while wearing his hat and veil. Window shadows for eyes and a gnawed-off nose opening into a screen porch and boards the color of cigarette ash and a slumped partial second story with tattery shingle tiles drooping off the roof edge. There were no lights. Frogs bleeped out in the marsh, like electric raindrops, and skeeters would cover your arm unless you kept swiping them off.

—Nobody's home, Leeli said in an exhausted tone.

—Maybe. It don't matter. The porch stair creaked and bowed to my step. The billowed-out screens were rusted through in patches, torn loose from the railing. Just pick out some rooms, I said. I'll see if anybody's here.

I left the others to creep around and scare the spiders and explored some. You couldn't find a grayer place, you searched in a cemetary. Every square inch and object had run out of time and stopped being what it once was. Phantom things that resembled tables and chairs and rugs and pictures on the walls and the walls themselves were just ghosts made of dust and habit and a gray smothery smell. The kitchen sink was gray and so were the stains on it. Peels of linoleum curled up from the floor like eucalyptus bark. The only bit of color I noticed was three custom car magazines poking from beneath an empty bookcase. Rickey's version of the redneck dream.

From down the hall came a gentle muttering. Around the corner I caught sight of a pale flickery glow escaping through a half-closed door. I pushed it open. A lounge chair faced a pint-sized color TV set on an orange crate. The chair was an island throne rising from an ocean of beer cans, pizza boxes, take-out cartons, grocery sacks, empty tins, condom packets, shrinkwrapped cookies, crumpled tissues, video cases, batteries. You name it, it was there. Stretched in the chair, wearing bib overalls, lording it over this his solitary realm, was the fucking vulture god of decay. He was thinner than the last I saw him, his beard about six inches longer, but he still had the worst combover in Central Florida. The dirt on his ankles made an argyle pattern. His right arm dangled off the chair arm, his fingers almost nobodies on their way to damnation. Credence and Lynard Skynard for the soundtrack. My daddy's kind of songs, but I liked them all the same. I found one cigarette left in my crumpled pack and lit up. It didn't taste a thing like movie smoke must taste, clean and savory, a working man's reward, but my exhales hazed the air so it looked old-fashioned and yellowy brown, 1970s air, air with some character, and I sat fingering the gun, trying to put my mind onto a future different from the sort promised by the movie I was in, but thinking mainly about the manager, what a strange thing it was for a man to come halfway around the world from a place where they had monkeys and elephants and shit to go with their nuclear bombs just to catch a bullet in a HoJos and die staring up at track lighting and styrofoam ceiling tile.

Rickey Wirgman, who I'd called my friend, was more of a brother fuck-up and former criminal associate, like a cousin you don't have much use for but deal with on occasion. His grandfather had left him some property on the edge of the marshlands near South Daytona, a collection of weathered frame buildings alongside a stretch of open water that grandpa, if not for a crack habit and some harsh words spoken to a fellow inmate in the Volusia County Jail that caused his history to take a sudden tragic turn, might have developed into a full-blown financial disaster. A fishing camp had been his thought. In the years since he'd inherited, Rickey had run a contest to see what would fall apart the fastest, himself or the roof he slept under. He sold off pieces of the land to survive and recreated with the finest dope and the nastiest hookers. The sheds and cabins were rotting away, but the marsh was pretty in the twilight. Black watercourses meandering through tall green grasses, here and there a tiny humped island thick with palms going to silhouettes in the soft gray light, and pelicans crossing in black flapping strings against a streak of rose along the horizon, like a caption in a cool language. Exotic-looking. A Discovery Channel place. The grass was tamped down around the relics of the fishing camp. Seemed like some huge, heavy thing had made an emergency landing, maybe a big jetliner bellying in, and the survivors had squatted where they'd been spilled until death had swallowed them too, and now their shelters were decaying. Scattered around in the higher grass behind the cabins were beat-up refrigerators and washing machines and stoves. They got you thinking it wasn't a plane had crashed, but one of those bird

HANDS UP! WHO WANTS TO DIE?

* * *

I'm not a complete fool. I understand it's all about pussy, but pussy must be a sickness with me, otherwise I cannot explain why I let myself get pulled back into a situation I knew was a dead loser. A psychiatrist might say I was hunting for just such a situation, but if Leeli had been one of the reverend's old gals, I wouldn't have wasted a second before putting her in the rear view. I admit self-destruction is the way of my life. The way of every life, maybe. But the style Leeli brought to her walk-off scene, switching her hips and arching her back and giving a sad, pouty look over her shoulder, psychology wasn't that huge a factor.

I told her to drive and funneled Ava, Carl, and Squire into the rear of the van, then climbed in behind the passenger seat so I could keep an eye on everybody. Squire was by the doors, legs kicked out, his head wobbling like he was listening to private music. Ava was next to the wheel hub, comforting Carl, who rested his good cheek on her shoulder.

—Get east, I said to Leeli. Use the interstate and keep it under the limit.

Ava asked, Where we going? It was loud in the van and she had to shout it.

—Friend of mine's place in South Daytona!

She thought about this and nodded gloomily.

—Wanna tell me what's going on? I pointed to Squire and then Carl.

She shook her head. Not now! She shifted to accomodate Carl's weight and said, I'd like my gun back!

—I like maple sugar on my oatmeal, I told her. But sometimes I gotta do without!

The sun was bouncing along just above the palm tops like a dragged bait, and the light was growing orangey, and a brown shadow gathered in the rear of the van. It was all calming somehow, the shadow and the rattling, droning speed. I felt submerged in it, a man sitting at the bottom of a swimming pool, unmindful of trouble in the air, and I worked the ride into a movie, not a big spectacular with sinister terrorist plots or world-shattering disasters, but a movie from back when stars used to play in crummy little stories about in. I headed the van toward the nearest exit and she dug her fingers into my thigh and asked where I was going.

— South fucking America if we can get that far, I said.

A pinch of time zipped by. Turn it around, she said.

— That's gonna happen.

— I mean it! You turn this thing right around!

— Fuck you going on about?

— I'm serious! She reached out with her left foot and stomped on the brake, nearly swerving me into a parked Camry. I'm not running out on my friends.

She kind of hiccupped over the word friends, but kept her gaze firm and determined.

— Your friends? You talking about the Munsters back there?

Her eyes flicked away.

— Oh, okay. You're talking about those twenty thousand friends. This ain't about twenty thousand dollars no more, Leeli. This here's about twenty-to-life.

— I don't care!

— You'll care when those lifer bitches with the tattooed mustaches start wanting to get cozy.

She opened the door, planted one foot on the asphalt. I'm not staying 'less you go back for Ava and them.

— Those motherfuckers gonna get us killled! They almost *got* us killed!

— Way I see it, you didn't act such a fool with that preacher, Carl wouldn't never done nothing!

I put my eyes out the windshield. A lost balloon was sailing off into the blue — it vanished as it crossed the sun. Damn it, Leeli! Get your ass back in here!

She slid down from the seat and stood in the glare, defiant as a dog off its chain.

I gunned the engine. I'm leaving!

She slammed the door shut.

— Something wrong with those people, I said. Man's shot in the face and it don't even phase him? Fuck is that? This ain't nothing we should be messing with.

She took off walking. Her round little butt looked real tasty in those shorts.

— Aw, Leeli! Come on back here, girl!

HANDS UP! WHO WANTS TO DIE?

* * *

There was some sort of promotion going on with the mall. The lot was more crowded than you'd expect. Jolly old farts wearing gaudy sport coats and blue Shriner-type hats were holding bunches of balloons on strings, handing them out to children and mommies, collecting money to cure some great evil that would never die, and two lanes of parking were used up by a carnival with a little ferris wheel, kiddie rides, game and snack stalls. Some high school girls strolled in a small pod, twelve tits in a row, those belonging to a hefty redhead nosing out a close race. They were eyed by a pack of high school boys whose thoughts of rape had likely gotten sly and civilized during hygiene class. Senior citizens dressed in peppy colors gazed soberly at the wheel. I reckon they were recalling greater wheels from the big glorious world that had died out from under them. Treacly music played—the same, it seemed, that played everywhere I traveled.

Ava's gun was stuck in my belt, under my shirt. Its weight made me walk taller than I should have felt. I held hands with Leeli, hoping to persuade folks we were a young couple hot for some corn dogs or whatever hell meat they were pushing at the carnival. We skirted the more populated area of the lot. I spotted a newish Ford van with smoked windows. We snuck up on it from the rear. Just as I was ready to pounce, Leeli warned me off. Standing a few cars over was a huddle of men in blue hats. These old fellows had ridded themselves of balloons. They were laughing, the nudge-nudge laughing men do when they hear a real good smutty joke. The fattest of them had a two-handed grip on his belly, like he was about to lift up a slab of fat and show them something even funnier. Of a sudden the men rested hands on each other's shoulders, forming a circle, and bowed their heads, praying, I supposed, for more balloons or for Jesus to cover the point spread against Satan or that one of the high school girls would lose her mind and fuck them.

Out front of the Home Depot was an old Chevy panel van. I busted the driver's window with the gun butt and hotwired it. The engine shook like the mounts were loose and made a tired, trebly noise until I got it idling. Leeli brushed glass off her seat and jumped

In the truck everybody talked at once, except for Squire. He was gazing out the passenger side window, having himself a fine vacation. Ava and Leeli fussed over Carl in the back seat, and I drove fast toward Ocala. I hadn't put a face on the wrongness of what happened, but it nibbled at the edges of a fucked-up angry fear that raised a red shadow in my brain and jammed spikes into my boneholes, making all my limbs want to stiffen and wiggle like a bug with a pin through its guts. Leeli urged me to drive faster and Ava said, Take us back to the motel! This all stirred in with Oh Gods and Carl repeating over and over in a sunny voice, Hands up who wants to die, shaping a child's song of the line. I told them to shut the fuck up, then I yelled it. For half a minute it was quiet. A big shopping mall come floating up on our left. I slowed and swung the car into it. Ava screeched, What're you doing? as I swerved into a parking slot away from the buildings, hidden by other cars from the highway. I switched off the engine. She clawed at my shoulder, cursing and giving orders.

I turned to her and saw that the manager's bullet had dug a furrow along Carl's jawline. The wound was oozing blood, yet he didn't seem to mind. I'm gonna find us another car, I said. But we ain't going back to no motel.

Ava objected to this and I said, Here's your keys. Go where the fuck you want. I'm getting the hell gone.

I climbed out and told Leeli to come along with me.

Ava caught Leeli's arm. I need her here!

—Well, I need a look-out, so fuck what you need!

—Take Squire, she said.

—Yeah, that'll help. Come on, Leeli.

Leeli hesitated.

A cop car whipped past on the highway, howling like a devil with a hotfoot.

—Goddamn it! Now! I said. You wanna wait around 'til he comes back for us?

Leeli hopped out and glanced uncertainly between me and Ava. She blinked and shivered as if the sun was killing her.

For the first time ever I saw a distinct lack of confidence in Ava's face. You better not leave us here! she said. I swear to God!

—I wasn't thinking on it, I said.

HANDS UP! WHO WANTS TO DIE?

left, clearing a path, and I went toward the door. That's when Carl shouted the magic words.

—Hands up! he said with sincere ferocity. Who wants to die?

The manager had retreated behind the cash register and Carl, beaming like a lottery winner, was pointing a blue steel automatic in his general direction, swinging the muzzle to cover the counter and a portion of window. People started hitting the ground, hiding in the booths, and wasn't more than a couple of seconds before the only ones standing were the five in our party and the manager. You could hear whispering and sobbing and the wheedle of some old pop song turned into a symphony, but it was stone quiet compared to how it had been. Ava slapped at her tote bag, gave it a squeeze, and that told me where Carl had got his shiny new toy.

—Give it to me, Carl, I said, easing toward him a step.

—Okay. He kept on swinging the gun back and forth kind of aimlessly, like it had a momentum that was carrying his arms through an arc.

—Give me the gun, Ava said. You don't need that gun now.

Squire was at her shoulder, nodding as if he firmly supported this idea, and Leeli, smart girl, was halfway out the door.

The manager made a move for something under the register. Ava and I both shouted a warning to Carl. I said, Watch it, man!, and Ava spoke what sounded like a word in a foreign language—I couldn't tell for sure because our shouts mixed together. Carl whipped the gun around and fired just before the manager fired, the explosions overlapping. Carl's head jerked, blood sprayed. His bullet kicked the manager into a buffet cart. He fell behind the counter. A few screams speared the quiet. Smoke lazied in the air. Somebody's lunch treat sizzled and blackened on the griddle. I stepped foward and snatched the gun from Carl. There was blood all over his face, but he was still smiling. Ava wrapped him in a hug and hustled him to the door. I had a quick look back of the counter. The manager was staring off into someplace I never want to see. Frightened eyes were locked on me from every direction, like forest animals peeping at a mangy tiger that had interrupted their play. I fired a shot into the ceiling and told them not to twitch forever and ran like hell.

* * *

Eventually, urged on by his outraged ladies, the reverend scooted out of the booth and ambled over. He clasped his hands at his belly, delivered us a patient look, and asked Carl if he wouldn't mind toning it down.

Carl beamed at him and said, Yes! A single mind!

Leeli said, Can't you can see the man ain't right! Ava offered an apology and I said, You best take your fat ass on back to the hen house, or they gonna need another rooster.

The reverend armored his face with a smile and looked down on me from a peak of blessed understanding. Young man, he said. Actually he said a good bit more, but the words young man were all I heeded. When I was five Reverend Nichols from the First Baptist told my mama having such a sweet little fellow as me by his side would be an asset when he was doing fund-raising, and since this gave her more time for drinking, she loaned me out to him on a regular basis. Young man, he'd say once we were alone, wanna sit my lap while I drive? Young man, I'm gonna open you to God's greatest gift. I didn't much appreciate anybody calling me young man, and I sure as hell didn't want it from a preacher. I caught him by the collar and yanked him down so he was gawking into the leavings of my chicken fried steak. The only thing I recall saying was, Cocksucking holy Joe motherfucker, but I know I expanded on that considerable. People were tugging at me, women were screaming, something struck the side of my head, but I was serene in the midst of it, talking to the reverend, showing him the ketchup-smeared edge of my steak knife.

Rougher hands grabbed me and the reverend broke free. Two guys wearing aprons wrangled me into the aisle, where we did some wrestling and grunting and swearing. A swung purse the size of a satchel knocked one guy off me. I clocked the other with a gut punch that cured him of upright and put him on his knees kissing the carpet like a devout Arab. Shouting people choked the aisle, a few wanting to get at me, the rest trying to get away. I heard Leeli cry, Maceo!, but I couldn't find her in the crowd, so I beelined for the exit, shoving aside Christian and heathen alike. The manager loomed ahead of me. A porky fellow in a maroon shirt and a black tie, his skin that spoiled pumpkin color comes either from a tanning booth or somewheres in India. A wedge of old ladies blocked him off to the pered urgently at him, probably telling him to pay attention or sit up straight. He stared cross-eyed into nowhere, dreaming of columbining the bunch of us. I winked at him, wanting him to know that some of us so-called adults could be dangerous haters, too, when forced to ooh and ahh over a glittery mess of edible sea bugs. This only got him hating me extra special. If somebody had slipped him a piece, they would've found me with my splattered head resting on a cellulite-riddled thigh.

After the boat ride we headed for a Howard Johnson's restaurant down the road from the resort. The reverend and his flock had beaten us there and were crammed into a circular booth across from ours. The ladies chattered away, the kid stared at his fries like they were a heap of golden brown logs on which he was roasting his mom in miniature. Part of my problem was I've been cursed with this inept paranoia that sees danger everywhere except where danger lies. Though I'd done nothing criminal recently, the reverend's presence made me feel criminally guilty. I fiddled with the suspicion that his turning up at the restaurant was police-related. That he'd recognized me for the perpetrator of a crime I'd committed and forgot. Now and then his fruity voice cut through the chatter. He was still going on about the damn fish.

— Did you notice, he asked, how the entire school turned as one? Indeed, all the actions of the underwater world seemed in concert, as though directed by a single mind. Is it such a leap to conceive that our actions are so directed?

Hell yes! would've been my answer, but Carl thought this was about the best thing he'd ever heard. He jumped around in his seat, repeating portions of the reverend's lesson and said to Ava, You see? See what I mean?, like these phrases connected with an argument they'd been having.

— I know, she said, and patted his hand to calm him.

— A single mind directed! he said loudly.

Several of the ladies were shooting pissy looks his way. Ava shushed him and said they'd talk about it later. But Carl wanted to talk about it right then and there. I'd never seen him so heated up. Whenever the reverend's voice carried to us, Carl would go to chuckling, spitting back the reverend's words, saying, Yes! Yes!, and sputtering other foolishness, giving this weird sort of affirmation, like he was a shouter in a retard church.

with me saying something forever stupid like, Somepin' wunnerful's gonna happen to them peaches, honey. Hillbilly Hallmark. I gave Leeli a kiss that sparked a shiver and she settled in against me.

—I could stand another beer, she said.
—Want me to fetch it?
—Naw, it's too much trouble.

Skeeters whined. A night bird said its name about three hundred times in a row. The TV inside the office flickered a wicked green, an evil blue, a blast of white, as if Mrs. Gammage was receiving communication from an unholy sphere. I wouldn't have much cared if the rest of everything was just this hot and black and quiet.

* * *

Squire seemed fine to me, especially for someone who looked to be a goner, but Ava was still acting mothery the next morning. Around noon she herded us into the car and drove to Silver Springs for, I guess, a give-Squire-love day. At a stall near the gift shop she bought a T-shirt with his face airbrushed on it by a genuine T-shirt artist. Squire had the good sense not to wear the thing. Wanna go see the tropical fish? she asked of Carl and Squire both. Squire said he didn't know, whatever, and Carl repeated the word fish until he figured out how to spray spittle when saying it. We crammed into a glass-bottomed boat with a mob of lumpy fiftyish women in baggy slacks and floral blouses. I assumed they were a church group, because they appeared to be the cut-rate harem belonging to this balding, gray-haired individual with a banker's belly and a sagging, doleful face, dressed like a Wall-mart dummy in slacks with an elastic waistband and a sweated-through sports shirt. A pretty blonde in a captain's hat steered the boat and as we glided across the springs, her voice blatted from the speakers, identifying whatever portion of nature's living rainbow we were then passing over. The man stood the whole trip, clutching a pole for balance, providing his own commenary and sneaking glances at Leeli, who was wearing short shorts. He was trying to make some general point relating to the fish. It had a chary Unitarian flavor, a serving of God and fried turnip slices. All the ladies nodded and favored him with doting gazes. Squashed between two of them was a chubby kid about fourteen who had the miserable air of a hostage. One of the women whis-

HANDS UP! WHO WANTS TO DIE?

galow. Leeli started to join up with them, but Ava waved her off and said she needed to tend Squire for a while. That brightened Leeli, but she watched until the door closed behind them.

—Don't none of this strike you peculiar? she asked.

—Pretty much everything strikes me peculiar. So I guess nothing does, really.

* * *

If I hadn't been consumed with getting Leeli into the bungalow and the two of us shaking the walls so hard, the framed picture would shudder off its veil of dust and the palmetto bugs would prepare for the fall of creation, I might've had room for some helpful thoughts. I don't suppose it matters, though. Chances are I wouldn't have reached any conclusion. If I had, either I wouldn't have acted on it or else it would have been the same half-assed conclusion I come to without even stretching my brain. Studying on things until you couldn't tell whether what you thought was what you wanted to think and all that—it wasn't my style. I had two ways of going at the world. One, I was a furnace of a man and everything I saw was viewed in terms of how it would do for fuel. The other, I was a pitiable creature who'd been walked on for so long there was a damn dog run wore down into my skull and whenever a shadow crossed my path, my instinct was to snap my teeth. Neither of those boys gave a sugary shit about situational fucking analysis.

Ava was kept busy that night tinkering with Squire's self-esteem. Least that's what I believed had sucked his fire down so low, his pilot light kicked off. It was like Leeli had been busted out of jail. She wanted one of everything with me. We come close to killing each other. Toward nine we took a break, borrowed Ava's car, and brought back catfish and puppies and fries. Halfway through our greasy feast, we went at it again, smearing fish juice all over the bed. It would've took oven cleaner to scour the sheets. Long about midnight we smoked cigarettes on the steps. Fireflies bloomed in the hazy dark. The breeze hauled a smell of night-booming cereus out from the shadows of the palms. A shine from the bulb over the office door fresh-tarred the blacktop. We had us one of those made-in-Nashville moments. Our arms around one another, heads together. Snap the photo, frame it with a heart, and stick in a word balloon about his girlfriend should have won the wet T-shirt contest. All the color had left him straightaway. His skin had the look of gray candlewax.

Mrs. Gammage snorted and snuffled some. Maybe she was seeing herself strapped into Old Sparky over to Raiford, or maybe she hadn't yet gotten that specific with self-pity and was tearing up because she felt the victim of a vast injustice—here she'd been protecting her precious petunias and now Jesus had gone and let her down despite all everything she'd done for him. I had in mind to tell her that feeling she was having that everything had tightened up around her and no matter how hard she tried to turn with it, the world was no longer a comfortable fit, and if she made a move to pry herself loose from that terrible grip, it'd pinch her off at the neck...I would have told her after a while it got to feel natural and she likely wouldn't know what to do things didn't feel that way. Before I could advise her of this, Ava came on the run and shooed us away, babbling about how Squire was prone to these fits and she'd handle it, just to leave her alone with him because when he woke up he was scared and she could gentle him. I returned to step-sitting out front of my bungalow and Mrs. Gammage streaked toward the office to recast the deadly prayer spell she'd been fixing to hurl at the universe. Ava kneeled to Squire, hiding his upper body from sight. My forty had gone warmish, but I chugged down several swallows and wiped the spill from my chin and looked back to the petunia bed just in time to see Squire sit bolt upright. It wasn't the kind of reaction you'd expect from someone smacked down by a fit. No wooziness or flailing about. It was like Ava had shot a few thousand volts through him.

Leeli had come out of Ava's bungalow, wearing white shorts and a green halter. She wandered over to me and sat on the stoop. What you think's wrong with Squire? she asked in a hushed voice.

—Boy's so slow, maybe his brain idles out every so often.

She stared at Ava and Squire as if she was trying to figure something out. I did some staring myself, digging my eyes under that halter. The heat cooked her scent strong. I leaned closer and did a hit. She glanced up and asked, What you doing?

—I wish I was smelling breakfast, I said.

Squire and Ava scrambled up, Squire gesturing like he was wanting to explain something of importance. They made for Ava's bun-

HANDS UP! WHO WANTS TO DIE?

beautify the grounds. Chop a few weeds, prune a shrub or two, cut back a climbing cactus from a palm trunk. He'd fuel his labors with glugs from a thermos that likely contained a libation stiffer than Gatorade. If he was feeling frisky he'd start his electric trimmer and hunt up stuff to trim. You could tell he loved that machine, the way he flourished it about. Watching him survey his property, hands on hips, his turkey-baster belly popped full out, it was my impression he was a happy man, though it was tough to understand why. Whenever he revved up the trimmer his wife would come to the office door and yell for him to quit making that noise. She was built short and squarish and commonly wore a dark brown housecoat. This sponsored the idea she might have given birth to the bungalows or was their spirit made flesh, or something of the sort. Her face was topped off by about a foot of forehead on which God had written a grim Commandment. I felt the air stir when she glared at me. Inside the office there was a Bible big as a microwave and I bet she would open it and pray for everythng around her to disappear.

    I was sitting outside my bungalow our second afternoon there, nursing a forty, when she come flying from the office and took a run at Squire. He'd fallen out on the grass near the highway, his head resting in a petunia bed. Mrs. Gammage screamed, Get outa my flowers, punching the ground with a lurching, stiff-gaited stride like an NFL guard with bad knees. Squire never moved, not even when she kicked him. She kicked him again. I wouldn't say I was spurred to action, but since I was technically supposed to be on Squire's side, I thought I should make a supportive gesture. Time I got myself on over to the petunias, she had stopped kicking and was bending to him and saying, Hey! Hey! She had a thin, bitter smell, like a bin of rutabagas. Squire's eyes were half-open, but only one iris showed.

    —'Pears like you killed him, I said.

    Mrs. Gammage staggered back from the petunia bed, gazing at Squire with an expression that crossed stricken with disgusted. He was already dead! I didn't do nothing coulda killed him.

    —You kicked him right in the side of his chest where the heart's on. That'll do 'er every time. It's a medical fact.

    I was just fucking with her, but Squire hadn't twitched and it dawned on me that he actually might be dead. His color was good, though. Only dead man I'd ever seen up close was this old boy got shot in the head outside the Surf Bar in Ormond Beach for arguing

LUCIUS SHEPARD

From Disneyworld the party train crossed the state to Ybor City, then up to Jacksonville and then back down to Silver Springs. Eleven days and we hadn't gone a mile toward Lauderdale. Often as not, whenever Leeli was with Ava and Carl, Squire would seek me out. He figured we were in the same boat, I expect. Whereas Carl had one trick, Squire was proficient in two. Like he was a grade up on Carl in Ava's pre-school. Mostly he desired to talk about how much pussy he'd been getting since a precocious early age, but it was plain he'd never gotten any that hadn't got him first. He recounted a string of fabulous conquests, each more of a joke than the last. A female jockey, a porn star, a TV actress, the girl who played center for the Dallas Sparks. They had the feel of lies he'd overheard in a bar and loved so much he'd taken them in and give them a new home. Tempted as I was to blow a hole in his picture window, I let him rave. Sooner or later he'd wind down and go to thinking about Ava. I didn't have to be a mind reader to know this. Ava thoughts stamped their brand on that boy's face. If I had thumped his head at those moments, it would've bonged like a bell.

* * *

In Siver Springs, instead of staying at the resort, we checked into a dump on a blue highway east of Ocala. A dozen frame bungalows painted beige wih dark brown trim and tarpaper roofs and screen doors tucked in among palmetto and Georgia pine. From the road they looked like the backdrop for a 1940s photograph of Grandma and Grandpa on the dashboard of their Model A, off to homestead down in Stark or Sanford, right before Grandma gave birth to the next gold-star-destiny generation of Scrogginses or Culpeppers or Inglethorpes. Up close you saw them different. Tarpaper hats tipped at shady angles over chunky, sallow faces with indifferent eyes, like Chinamen with sly intentions. The screens documented tragic insect stories. Palmetto bugs the size of clothespins scuttled from crack to crack. The sheets were maps of gray and yellow countries. Facing my bed was a framed picture so dusty I could lie back and make it anything I wanted. You smelled the toilet from the steps outside. The place fucking cried out for a shotgun murder.

Of an evening the owner, Mr. Gammage, a scrawny old geeze whose bermuda shorts hung like loose sail from his hipbones, would

HANDS UP! WHO WANTS TO DIE?

— Whatever you see, that's what it is. You know I ain't smart enough to fake nothing.

She didn't act like she believed this. Her lights dimmed and she lay quiet. She fingered my shirt button and appeared to be studying the stubble on my chin. I asked what she was thinking.

— Lots of things.

— Say one.

— I was wondering if anybody's smart enough to know they're faking and I was wishing we already had that twenty thousand.

— Anything else?

I was thinking you got a whole crowd of people paying rent in your skull. Different sizes, different ways of doing. But they all wearing the same face.

* * *

A woman starts to get deep on you, you know it's just the coming attraction for a head movie that'll be playing six shows daily in the weeks to come. She's evaluating her prospects and unless you're fool, you best do some evaluating your own self. Generally speaking, a commitment is being called for, but with Ava in the picture I wasn't sure how things were fitting together in Leeli's thoughts. She went to drowning in moods so wide, they'd wash over me from the next room. Sometimes she wanted me to be patient and other times she wanted me to haul her off to the monkey jungle. After playing mama's little helper at night, she needed daddy to straighten her out. I didn't have a good record when it come to treating female mental disease, but I managed it with Leeli. I gave her to know I was there for her like Oprah and Tarzan both. It surprised me that I was up to the task and when I meditated on this, I realized the feeling Leeli had spotted in me might be for real. A runty little weed sprouted from sandy soil — that was all it was. If it was going to survive, Jim Baker and Tammy Faye would have to drop in from TV heaven and manifest a miracle. But there it waved, baking under the sky of all the shit that had ever gone wrong with me, waggling its dried-up leaves, trying like hell to grow up and learn how to whistle. Puny as it was, it stood taller than any decision I could have made to chop it down.

—I was just letting you tell it.

—I know you're being sweet with me, and I appreciate it. But I'm wore out with sweetness. I could use a shot of male insensitivity. Can you handle that?

I grinned at her and said gruffly, Hell they talking about, woman?

Leeli sighed like those words had hit the spot. Ava'll stop right in the middle of things and explain what's going on. Anatomical stuff, y'know. And Carl he just sits there humming to himself.

—He don't say nothing back?

—Sometimes he asks can he go do something with Squire, and she'll say maybe later or naw it's not your time to be with Squire.

—See what I told you? He's a fucking retard.

—He's not dumb! Ava's always testing him or something. Asking him weird questions. He never gets a'one wrong. She'll ask him to do a sum and he does 'em in his head. Just snaps 'em off!

—Remember that Tom Cruise movie where his brother did all that? That guy was a retard.

—It's not just Carl. Ava, she's...

—What?

—She's a strong woman, is what it is. Sometimes I get a feeling I'm gonna drown in her, y'know. Like she's this tide rolling over me and when it goes out again, nothing's gonna be left of me. Leeli hung her chin onto her chest. I don't know I can do this for a month.

—Fine with me. Let's take the five and split.

The second hand must have galloped damn near ten times around the dial before she said, Chances this good don't come around but every so often. Let's give it a few days.

She come over to the foot of the bed and crawled up beside me and cuddled into my shoulder like she wanted to sleep. I did my best to be pillow and comforter, but the heat of her and my natural preoccupations got me all charged up. She reached her hand down and played with me a while, then lost interest and closed her eyes. Want me take care of that for you? she asked after another bit.

—We'll have our time, I said. Whyn't you rest?

She blinked and peered at me. Wide open, those brown eyes could be like a car coming at you with its high beams on. They left me dazed and fighting for the road.

—That a real feeling I see in there? she asked,

HANDS UP! WHO WANTS TO DIE?

fond memories years from now. It depressed me that I wasn't able to work such a change with my own miseries. Must be I come to Disneyworld too late in life for the enchantment to do its trick.

Close by the Pirates of the Caribbean, an elderly fat man with the word Jellybean embroidered on the chest of his overalls and dozens of jellybeans stuck on his straw cowboy hat had cordoned off a section of walkway and there created portraits of celebrities from thousands of — guess what? — jellybeans. He was working on his knees, dribbling jellybeans onto a rendering of the Statue of Liberty, which except for the spiky headdress looked a whole hell of a lot like his take on the fat Elvis. People stood around saying, Isn't that amazing. He seemed so jolly in his craft, I naturally wished him ill. Odds were he was a twelve-stepper who after a lifetime of domestic abuse visited upon wife and children had gone simple enough from Jesus and caffeine to believe this shit was a suitable atonement. A four-year-old howler with the mouse on his chest and a stalk of blue cotton candy in his fist broke free of his parents and came to stand by Jellybean. Way he held the candy to his mouth and screamed, you could easily picture him at twenty-one doing the same with a microphone and getting laid by supermodels. When his mama tried to drag him off, he endeared himself to me forever by ralphing all over Miss Liberty. Jellybean offered him grandpa consolation, but I caught a glint of good old murder in his eye.

We stayed at Disneyworld four more days. Leeli spent the nights with Ava and mornings with me. The rest of the hours we traveled as a pack. At these times the air got icy. Dinners became occasions of grand formality, long bouts of chewing and swallowing broken by courteous exchanges. Please pass the butter. Would you like another dessert? Can I bring you back something? Leeli had to make sure both Ava and I got our share of flirty glances and secret smiles, and the strain of it all roughed her up some. I learned to let her relax when she came back to our room. She would take two valium from a bottle Ava had given her and sit by the window, her breath ragged, like she was pushing herself to exhale. Finally she'd smile and say, Hi or How you doing?, as if she had just noticed me.

—I can't take much more of Carl, she said one day. It's not about him watching. I'm almost grateful he's there. It kinda makes it easier to switch off my head. But the talking they do…Jesus Lord! She glanced at me for a reaction. Am I boring you?

—I was you, hoss, I said, I'd polish up one of them special Disney smiles and waltz on outa here.

I guess he wasn't a total candy-ass. He had some size on him and I could tell he was weighing job security against the joys of bashing my face with in with one of those metal domes that kept the food warm. I thought about sucker-punching him just to see how far he'd fly, but he turned on his heel and headed for the door.

—Rock on, dude, I called after him.

I sat down to eat. Leeli gave me a God-you're-hopeless look. She bit into her toast with a snap, as if somehow it might do me an injury. We ate without talking for a while, then she said, It might be true what Ava told me. 'Bout the experiment. Carl and Squire are pretty strange.

—One's a retard, other don't know he's a retard. That ain't so strange.

She diddled the fork in her eggs. I can't figure why she'd tell me that story if it wasn't true.

I had to talk around a bite of steak. To make herself look like a big deal.

—People with the money she's got, they don't hafta do that.

—If they're freaks they do. I finally got the bite chewed. Say it's true. Fuck does it matter? We still get paid.

Leeli had built a little fence of eggs around her sausage patty. Nothing this good ever works out, she said, staring at the plate like she was considering making a rock garden out of her cottage fries. What I think's gonna happen and what does happen, there's always a mile of swamp 'tween the two.

—Yeah, well, I said. There is that.

* * *

With a step that was a shade perky for my tastes, Leeli ran off to tell Ava the news. For want of better occupation, I took my Disneyworld pass and went to experience America. As I waited on line the man behind me kept ramming my legs with his gray-headed mama who was sitting in a wheelchair, gripping the arms and scowling like a fury. Everywhere you turned you saw parents yelling at kids who were bawling about they didn't get this or that. Stuck in a photograph album, I supposed these same scenes would dredge up

HANDS UP! WHO WANTS TO DIE?

—She said it'd be okay 'long as you don't get crazy 'bout I'm sleeping with the both of you.

I turned this proposition over to see if it was missing a piece. I don't know, I said. I get these mood swings.

—Oh, really! I couldn't tell. She flounced down beside me, resting her chin on my chest. Can you deal with it? 'Cause if you can't, I might not do this. But I want that money! You imagine the party we could have on twenty thousand? I bet we can get more'n twenty, you ease back and lemme treat Ava right.

I hooked my thumb under the waistband of her panties and gave the elastic a snap. You a bad woman, ain'tcha?

—Goodness me! She batted her eyelashes. I don't know what in the world more I'm gonna have to do to prove it.

* * *

In the morning we had another conversation. It kicked off wrong when I said what bothered me was Ava offering twenty when she could have snagged Leeli for less. Once I got her cooled down, she said huffily, It's not like she was comparison shopping. She's took with me. Guess you'd have trouble understanding that.

—You know that ain't it. I'm just being a realist.

—That's what a realist is? A pea-brained Florida cracker?

—Damn, Leeli! Some guy offered me twenty grand to go party with him for a month, you'd think something was screwy.

—Maybe.

—Maybe my ass!

A polite room service knock ended this round. The waiter, a college boy with a forelock of frosted hair, rolled his cart to the table at the window, off-loaded Leeli's omelette and my breakfast steak, and stood waiting for his tip.

—I got no cash on me, I told him.

—You can add it to the bill, sir.

This was spoken like he was advising a backward child he'd stepped in shit. He had the kind of smug, fleshy face made me yearn to see it staring up from inside a roll of sheet plastic, dripping wet from a canal where he'd been swimming underwater for a week. I snatched the bill from him and wrote one billion dollars on the tip line. His eyes flicked to the amount and froze.

—Naw, I know why. She sat down on the bed, glum as old gravy, picked up the remote and went surfing, changing channels so fast, there was only little blurts of sound. Know what Ava told me? She says she works for the government. The FBI.

—No shit! I said. Is she a friend of Spiderman?

—She showed me her badge! Leeli bugged her eyes and stuck out her tongue.

—Give me ten bucks and I'll show you a badge. I can probably find one in the gift shop.

Leeli threw herself down on the pillow like she was trying to hurt herself. You wanna hear this or not?

—Sure. Lemme have it. I turned to lie facing her so she'd know I was listening, and rested a hand on her waist.

—She said she was an agent and Carl and Squire are in some sorta experiment. She's in charge of 'em. She says she'll pay me a ton of money to be part of it. The experiment.

—Want me to say what I'm thinking?

—I'm not an idiot! I know she likes me, and I know it could all be a story. But she's willing to pay twenty thousand dollars! For one month!

—You see the money?

Leeli gave a vigorous nod. I get five now, the rest after.

—Well, shit. I rolled onto my back. I guess this is goodbye.

—Not necessarily.

—Yeah, necessarily. I can't compete with someone throws around twenty thousand bucks.

She sat up cross-legged and muted the TV. Look, I'm not no shiny apple been sitting on the shelf like you think.

—That ain't what I think, I said, grumpy from losing out to a rich dyke.

—Then why you treating me like I don't know which end of a jar to open. I been with women. It ain't my favorite, but there's times I felt that way. And I can feel that way again. Enough to earn us twenty thousand dollars, I can.

The word us punched a hole in my overcast.

—I don't trust Ava, Leeli said. But with you along I don't have to trust her. So I told her you had to come with us.

—What'd she say?

rooms at the mouse's hotel. We'd have a few cocktails, go on some rides, and see what developed. This made Carl happy, but Squire and Leeli didn't seem to care. I sucked down a third forty on the ride over and after Ava checked us in, I told her I felt poorly and was going to my room.

— Me, too, said Leeli. I'm awful tired.

This surprised Ava as much as it did me. You sure? she said to Leeli. Space Mountain'll juice you right up.

— Naw, we'll catch y'all later. Leeli started walking so fast, she beat me to the elevator.

I had a shower while Leeli ordered room service cheeseburgers and Cokes. The food left me placid and sleepy. I laid out on the bed in my skivvies and Leeli stood at the window, her arms folded, stern of face, like she was taking stock of a brightly lit country she'd just done conquering.

— You don't have to worry 'bout me making a move, that's what's keeping you vertical, I said. I'm through for today.

She made a noise that didn't tell me much.

I grabbed the remote from the bedside table and found a wrestling show on TV. Wrestling hasn't been the same since the prime of Hulk Hogan and the Giant and Macho Man Savage, you ask me. Back in the day your superhero had a gut just like the asshole sitting next to you in the bar and so when you smacked him with a beer bottle, you had a greater sense of accomplishment. Now there was too many pretty boys and it was more tumbling and role-playing than the honest-to-God fake it once was.

Leeli wriggled out of her jeans. Ava gave me money to buy clothes, she said. Reckon we better do it soon.

— We can get some fine clothes here. Get us some mouse shirts and mouse hats with the ears. Maybe you can get some panties with the mouse on the crotch and wear 'em inside out.

She pulled off her tank top and threw it at me in a ball. You *always* have to be a shit?

— It was a fucking joke! Jesus!

She stared at me as if she didn't believe it.

— I swear, I said.

She held the stare a second longer. Damn! she said. Why do I like you?

— You want a honest answer?

—I suppose that's profound, but I'm just a dumb Florida Cracker. It goes right by me.

Ava flicked ash and sparks out the window. You might catch up to it one of these days, she said.

It struck me that Ava must be a lot older than I'd estimated, she was dating back in the 60s, but I didn't stay with the thought. I was a six pack along into a decent buzz and still feeling sour about Leeli, fully occupied with self-pity and scorn. When we stopped for gas I pulled Leeli aside, fed her all the I'm-sorry she could swallow and persuaded her to switch seats with Squire. I discovered a sensitive spot under her ear and before long I had her squirming pretty good, though each time my fingers traipsed near the old plantation home, she'd give them a spank. Squire began telling a lie about a beauty queen he'd gone with in high school and Ava shut him up quick, saying she needed to concentrate on the road. That clued me in she was upset about Leeli, and I felt satisfied in mind.

Scattered around the edges of Disneyworld were a number of shooting ranges where for a few dollars you could fire assault rifles. Given the encouragement this surely offered the freaks who flocked to the ranges, you had to wonder if the city fathers of Orlando didn't unconsciously long to see TV coverage of a giant blood-spattered mouse. While Carl and Squire were busy playing soldier at Buck's Guns and Sporting Gallery, me and Ava and Leeli walked to a nearby 7-11 and bought some forty-ouncers, one of which I chugged walking back to the parking lot. The girls sat talking on the hood of Ava's truck. I wasn't drunk enough to feel mean, but I felt separate from things. The cars racing along the six-lane were shiny toys with glaring headlights and dabs of meat inside. The strip malls lining the road were grimy slot-car accessories. The heat came from a neon tube inside my head and the starless orange-lit sky was a gasoline-soaked rag someone had throwed over the whole mess so's to hide it from company. What I'm saying, it wouldn't have taken much to upgrade me to mean. Ava was pitching hard at Leeli, touching her thigh, the back of her hair. I just kept working on my second forty. If I could drink fast enough, I wouldn't care what they did and I'd be able to ignore some deeper thoughts that were trying to gnaw out my brains like a squirrel with a nut meat.

When Squire and Carl returned, all hotted up from proving their marksmanship, Ava announced a surprise. She had reserved us with Squire, I dropped off the pace, lollygagging along. That's how Leeli wanted to play it, I told myself, to hell with her. I'd find myself a sweeter can of tuna. I started eye-fucking the bikini girls strolling past and when one made a smart-ass remark, getting her friends to laughing at me, I told her once she lost that babyfat she oughta try a real dick, but right now it'd likely be too much for her.

* * *

Ava drove south and then west on State Road 44 toward Orlando. She went to talking about the old days, the 60s, when there was so many UFOs in the sky—because of the rockets at the Cape, she guessed—you could see them from out on 44 every night. Boys useta take us down here to see 'em, she said, 'cause they thought we'd let 'em get fresh while we were stargazing. Leeli, who was riding shotgun next to Carl, said, I bet they were right, huh?
—'Course they were, Ava said, and they shared a laugh.
—You ever see any UFOs? Leeli asked.
—All the time! You look up in the sky, you couldn't help seeing 'em. Pretty soon what you thought was a group of stars would get to darting around, making these really sharp turns, flying in formation.
She asked Leeli to fish around in her tote bag and find her cigarettes. Once she got a smoke going, she said, Couple times we saw one real close.
—A flying saucer?
—Uh huh. We saw this one shoot a green light from its belly. Straight down to the ground.
—Maybe it was Santa Claus you saw, I suggested. Waving his green flashlight.
Ava took a glance back toward me. You don't believe in UFOs, Maceo?
—'Bout as much as I believe in liberty and justice for all.
—Don't listen to him, Leeli said. He's a contrary sort.
I told Leeli she didn't know squat about me and then said to Ava, Whatever you saw, wasn't no flying saucer. Ain't no sense to any of that business.
—That might be, Ava said. Most things don't make sense, especially you try and understand 'em too hard.

table and slipped him a twenty for his dry cleaning bill. Other folks put in their claim and once she had satisfied them, she sat back down and said to me, Temper like that, it's a wonder you still on the street.

Calmer now, I felt no call to answer. I gave her a fuck-you smile and popped one of Leeli's shrimp into my mouth. It was covered with grit that had blown up from the beach, which made it extra crunchy.

—You so smart, Ava said, whyn't you tell us how you'd handle the Joyland?

—Wouldn't nothing but a damn fool mess with it. Too many cops. Too many boyfriends might wanna play hero. You feel the need to rob something, head out on the freeway. You know the back roads along the exits, you can take down two gas stations easy and be sitting in a bar before the cops get motivated.

—I suppose it was your expertise landed you in prison.

—Oh I was a fool. No doubt about that. It don't mean I'm still a fool.

Challenged, I delivered a lecture on proper criminal procedure, most of it learned in Raiford, but salted in with personal experiences that I embellished for dramatic effect. You gotta terrorize a place, I told them. People ain't always scared, they see the gun. Sometimes they can't believe you're for real and they go to debating what to do. You don't want that, you want 'em scared. So you say something lets 'em know how scared they oughta be.

—Yeah? Squire said churlishly. Like what?

I made my hand into a gun and pointed it at his chest. Hands up! Who wants to die? You say that, it gets their attention every time.

I like that, Carl said, grinning. Hands up who wants to die?

—Takes the punch out of it, you say it with a smile, I said. Tell 'em like you mean it.

With that, Carl jumped up and snarled, Hands up! Who wants to die?'

The pregnant lady yipped and the people at the table behind me grabbed up their belongings and scooted. Ava pulled Carl down into his chair and I said to him, That'll get it done.

Leeli stood and said, Can we just go? Please!

We set off down the boardwalk toward the car and she fell into step with Ava and Carl. Irritated by this, not wanting to be stuck said, 'cause time to do it's when it's crowded. You walk on up and let 'em see your piece and grab them bags of money! He looked to Ava like he was expecting to have his belly rubbed. She smiled and dribbled salt from a packet onto her rings.

—You got a hard-on for quarters? I asked. They don't bag nothing but the change.

—You have people with you. Three or four of 'em so you can carry more.

—You think four loads of quarters divided four ways is more'n one load divided one way? You ain't been studying your arithmetic.

—You take the bills too, Squire said. Like, of course, he knew that.

—Where am I? I asked Leeli.

Her expression begged me to shut up.

—Seriously. Did we wake up somewhere's else this morning? Some other planet where stupid rules?

Carl chuckled and I said, Fuck is your problem, man? All you do's sit around and make fun of shit. What put you so high in the roost? Far as I can tell, Squire's your intellectual superior and he ain't got the brains of a box of popcorn.

—You the one's acting superior, Ava said, and forked up some slaw.

—Fuck, I am superior! Superior to this shit. Maybe it gets you wet listening to the criminal genius here, but it don't even give me a tickle.

Squire told me to watch my mouth, I was talking to a lady, and I said, Come on, you fucking chihuahua! Step to me!

Leeli caught my arm and said, Maceo! I jerked free and swatted my shrimp basket, backhanding it across the deck. People bespotted with ketchup splatter from the basket stared at us from the adjoining tables. The assistant manager, who could have passed for fourteen, looked like he was about to cry. Leeli was yelling at me, Squire was avoiding my eyes, Ava was calmly wiping her sleeve with a napkin. Carl giggled and said, Fucking chihuahua!

One of the citizens I'd splattered, a thick-necked, Hawaiian-shirt-wearing, Chevy-Suburban-driving son of the suburbs, his belly sagging like a hundred-year-old hammock, gave his pregnant wife a comforting pat on the shoulder and heaved up from his cheeseburger, but Ava saved his ass by intercepting him on the way to our

LUCIUS SHEPARD

* * *

    I hated Daytona, and not just because I was born there, though every time I drove through Holly Hills, redneck purgatory, and saw those little bunkerlike concrete homes with cracked jalousie windows and chain link fences and Big Wheels with faded colors buried in the front yard weeds, my wattles got all red and swollen. I also hated the beach, the kids who cruised it eight and nine to a convertible or rode around in ten-dollar-an hour rent-a-buggies, the bikini girls with their inch-deep tans and MTV eyes, the boys in Hilfiger suits with an old man's dream of financial security stuck like an ax into their brains at birth. I hated the fucking piped-in circus music that played along the boardwalk, sounding like it was made of sugar beets and red dye number seven. I hated the goddamn carnival rides and the heavy metal curses shouting from the arcades. I liked the ocean all right, liked the blue-green water inside the sandbar, the creamy ridges of foam the tide left along the margin, and the power of the combers, but I wished they rolled in to no shore. I hated the burger joints with their fried onion stink, their white plastic tables and chairs on a concrete deck, and walk-up windows manned by high school geeks with connect-the-dot acne puzzles on their foreheads, because it was at just such a joint I committed the error in judgment that earned me a nickel in Raiford, sauntering up to the service window so wired on crank, all I could smell was the inside of my nose, pulling a fifty dollar pistol, and before I could speak the magic words, two plainclothes cops who were drinking milkshakes at the time snuck up behind me and said to turn around real quick, they'd like that, and later in jail, Sgt. John True, a man apparently fascinated with me, visited my cell, the first of our many nights together, and said, When I was a kid I's just like you — meaning, I suppose, he no longer considered himself a dumbass hillbilly — prior to beating me unconscious. I carried a lot of anger relating to Daytona and that afternoon while we were sitting at a white plastic table on a concrete deck, staring at baskets of onion rings and fried shrimp so heavily breaded, eating one was like eating a hush puppy with a flavorless crunchy prize inside, I let angry out for exercise.

    Squire got things off to a start by going on about how easy it would be to knock over the Joyland Arcade. You gotta have balls, he

HANDS UP! WHO WANTS TO DIE?

tequila shots, we'd climbed aboard the party train. I remembered telling everybody about the beach house. From that I guess the idea had developed for Ava to drive me and Leeli to Lauderdale, making frequent stops for refreshment, with Ava paying the freight. They weren't going to welcome me back at the food mart when I turned up a week late for my shift, but that world was spinning me nowhere and I thought I might take a shot at separating Ava from some of the money she'd been throwing around. I worried about her going after Leeli, though. We'd only had us the one night, but Leeli and I seemed to recognize each other's zero score in life as only folks do who're born in a neighborhood where the most you aspire to is a double-wide and sufficient loose change to afford a couple of cases on the weekend. We'd both worn out our craziness to the point where we saw we might have us a nice little run and maybe avoid killing each other at the end. Once she loosened up and that sick-of-it-all waitress hardness drained from her face, I saw a sweet seam in her no one had bothered to mine.

I left Leeli sleeping and smoked in the breezeway of the motel, watching two rat-skinny children splash and squeak in the pool, while their two hundred pound plus mama, milky breasts and thighs and belly squeezed into inner-tube shapes by a lemon yellow bathing suit, lay on a lawn chair and simmered like a dumpling over a low flame. The drapes of Ava's room hung open a crack and I had a peek. All I saw of her was legs waving in the air and hands gripping onto a headboard. The rest was hidden underneath Squire. His pimply butt was just pumping up and down. Sitting straight in a chair beside the bed, like a schoolboy being taught a lesson, Carl was looking on with interest. Well, come get me Jesus, I said to myself. With Carl and Squire both bagging Ava, she wouldn't have much time for Leeli. I had to admire Squire's stamina, but he looked to be doing push-ups on a trampoline and if I was the boy's daddy I'd have advised him that women tend to enjoy some rhythmic variation. He finally fell off his stroke and rolled onto his back. Ava came up flushed and sweaty, hair sticking to her cheeks. She had a sip of water, spoke briefly to Carl, then straddled Squire and began more-or-less to treat him like he'd been treating her. I'd been feeling about ten cents on the dollar, but watching her work cleaned the crust off my brain. Being the gentleman I am, I decided to buy Leeli coffee and a Kripsy Kreme before checking out the rest of my parts.

ably hadn't done for Squire what he hoped. It made his face resemble a cream pie somebody drew a man-in-the moon face on, but he tried to sell the look as being the front door into the world of a badass individual with secrets you would want to know. It was kinda pathetic. He threw a couple of insults my way and when that didn't get a rise, he went on about how tight he was with Carl and Ava, how they'd been partying for two months solid, saying me and Leeli needed to get on board the party train, they'd sure show us time.

— Two month vacation must get in the way of your bartending, I said and he said, Huh?, then got flustered and came back with, Oh, yeah...Hell, I just work when we're there, y'know.

The juke box played the Dixie Chicks. Leeli squealed, clapped her hands, and did this slow, snaky hula, dancing like she was on stage at a titty bar and using Ava for the pole.

— We ain't hardly ever there, though. Squire said this like it was super important for me to understand. He started to spout more worthless bullshit, but I told him to hang onto the thought. I walked over to Ava and tapped her on the shoulder and said, 'Scuse me, buddy. Believe it's my turn. She flashed a condescending smile and backed off. Leeli kept her eyes closed like she didn't care what was going on, she was so lost in the music, but when I put my leg where Ava's hip had been she said, That was rude!

— Yeah she was, I said.

She punched me in the chest, but didn't leave off dry-humping my leg. Just 'cause we did the deed, don't you go waving no papers at me.

— That wasn't my intention.

She didn't hear and I said it again louder.

This ticked her off. Just what is your intention? she asked.

— I got a friend in Lauderdale lets me use his beach house. I thought we could drive down next weekend and see how it goes. But hey, you wanna fuck the old skank, do it.

— Well, maybe I will! She looped her arms about my neck and smiled me up. Or maybe I'll wait 'til after Lauderdale.

I thought the two of us were back on track, but when Ava decided to hit another bar, Leeli said in a cajoling voice, I'm having so much fun! Let's not go home yet! Wasn't until we wound up in a Daytona Beach motel on Saturday morning, sleeping in the room next to Ava's, that I realized somewhere in the middle of all those

HANDS UP! WHO WANTS TO DIE?

We piled out through the glass doors, both Carl and Squire heading toward the water. Fuck you think you going? I asked.
—Ava got her four-by-four parked down on the beach, Squire said.
I was staring at Ava and Leeli, who were still back at the glass doors. Leeli had her head down and Ava was talking. Something didn't sit right about the way they were together.
—Government don't care what goes on at the house no more, Squire said, apparently thinking I was off onto another track. We been partying here for years.

* * *

You know that kid's toy ball you can bounce and instead of coming straight back to your hand, it goes dribbling off along the floor or kicks off to the side? My expectations of the weekend had taken just that sort of wrong-angled bounce. After Leeli and I broke in the leather couch, I assumed we'd be heading over to my place, maybe coming up for air sometime Sunday. A shitkicker bar had for sure not been part of the plan.
The Dixieland was down on A1A, a concrete block eyesore with a neon sign on the roof that spelled the name in red and blue letters, except for the N was missing, which might have accounted for the gay boys who occasionally dropped in and left real quick. All the waitresses were decked out in Rebel caps and there were Confederate flags laminated on the table tops. The Friday night crowd was men in cowboy hats who had never set a horse and women with flakes of mascara clinging to their lashes and skirts so short you could see the tattooed butterflies, roses, hummingbirds and such advertising their little treasures whenever they hopped up onto a barstool. Some country & western goatboy was howling on the jukebox about the world owed him a living, while a few couples dragged around the dance floor, Ava and Leeli among them. Their relationship appeared to be deepening.
Carl fell in love with a digital beer display behind the bar that showed a bikini girl waterskiing. I was coming to understand the boy must have some empty rooms in his attic. He stood gawking at the thing like he was stoned on Jesus love. That left Squire and me alone at a table, sucking on our margueritas. Shaving his head prob-

Her face was full of bad days and wrong turns, the lines cutting her forehead and dragging down her mouth making it seem older than than the rest of her. Way the men tucked themselves in at her shoulders, you could tell she was queen of the hive.

Leeli clutched at my arm, breathing fast. Nobody said nothing. Finally I came out from behind the couch and tossed Leeli her panties. I stepped into my pants and feeling more confident with my junk covered, I said, Have yourself a show, did ya?

—Have yourself a show? the blonde man said, mocking me, and the baldy sniggered like a kid who'd seen his first dirty picture.

I pulled on my shirt. Y'know this here's government property? Y'all be in deep shit, I turn your asses in.

—You saying you the government? The woman's voice was a contralto drawl made me think of a dollop of honey hanging off the lip of a jar. You the first government man I seen got jailhouse ink on his arms. She turned to Leeli, who was tugging the tank top down over her breasts. How's about you, sweetcheeks? You in the government, too?

Leeli snatched up her jeans. You got no more right being here than we do!

The woman sniffed explosively, like a cat sneezing, and the bald man said, You can't get much more government than we are. Government's like mommy and daddy to us.

Leeli piped up, Well, whyn't you show us your ID?

The flow of feeling in the room was running high, like everyone was waiting for a direction to fly off in.

—Screw this, said the woman. We was just going for a drink. Y'all wanna come?

I was about to say we'd do our own drinking, but Leeli said, It's Marguerita Night over the Dixieland!, and soon everybody was saying stuff like, Looked like you was gonna fall out and God you scared the hell outa me and telling their names and their stories. Though he didn't seem up to the job, the blonde man, Carl, was the woman's husband. Her name was Ava and she owned a club in Boynton Beach where the bald man, Squire, worked as a bartender. I knew a kid name of Squire back in high school who was accused of having sex with a neighbor's collie. Much as I would have enjoyed bringing this up, I kept it to myself.

HANDS UP! WHO WANTS TO DIE?

—God, I could use something to drink, she said. I know there can't be nothing in the kitchen.

My carpenter's pants were puddled at the end of the couch. I undid the flap pockets and hauled out two wine coolers. What you want? I asked. Tropical Strawberry or Mango Surprise.

—I can't believe you carrying 'round wine coolers in your pocket.

—I hooked 'em off a truck when I was coming outa work.

We unscrewed the caps, clinked our bottles and drank.

—My name's Leeli, she said, sticking out her hand. I'm sorry but I forget yours.

—Maceo.

—That a family name? It's so unusual!

—It's for some guitar player my mama liked.

—Well, it's real unusual.

She seemed to be expecting me to take a turn, so I asked what a house was doing out there setting in a hole.

—Beats me. Government bought up all the land 'round here years ago. To keep people away from the Cape...'cause of the rockets, y'know? But I never knew nothing was here. My ex, his friend runs a helicopter tourist ride? I guess he saw it once.

—Maybe they opened it up for development, I said. And this here's the model home.

—Y'know, I bet you're right! She gave me a proud mama look, like my-ain't-you-smart!

I couldn't think of anything else to say, so I went to loving her up again. She started running hot and came astride me, but before she could settle herself, she let out a shriek and crawled over top the couch. I rolled my eyes back to see what had spooked her, said "Shit...Jesus!" and next thing I was hunkered behind the couch with Leeli, my heart banging in my chest.

Two men and a woman were hanging by the glass doors, nailing us with a six-eyed stare as clear in its negativity as a No Trespassing sign. The men were young, both a shade under six feet, dressed in slacks and T-shirts. A blonde and a baldy. They had the look of fitness sissies, like they might have pumped some iron and run a few laps, but never put the results to any spirited use. The woman wore cut-offs and an oversized denim shirt and carried a bulky tote bag. She was fortyish and big-boned, with wavy dark hair, and her body had a sexy looseness that would still draw its share of eye traffic.

and check out what's there, when everybody tells her it ain't nothing but sand fleas and Spanish bayonet, you say, Hell I'll go with you. Ten minutes later you're helping her jump down from a hurricane fence, risking a felony bust for a better view of those white panties gleaming against the strip of tanned skin that's showing between her jeans and her tank top. She falls into you, gives you a kiss and a half, and before you can wrap her up, she scoots off into the dark and you go stumbling after.

It don't take more than that to get shit started.

—Hey, I shouted. Come on back here!

She glanced at me over her shoulder, her grin shining under a moon fresh out of hiding, then she skipped off behind some scrub palmetto. I was trying to recall her name as I ran, then a frond whacked me in the face and I slipped to a knee in the soft sand. I spotted her moving along a rise, framed by low stars. Hell you going, girl? I said, coming up beside her.

She slapped at a skeeter on her neck and said, Lookit there.

The land was all dips and rises, an old dune top gone nappy with shrubs and beach grass, but down below was a scooped-out circular area, wide and deep enough to bury a mini-mall in. Dead center of it stood a ranch house with cream-colored block walls and a composite roof and glass doors. It was a giant banana, I couldn't have been more startled.

—I heard about there was a house here, she said. But I swear I didn't believe it!

We scrambled down the slope and tromped around the house, peering in windows. Some rooms were empty, others were partly furnished, and though I wouldn't have figured on it, the sliding door at the back was unlocked. I shoved it open and she put her hands over her head and got to snapping her fingers and hip-shaked across the threshold. A big leather sofa stood by its lonesome in the middle of the room. She struck a pose beside it, skinned off her jeans and showed me what I wanted. Wasn't long before we were sweating all over each other, grunting and huffing like hogs in a hurry, our teeth clicking together when we kissed. The cushions got so slippery, we slid off onto the floor afterward and lay twisted together. The moon came pale through the flyspecked glass, but it wasn't sufficient to light the corners of the room.

Hands Up!
Who Wants to Die?
Lucius Shepard

Shit happens, like they say. You know how it goes. The cops are looking at you for every nickel-and-dime robbery they can't solve, and the landlady hates your guts for no reason except she's a good Christian hater, and everything in the world is part of a clock you got to punch or else you'll be docked or fined or sentenced to listen to some ex-doper who thinks he has attained self-mastery explain your behavior as if the reasons you're a loser are a mystery that requires illumination. Otherwise it's been a kicked dog of a week. The boss man's had you stocking the refrigerator sections of the food mart, leaving you alone in the freezer while he sits and swaps Marine Corps stories with the guy supposed to be your helper, so you come off work half froze, looking for something to douse the meanness you're feeling, which could be a chore since you're a piss and a holler from being broke and New Smyrna Beach ain't exactly Vegas. Well, turns out to be your lucky night. Along about eight o'clock you wind up with a crew of rejects in a beach shack belongs to this fat old biker, snorting greasy homemade speed, swilling grape juice and vodka, with a windblown rain raising jazz beats from the tarpaper roof like brushes on cymbals. There's a woman with big brown eyes and punky peroxided hair who's a notch on the plain side of pretty, but she's got one of those black girl butts sometimes get stuck onto a white girl, and it's clear she's come down with the same feeling as you, so when the rain lets up and she says how she's got an itch to sneak onto the government property down the beach

Lucius Shepard

all for me, Dad, that terrible thing you did. I really try to believe it was all for me."

I'm comforted that my Sammy has had a good life. And much as I miss him and love him, I'm glad I've never seen his face staring in at me. Because there are lengths you have to go to for love, and places where you need to stop. I don't want Sammy to have to face the decisions I made.

I want him to be better.

IN PERPETUITY

years just…wandering. You've certainly shown me how much you love your son."

I closed my eyes. I was crying because of what I had done, and because even if I could rescue Sammy I had already failed him. I would never be someone of whom he could be proud.

When I opened my eyes again I was in the cell with my son.

"Daddy!" he yelped, jumping from his low bed, leaping into my arms, burying his face in my neck and soothing my pain with his tears. "Daddy, Daddy, I knew you'd come, I knew you didn't really go away!"

I wanted to tell him so much, so much that my thoughts jumbled and my mouth failed to work, but it did not matter because he was so happy to see me. *Wear a tooth guard when you're playing sport*, I needed to say, and *Helen's a lovely girl*, and *I'm so proud of your children, Sammy, I'm so, so proud.*

And, *I love you*. I needed to say that. But he knew already.

* * *

I am forever dying. *Proof enough,* the keeper had said, and Sammy was gone from that cell, long gone, and I was there instead, unmoving, frozen, blood mid-drip, eyes mid-blink, my own wretchedness apparent in the way I knelt, the slump of my shoulders and the dip of my head. *Proof enough.*

I am frozen in a moment of time so that those who occasionally come by and look cannot even see the moisture glittering on my eyes. For me, every second is an eternity in which I think about what I have done.

Sometimes, when the keeper is standing there looking at me, I wish I could ask him how long this will last. But even he must have some humanity to him. He does allow me my dreams.

* * *

"I'm a grandfather now, Dad. I haven't been to place flowers for a long time, and I've stopped looking for the door. Because the older I get, the more family I have to love and love me back, the more I think I can understand what happened. And I try to believe it was shaking his head, mocking me because he knew the truth. Perhaps he even created it.

"I have this," I said, offering him the jar.

He took it gingerly and stared through its old, cracked sides. "Ahhhh," he said, "very nice indeed. Yes, I'll place this one later. A pity she couldn't have been here herself, but…" He did something then, sent a thought flying, I felt it leave the room like a cold breath. Within seconds the curtain at the back of the room billowed and a little girl walked through. She looked tired and vacant, as if she was sleepwalking, but she knew where to go. She passed us by, sparing one glance for the keeper — there was hate there, intense and keen, but a deep, almost religious fear as well — before reaching the door and stepping out.

The street was clear. My car had gone and there were flowers tied to a nearby lamp post, sad tributes rotting in the sun.

"Was that…? But she's still young."

"Because I chose to keep her that way. Sweet young Helen. But now, you, your son, our arrangement. You may have helped someone else, but I have to ask you again: where is your proof of love? I'm very busy today, I really can't wait around here for long."

I slumped down to the floor, leaning back against the pool table I had seen him ironing his hand on yesterday. "I had it," I said. "I had it ready, I knew what to give you, but he stole it all away. The Green Man stole it all away."

"Oh dear," the keeper said, frowning and smiling again. He knew everything that had happened and enjoyed my pain. "Well, he's forgotten why he's out there. You can hardly blame him for trying to get back here any way he can."

"What *is* he out there for? What did you task him with? Why is he called the Green Man?"

The keeper leaned down close to me, and I smelled his breath. I wanted to die. People were dead because of me, families were grieving, and it had not done me any good.

It had not done me any good.

"That would be telling," the keeper said. And then he stood up and sighed, held his hands together, looked down at me where I bled onto his floor. "You really have been through an awful lot in such a short time, haven't you?" he said. "Some of my people spend

IN PERPETUITY

"What have I done?"

Elizabeth gurgled again, uttering no reply but speaking volumes. Her eyes, I could see so much in her eyes, and whether I was actually speaking to myself through her or not, she was right. There was disgust there, and fear, and also something insistent. She was *demanding* that I help her.

I knew now why she had never killed, never sat over somebody as they slept and slit their throat and collected what the keeper had charged her to collect. Because it was wrong.

I reached down and grabbed the jar from her hands, stepping over the leather-clad corpse of the girl and trying not to faint, or puke again, or turn and run into the road in an attempt to outpace what I had done. I was sure I heard laughing from somewhere, echoing as if trapped within a room. I looked up at the shop and the sign had changed to 'Open' once again.

Elizabeth growled at me and blinked rapidly a few times, and I leaned forward and placed the jar over her mouth. She stiffened for a second or two, and then the jar misted with her final breath. Her eyes remained open, staring into mine, and I think I saw a reflection of my memory of Sammy deep in there. Either that, or Elizabeth finally saw her little girl one more time before she died.

Somebody was shouting and trying to pull me away, but when I turned they stepped back.

"Leave me alone," I whispered. I would haunt their dreams forever.

Knocking at the shop door, I wondered whether anyone would see me when I stepped inside.

* * *

The shop was exactly as it had been the previous morning. There were no new additions to the ugly displays, although the coffins seemed to have slumped down somewhat lower, and there was now a space on the road kill shelf that would be filled very soon.

"You don't look too well," the keeper said.

"Give me my son."

"Do you have what I asked of you? Have you brought me proof of love?" He frowned and smiled at the same time, looking me over,

I could not see the Green Man.

Footsteps pounded concrete, another scream, the sound of a door slamming shut…and then for a few seconds, almost total silence. The engine ticked itself to death. Something was dripping, petrol or blood, and the girl on the car bonnet stared at me with one disbelieving eye. She might even have still been alive.

I clicked open the seatbelt and tumbled from the car, landing in the gutter. There was a small trail of blood running beneath me. I sat up and turned, looking back along the road, wishing I could forget. Two of the youths were dead, the one with the Mohican was trying to crawl with crushed legs, and where was the Green Man? Where?

I stood, holding onto the car, trying not to see the body on the bonnet as blood slicked the paintwork, slipping the girl down toward where Elizabeth lay crumpled against the wall. To my left the shop doorway was still there, but the sign had changed to 'Closed.' The keeper must surely be watching me, although I could see nothing past the drawn blinds. I stepped forward, expecting to find the Green Man's crumpled form pressed between the corner of the car and the wall, crushed there, burst open so that his sick fucking insides had spilled out, and I would pick up the photograph and the carving and the notebook of bad poems, wipe them free of his blood and go and knock at that door.

He was not there. Elizabeth stared up at me, shaking and twitching as she struggled to bring the jar up to her smashed mouth, but her arm was broken and useless.

No Green Man.

More footsteps.

He was running down the street, I saw him now, running and laughing and people could see him at last, he was pushing them out of the way if they had not already moved. And in his hands, waved above his head, were the things that could set Sammy free.

I knew then that I would never, ever catch him. I knew also that something was very wrong with me now, and it was not only the knife wounds in my stomach and the blood I spewed up into the gutter. It was something far, far worse than simply dying.

Elizabeth gurgled, and she blinked when I looked down at her.

The girl slid from the car bonnet and rested back against the wall, looking past the car and along the street at her friends.

People were running in to help now, the shock lifting.

IN PERPETUITY

kid trying to miss cracks in the pavement – he'd recognised me, and while the others were just screaming he looked confused as well.

Two seconds...

Elizabeth screamed, but I heard the sigh of the jar's lid being spun open. Something rattled beneath the car and it jumped slightly as the exhaust was ripped off. The wheel juddered in my hands. It tore to the right, struggling to steer away from the disaster facing it, the machine having more humanity than me for that split second, and I let the wheel turn because that was the natural thing to do, steer away, avoid the poor kids who'd come out of nowhere...

One second...

The Green Man would be turned away by the keeper, I was confident of that, but I could never be certain, *never*. That uncertainty held my hands straight. I would not get another chance. He was knocking at the door, I *recognised* that door, and it was the 'Open' sign that finally made up my mind.

I would not get another chance.

I closed my eyes and listened to the sickening sounds of death.

* * *

"I'm thirty-three now Dad. The age you were when Mum died. I've got a son and a daughter of my own, and I just know you'd love them so much. I tell them about their granddad and how he saved me, although when they ask how I find it difficult to explain. I'm not even sure myself; how do I tell my children? But I still go to look for the door sometimes on my own, though I never find it. I'm glad. I'm not sure I could just stay outside." I see Sammy, and it's like looking into a mirror. "I leave flowers here sometimes. The families do too, on the anniversary. I think it's only right."

I open my eyes.

We hit the wall next to the keeper's doorway. The seatbelt ripped into my neck and stomach, and I felt the wounds opening again, blood slick and warm against my skin. The car bounced back as Elizabeth grunted, exiting through the windscreen, passing straight over the body on the bonnet and striking the wall head-first. I heard her hit the ground as she dropped down between the wall and the corner of the car.

Somebody was screaming.

TIM LEBBON

We were several hundred yards from the keeper's shop.

* * *

"What would you do for love?" I asked.

"What do you mean?"

A car slowed in front of me and I swerved to avoid it, clipping its bumper and losing my own in a scream of metal and sparks. "How far would you go for love? For the love of your daughter? What wouldn't you do?"

"There's nothing..." she said, and then her voice trailed off as I aimed the car at the Green Man. He was running along the pavement, glancing back, dodging people where they walked their dogs or strolled hand in hand.

"Then why haven't you killed? Creep into a house at night, slit a throat, collect your sigh and set your daughter free?"

The car jumped its front wheels onto the pavement and I felt something tear lose inside me, flooding my insides with blood once again, bursting past the keeper's magical touch or perhaps obeying it to the full.

"I never even thought of it," she said.

I glanced across at this woman trapped by morality, cursed with this life because she could not think beyond what was right. Even after everything she had seen, all the truths laid bare and the impossibilities made real, still she was a good person.

"Then you'll never win."

The Green Man loomed large in the windscreen and his frown turned into a smile, just as I knew it would. I wondered whether those teenaged kids were still staying in the village, nursing hangovers and strange memories of the mad guy they'd tried to help yesterday. And they were, they were still here, because the Green Man suddenly moved ahead and he was amongst them, past them, reaching out to knock on the keeper's door even as my car bore down on the four youths, their eyes and mouths wide, limbs moving far too slowly as they tried to fling themselves out of my path.

There were three seconds when I could have changed my mind.

One of the girls had a pierced nose. The other showed bare midriff. The boy with the Mohican—he was the most likely to get away, I thought, because he'd been balancing on the kerb like a young

IN PERPETUITY

It was the largest flash of hope since I'd left Sammy to the keeper.

The car's underside hit the earth bank and the engine screamed before I took my foot from the gas. I was flung against the seatbelt, puking blood across the windscreen and dashboard. The pain was immense, driving me under for a few seconds and bringing brief, awful visions of Sammy screaming in his cell. *Now?* I thought. *Is that now?*

The car rocked for a moment and then tipped back, rolling its rear wheels onto the road.

Elizabeth had strained forward in her seat, spinning the top on her jar.

"He's not there," I hissed. "He's fooling me. Distracting me. We have to get back now, as soon as we can, go to the keeper before he reaches him."

The engine had stalled, and for the first few seconds after I turned the key it coughed and complained. And this is what the Green Man had wanted; for me to break the car and destroy my only means of reaching the keeper. He could travel by some other means, his speed proved that, but even though I had the car he still feared me. Which meant that I could beat him. It was not all hopeless.

And then the engine caught and reverse gear worked and the car whined and creaked its way fully back onto the road, obviously wounded but, like me, willing to fight on through the pain.

I drove quickly, dangerously, heading for the village where this had begun a day ago, though it felt like decades. And unlike when I had fled the place, the village seemed to appear around a corner too quickly. I was sure it was further, much further than I had driven. It was as if the place was eager to welcome me back.

The village was bustling, though I knew now that it never really slept. Elizabeth was making small, terrified noises in the passenger seat, clasping her empty jar and perhaps fearing that her quest had truly failed, she was back, she was back and the keeper would see her failure and keep her daughter forever.

If I had my way, her jar would be filled before long.

I drove into the village. Heads turned at the sight of my smashed car—some people were surprised, and others seemed to know just why I was here—and I saw the Green Man running along the pavement.

"Open the jar," I said to Elizabeth.

have been asleep. She held the jar in her lap, the skin of her fingers gray like old pottery.

The rising sun tried to blind me as I steered through the lanes. I drove at it, yearning for the safety that daytime had used to bring. Even after Anne died, the days had not been so bad. Night were quiet and promoted thought. Days were filled with Sammy. I was determined that they would be so again.

"I wonder if I'll always see," I said to myself, expecting no answer from the woman next to me and receiving none. *After Sammy*, I thought, *after I get him back, will I always see these people in the shadows? Will I always know more of reality than most?* There must be those who had succeeded, given the keeper what he wanted. He had a place full of impossible things.

I had stopped bleeding, but my stomach felt full and hard, and the knife wounds were still open. Perhaps the keeper's touch only went so far. I felt weak and tired, ready to lie down. It had only been one day. If the Green Man evaded me, if he fled and took those things with him, or if the keeper took one look at my proof of love and laughed…

I could be here a long, long time.

As if to lure us on, the Green Man appeared out of a hedge further along the road. He stood and stared me down, grinning, covered in freshly picked grass, ferns tucked into his clothes as if he were trying to become a part of the landscape. In his right hand he held the things he had stolen from me.

He did not seem to come closer as I drove faster. Instead he turned and walked back through the hedge, and as he vanished the car passed where he had been. I looked left and saw his shape moving in there, pushing through the undergrowth, and I slammed on the brakes and spun the car on the dew-slicked road. He was still pushing through — trapped, he's trapped in there! — so I gunned the engine, tried to judge just how deep the ditch was next to the road, and launched the car at the hedge. Just as the bonnet parted the bushes I saw something wrong with the Green Man's shadow. It was too regular, his movements too defined, too rigid, and I knew that it was not him in there at all, just the memory of him left behind to confuse me and make me waste time. As the car powered through the hedge and shattered the struggling shadow to the sunlight, I knew one thing for sure: *He's afraid that I can beat him!*

IN PERPETUITY

"Back," I said. "We're going back. We'll get him before he reaches the keeper. And if you help me, if you're here for me, I'll do my best to make sure you have his final breath."

She looked at me for a few seconds, eyes reflecting my hope with her own. "I didn't have to nudge you awake just now, you know. I could have sat here. I could have taken out my jar, and sat here, and waited."

"I'm not dying," I said. I did not know that for sure, but I meant it.

"How far away are we?"

"An hour, maybe more."

"An hour. Only an hour…" She drifted off, and I wondered how far she had wandered over the years. Perhaps she had always remained this close, looking for the dead and the about-to-die, and the realisation hit her only now. Her daughter was almost within shouting distance.

I started the car and headed off. When we found the main road I slowed down and drove carefully, not wanting to attract the attention of any police. The Green Man could travel quickly, and however he managed that I could not let him reach the keeper before me. I had no idea what would happen if he did. Whatever his forgotten quest was, would the keeper let him steal mine? I guessed so but hoped not.

Our chase was drawing attention. People stopped to watch us pass by, and I recognised some of them as the keeper's seekers, hollow desperate eyes, some carrying boxes or bags, many obviously mad. They seemed lost to crowds in the daylight. I had never seen so many people unseen and unnoticed, and the thought that they had always been there, moving through places and spaces where normal folk did not look, their respective searches so removed from normality that they were beyond sight…it frightened and humbled me. Perhaps ignorance truly is bliss.

We drove out of the city and into the country lanes. It was like moving into the wilds. Neither of us said anything, but I felt any dregs of safety being left behind, wrapping themselves around the normal people to protect and insulate them from the terrible truths we lived. Cool air blew through the smashed side windows, but Elizabeth did not seem to notice. Her eyes were open but she could

"He's on the main road," I said. "Heading east. He can't really have enough, can he? A picture, a lump of rock, a book? You've been searching for decades, I can't have found enough in a day?"

"Some tasks are harder than others," Elizabeth muttered. "I don't think the Green Man will ever finish his."

"Which is?"

"I never found out, but that's not the point. Can't you smell the doom on him?"

I closed my eyes again, welcoming the dark, comforted when I had no more rushes of the Green Man's thoughts. I felt alien enough in my own mind right now; I had no desire to be in someone else's.

I could not think of anything else, no more material items that would prove my love for Anne or Sammy any better than those stolen by the Green Man. Besides, I still did not know exactly what the keeper wanted. Proof of my love, proof of anyone's love, was all surely subjective. I could point him the way of charity, show him people who devoted themselves to others, claim that we are all still here because love triumphs in the end, regardless of wars and murder and death and hate, so much of which finds its way to us. Love wins out. And if I could believe this totally, perhaps I would find my way through.

Love wins out.

I wished it were Anne saying those words.

"I'm twenty-five, Dad," Sammy says. "I'm a musician. I'm working in America right now, but my heart's still in Europe along with Helen, my wife. She keeps it there for me. I know you'd be proud, I know you'd be happy, you and Mum together. Helen's a lovely girl…she will be if you save me. She is, she will be." I can see him, tall and more handsome than I had ever been, and before tears blur my vision I feel something so profound that it almost halts my heart: love. Total, unadulterated, unequivocal love for this, my son. He's so much a part of me and Anne, the sum of us and so much more.

"I go back and look for the door, sometimes," Sammy says. "I know I can't have dreamed it."

"Hey!" Elizabeth nudged me, shoved me against the door. I hissed in pain as the muscles in my stomach clenched, holding down the bloody vomit, holding myself together long enough to find my way back.

IN PERPETUITY

Instead I half walked, half ran to my car. Elizabeth made it into the passenger seat just as I pulled away. The Green Man had vanished, as I knew he would, but I drove anyway. In the golden morning light I saw invisible people looking for miracles. And I realised that I had found one myself.

"I should be dead," I said.

"The keeper has strange ways."

"I should be dead. I fell from a cliff yesterday. And he stabbed me today. I felt something die inside me."

Elizabeth shrugged but said no more.

Somehow my legs and feet worked, my hand found the gear stick, I did not crash. My stomach swilled with blood once again, my lungs throbbed and I felt slow bubbles popping at my nostrils. If I breathed through my mouth I tasted blood.

I saw him ten minutes later. Hurrying along a pavement. And even though he could not possibly have come this far on foot, I mounted the pavement and pressed down on the gas. His shadow was drawing level with a lamp post when it turned, and I saw the Green Man grinning as he flung himself sideways through a garden gate. I twisted the wheel sharply to the right and the car bounced back onto the road, the lamp post punching in both side doors. Elizabeth shook smashed glass from her hair, looking back to see whether I'd hit the Green Man. I pressed the brakes and looked in the mirror. The view shimmied as the car shuddered to a stop. No sign of him. He must have run through the garden, perhaps even into the house, and I would lose him.

"Shit!"

"He's heading east," she said.

"So?"

"East. Towards the keeper. Maybe he thinks he has enough."

The idea was crazy, but once uttered it played in my mind, even as I started off down the road away from the twitching curtains along the street. I found an isolated alleyway to park in, lowered the seat back and closed my eyes. And I could see the Green Man's feet hitting the pavement, feel his breath pounding in and out of my own ruined lungs, smell the stink of ages clinging to him like another layer of clothes. And then I knew what he thought of me. I jerked back in my seat. So much jealousy there. So much *hate*.

and leaned forward as I spewed what felt like a gallon of blood across the floor.

It felt as though I were there for hours, but it can only have been a few minutes. Eventually I was retching nothing but air. The cuts no longer gaped. I was feeling better. I let my shirt drop back down, not wanting to see or think about what I could not understand, content instead to stand and once again pursue that which I could: my only hope. My chance to save Sammy. The Green Man.

He knew where we were going before we got there. No amount of deception on my part would help, because he had been waiting here, ready to see me arrive before he stole what I had come for. Now he had the carving, the photograph, the bad poem, and even though I had started to suspect that these material things were less important than I imagined, still he was stealing. I could not show the keeper my dreams, could not let him view inside my head as I lay dying. I had to *give* him something.

"I'm coming," Elizabeth said, following me as I moved unsteadily onto the landing. Her surprise at my sudden recovery seemed to have waned quickly, and I remembered her words from earlier, how she had seen so much more. I had been here for a day, she had been here for decades. No wonder she was mad.

"Just keep that thing away from me," I said. "I'll smash it. You'll lose it, lose all hope. Or maybe next time I'll hold it to *your* mouth."

As I walked gingerly down the staircase—my stomach feeling hollow and not there, my upper body supported by nothing, hands grasping at air to support me—echoes came in, offering me peace and pieces of proof. If only I could retain memories and dreams...

I heard Sammy playing in the bath and Anne singing to him, hushing him to sleep when he had colic, and crying out in our bedroom on the night she conceived, Sammy again, running around downstairs and sliding across the living room after I'd laid timber flooring in there. All good times, all still here. I wanted so much to stay. Let these happy memories lull me to death.

Mourning the past, cursing the present, dreading the future, I stumbled down the final few stairs and fell out through the front door.

The Green Man was waiting for me. He stood at the neck of the cul de sac, reading my book of poetry, mocking me. Something bubbled in my lungs and I coughed up blood, but I did not go down.

IN PERPETUITY

bedroom door she made love to me, laughing and sighing and assuming that this was always the right thing.

And somewhere in that room Sammy was sixteen, confident and brash and full of my lost ambitions, still raging fires of aspiration rather than smoking embers that time had made them in me. "I'm going to be an actor, Dad," he said. "I'm going to be a contender, I'm going to shoot the devil in the back, I'm going to travel the world and help people and have adventures, like Cain in King Fu. I look for the door sometimes, Dad." And he was doing some of what he wanted, being a son who would make his father proud. I lost sight of him then because something blotted out the sun, something panting and excited, and for a second I thought that Anne had come back to me again, her image blurring with tears, and I felt hands on my stomach and chest, pressing and slipping in wetness…

It was Elizabeth. Her eyes were wide and frenzied, and still I could not see her clearly. I went to wipe my eyes and there was something hard in front of my face. I knocked it away and the glass jar skittered across the carpet, clanging hollowly as it hit the corner of the bed.

She hissed, crawled after the jar and hugged it to her chest, cooing as if it was her own lost daughter.

"Stay the fuck away from me!" I said, pushing myself into a sitting position. When I looked I could not believed that there was so much blood in me, enough to drench me from the chest down and spread across the cream carpet, soaking it deep crimson, a slick spreading from a holed tanker. "Just stay away," I said, quieter now. Shock was cutting in deeper than the knife.

Elizabeth stared at me wide-eyed. She looked so old that I could never age her. Any sense seemed to have fled. Along with Elizabeth there were things watching me inside that room, eyes less substantial than smoke, further away than the future.

Carefully I lifted my shirt and brushed my hand down over my stomach, clearing the blood. There were three rents in my skin, lipless mouths seeping blood like silent pleas. Even as I watched the flow slowed to a dribble, the blood thickening and darkening as it coagulated. I felt sick, and my stomach twitched involuntarily as its muscles cramped, working its contents up towards my mouth. The wounds pouted as I leaned over onto my side, and Elizabeth tensed like even though she knew she could not lie to me. For a second I thought it was pointless—this was stupid, this chase for tokens of love could never constitute proof, it could not be what the keeper sought—but then the anger came back, and I reached out to grab the book.

"That's mine!" I said.

The Green Man sidestepped and slowly, casually, pushed a long-bladed knife into my stomach.

The action did not register for a few seconds. My attention was on the book, that was all, the red cover faded by years of being forgotten. It seemed redder around his fingers where he grasped it tight, as if blood were leaking out to make the book his. I managed a clumsy step, wondering why the distance between me and the Green Man increased the closer I came. My fingertips actually brushed the tatty spine—for a second I had it, and I spied freedom and success somewhere in the vague, hallucinatory distance—but then the Green Man stepped back, tugged the knife from my clenched stomach muscles and thrust forward again. I heard the scraping of metal on bone, and that convinced me of what was happening.

I fell. I had hugged Anne against this wall when we were decorating the room, but now my blood stained the wallpaper, merging with traces of her left behind. I slid down, legs unable to hold my weight, as he withdrew the knife and stabbed me one more time. The knife passed straight between my ribs and struck something vital inside me, I felt it go, felt the pop and the cool rush of blood through my flesh, into my stomach, drowning my insides.

The Green Man grinned at me and then left the room. Yet still I was not alone. The space grew larger and distances faded, blending into one invisible horizon. The wallpaper was still there, the window and the wardrobes and the bed against the wall, but they were all endless, parts of a wider landscape now. And that landscape was not deserted. Anne was there in many ways, she peopled the place where I lay dying, and so many truths were made plain to me that I began to cry with the effort of understanding. There was nothing bad, nothing I could not have guessed or had not truly believed, but here things were so certain. The fact of her love for me, no longer relying simply on trust or hope, but now so definite. Here was proof, amorphous yet obvious in its intensity. Anne danced on our wedding night, strolled along a dusky shore on our honeymoon, and near the

IN PERPETUITY

and he turned to show me before disappearing into the spare bedroom.

"Are you going after him?" Elizabeth asked, and at last she was holding her jar, not trusting the time it would take to pluck it from the bag. She wanted death here today. She wished for it, she craved it, and there was little else that really concerned her. The lid of the jar muttered slightly, pressure from within or without.

I ran upstairs. Sammy had come down this way just yesterday, laughing and giggling as I chased him because he was still not dressed. I'd been impatient and flustered because it was taking too long to get ready. I may even have raised my voice. As I ran up now I pounded my feet in anger and shame. Elizabeth was suddenly forgotten, the memory of a shadow behind me. This was my house, and familiarity closed in, feigning safety. This place had been my refuge after Anne died. She was everywhere I looked — her memory scattered like dust — and that had comforted rather than upset me. I always liked the idea that she was still here, watching over me. I hoped her eyes were open now.

I burst into the spare bedroom. The Green Man was standing at the wardrobe with his back to me. He'd pulled down a box from the top shelf, dropped its contents across the floor, sifting with his foot. His long hair hung down either side of his face, shadowing the shadows. He moved like a shadow himself.

"You got here quicker than last time."

"Fuck you," I said. "This is my house. You're stealing my life. I don't care what you've forgotten...I hope it hurt, I hope it was a son or a loved one. I might have seen them in the keeper's rooms. Maybe it was that living corpse, crawling with insects and maggots and feeling every bite!" I despised what he was doing but my words, my attitude, shocked me still. This hateful manner felt so alien.

Lights swam about his head like fireflies. Even though the curtains were drawn light from outside lit up his face, and I could see so much more than I ever had in that room: dust furring the skirting, Sammy's skin and Anne's last breath combined; an echo of an old friend who had stayed here, a man who may have helped me had he still been alive; and the Green Man's rank breath filling the room, spreading something old and desperate and, essentially, sad.

He bent down and picked up the little hardback notebook I was looking for. It contained the bad poem that Anne had pretended to

I parked and ran across my front lawn. Elizabeth came after me for her own reasons, with her own mission in mind...and yet I was glad. Any company felt welcome here, whatever its objectives.

I paused at the front door. It was dark inside, I remembered coming home after Anne had died, dark then too, dark and foreboding and *wrong,* as if I should never have returned alone and the house itself had noticed an absence and frowned upon it. From inside came noise of the Green Man's destructive search, and I tried my best not to imagine where the book could be, certain now, convinced that he could see and use my mind, and I thought *fuck you,* and the noises stopped for a moment.

And then, with a laugh, they started again.

The house was an alien place. As I stepped inside the front door and looked down the hallway — the pictures on the holiday wall, the carpet, the telephone table with several of Anne's grandmother's Toby jugs standing guard — I could have been returning home after years at sea, decades away. Because the house was exactly as I remembered it...and yet things were so very different. The detail was stronger. Threadbare carpet, damp plasterwork, a dip in the ceiling, shadows moving where there should be no shadow or movement, echoes of my life playing back again and again. I closed my eyes but could not see less, so I opened them again and there he was, the Green Man, striding from the living room and nudging past me to head upstairs.

"Stop!" I said. He glanced around, his eyes awash with more shadows than my home. I wondered why they called him the Green Man. He mounted the stairs and started climbing, his only intention to tear my house apart until he found my book of bad poems, because that was what I'd returned for. Bad poems, and one bad poem that could be part of my proof of love.

I darted forward and grabbed his jacket, pulling hard. He grunted and turned, lashing out, catching me on the face with his fisted hand. I fell back and staggered against the front door screen, trying to shake the *stench* from my nose, the slickness from my cheek, the dizziness from my head. He must surely have been dead.

Halfway up now, and as I watched him climb I remembered where the book of poems lay hidden and forgotten. I could almost sense its pleasure as I thought of it, as if rediscovery had always been its game; but the real smile was on the face of the Green Man,

IN PERPETUITY

ink blending, words transmuting, gathering meaning and import as it lay hidden away from corrupting opinions.

"What poem?" Elizabeth muttered. She had slumped down in her seat as if unused to the bustle of the morning rush-hour.

"I wrote it..." I said, and then trailed off. I wrote, Anne hid it away. And now, looking for it, perhaps I was drawing the Green Man to it as well. "No poem," I said. "There's no poem." To think of it, perhaps that is all he required of me. The carving on the cliff and the photograph in poor Jean's house, he had stolen these after nothing more than a glimmer of an idea in my mind. Now, minutes away from home, I feared that he was coming closer again.

"How does the Green Man travel?" I asked. "How does he move around?"

"Same as you and me," Elizabeth said. "Same as everyone. Mostly."

"Mostly?"

She looked across at me. "There *are* other ways in the world. Most don't dare use them. He does."

As we turned into the cul de sac where I lived, the truth of her statement revealed itself all at once. Because my front door stood open, and disappearing inside—almost as if he'd been waiting to offer me that one glimpse—the Green Man. Other ways in the world, she had said, and I shuddered to think what routes he had trodden to reach here so quickly. There was an animal smell about the place, I could detect it even with the windows up, and the light was strange too. Not the clear light of morning, but tainted and grayed, as if this day had been left out in the open for too long.

"He's here!"

"This is where you live?"

"That house. He's here, he's in there already. How can that be? It was minutes ago I thought of coming here, only minutes, how the hell is he here already?" I looked at Elizabeth but she seemed not to have heard. Her eyes grew wider as her hands had strayed to the glass jar. She froze as I looked at her. I wondered what she could see of me now; whether it was my life or death that she imagined as she stared back into my eyes.

"I'm going," I said.

"I'm coming too."

"I'm thirteen now dad," Sammy says. "This is Helen. She's in my class at school and she likes martial arts movies too, and westerns. Cool, huh? I would have liked her if you'd let me, shared my first kiss with her, maybe more. She's really pretty." His voice is a teenager's croak, but it sounds as if his throat is constricted by tears. "I know these things don't usually last, but maybe one day she'd have been a part of your family. If you'd allowed it."

Something crashed by my ear, and I felt the impact on my head. *Hitting me*, I thought, *it's the Green Man caving in my skull with a hammer and he'll never have his proof now…unless he's looking for it inside. Trying to find the bits of my brain that matter, no pretence, no deceptions, love laid bare to the sunlight…*

I sat up and saw the petrol station attendant staring through the window. Her expression changed to one of disquiet as she backed away. She'd seen Elizabeth. She was not easy for me to look at, let alone someone who knew nothing of what and where we were.

"Inside my head," I said. "It's all inside my head."

And then I knew the next place we had to go, the next thing to try to collect.

"Wake up!" I shouted. Elizabeth stirred slowly, as if accustomed to being woken by violence. "We've got half a mile to drive," I said. "Half a mile to what I need. He *can't* beat us there, surely. I've only just realised. Only just thought of it."

"What?"

"The poem. I've only just remembered, it was so long ago. It came from inside me. Deep inside. Anne didn't really understand it or like it, but I think that's even better proof right there. The fact that I could show it to her and she didn't understand, and still it meant so much."

I twisted the ignition key and rammed the car into first. A motorbike swerved to avoid us as I pulled out onto the road and Elizabeth perked up, watching to see whether the rider would spin into a lamp post.

As I headed home, I tried to remember where the poem would be packed away. I had written it in a notebook, and it lay huddled between other bad poems that had bled from me over the course of a couple of years, revealing itself only to the back of a previous page. Anne had not liked it, true, but perhaps it had matured with age,

IN PERPETUITY

that was not normal stood out. People wandered the streets, more fleeting than shadows yet concrete to me, their purpose clear in all those frightened eyes caught in my headlights. Sometimes they ran, and once there was a thump as someone leaped onto the car, clawed at the roof, screaming as their nails flipped off and sprayed bloody droplets onto the windscreen. We passed a parked police car and the driver gave me a careless glance. I used the windscreen wipers to smear blood across the glass, giving the night a new hellish tinge.

The person fell from the roof and I saw a shadow fighting in the rear-view mirror.

"What the hell were *they* after?" I asked, but Elizabeth remained silent for the whole drive. I thought perhaps she had died, and I gently removed her jar from its bag and held it before her mouth. The glass misted and cleared, misted and cleared. I wondered whether she had thought of providing its fill, and knew that she must have.

I drove to areas where Anne and I had lived, partied, made love, shopped, drunk and visited friends. The town was as familiar to me as my own eyes, but at the same time I felt as though I were rediscovering it after decades away, living a whole night of nostalgia for a place I saw every day. Elizabeth snored gently beside me. Her history was long but her story short, a beginning and a middle with no end in sight. I pitied her, but it also disturbed me that she had come along. Surely it was not out of a desire to help? She must have seen something in my eyes, known that I was death walking, or a short walk to another death.

I could stop the car and kick her out here and now. But she would only find me again.

This world, these people, amazed me no more. In fact I felt little for them — a trace of pity, a tinge of disgust, a healthy dose of fear for something I had not been aware of until today — because my thoughts were for Sammy alone. A day had passed and another would go by quicker, another, and then the first week would be a milestone in the history of my loss, and then weeks would flow by easier like a baby's second, third and fourth real steps following the impossible first.

So I drove. And inspiration finally came with the dawn, after I parked the car in a garage forecourt and slipped easily into an uneasy doze.

the poor people like us suffer until we die. That's why there is no God."

"He has the one true cross."

"I never said Jesus didn't die for us," she said. "I just wonder if it worked. Maybe we killed him in more ways than we know."

"Believe what you like," I said, and Elizabeth turned to look at me, and she was amazed. She saw a man who had lost his son and seen his mother-in-law slaughtered on her kitchen floor, and still he kept his faith. Amazed, yes, but she also felt vaguely superior. She had been here longer.

"I do," she said. "After you've been here as long as me, you will too. I've seen more things than you can ever imagine. And amazing as they are, it's ironic how each one convinces me more that God is dead."

"So how do you explain them?" I had once spent months looking for a miracle, and when Anne finally died I knew, too late, that our final time together was what I had sought.

"The universe is a fucked up place. Humans are lucky enough to not usually see this, not fully, never clearly." She trailed off and I concentrated on my driving, my aims, the idea that had put me back in the car.

There was proof of my love out there, I had only to find it. Instead of wracking my brain, I would drive around the streets for the remainder of the night. There were places here that had seen our courtship, places we had been, things we had seen, and sooner or later something else would come to me. Location would reveal it in my mind, unearthing it from the grave where Anne's death had buried it. The smell of a tree, the sound of a stalking cat, the way the car bumped on a particular stretch of road, any one of these could inspire the memory of something that I could take to the keeper. And being so near, I would reach it before the Green Man. He would have no warning.

I would not let him steal the rest of my life away.

* * *

We drove until the traffic thinned to a few taxis and police cars, night deepened, and I realised for the first time just how much more was revealing itself to me. As normality went to bed, so everything

IN PERPETUITY

and even then speed would not be available to me when required. I thanked whatever Fate may have been watching over me that Jean's body had not yet been discovered. And then I wondered if that Fate was the keeper, and paranoia had him watching me again.

We paused at the end of my dead mother-in-law's street, hiding in the shadows between streetlamps, pushed into a hedge for added concealment. Elizabeth had followed me silently and effortlessly, so that from time to time I forgot she was with me. She kept her hands away from the jar on her belt. I was fine with that.

There was little activity in the street, and what I could hear and see and sense—inside and outside the houses—seemed relatively normal. No police sirens, no gawping neighbours. We walked from shadow to shadow until I heard those gentle piano strains still playing, and to the theme of Mozart we got into my car and left that murderous place.

At last I had time to feel pure rage toward the Green Man, not for what he had stolen but what he had done. And that belated fury shamed me terribly, to the point of tearing me away from myself, lessening my predicament, numbing the fear and dread I had lived with every second since leaving that impossible shop. He had killed, and I had been angry because he had stolen an old photograph. *Perhaps I could have saved her?* My self-loathing clouded my vision for a time, and I found yet more shame in the gratitude I felt for this.

I owed it to Jean to succeed, and when it was over and Sammy was back with me I would go to the police. They would track the keeper down somehow, and then the Green Man would be found as well. I would enjoy being at that bastard's trial. I would relish the look on his face when he was imprisoned for life. Mad he may be, but my blame still found him a deserving target.

"The police will never find him," Elizabeth said. "He's not of this place, not anymore. You should know that. You should know from the insight the keeper has given you."

"How do you...?" I began. Lights dazzled me, too many lights.

"You've been silent for so long. You *must* be thinking, and even after all this time, I remember what I thought about those first few weeks. I'd find her, somehow, whether I fulfilled my charge or not. Then I'd go to the police. Make him pay for what he'd done. Except sometimes people like him don't pay, they grow old and fat and sated on their own particular perversions, and they never pay, and

"But I've seen so many already!" I said. It had only been hours since I'd left him, *hours*. How many wanderers could Elizabeth have met through her decades of slow mourning?

"I've met so many more." She shrugged and I took my hands from her shoulders, looking into her sad eyes, hating that my own were reflected in there.

"I'll never do this," I said, turning away from her in despair. "I have no idea what I'm doing. I'm *useless!*"

Elizabeth shocked me then by coming to life. She pushed me against the hedge and breathed into my face. Her breath smelled of old times and places we should never know. I breathed deep.

"*Never* give up hope!" she said. "It's been hours, and already the Green Man is onto you. That means you're on the right track, because he sees you as someone who can get him back to the keeper. So don't you ever give up hope. Your son depends on you. You may have no idea what you're doing, but that doesn't mean it can't be done from instinct. You have to protect your son. You're still a man, a person, far more so than me, so that's what your blood is telling you now, your soul, the darkest corners of your mind are all rallying to save your son. It's human nature. It's *nature*. Survival instinct at its most basic. You have more hope than I've had in years." She turned away from me and I heard her tapping her glass jar with a ring on one of her fingers. She must have given up on whoever gave her that ring years ago. I was humbled that she refused to give up on me.

"I'm sorry," I said. It sounded and felt hollow, so I did not say it again.

"So where next?" she asked.

I closed my eyes and thought. Jean was there, the image of her alive and loving and dead and bloody combining in my mind's eye.

Sammy was there too.

Where next?

And then I knew.

"Not where," I said. "When. Come on."

* * *

I had no desire to go back to Jean's house, but I needed my car. Walking the streets at random would take weeks to cover the town,

IN PERPETUITY

Further down the street, away from the man's shouts, a shadow stepped from an alleyway a few steps ahead of me and walked in the same direction.

"Do you know love?" I asked. Elizabeth giggled behind me, but I tried to ignore the feeling that she knew something I did not.

The shape stopped and turned, and in the weak streetlight I saw a young man, younger than me but with age burned into his face. He began to cry. His tears were silent as they fell to the pavement, forming splashes of shadow on the concrete. His shoulders shook but he did not whimper, did not speak.

"One of us," Elizabeth whispered in my ear.

How could she know? I thought. But as I looked harder, so the truth of the statement manifested before me. The man did not belong on this street: his colours were out of synch, his presence an anachronism that seemed to ignore light and weight and the sounds of civilisation. He opened his hands and raised his sleeves, showing me the wounds of Christ that can only have been given in mockery, never received in hope. Whatever the keeper had asked of him it was too much. Too much for this man, and too much for me to take in.

"I know love," he said quietly, wincing as if speaking burst blisters inside his throat. He said no more, but turned and walked away, tying the buttons on his sleeves and never once looking back.

"Give me proof!" I shouted back, but he passed out of sight. I was glad. My own love was all I knew, and someone else's proof may be fake or meaningless. I could not return to the keeper with proof of which I was not totally convinced, something that may be false as a lover's smile…the authenticity of which is known to them, and them alone.

I turned to Elizabeth, held her shoulders and pressed her back into the hedge bordering the road. "How many are there?" I asked. "How many like us, wandering the streets?"

"Streets?" she asked, surprised. She did not seem perturbed by my behaviour. Indeed, she thinks of me as a poor, panicked young boy, younger than her daughter is now, if she's still alive. "More than just streets. Hillsides. Valleys. Sewers. Parks. Woodland. Shopping centres. We're everywhere. The keeper is old, and he's always been this way."

were eating the atmosphere. They had no idea about the truth of things. I could go in and tell them, point out just how much there was that they would never see. Like the shape in the corner by the bar, a toothed wraith from centuries before, perusing its flock. Or the things swimming in the air like fish out of water, ducking into and out of the patrons' mouths as they drank and laughed, eating of them as they ate the air. Perhaps they were cancers looking for a home. I pressed my lips close.

The noise increased suddenly as the front door opened and two girls emerged. They were teenagers, their attire begging attention, their eyes defiant and challenging as I approached them.

"Have you ever loved?" I said. "Do you have proof?"

"Fuck off, weirdo!" one of them said, setting the other one giggling. They shoved past me, burning my forearms with their cigarettes as they did so. I could smell the singed hair and bubbled skin, and the fact that one of the girls had recently had sex. Raucous laughter erupted inside the pub, perhaps at their departure.

No. Love was older than this.

I walked along the street, Elizabeth tagging along beside me. I sensed that she had much to say, but perhaps she realised that I had started something here. I had fired an arrow into the dark and had no idea where to was going to land, even though there lay my destination.

"Have you ever loved?" I asked an old woman walking her dog. She looked startled for a moment, but then something in my eyes must have convinced her that I was no threat.

"Oh yes," she said, nodding, walking on, her eyes graying as tears and time took her back to somewhere I could not see. But she's also thinking of me as she walks away, trying to come to terms with the strangeness in my eyes. It would have been terrible of me to pursue her, so I walked on again.

A man stood at the front door of a house, rapping on the wood. "Sue!" he shouted. "Sue!" He knocked again, shouted again. I stopped and stared over the garden hedge. The man stepped back and flung a stone at an upstairs window. Not a pebble; a stone. It *snicked* from the glass and left a bright line of white, like a scar already healed.

I could have asked this man, but it did not feel right.

IN PERPETUITY

us but let us be, as they would a breath of wind, a fallen leaf scratching along the street, a shadow hiding in a shop doorway. They didn't even growl.

The Green Man had been this way; I could smell blood in the air and I knew it was Jean's. But his trail was cooling with each passing minute. The blood was aging, the stench of his sweat old and musty rather than fresh and rank. And if I paused and breathed out slowly, I could hear his footsteps still echoing between buildings, fading, edging themselves eventually to nothing.

"What are you looking for?" Elizabeth asked.

"The man who stole from me," I said, but I knew before finishing the sentence that was not what she meant.

"What *really*?"

We paused outside a pub, static rocks in the river of life that flowed around us: the noise of enjoyment; the smell of food and drink; laughter soaking the air like that river's ebullient spray.

"*Really,* I'm looking for my son Sammy. The keeper has him, just as he has your daughter. It's only been since this afternoon. The keeper showed me his collection. He said that proof of love can give Sammy back to me."

She surprised me by reaching out and touching my cheek. Her fingers were rough and calloused, as if she had spent a lifetime looking under rocks. "That's not an easy one," she said.

"I have no idea what he really wants."

She pulled away. I was glad she kept her hand away from the bag on her belt. If I ever saw that — her eyes on me, hands opening the jar — I would have to run.

"Neither does he," Elizabeth said. "I've met someone looking for the first pacemaker, a woman searching for the sledge from Citizen Cain and a man collecting screams. The keeper makes demands, but I wonder if he ever knows what he's really asking for. Like me. How does he know what a final sigh will comprise? What will it be?"

Elizabeth continued talking but I had drifted off, staring through the pub window, its insides coloured by the old brewery name set in stained glass, and also by my perceptions of how far I already was from this reality. If I stayed out here for days more, weeks, years like Elizabeth, how different would I be if and when I finally had Sammy back? People inside were chewing at the air with their laughs. They light up her face. For a moment I saw the beautiful mother she had been so long ago.

Years. Decades. How desperate must she be?

"What's your name?" I asked.

"Elizabeth. What's yours?"

"I'm not telling you. I feel better that way."

She shrugged, smiled again. "I'll allow you that."

"How kind." I turned away and hurried to the back of the garden, feeling around in the dark for the gate latch. Elizabeth was behind me, I could feel her eyes concentrating on the back of my neck, perhaps finding some comfort in staring at something new to her old, old world.

I turned and took a final look at Jean's house. The kitchen light was still on, spilling through windows like the blood that had flowed from her body. The music was still playing. Perhaps the CD player had been set on 'repeat.' It seemed fitting that such beautiful, intricate music may be the warning sign to her neighbours that something was amiss.

I hoped that Jean lay still at last.

"I'm glad you didn't get here in time," I said to the tall woman. "I knew her. Her last breath was her own." *If she's breathed it*, I thought. I *had* to get away.

"But it wasn't," she said. "The Green Man saw to that. Strange, I don't think he's actually killed before. Not quite."

"He's getting further away." I set out along the lane between gardens.

"You won't catch him."

"Then why the *fuck* are you tagging along!"

"I want to fill my jar." Her reply was quiet, and in her calmness I discerned the utter obsession that kept her going. Years had passed and her daughter, if still alive, may be little more than a living mannequin by now, put to whatever use the keeper had found. Yet Elizabeth's single aim was still the fulfilment of her given quest. The final sigh of the dying. She kept the jar in a leather bag around her waist, tenting her jacket like a pregnant belly.

We walked in silence for half an hour. After emerging from the lane we kept to the main streets, blending in with the twilight and feeling the world flowing around us, unaware, uncaring. People saw us but did not respond. Dogs trotting along the pavement sniffed at

IN PERPETUITY

"I'm like him," she said, "except that I remember my quest. He'll never find his way back and his reward is lost forever. I may never fulfill my charge…and so my daughter is similarly lost to me. It's not fair. In a way he's luckier because of his madness. It's unfair."

"What are you looking for?" I asked.

"The final sigh of a violent death," she said. "He wants it in a jar. From a man, a woman or a child, he doesn't mind which. Maybe he'll unscrew the lid and breathe the sigh in. Perhaps he'll just put it on a shelf and forget about it. Nothing to him, everything to me. She's everything to me." The woman sobbed and her thin shoulders shook, but there were no tears reflected in the moonlight. Time had cried her dry.

"How long?" I asked.

"I don't know. Years? Decades? I'm never in time…I sometimes know when there's a murder, but I'm always too far away to catch the final breath. I'm nothing more than a ghoul. I seek murder but only find its aftermath."

"Do it yourself."

She seemed to freeze before me, like a tortured artist's vision splashed on the living canvas of Jean's garden. I heard her withheld breath and felt her tensed muscles. "Would you?"

I shook my head slowly. "I have to go."

"I'll come with you!"

The offer struck me as ridiculously kind, and a lump formed in my throat. She seemed to know what the Green Man was capable of, and yet she would accompany me as I tracked him down. And then I considered her true motives, how tied in they were to the keeper's demands on her, and the offer felt suddenly hollow.

When she looked at me, perhaps she saw murder.

"No, I'll—"

"You can't stop me," she said. "I can follow, I know where we are much better than you. You've seen some things already, I'm sure, seen the detail all around, stepped some way down the path the keeper gave you. But there's so much more yet to see and feel and taste. I've been there already."

"How do you know about murders?" I asked. "How do you seek out death?"

"Worried I can see a knife in your back?" she asked quietly, smiling, and although the smile should have been cruel it seemed to wondered. *Does he have any concept of next month, next year? Or is it all 'later' to him?*

"I'm sorry Jean," I muttered, hoping that she could no longer hear. The door slammed shut behind me, sucking in the light and giving me back to the night. I stood there for a few seconds, sniffing the air, listening, and in the distance I heard an area of silence, felt an aura of disquiet. That was where the Green Man must be.

"Am I too late?" a voice asked from the shadows. It was quiet, so low and wretched that it was androgynous. "I am, aren't I? Too late again. Could I really expect anything else."

"Who are you?" I hissed. I tried to appear taller than I actually was, wincing as wounds from my fall fought back, but maintaining the posture. The pain was deserved. Better still, it felt *right*. I should have been dead, after all.

"I'm always too late," the voice said, as if that could be an answer. A tall woman stepped away from the house, appearing from shadows I had thought were nothing more.

"I have to go," I said, unnerved.

"You won't catch him."

"Who?"

"Green Man. He's more removed from this world than any of us, and sometimes he slips even further. If you did get close he'd just…jump. Go so far out you wouldn't even see him."

I looked out beyond the garden and neighbouring houses. Out there was an element of my proof, part of the key that would rescue Sammy. The Green Man, his own quest long forgotten or lost, had taken on my own. The sense of uselessness was dreadful.

"I *have* to catch him," I said. Yet I waited there on Jean's patio — her pot plants' shadows were wilting, as if already aware of her death — and stared at this strange woman. Tall, dressed in dark clothes, black hair cropped short, her face was as white as the moon and equally melancholy. It seemed to reflect light from long ago, a time when things may have been all right.

She shook her head once and I heard the creak of her neck muscles, felt her short hair part the darkness, and she looked at me and saw a man as desperate as she. She thought my eyes were shaded and my soul hidden in greater darkness. I despaired at how quickly I had changed to these new ways.

IN PERPETUITY

I stood and ran to the door, feeling the slickness of blood beneath my feet. The next track began on the stereo.

"You bastard!" I shouted as I opened the door, but then borrowed light from the neighbours' houses quietened my voice. It was guilt that silenced me, the certainty that I had hauled Jean to this moment simply by calling her…perhaps even from the moment I thought of the photograph. She gasped again behind me but it must have been involuntary, a death rattle, she surely could not live, and it was hopeless me staying here now…

The murderer laughed one more time, though he may have been streets away by then. I knew without searching the house that he would have the photograph in his bloodied hand.

You're slowing down, the gruesome message on the wall read, scrawled over cigarette-yellowed magnolia paint. And so where next? What else could the Green Man see in my immediate future that I had not yet even considered? He'd already taken the carving, and stabbed Jean for the photograph.

He must have arrived minutes after she hung up the phone. Jean already knew that this single old image was important, vital, and her love for Sammy had helped her clasp it to her chest. She was no spring chicken but this intruder, haunted and haunting to look at, had not fazed her enough to give in. Perhaps he had mentioned me. Maybe he had ever told her whatever he knew of Sammy.

I had to go after him. There was a trail, I could smell it now, an unnatural taint on the air that had silenced barking dogs and made twitching curtains fall back into place. Whether I had a hope in Hell of catching the Green Man or not, it was essential that I follow him. If luck was on my side I would catch him unawares and take my possessions out of his grasp.

I stood on the threshold, undecided, torn between staying to watch her die and continuing onward. Looking again at the clotted writing on the wall, I could already perceive the final shape it would make. Food for thought for the police.

That decided me. The police would have to know — or they would find out — and I would be trapped. *No law,* the keeper had said. Jean would not want me being useless here when Sammy was still out there somewhere, awaiting my return but perhaps, hour by hour, trusting its certainty less and less. *How does a four-year-old think?* I

At the end of the hallway I could already see into the kitchen, and before I acknowledged or understood the writing on the wall I knew what it meant. Perhaps I had put it there by dialling Jean's number. *Down,* the word on the wall said, running from the tails of the 'w' and the feet of the 'n,' because it had been written in blood.

I could not move. To go forward would be to reveal the full message and the source of the dreadful ink. To back away would be to deny my responsibility. So for a few seconds I stood where I was, watching a bubble of blood slip down my dead wife's mother's kitchen tiles, slowing because it was already growing thick.

Someone laughed, and the back door from the kitchen to the garden slammed shut.

I did not even think about moving. It was as natural as breathing or eating, or loving my son. I leapt forward and held onto the door jamb, swinging around so that I faced the back door. The full message revealed itself as I did so—*You're slowing down!*—and then I saw something at my feet. Momentum took me forward, and there was rage there as well, because I already knew what had happened and why and who was to blame.

I stumbled over Jean's corpse and held my hands out to break my fall. But there was so much blood there, pooled and splashed and smeared by whoever had killed her, that I slipped forward and landed across her chest.

She gasped, a short, sharp exhalation that made me cry out.

"Jean, Jean, holy shit!" I pushed at the floor until I was kneeling, glanced at Jean, at the back door, at Jean again. She'd gasped but she was dead, she must be. If she *were* somehow still alive I would have wished her dead, the injuries were so severe. I looked back at the door again, and the bloody handprint on its frame drew me to my feet.

Jean gasped again, and a bloody bubble grew slowly from her nose before popping. She was alive. Barely, alive.

The hand that made that print had already thieved something from me, and now it was stealing more, fleeing with the memory of Jean's life already drying under its fingernails and in the crease of its lifeline.

He'd been laughing, and my last memory of Jean had been four weeks ago, when she had given Sammy a hug and kiss goodbye and he'd reached up and tweaked her nose and told her that he'd stolen it away.

IN PERPETUITY

I had not been to Jean's house for several weeks. She spoke to Sammy almost every day on the phone, but I always found excuses as to why we could not visit. They were empty and meaningless, more so because I loved Jean and bore her no ill will. Perhaps she reminded me too much of Anne. Or perhaps, not enough.

There were several lights on in her house, and music mumbled through the windows. I felt the reverberation of something classical, a soft string section coaxing me up the garden path with promises of hot tea and Jean's understanding smile. I would not tell her everything, I knew that, because however much she trusted me she could not keep this quiet and private. She would frown and nod and agree as I explained the need for secrecy, but once I left gone she would be on the 'phone to the police. Jean had lived a long life and seen her husband and daughter into their graves, but I was sure she had never seen anything beyond the world she knew. She had not walked the keeper's rooms and witnessed proof of how little we believed. She would not be able to understand.

I stood at the front door and reached for the bell, but smiled at the formality. It was my first smile since leaving the keeper's shop. It made me feel sick. I rang the bell anyway, and then tried the handle. The door slipped open and let me into the house.

"Jean!"

I could smell freshly-poured tea from the kitchen at the end of the hallway. She must have seen me pull up in the car. The music paused between tracks right then, and as I held my breath I heard the steady *pop pop pop* of trapped air escaping from beneath a hot mug.

"Jean! I'm here!"

She must have been cooking, because there were other smells from the kitchen. The sweet tang of burnt gas. Old grease on her oven. Blood.

"Jean?" I glanced into the living room before walking down the hallway. A cigarette had burnt down in the ashtray next to her favourite armchair, leaving behind a delicate skeleton of ash. The television was dead, screen hazed with a thick layer of dust, and a tatty paperback was steepled on the table beside her chair. Also on that table lay her cordless phone. My voice had shaken that earpiece not ten minutes earlier.

No proof in death. But there was little conviction in the thought. And for a second Anne was sitting next to me, scolding me for considering such foolishness.

I drove more carefully than ever after that, keeping to speed limits, expecting the dark to surprise me at any moment. As I drove into the city I became aware of the weight of things hiding beyond car lights. Before today I had known nothing in the night, other than golden flashes of car windscreens and garden hedges lit by headlights, the monochrome puddles of pavement around street lamps, the landscape startled into guilty immobility by lightning. Beyond, there was only more night. But now…

…now I can feel the solidity of reality hiding behind the dark, a truth unhindered by the lie of daylight, which itself is simply a trick of the eye. There are threats and promises out there, and promises of threats, skirting the oases of natural vision like tigers and bears at a camp fire, far enough away to stay hidden but close enough to make their presence felt. I felt eyes upon me, ears tracking my car motor and the motoring of my heart. There were fingers searching for me in the dark. Thoughts probed outward and found me wanting. I tried to close my mind, but I was not used to this way of thinking and really, truly, I was only a child here.

Yet people walked the streets and welcomed the night, unaware of what it held, the massive potential they could not perceive and the countless unknown things enjoying the cool night air with them. I had been one of these people this morning, and I knew that however much they tried to think up and out of themselves, in reality their thoughts were turned inwards. So far, in fact, that they almost reflected themselves, holding their originators in a spiralling trap of self-deception.

I had to ignore this new insight. But it was not easy. I drove along the town's main street and saw a child with a ghost at her shoulder, a shop built on an ancient graveyard which hummed with energy, a woman kissing a man in a shop doorway, a man who had horns and no face to kiss…but I drove on. Jean was waiting for me.

And Sammy was spending his first ever night alone.

* * *

IN PERPETUITY

It would not have returned if Sammy had died. We were already all but empty when the doctor told us that everything was going to be alright.

A nurse had taken a photograph of us at Sammy's bedside. I never knew why, but over the months and years following that night I wondered whether it was because she knew what she might capture. She worked with emotions, not just people, and perhaps she had known the magic of that place, wanted to retain some of it for herself. She had sent us a copy. It showed us not as a family but as a single, united whole. We were bonded by more than blood, right then. It was love that held us together.

We were all crying, so Jean kept the picture hidden away. It was too extraordinary to put on show.

"I can't lose him, Jean," I said, "not after Anne." There was a crackle and static stole her immediate response.

" — have to get it for you," she said.

"He thinks I've left him. He thinks I've abandoned him."

"I'm sure he knows that isn't the case, whatever has happened. Sammy's a bright boy. He's quiet, like his mum, but he thinks like her too. He'll know the reasons for whatever you've done, even if you think he can't."

A long line of cars passed in the opposite direction, headlights dazzling me. There was a flash in the sky above the hills to my left, bright as lightning but the wrong colour. Something dark fell from the boiling clouds' underbelly and skirted the hillside. A huge flying shape beat at the thermals and rose once again, belching fire, steaming its way into cover once more.

"There's so much more, Jean," I said. "So much more than what we know or believe. More than we even imagine."

Jean was silent again, and I began to think she had put down the phone.

"I think you should tell me when you get here," she said. "I'll get that photo. And I'll put the kettle on."

"Ten minutes, Jean," I said. I wanted her to stay but knew she had to go. We could talk when I arrived. I should concentrate on my driving; wrapping the car around a lamp post was not the way to help Sammy at all, even though…even though the accident's only cause would be my quest, driven by my utter, desperate love for him.

you why later, just please trust me, *please*. It's Sammy, Jean." I began to cry, and for a moment I thought it was raining. I even turned on the windscreen wipers, but they were powerless against my guilt. "He's all that matters."

Jean was silent, weighing up everything I had just told her. Anne had been like this. She was rarely wrong or misinformed in what she said, because she invested such effort and time thinking about things, letting her thoughts coalesce instead of bump together. Our arguments had often lasted for hours, consisting mostly of heavy silence. Like mother, like daughter.

"Are you sure you know what you're doing?" Jean said.

It was a question with no sensible answer, yet instilled with a trust I did not deserve. This world was a place I had never known existed, one where there was much, much more than normal people. Even now, with car lights blinding me at every curve in the road, I heard things moving in the fields.

"Yes," I said, "I'm positive."

There was another silence while Jean digested my lie. She knows it for what it is, but her real dilemma lies in trying to decide whether I am lying for the right reasons. She knows me as well as anyone — grief does that to people, lays them bare, strips their souls to scrutiny — and now, although she is confused and worried at my take on things, she knows that I am doing what I think is right.

"How far away are you?" she asked.

"Ten, fifteen minutes."

"I'll find it for you. See you soon."

It had never been the sort of photograph to grace a wall or sit on a sideboard or desk. Those were always safe, comfortable snaps of smiling faces and casual hugs, sunburnt cheeks and dopey smiles. Vacant images of people loved and perhaps lost, but empty nonetheless, harmless and fun, if melancholic at times. The photograph I wanted had been taken at the hospital when Sammy was two. He'd come out in a rash and we pressed a glass to his spots, neither of us remembering whether they should have faded away or not, and panic had been my guide as I drove to the hospital through rain-sodden midnight streets. For a couple of hours we were certain that our son had meningitis, and the whole world had been swallowed by the darkness outside, none of it mattering, most of it already vanished in readiness for the grave news we both expected.

IN PERPETUITY

There was more proof out there, waiting to be found. The photograph was next. Like the carving it was something I had not thought about for years, yet now its place in my collage of proof was so obvious. A good photo holds and echoes lifetimes, that's what my mother used to say. It was the reason Anne and I had never bought a video camera to record Sammy's early life; we'd wanted photo albums. His smiles frozen, those milestones retained forever for us to see. And sometimes, only rarely, everything that we were was caught within the lens. Just once I could remember, all three of us.

I tapped in the phone number as I drove. For a few seconds I wondered whether my mobile would work here, between many places and beyond most, but it rang and was answered.

"Hello?"

"Jean," I said. "It's me. I have to see you, I'm in trouble."

"Oh God..."she said. Nothing else. I did not even hear her breathing, and for a panicked few seconds I thought of the Green Man. Somehow he had known of the carving. That was something I'd been trying to ignore up until now, shuffled away in the 'To Be Considered Later' part of my mind along with the fact that I'd survived the fall relatively unhurt, and those injuries I had picked up now seemed far less serious than even half an hour ago.

He'd known of the carving, and maybe now he knew of the photo.

"Jean, I need to borrow a photo. That one of me and Anne and Sammy at the hospital, the one-"

"Oh Christ, is Sammy missing?"

That threw me. I even swerved the car, hissing across the gravel at the roadside.

"How do you know?" I whispered.

"As soon as you rang I had a bad feeling." She was Anne's mother. She still treated me like a son. And, like a bad son, I took her for granted far too much. "I don't know," she continued. "I've not been able to do anything all afternoon. I rang but I remembered you were taking Sammy out for the day. The police, have you called-"

"No law," I said. That brought the keeper's face flashing back at me, and I didn't like that. The thought that he was thinking about me, listening in, actively following everything that was happening— "No law, Jean. It's something I have to handle on my own, I'll tell needed. The carving was a portion, and there were more to gather before I could join them together, make them react and give the keeper what he had asked for.

Another idea came. The fall had perhaps cleared my confusion like a windstorm through a dusty attic; the impact, maybe, knocking in a knowledge I had only been grasping at up to now.

I knew what I needed next.

* * *

On the way I passed a police car. It was cruising, lights off, perhaps trawling for a final speeding ticket to fill their quota for the day. I almost flashed them down. I would pull them over and go to the driver's window, lean in, breathe in all that had happened to me over the past few hours. The shop, Sammy, the bag of heads, the demand, the door I could not touch, the one true cross, cross at its incarceration, the Green Man, my fall from the cliff —

— and why my bruises were fading, not expanding. And why my bleeding cuts had already scabbed over. I could sense the pain, smell it, taste it, but because I was so in awe of what my senses knew, I was also certain of my recovery. A rib may have been broken, but I could hear it knitting. For now, I could not think about these things.

I'd wave them down and tell them all I could. There was nothing else to do.

No law, I remembered, and the voice was with me in the car. I spun around but there was no one there. The keeper was thinking of me then, sitting at his desk puffing at another cigar, feet crossed on the huge open book, my name scratched in there already, a scrawl of a beginning with an ambiguous middle and an ending waiting to be written.

No law.

I pressed my foot on the gas and drove on. I had to be the author of my life, until I next saw the keeper. I could not let him ghost me. That would take Sammy away and I would forget myself forever, a lost identity wandering the streets, struggling to remember a dead family, their memory chased every day and night to the bottom of a bottle.

IN PERPETUITY

a sweet. He likes Jelly Babies, just like me! And his granddad was in the army too, *and* he likes Willard Price books and Thunderbirds, and we make friends."

Silence for a time. Darkness and silence. I can hear a breath being held and the space between heartbeats, and I wonder if they will go on forever, potential winding incessantly until it folds in on itself and this vision withers and dies.

But Sammy is there again.

"Me and Jack will be best of friends, Dad," he says. "If you let us."

If I let them? Why wouldn't I? Sammy is a growing lad, no reason why...

He's four and a half.

I open my eyes. I hear the Green Man's thought, even though he must surely be long-gone by now: *another one dead*.

I was lying on my back on the ground, the dusky sky filling half my field of vision, the cliff face the other. The sky was beautiful, the cliff face angry that I had even tried better it. Its ledges scowled, the cracks running vertically were slit eyes that closed even as I looked at them, hiding itself away from me once again. Shadows merged and softened its expression as the sun dipped in the west.

Pain kept me bright. I sat up and agonies coursed through my body, lighting my limbs and chest and neck, exploding in my head. I groaned out loud, and it was louder than I would have liked. The darkness was there, and anything could be hiding within it, listening for me. I had seen that in the keeper's shop, the fact that everything was out there should we but choose to acknowledge it. He had given me a key, a doorway to the locked routes of my mind, but by doing so he had also opened me up to their dangers and threats.

I should have been dead. The top of the cliff was high in the sky, and I should have been dead.

I should be dead!

There were bumps and bruises and cuts, half my body was stiff with dried blood, sticky where my movements started the bleeding afresh, but I was still very much alive.

I fell...I fell a hundred feet!

Yet I could still taste the cold and hear the mysterious distance.

The Green Man had stolen what was mine, but if he was already seeking the keeper he would be fooled. He only had a part of what I

I started down after him. The thought of what he was stealing urged me into action. I actually wanted to see it so much, I *needed* to see it, because not only was that carving old proof of my love for Anne…it was proof of myself. A confirmation of my existence, my past and history, and evidence of that would make what was happening in the present easier to handle. There was a whole history to me, not just the panicked, useless here and now.

I moved far slower than the Green Man, trying to never have more than one foot or one hand away from the rock at any one time. The thief was shifting with the speed and grace of a spider, whereas I was the slug. So thinking, my hand slipped into a crack and found something cool and wet in there. I drew it out quickly, gasping, hearing and sensing the animal shock of whatever I had touched. I slipped down a few feet. It wasn't until I kept slipping that the shock really kicked in; the realisation that my heart had stuttered and my fists opened and I had relinquished my trust in the rock.

I'm here and there, I think, *at the back of beyond and the forefront of things, and I'm already sure that this is not a place where normality is what I'm used to.* I grab at the rock and see Sammy's face, older than I remember it, sadder, as if all he knows of me are his memories of my abandoning him with the keeper.

My right foot struck a rock and tumbled me out into the air, and I was truly falling. Distance and orientation left me. My views span, but two sights stayed with me and accompanied me down: the village across the valley, larger than it should be, more bulbous, like a cancer that had jumped several years of growth; and the face of the Green Man as I fell past him. Turned to look at me. Knowing I was falling. Nothing in his eyes, no guilt, no pity. Not even victory.

As I struck the ground, I felt every twist of pain.

* * *

"Dad," Sammy says.
Dad. Not Daddy.
"This is me when I'm nine. I'm with my friends in town and there's this boy, a bit older than us, he's got an earring and a leather jacket and he's only ten. He pretends he's the Man, and most of us are scared of him, but I remember what you and Mum told me, Dad, to not judge people by their appearances. I talk to Jack and offer him

IN PERPETUITY

He kept tapping, harder now, faster. "I just steal," he said. His voice was gruff, as if unused. His clothes were torn, his hair knotted with filth, and he had a long beard that must have been home to things. He had been on the outside for so long that he seemed to have forgotten himself.

I knelt, edged backwards over the cliff and planted my toes against the rockface. It was actually about ten degrees from vertical, but the memory of exquisite danger came back hard. I stood there for a few seconds, my arms stretched out across horizontal ground as if to keep hold of safety. I did not want to let go. I had no idea what I would do once I got down there.

"Please," I whispered. "I need it for my son." But the words must have been swallowed by the ground before me, because the man's only response was to tap harder at the rock.

I heard the patter of small stones tumbling down the cliff. "No!" He'd broken it, shattered my clumsy heart and torn our names apart. They would never be found now, not in a million years could I gather the stones and shards and piece it back together. It would be like grabbing a handful of air and trying to reconstruct Anne's final breath.

"Got it!" he said. I looked down over my shoulder and he was mocking me. Not content with stealing, he was waving a fistful of stone at me, a small rock faced with my expression of love for my dead wife.

"That is mine!" I hissed, the anger pure and enlivening. I felt so *wronged*.

"Which means it's now mine." And then the Green Man began to scurry down the cliff. He descended incredibly quickly, using only one hand, the other retaining its grip on the rock. He stared down at his feet as he went, effectively dismissing me. There was a mole on the back of his neck. His crown was thinning, showing browned scalp beneath. He'd lost a finger on his left hand, ages ago, and I wondered if he had once been a carpenter. He must have loved things then, coaxed shapes from wood, taken time, taken care. He must have been a normal man once.

"What did you lose?" I asked. The Green Man did not seem to hear. He continued his descent, jumping down several feet from one ledge to the next, nails scraping on the rock face so harshly that I felt the vibration through my toes and fingertips.

was barely a conscious decision, simply something I had to do next, like breathing or blinking.

Tap tap tap.

He *had* been laughing. Because he was here to steal away part of my proof, take a small part of what I could use to save Sammy. The reasons hardly mattered. The fact that it was happening gave me the only impetus I needed. I did not let tiredness or pain slow me down, and the raw anger went to speed me up. A pair of birds were startled from the heather to my left, and I heard their feathers stroking the air as they drifted away. They spoke to each other as they flew. I could have known what they were saying, it was almost within my reach, yet right then it would not have been of interest.

I reached the summit and the world fell away. I was looking out over the countryside I knew so well, grateful to see roads and electricity pylons and the smudge of a village in the distance. Anne and I had eaten at a pub' there once, sitting outside in the summer heat and swapping her cheese for my slice of ham. We had often shared meals. There was little we called our own.

Yet there were differences here, and they disturbed me greatly. The village looked larger than it should, some of the buildings taller. And the landscape itself had changed. Like a face grown old, its proportions were now subtly different, the rises higher, the dips deeper.

Tap tap tap.

I looked down and there he was, standing on the narrow ledge fifteen feet below me, one hand holding a small hammer, the other tracing a chisel against the carving I had not seen for years. I almost leaned out to take a look. It was mine, I had put it there and I owned it, and the need to see was great. But then the man looked up at me and grinned — rotten teeth, eyes so empty that I wondered how he could still be alive — and I knew I had to climb down. He sees me and hates me, he sees purpose and a love still burning strong. But he feels nothing because there is nothing to feel, no past, no history, no course of action other than to steal someone else's route back to the keeper.

"That's mine!" I called down. "I came here for that!"

"Stake a claim on the rock of the world, do you?" the Green Man said.

"Do you?"

IN PERPETUITY

seemed not to hear me any more. He had even slowed somewhat, his attitude calmer now. His shoulders were not so tense, his breath came easier...and perhaps he gave an occasional giggle.

Why should he be laughing?

He could help me, I think, *if I tell him what I'm doing here maybe he'll help me find the carving, chisel it out, preserve my romantic intentions from so long ago.*

I tripped, stumbled forward and hit the ground hard enough to wind myself. My hands sank into the soft loam, and I felt things moving beneath my palms and between my fingers. The living earth, the mud awash with life, felt more keenly now, smelled and heard and as I looked down, seen. I could *see* the ground moving around me, such was the potential it held. The history, too. It held the past like the coveted lushness of a recently-buried corpse.

When I looked up the man had vanished. I hurried on, passing rocks I remembered from my last time here, years ago. My visit from then was clear, the intention certain. Déjà vu struck me hard as a breath of wind blew dandelion seeds across my path. I looked left and saw a bird drifting low across the hillside. Down by my feet, a scrap of sheep's wool lay tangled in a thistle, all as it had been years ago. I even had the same tools in my pocket, the chisel and hammer...but inside, I was so different.

I sighed as the déjà vu drifted away on the breeze, and then I heard a bird calling from somewhere higher up. A bird of prey, I thought. It was powerful and confident. But I had never heard a call like this. It would not have surprised me to see an unknown species hovering up there. I looked around cautiously, and although the calling continued I could see nothing.

Detail came in at me again, and I realised that I was hearing two sounds, not one. Metal on metal; and metal on stone.

Tap tap tap, as the man ahead of me tried to carve something from the cliff face.

There could be no other reason for him being here. Or if there were, the coincidence would be huge. Coincidences happened, I knew that — I believed in much more right then than I had mere hours before — but on this scale it would be unthinkable.

He was the Green Man, here to steal.

I ran. If this really *was* the Green Man, and if the head collector had been right, then he was dangerous. Yet I had to confront him. It by standing here. Once I moved it would be under threat again. For now I had control over this thing's life and death, even though I had never seen it before.

I probably killed things walking from the car, but if it changed the world I would never know.

And then Sammy called out to me and I saw nothing. Strange that his voice sounded so loud even though he was forty miles behind me. "Daddy," he said, not calling or crying, just talking. "Daddy, I'm seven now; I've been playing football for the school team. My knees are scraped and I've knocked out a tooth, but I don't care because I scored the winning goal and the tooth fairy will leave me a fiver."

"You're a very clever boy," I said, and my voice spread across the hillside and startled a big bird into flight. It was a buzzard or a goshawk, and as it took off I saw something squirming in its talons. For an instant it looked as if the victim wore some sort of clothing, but it must have been a splash of blood.

I started walking up the hillside. This place had the reputation of being a favourite suicide spot, although I could not recall ever hearing of anyone jumping. Maybe it was too beautiful. Perhaps here, suicides never quite happened.

The ground shimmered, wavering in and out of focus as if through tears, but I was not crying. It kicked lightly against my feet. I wondered if I was feeling the world's heartbeat.

I looked up again, and there was someone running up the hillside ahead of me.

He was not dressed in green, and as he glanced back down at me his face looked pale, almost white. Yet I was terrified. He had not been here moments before, and now he was above me, legs cutting through the bracken as he ran for the summit and the potential plunge beyond. He was two hundred feet away, yet I could hear his panting, smell his sweat, almost feel the itch of rough cloth against skin as he increased the distance between us.

"Wait!" I called. The man surprised me by stopping and turning around. He leaned forward and rested his hands on his knees, gasping for air. "Wait!" I said again, the word redundant now that he was still.

I started up the slope, but my movement set him running again. I shouted, called, tried to be friendly and then threatening, but he

IN PERPETUITY

A ghost from the past hit me right then, and suddenly I knew where to begin.

*   *   *

There was still time before the sun went down. I had maybe an hour to drive up the gentle hillside and then climb the final steeper two hundred feet to the summit. On the other side, where part of the hill had fallen away in some million-year-old cataclysm, mine and Anne's names faced out across the lowlands of Monmouth. A foolish greeting-card heart wrapped them together, intent so much more complex than execution. No one ever saw them, but that had not been the point. I had carved them in rock in the hope that they would become as timeless. A teenaged idea of romance, when love exulted in physical form was love made stronger. I smiled as I remembered climbing down the cliff face, heart thudding, sweat tickling my sides as if to make me lose my grip. It was thrilling and tempting, that chance-taking, and I had felt naked and so alone. Anne had been in college. It was all my own effort, and I had fully intended bringing her up here to show her my handiwork, show her just how far my love for her went. For one reason or another, however, days and weeks passed by, and eventually I decided that the carving was best left unseen. It was my own private statement and eventually it faded from my mind, as if worn by an aeon of erosion.

I had not thought of that carving since Anne's death.

As I parked and stepped from the car I was assaulted by detail once again. The sun came in low over the hillsides, dazzling me and giving me clarity of vision at the same time. It was as if its fresh, filtered light was washing my eyes, clearing out the cobwebbed corners where traditional vision held sway and truth was hidden away. Looking down at my shoes I could see the teeming life around them. Wood ants scurried through pine needles, both blown here by the wind. They moved with purpose even though they may have been lost. Some carried leaves, others locked antennae in brief embraces. I wondered what they shared, and for a terrifying instant I thought I could know. But tiny and insignificant as they were, the working of their minds was way beyond me. There were woodlice too, an earwig, a grub squirming its way blindly between grass stalks and danger. Perhaps I was shielding it from a bird's attention simply even smile, but it was that familiarity and acceptance that made me feel so loved. Anne's drawing was my favourite of them all, although each inspired different memories, smells and sounds and rich golden days which, at the time, had seemed nothing special at all. Fate contrives on occasion to make the normal extraordinary. If only we could recognise those times when we were there, not years later.

Two paintings away from my dead wife's drawing was a photograph of a harbour wall in Cornwall, the sun slipping down behind craggy cliffs and setting fire to the oily waters. I could remember taking that picture, turning to Anne, kissing her, telling her how proud I was…simply how proud. Like déjà vu in the making, that brief and seemingly normal moment springs back at me now so that I can smell the sea, feel the weakening sun on the right side of my face, a cool breeze on the left. I turn, alone in my hallway, and although Anne is not there my memory conjures her smile and the taste of her lips.

I walked upstairs and outside our bedroom was a place where her smell so often lingered. Perhaps her perfume was in the carpet or ingrained in the walls themselves. I could almost hear the perfume bottle being shaken, see the haze of spray drifting in the afternoon sunlight. I began to cry and even that brought a memory; Anne holding me when news of my grandmother's death came through. And my own lonely tears, shed so often in this room as night hugged me close, cried into the pillow so that Sammy did not hear them and come running, asking why are you crying again, Daddy?

Still I had no proof.

I looked at the ring on my finger; metal, that was all. Mouldable, meltable, easy to lose, a token rather than a product of our love. A wedding band signifies the traditional, not the spiritual. I had never taken it off, but that meant nothing.

Sitting on the top stair, looking down at the empty hallway and hearing the empty house around me, I began to have an idea of what I had to do. I could not catch a kiss, or the component parts of a muttered *I love you* long since stolen by the winds and shattered against distant hillsides. But just as love itself is not one thing but many, so its proof would need to be a collage. Physical, spiritual and imaginary, all these pieces would go to make up a big picture, just as devotion, attraction, respect and a dozen more subtle aspects combine for love. I would have to make a collection.

IN PERPETUITY

were. A hummingbird drinking nectar, where there should only be sparrows and blue tits eating seed. A shape staring at me from the darkened window of a neighbour's house, glass smudged with too much breathing. Two dogs in the next door garden, mirror images, tails swinging at the same time…every hair, every whisker distinct, and all of them exactly the same. My mind was holding a mirror up to this world and reflecting reality back, telling me to accept, to believe. I realised no sense of glee that I had to inhabit both sides to save Sammy.

I stood and stalked the ground floor of my home, full of empty spaces now without Sammy's shouting, his chattering, the rumble of toy cars on the timber floor, the crash of book towers being built and demolished, whole worlds making up his game. And suddenly, being home alone, Anne was more there than she had been since her death. She may as well have been breathing the same air.

There was a spread of paint on the dining room wall that did not match the rest, and Anne grinned at me and said, *You just have to leave your mark everywhere, don't you?* I smiled and shook my head at the memory, and a second later she was sitting at the table, eating the meal I cooked for our first anniversary. She smiled across at me and nodded appreciatively. There was a smudge of food on her chin but I did not say anything, we didn't know each other that well yet, life was still an adventure of discovery and the future was luscious and long.

Anne was pregnant with Sammy right then, although neither of us knows it at the time.

I turned and left the dining room. In the hallway was what we used to call our holiday wall, a place where we hung photographs and paintings and etchings from the places we had been together. One of the frames held a sketch that Anne had made of a Saracen watchtower on Italy's Neapolitan coast. It was not a very good drawing — it had been the end of her brief foray into doomed artistic ambition — but I loved it more because of that. I stared at the picture, and I could see Anne sitting on a chair in a pavement café, brow furrowed and hand dancing across the paper as she tried to bring the image to life. Her stomach was full and round with our child. There is a drop of ice cream splashed on her chest from moments before, slowly running its way down between her breasts, and I reached over and wipe it away with a delicate stroke. She did not

I had seen and they could not imagine. I saw a man driving an MR2, shaving cuts lined on his cheek like claws marks, or scratches impersonating razor slashes. A white van was spotted here and there with bloody stains, most of them smaller than cigarette burns, probably rust but perhaps blood, evidence of a careless dog or a recent hit and run. In a new Mini, a woman frantically frigged herself with one hand and steered with the other, nodding her head slowly up and down while she kept to fifty in the slow lane. I saw all this, and more.

"Daddy!" Sammy calls. "Look Daddy, I'm riding my bike!" I have been at work all day and I've missed this milestone; it's been witnessed only by Anne's mother Jean. "He's riding his bike!" she says. I smile and nod. Sammy is wobbling in an uneven circuit of the garden, joy in his eyes, a sense of achievement in the way he glances up at me every few seconds. He is six years old.

"What the fuck," I whispered, and the image vanished, washed away by a new rush of tears.

I went home. The house was more detailed than it had ever been. The street wavered in heat-haze, and with each flicker of my eyes I could see something more, something extra. It was as if layer upon layer of lies were being peeled back, sheets of air ripping it away until I could see reality peering out from beyond. My front lawn held hillocks and hummocks and battlegrounds for ants and woodlice. Acid evidence of their encounters seared the grass. The corpse of a small slug lay beneath a piece of tree bark, stinking and humming with microscopic life.

Detail, detail, so much detail came at me without my being able to filter it. I had stopped lying to myself, but it was all too much. Sensing more let me understand less.

I tumbled through the front door, ignoring my neighbours where they stood like wax dummies, staring at my red eyes and the empty space around me where Sammy should have been. It was none of their business. How dare they even think about asking.

In the dining room at the back of the house I sat at the French doors, keeping them closed. There was too much going on out there. I had to think. I had to plan. I had to prove love and get my young son back.

Each time I considered returning to the village and breaking into the shop, I saw something else that reminded me of how things now

IN PERPETUITY

But he had been out here for a long, long time. Why would he jeopardise his reward for me?

"How long have you been looking?" I asked.

He seemed confused for a few seconds, shrugging the sack higher onto his back and paying no attention to the whispering coming from within. "Long enough to find these," he said.

He turned away from me for good. He did not turn or pause or wave, and so I closed my eyes and turned my face to the sky. The sun felt good on my skin, but after a few seconds it began to burn like bad memories. I had enough of them, and I wished for no more.

When I looked back, the head-man had vanished. The road was long and flat, and although there were ditches and undergrowth on either side I did not believe he had hidden himself away. The distance shimmered with heat haze, liquefying the way I had come and the man had gone, turning it indistinct. I blinked again, but the haze grew thicker.

Noises came at me from across the fields, through the woods, beyond the hills. At first I thought they were the voices of giants — grumbling as they awoke, moaning as they hauled themselves up out of the ground and climbed the hills — but then a lorry came around the corner, a helicopter buzzed by high overhead, and within thirty seconds I came to recognise my surroundings.

Cars passed me by, occupants sparing me bored or vaguely curious glances. Perhaps they saw that I had been crying. Maybe some of them realised, in the couple of seconds they had to see, that I was not as wholly here as they.

The motorway was nearby. I had to sit down, plan, think about what had happened and how best to rescue Sammy. I thought that home, a thirty minute drive from here, would be the best place to do so.

Now I had a plan. But desperate as I was, I could not know just how much had changed.

* * *

The journey home was haunted by strangeness. Thoughts of the Green Man and the bag of heads and the lost woman intruded, casting themselves alongside careless lorry drivers, angry sports cars and people stuck inside their own little worlds, staring into distances and over. Perhaps they were the final words they had spoken before their decapitation.

It was impossible. They should not be here, just as everything I had seen in the keeper's shop could not be. I had been duped, drugged, driven temporarily insane by Sammy's disappearance, and now here I was miles away, talking to a madman. He had picked up his sack and slung it over his shoulder, and there could be anything in there.

Above the hills I saw a plane trail drawing slowly westward. Reality.

"I need to go back and get him," I said. I was speaking to myself. "I should call the police, tell them, then find him and—"

"No!" the man said. "You go back looking and you'll be looking forever. You'll lose sight of what you have to do...which is exactly what the keeper says. He never lets anyone return without whatever it is he's sent them to find. He's not that kind of collector. He doesn't take failure."

I thought of the sad, bedraggled woman I had seen in the village, dead but walking, forever lost even though she knew exactly where she was.

"I have to go," the head-man said, almost apologetically. "I've finished, now. I have to find him again."

I felt a rush of jealousy, warm in my guts and cold in my head. The man walked away and he had found his charge—the heads of famous dead people—and however impossible that was, at least they had been a physical, tactile request.

The keeper's challenge to me, however...even if Anne were still alive, where was my *proof*?

"One more bit of advice," the head-man said. He turned and he had changed, his skin more flushed, eyes wider and a subtly different shade of blue. He looked like a final chapter, and the broken veins in his eyes were maps of where he had been. "Keep away from the Green Man. He's lost, but still out there. He's gone mad, forgotten his quest, so he tries to steal from others. Just...stay away from him."

"Green Man?" I said, only more confused.

He looked back one more time, standing there in the road between me and my son. I could ask him to rescue Sammy, I thought. I could go back with him and when the keeper lets him in...

IN PERPETUITY

tears as always, but I needed the love we had felt to be fresh and rich.

I *needed* her.

I needed my dead wife.

And then a man ran along the road with a sack full of heads over his shoulder.

* * *

"Have you come to collect me?" he said.

"No." I knew there were heads in the sack; I could hear them talking. Several different voices muttered the same short sentences, again and again. It was a light hessian sack, stained red. It dripped.

"Oh," the man said, face dropping. "Only, I've been walking a long time, and I think it's time I got to the shop."

"Who are you?"

He looked instantly suspicious. "Who are you to want to know?"

I shook my head and stood up. "I need to go," I said.

"No! Wait! You have to see, are you from him? You have to see." He shrugged the sack from his shoulder and upended it on the verge next to my car. "I have as many as I could find," he said. "Is it enough? Do I get it, do I get what I was promised?"

He wittered on and I let him, I could not stop him, I was too busy recognising the heads rolling and spinning and coming to a stop at my feet. Jayne Mansfield, a milky Ian Holm, David Warner still muttering omens under his breath, a head wearing a hockey mask and someone who had surely once been a princess.

"Do I get my reward?" he asked again.

"But these have been dead for years," I said, feeling naïve and childish in my assumptions. I had been in the keeper's rooms. I had seen his displays.

"You're new," the man said, obviously disappointed. "Oh. Well, you'll soon see. What has he promised you?"

"My son," I muttered, but I said no more. My quest felt foolish, and I was certain that this man could not help me. He looked like he'd been out here for a long time.

He gathered his heads, picking them up by the hair and dropping them back into the sack. Still they muttered, the same phrases over reflection of the uneven road surface, and it was just possible there were no two trees in there even approaching a similar height.

I was seeing more.

I glanced at the car's dashboard and every number on the speedometer registered, every crease in the cheap plastic trim was a size, length and shape of its own. The motor rumbled, and I could distinguish the slick hush of pistons from the whirr of the drive shaft. The crackling of tyres on the hot road surface changed sporadically as I ran over a snail, a leaf, a puddle of pitch melted by the blazing sun. Smells parted and gave themselves to me individually, and I felt as if I had a dozen nostrils acting independently, not two. I breathed in deeply and smelled bluebells in the woods, the corpse of a hedgehog by the road and the sweat of a running man.

I was seeing, experiencing and understanding more, much more. Everything was being fed to my conscious mind, not filtered and sorted into important and unimportant, foreground and background. For a few seconds the sensory input was too great and I felt faint. Wheels growled as they encountered grit at the edge of the road. Opening my eyes and biting the inside of my cheek, I tasted blood. I was still in an unknown wilderness. And there *is* no wilderness; not in the here and now, at least.

I pulled over, trying to ignore the weight pulling me back. The gravity of my abandonment drew at every cell in my body, every slight electrical impulse in my nerves and muscles and brain. I could almost sense Sammy far back through the hills and rock and underground caverns, as if his presence were so strong that mere physicality could not hinder its effect nor tarnish its glow. He is sitting there now, still crying and afraid and wondering why his father has not come to rescue him from this room, where water drips down one wall as if the building is crying in sympathy.

I jumped from the car, suddenly sick and cold and needing to sit and look out across the countryside. The engine ticked behind me as it cooled, and I imagined the sounds a body may make soon after death, the gurgles and farts and sighs as if the soul could mourn its own demise.

Anne had been dead for two years, but she was always here. She was present in my actions, my beliefs, my morals, my faith, my behaviour and my habits — more than anything, her memory was a pleasant habit — and now I sat and actively thought of her. It brought

IN PERPETUITY

"I'll give you access," the shopkeeper said. "To your hidden thoughts and the places they lead. To pathways that most people cannot or will not see. I'll give you vision."

And he reached out and touched me for the very first time.

* * *

Twenty minutes after passing the village outskirts, I was still driving through countryside.

Monmouthshire is a beautiful part of the world, but it is hardly wilderness. There are country lanes that seem to lead to places unvisited for years, hillsides and valleys seen only if one abandons the car and proceeds on foot, and here and there stand dilapidated houses and farms buried by vegetation and time, echoing with memories of the dead and stories too long forgotten to ever be told again. The spirits of Romans wander these vales and meadows, the clinking of their armour quieter now than the tinkling woodland streams, subsumed beneath the waters just as their true selves lie buried in the earth, hidden in graves lost millennia ago. So the place is wild, true, but not wilderness. There is little of that left on the planet, and none here. The roads are short, the distance between neighbouring villages and towns small. I had been driving hard, and by now I must have covered almost twenty miles. I should have been out of the county. I should have found civilisation.

Instead, more hills and valleys surrounded me, and wild woods hunkered down on hillsides with no evidence of planned planting. I searched for electricity pylons and plane trails in the sky, but there were none. There were no road signs, either, and the road was more contoured than before, raised and dipped all over, every imperfection exaggerated and put on display.

Looking back up at the wooded hillside, I saw not only trees: there were ash, oak and sycamore, interspersed here and there with rashes of tall, thin pine. Branches raised up and pointed down, to and away from the sun, and even from this distance I could see that the leaves held no uniformity of shape. A willow hung curtains of colour at the lower edge of the forest and two dead, lightning-struck trees were the skeletal hands of the earth, trying to push up and out of the smothering woodland. The canopy was like an amplified leather thong hung around his neck bearing several large teeth. They clinked together as he moved and spat a tiny flame, and I knew they were from a dragon. This man was beyond belief.

"That's all you need to give me," he said.

"I loved my wife."

"Prove that to me."

"Sammy is the proof. He's our love made real. Now give him back to me."

The keeper shook his head. "Not good enough. And besides...I can't keep words on display. I can't catch your alleged love for your wife and hold it captive, to muse upon as I grow even older. What would the sabre-tooth think of me listening to nothing? How can I sit before Dracula's lower jaw bone and feign interest in meaningless, long-gone echoes? No. I need something. Something physical, tangible."

"I loved my wife," I said again, and he sees that this is the truth, he looks inside my head and sees the frantic memories of Anne that have been coalescing over the past few minutes. He sees and believes but it is not enough for him. He needs something *tangible*...and stealing my thoughts is way below that.

"I know," he said, almost with pity. "But I need to know forever."

A car passed by outside, a child shouted, a dog barked. Normality mocked me.

"Now you can leave." He looked down at a blank sheet of paper and started to write, dismissing me entirely.

His attitude disarmed me and I slumped to my knees in front of the desk. I watched the keeper write, saw my name appear in a beautiful script on old parchment-like paper, bleeding from his pen as if passing out of his mind, down his arms and through his fingertips.

I had never told him my name.

He looked up. "Are you still here?"

"How long do I have?" I asked.

He shrugged. "How old are you? Do you look after yourself, are you healthy? Looks to me like you may have forty, fifty years in you yet."

"I don't know where to look, what to find, who to ask. I have no idea where to go."

IN PERPETUITY

up at the time-yellowed ceiling and sighed, then leant forward like an excited child. "The fleece, did you see the fleece?"

I shook my head, although I could remember little of that strange walk now. I was concentrating on just one impossible exhibit, unbearable to recall: Sammy locked in the room. The door shifting from my hand, as if diffracted through water. Sammy was my one true treasure.

"Pity. Well, there's more that I want of course, much more. The Grail would be nice...I have a corner where it would look very effective." He grinned, and for the first time something savage showed through. I was almost pleased. "There's someone out looking for that right now," he said, sifting a sheaf of papers and perusing a book I could not see. "Ah yes...more than one, in fact. I suspect they may be some time."

"Me," I said. "What do you want me to find? Tell me what and how and I'll go. I don't care about your habits or your collection or how the hell you came to be here, today, just when I brought Sammy to visit."

"Fate," he said.

"I don't believe in fate."

The keeper shrugged. "It doesn't need your belief. Unlike God, it works just as well without."

I stood, ready to leap across the desk. He was playing with me, like a cat toying with a mouse before the kill.

"Find me proof of love," the keeper said. His words hung in the air between us for a few seconds, sinking slowly in. And then that saccharine smile again, like an evangelist or a talk-show host. "I apologise, of course. I appear to be turning abstract in my old age."

"Proof of love." I stared at him, waiting for the smile to break into a laugh, his façade to fracture and the truth to come tumbling out. And once started, my mind continued down that route. I looked around for the hidden camera — what foul TV programme had they dreamed up now, how many deluded and brainwashed sheep-people were phoning in their votes on my fate? — but there was no camera and I had never felt so alone.

The keeper gathered some papers from his desk and knocked them into a pile. None of them were the same size. He wore a ring on every finger, all of them different grades of gold, silver, platinum and other metals, no two colours the same, each design unique. A

"I have many things and want more. I'm a collector and an admirer, an artist and a consumer. I covet what I have not and treasure what I have, because I respect the stranger things in life. Sometimes, so strange. Sometimes too strange to be. But I've never let that rein in my desires." The keeper puffed on his cigar and gave more smoke to the room. I felt queasy. "This is when you ask me what they are," he said mildly. His mouth made a *pop, pop* noise as he obscured the room.

"You have my son in a locked room," I said, my throat clogging, eyes stinging. "You think I give a shit about your desires?"

The keeper sat forward and took the cigar from his mouth. His face seemed to part the smoke as he leaned across his desk toward me, eyelids drooping, the smile as sick and sincere as ever. "Oh, I think you do," he said. "You've seen what I have and you believe in me. That's a good start. Better than most. And while your child cries out for the father who's left him, try to tell me there isn't a little part of you that's *fascinated* with me!"

I shook my head but smoke shapes spoke of my lie, dancing in amusement as swirls of air stroked my still-damp cheeks.

Those things he had out there…such things! And still he wanted more.

"You're a magician?" I asked.

He snorted. "That's like saying you're a master of life, simply because you live. No. I see and accept more of the world than most, that's all."

"How does that help me get my son back?"

"You'll see more soon, too. You'll accept. I want you to find me a new addition to my collection."

"And if I bring it to you?"

"Yes. Your son. Of course!" His voice vented outrage at any hint of mistrust. Again, I believed.

"What do you want me to find?"

He sat back in his chair once more. It creaked and sighed as he rested his feet on the desk. I wondered how many times he had done this before.

"Well, I have many things, as you've seen. Some of them you will have recognised, some perhaps not. The cross that Christ was crucified on…that took some finding, and some getting." He stared

IN PERPETUITY

"You'll never forget him," she whispered. "And you'll never see him again."

"I have to! He has my son, locked up crying and thinking I've left him…" Tears came then, and I wished my guilt could be purged with them. Instead they seemed to feed it and lend it strength.

"I'll keep looking," the woman said. "I'll just keep looking. One day he'll slip; one day I'll see the door." She stood and walked away.

"Wait!" I jumped from the car and followed her across the road, running the last few steps as a car honked. I met the woman on the far pavement and reached out to grab her. She evaded my grasp without moving.

"Been looking a long time," she said. "Never found what I was sent for. He has my daughter." Her eyes, deep and dark and all but dead, seemed to deepen more, like the zoom lens of a camera. "I'll see her again, just one more time…"

She moved away and I could not stop her. The same young family she had paused by minutes before had turned around, and now they passed us by. The father gave me a look loaded with suspicion. The woman brushed by his shoulder without him even noticing.

I watched her leave, wending her way along the pavement and turning eventually into a car park shielded by trees. Tears still blurred my eyes, but they could not explain how the woman seemed to skip and jump across the street, as if the scene were part of a jumpy old cine 8 film.

When she had gone, the street was normal once more.

I got into my car and drove from that village. I drove at breakneck speeds along country lanes, and in the back there was Sammy's booster seat, a plastic dinosaur he'd been playing with that morning, a shower of crisps speckling the seat, a half-empty bottle of water which he would never finish…

I thought of that lonely woman, wandering the streets as if that was all she had ever done, her body and clothes and eyes making her invisible to people around her. Because she was somewhere else, somewhere not here, in a place where the keeper had sent her. And where she had found nothing.

She was somewhere I had to go.

* * *

TIM LEBBON

* * *

I had not even left the village before I saw someone who would know me.

The woman was walking along the pavement, glancing into shop windows, pausing to stare at the sky, but I knew from the instant I clapped eyes on her that she was out of place here, out of time. Her clothes were old, tattered and grubby. Her blouse was ripped and bloodied, an old denim jacket draped around her shoulders bearing signs of some ferocious attack. She only wore one shoe; her other foot was clod with blood, and it left a single trail of red footprints along the hot pavement. No one saw them but me.

She passed a young family — sporty father, sexy mother, cute little girl with a chocolate beard — and paused. They walked away without acknowledging her, and even though the father moved to one side to let the woman pass, I was certain he had not actually seen her.

She looked at the sky again and seemed to sigh, shoulders drooping, cheeks glistening with tears or blood.

I rolled the car to a stop and sat there unmoving, wondering whether I knew this woman. I had never seen her before, but the way she blinked and stroked her ear inspired déjà vu, ten seconds, twenty, such a long spell that I felt giddy with possibilities. I clasped the wheel tightly and closed my eyes, and when I opened them again the woman was walking toward me. Staring. Seeing me through the sun-glare from the car windscreen.

"Have you seen him?" she asked. Her voice was like a fox's yap in the night, secretive and instantly lost.

"The keeper?" I asked.

"Of course, the keeper." She sat in the road and rested her forehead on my door. A car approached but the woman seemed unconcerned. It swerved to avoid her without its horn sounding, and with no angry look from the driver.

"So long," she said. "I've been looking for so long..."

I leaned against the door so that I could look out the window, and she looked up at me quickly and smoothly. She knew that I had just left him, she could smell him on me, that stench of cigar smoke and calm deceitfulness. She saw the terror of him in my eyes, and I blinked to try to clear the memory of him.

IN PERPETUITY

though the walls still sprouted miracles and impossibilities, I looked at the keeper. I could read nothing in his face other than enjoyment.

"You've seen my display," he said. "You've seen the things I have in there."

"They're not real," I said, but it was a lie in my throat. I flushed and looked away from him.

"I think you know they are." He opened a small wooden box and, ridiculously, offered me a cigar. I refused. He chose one, clipped the end and lit it, taking care to puff as much as he could to fog the room. It did not cloud my vision. I could see him just as well, and I would remember his eyes as long as I lived.

"You've seen *Fargo?*" he asked.

"Huh?"

"The film, *Fargo?* You've seen it?"

I nodded.

"Last year I took a child from a car and told its mother that I wanted the money the criminals had buried in that film. She flew to the 'States to look for it. She went to Fargo and froze to death."

I could only frown. There was nothing else to do. I could not, do not understand.

"Don't die on your quest," he said. "If she'd worn warm clothing, gone prepared, she might yet be alive. And the child might not be where it is now...wearing what it is."

"What quest? I'm going nowhere, you have my son, I have you in my eyes, I'm not going anywhere without him."

"No law," the keeper said quietly. He had seen into my mind, that flicker of an idea about leaving here and going straight to the police. "Tell no one of this. I'll know if you do. If they come looking — if they think they can find me just by looking — I'll know."

"What quest?" It was barely a whisper, because I was beginning to see the hopelessness of this. He had me, trapped not by strength but by the surreal, imprisoned in some strange psychotic dream where truth was a lie and everything unreal was as real as my loss. I thought of the cross I had seen out there and felt the holy truth of it. And Sammy, sitting in his room as he cried and wished for me, wished I could go and find him.

"I want him back," I said. It was an admission of defeat.

"Good," the keeper said. He stood to move his game one step forward.

So I left my son and followed the old man, ready to hear what he had to say. We passed more displays—cages and tanks and echoes and smoke-filled rooms and chattering artefacts—but I ignored them all. I concentrated on the back of his neck, seeing the lines worn in by years of looking up. He was a little man. I wondered how strong he really was.

"Here," he said eventually, turning left and shifting a curtain from a doorway. He motioned me through and I did not pause, not for an instant. If he wanted Sammy and me locked away together he would have had us. I could not have protected myself. My only hope was that he was telling the truth.

"Come into my office," the keeper said, giggling as he dropped the curtain behind him and entered the room.

Outside, the village street. It was still sunny. There were a man and kid across the road, paused on the pavement as the man knelt and wiped ice cream from the boy's shirt. The boy—not much older than Sammy, maybe five or six—continued licking his ice cream cone, smiling wickedly as another chocolate blob dripped down onto his dad's hand. The father looked up and growled, held his son's arms, shook him and buried his face between his shoulder and neck to give a playful bite. The boy put his head back and laughed. Sunshine glittered from his ice cream tongue. His dad was bald, his scalp pink from the long hot day he had spent with his boy. A happy day. A day without concerns.

Half an hour earlier, that had been me.

"Where's Sammy?" I said, turning to look at the curtain.

"He's not back there," the keeper said. He shuffled around and sat behind the desk taking up half of the room. It was a chaos of paper and envelopes. I tried to see the addresses on some of them but they were all the same, and equally nonsensical. They had no street, town or city names, and the intendees were little more than smudged scrawls.

"Then where?" I said.

"He's waiting for you."

"Waiting for me to do what?"

"To find something for me."

I saw that strange room again, long as the world, shrunken to nothing at the end by perspective, fading into time and space even into a grimace of agony. People had done bad things to me before, but never to my son. This feeling, this anger, was fresh and new and primal. It felt good.

I *growled*. Veins raised on my forearms as I squeezed harder, feeling pinches of the man's flesh caught in his rumpled shirt. He did not seem to notice or care.

"The more you hurt me, the more your son will feel that hurt."

Sammy had stopped shouting but it was replaced with a cry, something worse than the shouting because I recognised it. He was in pain. If he'd been play-acting the cry would have been loud and forced.

I let go of the keeper and sprang to the door. It shivered away from me as if suddenly swallowed by a heat haze, a mirage formed from the heat of my anger and fear. Yet I could see through the viewing panel. Sammy was still on the bed, but he'd shifted until he was leaning back against the wall, brushing at his chest as if to wave off a wasp or fly that had landed there. There was no insect. There *had* been my own hands on the keeper's shirt...perhaps that was it.

"Daddy," Sammy said again, and my heart broke, I *felt* it. I've heard the expression before, but now I sense the rupture, feel the coolness of shock and then the white-hot rage as blood floods my chest cavity, my insides, drowning me in grief quicker than I can choke.

I turned to the keeper. "I want him back."

"And you'll have him," the old man said. "I'm almost certain of that. Come with me, I'll tell you how." He turned and walked away, further along this wide room that I knew could not be, without a single backward glance.

I suppose that was when I gave in and realised that he had me. Any normal person would have remained behind with their son, tried to get through the door, ignoring the impossible flexing and distortion as their love blinded them to the intolerable and insulated disbelief. But the irony was that no normal person would have seen this. I may have been normal half an hour before, but I had witnessed things, felt things, which destroyed normality as surely as a dream given life. I had seen the one true cross and known it to be genuine, smelled sabre-toothed tiger faeces and not even touched my nose to question the scent. I had queried nothing. That made me not normal.

I saw something else long before we drew level. It struck me and held my attention, obvious, unmistakeable, but when the keeper spoke its name I sank to my knees. Not in worship, but in fear.

The one true cross.

He moved on quickly, as if there were more important exhibits deeper in the room.

Pacing a cage, too large to be inside but here nonetheless, a sabre-toothed tiger. It looked at me with pale, wan eyes, dipped its head and strode one way, dipped again as it came back. There was madness in its gait.

Turned to the wall, sitting on a table, an open suitcase cast its unknowable golden glow against damp stone.

More things, more, and the shop's name suddenly held meaning as I remembered the quote from Hamlet. I looked at the back of the keeper's neck, within easy reach of my hands, and suffered the same indecision as that Danish prince.

"A door," the keeper said. He stopped and looked back at me, his arms crossed, waiting.

There was a glass viewing panel and I looked in, saw Sammy huddled on a dirty bed. He had been crying for a long time.

"Sammy!" I shouted, reaching to bang the door and grab his attention. The door drew back from me, like someone drawing in their stomach muscles. "Sammy!" I said, quieter this time, but he merely looked across the room at the far wall, lost, forlorn, forgotten, shoulders shuddering and bottom lip protruding.

I cried. It did no good, there was no power in my tears, but I could not hold them back.

And a few seconds after the tears, came anger.

"Give him back to me!" I hissed. I launched myself at the keeper. My hands were clawed to grab, my heart aching to give pain, but as my fingertips brushed his thick shirt Sammy cried out.

"Daddy!"

I held on to the keeper, pulling him toward me so that I could head-butt him in the face. I wanted to break his nose, see his blood. I abhor violence, and this rage was a thrilling shock to my system.

"*Daddy!*" Sammy shouted again, his voice cutting into me, misting my vision red with furious tears.

"You're only making things worse," the keeper said. He was still smiling. I wanted to rip off his face, turn that smile upside down

IN PERPETUITY

He paused beside a glazed picture frame. It held a neatly written one-page letter, an admittance of guilt and dishonesty, signed Lucan.

"I almost had the man himself, but he's a slippery beast." The keeper gave me his smile, sickening in sincerity. "Must be all that seaweed."

He walked on and I followed on behind. The corridor opened out until we were walking down the middle of a long, high-ceilinged room. It was huge, its end lost in a haze of perspective, and it could never be here. The shop Sammy and I had entered had been sandwiched between two others, small, a dwelling house with a converted downstairs. Not this place, this somewhere else. Its crannies were lit with gas lanterns hung from impossible heights, the light too strong and even to be only from them. The floor was covered with old carpet, worn in places by countless footfalls until the darkly stained floor showed through. There were smells...they were familiar, the whole rank stew of them, but I could place none. Individually they seemed to conjure secret memories I could not consciously recall; images and places and people and comments and feelings I must have experienced once, such was the sense of familiarity. But they remained unknown to me.

"Look," he said, and "Look," raising his left hand, his right, pointing up and down at the strange exhibits hanging and lying and living in this place. And quickly, shockingly, I began to realise that I was somewhere else. I had moved on, sideways, aslant, and the things I saw here...they were genuine. I believed that instantly and without doubt, as if the air itself were a truth drug and the keeper and I were breathing deep.

A glass case containing the smashed skull and torn brains of Kennedy, still glistening and wet, unclotted, sitting there like the incorruptible remains of a saint.

Further on, hanging in mid air with no visible means of support, something that looked like a blinded eyeball plucked from its socket. *Hitler's testicle,* the keeper whispered, and I believed him.

Sitting on a wide wooden bookcase were a collection of bones, skull ridged and distorted, ribs twisted as if melted and reset a dozen times. The skeleton of an Orc. It even displayed battle damage, knots smashed from the pelvic bone by the repeated impact of an axe.

I had to go. There was nothing I could do here, not any more, because my life had changed in the last hour. It was more than realisation or experience, it was something fundamental about my existence that had drawn previously held truths from my mind and diced them, hacked them, slaughtered them on the threadbare carpeted floor of the keeper's back room. I'd watched them die, those beliefs, heard their final whimpers through ears still echoing with my young son's pleas for help. Those cries were imagined — nothing could get through that door, not sound, not smell, not me — but they were no less cutting because of that. I had failed him. It was my job to look after Sammy, he was my boy my blood my son and I had failed him. I had left him.

But there was no other way. I believed what had happened, what the keeper had told me and demanded of me. Later I would question this instant belief but right then, right now, there were places I had to be.

I slid down the grass bank and ran to my car. It was hot in the afternoon sun. It needed a wash. I saw Sammy's handprints where he had insisted on opening and closing the door for himself, always learning, always striving for experience and knowledge, *Daddy, why is glass hard, where are the dead people, is there a dinosaur in the sea...?* The car was familiar and unaltered over the last hour, so I clung to it and hoped it may change things back. It did not. Sammy remained not there.

Sammy! I heard from the distance, but if it was still the skinhead it was an echo at most. They were only trying to help, and I should have stayed to thank them, but I had to go. I had to leave and find the pathways that most people could or not would see. The keeper had given me the key. There was nothing in my pockets, my hands, around my neck, but somehow he had given me the key.

I looked across the river at the ruined cathedral that was this village's life-blood, and for a moment I saw a colour I did not know.

* * *

"I have many things," the keeper said as I pushed the curtain aside and followed him in. Sammy's cries had ended without echo. "Many, many things. Here. See this."

IN PERPETUITY

"You'll see him dead, of course," the shopkeeper said, holding the curtain aside as an invitation. "Here and there. Now and then."

Where is Sammy? Where am I?

"Somewhere neither here nor there," the shopkeeper said. "This is my place, my real place. I'm the keeper of it. Come inside if you want to help your son, and I'll tell you what you have to do."

"Tell me now," I said.

The keeper shook his head, face still holding that smile, begging to be melted off with a blowtorch. And I would. When this was over, when I had Sammy back, I would go along with this madman's demand for no law and assert my own.

The smile broadened slightly, and he knew what I was thinking. "Come," he said.

"No. Tell me now. Tell me, or I put a chair through your window and leave."

He knew I would not. He knew I *could* not, not without my son. He disappeared behind the curtain, laughing softly as I heard Sammy crying out for his daddy.

* * *

It is panic now, but a panic somewhat tamed by the memory flying at me. I cry. I sob. And I think of the things the keeper had said.

No law, he said. *Any interruption from outside, any efforts to reveal the truth, and you will never see your son alive again.*

I froze on the edge of the pavement, the car park down the slope before me, the road behind, the row of shops and cafes staring at my back. 'More Things' was not there. Maybe it was further along the street, or in an alleyway I had forgotten fleeing only minutes before. But I thought not.

"Sammy!" I heard from my left. The skinhead and his friend were at a junction in the road, hands cupped to their mouth, their shouts so desperate that they could well have been my own.

I wondered whether asking them for help had been revealing the truth. Maybe even now the keeper was opening the door I could not touch, smiling his benevolent smile as Sammy cried out for me, drew back from the little old man, knowing danger when he saw it...

Sammy pouted and frowned heavily for a moment—his not-on-your-life look—but then he saw how serious I was. In that moment, that final moment, I think even Sammy knew just how much trouble we were in. He moved quickly to the door.

"Daddy!" he said, tugging at the handle with a kid's conviction that it would do exactly what he wanted it to do, and *now*. "It won't open!"

"Want sweeties, Sammy?" the shopkeeper asked.

"No, he doesn't!" I said.

"No, thank you," Sammy said. "Daddy said I mustn't. Not from strangers or nasty people."

The shopkeeper turned back to me, not bothering to correct Sammy's depiction of him. "If you want him back," he said, "I need you to find something for me."

Everything shifted. Minutely, almost imperceptibly; I felt it in my bones, my cells, although I did not actually see or hear or feel any movement at all. The change was instantaneous, so fast that my senses dizzied themselves catching up.

One second he was there, the next he had vanished.

Sammy.

"Sammy?"

"Let me show you," the shopkeeper said. He made to walk past me, a faint smile holding his lips up. He stank. Dirt and grime and sweat and worse, a miasma of stenches I had not noticed upon entering the shop. The road kill had gone rotten, slicking a greenish mess down the wall. The broken coffin had spewed its content across the floor. It wore a dress.

Sammy had gone.

"Where's my son?" I hissed.

"As I said…let me show you. Listen to me and you'll know." He held up his hand and pointed, a filthy fingernail aimed straight between my eyes. "But no law. Any interruption from outside, any efforts to reveal the truth, and you will never see your son alive again." He walked past me and pushed aside a dark curtain hiding a doorway. The weight of further rooms beyond was immense.

I was speechless, actionless, stunned by how things had changed and how outside, everything seemed so normal. Cars passing by, people sitting on a wall eating bags of chips, fluffy clouds dancing across the sky. All the same but an infinity away.

IN PERPETUITY

Sammy turned around and pointed down at the carvings, eyes wide, a big grin on his face. "Horses!" he said. "Pigs! Daddy, pigs and horses!" From where I stood they were not likenesses of anything known.

"No law," the shopkeeper said for the third time, and he placed the iron on its base and turned to look at Sammy.

I moved towards my son. The shopkeeper raised a hand and I felt stupidly threatened; stupid because he was hardly there, little more than five feet tall and probably a measly nine stones to my sixteen. His hand was red-raw from the iron. I felt the heat coming off him in sickly waves, but he did not seem to be in pain.

"Sammy, get out," I said. "We're going now. We're going for an ice cream!"

"No," the shopkeeper said, "you're not."

"What is this?" I asked again rhetorically, totally believing what he said. We were not leaving. The mere possibility of going for an ice cream was almost laughable. The view from the window was of a country I had never visited, a place I could never go. The shop felt darker, heavier, deeper than it had when we had entered five minutes before. Sun shone through the windows stronger than ever, but it was as if a haze of dust had been lifted from the floor, vision tinted with a sepia brush.

"This is something far removed," the small man replied. He smiled. It was a pleasant smile, toothy and fresh and it touched his eyes like all good smiles should. There was nothing unkind about it at all, and for a moment I wondered just why I was worried, why I'd concerned myself with a few strange exhibits, he was a little quirky, that was all, and quirkiness was needed to make a living in a place like this, so much competition in the village, so many others trying to ensnare the tourists.

It was a good smile. An easy smile.

But it was ancient.

"Sammy, out you go, son," I said. "Wait for me on the pavement." Sammy was standing by the window, not far from the counter and the exit. The shopkeeper was in the middle of the shop, the central exhibit in a place lined with strange wares. I stood to one side, next to ranks of loaded book cases, shelves sagging like a fat man's jowls, tomes askew.

As more memories sliced through my shock, forcing the truth into parts of my brain that were surely never designed to deal with such things, I remembered Sammy locked in that room. His eyes staring out, my vision blurred with tears that may have been mine, or his.

And he's thinking of me, seeing me, wondering why I've left him in such a place.

He's *missing* me.

Fleeing is all I can do to help.

* * *

"No law," the shopkeeper said.

It was at that precise moment when I knew something was amiss. Sammy was at the window display, looking down at the wood carvings that had so grabbed his attention as we walked by outside. His eyes were wide as he took in whole new worlds. I was browsing the books, dusty old tomes I had never heard of before, used to fill old oaken bookcases to give the place some warmth. There seemed to be several copies of the same book there, though the title refused to imprint itself on my mind.

The shopkeeper was ironing his hand on an old pool table.

"No law," he said again, turning his hand and pressing his palm. There was hissing and steam. When he took the iron away there were no markings on his skin, no burns, no lifeline.

Everything changed. Not visibly — there was no movement, no shift in things — but I noticed things I had not seen before. A display of recently acquired road kill graced one shelf behind the counter, dripping slow red stalactites to the floor. A cat gazed at me with glazed eyes. A hedgehog bristled, guts hanging out of its arse. A magpie pointed one sad wing skyward, mourning its loss. Further along the wall a row of six coffins were stacked upright, timbers blackened and weakened by long submersion in the soil, the wet mud spilled around their bases holding treadless, nameless footprints. One had ruptured, and I saw something white trying to break free.

"What is this?" I whispered, not intending the shopkeeper to hear. He was ironing his other hand now, watching me as I glanced over at Sammy. "Son!" I said.

IN PERPETUITY

"Sammy, right?"

I nodded. The skinhead ran back across the road, signalled down the bank at someone in the car park below and turned back to me. "Where'd you last see him?"

"In a shop," I said, raising my voice as a car passed by, its inhabitants unknowing and uncaring. "An antique shop, but with lots of other stuff. It was called 'More Things.' I think. But I'm not sure..." I trailed off, ran along the street for a few seconds and tried the front door of a house. It was locked. Nobody came to open it. Fear presses in, panic, a terrible need to do something, *something*. "I'm not sure where it is now," I said.

I looked back across the road and three other youths had joined the skinhead, a boy and two girls, similarly attired in metal and leather and honest attitude. They huddled together for a few seconds and I was suddenly, inexplicably certain that they would step apart and there would be Sammy, laughing as they laughed at this cruel joke, but at least is *was* a joke, only a gag, at least he would still be *there*.

"Sammy!" they yelled, a couple going either way along the street. "Sammy, your dad's looking for you! Sammy!"

Their voiced faded, I crossed the street and looked down at the car park, and I was surprised that I could still see my car. The fact that my son was missing had not changed the way it looked one bit.

Shop's gone, I thought. *Car's still there.* It is truly panic now, but then fragmented memory starts to swing in and take a stab at me, a foe parrying and prodding until my defences are totally clear.

I'll give you access, the shopkeeper had said. *To your hidden thoughts and the places they lead. To pathways that most people cannot or will not see. I'll give you vision.* But that was later, after Sammy had been taken and the keeper had charged me with my task, something I was still not sure of, a puzzle like a jigsaw thrown to the wind, waiting to land and be turned up the correct way. Right now I didn't even possess the corners.

"Sammy!" a voice called in the distance.

"Proof of love," I said, trying the words in my mouth, discovering that they sounded less ridiculous than they should have by any sane benchmark. *Access,* the keeper had said. *To pathways.*

I wondered where they led.

chocolate buttons he'd kept in his pocket—they'd be melted mush by now, all the better to make a mess for his poor dad to clean up—and he'd laugh as he heard me fading out and fading in as I ran back and forth, because now I was panicking, retracing my steps, passing the place where the shop had been and should be again and again and-

"Sammy!"

First signs of madness there. My voice was louder, surreptitious glances from others in the street changing to longer, blatant stares. One of them crossed the road and approached me, holding back as I leapt at a six-foot timber fence, pulled myself up, straining to see over, looking for the shop.

A garden. Kids' toys scattered about, a well-manicured lawn, a dog taking a shit in a flower border, glancing back at me as if offended at my intrusion.

I dropped back to the pavement and muttered my son's name under my breath. It came as a gasp.

"You got a problem, mate?" The guy was a punk, purple Mohican out of place amongst the antique shops and cream tea parlours of the little village, too colourful to be seen against the wan grayness of the centuries-old tumbled down cathedral by the river. A tattoo of a dragon crawled out of his black tee-shirt and a silver Celtic ring pierced his nose, and I remembered a story my old headmaster once told me at primary school. He was long-since dead, that wonderful man, but his words had stuck with me, the tale of a leather-clad, heavily tattooed and pierced biker pausing in a multi-storey car park and going back up the stairs to help a woman with two kids and a buggy. Don't judge people by their appearances, the story had ended, the moral hammered in but utterly memorable, something he said would be with me for ages and had been forever.

"Yeah." I ran further along the street, jumped at a stone wall and saw an old man washing his car before I slid back down. The stone snagged my jeans and scraped my legs. If only my senses were as keen as my pain, I may have perceived that something was wrong early enough, soon enough...

The skinhead had wandered after me, frowning. He looked very young. The tattoo was vivid and fresh.

Sammy was four-and-a-half.

"My son's missing," I managed to whisper.

In Perpetuity
Tim Lebbon

Have you ever lost something? I don't mean your keys or your voice or something you've always meant to shed, like your virginity or that smoking monkey on your back. And I don't mean something less quantifiable, like losing your nerve in a darkened street-fight or forgetting an important fact about someone: their name; their age; their reason for being in your bed.

I mean something precious, loved and protected.

Your son, for instance. Your own flesh and blood. Have you ever lost your son?

* * *

"Sammy? Sammy?"

For now it remains a vaguely worried shout, tinged with embarrassment at the people glancing up from across the street and tempered by the thought that I must be mistaken, I *must* be, because stuff like this just doesn't happen.

"Sammy!"

He had come out of the shop and sneaked away, that was it, hide and seek, slipped across the street and found his way down the steps to the car park and river. He was only four-and-a-half, but he was resourceful and mischievous and perfectly capable of hiding down there behind a bush, giggling as he listened to me slowly but surely going mad up here on the street. He would eat those last few

Tim Lebbon

Soon, they would be lifted off this rock. She would abdicate, turn the iron crown over to the goats. Placating them with chocolate bars, which they ate wrappers and all, she had already come to a truce with her vicious subjects.

Jeperson was comfortable, not complaining of his injuries.

She supposed she was bruised and battered, too. Two of her fingers bent the wrong way and she couldn't feel them.

Stacy sat by the Man From the Diogenes Club.

He handed her a Bounty. Sewell Head's back-up stash of sweets had been in the Sea King.

She ripped the paper and bit off a chunk. Chewing hurt. She thought she'd lost a filling—though not, Lord willing, any of her precious back teeth—while being knocked about.

"What's down there now?" she asked.

"A mess. And dead people. Mostly water, though. The apports haven't lasted in coherent form. Adam Onions missed his chance to study a unique set of phenomena."

The rescue helicopter approached the island.

"It'll be good to be back," she said.

"It is good," he responded, eyes flashing bright silver.

SWELLHEAD

guts of Skerra. White shreds that might have been ghost-goons were whipped around inside the torrent. A mini-jeep was tossed out of the maelstrom like a dinky toy, smashing against the cave-wall.

Water got under the lift-platform and raised it higher.

Stacy yelled as if on a fairground ride.

The guardrails were like liquorice sticks pulled out of shape. The platform itself felt rubbery and melted in patches.

Richard took Stacy's hand and held fast.

He tried to believe again in Swellhead's world. Where a hero might survive something like this. Where the valiant were rewarded.

Not only was Stacy Droning of Skerra but the new trivia champion. She had remembered, no *intuited,* that Head hadn't know the answer to the easy pop music question Really-a-Good-Bloke Rory had raised.

Of course, he could have been peeved enough to look it up in his *Guinness Book of Hit Singles* in the meantime. Then, things would have been different.

The Blowhole grew bigger as they were forced up at it.

He patted her hand, well done.

The platform threw them up into the open air.

They tumbled down the hillside, away from the water-spout that rose high as if geysered, demonstrating how the Blowhole got its name.

Jagged stone scraped his side. He heard Stacy swear.

It was not too late in the day to break his neck.

He came to rest in a tangle of limbs, wet clothes twisted, and looked up at pre-dawn sky. Dramatic clouds were incarnadine as red washed over his vision.

A bearded face, upside-down, obtruded into his eyeline. And neighed rather nastily.

He shooed away the goat.

13

After a bare five hours of morning, Skerra day was almost over.

The radio crackled, but neither Stacy nor Jeperson were inclined to climb back inside the Sea King to answer it.

A rescue chopper was on its way.

The walls themselves slumped, running down in waves like a dropped curtain. Glistening rock showed through.

They had to get to the Blowhole.

12

Sewell Head was dead and Swellhead sucked back into the void from which he had come, but the Talent was still here. Breaking a pot doesn't make the jam disappear. The complex, the huge apport, was collapsing, resolving itself to its physical components — salt and water, mostly — but it would take time. Perhaps traces would remain forever.

In a way, Richard hoped so.

Without Swellhead's belief, rigidly suppressed but devout, that every villain must be bested by an arch-nemesis, Richard felt again like a broken old man. He was sure bones had snapped inside him, but the soaking chilled him so much that he could not yet tell how badly he was hurt.

He was back in the world again.

Perhaps Fred was right and he never should have left. If he had stayed in the game, knocking heads with dolts like Onions, perhaps this would have been handled differently. Good people and bad might still be alive, including Adam Onions. There might have been a place for a Talent like Sewell Head, even if it was as the cleverest shop assistant in the universe.

His feet kept working as Stacy helped him through corridors. The lighting was uniformly dim and dying. The carpeting was sludge.

They made it to the lift platform.

"If you can still fly, it'd be a useful back-up," she said, hammering the up control.

He shook his head, too racked to explain.

The platform rose.

Stacy gasped.

Richard shifted — agonies shooting through him — to look.

Beyond the guardrail, he saw the great cavern. The big dish was bent out of shape like an origami structure trampled by Godzilla, and washed back up its tunnel by waters that still poured into the

00:01:00

Not in the last minute, the last second!

00:00:01.

Swellhead was stricken, Sewell Head looking through his eyes, under his Heath Robinson-Jack Kirby hair-dryer. She could tell he was aware of his own absurdity.

"Kylie," she said, putting him out of his misery.

With a sad, should-have-known look, Head slumped. His head exploded in a shower of red fragments.

00:00:00.

Jeperson fell, landing on the edge of the trap, falling the right way, away from the hole.

00:00:00:00:00:00.

The zeroes were eggshapes.

Stacy looked for Persephone Gill, and found her dead, a dagger-wedge of Sewell Head's skullbone stuck in her eye, spearing into her brain.

The tremors were more sustained. The floor was bucking under her. She scrabbled to help Jeperson to his feet.

He was looking around, confused.

"It's all still here," he said. "I thought it'd just go pop and be gone."

The computers kicked their spools, unreeling tape across the control room, and sparked showers that set many little fires. The whitesuits were phantoms, coming apart and forgotten, or slumped corpses.

"It won't be here much longer," she said.

Somewhere in the complex was an almighty crash. Everything shook, and there was a huge roaring.

A spout of saltwater rose gusherlike from the trapdoor, tossing remnants of Onions and de Maltby, along with sleek black toothy things, up against the ceiling of the control room, battering away asbestos tile to show bare rock. Water showered all around. Stacy had to fight to keep her footing and hold of Jeperson.

"The Kjempestrupe just poured in," he said. "Head was keeping it out through force of will."

She dragged him from the control room, a wash of water around their feet, into the Head Room.

The trophies on the walls were fake now, moulting papier mâché.

But this could be a post-modern, ironic story. A despairing, millennial vision in which the baddie triumphs.

00:25:01.

Swellhead was radiant. His musak was playing 'All You Need is Love,' whale-songs, a football crowd version of 'You'll Never Walk Alone' and the '1812 Overture' all at once.

00:20:00.

"Trivia Man, what is transhumance?" asked Jeperson.

"A form of Swiss crop rotation," he responded.

00:15:01.

"You ask him one," Jeperson thought to her.

She didn't think that would work. Everything was in Head's head. *Everything*. History, geography, maths, physics, mythology, archaeology — the whole core syllabus.

"His specialist subject is Popular Music *Since* 1973..."

00:10:00

A beam rose from the dish, so intense that the video hook-up couldn't handle it. It whited across the screen. It was on its way to the moon, and then would come back to break against the whole world.

Head's lips twitched. She'd seen that before, in Really-a-Good-Bloke Rory's office. She recognised the look from hours of suspects lying to her, the "tell" that meant she'd found a button she should press again.

00:05:01.

"Who had a hit with 'Lucky Lucky Lucky'?" she asked, praying.

00:04:00.

No instant response.

00:03:01.

"Come on," said Richard, "even I know that! She was in *Moulin Rouge!*"

00:03:00.

"No clues," shrieked Sewell Head, furious.

00:02:01.

The big picture fragmented and fell. A glimpse of Kylie Minogue's face appeared and disappeared in the white static.

00:01:01.

Only the numbers, now in black on white, remained. There was a rumbling in the earth, shaking the floor and the walls.

Actually, he had never levitated before.

He was siphoning Swellhead's Talent, the villain's belief in the worthiness of his foe. It was why Richard had actually felt stronger, sharper in the complex. Swellhead needed an antagonist who could put up a fight. This story needed a hero, and Richard was elected.

Given time, Swellhead would notice.

00:55:01.

But there was not much time.

00:55:00.

"You know how the story goes," said Richard...

Klaxons were sounding.

"...the villain is always *thwarted*..."

00:50:00.

"...in the last minute."

11

No one had told her Richard Jeperson could fly. All her doubts vanished: this was a man to follow into the jungle.

00:45:01.

She found her knife and threw it at Swellhead. It struck an invisible barrier feet away from him and bounced, falling into the trap along with Adam Onions and Viscount de Maltby.

00:40:00.

Jeperson floated upwards. She saw strain in his face. A trickle of black sweat ran beside his eye, slid down a groove in his cheek, dropped from his chin. The black, she realised, was hair dye.

00:35:01.

On the big screen, the dish transmitted a preliminary signal skywards, visible waves of radiant force emanating from its centre.

00:30:00.

"In the last minute," Jeperson had said. Not "at the last minute." She'd instinctively grasped what the Man From the Diogenes Club meant. Somehow, Sewell Head had cast himself in his own movie. She knew from experience that every neighbourhood drug peddler and receiver of stolen DVD players fancied himself as a Bond villain. Head just had the brain-juice to make it so.

more control. As it was, Richard's earlier criticism held: the illusion didn't have enough detail.

Too many ghosts.

A comparatively weak lever can unseat a monument.

02:00:00.

But maybe not within two minutes.

He finished chanting.

Everything was clear.

"Sewell," he asked, "why did you choose to be a diabolical mastermind?"

Swellhead had no answer.

"Villains have more fun, I suppose?" ventured Richard. "But you must have seen the flaw? Remember the coat? It's what brought us all here. Our blood was on it, and this place was a ruin. This happened before, and you were thwarted. Good word, that. 'Thwarted.' Has the old melodramatic tone. Like 'foiled,' 'bested,' 'vanquished.'"

01:39:01.

The faintest line of concern appeared between Swellhead's brows. His helmet-lights flashed faster, in more complex patterns.

"That was somewhen else," Swellhead said.

He gestured.

De Maltby, deadly hand raised to swipe off Richard's head, stepped forward.

At the same time, just to make doubly sure, or perhaps through a split-second indecision, Swellhead flicked his switch.

A wasteful gesture. Counter-productive.

The floor opened. De Maltby tumbled into the darkness.

Cold wafted up, but Richard hung suspended in the air.

01:02:01.

"Didn't I mention I could do this?"

It was not easy. Richard felt a strain in his back-brain far worse than anything he had put his spine through.

He unlotused in mid-air, letting his legs dangle, extending his arms crucifashion.

Beneath him, there was a whirring and screeching. De Maltby's prosthetic killing arm outlived him by seconds, cutting through something from the inside, parting black slime, spilling knotty gut. The rising stench was dreadful.

Richard tried to make his pose seem effortless.

SWELLHEAD

"Sod this for a game of tin soldiers," said the Man From I-Psi-T, turning to leave the control room. "I'm radioing in from the helicopter."

Onions walked across the room.

Swellhead flipped a tiny switch.

The floor opened up under Onions. With a look of resigned irritation, he fell into the chasm. A splash, thrashing, screams.

"I enjoyed that," said Swellhead.

03:46.01.

The hatch sprung closed.

Richard walked onto the trapdoor section of the floor.

"Stacy, if you'd help me," he said. "I need to sit down."

She was by his side, holding his arm as he sank. His back spasmed and he felt his joints creak. She helped him to the floor.

"This will be tricky. I need to lotus."

She pulled off his boots — he wore wasp-striped socks — and helped him tuck his feet into the crooks of his knees. He pressed his palms together and settled, trying to find a focus.

Swellhead observed all this, almost with interest.

02:55:00.

"What do you plan now, Mr. Jeperson? Have you reached the stage of acceptance?"

Richard chuckled.

"No, I intend to out-think you."

Richard sub-vocalised a mantra. Not very fashionable these days, but still effective.

He thought of a spiral, let it whirl around him.

Pains and aches faded, a pleasant side-effect. The whitesuits were wispier, more ghostly. He could tell which ones had Captain Vernon's team inside, and which were made up from whole cloth.

He gained a precise sense of where he was in relation to the complex, to the living and half-living things all around.

He had a Talent too.

02:02:01.

He was nothing compared to Swellhead, but at least knew what he was doing. If the late Adam Onions had put the possibly late Sewell Head through the full battery of tests, or let the Americans or Tibetans have a crack at him, then Swellhead might have had even

"Congratulations," said Jeperson. "The iron crown is yours."

Having defeated Persephone Gill in single combat, Stacy supposed she had the right, for the next five and a half minutes, to call herself the Droning of Skerra.

She didn't feel like a princess.

10

05:31:01.

Though Swellhead looked unconcerned, Richard saw a crack.

De Maltby, silver fist whirring with knives, stepped past Miss Gill and squared up to Stacy.

"Stand down," Richard thought.

Stacy — good girl! — held her empty hands out and backed off.

De Maltby lowered his deadly gauntlet.

Swellhead settled in his chair and tapped a series of buttons. He smiled serenely as a helmet descended from the ceiling on a thick rope of wires and settled around his dome. A rim of lights on the helmet began to flash.

04:52:01.

Richard gathered Swellhead was charging the machine. His brain was a key component. Anything powerful enough to *will* a moonbase into existence ought to be subject to the strictest international controls.

Whatever happened, Richard did not intend this apported apparatus, or this unmatched Talent, to be put at the disposal of Really-a-Good-Bloke Rory and the Deputy Minister for Heritage and Sport. Their overwhelming Opinion, shaped by focus groups and policy studies and target figures and budget assessments, would probably make for a worse world than the supervillain fantasy hatching inside Swellhead's egg-dome skull.

04:26.00.

Adam Onions had been close to boiling over for hours. Now, he stepped forward.

"Really, Mr. Head, what do you think you're doing?"

Swellhead swivelled his chair to look at Onions, umbilical wires stretching.

The mask made it impossible to tell whether Miss Kill was hurt. Stacy tasted her own blood.

She got close to Miss Kill, pressing her body against her opponent — it's hard to hit someone who's practically hugging you — and getting a hold on her hair, which she yanked hard. Any woman who remembered playground scraps knew how effective a solid hair-pull could be at disabling a trouble-maker. She always advised her pupils that it was better to be mugged by someone with crustylocks than a baldie (for skinheads, she recommended a nailfile across the scalp — those cuts bleed like fountains).

Miss Kill's head went back as Stacy pulled, but no scream came through the mask.

Pincer-grips came at Stacy's sides, long-nailed thumbs stabbing between ribs, vice-pressure fingertips digging into her back. She was lifted off her feet and held out at arms' length.

She tried battering Miss Kill's hands, but only bruised her own fists.

06:00:00.

She was sure Miss Kill's thumbs were knuckle-deep in her torso.

She looked down at the impassive pretty-doll face. Red and black blotches swarmed across her vision. Whatever happened at 00:00:00, she wouldn't be here to go through it.

Probably a mercy.

Miss Kill's stiff lips might have smiled.

Furious, using a move she only ever recommended with caution ("tends to hurt you as much as him"), she executed the classic Glasgow kiss, known in London as "nutting." She rammed her forehead against the bridge of Miss Kill's nose. The argument for this is that bony skull bests nose-cartilage as often as paper wraps stone. It might not apply to a mask.

An almighty *crack!* sounded through her head.

She was let go, and Miss Kill staggered back. Stacy had blood in her eyes, mostly her own.

Miss Kill held her mask to her face. It was split across.

"Percy," shouted Jeperson.

The mask fell away. Persephone Gill looked as if she'd woken suddenly from a bad dream. Her bloody face wasn't a mask, but mobile with an incipient scream.

05:32:00.

And she wasn't sold on being an assassin. That hadn't been what Fred Regent hauled her off shift for. She'd never signed up for that. Whenever it came up at the Police Federation, she voted against ordinary coppers carrying firearms or even stun-guns. That wasn't how she wanted the world to be.

But no one was listening to her now.

07:36:00.

She waded through ghosts. They moved slowly. Guns spat floating, easily-dodgable blobules.

Then a regular-speed kick winded her.

Her knife skittered off on the floor.

She bent double, trying not to retch.

Miss Kill, the masked Persephone Gill, walked around her. She wore a long dress slit to the thighs, and the gold spike-heeled pumps modelled by a well-dressed skeleton. Above her mask, her hair was done in a topknot with a flowing tail.

Stacy tensed, anticipating the kick at her side.

Miss Kill looked to Swellhead. For applause?

Stacy braced both hands against the floor and swept-kicked Miss Kill's legs out from under her. A simple, textbook self-defence move.

The masked girl went up arse over tit.

In mid-air, she flipped, regained balance on her points. She wheeled round, ponytail whipping out.

Stacy was on her feet now.

A lot of her pupils expected *Crouching Tiger* business, which she always patiently explained required a team of effects experts and hidden wires — hardly practical when a yob shoves you against a wall by a cash machine.

Miss Kill might actually have been on wires. She tucked one foot against her knee and flew straight at Stacy's face like Peter Pan, arm stretched out, fingers pyramided into a killing point.

06:32:01.

Stacy ducked and thumped upwards at Miss Kill's silk-covered stomach. She couldn't get the leverage for a forceful blow, but had the satisfaction of connecting.

Miss Kill touched down and slapped Stacy, open-handed, contemptuous.

It smarted and kinked her head almost off her neck. She responded with rib-punches that had no effect.

SWELLHEAD

the life of a South American tribesman or a market-trader in Kuala Lumpur or a teenage girl in California. The vast bulk of humanity will be milling extras, barely templates, low-resolution, bad painted backdrops. Most of your world won't be real enough."

09:34.00.

"I know best," said Swellhead, almost benignly.

"Penny in the slot, Trivia Man," said Richard. "Alfonso the Wise, King of Castille…"

"1221-1284."

"That's the fellow. Most famous saying of…?"

"'If I had been present at the Creation, I would have given some useful hints for the better arrangement of the Universe.'"

"Alfonso wasn't being the Wise when he said that, he was being the Funny. Alfonso the Wise-Cracker. It's supposed to be a joke, to expose hubris."

"That's not Fact, that's Opinion. Too debatable for a quiz question."

08:57:01.

"Not in nine minutes it won't be. There'll be only one Opinion. Do you really want to live in that world?"

"So long as it's the right Opinion."

"Yours."

"Absolutely."

"You'll be on your own. Despite all these masks and ghosts and puppets, completely alone."

A tiny glimpse of Sewell Head came through.

"I'm used to it," he said.

08:02:01.

So much for Reason. His only back-up plan was Violence.

"Stacy," he thought, loud enough for all the ghosts to hear, "now!"

9

07:54:01.

She pulled off her transparent gauntlet and gripped the knife.

As she shrugged, ghostfingers sank through her arms, giving her a bone-scraping tingle she hoped never to feel again.

She hadn't followed Jeperson's argument.

"Detective Sergeant," said Swellhead, "so kind of you to join us. You are our final guest."

11:50:01.

Hands, unghostly, gripped her arms.

Jeperson looked at her, with sympathy.

"If you get a chance," he thought, "kill him."

8

"If you can," Richard added, damping the thought so Stacy would not pick it up. It was horribly possible that Swellhead had such control over the situation that any holes in him would heal instantly.

11:34:00.

He felt something cold against his palm. No, he was feeling through Stacy, something cold against her palm.

A blade.

Such a small thing.

"Isn't this about the time when you call up the Prime Minister or the President of the United States or the Secret Ruling Council of the League of Pata-Nations to make your demands?"

"This isn't extortion, Mr. Jeperson. This is inevitability."

Richard was worried. The many memories that had plagued him earlier were like dreams, almost forgotten on waking, leaving only incoherent images and impressions. He had no idea what Fred Regent looked like as an older man.

The past was a blank.

Only this countdown was real.

The musak began to play 'Welcome to My World,' the Jim Reeves recording with psychedelia mixed in.

10:56:00.

"Listen, Head," he said, trying to get through, "even you aren't big enough to do this. I've no doubt you can rearrange all of us here, perhaps even all over the world, but you'll be spread too thin. Where you are, in your mind empire, it'll be a satisfying illusion, cartoonish but still convincing. But the further away from you, the sketchier the effect will be. No one can encompass the universe in his skull. You know a great deal in theory, but you can't really imagine, say,

SWELLHEAD

count had a strange shining mechanical glove. Persephone Gill wore a wax mask. They weren't completely changed (like Head), but they were different—redressed and redirected.

She didn't risk signalling Jeperson, but he looked directly at her.

She remembered he could sometimes tell what she was thinking.

"What the...?!" she thought, hard.

"Meet Swellhead," thought Jeperson, clearly in her mind. "And watch out for Miss Kill."

Stacy had a panic stab that Persephone—Miss Kill!—was staring straight through her faceplate, but it passed.

Sewell Head—Swellhead—climbed into his favourite chair.

13:34:01.

Whatever was due to happen at 00:00:00 was unlikely to be good.

She had flashes of the possibilities: all the world's nuclear arsenals activated at once, space weapons searing every patch of arable land on the planet, the activation of super-anthrax engineered to wipe out all non H-logoed lifeforms, fomented tidal waves and cyclones washing over continents. War, famine, pestilence and death.

12:43:00.

Swellhead fisted his forehead.

All the drones returned salute—de Maltby even raising his unwieldy prosthetic. Stacy was a moment out of sync, and mashed the rim of her faceplate painfully against her nut.

"Friends," began Swellhead. "We are on the brink of a great venture. In less than a quarter of an hour, the world will be neat and tidy. I should like you all to take a moment to pray..."

She wasn't surprised he turned out to be some species of religious crank.

"...to me."

"Good grief!" she thought.

"It's worse than that," came Jeperson's mind-voice.

The drones all took off their helmets and bowed their heads.

Stacy had no choice but to follow suit and hope not to be noticed. The unfamiliar helmet arrangement didn't unscrew easily. She made a comical bumble of the business of getting loose, then got her hair in her eyes.

The other whitesuits had colourless faces and hair. Ghosts.

"Yes, without anyone noticing," Swellhead answered the unasked question. "Clever, isn't it?"

A technician came up, thumped his forehead, and gave a silent report.

"It will take some minutes to align our dish with the one on the moon," said Swellhead. "We should go to the control room. You'll find the next phase of the process fascinating."

Richard looked up at the stars.

Then at the man he was afraid could change their alignments.

"He's a Talent," Onions had said. "Off the scale."

7

She stood at a console in the control room and tried to look busy. It wasn't too difficult, since ghost activity consisted mostly of silently checking dials and read-outs.

The room had changed. The computers were all back in place, and working. Big reels whirred back and forth. Tickertape stuttered out of slots. Lights flashed and beeped.

The big screen was uncracked and showed a televised picture.

Stacy saw the dish hauled into position and the ceiling open. Tiny white figures watched. It looked like an outtake from *Thunderbirds*. An amazingly detailed miniature, imperfect because of the impossibility of scaling down water.

The screen split into quadrants: one showed the dish; two had postcard views of the White House and Number Ten Downing Street; and one was a complicated animated diagram showing the Big Dish, the Earth and Moon, some sort of moon complex and a lot of dotted lines for trajectories. The White House was replaced by scrolling numbers, like logarithm tables. A giant H-egg logo appeared in the middle of the screen, expanding to overlay all four quadrants.

A digital clock flashed on at 15:00:00 and began to count down.

She looked around, hoping to see a plug she could pull.

Doors shushed open and Sewell Head walked in. No, someone who looked like Sewell Head walked in. This man had a different presence.

Jeperson and Onions were with him, and de Maltby and the Droning. The first two were prisoners, the latter guards. The Vis-

SWELLHEAD

dling the vast device about a quarter of a mile, deeper into the Earth, was a major operation.

A whitesuit was caught in the machine, turned to a red smear. No one commented. Richard had flash-visions: slaves hauling pyramid blocks, worshippers ground under the juggernaut.

The deeper they went, the colder and wetter it was. Bare rock walls cascaded with water, which sluiced away through new-carved streams. Great crude wheels turned to keep the system flushing. Gusts of steam periodically escaped from a valve, with a dreadful whistling.

In addition to the grinding of the wheels on rails, a greater roaring filled the cavern. The air tasted of salt.

"We are directly under the Kjempestrupe," announced Swellhead.

A goon handed out white, H-logoed sou'westers. Swellhead, Richard and Onions put them on.

Richard looked up at the rock ceiling. A hole appeared, water falling through, and then irised open.

He gasped, expecting a heavy gush as sea flooded in. The black hole expanded. Then Richard saw night sky. Above the dish was a big liquid funnel. The sea was kept from pouring through the hole by the mighty force of the whirlpool, augmented by Swellhead's mightier self-belief. Water fell, but no more than a heavy rainfall.

At Swellhead's command, banks of switches were thrown. The dish lit up.

Richard felt heat. Water on the face of the dish sizzled and evaporated. Then the fall stopped. Richard doffed the sou'wester.

"You've turned off the rain," said Onions, awed.

"Merely bored a hole in the cloud cover," explained Swellhead. "A necessary preliminary."

A shilling-bright full moon shone. A thousand points of starlight were caught and reflected in the revolving rings of the Kjempestrupe. Flashing marker buoys whizzed around on their swift courses, held by centrifugal force against the vertical surfaces.

"What are you using to rebroadcast?" Richard asked. "A ring of satellites?"

"Another dish, on the moon. I've run a covert space program to set up the installation."

Onions snorted disbelief.

players and had to act out the role of diabolical mastermind. That was a chink of hope—villains always lose.

"It'll make things neat and tidy," said Swellhead.

"In your terms, it'll amplify his Talent," Richard told Onions.

"Very perceptive," said Swellhead.

"He's going to overwrite reality."

"That's ridiculous."

"Look around, Adam. It's been ridiculous all along, but here it is. In an infinite number of possibles, many of them will be extremely improbable. Is this that much stranger than regular reality?"

"Yes."

"Then you haven't been paying attention."

"I'm a scientist, not some cracked guru."

"An old argument."

As Richard and Onions squabbled, Swellhead beamed.

Richard tried to reserve part of his mind for thinking this through. There was still Stacy.

"Don't think I've forgotten Sergeant Cotterill," said Swellhead. "I'm sure she'll pop up eventually. Miss Kill and Viscount de Maltby will see to her. She'll make a fine addition to my Head Room."

Richard told himself it was not a mind-link, like the one he was forging with Stacy. Swellhead had a knack for following thought processes through deduction and inference.

The Big Dish moved. Ancient gimbals screamed.

Slowly, the array trundled on its railbed, dish angling upwards. The rails sloped down, into a tunnel under the sea-bed. A mini-jeep drove up, and Swellhead took the front passenger seat. De Maltby indicated that Richard and Onions should get up on the rear section, and prodded Onions with his inert hand to hurry him along. The Man From I-Psi-T had a slight shock and hopped up on the trolley. Richard needed a hand to clamber up. His back and legs were giving him severe gyp.

After the exertion, he suffered from cold caresses and whisper kisses and was tempted just to drift away. It took several moments to get his mind back on track. When he was able to pay attention again, the mini-jeep was apace with the dish. Crews with big brooms swept the rails ahead of the array. Wire-strung whitesuits clambered monkeylike on the face of the dish, checking and cleaning. Trun-

SWELLHEAD

5

Stacy tried to imagine a cutaway diagram of Skerra, but found the mental map of the complex made her head hurt. It probably didn't add up anyway. She wasn't sure there was room under the island for all this.

She found herself back in the sculpture garden.

Something was missing.

By the Easter Island-look Sewell Head lay the elegant skeleton, black-handled blade stuck in its skull. The mask it had worn was missing.

Stacy plucked the knife. It was about three inches long. Whisper-touching her thumb to the blade, she sliced open her gauntlet.

It wasn't a machine gun, but it was something.

She'd only had an afternoon of firearms training, anyway. A knife ought to be more use. She had taken, and now taught, an evening class in women's self-defence. To demonstrate the proper countermove for knife-attack, twisting a wooden sticker out of a volunteer's grip, she'd picked up dirty-fighting skills. She usually had to cheat on the final exams, letting pupils take the sticker away from her when she knew she could easily get it against their throats.

Blade out, she entered the hallway of heads.

Stalking past, she tried to conquer the impression that the trophies were looking at her.

She was at the point of peering into the control room, when a bloody stare caught her attention.

There was a new trophy, crudely hacked and inexpertly mounted.

AIRCREWMAN VICTOR KYDD, SKERRA, 2003, MACHETE.

She swore, furious and grief-shocked.

6

"But what's it *for*?" asked Onions. "What does it do?"

Richard wondered if Swellhead would go back on his word and explain his grand design. Possibly, he was as trapped as all other

Richard was not surprised.

The dead bodies were all up and about, flesh on their bones. Some had dwindling red-stains or contracting black holes in their jumpsuits. One passed by: a network of cracks in his faceplate disappearing as if the film were running backwards at double-speed.

As Swellhead stepped off the lift-platform, the white ghosts turned and thumped their foreheads in salute.

Respectfully, he returned the gesture.

Activity all around. Busy, busy ghosts. Technicians, lab coats flapping, ran silent diagnostic tests at banks of controls. White jeep-cum-golfcart vehicles trundled without colliding, like well-controlled model trains, some dragging trailers of white, H-logoed barrels. Mechanics with dark stains on their uniforms oiled the rails on which the Big Dish ran.

"All very satisfactory," said Swellhead.

A pipeline burst across the floor, slithering like a serpent, coughing out thick black liquid. A clean-up crew descended automatically, spraying foam on the spill, tethering and repairing the line.

This crisis did not impinge on Swellhead's calm.

Richard looked up, towards the Blowhole.

...a hundred black figures rappelling down, firebursts in the air all around, the roar of attack choppers...

He could not count on that this time.

In the 1973 of his phantom memory, Edwin Winthrop was waiting at the Club, monitoring all frequencies. An SAS strike force was scrambled and at ready in a secret base in the Orkneys. At Richard's signal, Swellhead's complex would be attacked, breached and overwhelmed.

Here and now, Really-a-Good-Bloke Rory was snug in bed waiting for a report about intellectual salvage rights that would win him bonus points with his minister. Morag Duff could no more authorise a military attack on Skerra than she could get reform of the Common Agricultural Policy through the EU.

Soon, the government would be irrelevant.

All governments. All churches. All beliefs. All aesthetics.

Everything.

The whole world would be living inside Sewell Head's head.

SWELLHEAD

pad by the door, which opened noiselessly. She found a large suit and wriggled into it. A groin-to-throat seal had to be pressed closed with a toggle-zip affair of unfamiliar design. The garment bulged everywhere, but could be belted in. Plastic bootees went over her boots. She replaced her gloves with gauntlets that clipped easily to the sleeves. The helmet screwed into a collar-ring.

Though opaque from outside, the faceplate was transparent for the wearer.

Cool.

As the helmet locked, a red display lit up at the lower right of her vision. The H logo hatched, and figures she didn't understand scrolled.

All she needed was one of those machine-gun things.

The weapons weren't stored here, though.

Returning to the corridor, she strode on, trying to project purposefulness.

She thought she was walking into a mirrored barrier. It was only an identically-dressed figure coming the other way.

The ghost made a salute, a fist pressed to the forehead.

Inside her helmet, Stacy struggled not to laugh. On her manor, the gesture was slang for "knob-head."

She returned the salute, Harpo mirroring Groucho.

The other whitesuit stepped aside to let her pass.

Another jogging platoon passed. They all turned and gave her the knob-head salute, which she returned.

When they were out of sight, she stopped, bent over and grabbed her knees, painful spasms in her gut. She had to laugh. An odd out-of-body feeling suggested remotely that she was on the point of genuine hysterics.

Tears leaked down her face. She clanged a gauntlet against her faceplate trying to wipe them.

Her own barking laughs filled her helmet.

She realised she was shaking with terror.

4

The Big Dish was healed. Its H shone as if new-painted.

The soot-patches on the walls had shrunk. They were disappearing like condensation on a warm morning.

De Maltby's silver hand began to whirr. Revolving needles protruded from the knuckles.

Swellhead calmed down and wagged a finger.

"Very clever, but you can't distract me."

He snapped his fingers. The musak billowed: 'These Boots Were Made for Walking.'

Miss Kill danced, mask making her seem like a robot.

She wound around the impassive Swellhead, then de Maltby, then took a solo spot. She was very good, had all the moves, and each air-kick had a force that could have broken bones. At the end of every chorus, she broke something: arm crushing through a wrought-iron table, heel battering a chair out of shape.

...one of these days, these boots are gonna...

Richard's old wounds ached just to watch her.

...walk all over You!

She finished her routine. Swellhead applauded. So did de Maltby, very carefully.

Sincerely, Richard joined in.

"I think it's time to go up and visit the Big Dish," said Swellhead. "What do you think?"

Richard nodded.

Endgame. With people-pieces.

3

The complex had changed while she was topside.

Now, it was fully operational. If Stacy touched the walls, she felt vibration. As she'd guessed, vast machines buried below Skerra were turning over. Energy thrummed throughout Head Office.

And there were staff.

She pressed into an alcove as white-suited soldiers jogged by.

Ghosts? Or woken from deep-freeze?

She was in an area of the complex they hadn't toured earlier. Corridors curved but had no corners. Through glass doors, she saw illuminated rooms where scientific processes were being carried out. Most involved large, bubbling tanks of different-coloured liquids.

One room contained nothing but ghosts, row upon row of clothes-hangers draped with the white jumpsuits. She knuckle-punched a

SWELLHEAD

"That's not strictly true," he said. "This whole complex is a ghost, not of a person but a thought. An idea you had, Mr Head. Maybe you had it in another place, where you were an international mastermind with a cadre of loyalist goons at your command. Maybe you had it while you stood behind the confectionary counter, your wonderful brain switched onto another track by years of breathing in chocolate dust. Dreams can come true. That's what magic does. And you're not one of 'Pronounced "Eyesight"'s Talents. You're a natural-born magician. Onions would say it was all down to chemicals in your brain. Others would give you a pointy hat and call you a wizard. We both know it doesn't matter what you are."

Swellhead clapped, slowly.

"Quite right, Mr. Jeperson. What matters is what I can do."

"Which is...?" demanded Onions.

Swellhead nibbled the corner of a bon-bon, almost flirtatiously. "Ah, wouldn't you like to know?"

"Will you get someone to write you a theme song?" Richard asked. "'*Swellhead, Swellhead, on sweeties fed, he'll leave you dead...*' Or how about: '*You should have stayed in bed, it's got to be said, you'll fear to tread, after...The Man with the Swollen Head*'"

"You know, that's not a bad idea. Miss Kill, who should I hire? John Barry? Burt Bacharach? Stephen Sondheim?"

Swellhead took music seriously. Richard remembered Ken Dodd, slaughtered and mounted for hogging the Number One spot with a dreadful ballad.

"Percy is twenty-one years old," he said. "She'd want N'Sync or Robbie Williams or Eminem."

Swellhead's brows contracted, then relaxed.

"Trivia Man, are you still in there?" Richard asked. "Your Specialist Subject is Popular Music *Since* 1973..."

"Soon, all that will be forgotten. In my reality, we have proper music."

"You can hear the lyrics and hum the tunes, eh?"

Swellhead looked almost offended. "Yes, why not?"

"Don't ask me. I'm probably sixty-five. I haven't *liked* a chart-topper since Mary Hopkin. That's the point of pop music. It's irrelevant to us oldies, just as we're irrelevant to it. No matter what you do to the world, you won't change that."

Swellhead was a little flustered.

"Do your feet suffer from bo-*nye*-ons?" snapped Swellhead. "As anyone who's faced me in a pub quiz damn well understands, I know my onions!"

The little bald man was transformed. His forehead bulged, as if extra brains packed his cranial cavity. He still chewed, popping Belgian chocolates like a pep pill addict. He radiated the sort of confidence you get when you know fanatical devotees are on hand, prepared to murder at your whim or die to protect you.

Miss Kill and de Maltby were solid presences, as were some of the whitesuits — Vernon and his team? — but there were phantoms as well, coalescing, gaining substance. The complex was coming to life, each section getting noisier, busier as its inhabitants grew corporeal, purposeful. From Swellhead's swollen head flowed a conviction that gave his world hard edges.

"I'm not sure where you fit in," Swellhead told Onions. "But unless you give me reason to have you eliminated, it'll be interesting to find out. As the world rearranges, everyone in it will be affected. Maybe you'll fade, become one of the ghosts you've been chasing. That'd be an appreciable irony."

Onions tried to stand, but Miss Kill laid a slim hand on his shoulder.

Richard could not see Persephone Gill any more. Just the woman in the mask whose fingers and feet were weapons as deadly as de Maltby's silver-knived hand attachment.

He remembered Miss Kill.

...thrown off balance by that revolving restaurant, he realised the thief hadn't trapped herself by fleeing to the top of the tower, that she had a prepared exit...

And, later...

...a struggle in the sculpture garden, taking blows to the chest and face, twisting on the astroturf to roll out of the way of a stabbing spike-heel aimed at his eye, an accurately-thrown knife...

Did she remember? She would not leave that opening twice. And he was thirty years older, slower. Even a simple breakfall would probably throw out his back and leave him flapping like a fish, easy to skewer with a deliberate stab of a stiletto.

"Just for the record, Onions," said Swellhead. "There are no ghosts."

The pain in Richard's head kinked, then shut off.

SWELLHEAD

Somewhen where Sewell Head was an industrial giant/diabolical mastermind (not a counter clerk in a sweetshop), Richard had been responsible for undoing his colossal schemes. At great personal cost.

Scalpels of pain slid behind his eyes.

The overlaps and contradictions hurt. From remembering too little, he switched to remembering too much. He was not struck by memories from two lives, but dozens...

...*the 'Horst Wessel Lied' played over and over as German athletes won Gold Medal after Gold Medal at a 1956 London Olympiad.*

...*tracking a psychic assassin through the crowds at the Glastonbury Festival in 1969, saving the life of a future Prime Minister.*

...*arguing through an interpreter with an* Okhrana *man about screening the guests at a Royal wedding in St Petersburg in 1972.*

...*an Embassy siege in 1980, negotiating with vampire terrorists demanding Transylvania as a homeland.*

...*a kidnapped London mayor replaced by a perfidious impostor in 1999.*

...*under torture in 2001, compelled by arachnid overlords to betray a human resistance cell in Highgate.*

...*Biplanes battling over a London of 2003, the city radiating out not from Buckingham Palace (which was missing) but from the Tower...*

In all the lives he had led, that other Richard Jepersons had led, there were no memories before 1945. The blank that had been with him all his adult life was a constant.

"Come back, Mr. Jeperson," said Sewell Head, chuckling.

For a terrifying moment, he was not sure which Richard he was, which *world* this was...

"With concentration, I found I could compartmentalise continua. Of course, I have Eighth Stage Asperger's. As syndromes go, it's one of the more useful ones. Your partial amnesia is not going to be an effective substitute."

"What is all this nonsense?" demanded Onions, getting annoyed again. He had been in shock since Yoland's death, hankie blotting his messy scalp-wound, sulking about the turn his expedition had taken, warily eyeing the maskfaced Miss Kill. Now, he was ready to reassert himself.

"You're not part of the backstory, Onions," said Swellhead, pronouncing the name like the vegetable.

"O-*nye*-ons," corrected Onions, automatically.

Angry, guilty and scared, she knew she had to go further into this dark place and find Jeperson and the others.

The prospect did not appeal.

2

"Traditionally, I should explain everything to you," said Swellhead. "But I am not one of those inadequates who needs the respect of his enemies. I don't mind toiling in the dark. My achievements are their own satisfaction. I don't demand that the whole world recognise how clever I am. Indeed, in the end, no one will know what I've done. Possibly, when the story is rewritten I will myself be unaware of how much I have accomplished. That's still undetermined. Mr. Jeperson, how's your memory? Giving you a headache?"

Swellhead was right.

It was increasingly hard to concentrate.

The gaps were filling in, but not comfortably. Now, Richard remembered...

...*a briefing from Edwin Winthrop, in 1973, about the interest the Diogenes Club was being forced to take in Sewell Head Industries.*

...*a woman in a leotard and mask, leaping from the revolving restaurant of the Post Office Tower to a SHI advertising blimp, absconding with vital components of a communication satellite relay.*

...*a game of chess at a Surrey estate, played with real people and electrified board squares.*

...*Fred Regent's headless body dumped on Richard's Chelsea doorstep, with a note, "he lost his head over a girl'.*

...*wearing a white jumpsuit and faceplate, mingling with minions.*

...*black-clad SAS men abseiling down the Blowhole.*

...*a firefight around the Big Dish.*

...*duels, deaths...*

It was fragmentary and did not fit facts he was sure of. Fred Regent was not dead. The revolving restaurant shut down in 1971 after a bomb attack by the Angry Brigade. There had never been a Sewell Head Industries.

These were not his memories, but those of another Richard Jeperson.

SWELLHEAD

The rope was free. It whipped away, well out of reach.

She was on her own. The business of getting both feet firmly on the ledge was tricky enough, but then she had to stand up and turn around to face the door. She took a hold of the chain, which crumbled to rust-flakes and fell apart. Angrily, she extracted the bolt-cutters from her underwear, minded to toss the bloody tool into the sea.

Then, sense prevailed. She might need them as a bludgeon. Or nail-clippers.

The door had a handle, like an old-fashioned freezer. She expected it to come off in her grip, but it was firm. There was no keyhole, so even if she'd had a full set of picks they'd be no use. She wrenched the handle, feeling a catch go free, and pushed.

The door didn't move.

She pushed again and realised the door opened outwards. It wasn't a convenient set-up. In order to pull, she had to lean away from the cliff and risk the fall. In opening, the door swept the ledge she was standing on. She had to ease herself around it, dangling for horrible seconds. Hinges strained and complained. A blast of warm air shot out at her.

If the hinges broke, she was dead.

Clumsily and in a tangle, she managed it.

She wound up inside a dark place, looking out, with solid floor under her.

Peeling off her gloves, she found slight weals across her palms, but not the churning open wounds she expected. She pulled her shirt out of her waistband and bent to wipe rain out of her eyes. She ran her fingers through her hair, wiping runnels of cold water back across her skull and down her neck and spine.

She was inside, not exactly safe.

What about Kydd? She yelled his name.

No response.

Frustrated, she clanged on the metal door with the bolt-cutters, as if sounding a dinner gong.

She poked her head out and looked up.

All she got was wet again.

The fringe of light still shone, marking the cliff-edge. Then, it shut off.

There was no reason for Kydd to turn out the lights.

elements and thoroughly battered against rock on her plunge to be sucked under whirling waves and marr-i-ed to a mer-my-id at the bottom of the deep blue sea. Neither appealed. Climbing down had been hard and, with no feeling at all in her hands, climbing up would be much harder. The thought of going untethered opened a cold wet anemone in the pit of her stomach which she recognised as stark terror.

She gave Kydd another wave, pointing down, shouting "more rope'.

Kydd's face disappeared as he stood up.

She thanked a power higher than the Chief Constable that her message had been received. She wound herself around the rope, entwining it with both arms, gripping with thighs, knees and heels.

A little give came and she lurched downwards.

Her cheek pressed against metal.

She lurched down again, way too fast, and scraped over rock. Her feet scrabbled for perches. The cliff sloped out a little and she stopped falling. The rope was loose above her.

Had something happened to Kydd?

She tugged the rope. Yards of it came free.

If something had happened to Kydd, that something's attention would be on her next.

She relaxed her grip on the rope, still keeping it between her and the cliff, and experimentally reached upwards. Her hand crested a ledge — the door-ledge! — and she got a reasonable hold. She raised her other hand and let her whole weight hang from the ledge.

The bloody bolt-cutters shifted again, handle twisting her knickers, business-end pressed into her belly. She thought for a moment she was gutted and bleeding, but it was just the freezing metal against her soft tummy.

Her first attempt at lifting herself was pathetic. Her elbows wouldn't bend. She just succeeded in fraying pebbles from the ledge.

She couldn't think of Kydd.

Ordering herself to do better, she hefted herself up, getting her torso over the ledge, then her bottom. She was sitting, looking out at the dark sea, getting another faceful of rain.

A dim white circle foamed on the waters. The Kjempestrupe. Never mind that, anyone who braved this cliff was a worthy consort for the Droning of Skerra. Not that she fancied Persephone Gill.

SWELLHEAD

Thirty feet below the edge of the cliff, she needed a rest and found a ledge. Rope wound around her arm, she leaned against wet rock. It was raining again. The wind aimed marble-sized drops at her eyes. Her beret was snatched away, which meant her face was now also lashed by her own wet hair. She'd liked that beret.

Forty feet below the edge of the cliff, with fifteen feet of rope flapping below the section pinched off between her boot-insteps, she remembered an old school exercise about judging height by counting seconds as something fell and multiplying by ten. She clawed a rock free, held it out, and dropped it. After six seconds (sixty feet?), it bounced off an outcrop. If it splashed down, she couldn't make out the individual noise amid the roar of surf. So she was no wiser.

Fifty feet below the edge of the cliff, with hands on fire and (she thought) ripped bloody inside her gloves, it occurred to her that the door might be locked as well as chained. With burglar tools it wasn't especially legal for a policewoman to carry, she could crack most household locks. They'd done a seminar on it at Hendon. However, one-handed, in darkness, lashed by wind and rain, clinging to a precipice and pretty bloody fed up, she wasn't confident that she could use what was in her pockets (tube of mints, some tissues, flat-keys, coral lipstick, mobile) to effect an entry.

Fifty-five feet below the edge of the cliff, she found she was still not level with the door. She didn't know how that was possible, but here she was—toes scraping the upper edge of the metal.

She tried shouting to Kydd, but couldn't hear herself.

Looking up, she saw his face peering over, waving encouragingly. From his angle, he might not be able to see her problem.

Off to the side, beyond the light, she had a sense of other faces looking over the cliff at her, white-bearded, evil-eyed and horned. She decided she really hated goats.

All she needed was for Kydd to uncleat the rope and give her five more feet.

She waited, hoping the penny would drop. No such luck.

Her choices were: a) climb all the way back up and ask politely for a longer rope, then hope the door didn't sneakily work its way down the cliff another five or ten feet; or b) go off-rope and make her own way down to the ledge, trusting her luck not to lose grip, rely unwisely on an unsafe hold or be plucked from the cliff by the

Kydd fetched a reel from the ATV and fed blue nylon rope over the cliff. At first, the rope was caught by the wind and blown almost out of his hands. He tied a three-litre plastic carton of milk to the end, threading the rope through the handle and confidently tying a seaman's knot. That gave enough weight. The carton bumped against rock as Kydd lowered the rope.

Stacy directed the lights, all too conscious that chunks of this cliff had been joining the seabed for millennia. Where she was standing would eventually fall, ten minutes or a hundred years from now.

The carton bounced against the door.

"Fifty-five feet," said Kydd. The rope had red rings every five feet.

"No distance at all," she said, not believing it.

Kydd gave Stacy the rope, then took the reel away, unspooling until he was back at the ATV. The reel fitted into a catch on the vehicle and fastened tight. The Aircrewman cleated the rope to prevent further unspooling. He signalled and Stacy let the rope go. It twanged and bit into the cliff-edge, carving its own groove.

A big gust of wind came, staggering Stacy sideways. She heard an explosion.

Looking over, she saw the carton had burst. Milk splattered against the door, and dribbled in runnels. The rope caught in its groove, and whipped about.

"Never mind," said Kydd. "We'll weight it down."

That wasn't a comfort. Stacy imagined a red splatter against the cliff.

"I'll go first, miss."

"I'd rather you were up here keeping the rope secure," she said.

"Fair enough."

Kydd fetched bolt-cutters from the ATV. Stacy hooked them over her waistband.

She wished he'd argued more.

Ten feet below the edge of the cliff, she decided her gloves and boots weren't thick enough. The bolt-cutters shifted, pressing an ice-cold metal handle against her thigh.

Twenty feet below the edge of the cliff, she remembered the Blowhole's stone grinders and wondered if any sections of rockface were devices like that. She kept kicking at stones which fell.

SWELLHEAD

with each other. Onions should perhaps have distributed the equipment before venturing below. She'd mention it at the official inquiry.

"There must be another entrance," she said.

Kydd didn't respond.

"I mean, the place is huge. The Mysterious They can't just have used the Blowhole. There must be other ways in and out."

Skerra Landsby was underwater. Any entrances there would be flooded.

That left the rockface.

Stacy climbed the ATV and directed the searchlights. White shaggy flanks were caught in beams. Goats hurried away. Kydd got into the driving seat and they bumped across a hundred yards of grass, halting a safe distance from crumbling cliff-edge.

She wasn't looking forward to this.

Hopping down from the vehicle, she was surprised to find the rumbling persisted. They were well away from the Blowhole. She knelt and put her hand on the ground, pressing. The long grass was wet, cold and irritatingly scratchy. The earth was warmer and vibrating. She felt it in her fillings. A thrumm, too low for human ears but still bone-rattling, goat-maddening. A big machine, she thought, buried deep.

Kydd unhooked the searchlights, which were on extensible flexes, and carried them to the cliff-edge. He whistled.

Stacy joined him and looked down.

"Christ on a bike!"

"Yes, miss."

Hundreds — thousands? — of feet below, the sea churned white. Foam swirled around black rock chunks. Mad waves hammered into eroded caves and frothed out again. It looked like God's washing machine.

Kydd tried to play the light on the cliff itself.

It wasn't sheer rockface but battered and broken, with many obvious paths and handholds. It was impossible to tell which were reliable, and which dangerously loose.

"There, miss," said Kydd, pointing.

It was a metal door, flush with the rock. Once it had led to a natural balcony, but most of that was broken off, leaving only a vestigial ledge. The door was fastened by a chain.

KIM NEWMAN

Act III: A Game of Tin Soldiers

1

When Stacy and Kydd got back to the Blowhole, things were changed.

Kydd had driven the all-terrain vehicle up from the landing site. Powerful searchlights, fitted on the roll-bar, lit up the area.

A rumbling, grinding noise came from the Blowhole.

Stacy peered into the cavity. Rings of jagged rock revolved at different speeds. The dangling rope ladder jounced around, shredded.

The Blowhole was working like a giant kitchen disposal device.

"A good thing that didn't start up while we were on the ladder."

"Yes, miss," agreed Kydd, as unsurprised by this turn as everything else. Either the Aircrewman had been more fully briefed or he'd learned to accept literally anything. It could be something the Navy put in the tea.

Goats lurked in the dark, making low, threatening noises. She had no idea whether this was natural: she'd never seen a goat in the wild before, or even on a farm. It was about half past eight: she should either be two hours into a night-shift or an evening in front of the telly. Maybe out at a film or a pub or club.

The searchlights made the grass a vivid yellow-green. Her breath frosted like steam. Beyond the light, everything was midnight dark. No sodium-orange streetlamps, passing car beams, curtained but lit-up windows, twenty-four-hour supermarkets, electric signage. Cloud cover must be thick, because there were no stars.

This was not ideal.

She checked her mobile. No signal and nobody to call anyway.

Among the gear on the ATV was a communications centre: headsets for the whole party, so the team could remain in constant touch

SWELLHEAD

Head was busy making up to his Miss Kill, with an eye on Richard.

He was expecting trouble from Richard. He might not have considered Yoland. If nothing else, this was all the work of a monumental solipsist, someone who considers himself alone at the centre of the universe.

Yoland shifted, getting a good grip on his laptop, the only proven bludgeon to hand.

Onions blinked. Head saw.

Yoland launched himself from his seat with a war-cry. Nimbly, elegantly, Head was out of the way.

Miss Kill kicked Yoland in the face, pirouetting like a dancer.

Yoland grabbed his laptop and ran across the courtyard, dodging the lumbering figures in white.

Head was mildly irritated.

Yoland whirled up the spiral staircase and made it to the landing.

Then a door opened and a man came out. It was de Maltby, wearing a white jumpsuit and milk-white goggles, an elaborate silver glove over his injured hand.

The glove buzzed and passed into Yoland's chest.

The weapons inspector's eyes reddened.

De Maltby raised his arm, lifting Yoland off his feet. He dangled the twitching man over the edge of the balcony. Bloody rain pattered onto the courtyard, along with one of Yoland's shoes.

The pilot withdrew his gloved hand, which was lined with tiny whirring blades. Yoland slid off de Maltby's arm and fell, landing with a thump. His body leaked.

De Maltby produced a large monogrammed handkerchief and fastidiously wiped his mechanical hand.

"Now, honoured guests," said Swellhead, addressing himself to Richard and Onions, "let me give you some ground-rules for maintaining my even temper and not abusing my hospitality."

Richard had heard him say that before.

Head smiled, and nodded at him.

"Yes, that's right," he said. "Here we go again."

Guns were pointed at them.

"The place has been run on a skeleton staff," said Head. "But that will change now."

Miss Gill stood up and said "it's time you stopped playing silly buggers."

Head walked over to her. She was inches taller, but could not look him in the eye.

"Who are all these people?" she demanded, "and where have they been hiding?"

Head took her hand and kissed it, bowing at the waist.

"The Droning of Skerra," he said. "Miss Kill, you are my guest. Your every comfort will be seen to."

He made a signal. One of his jumpsuited goons brought over an attaché case.

"This, my dear, is a gift," said Head. "From me to you."

He held the case and thumbed the catches. It sprung open, with a slight hiss.

Miss Gill folded back some translucent paper and picked up a mask. It was wax and bore her own face.

Richard had seen the like before, on the corpse in the sculpture garden.

"Let me help you," cooed Head, raising the mask to her face.

Miss Gill didn't struggle.

"It feels funny," she said.

"Only for a moment."

Head took his fingers away. The mask was fixed to Miss Gill's face. She touched it herself. The wax fit perfectly around her eyes and mouth. She was disguised as herself, but without expression.

"There," said Head. "That's nice and tidy. You'll always be pretty now, Miss Kill. You'll always be a proper princess for this island."

A giggle leaked through the mask, somehow terrifying.

"Oh, Swellhead," said "Miss Kill," girlish and imbecilic, "you aren't half clever."

Head stroked her stiff cheek.

Onions was still groggy, and thus more useless than usual. Richard wondered if he could count on Yoland? The weapons inspector showed signs of open-mindedness. He was quick enough to sense changes in the psychic temperature, and ought to be attuned to rapid reassessments of dangerous situations.

SWELLHEAD

"I beg your pardon."

Head struck Onions across the face with the laptop, cracking the casing, and knocking the Man From I-Psi-T out of his chair.

Miss Gill's mouth gaped in an O of surprise.

Onions was astonished, and bleeding from the scalp.

Head gave Yoland back his computer.

"Mr. Jeperson," said Head, quietly, politely. "Would you care to try to kill me now?"

Richard knew he should. It would cut the Gordian knot.

Sewell Head—Swellhead—opened his hands and tilted his head back. A tiny bulge in the frog-fold between his mouth and collar was his chin. A forceful blow struck below the bulge would crush his larynx and end everything.

Long seconds stretched.

Richard made no move. The ghost of the pub quiz champion who was content to work in a sweetshop was still before him, displaced by an apported personality but perhaps not lost forever.

"I thought as much," said Head, turning his back. "You are weak. It is why you will not win this day."

Swellhead was acting as if he owned the place, which—of course—he did.

"Not killing people on the offchance it'll solve a problem is just one of those habits," Richard remarked. "Maybe it's one of the things that makes me better than you."

Head wheeled, eyes flashing fury.

"Yes, Mr. Swellhead, I said *better*."

"Is that a challenge?"

"If you choose to deem so."

Head was tempted, but decided against it.

"You're a spent force, Mr. Jeperson, a distraction. Momentous business is being conducted. Maybe we shall settle things later."

Onions got himself together and crawled back to his chair.

Yoland and Miss Gill were lost.

Head raised a hand in a signal.

Other people emerged from around the courtyard. They wore white jumpsuits and faceguards, and carried H-logo weapons. They were not phantoms like the thing in the hallway, but substantial, physical beings.

Perhaps they perceived Richard and the others as ghosts?

"No, this isn't fake old," said Richard. "It was built in the 1960s and it wasn't here until this year. Both statements, irreconcilable as they are, hold water."

"You're raving, Jeperson. And you're well off-topic. Next on the agenda…"

"Listen to me, Adam. It's important. *This whole place is an apport!*"

7

"As I said," continued Onions, "next on the agenda…"

Richard tried to appeal to the others.

"We're inside a big ghost. That's not a safe thing."

Yoland and Miss Gill did not seem bothered. This was so outside their experience that it didn't sink in.

Head was thinking.

Richard really did not like that.

"I've drawn up a rota," said Onions. "To keep watch for phenomena. Each should be logged and categorised."

"Phenomena!" shouted Richard. "You're sitting on a phenomenon…" (he kicked the deckchair) "…under a phenomenon…" (he slapped the umbrella) "…inside the *fenomenoni di tutti fenomena*, this whole place!"

Richard's outburst echoed. He was breathing heavily.

Head walked towards the table, taking tiny steps.

He was craning, twisting his head from side to side as if trying to work a crick out of his neck. Or trying to get his skull to fit properly onto his spinal column.

"May I see that?" he asked, indicating Yoland's laptop.

He took the gadget and peered at it.

"Have we missed something?" asked Yoland. "All the details of the visits to Skerra are in the memory. You can click on the reports and read what went into the secret files."

Head was not scanning the information on the screen. He held the computer as if it was the first he had ever seen, turned it over to examine the ports in the case, brushed his fingers over the keyboard.

"Ingenious," he smiled. "Compact."

"If we might press on," said Onions.

"Silence," said Head, firmly.

SWELLHEAD

"No, you won't tell me? Or no, they never peeped? See, now I'm confusing myself."

"According to reports, this place wasn't here in 1974, 1984, 1994 or 1996."

"Thank you for your directness, Mr. Yoland."

"The reports must be wrong," said Onions. "It's not impossible to suborn officials."

"Indeed it isn't. But I'll bet you checked out the names on the papers. Did extensive re-interviews? With persuasive methods? I'm right again, aren't I? I could get used to this. Is it how you feel in quiz contests, Mr. Head? When you know all the answers. So, to return to the impossible factor, what we have is a vast installation that evidence suggests has been here for at least thirty years but which can't have been here as recently as 1996? Do we agree?"

"Is this some sort of *Omphalos* argument, Jeperson?"

"The benefits of a classical education. Mr. Head, could you expand on Adam's reference for those among us unfamiliar with the works of Philip Henry Gosse."

Head was silent. He loomed, face craning forward.

His eyes were intense, wary, cunning. As if he had just awoken among strangers.

"Come on, Swellhead," joshed Yoland. "Penny in the slot."

"The *Omphalos* argument," began Head, tone unfamiliar — not a blank recital, but impassioned, "was advanced in the nineteenth century by fundamentalist Christians in reaction to archaeological evidence that the world is older than the Biblical date of 4004 BC. Gosse, among others, put forward the notion that God created the Earth complete with a fossil record of creatures that never existed just as He created Adam and Eve with belly-buttons — the word *"omphalos"* is classical Greek for navel — indicative of conventional birth."

"You're saying that this place was whipped up in the last few years," said Yoland. "But *faked* to seem older? Pirelli calendar and all? It still doesn't solve my problem. No matter when the complex was built, it'd have been impossible to do it in secret."

Head was smiling at Richard, nastily.

The man was *remembering*. Something trickled inside Richard's mind, trying to take shape.

"I see there was a naval exercise here in 1996. We must have been thinking of invading an island. No, it's the other way about. There was a worry that Spain might take the presence of Israeli or Moroccan tourists on Gibralatar as violation of the fifth paragraph of Article Ten of the Treaty of Utrecht and pull a Galtieri. It seemed like a sensible idea to play out a 'liberation scenario.' You'll be relieved to learn we showed Johnny Spaniard he couldn't hold the Rock for long."

"Shouldn't the Navy have asked me first?" protested the Droning of Skerra.

"You might have a case for invoking a UN sanction against the British Crown for invading your sovereign territory, but I doubt you'd get very far."

"All this is still classified, Jeperson," said Onions. "You didn't need to know."

Head stood erect, hands behind him. For a moment, he wavered.

Something was different about his eyes. As if the taxidermist had the wrong reference.

"Jeperson?" said Onions, irritated.

"Yes, where was I? History of Skerra visitations: 1944 to the present day. Got it? Now, you may be right in that we didn't need to know about the germ warfare or the relief of the Rock, but it is certainly relevant that, far from being an unvisited and forgotten protrusion in a far northern sea, Skerra has been only marginally less congested than Piccadilly Circus at ten o'clock on a Saturday night. You'll have all the reports filed after the bio-weapons tests and the naval exercise?"

Yoland nodded.

"And what don't they say?"

Yoland frowned.

"Pardon me, that's a confusing question form. But I'll lay you a tenner in old money that no one who trod on Skerra before Captain Vernon's team — and I haven't forgotten them, Adam — ever reported a dirty great underground complex in the caverns. Not that easy to miss. And don't tell me those thorough mad science wallahs or resourceful jack tars stayed topside and never so much as peeped down the Blowhole."

"No," said Onions.

SWELLHEAD

"Whose name is on everything here. Whose initial marks everything."

Head thumped his chest. The place was getting to him too. It could be that he had the most to gain from it.

"We'll come to that in a minute," said Onions.

"Can I be the one to talk about the impossible?" said Richard.

"I think that falls under the 'bloody obvious' category, Jeperson," said Onions. "The impossible is our daily bread, remember? Even the amateur dabblers of the Diogenes Club."

"I don't mean the unexplained, the supernatural. Ghosties and ghoulies. I mean evidence of things we know did not happen. Fred Regent was not decapitated in 1972. Ray Bradbury did not write *2001*. Sewell Head did not broker the meet between Nixon and Elvis."

"That photo's in your room too?" said Yoland.

"A corporation that has never existed did not build an underground complex on Skerra in the late sixties. A small war was not fought here in February, 1973. Mr Head and I did not bleed all over my third-best coat in that control room."

Head said nothing.

"I know you'll be thoroughly prepared," said Richard. "You'll have a record of everyone who has set foot on Skerra between the evacuation of '32 and our arrival this morning?"

Onions flinched, minutely. Yoland looked at his computer screen.

"I see that information is available."

Richard pulled Yoland's laptop across the table.

"That's interesting," he said. "Miss Gill, when your father bought Skerra, did anyone tell him that Winston Churchill used it for anthrax experiments?"

Miss Gill was aghast. "Bloody hell they did!"

"Those Skerran goats must be the hardiest creatures on Earth. They were supposed to have been wiped out by bio-warfare in 1944. The spores were active and deadly in "57, when a trawler off its course ran aground. There were deaths. The team from Porton Down who visit every ten years reported non-lethal traces in 1964 and no danger at all in 1974, 1984 and 1994. No danger from anthrax that is. In '84, there was a fatality due to goat attack. I suppose this jaunt is incidentally supposed to take the place of the scheduled check-up?"

Yoland nodded. "It's perfectly safe now."

Richard scrolled down.

No one wanted to debate that. Yet.

"Yoland, can you give us your preliminary report?" said Onions. "You've a different remit here."

Richard had wondered about that. What did Morag Duff and Really-a-Good-Bloke Rory expect to get out of this expedition? People like them always thought of "practical applications." I-Psi-T was Min of Def-funded, too.

Yoland shut his computer. "Too early to say, but I think there are things here of immense worth."

Miss Gill clapped her hands and threatened to laugh again.

"Yes, monetary worth," said Yoland. "But more than that. Mr Jeperson, you asked about the power source. I've ferreted about a bit and it's definitely tidal. We have nothing like it. And the equipment we've seen is a paradox. A lot of it is bakelite and solder antique, but there are shortcuts I don't understand. This place is thirty years old, but whoever built it was forty or fifty years ahead of their time. Handicapped by the tools available, but spooky brilliant. My guess is that a handful of circuit-boards from the control room could yield patents that would bring in millions of euros a year. You know my field. Weapons. I've been tinkering with one of those machine-pistol jobbies, the things with funny magazines. It's not like any small-arm I've ever seen. Recoilless, silenced, and fires pellets that expand in the air. And we haven't cracked the puzzle of the big dish. I reckon it does *something* interesting. Whoever ends up with ownership is going to be, ah, enormously at an advantage."

"'Whoever?'" protested Miss Gill. "Daddy paid good money for Skerra."

"For the island, not what's under it."

"So, who else's is it? The Skerrans are all gone. And this isn't Britain. It's an independent country and I can make up my own laws."

Richard saw Yoland and Miss Gill were being seduced. Knowledge, money, power, justification, intrigue. Even Onions, with quantifiable results that could not be dismissed, was half in love with the complex.

He wondered when Stacy and Kydd would get back. Of the party, they were the two he trusted most.

"You're forgetting something," said Head.

"What?" asked Miss Gill and Yoland, together.

SWELLHEAD

"No, that's *Nineteen Eighty-Four*," put in Yoland. "*2001* is...it's on the tip of my tongue. Wait a minute, we've got the triviameister here. Swellhead, who wrote *2001*?"

"Arthur C. Clarke," said Head, dully, not turning round.

The world settled again, and Richard nodded.

"That's decided then."

"What are you on about, Jeperson? This is no time..."

Richard produced the book. Onions looked at it, puzzled. Then saw the names on the cover. He passed it to Yoland, whose instinct was to turn to the last page.

"How does it end?" Yoland asked Head.

"'For though he was master of the world, he was not quite sure of what to do next,'" recited Head. "'But he would thing of something.'"

"*Wrong-g-g-g!*" said Yoland. "'Then, as the moon watched, the Star Child left the wilderness behind and walked into the town.'"

Head turned, almost angry.

Richard realised the little man could not bear to be mistaken.

"Let me see that," he said.

Yoland tossed him the book. He looked through it roughly, breaking the thirty-five-year-old spine.

"This isn't right," he said.

He tore the book in half and threw the pages away.

Richard had a pang of loss and fury. Then he remembered the insinuating gun. The book was best out of reach. It had been a dangerous temptation.

There must be books in all the rooms. Maybe LP records.

Best not think of that.

"Nothing is right here," said Richard. "This is not a natural place."

"If there's a prize for speaking the bloody obvious," said Miss Gill, "the old hippie just took it home."

"Just because a thing is bloody obvious doesn't mean it shouldn't be spoken."

"Could you please stop bickering," said Onions. "And pay attention."

Onions slapped his agenda on the table.

"Now," he said, "observations, please."

"This is treasure trove, right?" said Miss Gill. "But on my land. So I own it."

Somewhere under Skerra, there must be a cinema.

He killed the thought and looked at the mirrored cabinet.

Behind his old eyes, there were lacunae. Maybe Ray Bradbury had written *2001,* and it had slipped his mind, liquid misinformation rushing in to fill the hole. Maybe Sewell Head had mounted Fred Regent's head on a board thirty years ago, and the decades Richard remembered were a protracted psychotic episode, born of guilt at being unable to keep his friend alive.

He took the vial of cocaine from the drugs kit and thought about it.

Circles, he realised. He was beginning to think in circles.

But there was something else. The sense of *wrongness* was still there, but other senses crowded in. He was thinking more clearly, with fewer of his memory lapses. He even felt better, long-settled aches lifting from his limbs. The air down here was good for him. He had not expected that.

Was this another trap?

He left the room, sealed it behind him, and walked along the balcony to a white filigree spiral staircase.

Assuming that Stacy and Kydd were not back and de Maltby excused, Richard was the last to make it to Onions's meeting.

They were assembled in a gazebo affair at the centre of the court, sat on folding chairs around a wrought-iron table under a giant candy-striped umbrella. Yoland had a laptop computer fired up. Miss Gill had changed into a Skerra tartan designer skirt with matching sash. Onions had an agenda drawn up and was checking it over.

Sewell Head stood a few feet away, back to the others, looking up.

"I was listing the types of phenomenon observed here," said Onions. "Spectral figures, ectoplasmic spores, hot spots, cold spots, cyclic apparitions, aural and visual manifestations..."

"Apports," prompted Richard.

"Of course, apports."

"Lots of 'em. Adam, who wrote *2001?*"

Onions frowned.

"I know that one," said Miss Gill. "George Orwell."

Richard felt his mind crack again.

thors. The first chapter began "When Heywood Floyd was a boy in the mid-West he used to go out and look at the stars at night and wonder about them." Reluctantly, he closed the book and slipped it into his pocket. A drawer that pulled out from under the bed had an array of gleaming silver-steel, H-stamped weapons — automatic pistols, clips of ammunition, combat knives, a samurai sword.

A fizzing cut through the musak.

He looked at the telescreen. It had come to life, or at least static.

The swirls resolved into a blurry H logo, then the letter faded and the oval shield grew brighter. Richard fancied eyes and a smile.

He picked out one of the pistols, rammed a clip into the butt, slipped off the safety and shot the screen. The tube imploded with a cough of smoke. In the sparking wreckage, a necklike attachment craned — it ended in a blinking lens.

There was a sharp rap at his door.

"Come in, it's not locked."

Onions, free of his gadget belt, tentatively looked round the door.

"I shot the screen, Adam. A pre-emptive strike. It was trying to get to me."

Onions humoured him and pressed on.

"Meeting in the courtyard in five minutes, Jeperson. We need to hash out a schedule for the investigation."

Onions withdrew.

Richard hefted the automatic pistol. As a rule, he disliked guns, but this had a satisfyingly heavy feel. It hadn't kicked when fired, and the noise — the thing he hated most about using firearms — had been damped somehow. His ears still rang from the shot de Maltby had fired in the trophy hall, but his own more recent discharge had wiped itself out. He turned the gun over in his hands, getting the heft of it.

Then he put it down and went to wash his hands.

He didn't even like using the water in this room, let alone the weaponry. The gun had been on its best behaviour, endeavouring to win his confidence, wheedling to get holster-close to his heart. He had no doubt that if he trusted the thing, it would turn traitor. Worse still was the *2001* paperback, which whispered "read me, read me" in his ear. He would happily burn the negatives of every movie Steven Spielberg ever directed to get into a screening of this *Space Odyssey*.

this sector offered rooms arranged like an American motel, in balconied tiers. Instead of sky, the central courtyard had naked rock. Garden furniture was scattered around, but there were no corpses.

Stacy and Kydd had gone topside, to fetch supplies from the Sea King.

De Maltby was in drugged sleep, but otherwise stable.

Richard checked the room he had staked for himself. It was anonymous Scandinavian moderne, with clown paintings in place of windows and piped-in dabba-dabba-dabba musak. A duvet lay on the drum-tight fitted sheet of the single bed. At first, he thought the bedding a uniform gray, but his touch disturbed a thin layer of dust. The duvet cover and pillowcase were white, imprinted with the bright yellow H logo.

The door had an airtight seal. Ventilation and heat came through grilles in the walls. Besides clown paintings, decor extended to a framed photograph of a young, Kupperberg-suited Sewell Head with his arms around a couple of sweaty Americans who proved, on close examination, to be Richard Nixon and Elvis Presley. The Prezz and the King both looked up to Zen Master of Quantum Cleverness.

An en-suite bathroom offered a plexiglass shower booth and stainless steel toilet and washstand. He ran the taps and got hot and cold water. After bursts of rusty-red, the flow ran clean. He tasted the cold and found it drinkable. He assumed there was a desalination plant somewhere in the complex, converting seawater. A bathroom cabinet contained a solidified tube of unbranded toothpaste, a blister-pack of contraceptive pills and a bottle of Breck shampoo. A H-logoed sampler kit contained syrettes, vials of powder marked "heroin" and "cocaine', and purple lozenges stamped "Lovely Shining Dream'.

The musak—José Feliciano playing the Doors' greatest hits—came through the speakers of a large telescreen inset into the wall opposite the bed. There were no on-off or channel controls, and no handset. Whoever lived here listened to and watched whatever the master programmer gave them.

A wardrobe contained three identical lab-coats and dispenser-packs of disposable plastic bootees and mittens. A bedside table had unread paperbacks of *Valley of the Dolls* and *Airport* with early seventies covers. He also found the *2001* movie tie-in, and raised an eyebrow to see Ray Bradbury and Stanley Kubrick listed as co-au-

"That's what puzzled us when Vernon's report came in," said Onions. "We found Mr Head very easily. He's in the phone book. There's only one of him."

Richard wondered if that was strictly true.

"And we know, in exhaustive detail, what he's done with his life. There just isn't any gap in which he could have done this..."

Onions spread his hands, indicating everything in this complex.

"Some obsessive trivia quiz fan did all this *for* him?" said Miss Gill. "I find that impossible to believe."

Head's fingers hovered over buttons.

Kydd stood by the dais, de Maltby's gun tucked into his belt, at attention.

"What's it all *for*?" asked Stacy.

"That's an interesting question," said Yoland, "and I can make a range of guesses. But the big question is 'how's it all here?'"

The techie was in his element, getting up to speed.

"This couldn't have been built in secret," said Yoland. "It's a major construction project. Hundreds, maybe thousands of men would have had to work on it. Think of all the raw materials that must have been transported here, to an abandoned island. There'd have had to be a non-stop back-and-forth on the sea-lanes. Where are the ships' logs, flight-plans, invoices, bills of lading, pay-slips? This is a small underground city. Supplying must have been a mammoth operation. It would all have gone on in the public eye. Millions of pounds must have been spent. Multiples of millions. There may be no Sewell Head Industries, but something wealthier than most countries created this place."

Richard remembered how he had felt when he saw the apported coat, how he had instinctively avoided touching it, how it had been an affront to his sense of the way the universe fit together. He was feeling the same thing again, on a colossal scale.

This *whole place* was *wrong*.

6

They made camp three levels above the control room, in a block Richard guessed was accommodation for SHI executives. Spartan barracks and dormitories were provided for jumpsuit drones, but drawn to it for a moment, but he forced himself to look away. It was too easy to see shapes in static.

"Clock this," said Stacy.

She picked up a cardboard file-folder, embossed with the familiar H. Under the oval, in a retro-futurist typeface, were the words "Sewell Head Industries'. Yoland took it and passed it around.

"You're a captain of industry, Swellhead?" said Miss Gill. "I thought you worked in a sweetshop."

Head found a control panel in the arm of his chair. The designer must have been a *Star Trek* fan. Head pressed a button: lights came on at the base of his dais and in a circle overhead, catching him in a shaft of brightness.

"This is all new to me," he said.

"But you know where the light-switches are," said Yoland.

"Which button opens the trapdoor to the alligator pits?" asked Miss Gill. "Or do you prefer piranhas?"

Head was thoughtful. He stabbed another button.

A section of the floor flapped downwards. Richard was suddenly at the edge of a hole. A foul smell wafted up. Richard tottered but Stacy pulled him back from the brink. He slipped. A sharp stab of terror went through him as he felt Stacy going over too.

"Got you, miss," said Kydd. He had stepped in to grab her around the waist.

It took some doing, but they were all restored to safety.

"I'm so sorry," said Head. "I didn't think."

The bottom of the pit was dark and liquid. And inhabited.

"Best not fiddle with the toys anymore," said Richard.

"Quite right," said Head, mildly.

He didn't get out of his chair though. More and more, he looked comfortable.

"What *is* this place?" asked Miss Gill.

"Head Office," said Head.

"Very clever," said Richard. "But you'd have to be clever, wouldn't you?"

Head sat, impassive.

"There is no Sewell Head Industries," said Yoland. "At least not off this island. Never has been."

Head nodded.

SWELLHEAD

Banks of computers stacked against a wall — bulky cabinets wired together, each the size of a fridge-freezer, with exposed spools of tape and letterbox slots for punchcards and print-outs.

"Pre-silicon chip," said Yoland, stroking a machine. "Installed in the late 1960s, maybe early seventies."

Richard picked up a Pirelli calendar from a strew of papers on the floor. A naked woman snarled, holding a scary African mask next to her face. The photograph was manipulated to shade into a drawing at the extremities.

"Might I take a wild guess and suggest this facility was abandoned sometime in February, 1973?"

"That sounds about right," said Yoland. "What was happening then?"

"Oil crisis. Power cuts. Television shut down at half-past-ten. IRA mainland bombing campaign."

"All that never happened," said Miss Gill, born 1983. "He's getting the seventies confused with the War. People his age were all on drugs."

Richard was more amused than offended.

Yoland twiddled some knobs on a console.

"Does it still work?" asked Stacy.

"Unlikely," said the weapons inspector. "These old jobs were as dicky as Christmas tree lights."

One wall was given over to a gray and dead display screen, a stitching of bullet-holes across the glass.

There had been fighting in here. Some cabinets were overturned and ruptured, bleeding wires and circuit-boards.

"I told a lie," said Yoland, holding up a component. "This *is* a silicon chip. Or some sort of prehistoric ancestor. Ceramic, micro-printed. It's the size of my thumb, but it's definitely a chip. Whoever put this together was way ahead of the game."

The tile floor was patchwork-quilted with spilled files, strews of punchcards and streamers of magnetic tape.

This, Richard knew, was where his coat had been found.

Head walked up to a black swivel chair on a dais. He sat in it and whirled around like a child, legs pointing out. As the chair revolved, gears clicked. The big screen hummed and warmed up. Behind spiderweb of cracks, static buzzed. Richard's attention was tape isn't a medium of recording but of transmission. Whatever haunts here will try to affect us, to work on our weaknesses. It's already begun, subtly and, ah, not to subtly. From now on, be alert, open, on your guard. I needn't say we shouldn't go wandering off alone. Always know where everyone else is. Fix on that. It'll help you when there are others among us. Beware of circles—physical circles, mental circles. The place would like us to go round on its little rails. Haunted houses are traps and tests. The bad ones, that is, and this is certainly one of those. Adam, give a heads-up whenever your needles twitch. It'd help if we knew something was coming before it arrived. We've seen what can happen. Let's not let it happen again."

Onions opened his mouth, as if he had a long, prepared answer.

"Let's move on," said Richard, cutting him off.

Kydd relieved Yoland of de Maltby's side-arm with "I'd best look after that, sir." The Aircrewman helped the doped pilot stand, making sure he could walk without falling over himself.

Before leaving the hallway, Richard looked at the Fred trophy. It was the best-preserved of the modern collection, as if curing methods had improved between 1953 and 1972. It was a real severed head, very deathlike, and was somehow really Fred, hair close-cropped, mouth open. Fred as he had been as a young plod in 1972, not the top cop Richard had seen two days ago at Euston.

The eyes were blue not hazel: they were taxidermist's glass, a detail mistaken by whoever prepared the head for display.

Staring into Fred's wrong eyes made Richard queasy.

But determined. Being shut up, inside himself, inside his home, had been a mistake.

If this was out here all along, he should have been in the world.

Skerra was his problem.

5

They were in a control room.

Yoland whistled in astonished amusement.

"Vintage," he declared.

flat against a wall, Ken Dodd gurning over his shoulder as he fiddled with his doodad.

De Maltby stopped kicking and Kydd got a proper tourniquet around his arm. The blobule hadn't gone through the pilot's hand, but dissipated on impact, turning to nasty black gunge. Kydd washed out the wound with bottled water and slapped on a pressure bandage.

"...*uhhhm*...hurts," said de Maltby, redundantly. He shook his head and grit his teeth.

The pilot was in no shape to fly them off Skerra. Richard hadn't qualified on a helicopter in twenty-five years. Unless someone else in the party had hidden talents, they were stuck here until they could be rescued.

De Maltby relaxed, eyes fluttering shut.

If the viscount had shifted a bit more to the left, his lesser relations would have bumped up in the line of succession. The Royal Navy would have had to do some embarrassing explaining to the Royal Family.

Miss Gill got up and angrily aimed a finger at Onions.

"You said it was an after-image! You said it couldn't harm us!"

Onions tried to show her a read-out. She wasn't interested.

"Where are the proper experts who're supposed to protect us?" she demanded. "I was promised a crack team of up-for-anything sailors armed to the teeth and ready to throw up a ring of fire and steel around us. All I've got are useless old weirdoes and a bloody meter maid. I didn't come here to be shot at."

Stacy, the "meter maid," cocked her gunfinger and pointed it at the back of Miss Gill's head. Richard gave her the nod and she put it away.

"It's extremely rare that a manifestation causes injury."

"Tell *him* that."

De Maltby was smiling now, morphine kicking in.

Miss Gill and Onions glared at each other.

"Listen to me," announced Richard. "This is a haunted house. Bigger than most, but still a haunted house. Adam's little gadgets are all well and good, but what is going on here isn't just an atmospheric phenomenon, like weather. It's reactive and it's directed. A show is being put on for us. But we aren't just an audience, we're targets. The place is inhabited, ensouled. Make no mistake, the stone

A red wound flowered on the ghost's chest, unfolding like one of those pellets that become roses when dropped into water. It was knocked off its feet and floated upwards, legs trailing and dissipating.

Stacy, astonished, raised her finger and blew on the tip.

"Temperature is down ten degrees centigrade," said Onions. "It's sucking heat, converting it to matter."

The ghost's phantom gun kicked. Black blobules coughed from the barrel and lobbed through space. Yoland bent out of their path, knocking Miss Gill down, covering her against the floor.

Sewell Head, fascinated, turned, watching ghost bullets pass by him. They left visible ripples in the air. Head prodded one of the wakes with a long finger, and twirled it into a nebula-shape.

Stacy drew both index fingers and popped like Wyatt Earp emptying his six-shooters into Old Man Clanton. The ghost jittered and staggered.

The blobules still swam through thick air.

De Maltby fired his real gun. The report was appallingly loud, but the shot did less to the ghost than Stacy's pretend bullets.

De Maltby stuck out a hand to steady himself as he took aim again. One of the blobules collided with his palm.

Everything sped up. The ghoststuff fell like rain, splashing the carpet in a splatter, leaving a Hiroshima blast shadow.

The single shot still resounded, an assault on the ears.

Another scream exploded, not ghostly.

De Maltby's left hand was a red ruin, fingers stiff and shaking, blood welling from a ragged black hole. He dropped his gun.

"Now that was bloody stupid," said Richard.

The viscount gripped his wrist and fell, swallowing yelps of pain. He thrashed a little and swore a lot. The barracks vocabulary set ill with his plummy accent. Kydd got to the pilot's side with a battlefield med-kit. Richard helped Stacy pin de Maltby down as the Aircrewman prepared a syringe, drawing from an ampoule of morphine. Stacy skinned de Maltby's sleeve and held his arm steady so Kydd could get the shot in him.

Yoland had picked up de Maltby's dropped gun; he aimed at the doorway. Head still stood out in the open, puzzled. Miss Gill was in a crouch by Yoland, presenting a small target. Onions was

His hands knotted into fists.

Time passed inside his mind.

He forced himself out of fugue, and realised everyone else had heard the scream, which still echoed.

No, not echoed — continued.

Another dramatic situation.

4

"It's in here," said Onions, his LEDs readings flashing angry red.

The scream careened about the hallway like a pinball. There was an associated visual phenomenon, a ragged freeform shadow that darted in a zigzag. It caught Kydd out in the open and passed through him with a ripping sound. The Aircrewman patted his chest.

"That wasn't half a funny feeling," he said. "Warm and wet."

Richard was pressed against the wall, Stacy by him. He tried to follow the shadow, but it flickered too swiftly.

"Nothing to be afraid of," announced Onions. "It's an after-image. It's not happening now. It's long gone. Just a recording on the Stone Tape."

The wall was trembling. Richard wondered how dormant that volcano was.

At the end of the hallway a door flapped open and a figure lurched in view, like a target at an army shooting range. A person of indeterminate sex in a white coat and hardhat, opaque white visor over the face, loose white polythene bootees and mittens tied over the extremities. It held one of the unfinished-looking guns that had been in the hands of the corpses in the cavern.

The apparition moved at half-speed and was silent.

Onions pointed his doodad at the white figure. Its edges blurred and Richard saw the knees kink as if the thing were a hologram projected on drifting mist.

"Now, *that's* a ghost," said Stacy.

The figure's movements slowed. It was wheeling about, bringing its gun to bear on the hallway. The outlines were smeared completely now, bleeding into the background. Even the gun was soft, barrel and magazine floppy.

Stacy made a gunfinger and popped her mouth.

KIM NEWMAN

Sewell Head was getting excited by his nostalgia wallow. He came to a nearly-preserved head wearing an army cap.

<small>Sergeant Arthur Grimshaw, Walmington-on-Sea Barracks, 1960, .303 bullet in cranium.</small>

"When I did my National Service, there was a very loud sergeant called 'Grimmy.' Used to get into a lather about close-order drill. Said I had two left feet. Always had me peeling mountains of blessed spuds. You know, I think this really is 'Grimmy.' He's still frowning, and red in the face."

Stacy tugged Richard's sleeve.

"Richard," she whispered, urgently, "I went through the files on Head. School, family background, National Service, employment history, the lot. Boring as Bognor on a wet bank holiday. If his past were littered with headless corpses, it'd show up. Surely?"

After Grimshaw in 1960, the names meant less to Head.

"Professor Etienne Bolin, the particle physicist. I've heard of him, but who hasn't. Ken Dodd, the comedian. I always found him more irritating than funny. Scary clowns were a phobia of mine when I was little. And do you remember that ghastly pop song that was on everywhere you listened for months in 1965? 'Tears for Souvenirs.' Put me off *Top of the Pops* for life."

Yoland gave a sympathetic ugh.

Richard and Stacy looked at the preserved pop-eyed, crooked-teethed Ken Dodd trophy.

"Now *he's* not beheaded," said Stacy. "He was in that Kenneth Branagh *Hamlet* film."

"This does look like him, circa 1965, though. As if he were cut off in his prime."

"'Tears for Souvenirs.' Can't say I've heard of it."

"You haven't missed much."

They were nearly at the end of the Trophy Hall.

"And this fellow means nothing to me," announced Head.

<small>Frederick Regent, The Diogenes Club, 1972, decapitation via monofilament.</small>

Richard heard the ghost of a scream.

SWELLHEAD

Head made a swishing motion, whipping an imaginary cane.

"The strange thing was that I was an obedient boy, got my homework in on time, never ran in the quad or talked out of turn. But, every few weeks, 'Whacker' found reason to chastise me. 'Six of the best, Swellhead, six of the best!' Looking back, I think he was one of those sad fellows who got pleasure from caning small boys. It wouldn't be allowed these days."

The nail had been pounded into the skull in the centre of the forehead. Dents around the nailhead showed that a few hammerblows had missed.

Richard looked from the Tuomey-Rees trophy to the others.

"Do any other names mean anything to you, Mr Head?"

Head scuttled down the hallway, examining plates.

MORRIS "BASHER" CROPSHAW, HOLLY NOOK
RECREATION GROUNDS, 1954, PENKNIFE IN OCCIPITAL HOLLOW.

"There *was* a boy called Basher Something. Lived three doors down. Always hanging about on the corner when I was coming home from school. Very high-spirited, boisterous, got into scrapes. He took my satchel once and never gave it back. My homework was in it. "Whacker" striped my bottom for that."

Head came to a trophy with fine red hair done up in a topknot with a big blue bow. The face was shrivelled.

"Here's another old friend," said Head.

MELANIE POTTER, HOLLY NOOK YOUTH CLUB, 1956, CRUSHED HYOID.

"Pretty girl, but not very friendly. She danced with me once. To win a bet with Mavis Bryant. Oh, how funny!"

MAVIS BRYANT, "BRYANT THE TYRANT," HOLLY NOOK
YOUTH CLUB, 1956, MULTIPLE SIMPLE FRACTURES.

"Have you noticed how that happens? You don't think of someone in nearly fifty years and then when you do their name comes up in some completely unconnected manner."

Richard noticed stricken looks among the party. Even Onions was taken aback.

3

The hallway was lined with heads, mounted on shields fixed to the walls. Some were skulls, ancient and cracked. Others were poorly preserved, features dripping like wax. A few were disturbingly lifelike.

Under each trophy, museum-plates gave details. Richard looked at the prize of the collection.

AUSTRALOPITHECINE, STIRKFONTEIN CAVES, C. 3M B.C., AXE-BITE.

It was just a partial cranium, with a jagged gash. Most of the others were of far more recent vintage.

He considered the next trophy.

R.J. TUOMEY-REES, MA CANTAB, 1953, SIX-INCH NAIL EMBEDDED.

"Six-inch nail embedded," said Miss Gill. "It bloody is, too. Gruesome!"

Tuomey-Rees was one of the incompletes, flaps of dried meat over gray bone. A lot of goldwork in his teeth.

"'Could do better if he tried,'" said Sewell Head.

The little man looked into the empty eyesockets.

Everyone stared at Head.

"My Second Year form-master at Coal Hill Secondary Modern was called Tuomey-Rees," Head explained.

"He didn't happen to disappear in 1953, did he?" asked Stacy.

"Not at all," said Head, missing any accusation. "He was still flapping about in his blessed mortar-board and gown in '57, when I left school. Tuomey-Rees was a most humorous fellow. 'With your name, young Sewell, you should be, ahem, *Head of the Class.*' He gave me my nickname. He would say, 'don't get a *swellhead,* Sewell Head!' Soon they were all calling me 'Swellhead.' Very amusing."

It was the longest speech Richard had heard from Head.

"Happy days," mused Head. "The tuck shop, playground japes, Nurse dosing for nits. And 'Whacker' Tuomey-Rees. That was *his* nickname, 'Whacker.'"

SWELLHEAD

"I should say somebody has a big head," said Miss Gill, more pettish than amused now.

Sewell Head said nothing. Next to these three-dimensional images of himself, he seemed insubstantial, as if he were the third-generation copy and the artworks the original.

At the base of a Soviet-style statue of Head heroic in overalls and hardhat was the skeleton of a woman, laid out like a sacrifice. A long white evening dress clung to bones. At first, Richard assumed her head was miraculously intact, then he realised she had worn a wax mask. The doll-face was cracked across, pinned to the skull by a black-handled throwing-knife.

"I'd kill for those shoes," said Miss Gill.

The spike heels were at least six inches. Gold filigree bands wound up almost to the knees; they curled slackly around unclad shinbones.

"Feel free," said Head. "They're your size."

Miss Gill looked at the little man as if seeing him for the first time. He was past his insubstantial phase. The likenesses reflected back on the original, lending him a charisma that had gone unnoticed.

Richard knew Onions wasn't pointing his doodad in the right direction.

At the end of the path, doors opened.

Head passed through, followed by Miss Gill and de Maltby.

There had been an uneasy shift of authority within the group.

"Adam," he said. "Don't let this get away from you."

Onions had been looking at the dead woman. He reacted to Richard as if slapped.

"I don't know what you mean, Jeperson. I am in complete control."

"Could have fooled me," thought Stacy.

"What are you smiling at?" snapped Onions.

Richard did not explain. There were so many voices in his head here that it was a delight that at least one was friendly.

Onions, grumpy, stamped off towards the open doors.

Miss Gill honked astonished laughter. You had to have unearned wealth to get away with a bray like that.

On a brushed steel plinth was an eight-foot tall marble egg, carved with Humpty Dumpty features.

It was a monumental bust of Sewell Head.

2

"Someone's got some bloody explaining to do!" said Miss Gill, through snorts of aghast hilarity. "I mean, whose island is this?"

Head looked up at his own face, curious. Richard could tell the little man wanted to touch the marble but was afraid to. He had chocolate on his fingers and did not want to spoil the surface.

"You're the pub quiz king, Head," said Onions. "Any answers?"

Head said nothing. Onions pointed his doodad at the sculpture and pressed buttons.

"He doesn't remember," said Richard.

Onions wheeled on him, hostile.

"He doesn't *want* to remember. Like you, Jeperson."

"Back off," said Stacy, protective, eye on de Maltby's gun.

Onions, surprised, did. He wasn't handling this well.

"I *don't* remember," admitted Richard. "It's not a choice. It's a condition. There is more here than we see. More than you can quantify, Adam."

Onions huffed. An old argument was in the offing.

Stacy had stepped in for him. He squeezed her arm as silent thanks. They had an understanding now.

With her strength, he wasn't so feeble.

Beyond the monumental bust was a sculpture garden, with astroturf for grass and subdued lighting. A path wound between a dozen pieces, all representing the same subject — Sewell Head. Some were naturalistic, showing a younger man than the shuffling original, crudely attempting to convey dynamic presence; some were completely stylised, just H-stamped ovals; one was a mobile on which twenty or so transparent crystalline eggs were arranged to represent the atomic structure of an element unknown to science; another was a parody Easter Island head, eggskull elongated and eyes exaggerated.

SWELLHEAD

Richard shrugged. "Just trying to help," he told Stacy.

Yoland, Kydd and Miss Gill padded after the others.

Richard hung back, mind open, all receivers alert. The place was shrieking at him now. Stacy touched his shoulder, carefully.

"We'll be left behind," she said, gently.

He looked into her face, glimpsing skull under skin. He saw for an X-ray instant the back-teeth she would not sacrifice for a career, sensed the sparking synapses of her admirable brain. Fred had not assigned his minder casually. He had a spasm of fear for her. This place was dangerous.

Between seconds, he had a flash — more than a vision, it came with sound, smell, temperature. The corridor was swept by a blossom of fire. The stutter of gunfire was tinnitis, cutting through his skull. His skin broiled, his hair crisped.

"Richard," Stacy said, snapping her fingers under his nose, "come out of it."

He did. His face tingled, his ears rang. Otherwise, he was fine.

"Who am I?" she asked.

He knew who he was. He knew who she was. He knew where this was.

Though exposed, he was growing stronger again.

"You are an arresting woman," he said, startling a smile out of her.

The sound system burbled 'Let the Sunshine In' scrambled with 'Spanish Flea.'

At least she was starting to trust him. Refreshing as it was to be treated bluntly like a mad old relic, the tonic lost its effectiveness after a few doses.

"Flaming Nora!" screamed Miss Gill.

The others were out of sight, beyond a turn in the corridor.

"That's a call to investigate," he told Stacy. "A good many dramatic situations begin with screaming."

"That's from *Barbarella*," she said, making him feel younger. "My dad's favourite film," she added, rubbing it in that he was ancient.

Miss Gill's scream segued into a nails-down-a-blackboard laugh.

At a trot, they rounded the corner. The floor was lush as an executive suite, though the nap was moistly squishy, mouldy in patches. The carpet pattern consisted of tiny interlocking H symbols.

They found the others, gaping up as if at an art exhibit.

Others followed his example and took off their heavy-weather gear.

The Detective Sergeant wore brown corduroy trousers and a zip-up matching waistcoat.

"Very practical," he commented.

She took an onion-seller's beret from a pocket and tucked her hair into it.

"This is my arresting outfit," she said. "Your average villain tends to leg it if a bloke with size-eleven boots gets within spitting distance, but he'll hang about like a prat if someone blonde asks him the way to Acacia Avenue. Most bollockbrains still give out bullshit directions after they're cuffed and in the van."

The guardrail automatically folded into the floor of the platform.

Ahead was a plate glass barrier, studded with white star-shaped opacities. Beyond was a reception area and a corridor. With a hiss, the glass was withdrawn into the ceiling. No one wanted to step under it — the glass would make a very servicable guillotine.

A concealed sound system began to tinkle, 'Aquarius' from *Hair* played in the style of Herb Alpert and the Tijuana Brass.

Miss Gill mewed surprise, then said "It's not exactly Chris De Burgh."

"Why did Chris De Burgh cross the road?" asked Stacy. Miss Gill shook her head. "*To get to the middle.* Boom-boom."

Yoland and de Maltby laughed and Onions looked impatient. Miss Gill took the joke as a personal dig, which Richard assumed Stacy intended. Head, he noted, was puzzled. That was worth filing away.

It was Onions's place to press on. Richard waited for him.

The Man From I-Psi-T was fazed, not eager to venture further. Richard heard susurrus under the musak.

Ghosts.

Head made the first move and wandered off the lift-bed platform.

That jolted Onions out of his reverie. He nodded to de Maltby and followed Head.

Richard saw the pilot had his sidearm out.

"I'd put that away if I were you," cautioned Richard. "Someone'll only get hurt."

"*Uhhhhm,*" said de Maltby, affecting not to hear the advice.

SWELLHEAD

"Not necessarily. Whatever happened here isn't finished. If it were, our presence wouldn't be required."

"That's what I like about you, Jeperson," said Onions. "Always reasons to be cheerful."

"If you think I like making ominous pronouncements..."

Onions's belt beeped an interruption. He examined himself to find the gadget which had sounded out of turn.

The lift platform was level with the cavern floor. The dish towered hundreds of feet above them, lights shining through holes where plates were missing. Fighting had been fierce around the lift-bed. Many skeletons were spilled about, dusty brown-black stains on their uniforms, obvious bullet-holes in skulls.

"It's a mess," said Head, intently. "It should be tidied."

For Head, Richard realised, H stood for Home.

The lift sank below the floor. Yoland looked at the control handset and found nothing besides simple up and down buttons.

They descended several further levels.

Suddenly, it was dark. Then light again. As the lift sank, circuits connected. Overhead striplights tried to come on. Some panels buzzed and flashed and died, others sparked dangerously. Whole sections lit up perfectly, as if installed yesterday.

Richard had a sense of corridors winding into successive layers of labyrinth. Admin offices, supply areas, living quarters, cafeterias, recreation facilities, laboratories, lecture halls, testing grounds, museums, toilet facilities, information storage. No bare rock, but metalled walls, rubberised floor, heating and ventilation ducts (note to infiltrators: suitable for crawling through). Framed pictures were designed to seem like windows, the sort of touch you only got after expensive consultation.

They were deep underground, deep under the sea. Below the sea-bed, probably. He had a sense of enormous weight pressing in.

Without so much as a judder, the platform stopped.

Here, it was more than warm. The atmosphere was humid, tropical. Richard doffed his sou'wester and poncho, then unzipped his flightsuit, which came away in sections. Underneath, he wore thigh-flied scarlet buccaneer britches and a lemon-yellow bumfreezer jacket buttoned to the throat, with an explosive cravat of red lace. He plumped the black silk rose in his lapel.

"Fab threads," said Stacy, satirically.

"I don't have any readings," said Onions, tapping his doodad. A lone light flashed red. "Except that. Variation in atmospheric pressure. Entirely natural phenomenon in a cave this size."

It was what Richard had expected.

Onions cooed over his gizmo. Richard had a flash of Professor Calculus in the *Tintin* books—swinging his plumb-bob and muttering "a little more to the west." Of course, he turned out to be right.

Everyone else—except Head, who was chewing placidly on a cud of fudge—craned over the low guardrail and peered out at the cavern, looking for movement where there was none.

"What's that thing?" Stacy asked. "The giant satellite dish?"

"A transmitter," said Yoland. "It was gimbal-mounted, and on those rails. A nice bit of workmanship, if obsolete. Now, nanotech is sexy. Next generation isn't worth gasping at unless it's tinier than the last. But once upon a time, your equipment had to be *monumental* to attract funding."

"What did it transmit?" asked Stacy.

"Two-year-old episodes of sit-coms you didn't watch on their first run," suggested Richard. "Championship dwarf-tossing from Glamorgan? Those radio broadcasts that teach alien invaders to speak English with BBC accents?"

Yoland shook his head, but did not venture an opinion.

As they neared the cavern floor, the corpses were more obvious. Skeletons in white H-on-the-left-tit jumpsuits. H-logoed dome hardhats chin-strapped to clean skulls.

Kydd whistled. The Aircrewman was the only one among them who had served in a shooting war.

"Those people have been dead for a long time," said Stacy.

"Decades," Richard agreed.

The skeletons had died clutching automatic weapons with fold-out tube-frame H-stamped stocks and unfamiliar horizontal magazines.

"Did they turn on each other?" asked Stacy. "I see only one type of uniform."

Among the jumpsuits were a few dead people in labcoats, full-skirted like spaghetti western dusters, and oversized peaked caps. Not officers, but technicians, scientists, supervisors.

"The other side took away their dead," deduced Richard.

"The winners," said Yoland.

SWELLHEAD

The doors had opened at the sound of Sewell Head's cough. Had anyone else noticed that?

Yes. Head had. *Naturellement*.

Richard perceived he had not been entirely right about the immunity of the rest of the party. This place affected Head. Onions spent far too little time thinking about the problem of Sewell Head.

If only it were easier to concentrate.

Onions had his suitcase open. Instruments nestled in foam-rubber padding. He took off his anorak to reveal a utility belt and braces, tailored to fit when he had been a stone or two lighter. He had home-bored a frayed extra buckle-hole to loosen a harness which still cut into his tummy. Expertly, the Man From I-Psi-T transferred his precious gadgets from compartments in the case to holsters on the harness. A complex doodad, which resembled the universal remote for a multi-function entertainment system, strapped watchlike to his wrist. Onions entered a code on the keypad and the doodad beeped to life. Green, orange and red LEDs lit up.

"Prepared for the unknown, Adam?"

"It's only the as-yet unquantified."

Richard looked out at the cavern.

The *wrongness* of it all was nauseating, an electric thrill. With his gadgets, Onions could doubtless measure the condition as an increase in ozone levels or ambient charge or some such jargon. Richard did not doubt the physical effects were quantifiable. He just thought figures did not really help.

As they neared the bottom, he saw bulletpocks on rock and concrete.

"This was a battlefield," he announced.

Under the thrumm of the generators and the grind of the lift-platform, he again heard ghost gunfire, shouts. An explosion, mid-air, very near.

Spectre shrapnel shot through his mind.

Stacy was at his side, holding him up. He was momentarily riddled with scraps of hot pain. Then it was gone.

"You felt something?" she asked.

"Is it all coming back?" demanded Onions.

"Not a memory," Richard said. "Ghosts. Everywhere, ghosts."

The others could not feel anything yet.

The cavern was of a size that would suit a collector of fully-inflated antique Zeppelins. Natural rock formations had been shaped to accommodate the base. The floor was levelled and metalled, marked off like a runway or a launch-pad. The place was littered with white mini-jeeps, uniformed bodies and hard-to-identify machines. Concrete bunkers and blockhouses surrounded the ruin of a large, rail-mounted device with a Jodrell Bank-sized circular array. There had been a major fire here—a thick layer of soot blackened a swathe of wall and roof, and half the big dish was burned through to the frame. A forklift truck had been driven into a gantry and brought the structure down.

Deja-vu made Richard's knees and ankles weak.

He saw shadows flitting about the cavern-floor, from cover to cover. Distant alarums of machine-age battle sounded: klaxons, automatic weapons fire, warning bells and whistles, shouts of pain.

The others were immune to such phenomena. For now.

His coat had been found here, covered with his blood. Any deja-vu could be down to the circumstance that he really *had* been here before. No, it would not wash. He was used to holes in his memory, but here there was a hole in *everyone's* memory. If he had been here before, it would have made the secret history books. Limiting the circulation of information on an eyes-only basis paradoxically means preserving it.

Richard gripped the guardrail for support. He missed his white room, the neutral calm. This trip had disturbed his carefully-maintained equilibrium. He had been preserved in his home; exposed to open air, he worried the decay he had staved off would catch up with him.

Everything hurt.

A colophon appeared all over the place: a yellow capital H, bent in at the corners to fit a white oval shield. It was huge, if half-burned, on the face of the array, and in miniature on everything else. The oviform pommels on the guardrails were three-dimensional versions of the same logo.

"What's the H for?" asked Stacy. "Hers?" she suggested, thumbing at the awestruck Miss Gill. "Hellfire Club? Hugeness? Hidey-Hole?"

"H'egg?" suggested de Maltby.

"Head," said Head, touching one of the egg-shapes.

SWELLHEAD

Act II: Head Office

1

After the murderous wind and rain topside, the cavern was pleasantly temperate.

Though rusty on cutting edge high-tech, Richard Jeperson had seen the inside of enough military-industrial complexes to recognise the installation under Skerra as private enterprise rather than government. It was designed first to impress visiting shareholders, then to be a work environment.

Once the party had stopped exclaiming and clattering, he heard the thrumm of big engines somewhere below.

"Just heating and lighting this must suck an enormous wattage," he mused. "And we're well off the national grid. What d'you reckon, Yoland?"

The weapons inspector was thinking it through. "Geo-thermal, from the volcanic fault? That'd be extremely high risk. Ask the Pompeiians. My gut says it's the sea."

"Waves?"

"Could be. If they've found a way to harness the big whirlpool, that'd be something...exciting."

Huge banks of Wembley floodlights hung under the bare rock roof.

The entrance doors had led them onto a railed-off metal platform that was also a lift.

"Don't touch any controls..."

Onions issued his order while on his knees. He was entering the code to open his suitcase. Yoland ignored the dictate and picked up a plastic handset at the end of a python of insulated wire. He thumped the big button with the down arrow. Smoothly, without a lurch, the platform began to descend.

It had started to rain. The wind was so fierce that pellets of water came at them horizontally, or even from below.

"We should get out of this weather," said Persephone Gill. "Seriously."

"So speaks the classical Queen of the Underworld," said Jeperson.

"Also known as 'Proserpina,'" footnoted Head.

"Our business is down there, Adam," said Jeperson. "It is why we're here."

Onions made show of thinking it over.

"Until we find out what happened to Captain Vernon's team, I don't think we should risk..."

"We won't find out by standing up here catching our deaths," said Jeperson. "I deduce from this ladder that the estimable Captain and his hardy tars are quite likely down below."

"They were ordered to stay..."

Jeperson silenced him with a look.

"In case you'd forgotten, we're the professionals in this field. We're the psychic detectives, the occult adventurers, the ghost-hunters. And this hole leads to a haunted place. It's where we should be."

Jeperson bent to grasp the ladder and get his foot on a rung. His moon boot slipped, and Kydd grabbed his arm.

"Thank you," said Jeperson. "Nearly a nasty accident."

With Onions's torchlight on him, Jeperson made his way down the Blowhole. The reflective strips on his poncho shone red.

Kydd followed.

Onions reluctantly surrendered his torch to Stacy, which meant she'd have to go last. Before descending, Onions fastened a rope to his suitcase and lowered it to the temporary custody of Kydd. Once the others had touched bottom, she dropped the torch, which Onions managed to catch.

By the time she was at the foot of the ladder, the others were arguing about underground breezes. Though shielded from the worst of the rain and wind, there was a definite air current.

Onions played torchlight across ancient rock.

For a moment, Stacy assumed Captain Vernon's initial report had been a complete wind-up. This was just a hole in an island.

Then Sewell Head coughed.

And the rock walls parted with a metallic clang.

Bright, artificial light struck them blind.

She didn't want to laugh, but his boyish look of querying innocence tickled her.

"That's better. You were a smiler, not a pouter."

It was true. She had always been photographed showing her teeth. She thought that was why the agency made a fuss about them.

"Besides, I'm here, aren't I?" said Jeperson. "I could have thrown a pillow over my head, but I'm on the way to Skerra like the rest of our merry band."

"Have you been to the island before?"

"I don't know. Possibly."

9

The Blowhole was the highest point on Skerra. It looked like a volcanic crater, but the file said it was man-made, a vertical shaft sunk from the levelled-off plateau abutting the cliff into the water-carved caverns below. Steps hewn into the rock wound around the hole, though a post-it note on the page advised against attempting any descent without climbing gear.

Adam Onions, big orange suitcase fetched from the Sea King, stood at the lip of the Blowhole and pointed his torch down.

The "steps" were a wet-looking groove around the shaft. However, a ladder—orange rope and silver treads—dangled, secured to the rock by pitons.

"'Arne Saknussemm, His Sign,'" quoted Jeperson.

"Beg your pardon?" said Onions.

"*Voyage au centre de la terre,* Jules Verne," explained Sewell Head, the trivia champion, "1863, expanded 1867; translated, anonymously, into English as *Journey to the Centre of the Earth,* 1872."

"Also a film with James Mason," Kydd added.

"I'm *so* glad that's cleared up," said Onions.

Head scrunched the wrapper from a large bar of Cadbury's fruit and nut, held it over the Blowhole, and dropped it. Weighted by silver foil, it spiralled downwards, then an underground gust caught it and disappeared. For a moment, Stacy didn't know why her spine prickled. Then she realised the chocolate wrapper had been *sucked* rather than blown.

Pall Mall. Those who could be pensioned off, were. Some others were kept out of it with the threat of prosecution or worse. Fred was seconded back to his original job and began his long slow climb at the Yard. I, ah, had several *episodes* which did me no credit. There is such a thing as feeling too deeply. Mrs Empty, you'll gather, scrapped the South Atlantic gunboats too. You know how that played out."

"Where does Onions come into it?"

"O-*nye*-ons? He's a scientist, you know. Not a crackpot. Well, just because the Diogenes Club was out of commission didn't mean that the vast and strange forces of the world slacked off. There were still ghosties and ghoulies. And some official response was required. 'Pronounced "Eyesight"' was a typical Thatcher body — not responsible to parliament, a huge drain on public money, and with barely a result to show for it. But it is *scientific*. It's a wonder they didn't try to sell shares. Onions publishes enough to keep tenure and submits reports on the practical applications of the paranormal. John Major's man originally, he's very New Labour now. The woman who left her cap at that meeting is covertly the Minister for All Things Weird. 'Heritage and Sport' is a euphemism, of course. The last Big Idea was that economic blackspots were under ancient curses. Focus groups were quizzed as to how to lift the gloom. They came up with the Millennium Dome. One could be forgiven for weeping. The whole apparatus trundles along, most of the time. It has managed tolerably without me."

"And you? You left it all behind?"

"Took my bat and ball and repaired to Cheyne Walk. It was a relief, really — not having to *feel* anything any more."

He made her angry again. It was all very well to sneer at Onions and the government and the bloody dome. If he'd done anything in the last twenty-five years except stare at white walls and feed the cats, she might have been more inclined to sympathise.

"Good point," he said.

He had picked up her thoughts. It was like ice-points in her heart.

"I'm sorry," he said, genuinely. "We're just in tune. Fred knew we would be. You haven't tumbled yet."

"But I will?"

"Don't be peeved. It's not so terrible. What harm can I be, I'm a bitter old recluse, totally ineffectual and probably on drugs."

SWELLHEAD

"When I was under Winthrop, adventuring with Fred, successive governments were fractious. This is what happens when you become Prime Minister, or used to anyway. Just after you've had tea with the Queen and been given the launch codes for the independent nuclear deterrent, the Man From the Diogenes Club presents you with irrefutable evidence that there are more things in Heaven and Earth than came up on *Any Questions?* during the election campaign. If you're very polite, the Man tells you who Jack the Ripper was, what happened to the *Mary Celeste* and where that thing at Roswell the Yanks are so bloody sure is an alien spacecraft actually comes from. PMs shudder and stick their heads in the sand. The Diogenes Club is then left to get on with defending the realm from ghosties and ghoulies."

She thought of pressing him on the identity of Jack the Ripper, but the moment passed.

"Winthrop did Wilson and Heath. Your darlin' Harold grumbled a bit but sat up straight when he was shown a genuine fifteenth century manuscript describing the course late twentieth century history would take if British troops were committed to fight in Vietnam. Ted Heath got very enthusiastic and interested in curses and banes in the context of industrial relations, then bothered Winthrop with 'suggestions.' By the time Jim Callahan took over, Winthrop was gone and I wound up with the thankless task. Actually, that's inaccurate. Callahan said thank you very much. I told him that the chicken entrails suggested it might be an idea to keep a gunboat or two near the Falklands, and he said right-o. Otherwise, he continued as if we didn't exist. Which was as it should be. Then, in 1979...I bet you can guess the rest."

"Margaret Thatcher."

Jeperson raised his glass in toast.

"Got it in one, Stacy. Margaret Hilda Roberts Boadicca Thatcher. Not so much a new broom as a new defoliant."

"She refused to believe in anything?"

Jeperson smiled.

"Oh no. She knew it all before-hand. She had *associations*. The Club was never alone in its interests. It always had powerful rivals, and Mrs Empty...Mistress M. T....was a sponsee of the worst of 'em. There was talk of privatisation, but in the end she went for dismantling us, tearing up the historic charter, boarding up the premises in

So that was how he lost his hair!

"Diogenes was the philosopher who lived in the barrel," she said, "told Alexander to get out of his light."

Jeperson raised an eyebrow.

"I've been on trivia teams too," she said. "But what *is* the Diogenes Club? Everyone goes on as if it were famous, but I'd never heard of it."

"The original idea was to be obscure. It was a club for the unclubbable. Also, a trunk of our family tree of intelligence agencies. It was there for all the business the other plods weren't comfy with. Businesses like Misery Maudsley. That'd have been a Diogenes show in my day. Angel Down, Sussex. Tomorrow Town. The Seven Stars. Many other matters mysterious and malign. Few of which mean anything to the general public. Part of the game has always been protecting the Great British from knowledge deemed likely to send them off their collective nut."

"In my experience, the general public can cope with a lot."

"Maybe so," he said, swivelling his eyes to peer at her, thinking. "However, for more than a hundred years, the Diogenes Club was a court of last resort. The Ruling Cabal were the original 'spooks.' Before me, the Club harboured others with special interests. Mycroft Holmes, Charles Beauregard, Henry Merivale. Women, too: the Diogenes was the first gentleman's club to go co-ed. Katharine Reed, Catriona Kaye, Dion Fortune. My immediate sponsors were my adoptive father, Geoffrey Jeperson, and Beauregard's protégé, Edwin Winthrop. My intention was that Fred and...and another person, unknown to you...should succeed me. It didn't work out like that."

"What happened?"

"Nothing dramatic. Drip-drip-drip of history. Some might blame Arthur Conan Doyle. He let Dr Watson put in print the observation that Mycroft Holmes not only worked for the British Government but 'on some occasions, *was* the British Government.' Naturally, that earned a black demerit in Whitehall. Steps were taken to ensure that those occasions never reoccaised. Winston Churchill spent years trying to set limits on the remit of the Diogenes Club. He was a man for fixations, hanging onto Hitler, standing up to India (pardon me, t'wixt and about) and curbing that blasted Club."

Jeperson frowned and somehow made his face Churchillian. He laughed, breaking the illusion, and refilled his glass.

SWELLHEAD

frowned a little, but plodded off up the wooden hill to Bedfordshire without complaint.

This was the first time she had been alone with her charge since leaving his house thirty hours previously.

She still didn't know what to make of him.

"And who might you be, my dear?" he asked.

The snug was warm, but the question chilled her.

"Ah," said Jeperson. "We've met. Pardon me…"

He shut his eyes and massaged his temples. Then, he clicked his fingers.

"All present and correct, Stacy. Fearfully sorry to give you a fright."

The knot inside her relaxed. Jeperson was so spry and mercurial it was too easy to forget his fragilities.

He insisted on killing a bottle of thirty-year-old Scotch. After two busy days, a single tot made her head swim and she was seeing shapes in the fire. But he drank steadily without seeming more or less affected.

By firelight, his face was dramatic, almost pantomimish.

"CI Regent told me to catch up on my secret history," she ventured.

"Sound advice."

"But if it's secret…"

"I see your problem. Don't you have that welcomed-to-the-inner-circle feeling yet? Corridors of power, meetings with mandarins, transport laid on, Royals and Nobs, accommodation to order. It's very different from chasing villains and making court dates."

"I still get the impression I've not been *told* anything."

Jeperson chuckled. "I've been in this game as long as I can remember, and I mean literally, and I feel like that too. Of course, I'm supposed to be super-sensitive. I don't need to be *told*, because I have to keep on proving that I'm still sharp. I have to intuit, feel, *scry*…"

He waved his fingers.

"You and CI…you and Fred…used to work like this? In the seventies?"

"Not quite like this, though he also came to the Diogenes Club from the Met. Only just out of uniform. Shaved his head to go undercover with a bovver gang."

dered if she'd packed enough warm clothes. Before she boarded the train, her guv'nor took her aside, nodded at Jeperson, and said "he's special, take care of him." She agreed he was and promised she would.

The first leg didn't even get them half-way to Skerra. At Edinburgh Airport, they breakfasted and Persephone Gill joined the party, with luggage. A private jet, a luxurious waiting room with wings, flew them to Thurso, almost as far north on the Mainland as John O'Groats. Stacy had never been to Scotland before. Edinburgh seemed essentially London with different accents. Only after flying over green glens and glinting thin lochs for tedious hours did she have a real sense of being hideously off her patch.

If she'd been asked yesterday where Thurso was, she'd have ventured a guess at Antarctica; she wasn't sure now that she'd have been wrong. At home, whether in her flat or on duty, she knew how to get tampax, small-arms ammunition or last Thursday's daily papers at three in the morning. Here, she wasn't even sure what to ask for when she needed directions to the Ladies.

In Thurso, mid-afternoon, they all had complete medical check-ups at the Air Sea Rescue station clinic. She got a five-minute once-over and a nurse congratulated her on not being pregnant and having all her limbs. Jeperson was in with the woman for an hour and a half. Everyone else sat around a reception area. Sewell Head offered round Fisherman's Friends, and hers went tasteless during the wait. When let free, Jeperson shrugged an apology. He kissed the nurse's hand; she gave him a seal approval that struck Stacy as a lot more personal than the one everyone else in the party had stamped on their file.

Then they were all put in a "guest house," opened especially out of season. Before dinner, Viscount Henry de Maltby made himself known. He looked with disdain down Persephone's dress, said "*uhhhm*" several times, then had a huddle with Adam Onions to go over charts and reports. Aircrewman Kydd was there, too; rubber-faced and cheery, Falklands and Gulf War I insignia on his jersey shoulder.

"Better get an early night," suggested Onions.

That made Jeperson decide to stay up by the fire in the snug. Stacy's prime directive was to be his minder so she did too. Onions here before and scoped out the potential dangers. That was out the window.

"What do you suppose happened?" Persephone asked her.

"Nothing good."

The Droning of Skerra chewed that over. As the expedition's volunteer, she must be kicking herself. Really-a-Good-Bloke Rory had decided they ought to ask Persephone before camping out on her island. She'd given in to a whim, insisting she be taken along to check out her realm. Ascot was a wash this year, evidently.

Onions and Yoland climbed a wall which extended into the sea and walked out across the waves. Onions shone his torch at the A-Boat, which was in a sorry state, hull shattered below the waterline.

"We should be below," said Jeperson.

"Out of this bloody weather," put in Persephone. "Too right."

Head skinned the wrapper from a Twix and bit off both biscuit fingers at once.

"My understanding," said Jeperson, calling out to Onions, "was that all the observed manifestations were in the caverns. Up here, it's just wind and goats."

Yoland and Onions stuck out their arms like tightrope walkers and came back to shore, footing wobbly on none-too-secure stones. Yoland took a run at the last few feet and jumped onto dry land.

Onions made a show of coming to a decision.

"We should make our way to the Blowhole," he said.

Jeperson refrained from pointing out that he had made that suggestion when it was still light.

"Lead on," said Stacy.

Onions looked at his map and strode uphill.

Before his light got too far away, everyone fell in behind him.

8

CI Regent had turned up at Euston to see the party off on the midnight sleeper for Edinburgh. While Really-a-Good-Bloke Rory issued "non-optional suggestions" to the man from "Pronounced 'Eyesight'" and Sewell Head filled a carrier-bag with sweeties, Regent had a moment with Richard Jeperson. Stacy gathered they hadn't talked in over ten years. She hung back tactfully and won-

"We discourage that sort of talk, but yes...some other continuum, where things are put together differently. That clock is interesting. Turned up in a bus station in Eastbourne. We have it on the surveillance camera. Not there one instant, there the next. Its insides are the bones of small animals we can't identify, fit together with sticky gum we can't analyse, generating a small but quantifiable electric current. Because it didn't keep very good time, we thought it was something *disguised* as a clock. Then Mr. Head worked out that it keeps perfect time, if hours were to ebb and flow like the tides, getting longer then shorter again. The cycle is beyond me but he says it makes perfect sense."

Head nodded.

"So this is *pretending* to be your coat?" she asked Jeperson.

"No, this isn't like the clock. This *is* my coat. Messrs. Drecker and Coote, Savile Row and Carnaby Street. Made to my order in 1968. And this is my coat too. It has just come here by a different route."

"A rough route, by the looks of it," said Rory. "We DNA-tested the blood."

"Some of it's yours," said Onions, enjoying the thought.

"And the rest of it's mine," put in Sewell Head.

7

Skerra Landsby barely qualified as a ruin. All the buildings were roofless, and most of the walls had fallen. A War Memorial (Boer, 1914-18) was a brass plaque, names unreadable, plinth aswarm with bubblewrap seaweed. Stacy remembered mindlessly happy childhood days at Southend-on-Sea, bursting the little brown bags between thumb and forefinger, jimmying whelks off rocks with her Swiss army knife.

More collapsed tents flapped in the wind, tethered by skewers.

Onions's torch was the only light.

There was supposed to be a Royal Navy assault team here, despatched under cover of a training exercise, kitted out with arms to last through a small war. Her understanding was that the boffins' security would be provided by Captain Vernon's mob, who had been

SWELLHEAD

"Nothing in the constitution says everyone should be ambitious," continued Rory. "We dug out his old report book from Coal Hill Secondary Modern. Min Inf keeps copies of those, you know. I burned mine. Forgotten what your netball teacher thought of you, Detective Sergeant? We could find out. Any guesses which phrase came up all the time in young Sewell Head's reports? All his teachers said it. Over and over."

Jeperson stroked his moustaches. He nodded to Stacy.

"Could do better if he tried," she said, flatly.

Rory thumped the desk in delight.

"Spot bloody-on. Give *Juliet Bravo* a cuddly panda. Cripes, the brainpower in this room! Find a way to harness it, and we could light up Blackpool's Golden Mile."

Jeperson gave Rory a penetrating look, then left Head in his corner.

He took off his coat and threw it on the table. It flopped over Morag Duff's minidisc recorder, and lay like the king's deer tossed dead onto Guy of Gisbourne's table by Robin Hood.

"Adam," said Jeperson, seriously, "tell me about the apport."

Rory tried a "now-we-come-to-brass-tacks" chuckle but it died.

Onions looked at the coat. Stacy unrolled the brown paper and let the other coat (the same coat?) lie next to the original (copy?).

Onions bit his lower lip.

"Yes," said Jeperson, insistently, "they're the same. Not in the way two peas in a pod are the same, but in the way one unique special never-to-be-repeated, once-in-a-lifetime pea is the same as itself."

"What's an apport?" Stacy asked.

"A physical object manifested supernaturally," said Sewell Head.

"Rabbit out of a hat," footnoted Jeperson.

"At I-Psi-T, we've documented the phenomenon extensively," said Onions. "Apports are often household items. Inanimate. We have a collection. Hairbrushes, fireplace pokers, a clock with mangled guts. One theory is that they slip through wormholes, travel in time. Miss 1893 loses her garter and it pops up a hundred years later, to the bewilderment of all concerned. Others don't obviously come from the past or future but from somewhere else."

"Dimension Xxxx," said Jeperson in a hollow, echoey, radio announcer voice.

interesting Facts. Fifty, a hundred quid on the table. Side-bets with everyone in the bar to bump up the total stake. Quiz gets serious, one-on-one, make-your-mind-up-time. Our Mr. Head suddenly switches on like a toaster, goes from wondering if 'Lucky Lucky Lucky' was a hit for Bananarama..."

Head's lips twitched, a downturn at one side, peculiar pain in his glassy eye.

"...to rattling off the fifth paragraph of Article Ten of the Treaty of Utrecht of 1713..."

"And Her Britannic Majesty," said Sewell Head, conquering panic and rising to the occasion, "at the request of the Catholic King, does consent and agree, that no leave shall be given under any pretence whatsoever, either to Jews or Moors, to reside or have their dwellings in the said town of Gibraltar; and that no refuge or shelter shall be allowed to any Moorish ships of war in the harbour of the said town, whereby the communication between Spain and Ceuta may be obstructed, or the coasts of Spain be infested by the excursions of the Moors."

Rory laughed and pointed.

"I love this guy. Penny in the slot. He knows the answer. Anyway, by the end of the evening, Local Hero is bleeding from the arse, fallen faces all round the room. Our Mr. Head is off with a fistful of notes. And that's another pub off the list. They call him the Triv Terminator."

"It's not a memory trick," said Onions, warming. "He's not some autistic savant with a set of encyclopaedias. He's a puzzle-solver. We've never tested anything like him. He's a Talent. Off the scale."

Head shrugged modestly.

"I like to think things through," he said. "Make everything neat and tidy."

"Call him the Zen Master of Quantum Cleverness," said Rory.

"Duke have offered the dean's left nut for a free run at him," said Onions. "The Tibetans have their antennae a-twitch. He could take the field up to the next level. Scientifically verifiable. None of your 'feelings' and 'intuitions,' Jeperson. Cold, hard, steely data. And he can do it every time, under laboratory conditions."

Jeperson looked down at the little man.

"He works in a sweetshop," said Rory.

Onions gave a what-a-waste sigh.

livery systems for,' how did you put it, 'geography parcels and history parcels?'"

Yoland shook his head. "'Physics packages, chemistry packages or biology packages.'"

"In the long run, you're more right than you know," Jeperson told Rory. "It comes down to geography and history."

"Very true. Take a pew."

Jeperson walked round the room. He picked up the tam o'shanter and put it down again.

Yoland looked at the man from the Diogenes Club as if he might detonate.

At the opposite end of the table, a secretary sat with an open laptop, fingers poised over the keyboard. Jeperson smiled at her, acknowledging her presence with a little wave. She did not respond.

Jeperson found an odd little old man sat in the corner, away from the table, reading a book. A strange look arced between them.

"Don't mind him," said Rory. "That's Sewell Head."

"Swellhead," mumbled the little man.

Jeperson shook his hand, warmly.

Head was bald, with an odd, dome-shaped skull, no chin to speak of and flattish wet eyes. The sleeves of his shabby overcoat were too long for his childish hands. A knit scarf was wrapped several times around his neck, so his head nestled like an Easter egg in its presentation bow.

"He was Brain of Britain a while back," said Rory.

Head gave a puzzling smile, one Stacy had never seen demonstrated in a photograph. Almost lipless, he had a lot of extra teeth. He had eaten chocolate recently.

"Mr Head is Adam's discovery," said the civil servant.

"What's your IQ, Jeperson?" asked Onions. "Off the scale? Next to Sewell Head, you're a cretin. So am I. Technically, he's the cleverest man in England. Top Five in the world."

"Barred from pub trivia contests throughout the home counties," put in Rory. "You used to hustle, didn't you, old son? Guys, he would go in alone on quiz night, nurse a gin and it, then bungle a couple of easy ones. 'Who won the World Cup in 1966?' 'Was that perhaps Italy?' Big laughs. Then he'd get a bit tipsy. *Apparently,* tipsy. Come over all shirty, insist on a big money bet with Local Hero. You know the type, Captain Know-It-All, memorised his *Guinness Book of Un-*

were behind it, peeking through hidden eyeholes. This was the apparatus of the secret state, and spooks loved these games.

Jeperson was a study in suppressed excitement, alert to the point of hypertension, given to chewing on a knuckle. He had been in deep thought during the drive over.

Now, he took in the room. Three men sat like wise monkeys.

"Adam," Jeperson acknowledged the alpha ape, hear-no-evil.

"Richard Jeperson," grunted the bearish man. "We *are* calling out the reserves."

Stacy pulled out a chair for Jeperson, who insisted she take it. She ended up sitting across from the big man. He looked like a rugby player five years into beery middle-age, a slackening mountain in a baggy suit.

"This is Adam Onions," said Jeperson.

"O-*nye*-ons," he corrected. "Nothing to do with the vegetable. A whole different etymology."

"He is from the Institute of Something Trickology."

"I-Psi-T. Pronounced "Eyesight." The Institute of Psi Tech. Director of same."

Onions' eyes took in her chest. She didn't need to be psychic to know what he thought of her.

"I'm Stacy Cotterill. *Detective Sergeant*."

Onions did a not-a-secretary-then take. She'd seen that before.

"I don't know these other fellows, I'm afraid," said Jeperson.

"Call me Rory," said see-no-evil, a chunky cardigan chap who reminded her of an eager young vicar she'd arrested for molesting elderly parishioners. "I'm a civil servant, but don't hold it against me. I'm really a good bloke."

Rory smiled, delivering what Stacy recognised from her modelling days as Benign Variant Two. She wondered if he was working from the book they'd had at her agency, *101 Expression for All Occasions*.

"And this is Franklin Yoland…"

Say-no-evil put up his hand. He had a tan and lush lips.

"He's one of those Weapons Inspectors you hear so much about. Nothing he doesn't know about whizz-bangs, nerve gases and anthrax spores. Up on all the latest euphemisms. Made us laugh earlier…what was it, Frank? Yes, he was describing missiles as 'de-

SWELLHEAD

Stacy jogged down, miraculously avoiding a twisted ankle. She joined Jeperson in hauling the "bat" off Onions. It was a tent, trailing guy-ropes and skewers, poles snapped.

Kydd had drawn his revolver and assumed the stance. Now, with Onions free of the tent and sat on the ground, Kydd's gun was aimed at his head. He waved it aside, red-faced, hair stuck up in an undignified crown.

"You have been attacked by an item of rogue camping equipment," said Jeperson.

He helped Onions stand up.

The wind caught the tent again. It hurtled off like a crooked kite, chasing after Persephone's scarf.

Onions patted his hair and twisted inside his anorak, realigning the hip-pockets with his hips.

"Vernon was supposed to set up camp," he said.

Jeperson laid a hand on Onions's shoulder.

"Vernon is gone, Adam."

"We have to look."

Jeperson nodded and let Onions continue.

"Don't know what they're talking about half the time," Persephone said to her.

Stacy thought that was a fair average.

Onions had been right about one thing. It was getting dark.

6

The briefing was not at the Yard, but in Whitehall. From the yellowed ceiling, Stacy guessed the panelled, windowless committee chamber had been one of the legendary "smoke-filled rooms." New Labour had taken out the ashtrays and put up "thank you for not smoking" signs.

Notional chairperson was Morag Duff, Deputy Minister for Heritage and Sport, who didn't actually appear. A sound-activated minidisc recorder lay on her blotter at the head of the table. A tartan tam-o-shanter perched on the back of a chair, suggesting that the Deputy Minister had been here but just popped out.

Stacy looked at the Walter Sickert on the wall—saved from Patricia Cornwell by public subscription—and wondered if Duff

Stacy didn't point out that unless he wanted to become Persephone's sole subject he'd have to take the return trip.

"Should I get some grub up?" Kydd asked Jeperson.

"A very civilised notion."

"No time for that," said Onions, coming back. "We need to find Captain Vernon. I don't mind saying I'm worried about the A-Boat."

"Lost with all hands," said Jeperson.

"You can't know that."

"Quite right, Onions. I can't. But I do."

"Vernon had a six-man team."

"They're gone. Forget them."

Onions frowned. Jeperson lost interest and drifted away, towards Sewell Head. The little man hadn't brought a hat, and was trying to protect his bald dome with his hands. Jeperson gave him a knit-cap he had spare. Head smiled weak thanks.

Stacy noticed Jeperson was the only one who could talk with Sewell Head. She worried that they shared more with each other than anyone else here.

"We should get to the village," said Onions.

"The Blowhole, surely," ventured Jeperson.

Onions ignored him and strode downslope, expecting to be followed. Jeperson gave Stacy a look, then shrugged and plodded carefully after the Man From I-Psi-T. Stacy let the others get moving before taking up the rear.

De Maltby stayed with the Sea King, but Kydd came along.

A mean-eyed goat peered through a hole in the wall, cynically examining the newcomers. If war came, it'd be a toss-up who'd get eaten and who'd get to eat.

After only a few steps into merciless wind, down a field that inclined enough for a ski-slope, Stacy couldn't feel her face but was hobbled by pain in her ankles. She wished she had a city around her.

Onions paused to look at his flip-book.

A large blue bat attacked him, all spiny frame and enveloping membranes. He was wrapped in an instant, and spun off balance.

Sewell Head threw himself face-down in the dirt. Maltesers bled from his pockets.

Onions yelled from inside his blue cocoon.

"Shoot it, shoot it."

He seemed to flinch from daylight, from the outside world. Then he looked at her parcel.

"No choice," he said, striding through the doorway.

They left the house. Jeperson did not lock up behind them.

5

"It's your island, Miss Gill," Jeperson said to Persephone. "You be Neil Armstrong."

Stacy noted Onions sulking whenever Jeperson acted as if he were in charge. The Man From I-Psi-T needed to feel he was tour operator for this jaunt.

At Jeperson's nod, Kydd hauled the handle and swung open the door. The temperature in the back of the Sea King plunged.

"Best not," said Onions.

Persephone had unstrapped herself. Ignoring Onions, she slid across the floor and out of the helicopter.

"Mind the goats," Stacy advised.

Through the door, Stacy watched the Droning of Skerra stamp around, doing the hunting set version of t'ai chi — thumping the heels of her green wellies against grassy sod, flexing her back and thighs as if she were on horseback, and struggling against the wind to tie a Hermés scarf around her hair. She lost the scarf, which was sucked upwards by an invisible Kjempestrupe.

Nothing killed Persephone, so Stacy assumed it was all right to get out of the transport. She took off her ear-baffles and undid all the straps.

Jeperson made a "ladies first" bow. Stacy dangled her legs out of the helicopter, then took the jump. She realised how stiff she'd become and uncrooked her back.

Wind slashed her face.

Onions thumped onto the turf beside her, and strode off purposefully. Kydd helped the others leave the Sea King. De Maltby clambered down, snug in his flight-suit and helmet.

Yoland was on his knees, grateful for solid ground under him, grasping handfuls of Skerra.

"I wouldn't do that again in a hurry," he said, smiling.

The sound system was playing 'Rocky Raccoon.'

Jeperson looked at the makers' label. He held the coat against himself, mouth open in astonishment.

"This is..."

"Yours. We traced it through your tailor. They had the record on a hand-written card in a box in the basement. You bought it in 1968, about the time this album came out."

Jeperson shook his head. He was trembling, garment shaking in his grip. She thought he might have the beginnings of a seizure.

"It's the same cut as that one there," she added, nodding at the settee.

The kitten had escaped from its pocket and was trying claws out on the silk lining.

"I don't own two of *anything*. This *is* that coat over there. Where was this found?"

"You'd better come with me to the Yard."

Jeperson laid the coat down next to its identical twin.

"To help you with your enquiries," he said, frowning hard. "I think I better had. This, Stacy, is serious. This makes 'Misery' Maudsley look like a purse-snatching in Safeway's car-park. There isn't room in the world for two of this."

"I have a car waiting," she said.

He picked up his coat, the one she hadn't brought, dislodging the kitten. It nosed the döppelgarment, thought better of it, and dashed from the room. Jeperson slipped an arm into one sleeve, but needed her help with the other. His shoulder shook, almost spasming.

For a moment, he did look his age.

"You'd better bring *that*," he said, finger aimed at the surplus coat. "Wrap it up again. It should be sealed in lead, but sturdy brown paper will have to do."

She knew she was not suggestible. But she no more wanted to touch the coat than the kitten had, or Jeperson did.

Still, she picked up the paper, using it like an oven-glove, and took hold of the coat, wrapping it tight against the possibility that its arms might come to life and throttle her.

At the doorstep, Jeperson hesitated.

"It's been a very long time," he said, weakly. "I don't know if I can..."

Jeperson shook his head.

"So anyone could breeze along and filch the tomes? That's like tossing a sackful of loaded revolvers into a playgroup. Never have happened in my day."

He was enthused for a moment. Then he stopped.

"But I'm out of it. As you'll have gathered."

She said nothing. Jeperson wandered around his white room, touching things, looking away from her.

"It's all *parapsychology* now," he said. "Target figures and year-end reports and jolly-promising-results-minister. We had *mysteries*, Stacy. Riddles of the sphinx, conundrums of the incalculable. Not parapsychology, but parapsychedelia. Not phenomena, not anomalies, not quantum metaphysics, but *magic…enchantment…deviltry!*"

He stood by the table, fingers drumming on brown paper.

He looked at her, eyes piercing, looked at the package, bit the end of his moustache, looked at her again.

"What's in the parcel?"

"I thought you said you were out of it."

"*Minx!* What's in the parcel?"

"You of all people should know what they say about cats and curiosity."

Jeperson picked up the parcel, like a six-year-old with a present on Christmas Eve. He shook it, and held it to his ear.

"Very light for its size. Not a case of wine or an occasional table, then."

He squeezed and crackled.

"Feels fabricky. Like a blanket. Or a party frock."

He tweaked something through the paper.

"Brass buttons. It's a coat. I've guessed. I'm right, aren't I? A coat, found in evidence. Bullet-holes and bloodstains."

His mood switched, from playful to serious. She felt a chill.

"I'm right about that, too," he said, sober.

"Open it," she urged.

"Very well," he decided. "For you. Because you told me about Maudsley's eyes. But no commitment. This is not going to be Richard Jeperson Rides Again."

He slipped a tiny blade out of his sleeve and snipped the string. The paper fell away and he held a stiff, grayish green coat. There were bulletholes in the left sleeve and the hip pocket. And old blood.

Whatever threatens the fabric of our reality will prove a nice change from playing solitaire with rhine cards or theorising undetectable assassinations or whatever Adam Onions's little helpers do to justify their expenses claims."

She waved him to a halt.

"This is too much for me, Mr. Jeperson..."

"Richard, please..."

"This is too much for me, *Richard*. Until this morning, I'd never heard of you or the Diogenes Club and I'm really not up to speed. CI Regent..."

"Fred..."

"*CI Regent* has requested that I work with you."

"Very clever. Chuck the old dog a dolly-mixture and creep up with the muzzle."

Hot-cheeked, she stood up.

"You resent that," he said.

"They told me you were perceptive."

He was up too, close to her, hands around hers, radiating sincerity.

"I apologise. I forget myself. As I mentioned."

She damped her momentary anger. But she wasn't ready to trust this dinosaur.

"Fred Regent wouldn't have sent you round if you were only blonde. You collared 'Misery' Maudsley, did you not? Fred must have fought hard to keep that little brouhaha out of Onions's remit. Tell me, it wasn't in any of the papers, but...when you slapped the cuffs on him, was Maudsley doing something with his eyes, something more than looking at you?"

She remembered. A squirming. Like REM dreamtwitches, but with the eyes wide open.

"I thought so," said Richard, wheeling across the room. "Maggots. Little tiny maggots, hatched and hungry. An inconvenience, at the least. Always the problem with reanimation by force of will. Any qualified *houngan* cures the corpse before raising the *zombi*. Still, Maudsley got his job done. What happened to his books? Mislaid in the evidence room as usual?"

"Everything from the house went. There was no court case pending, so the coroner brought in an open verdict. Maudsley's stuff got tossed into a skip."

interesting Englishman. Unlike me. I'm foreign, you know. Non-specific, but foreign."

He slipped back the cuff of his kaftan, to show a blue tattooed number.

"Adopted by an Englishman, adopted by the Club. Raised for the position, as it were. I'm a foundling of War. I must have had a name and a nationality before 1945, but the cylinders don't fire up here."

He tapped his temple.

"Nothing before the Liberation. A few other gaps, sadly. It's been a crowded life, so I have had to forget things to make room. Wish I could have planned better. I remember a great many things it would make sense to forget. But not…"

He let the thought dangle and opened a door.

The white study was striplit. Windowpanes were whitewashed to match the walls, ceiling and carpet. A large picture hung opposite, canvas as blankly white as the frame. A milk-white shelving unit contained books with white, featureless spines. Soft white plastic cubes formed a settee along one wall and chairs around the room. Hard white plastic boxes made a desk and tables. A perfect-bound magazine for the blind, glossy pages stamped with Braille, lay open on a low table. A towering sound system, white as a fridge, played 'Happiness is a Warm Gun.' The almost-invisible CD jewel-case on the floor reminded her the song was from the *White Album*.

"This is a visually sterile environment," Jeperson explained. "I need it sometimes. There is too much information out there to process comfortably. I have an open mind. That's my gift and curse."

Jeperson sat, arms laid along the back of the settee, shrugging out of his coat, long legs crossed. He motioned her to do make herself comfortable. She put her parcel on the low table, a violent intrusion of brown, and sat on a stool.

"Is that a present? For me?"

"CI Regent asked me to bring it to you."

"Ah-ha. It's evidence, isn't it? This is a *case*. You know I'm retired? I don't consult or sleuth or intuit or adventure. Not my decision. Things changed. Certain elements among our rulers made judgements. The Diogenes Club closed its doors. I am given to understand that some quango took over our duties. You can probably reach them in a unit on an industrial estate in Wolverhampton.

He spoke like a theatrical knight, but his eyes were lively. She could imagine him headlining the Glastonbury Festival in 1972 or playing Don Quixote in a silent movie.

She introduced herself as DS Cotterill.

"Stacy," he said, surprising her. "Interesting career."

She was surprised he kept up with New Scotland Yard.

"Teenage model, then policewoman. Why the change?"

Almost no one mentioned it any more. At Hendon Police College, she had done extreme things to blokes who thought it funny to go on about her after-school job. Jeperson had wrong-footed her, though he seemed genuinely interested rather than attempting a put-down.

"It's no life for a grown woman without an eating disorder," she said, uncomfortable. "And the agency dropped me when I refused to have my back-teeth pulled. It was supposed to make my face look thinner."

He cocked his head to one side, then the other, considering her face.

"I bet they wanted to keep the teeth."

"As a matter of fact they did. All the girls' teeth. In jam-jars in a cupboard, individually labelled. In solutions of brine."

"Better than a contract. You're well out of that."

Jeperson looked at her face first and last. Which made him different from ninety-five percent of men. That shouldn't be a surprise; everything about him was different. She found herself almost disarmed, then remembered he was mad.

"Come through to the study," he said, dislodging the Siamese, who streaked squirrel-fast up branches to the second-floor landing. The plant was a spreading green apocalypse, a tree that became a vine when it suited. It was stapled to the wall in several crucial places.

"Would you believe this began as a cutting? From *yggdrasil*, the Norse world-tree. A gift to the Diogenes Club from William Morris in the days of gaslight and pea-soup fogs. When Mycroft Holmes sat on the Ruling Cabal. Brother of the more famous. Charles Beauregard lived in this house then. You wouldn't have heard of him, though some scholar has been struggling to research a biography for years. I met Beauregard once, when I was a little lad. Nearly a hundred, but kept *au fait* with the comings and goings. A very

SWELLHEAD

The clear glass pupil of the Egyptian eye darkened. A real eye looked out at her: startling silver-flecked blue-gray iris trapped in veinous cobweb.

She held up her warrant-card.

"Come on in," boomed a voice. "S'not locked."

She took the handle and pushed the door, which resisted. A small avalanche of newspapers, pizza menus, minicab cards, AOL start-up discs, estate agent's brochures and letters from the council shifted, was ground under, then stopped the door dead at half-open.

Stacy turned sideways and slipped into the house.

She smelled incense, sweet and heavy. The long, narrow, crowded foyer rose three storeys to a murky glass roof. Potted plants exploded from tubs and grew up banisters, reaching tendrils toward the distant sun. Odd objects were piled at random: books of all formats and thicknesses, primitive masks, fancy dress finery, dissected animals under glass domes, unsleeved vinyl records, unnameable musical instruments, ancient valve wirelesses in various states of dismantlement, obscure statuary. And multiple cats — which explained the milk. They roamed free, clambering and searching.

"You must be from Fred."

Richard Jeperson stood before her: tall, thin and gaunt. He could have been any age, but working it out from the backstory — child in the War, career in the 1970s — Stacy knew he must be in his mid-sixties. When younger, he'd looked older; now, he just looked himself. Dramatic streaks ran through the Zapata moustache, but the long fall of tight curls was glossily black. He had the pale skin of someone who's stayed indoors for decades, deep-etched around those silver-flashing eyes but unslack under the chin, unspotted on the backs of his hands.

A Persian kitten peeped out of a pocket and a Siamese cat perched on his shoulder like Long John Silver's parrot. He wore suede winkle-picker shoes, pinstripe city gent trousers, a turquoise kaftan tunic belted with a sash, and, as if to offset the Siamese, a gold-frogged green velvet great-coat over his other shoulder, pocket unflapped so the kitten could breathe.

"You expected Howard Hughes fingernails and a Ben Gunn beard?"

As the Sea King descended, propwash whipped grass into crop circles. De Maltby searched for a likely landing spot.

Onions waved downwards, indicating to the pilot the urgency of making ground.

Even as they hovered, the island slipped out from under the Sea King. De Maltby had to fight strong winds to avoid dipping in the drink. An intermittent stone wall rimmed what had once been a field. De Maltby put the Sea King down by it. After the rotors stopped, there was still whirring — the wind, trying to wipe the island into the sea.

"I own this carbuncle," said Persephone Gill. "Any offers? I'd have to abdicate, but I think I could be persuaded by any convincing bid. A bean and a button?"

Stacy wasn't tempted. Even if owning Skerra meant being able to call herself a princess.

"Let's get out and find camp," said Onions. "It'll be dark soon."

It wasn't quite lunch-time and night was about to fall.

No wonder Princess Percy wasn't surprised by the lack of potential buyers.

4

In Chelsea, Stacy told her driver to wait in the car and searched for the address she'd been given. She had the brown-paper parcel under her arm.

The house didn't show a street-number. Inset in the front door, where neighbours had number-plates, was an art nouveau stained-glass panel with an Ancient Egyptian eye motif.

When Stacy thumbed the button, a bell jangled inside the house. Shadows shifted.

She noticed the milk — eight bottles — hadn't been taken in. A rain-eaten roll of free newspaper was rammed into the letter-slit, drooping like a fag from the mouth of a charlady in a 1970s ITV sit-com. Freesheets were the burglars' friend — you couldn't stop them when you went on holiday. From the looks of this place, the home-owner never went on holiday. She wondered why CI Regent thought he'd stir himself now.

SWELLHEAD

Being a princess evidently wore thin.

"And any woman who wants to challenge for the iron crown has to face you in single combat," Jeperson added.

"They're welcome to try."

The Sea King circled the whirlpool, clockwise to its anticlockwise. It was too much for Yoland, who finally spewed. Aircrewman Kydd tactfully provided a paper bag.

"Does he have to?" asked Persephone, infinitely weary.

"Yes, love, he does," said Kydd.

The Droning of Skerra didn't care to be addressed as "love." Kydd was too busy tidying up after Yoland to notice her moué of annoyance.

"Better out than in, sir," said Kydd, with cheery deference.

Yoland nodded something like thanks.

The helicopter passed over the Kjempestrupe and approached the island. Skerra was a volcanic extrusion, originally expelled through a hernia in the planet's crust, bursting molten above the seas to solidify like an igneous loaf, then shaped and sculpted by unrelenting wind and water. When the satellite pictures came in, the first theory was that the volcano was active again. Met office wags nicknamed it "McKrakatoa."

The squared-off cliffside had been gouged out by millennia of brutally battering waves. A torrent poured into the vast cavemouth and washed back out again as froth. The island was hollow, like a decayed tooth. It should eventually collapse on its caverns and become rocks strewn across the seabed, lamented by no one but map-maintainers and reduced-to-commoner female Gills.

The ridge of the cliff whizzed below.

There wasn't a tree on the island, though its upper slopes were infested with long, thick grass. Survivalist goats had persisted after the people left, the toughest specimens emerging from some cave-shelters to reclaim the surface. Their savage descendants looked to the sky as the helicopter passed overhead, but did not abandon tussock-chewing to run for cover. DeMaltby and Kydd had been issued small arms, but Stacy fancied Skerran goats likely resistant to everything this side of depleted uranium shells. They were a prison population: faces smashed by headbutting hornfights, flanks ripped by scars like tattoos, each lifer the perpetrator of multiple rapes and dreeps.

The hardy, vicious flocks of goats that supported the local economy and ecosystem (and fashion statements) declined over the centuries and were all but extinct by 1932, when the last remaining islanders were evacuated to unimaginable Southlands. This emergency measure led to the dumping of a knot of insular, Innsmouth-featured folk in a Glasgow slum. Their descendents were allegedly the city's most violent criminal gang. One of the few surviving words of the Skerran tongue was 'dreep,' underworld slang for an especially horrific form of murder-by-torture.

Sir Piers Gill (né Paddy Kill) had bought Skerra from another private owner when Persephone was six, so his daughter could legitimately call herself a princess. This was the first time the Droning had come within five hundred miles of her island realm.

Stacy saw where waves washed the incline. Rising seas had swallowed the harbour decades ago. Choppy waters swirled around the few stone skeletons that remained of Skerra Landsby, the abandoned village.

"Look," said Onions, "the A-Boat."

It was caught in among the shattered buildings, on its side, mostly underwater. If the hull hadn't been rust-red, the boat would have passed for a reef.

Onions whistled.

"How the hell did that happen?"

"Strange waters," commented Richard Jeperson. "Look at the whirlpools."

There were three around the village end of Skerra, spinning like submarine Tasmanian Devils, and a far larger maelstrom to the north.

"The Kjempestrupe," said Jeperson. "It's as if God pulled the plug."

For the first time, Mr Head took an interest. He closed his *Petesuchis* and peered out the window.

The Kjempestrupe was a funnel in the sea. It seemed bottomless, spiral walls of whirling water keeping open an impossible chasm.

"Any man who wants to marry you is supposed to brave that in a coracle," Jeperson told Persephone. "Otherwise he's not fit to be consort to the Droning of Skerra."

Persephone looked as if she had heard the legend so many times it wasn't even worth commenting on.

SWELLHEAD

"Come off it, Ellbee," she said. "I happened to be in the office with a clearish desk when the guv'nor wanted a parcel delivered to Chelsea. End of story."

"Mind how you tread in the dark, Stace."

Somebody else who had lived in Cheyne Walk was Bram Stoker. Stacy remembered the peasant pressing her crucifix on the young man on his way to Castle Dracula.

This wasn't how she usually thought of Sergeant Ellbee. She put his theory into practice and adjusted to accept it.

In the car on the way to Chelsea, the driver didn't speak to her.

The only thing Maudsley had said as she was bringing him in was "a cavern, far North." She had thought it random sparking in a broken brain, not even addressed to her.

Now, she wondered if Misery had known about Skerra.

3

At first sighting, the island was a greenish thumbnail barely stuck out of the sea. Then, as the helicopter neared, Skerra looked more like a sinking aircraft carrier: an oblong wedge rising steeply, sloping deck sliding into the ocean, barnacled stern lifted clear of the water.

They circled. Stacy got a good look at the place.

Skerra was a British Isle, but only for cartographers' convenience. Too far North to be a Shetland (let alone an Orkney), the outcrop lay alone and desolate in cold gray water between Iceland and the Norwegian coast. As much, or as little, Scandinavian as Scots, a case could be made for calling it the Easternmost Faroe. In the reign of Macbeth (yes, that one), Skerra had been gifted to Scotland among the dowry of the Princess of Denmark. An agreed reciprocal tribute went unpaid, so the transfer of sovereignty was moot. If either crown had regarded it as a possession rather than a dependency, Skerra might have become a mediaeval Schleswig-Holstein Question. As it was, Dunsinane and Elsinore remained barely aware that such a place existed. The islanders looked to their own matrilineal monarchy.

The title of Droning still existed, but the Skerrans didn't.

"Not with *his* haircut. Richard Jeperson was a private consultant. A spook. The spooks' spook, in fact. Ever hear of the Diogenes Club?"

She hadn't.

"Read your Sherlock Holmes, girl."

She had the feeling everyone knew more than she did. Regent had given her the bare bones and a large brown-paper parcel tied with pink string.

"Diogenes wasn't a club, really," continued Ellbee. "It was a Department of Dead Ends. Like our old, pre-PC Bureau of Queer Complaints. That was nothing to do with policing Gay Pride marches. Know why the CI's thrown you this scrap? Fred's had an eagle eye on you ever since the Maudsley murders."

Stacy didn't think the case was her finest hour. It had seemed a simple, if gruesome triple homicide. A middle-aged man found in a fugue state in his own home, sitting amid the remains of three diced street kids. Evidence indicated that the vics, all well-known to the courts, had entered the premises with unlawful intent and received something very like just desserts. A history of ill-will existed between the district's druggies and the reclusive householder, Mantan "Misery" Maudsley.

Before the likely perpetrator could be roused enough to understand formal charge, Maudsley perished in his cell. Not just died, *perished*. Autopsy suggested he'd been dead for three weeks at the time of arrest. When Stacy had met Maudsley, he wasn't speaking much or smelling fresh but had been capable of walking about. The file was still open.

"Some plods go through a whole career without anything like 'Misery' Maudsley," said Ellbee. "Others clock Scooby-Doo cases every week but never tumble to the way the world *really* works. You took it in, Stace. Adjusted to accept it. When he was with Diogenes and Richard Jeperson, that was Fred Regent's special knack. He thinks you've got something similar."

She remembered the sick, clear atmosphere after the Maudsley case, the way station-mates treated her differently, the eagerness of her shift commander to get her onto something else quickly. It wasn't something she had enjoyed at all. She didn't relish the prospect of anything more in that line.

2

Two days earlier, DS Cotterill learned she was to be despatched to the blue plaque jungle of London, SW3. In New Scotland Yard, CI Frederick Regent ran off a list of who else had lived in Cheyne Walk, Chelsea.

"Isambard Kingdom Brunel, George Eliot, Turner, Mrs Gaskell, Whistler (of 's Mother fame), Dante Gabriel Rosetti, a bunch of other pre-raphs, Thomas Carnacki, Henry James. With Carlyle round the corner in Cheyne Row."

Stacy said she'd heard of them all, except Carnacki.

"Carnacki the Ghost-Finder, Cotterill," her guv'nor said. "Secret history. Bone up on it."

Easier said than done.

It struck her that the guv'nor either wished he was going out on this call himself or was profoundly grateful seniority kept him snug in his office. Or both at the same time. Regent was a funny specimen of top cop. Higher-ups didn't often let him do telly interviews. Gossip at the Met was that he was the only senior officer ever to turn down a CBE, nearly get married to Diana Rigg and earn the honour of laying the wreath on Joey Grimaldi's grave at the annual Clowns" Service at Holy Trinity Church in Dalston.

Stacy didn't fully realise how out of the ordinary the errand was until Regent told her to take a chit to Sergeant Ellbee, who would scare her up a driver and car. That luxury was a first in her career.

Ellbee recognised the address and laughed.

"Haven't seen that one in an age, Stace," said the sergeant, who had a London Welsh accent. "Surprised Jeperson is still alive, what with all he went through. Put the guv'nor through, too. How do you think Fred Regent lost his hair?"

It wasn't something she'd ever considered.

"The famous Richard Jeperson," clucked Ellbee. "Name from the seventies. Sixties, even. Fab crazy gear, man. Austin Powers era. Watch out he doesn't try to shag you, baby."

"Was he a copper?"

Dante) reckoned the Viscount more or less Royal than the Droning of Skerra, but in this party of geniuses and idiots he was the one Stacy felt herself level with in the middling cleverness bracket. Shame his Hapsburg lip was so developed that it resembled a facial foreskin.

With a wink, Kydd handed her a mug of English breakfast. It was a plastic beaker with a childproof top. She nodded thanks and drank.

The tea hit the spot.

"Perhaps you should look in your big orange suitcase," Jeperson suggested to Onions. "Check if your anemometers are all in order."

After consideration, Onions got back to his seat. He was most particular about his kit, which indeed came in a big orange suitcase. Jeperson said it was full of ghost-hunting gear.

They shared the troop compartment with an all-terrain vehicle, weighted down by neatly-stowed supplies and equipment. The ATV occasionally shifted on its tethers. If it got loose, it would crush them all.

The intercom crackled.

"Skerra up ahead," said de Maltby, sounding uncannily like his great-great uncle abdicating from the throne. "We should be aground in...*uhhhm*...about ten minutes."

Yoland thanked the gods but had to gulp back his silent words. He waved away Kydd's tea.

"Exciting, isn't it?" Jeperson said to her. "Venturing into unknown territory."

She wasn't exactly sure how she felt.

"Look, sir, you can see the island."

Kydd pointed out of a window. Jeperson casually turned to glance at Skerra. Onions lurched from his seat, again hanging apelike from strapholds, and peered at the seascape, searching for their destination.

"There," said Jeperson. "Such a tiny scrap of rock."

The only thing this assignment had in common with regular police work was that Stacy had the usual feeling of coming in late and having to pick up story threads before she could make any progress.

If she was to cope with Skerra, she needed to catch up.

her Richard Jeperson knew more arcane facts than anyone alive, but that whole years were missing from his memory banks. Stacy supposed that if she lost her primary school years or Thatcher's second term, she'd be as concerned as Jeperson with accessing what was left in her skull. Still, he wasn't someone she was comfortable around. She wondered again why she'd drawn this duty.

"What's that?" asked Onions, voice raised.

"Nothing important," said Jeperson, dismissing the inquiry with a flutter of long fingers. "Are we there yet?"

Jeperson perfectly mimicked the stereotypical whine of a bored child on a long car journey. His prog rock moustache, coal-black but flashed white at the corners, twitched with amusement.

It took Onions long seconds to tumble that he was being spoofed. He looked at the plastic-wrapped chart in his mittened paws before he got the joke, then made a sour face.

"Very mature," he commented.

Jeperson gave Stacy a private eyebrow-wiggle. She almost warmed to him.

Onions detached himself from the webbing and, unsteady as an astronaut going EVA, hauled himself down the compartment to confer with (ie: nag) Lieutenant de Maltby.

"Cuppa char, sir?" asked Aircrewman Kydd, a cockney gnome. His duties obviously included keeping the passengers from distracting the driver while the bus was in motion.

Kydd held out a thermos, face arranged into a feral smile.

Onions hung from hand-holds, unsure.

"I'd care for some tea, if that's all right," said Jeperson. "And maybe the ladies…"

Kydd, who knew a proper gent when he saw one, delivered a real smile and a salute. He had different flasks for English breakfast, orange pekoe and lapsang souchong.

"Best not bother the Viscount," Jeperson told Onions. "He probably has a lot on his mind, what with avoiding diplomatic offence to our esteemed allies in Oslo or Reykjavik. Last thing we need is another Cod War."

Lieutenant de Maltby was Viscount Henry de Maltby, somewhere in the mid-thirties in line of succession to the throne. He had the House of Windsor habit of being unable to string together a sentence without saying *uhhhm*. It was not settled whether Debrett (or

Onions ("O-*nye*-ons," he had insisted, understandably) looked up, as if jolting awake inside his expensive parka. Stacy noticed he always kept half an eye on Jeperson, like a bear sharing a cave with a languid adder. Onions adjusted his baffles, exposing an ear.

She glanced around. None of the others were interested.

Mr Head munched a Lion bar, fixated on *Petesuchis,* a high-end crossword magazine. The little man, whose boiled egg baldpate and wide watery eyes suggested something without bones, did not fill in a puzzle, just solved all the clues mentally, left the grid virginal, and proceeded to the next, more challenging page. Onions had told her *Petesuchis* scorned newsstand distribution. The publishers set an entrance exam for the subscription list, charging on a sliding scale, lower price for higher grades. Adam Onions paid a thousand pounds a year for thirteen slim numbers; Sewell Head got his for free.

Persephone Gill, the Droning of Skerra, wore tiny walkman earclips under her baffles, nodding serenely to something bland. Once she got past the notations in "Percy" Gill's file ("21 years old, inheritrice of the most unearned wealth in the United Kingdom, no educational qualifications"), Stacy was still venomously glad the girl had been voted out of the mansion at the first cull of Channel 4's *Posh Big Brother.*

Franklin Yoland, the tech guy, gripped his webbing, white-faced and praying for deliverance. He suffered from airsickness and flight terrors, perhaps not ideal qualities in an editor of *Jane's Book of Air-Launched Weapons.*

"I'd been trying to remember," Jeperson explained to Stacy. "You know what it's like when you have something in your head but can't fish it out. The name of a tune you hear in a fresh arrangement. The new capital city of a country that's changed its name. Whether Dante ranks virtuous pagans above or below Christian hypocrites in Hell. Pidgin English for 'helicopter.'"

Through a floor-set plexiglass bubble that sealed a gunport, she saw the arrowheaded shadow of the Royal Navy Sea King Mk4 rushing across the Norwegian Sea at 100 knots. Crescents of sunglint flashed on roofslate gray waters. Lieutenant de Maltby, the pilot, flew almost at wave-level, under radar.

"Bloodybuggerinmixmaster blong Jesus Christ."

Jeperson nodded to himself, happy that his pidgin vocabulary was filed away neatly. In London, Chief Inspector Regent had told

Swellhead
Kim Newman

Act I: "Arne Saknussemm, His Sign"

1

"Bloodybuggerinmixmaster..." said Richard Jeperson.

Detective Sergeant Stacy Cotterill looked across the troop compartment at the Man From the Diogenes Club. Since take-off from the Air-Sea Rescue helipad, he'd been sitting quietly, secured by webbing which reminded her of a strait-jacket. He wore a dayglo orange oilskin poncho with reflective road safety trim, folded newspaper hat that was actually a PVC sou'wester with a novelty design, padded plaid jumpsuit with multiple pockets and pouches, and lemon-yellow moon boots with chemical lights in the heels.

For his first enigmatic pronouncement in hours, Jeperson didn't seem to need to raise his voice. Stacy heard him clearly over the chopping whirr of rotors, through the big blue baffles everyone wore to protect their ears.

"...blong Jesus Christ," Jeperson added, emphatically.

She wondered if, in addition to everything she'd been briefed on, the old man had Tourette's Syndrome.

Kim Newman

those grittier corners the tourists rarely see. At the heart of the story is Maceo, an ex-con and doomed loner whose faulty instincts lead him from one predicament to another. His troubles begin in earnest when he and Leeli, his newfound girlfriend, meet up with a strange, otherworldly "family" dominated by the ageless, sexually voracious Ava. The result of this conjunction of volatile forces is a haunting, enigmatic story — Jim Thompson meets the Twilight Zone — that no one but Shepard could have written.

These three powerful stories are as different from one another as any three stories could be — different in tone, theme, technique, setting, and perspective. Together, they add up to a multi-faceted celebration of contemporary fantasy at its darkest and most developed. The stories you are about to encounter may unsettle and disturb you. But they will also, I believe, delight and entertain you, and take you to places you have never visited before.

Here, then, without further interruption, is *Night Visions 11*.

Enjoy.

INTRODUCTION

ture of Life As We Know It. James Bond fans will find themselves on very familiar ground in this one.

Tim Lebbon, the youngest contributor here, was born in London in 1969 and currently resides in South Wales. In a remarkably short time, he has amassed a large, uncompromising body of fiction, and has built a solid reputation as one of the rising stars of contemporary horror. Lebbon is, in the truest sense of the term, a horror writer. His stories deal with loss and survival, love and commitment, madness and despair. They confront without flinching the brutal, sometimes enigmatic forces that can erupt without warning into the most stable and settled of lives. Readers interested in horror fiction with teeth should check out his superb collection of short fiction, *As the Sun Goes Down,* his deeply unsettling full-length novel, *Face,* and his exemplary collection of novellas, *White and Other Tales of Ruin.* This, as they say, is the real, unadulterated thing.

Lebbon's contribution to *Night Visions,* "In Perpetuity," is an authentically nightmarish account of a decent, ordinary man who has recently lost his wife, and who finds himself in imminent danger of losing his only son. The story begins when Lebbon's hero wanders into a picturesque antique shop with his four-year-old son, Sammy. Before he leaves, he will watch as Sam is kidnapped by a crazed "collector" with unnatural powers, and will find himself launched on a strange, perhaps impossible, quest. "In Perpetuity" is a raw, painful story, and it poses questions most of us will never have to face, such as: How far would you go in the name of love?

Our final contributor, Lucius Shepard, was born in Lynchburg, Virginia in 1947. On the evidence of his fiction, however, he appears to have lived in or visited almost every corner of the civilized — and not so civilized — world. A superb stylist and a consummate observer, Shepard writes fiction that is beautiful, passionate, brutal, ironic, and always fully engaged. His stories move with equal authority from Seattle to Central America, from Nantucket to New Orleans, from Mexico to the fragmented societies of post-Soviet Russia. At its frequent best, as in "Salvador," "Delta Sly Honey," and the Nebula Award-winning "R & R," his work is as vivid and evocative as anything being written in America today.

Shepard's *Night Visions* novella, "Hands Up! Who Wants to Die?", is a tale of sex, violence, and damnation that ranges up and down the state of Florida, from the sanitized preserves of DisneyWorld to

BILL SHEEHAN

Other recent, memorable examples include "Needing Ghosts" by Ramsey Campbell, "Cleopatra Brimstone" by Elizabeth Hand, "The Hellbound Heart" by Clive Barker, "Father Panic's Opera Macabre" by Thomas Tessier, "The Skin Trade" by George R. R. Martin, "Carrion Comfort" (in its original incarnation) by Dan Simmons, and virtually the entire contents of the millennial anthology, *Revelations*, edited by Douglas E. Winter. The list extends indefinitely, and contains numerous stories by the three contributors represented here: Kim Newman, Tim Lebbon, and Lucius Shepard.

Kim Newman, a dapper, London-based novelist born in 1959, must, by now, be sick to death of being described as "clever." He is, it must be said, extremely clever, and has produced an impressive—and utterly unique—body of work. But Newman is more than merely clever. He is a formidable storyteller with a wickedly satirical eye and a gift for fluent, fast-paced narratives. He also possesses a bottomless familiarity with the history of popular culture in the 20th century. He is probably best known for the *Anno Dracula* novels, which present an ingeniously sustained portrait of a world in which Dracula defeats Van Helsing and his cohorts, and engenders a society in which vampirism not only survives, but flourishes. He has also written a remarkable portrait of a modern Faustian bargain (*The Quorum*), an episodic, hugely entertaining pulp adventure (*Seven Stars*), and an inexhaustible choose-your-own-adventure novel (*Life's Lottery*) in which the reader makes choices that determine the direction the book's many narratives will take. Newman's novels and stories comprise a loose but coherent fictional universe. They are dense with interconnections and pop culture references, and are a consistent pleasure to read.

Newman's contribution to *Night Visions 11* is "Swellhead," a bravura piece of storytelling featuring Richard Jeperson, hero of such earlier adventures as "Tomorrow Town" and "Egyptian Avenue." Jeperson, a member in good standing of Newman's ubiquitous Diogenes Club, is a consulting investigator drawn repeatedly into weird, uncanny situations. Jeperson's previous investigations have all taken place in the 1970s. This time out, Newman sets his story in 2003, dragging an aging—but still stylish—Jeperson out of retirement, placing him on the storm-wracked island of Skerra, and setting in motion a hallucinatory conflict which will determine the fu-

Introduction
Bill Sheehan

Welcome to the latest installment of the newly revived *Night Visions* series. Like its predecessors, *Night Visions 11* offers a generous selection of original work by three gifted — and very different — writers. Unlike its predecessors, this latest volume consists solely of novella-length stories, each of them the product of a master of the form.

In many respects, the novella is among the most satisfying of all narrative modes, combining the range and complexity of the novel with the brevity and heightened focus of the short story. Henry James, who created such sublime examples of the form as *The Turn of the Screw*, referred to it as "the blest nouvelle." Peter Straub, commenting on his own literary preferences, has said that novellas "have a special place in my affections. [They] allow me to relax into characters and voices too intense, too singular, and too limited to support an entire novel, so in a way they encourage a kind of experimentation not advisable in the longer form."

In recent years, the horror field has been graced with an unusual number of first-rate, darkly disturbing novellas. Straub himself, in collections like *Houses Without Doors* and *Magic Terror*, has given us *Mrs. God*, "Bunny is Good Bread," and "The Juniper Tree," among many others. Stephen King, a writer with a profound affinity for the epic, has published some of his finest work in the novella collections *Different Seasons* and *Four Past Midnight*. T.E.D. Klein's *Dark Gods* contains a quartet of masterful novellas, among them "Children of the Kingdom" and the award-winning "Nadelman's God."

For Janice, Eileen, and Molly,
who help hold back the night

TABLE OF CONTENTS

Bill Sheehan

Introduction · 9

Kim Newman

Swellhead · 13

Tim Lebbon

In Perpetuity · 109

Lucius Shepard

Hands Up! Who Wants to Die? · 181

Night Visions 11
Copyright © 2004 by Subterranean Press.
All rights reserved.

Interior design
Copyright © 2004 by Tim Holt.

"Introduction" Copyright © 2004 by Bill Sheehan.
"Swellhead" Copyright © 2004 by Kim Newman.
"In Perpetuity" Copyright © 2004 by Tim Lebbon.
"Hands Up! Who Wants to Die?" Copyright © 2004 by Lucius Shepard.

FIRST EDITION

Trade edition ISBN
1-93081-94-8

Limited edition ISBN
1-931081-95-6

Subterranean Press
P.O. Box 190106
Burton, MI 48519

email:
subpress@earthlink.net

website:
www.subterraneanpress.com

edited by

Bill Sheehan

all original stories by

Kim Newman

Tim Lebbon

Lucius Shepard

Subterranean Press · 2004

Night Visions 11